THE LIFTED VEIL

THE LIFTED VEIL

The Book of Fantastic Literature by Women
1800—World War II

Edited and Introduced by
A. Susan Williams

Carroll & Graf Publishers, Inc.
New York

First published in Great Britain by Xanadu Publications Limited 1992.
First published in the United States of America by Carroll & Graf
Publishers, Inc. 1992, by arrangement with Xanadu Publications
Limited.

Carroll & Graf Publishers Inc.,
260 Fifth Avenue,
New York, NY 10001.

Library of Congress Cataloging-in-Publication Data is available.

ISBN 0-88184-913-8

Manufactured in Great Britain.

Contents

Contents

Introduction

Not long ago, space travel and genetic engineering were the stuff of fantasy. But today, they are a familiar part of our reality. It is as if there has been a narrowing of the gap between what is real and what is fantastic. This process has influenced many aspects of our life, not least the development of fiction. 'It is by now commonplace,' observes Doris Lessing, 'to say that novelists everywhere are breaking the bonds of the realistic novel because what we all see around us becomes daily wilder, more fantastic, incredible.'[1]

More and more writers and readers of fiction are being drawn to the fantastic. '[Our] narrative fiction,' claims Ursula Le Guin, 'has been going slowly and vaguely and massively . . . in one direction, and that direction is the way of fantasy.'[2] Every form of this kind of literature—science fiction, stories of ghosts and the supernatural, tales of magic and vampires, fairy stories and weird horror—can be found in bookshops and libraries. Literary critics[3] have started to take fantasy seriously and students are taking examinations on science fiction.

Until recently, fantasy was kept firmly on the margins of literary culture. It was seen as childish and time-wasting, so ineligible for membership to the exclusive club of Great Literature Written in English. No wonder, then, that so many people have different opinions about what makes a piece of fiction qualify as fantasy. 'Because ghosts inhabit, or haunt, one part of the vast domain of fantastic literature,' writes Le Guin, '. . . people familiar with that corner of it call the whole thing Ghost Stories, or Horror Tales; just as others call it Fairyland after the part of it they know or love best, and others call it Science Fiction, and others call it Stuff and Nonsense.'[4]

So what is fantasy? Perhaps, like some other 'first explorers in new territory'[5], as one scholar of fantasy describes herself, we should turn to a dictionary[6] for help. The word 'fantasy' comes from the Greek noun 'φαντασια', which means 'appearance (later, phantom), faculty of imagination'. From its earliest uses in English, 'fantasy' has been associated with 'imagination' and 'fancy'. It now signifies the use of the imagination to form 'representations of things not actually present', running from 'caprice, a whim', all the way to 'visionary fancy'.[7] In general terms, then, the meaning of fantasy appears to lie in its difference from reality.

In the more specific area of fantasy fiction, this meaning is equally applicable. Fantasy writing is different from the type of fiction that is called 'realist'. A realist novel or story (like Charles Dickens's *Oliver Twist* or George Eliot's *Middlemarch*) is 'mimetic' in type, which means that it assumes an equivalence between its fictional world and the 'real' world outside the text. In fantasy, however, there is serious doubt about the possibility of such an equivalence. The closure that is typical of the realist novel does not occur in fantasy. On the contrary, fantasy resists closure and opens up questions and possibilities. E. M. Forster put it like this: 'The other novelists say "Here is something that might occur in your lives", the fantasist "Here is something that could not occur".'[8]

Women writers have been attracted to fantasy from the early days of the development of the novel. 'It is a sobering blow to the male ego', admits one male critic, 'that what must rank as the single most influential novel in the history of weird fiction, *Frankenstein*, (1818), was written by a young woman: Mary Wollstonecraft Shelley.'[9] Even before Shelley's birth, women were writing weird fiction. Clara Reeve's *The Champion of Virtue* (1777) was the first deliberate attempt at a Gothic—or 'terror'—novel along the lines established in 1764 by Horace Walpole's *The Castle of Otranto*. Her book was followed by many other efforts by women, with titles like Eliza Parson's *The Mysterious Warning: A German Tale in Four Volumes* (1796). Ann Radcliffe's Gothic novels[10] of the 1790s were largely responsible for the immense popularity of the genre between 1790 and 1820.

The nineteenth century was the heyday of the realist novel in England. Nonetheless, as we see from the Gothic ingredients in Charlotte Bronte's *Jane Eyre* (1847) and Emily Bronte's *Wuthering Heights* (1847), fantasy continued to make its mark on prose fiction. In the middle of the nineteenth century, a woman called Catherine Crowe published *Night-side of Nature* (1848), a volume of stories about the supernatural that were supposed to be true. It 'captured the public's interest . . . for the most succinct and pointed horrors of the short story'[11] and encouraged the rapid production of short ghost stories on both sides of the Atlantic. Some of the best were written by Amelia Edwards and Elizabeth Gaskell in England and by Harriet Beecher Stowe and Elizabeth Stuart Phelps in the USA.

One admirer of Gaskell's ghost fiction claims that, 'the female writers [between Poe and Sheridan Le Fanu] kept the horror story alive and raised it to new levels'.[12] But most women authors of the fantastic were anxious to conceal their accomplishments. Louisa May Alcott, who readily published novels like *Little Women* (1868) and *Good Wives* (1869) under her own name, wrote her more sensational fiction—like the Gothic tale, *Pauline's Passion and Punishment* (1862)—under the pseudonym of A. M. Barnard. E[dith] Nesbit was equally reticent about her horror stories, preferring to give the impression that they were written by a man.[13] To this day, few people are aware that the famous author of *Five Children and It* (1902) also wrote horror fantasy.

In the early twentieth century, many women writers of fantasy felt the doubt and confusion of the modernist period. Charlotte Perkins Gilman was particularly concerned about the oppression of women in American society. In her well-known story, *The Yellow Wallpaper* (1899), she traces the journey into an alternative reality of a woman trapped in a repressive marriage. The bitter and painful reality of women living in a world run by men is a recurrent theme in stories by Willa Cather, Edith Wharton and May Sinclair.

In the 1930s, 'Isak' Dinesen (Karen Blixen) wrote a set of stories that she described as 'Gothic'. They are more disturbing than frightening, which was the hallmark of the Gothic fiction of the eighteenth century. They convey a keen sense of unease about the decay of the old world and the emerging values of the new society. By the middle of the century, this 'New Gothic' style was being developed to sinister effect by Elizabeth Bowen, Shirley Jackson and Daphne du Maurier. Their chilling stories probe the underlying violence in human relationships and the nature of fear. More recently, Angela Carter, Tanith Lee, Emma Tennant and Carol Emshwiller have written a kind of weird fantasy that works within the Gothic tradition but is highly original. It draws for its effects on surreal explorations of sexuality and visions of an apocalyptic future.[14]

Most people agree that Mary Shelley, the author of *Frankenstein, or the Modern Prometheus* (1818) and *The Last Man* (1826), founded the genre of science fiction. Yet SF has been considered a male interest for most of the twentieth century. It has also been dominated by men. '[A]part from the golden moment in the seventies[15] when the likes of Le Guin, Cherryh, Tiptree and Russ sprang into prominence,' notes one SF enthusiast, women have been 'outnumbered by men in a proportion that would be scandalous among Booker Prize contenders.'[16] In the first half of this century, many women writers— such as C. L. Moore, Leigh Brackett and C. J. Cherryh—used a pseudonym or a form of their name that would give the impression they were men. Presumably, this was their best chance of being published and read.

The difficulties for women writers of SF have not disappeared. As recently as 1969, *Playboy* persuaded Ursula Le Guin to sign *Nine Lives* as U. K. Le Guin (she later regretted this decision to conceal her gender). It is becoming less of a handicap, though, to be a woman. Support is available from the new women's publishing houses, such as The Women's Press, which is determined to 'challenge male domination of the science fiction tradition itself'.[17] But in any case, women have at last entered the mainstream of SF. Writers like Lessing, Le Guin, Joanna Russ, Mary Gentle and Suzy McKee Charnas are at the forefront of the creative development of the genre. Many SF novels by women are bestsellers: few male authors can match the popularity of Marion Zimmer Bradley, the creator of the 'Darkover' novels, or of Anne McCaffrey, the chronicler of the legends of Pern.

It has been argued that women's writing is different from men's, most notably in the area of SF. The case of James Tiptree Jr.[18], however, exposes the danger of making such an assumption. One so-called 'expert' on science fiction stated that, 'It has been suggested that Tiptree is a female, a theory that I find absurd, for there is to me something *ineluctably masculine* about Tiptree's writing. I don't think the novels of Jane Austen could have been written by a man nor the stories of Ernest Hemingway by a woman [emphasis added].'[19] Whether or not he was right about Austen and Hemingway, it is impossible to know. But he was certainly wrong about Tiptree, who later revealed that 'he' was Alice Sheldon.

Le Guin is right, therefore, to warn us to think carefully about 'all the stuff that has been written about "feminine style", about its inferiority or superiority to "masculine style", about the necessary, obligatory difference of the two.'[20] It does seem, though, that women writers of fantasy—generally speaking—have different interests and aims from their male colleagues. This is most obvious in science fiction. Stories by a number of male authors have portrayed men who were 'either slab-jawed heroes or else stiff-jointed puppets who delivered scientific lectures, and the women, when there were any, were fluttery little things who ran about shrieking and screaming to be rescued from monsters.'[21] These women are unremarkable, apart from their very weak brains and skimpy underwear. The men are at the centre of the story and control events; the women are the peripheral objects of their desire and chivalry.

This kind of gender-based allocation of roles sometimes occurs in SF by women, especially when the author is trying to imitate a popular style. But as a rule, female characters created by women are active, intelligent and fully clothed. They might not be as heroic as C. L. Moore's Jirel of Joiry, a brave warrior queen of the fifteenth century, but they are placed firmly at the centre of plot. Sometimes they share the centre with men, as in Marge Piercy's *Woman on the Edge of Time* (1976)[22] and Margaret Atwood's *The Handmaid's Tale* (1985). At other times, the men are relegated to the margins of the story, as in Joanna Russ's *The Female Man* (1975).

Fantasy is ideal, of course, for any exploration of the social construction of gender. Virginia Woolf's *Orlando* (1928) is just such an exploration. It tells the story of an androgynous person from the time of the sixteenth century (when a man) to 1928 (when a woman). In *The Left Hand of Darkness* (1969), Ursula Le Guin 'eliminated gender, to find out what was left'[23], by creating androgynous beings who have no sexuality except during the oestrus period of 'kemmer' (when they become, briefly, a man or a woman). 'When you meet a Gethenian,' observes the female Investigator of the first Ekumenical landing party, 'you cannot and must not do what a bisexual naturally does, which is to cast him in the role of Man or Woman, while adopting towards him a corresponding role dependent on your expectations of the patterned or possible interactions between persons of the opposite sex.'[24]

Utopian fantasies by women include Rokeya Sakhawat Hossain's *Sultana's Dream* (1905), a vision of an Indian society where women and men live as equals. Charlotte Perkins Gilman's *Herland* (1915)

and Alice Sheldon's *Houston, Houston, Do You Read?* (1976) describe
a female separatist utopia. Joanna Russ's *The Female Man* (1975)
celebrates the freedom enjoyed by women on a planet where no men
have existed for hundred of years—

> There's no being *out too late* in Whileaway, or *up too early*, or *in the wrong
> part of town*, or *unescorted*. You cannot fall out of the kinship web and become
> sexual prey for strangers—the web is world-wide. In all of Whileaway there is no
> one . . . who will follow you and try to embarrass you by whispering obscenities
> in your ear, no one who will attempt to rape you, no one who will warn you of
> the dangers of the street, no one who will stand on street-corners, hot-eyed and
> vicious, jingling loose change in his pants pocket, bitterly bitterly sure that you're
> a cheap floozy, hot and wild, who likes it, who can't say no, who's making a mint
> off it, who inspires him with nothing but disgust, and wants to drive him crazy.[25]

Such fantasies can be contrasted with dystopian futures like Suzy
McKee Charnas's *Walk to the End of the World* (1974), in which
women are viciously suppressed. Zoe Fairbairns's *Benefits* (1979) and
Margaret Atwood's *The Handmaid's Tale* show efforts by men in
a future society to exert a horrible control over women's minds
and bodies. In these dystopias, the authors are trying to educate
their readers by exaggerating for effect some repressive aspects of
contemporary society. They are exploiting the 'particular advantages
of science fiction [and fantasy] for feminists: . . . a licence to play
around with the interface between "nature" and "culture".'[26]

The past few decades have seen the publication of several excellent
anthologies of fantasy fiction by women. In 1967, Peter Haining
produced *Gentlewomen of Evil*[27], a collection of 'rare supernatural
stories from the pens of Victorian ladies'. Anthologies like *Women
of Wonder, More Women of Wonder*[28] and *Aurora: Beyond Equality*[29]
made women's fantasy more easily available in the 1970s. Paperbacks
like *Despatches from the Frontiers of the Female Mind*[30] (1985) and a
selection of weird horror tales called *Skin of the Soul*[31] (1990) have
continued this trend.

What is missing, though, is a 'grand' anthology that reflects the
range, quality and innovative nature of women's fantasy writing.
The larger anthologies of fantasy that are on sale contain few or
no stories by women and are almost palpably dominated by male
writing—'without making a Special Issue of it, or even the slightest
assumption that . . . [they] presumed to sum up or even illuminate
the Male Experience'[32]. An anthology like *The Book of Fantasy*, for

example, which boasts a list of eighty-one selections, offers no more than a handful of stories by women. The impression given is that only men are capable of *serious* fantasy.

This Book of Fantasy Stories by Women refutes such an impression beyond any doubt. It contains a wide range of fantasy fiction, written between the start of the nineteenth century and the outbreak of the Second World War. The only limits on choice have been that each piece should be in the form of a short story, that it should have been written in English and that it should be of the highest quality. The structure of the book is chronological, so as to give some idea of the development of this kind of fiction.

Initially, it was planned to include stories from the post-war period in this book. So many excellent stories were uncovered, however, that it became necessary to divide the collection into two volumes. A second Book of Fantasy Stories by Women is forthcoming, which will bring the anthology up to date. Together, the two books seek to answer the question raised by Joanna Russ in *The Female Man*—'I think it's a legend that half the population is female; where on earth are they keeping them all?'[33]

---

[1] from her introduction to *Shikasta*, the first novel in her series of speculative fiction, *Canopus in Argos: Archives* (1979; rpt. London: Granada, 1981), p. 8.

[2] Le Guin further suggests that, 'Our society—global, multilingual, enormously irrational—can perhaps describe itself only in the global, intuitional language of fantasy.' From her 'Introduction' to *The Book of Fantasy*, eds. Jorge Luis Borges, S. Ocampo and A. B. Cesares (London: Xanadu, 1988), p. 12.

[3] notably Tzvetan Todorov's *The Fantastic. A Structural Approach to a Literary Genre*, (1970; rpt. and trans. Ithaca, NY: Cornell UP, 1975), the first major work on fantasy and a fascinating attempt at developing a structuralist 'poetics of the fantastic' with a 'scientific' approach. 'There is an uncanny phenomenon,' explains Todorov, 'which we can explain in two fashions, by types of natural causes and supernatural causes. The possibility of a hesitation between the two creates the fantastic effect.' (p. 12). In other words, the fantastic is located on the frontier of two genres—fantasy fiction exists in the moment, however long, of the hesitation between the possibility of natural causes and supernatural causes. Ann Radcliffe's *The Mysteries of Udolpho*, (1794), for example, which centres much of its plot on apparently supernatural events, produces a fantastic effect up to the point where we are assured that there is a rational explanation for these weird events; but at this moment, the novel becomes *uncanny*. Horace Walpole's *The Castle of Otranto*, (1764), produces a fantastic effect up to the point where it is obvious that we must rely on the supernatural to find an explanation of events; the novel can then be described as *marvellous*.

Todorov's work encouraged a second generation of critical theorists of fantasy, who are exploring links between fantasy writing and psychoanalytic and cultural theory.

One of these, Rosemary Jackson, acknowledges her debt to Todorov's book, which she describes as 'The most important and influential critical study of fantasy of [the] post-Romantic period . . . The value of Todorov's work in encouraging serious critical engagement with a form of literature which had been dismissed as being rather frivolous or foolish cannot be over-estimated . . . .' From *Fantasy. The Literature of Subversion* (1981; rpt. London: Routledge, 1988) p. 5.

4 'Introduction' to *The Book of Fantasy*, p. 10.

5 Kathryn Hume, *Fantasy and Mimesis, Responses to Reality in Western Literature* (London: Methuen, 1984), p. xv.

6 in this case, the Oxford English Dictionary.

7 Today's use of the word 'fantasy' is actually much more complex, because of the multiplicity of its meanings. The specific uses of the word in the field of psychology, for example, have had a marked influence on most people's understanding of the word, often leading to a vague association of the word with sexual imaginings. Still more confusing is the fact that 'fantastic' as an evaluation today has opposite meanings: 'terrific', as well as 'silly' and 'absurd'.

8 E. M. Forster, *Aspects of the Novel* (Pelican, 1962), p. 113. Forster's Clark lectures of 1927 were later made into the book, *Aspects of the Novel*, which contains the only serious study of modern fantasy before Todorov's work in 1970. It describes fantasy as one of the seven important aspects of the novel.

9 Michael Ashley, *Mrs Gaskell's Tales of Mystery and Horror* (London: Victor Gollancz, 1978), p. 11.

10 A mark of Radcliffe's success is the fact that her *Mysteries of Udolpho*, (1794), was satirised in Jane Austen's *Northanger Abbey*, (1818). Radcliffe showed in her work that there is always a natural explanation for events which appear initially to be supernatural. Nonetheless, the *possibility* of the supernatural is the basis of each of her plots.

11 'Introduction' by Colin Wilson to Catherine Crowe, *The Night-side of Nature; or, Ghosts and Ghost-seers* (1848; rpt. Wellingborough: The Aquarian Press, 1986), p. 12

12 Michael Ashley, ed. *Mrs Gaskell's Tales of Mystery and Horror* (London: Victor Gollancz, 1978), p. 11.

13 She gave this impression by limiting her first name to its initial—as in E. Nesbit and E. Bland (Bland was her husband's name). Her choice of a male first person to narrate many of her horror stories was also suggestive of male authorship.

14 The heroine of Tennant's *The Crack*, (1973), for example, is the only bunny left at the Playboy Club after London has been divided in half by the drying up of the Thames.

15 this 'golden moment' coincides (but surely this is not a coincidence?) with the resurgence of the women's movement in the 1960s and 1970s.

16 Lee Montgomerie, 'Interface' in *Interzone. Science Fiction and Fantasy* (Dec. 1990, No 42) p. 4.

17 Statement made by The Women's Press in Lisa Tuttle, *A Spaceship Built of Stone and other stories* (London: The Women's Press, 1987).

18 This respected SF writer chose a brand-name of jam as her pseudonym!

19 Quoted in Ursula Le Guin, 'Introduction to *Star Songs of an Old Primate*', 1978, rpt. in Le Guin, *The Language of the Night, Essays on Fantasy and Science Fiction*, ed. Susan Wood (1979; rpt. London: The Women's Press, 1989), p. 158.

20 *ibid*, pp. 158–159.

21 *Robert Silverberg's Worlds of Wonder* (London: Victor Gollancz, 1988), p. 126.

22 the heroine of this novel is a poor Chicana woman, who has been incarcerated in a mental hospital; such a character—poor, female, Chicana, and diagnosed as mentally ill—would not qualify for much attention in mainstream science fiction.

[23] Ursula Le Guin, 'Is Gender Necessary?', 1976, in *The Language of the Night*, p. 138.

[24] Ursula Le Guin, *The Left Hand of Darkness* (1969; rpt. London: Futura, 1989), p. 85. When writing the novel Le Guin chose to call a Gethenian 'he', regarding it as the generic pronoun. Later, she believed that this had been a mistake, since 'the so-called generic pronoun he/him/his . . . does in fact exclude women from discourse.' From 'Redux', 1988, (*The Language of the Night*), p. 145.

[25] Joanna Russ, *The Female Man* (1975; rpt. London: The Women's Press, 1985), pp. 81–82.

[26] Ann Oakley, *Subject Women* (Oxford: Martin Robertson, 1981), p. 340.

[27] London: Robert Hale.

[28] edited by Pamela Sargent (Penguin), 1974 and 1976.

[29] edited by Vonda McIntyre and Susan J. Anderson (Greenwich, Conn: Fawcett), 1977.

[30] edited by Jen Green and Sarah Lefanu.

[31] edited by Lisa Tuttle.

[32] this is part of a clever explanation by the editor of *Interzone* of the decision to devote an entire issue (Dec. 1990) to fantasy writing by women. 'It is with more embarrassment than pride,' writes Lee Montgomerie, 'that we introduce our first all-female issue, indeed our first ever issue with even a preponderance of women writers. We have published many an all-male edition of *Interzone* without making a Special Issue of it, or even the slightest assumption that, say, *Interzones* 35, 36 and 37, a deplorable trilogy of unabashed masculine mag-hogging, presumed to sum up or even illuminate the Male Experience.' Montgomerie adds, 'Women in science fiction appear to be a beleaguered minority. Is it any wonder that many of the story titles in this issue read like chapter headings from a survival guide for the undercover agent in a hostile alien culture?[!]' (p. 4).

[33] *The Female Man*, p. 204.

c. 1806

The Spectre;

or,

The Ruins of Belfont Priory

SARAH WILKINSON

In the reign of our eighth Henry, when the religious houses were suppressed, and their treasures seized by the monarch, Belfont Priory, was among the number of those who vainly resisted the command, and by an appeal to Rome, endeavoured to keep possession of their domain, which was extensive, and liberally endowed. This served no other purpose but to draw down on their heads the vengeance of their irritated sovereign: they were forced to seek shelter in another foil, and a great part of the Priory was levelled to the ground. The lands they possessed from the founder of the order were sold; but the edifice remained a stately ruin, unnoticed by the rich, and shunned by the peasantry, who entertained a firm belief that it was haunted—not the most courageous among them could be prevailed upon to pass by it after sun-set. In this manner it remained till the reign of Elizabeth; when she made a grant of the Priory to Cecil Lord Burleigh; but his lordship being in possession of several magnificent seats, he did not chuse to incur the expence of rendering it fit for the reception of his family.

Soon after this period, Theodore Montgomery left his native country (Scotland) to seek a shelter from his vindictive relations in England. This brave youth was the heir of Earl Gowen, a Scotch nobleman of great wealth and power. His son, by espousing Matilda Maxwell, (a young lady endowed with mental perfections as well as personal beauty, but no fortune) incurred his displeasure, as well as the rest of his relatives; for the family had set their hearts on his marrying the heiress of the Earl of Glencoe. The unfortunate Montgomery and his beloved Matilda, were persecuted with every action cruelty could invent, or malice suggest; wearied out with being drove from place to place, they resolved to seek a refuge in England.

By the sale of some valuables they possessed, they raised money sufficient to carry their scheme into execution, and they set out on their journey, with only two domestics, on whose fidelity they were conscious they could depend. They arrived at the metropolis without any particular occurrence or discovery taking place. Montgomery immediately made himself known to Lord Burleigh, to whose lady his wife was distantly related, and informed him of his marriage, and subsequent misfortunes.

Lord Burleigh assured him of his protection, till he could be reconciled to his family; and that he would maintain an inviolable secrecy in regard to their retreat, and he informed them of the ruinated Priory. They accepted the proposal with joy, and the next morning began their tour of Cornwall. The beautiful scenery of the surrounding country enlivened their spirits, and they felt happy in their exile. When they arrived at Truro they discharged the carriage and attendants, and proceeded on foot till they came to the Priory. It was near eight in the evening when they entered the avenue that led to the gates—the surrounding objects could scarce be distinguished through the gloom that now pervaded, and the tall trees waving over their heads, inspired them with melancholy sensations, which the ruins they approached to was not formed to dispel. Theodore led the way to the habitable part, according to the account he had received from Lord Burleigh, and entered a wooden arch of the most antique appearance; it led to a small door—he placed the key which was given him, in the lock, and with difficulty opened it: they struck a light, and kindled their torches, when they found themselves in a large hall, with painted windows, and a vaulted roof; from this place there opened several doors and passages, that led to the interior of the building—upon examining they found that this part that was left undemolished was the offices of the Priory, and not immediately joined to the edifice, and therefore escaped devastation, as the ravagers thought it unnecessary to search for treasures in a part appropriated to domestic purposes. To their extreme consolation they found the furniture yet remained, though covered with rust and dirt.

Donald gathered such materials as he could then find at hand, and made a fire in one of the rooms that looked more comfortable than the rest, and here they set down to rest from their fatigue, and to air such things as they could collect for their bedding. After a repast on some cold provisions they had brought with them, they retired to rest; and for that night they resolved to lay their different mattresses in the same room, that they might be near each other. Wearied with their journey, sleep soon sealed their eyes, and the thoughts of their new situation did not hinder their repose: it was late the next morning when they arose, nor felt no traces from their fatigue; they employed that day in making their habitation comfortable, and succeeded beyond their hopes—they compleated three bed rooms, a parlour, and a kitchen, in a neat, though antique style, and piled up the lumber in a large dismal room they did not like to use.

They agreed that Donald should go every week to the next town, to purchase provisions, at the dusk of evening, and return as privately as was possible.

As soon as their necessary arrangements were made they spent their time in exploring the ruins. The great hall was still left; it was about seventy feet long and thirty-four broad, and the height was seventeen feet. On the North side there was an ascent to this place, by a direct stair-case, about two yards wide; the roof was vaulted, and supported by twenty arches, which rose gradually one above another, till you entered the hall. Opposite the stair-case, on the South side of the room was a chimney, about twelve feet wide; on each side of the fire-place was two large gothic windows, adorned with sculptures of fruit and leaves. On each side of the hall were eight triangular pillars, placed at equal distances, and supported by three busts: the grandeur of the architecture inspired them with delight. The chambers which led from this place were now levelled with the ground, or only a part of the walls remained standing. They now descended the noble stair-case, and crossing the court yard of the ruins entered the chapel, but only a small part remained in its former state—they examined what monuments was in their view, and Theodore was much surprised to observe on a stone, scarcely legible, the titles of Earl Gowen joined to that of Belfont, but the rest of the inscription, (and which consisted of many lines) was too much injured by time for him to decypher; after much study and pains, he was obliged, with much chagrin, to give up the pursuit, and rest in ignorance. Leaving the chapel and turning to the left, they came to the library—the principal of the books had been removed and only a few volumes were left on the shelves, but this was a pleasing acquisition to Theodore and Matilda; they were just going to retire, when Blanche pulled open a small oak door, which had escaped the notice of her mistress, and uttering a loud scream, fell on the floor! Donald flew to her assistance, but on casting his eyes towards the place that had caused her such alarm, he became in no better plight than the terrified damsel—his whole frame shook like an aspen leaf, and his eyes glared with a frightful wildness—the gentle Matilda clung to Theodore's arm, and besought him to protect her; he gently carried her back to the habitable apartments, and placing her in a great chair, he returned to his servants, whom, he found in the same posture he had left them, but to his astonishment the door had closed without aid. He assisted Donald to rise, who resuming his wonted frame of mind at the presence of his master, he assisted in conveying Blanche (who still remained in a state of insensibility) to Matilda, who saw them return with pleasure. As soon as the domestics were recovered from their fright, Theodore desired they would relate the cause of it. Blanche said, that as soon as she pulled open the door, an erect tall figure met her view, approached towards her, and waved one of its hands; that its visage was a deadly white, with terrible large eyes! Donald corroborated this account, with the addition of its having a blood-stained sword in its right-hand, which it brandished with a menacing air. 'Mercy on me!' re-echoed Blanche, 'so it had, I remember, but the fright has deprived me of my senses—Oh, it was a terrible Spectre!'

Theodore now ordered Donald to follow him, that they might search the ruins, to see if the object of their alarm still continued; the trembling Blanche flung herself on her knees before Theodore, 'O! my lord' said the maiden, 'I conjure you not to go, if the ghost should murder you and Donald, what will become of me and my dear lady!'

Theodore smiled at the artless simplicity of the affectionate girl, but would not be dissuaded from his purpose, and commanded Donald, who stood like a motionless statue, to accompany him without further delay to the hall.

Matilda now arose from her seat and declared her resolution to go with them, saying that her fears for the safety of her lord would not permit her to remain behind.

Her beloved husband after some gentle remonstrances yielded to her request, and Blanche, who was ashamed to appear less heroic than her mistress, joined the party, and they proceeded to the library; Donald exclaiming all the way, that he would rather face a regiment of Frenchmen than one Spectre—'I never was a coward' said the man, (and in this he spake truth, for he had shewn several instances of valour), 'but I hate these supernatural beings.' 'Peace, you blockhead' said Theodore hastily, as they came to the oak door, which he flung open, while his lady and servants gave a sudden start occasioned by their apprehensions, which were now arrived at the highest pitch; nought appeared, and all was silent as the grave.

The party entered, and they proceeded to investigate the furniture, which appeared more ancient than any they had yet met with in the Priory; the hangings were of rich tapestry, on which were exquisitely displayed several passages of historical tradition, the whole bordered with a lovely wreath of flowers; the chairs were made to correspond with the work, but the tables were of a beautiful carved wood of the most curious form. At one end stood a large folding press of ebony, which Theodore opened—his blood curdled with horror at the dreadful scene which presented itself to his view: no less than three decayed human bodies hung up in this place!—at the bottom of the press was a dagger, with a handle of solid gold, embossed with various characters; from the appearance of the blade, he had no doubt but it was that with which the murder had been committed.

The murdered persons, by the remains of their dress that was not effaced by the all-subduing hand of time, appeared to be of high rank in life: there was a gentleman, a lady, and a little boy, apparently about seven years of age—the assassins did not appear to be of the common stamp, to whom plunder would have been a chief object, for there were several ornaments of considerable value left on their persons; the most conspicuous was a diamond cross, that was suspended by a chain of gold, to the bosom of the lady—after a minute search nothing could be found to elucidate the mystery, who was the assassin, and they returned to their apartments overwhelmed with horror; the dreadful knowledge they had obtained made the asylum they had once deemed so comfortable, hateful to them, and disturbed their repose, but necessity obliged them to continue in their retreat.

One evening, when Donald had accompanied his master to the next town, to purchase some few articles, that they wanted, they were much delighted with the various conversations they heard about the haunted Priory: lights had been seen, and the figures of men and women walking in the ruins; all which was judged to be supernatural, and every account much exaggerated—some affirmed that the spectres had no heads, and some that they were above a dozen in the ghostly party. Theodore demanded of one of them who seemed the most loquacious, what reason was given for the reappearance of those, who by divine and natural laws, ought to rest in the quiet sepulchre; the man (who proved to be the village notary) informed him that the Priory was not built till the reign of Edward the IVth, in the year 1463, by Robert Earl of Belfont, who was a powerful man, and in great favour with the monarch, to whom he was a faithful subject, and vigilant in his cause against the house of Lancaster, and was one of the chief in hurling the unfortunate Henry the VIth from the regal dignity. This building was erected for the performance of a vow he had made in the field of battle, so to do, if God granted him victory over the enemies of his sovereign: this proved to be decisive in favour of the York line, and the Earl fulfilled his religious promise. He endowed it with munificence, and the edifice was supposed to be the most beautiful structure of any religious house in the kingdom. The Earl lived to a very advanced age, but at the time the vile Duke of Gloucester ascended the throne, he retired from the world in disgust, and became one of the brethren of Belfont Priory.

Thus he continued exercising the prescribed rules with the most rigid exactness, till the decease of Hugh de Burgh, the Prior, when he was elected in his room, by universal consent, and died much lamented; he was buried in the chapel, but the monument is now enclosed in the mass of ruins. His son succeeded him in the earldom; he was the worst of tyrants—arrogant, cruel, and vindictive: he espoused Lady Margaret, a daughter of the Earl of Gowen—(Theodore could not avoid a convulsive start) this lady expired in giving birth to their first child, a daughter who received the name of Avisa; the Earl was chagrined in not having a male heir to his titles and estates, and deplored that circumstance more than the loss of his amiable spouse—he entered into second nuptials in a few months after this fatal event, and had no offspring, and the Earl and Countess lived in a very discontented manner; she died some years before her husband, not without some suspicion of poison being given to her in some wine.

The lovely Avisa was much neglected by her father, and long before his death retired into a convent at Sheen, where she remained till she had attained her thirtieth year. The Earl on his being informed by his physicians that he had not many hours to live, declared a nephew of his first wife lady Margaret, his heir in case he espoused Avisa, and a dispensation could be procured from Rome to emancipate her vows. This was accordingly done, but neither the young Earl of Gowen nor Avisa was forward for the marriage; they were both handsome and agreeable, but they had not a mutual inclination for each other. The Earl had fixed his affections elsewhere, but as he could not have the estate without complying with the will of his late uncle, therefore he chose to dissemble and espoused the heiress; they lived near seven years in the utmost harmony with each other. The Earl possessed a noble and elevated mind, and he scorned to behave ill to the amiable countess, he strove to forget his first love, and paid Avisa the most assiduous attention, while she on her part returned his kindness with duty and complacence. About this period of time, Gowen introduced at his castle Sir Leopold de Courcy, who had arrived unexpectedly from Germany—upon his entering the room where Avisa was sitting working tapestry with her women, she raised her eyes, and on beholding the graceful knight, fell from her seat and fainted; the Earl was much shocked, but the lady attributing her emotion to a sudden and violent indisposition, he was satisfied, and she retired to her chamber.

After some time spent in conversation on different subjects, the alarm of the countess on the entrance of his friend, recurred to the memory of the still doubting husband. 'Pray Sir Leopold' said the Earl, 'did you ever visit the late Earl of Belfont the last time you honoured our native land with your presence?' The knight answered in the affirmative. 'Perhaps' said his friend, 'you were then acquainted with lady Avisa his daughter?' Sir Leopold replied he had never seen her to his knowledge: 'But why that question' continued the knight? 'Nothing particular' said the Earl, with some hesitation, 'I only thought you and my lady might probably have been acquainted before.' Here the entrance of dinner interrupted their conversation. One of the domestics brought word that the countess was too ill to appear at table, and the rest of the company being arrived, they sat down to the sumptuous repast. On this very day was the Priory of Belfont destroyed by an edict from his Majesty, when it had only stood seventy-four years.—The Earl who was a most zealous reformer, heard the news without the least regret; besides, to his extreme consolation, the large sums he was charged with annually, by the will of Robert, the founder of the Priory, he was now freed from obligation to pay—but the case was far different with lady Gowen, she venerated this, and all religious houses, and was for some time inconsolable. The offices of the Priory, the principal hall, and a large room which had been the chamber of the superior, was still left, and his lordship applied to the king for leave to make it a temporary residence in the hunting season; this was readily obtained, for the Gowens had always been favorites with the Henries, for their strict adherence to the Lancaster family. But fate so ordained that the Earl never enjoyed the privilege he obtained—in less than three months after the arrival of Sir Leopold, Gowen was obliged to attend his monarch on account of his marriage with Ann of Cleves. Being one night (during his stay at the court) invited to a splendid banquet—towards the end of the entertainment, the gentlemen got a little inebriated with drinking the health of their majesties. Lord Weston facetiously rallied the Earl upon entertaining one who had been the paramour of his wife. Lord Gowen waited on that nobleman the next day, declared his ignorance of the circumstance to which he had alluded the preceding evening, and desired an explanation, which Lord Weston gave him in the following words: Sir Leopold de Courcy for a length of time paid his addresses to the heiress of Belfont; but the Earl refused his consent, declaring he had other views for his daughter, and desiring the knight to discontinue his visits; this proved a great affliction to Leopold and Avisa, but they contrived private meetings at the house of the lady's nurse, which continued for some length of time, till one of the herdsmen informed Lord Belfont of the affair, and Avisa was confined to her chamber, and soon after sent to the monastery at Sheen; and Sir Leopold finding all his schemes for recovering his mistress frustrated, retired to his own country, where he soon after met with a rich widow whom he espoused. Here the Earl of Gowen interrupted him, with remarking that he well knew the lady, and that he first became acquainted with Sir Leopold at the celebration of their nuptials at the Spa—to this he added that Lady de Courcy being dead, was the reason of the knight's return to England, in order to alleviate his grief. Lord Weston resumed his discourse by informing the Earl that Lady Avisa was only placed in the convent as a boarder, but on receiving the account of Leopold's marriage, she insisted on taking the veil, which she did in utter disregard of the commands of Belfont to the contrary, and he was so much exasperated at the conduct of his daughter, that he never went to the grate to visit her during the many years she survived this transaction. 'But I never heard, said Lord Weston, that any thing criminal had been suspected between the lovers, and I hope their actions now will be dictated by honor and rectitude.' Here the noblemen parted, and the Earl of Gowen went back to his lodgings in a frame of mind, the most wretched that can be conceived. 'But here it may be necessary to inform you', said the notary, 'that Lord Weston was a relation of the late Earl's second wife, and was better acquainted with the affairs of the family than the nephew Earl Gowen, who had resided in Scotland, till his nuptials with Avisa.' By this time Theodore and his companion had arrived at the end of the village; the night was drawing on apace, and made his further stay dangerous to himself and distressing to the feelings of Lady Matilda, who doubtless would be alarmed at his unusual delay. He therefore informed the notary that he was anxious to get to his abode, which lay in a distant village. But that he was so much interested in the story he had been so obliging to relate, that he would meet him at the inn to hear the remainder of the narrative, any time he would be pleased to mention; the notary appointed to-morrow evening, and they parted.

Theodore and Donald made the best of their way across the forest, till they arrived at the Priory, where they were received with pleasure by the Lady Matilda and her faithful Blanche, to whom Theodore, related what had just been told by the notary. 'I now find', said he, 'the reason of the tombstone in the chapel, bearing the names and quartered arms of the families of Belfont and Gowen, and tho' so closely connected by two marriages, the dreadful scenes that doubtless occurred, prevented my father from mentioning the affinity between them, for I often remarked he did not like to talk of his ancestors.'

The next evening Theodore repaired to the inn, and found the notary true to his appointment, and resumed the thread of his discourse as fellows; Earl Gowen as soon as he could retire from the court with propriety, returned to Belfont castle, which was situated some miles distant from the Priory, at the town of Launceston; he resolved on his journey how he should act in consequence of the news he had heard. To deny Sir Leopold to continue his visit at the castle, without assigning the reasons of the act would appear like a breach of hospitality. He was assured in his own mind that the intentions of the knight were not honorable, or he would not have denied being acquainted with Lady Gowen. But he acquitted Avisa of entering any knowledge of the arrival of Sir Leopold, and he determined to challenge him to single combat, and wipe out the blot his honor had sustained. The Earl travelled with such speed that he arrived at the castle much sooner than expected by the inhabitants, who appeared agitated and surprised. The Earl leaped from his proud steed and eagerly inquired of the domestics the cause of the consternation so visible in their countenances, but could obtain no satisfactory answer. He was proceeding to the apartment of his Lady, when the groom of the chambers with some hesitation informed him that Lady Gowen had left the castle the preceeding evening, in company with Sir Leopold, and the young Lord Montgomery, with only two attendants, that belonged to the knight; when they went, they told him they were going to view the mines; and when he found it dark, and they did not return he became uneasy, and accompanied by some of the domestics, he went in search of them, fearful some dreadful accident had occurred; but all his inquiries were in vain, and he was certain they had not been at the mines, nor could he get any intelligence of them.

The Earl gave himself up to the most violent paroxysms of rage, vowing revenge on his perfidious wife, and false friend. He dispatched his vassals every road he could think on, mounted on fleet coursers to pursue them, but all his endeavors were useless, and filled him with despair.

Bitterly did he reproach himself for espousing Lady Avisa, and forsaking Lady Julia Malcolm, who was the real object of his affections, and to whom he had often made the most solemn declarations of his love. He regarded his misfortunes as the dispensation of heaven, as a just reward for his perjury, and he cursed the Belfont estates as the means of his undoing.

Some weeks passed and no tidings were obtained of the fugitives, till Roland one of the Earl's huntsmen brought intelligence of a surprising nature: he related that being in pursuit of his game, chance led him near the Priory, just as there came on a violent shower of hail; he was alone, and tho' he wished to seek shelter from the inclemency of the weather, he was not fond of entering the ruins, as it was reported by the peasantry that since the edifice was demolished, the ghost of the founder was seen wandering about the windings of the ruins: but the storm continued with such violence he had no choice left, and he stood under a large portico. He had not been in this retreat many minutes, when he heard the voices of different persons as if conversing at some distance; this rather startled him, but presently it recurred to him that it might be some travellers, who like himself, had sought shelter from the weather; and he resolved to search for them, that he might join their party. He dismounted from his horse, and fastening it at the image that remained in the wall, he attentively listened from whence the sound proceeded, and he ascended the noble stair-case, and entered the hall, the persons appeared to be in a room beyond. Roland called to mind that some furniture had been moved there from the castle, in order to render that room fit for the reception of his master in the hunting season, and he thought that was the reason for their choosing that apartment, which lady Avisa had fitted up with exquisite taste. He was just going to enter the door, when to his extreme terror and surprise, he became sensible that one of the persons was Sir Leopold De Courcy. Resuming his courage, he peeped through the crevice of the door, and beheld the knight, Lady Gowen, and her son, with the two attendants: he understood from their conversation that they had concealed themselves in that retreat ever since they left Belfont Priory, but that night they meant to begin their journey, they was to depart at the mid hour, and a suit of man's apparel had been provided for the Lady, which she was to wear till they arrived at Germany. The man with difficulty escaped unseen; for Sir Leopold entered the hall the moment Roland had gained the stairs; he mounted his horse and made a precipitate flight, for he had no doubt of being assassinated, was he caught in that place. The Earl rewarded the huntsman for his fidelity, and commanded him to keep the affair secret from his fellows. About nine in the evening Earl Gowen, privately quitted the castle, and repaird to the ruined Priory; he arrived there just as the clock of the adjacent village announced the eleventh hour. He proceeded cautiously to the hall, the door of the inner apartment was open, and he had a full view of his lady, and the treacherous knight; he was persuading her to put on the attire he procured for her, to which she appeared to acquiesce with reluctance, but at last consented, telling him with most affectionate air that she would sacrifice her life to oblige him.

Sir Leopold embraced her and remarked the hour was drawing near, that he fondly hoped would rescue them from their irksome solitude, and from the fear of being surprised by their enemies. Lady Gowen returned an answer so endearing, that the Earl could no longer restrain his vengeance, he rushed into the room and plunged a dagger in her breast, surprise had unnerved the arm of Sir Leopold, but recovering from his stupor, he drew his sword and made a furious thrust at the unfortunate husband, but missed his aim, and received a mortal wound from the weapon, still reeking with the blood of his mistress.

Sir Leopold staggered a few paces, and exclaiming he would not fall unrevenged, ran his sword through the heart of the child, (Lord Montgomery) who was sleeping on a seat in a little travelling dress, he uttered not a word, but instantly his pure unspotted soul winged its way from its earthly tenement, and flew to the realms of bliss. The Earl was almost in a state of distraction, his revenge had been dear bought; he loved his son with the most enthusiastic fondness, and beheld the fatal stroke with horror that beggars all description, he placed the hapless victim in an oak press, and locking the door, rushed with dire frenzy from the scene of blood. He regained his castle in safety, tho' crossing one of the courts he heard the trampling of horses in the track that led to the Priory; he remembered for what purpose they were going, and a transient wish came across his mind that their escape had not been prevented; agony of woe, and the most heart-rendering sensations for the loss of his beloved boy, soon affected his brain, and he became a miserable maniac, in which state he continued near three years, during which time he uttered the most dreadful expressions. Roland was the only one of his attendants that believed his ravings about murder, but he kept the fatal secret confided to his own bosom.

About a week before the death of the unfortunate Earl, he became sensible, and sending for a priest made a public confession; the case was immediately reported to the king, who ordered every attention to be paid to Gowen, and duly considering the unfortunate and aggravating circumstances of the case, he granted him a full pardon under his seal, in case he should recover his health. But the estates of the Belfont family were seized by the crown, but had no interference with that of the Gowens. The Earl just lived to receive the pardon, uttered a petition to Heaven and expired. By his own desire he was privately interred amid the ruins of the chapel belonging to the

Priory. He was succeeded in his estates at Scotland, by his brother Adolphus. For what cause I know not, but the monarch ordered the bodies of the murdered persons to remain unburied, and their spirits are frequently seen hovering about the spot. Here the notary finished his sad relation, with a wish that they might be permitted to have the funeral rites performed. After some mutual civilities passing they parted, and Theodore resolved in his own mind the dreadful circumstances, and sincerely deplored the fate of his ancestors.

The small circle that composed their family were sitting round the cheerful fire, attentively listening to Theodore's recital of the account the notary had given. Matilda shuddered at the horrid tale, while the hair of the two domestics stood erect on their heads; they drew their chairs close to their superiors, and shewed every symptom of terror. Theodore had just concluded his narration, and was telling Donald to fetch a bottle of wine from the chest, that by an enlivening glass they might exhilarate their spirits, and disperse the gloom that overspread each visage. Donald was preparing to obey the commands of his master, when the door of their apartment (which was always bolted with care on the inside, as soon as they were assembled for the evening) flew suddenly open, grated on its hinges, and then shut again with violent force; this was repeated three times, and then all was silent as before. Theodore was the first that recovered from the shock and confusion, into which this affair had thrown them—when he endeavored to calm their apprehensions, by assuring them that they had neglected to secure the door, which was thus blown by the winds. He advanced to examine it, with a firm believe that he should find the bolts undrawn—but how was he staggered to behold it completely fastened in the usual manner; the most extreme terror took possession of each of these unhappy fugitives.—Lady Matilda declared that she would rather beg her bread, than continue in a place so replete with horror. They passed the night with the most dreadful apprehensions, listening to every sound with acute misery, but nothing further happened to disturb them. They arose early the next morning weary and ill for want of rest, and they determined to seek a more comfortable asylum without loss of time. All that day the rain poured in torrents, and detained Theodore and his servant from taking the rout that was intended.

From the unfavorable state of the weather, it was not possible for them to remove from the Priory, and Theodore to calm the apprehensions of Matilda, determined with the assistance of Donald, to inter the remains of the guilty victims and the innocent child, in one of the aisles of the ruinated chapel. He sent his servant to procure a pick axe and a spade; and placing their remains in an old chest, they performed the duty so necessary to the obsequies of the dead.

Theodore endeavored to persuade his Lady and the domestics to remain some time longer in their present abode, in hopes that now the dreadful spectacle was removed, they should be permitted to rest in peace: after some arguments on both sides, they consented to his proposal, and endeavored to arm themselves with fortitude.

The moon now shone with resplendent brightness, and the season of the year was uncommonly fine and warm. Theodore and Matilda often roved about the grounds, while their faithful attendants, who entertained a sincere affection for each other, followed at a distance. In one of these nocturnal rambles, they wandered insensibly a great distance from their abode; the striking of the clock in the neighbouring town, warned them it was the much dreaded hour of midnight, and they returned towards the Priory with as much haste as they could possibly effect: they had just gained the ruins when the Spectre who appeared to the view of Donald and Blanche, on their first entering the hall, crossed the path, uttering a most dismal groan, and surveying the party with a scrutinizing eye, and then vanished from their view. They proceeded slowly on without uttering a word, so great was their affright, which was still more augmented when ascending the stairs that led to the room where they commonly sat, the same figure impeded their passing to it, by planting itself in the narrow passage. Theodore disengaging himself from the grasp of the terrified Matilda, and advancing boldly towards the Spectre, conjured him, by every sacred obligation, to relate the reason of its thus bursting from the confines of the dead, and haunting that abode of horror. The Spectre, in a solemn voice, commanded him to follow, and turned down another winding of the passage, while Theodore followed in silent awe, yet resolved to obey the summons, and learn, if possible, the dreadful mystery. His ghostly conductor led the way down a narrow flight of stairs, while a blue flame cast a faint light on the surrounding objects. At the bottom of the descent they entered a spacious vault; in the middle of the place was a broad square stone, here the Spectre stopt, and addressed the youth:

'Behold! thou heir of Gowen, the wandering spirit of Robert, lord of all Belfont's rich domains; whose deeds of benevolence endeared him to his vassals—but know, he was a murderer!' Theodore uttered a deep sigh—the Spectre proceeded. 'My elder brother was a noble youth. We beheld each other with the most affectionate regard, nor had we a sentiment we concealed; all was candor and fraternal love. I had just entered my eighteenth year when, unfortunately, I fell violently in love with the fair Elizabeth, niece of the Duke of Somerset, who, unknown to me, was previously engaged to my brother. I soon made a declaration of my affection, which she refused. Shortly after I learned the cause of her refusal was because she favored my brother. From that hour jealousy, deadly hate, and revenge, took possession of my soul: I hired four ruffians, who way laid him in a private path; he made a brave resistance, but fell, covered with wounds—they dug a deep hole, and hid the cruel deed from the eyes of mortals. Never was the dire murder discovered, I even concealed it from my confessor; but my conscience burthened with the sin, was a torment to me. Some years after I obtained the hand of Elizabeth, who yielded with much reluctance to the wishes of the Duke, who was anxious for a union with our family. Heaven did not smile propitious on a marriage founded on blood. Elizabeth died the second year of our nuptials, in giving birth to my son. The annals of my race, are they not stained with murder, dishonor, and most horrid deeds? In you, noble Theodore, the virtues of my brother live again. Remove his stone; dig some feet down, and there you will find the skeleton of the hapless Edward! Pay funeral honors to it—have masses said for the repose of my soul, and then shall my perturbed spirit have the rest so long denied it. According to my vow in the civil wars, I erected this Priory, and I chose the spot when the murder had been done, in hopes to expiate the fault—Curst fratricide!'

Here the spirit of Earl Robert vanished, with the most dreadful groans, and the blue flame gradually faded away. Theodore was left in total darkness—he groped round the walls in hopes to find the passage by which the Spectre conducted him to the dismal vault, but his endeavors were unsuccessful: in vain he made the place ring with his voice, he was only answered by the echo resounding from the lofty roof, and he began to feel the most terrific apprehensions for his fate, when he found his hand grasped by another of the most icy coldness—this invisible agent led, or rather pulled him forcibly to a considerable distance, and the youth presently perceived that he was in a narrow passage by which he entered the vault: this circumstance revived his drooping spirits, and he began to think that the same Spectre led him, though veiled in darkness from his sight, and he felt perfect confidence in his conductor. His feet now stumbled against the winding stairs, and to his great joy, he found that he was near his own apartments and his beloved Matilda, whose distress at his absence he well knew would be excruciating. The cold hand let go his hold; a slow mournful voice exclaimed. 'I can go no further—this is the utmost step of my limited bounds; proceed, and all good angels guard you.' The tone was far different from that of Earl Robert. Theodore was lost in amazement—a great light now shone behind him, he turned round, and beheld a sight that filled him at once with pity and horror: the ghost of the murdered Edward (for such it doubtless was) stood at some distance! his body covered with wounds, and one large gash in his forehead, from which the blood still appeared to flow in copious streams. Montgomery's eyes were fixed on the dreadful spectacle, but the view was but transient, it instantly disappeared from his sight, and with a soft sigh exclaimed, 'Theodore! the only remaining hope of two noble families, fulfill the request of my murderer—the deed will amply repay you.'

Theodore was obliged to stop some moments to recover his surprise, when he hastened on and entered their apartments in safety. The two domestics were endeavouring to conceal their own apprehensions, and to give comfort to their afflicted mistress, but in vain, grief had taken possession of her soul, and she declared her Theodore was lost for ever; at this instant he appeared and fondly clasped her in his arms. Overpowered with the pleasing surprise, she fainted, while Donald and Blanche knelt down and returned their thanks to heaven with fervor, that their beloved master was restored to them in safety. As soon as lady Matilda was restored to life, and the serenity of the family restored, Theodore complied with their anxious requests, and acquainted them with every particular that had occurred during his painful absence: he concluded his account with a wish that he could perform the injunctions he had received from the hapless spectres, but was fearful of involving themselves in ruin, as such a step must of necessity disclose to his cruel and relentless father where they had sought a retreat from the dread of his power, and he might form some dire project of tearing from him, his beloved Matilda, whose situation now required more tenderness than ever.

Matilda besought him to let no concern for her, however just, deter him from an act, which heaven must approve, and in its own time reward.

'Pray my Lord' (said the artless Donald, with a simplicity that forced a smile from Theodore,) 'pray my Lord bury the ghost, or else he may seek for revenge and tear you to pieces!'

After various resolutions on the subject, they agreed that they ought to take no step of consequence without Lord Burleigh's concurrence, and to refer the matter to him. Theodore arose early the next morning, and equipping himself in the disguise he travelled in, took an affectionate leave of Matilda, and mounting his horse rode to Launceston attended by Donald—here he met with a proper vehicle to convey him to the metropolis; he sent his faithful servant back to the Priory, giving him strict charge to take great care of his Lady and Blanche during his absence, which he would make as short as possible.

He arrived at Lord Burleigh's without meeting with any incident on the road worth recording; he was received by that nobleman with every mark of friendly attention—but nought can equal the surprise of Cecil, when he was informed of the reason of the visit, he was no stranger to the murder of Sir Leopold de Courcy and the Countess of Gowen, but of the rest he was ignorant, and he admired the inscrutable ways of providence, in bringing hidden murder to light. 'I have now', said the Earl, 'as great a surprise in store for you as that you have been communicating to me; let me now congratulate you upon your accession to wealth, splendor, and title.' 'Explain yourself my Lord' said the astonished Theodore! Lord Burleigh informed him that he that morning received an account of the decease of the Earl of Gowen, that he expressed before his death, the most sincere repentance of his ill treatment to his son and his amiable lady, to whom he had written with his own hand, intreating her not to hate his memory. 'I know the virtues of your Matilda so well' added Lord Burleigh, 'that I am sure she will banish all resentment from her breast; your father has left you all he possessed, nor have I been idle in your favor, I have implored our beloved queen, and she has ratified my grant of all the lands of the Priory and castle of Belfont to your Lady, which I now hold as a gift from my sovereign:

you took Matilda without a portion in preference to the rich heiress of Glencoe; you have endured poverty and misery for the sake of each other, and now you are rewarded. I never meant one of our family to be portionless, but I resolved to conceal my intentions and try your virtues and sentiments, they have exceeded my fondest hopes, and behold in me a firm friend, that loves you equal with his own children; here are the deeds of the estates, they are your own, and with regard to the supernatural visit you have received, you are at liberty to act as your wishes prompt you.' Theodore was not slow in expressing his gratitude. As soon as he had been to the court and paid his devoirs to his sovereign, he returned to Cornwall.

Matilda could not suppress her tears when informed of the death of the Earl, and the alteration of his sentiments in her favor, and sincerely regretted he had not survived, once more to behold and bless them. These affectionate remarks endeared her to her amiable husband, who felt the same regret as herself, at the death of the Earl, whom he revered, notwithstanding the cruel treatment he had received; and even this was forgot when he heard the love he expressed for him, before he breathed his last.

The notary was the first person to whom Theodore revealed his rank; the hair of the old man stood erect with terror when informed of the Spectres that had appeared to the Earl, and Theodore was obliged to exert all his eloquence to persuade him to return with him to the Priory; at last he consented, and accompanied the Earl, with many apologies for the freedom he had formerly treated him with. 'Continue it, I beseech you' said Theodore; 'sincerity is what I esteem.'

Donald had procured two men, and by the aid of torches they descended the winding stairs, and pursuing the way the Spectre had shewn Theodore, they arrived at the vault.

The Earl led them to the stone, which they removed, and dug a good depth before they came to the object of their search. The skeleton was much decayed, but the head was most perfect; the Earl minutely examined it and could plainly perceive that it had a deep wound in its forehead, corresponding with the second Spectre he had seen.

They carefully placed the remains in a coffin they had brought with them; and while they was performing this duty, they heard the most sweet and solemn music, which shewed how highly acceptable was this service to their wandering manes.

The next day the funeral took place at Launceston, with great pomp and magnificence, and an elegant monument was erected in Launceston church, to the memory of Lord Edward—on which was engraved the melancholy story of the two brothers.

Theodore, on clearing the ruins of the Priory, discovered an iron chest, containing an immense quantity of gold and jewels; there was a parchment enclosed therein, which described it to be the property of Hugh de Burgh, the first Prior of the foundation, who on his renouncing the world, being offended by his relations buried his wealth, and bequeathed it to them that should be so fortunate as to discover it. Thus by a singular whim of the Prior, Theodore became possessed of a valuable treasure, which he set aside for liberal purposes. He built a noble mansion, on the site of Belfont Priory, at which he resided some months every year, and never felt the least disturbance from any supernatural visitors; all was peace and tranquillity, and the unhappy spirits no longer wandered to disturb the repose of mortals.

Theodore and Matilda were blest with a lovely and dutiful offspring. They were revered by the tenants and domestics, and lived respected and happy, to extreme old age; they died within a few days of each other, and even that short space was painful to the surviver.

Donald and Blanche married soon after Theodore came to the Earldom, who settled them in a valuable farm in Scotland; and ever retained, with his Matilda, a sincere regard for these faithful domestics.

1833

The Mortal Immortal, A Tale

MARY SHELLEY

July 16, 1833.—This is a memorable anniversary for me; on it I complete my three hundred and twenty-third year!

The Wandering Jew?—certainly not. More than eighteen centuries have passed over his head. In comparison with him, I am a very young Immortal.

Am I, then, immortal? This is a question which I have asked myself, by day and night, for now three hundred and three years, and yet cannot answer it. I detected a gray hair amidst my brown locks this very day—that surely signifies decay. Yet it may have remained concealed there for three hundred years—for some persons have become entirely white-headed before twenty years of age.

I will tell my story, and my reader shall judge for me. I will tell my story, and so contrive to pass some few hours of long eternity, become so wearisome to me. For ever! Can it be? to live for ever! I have heard of enchantments, in which the victims were plunged into a deep sleep, to wake, after a hundred years, as fresh as ever: I have heard of the Seven Sleepers—thus to be immortal would not be so burthensome: but, oh! the weight of never-ending time—the tedious passage of the still-succeeding hours! How happy was the fabled Nourjahad!—But to my task.

All the world has heard of Cornelius Agrippa. His memory is as immortal as his arts have made me. All the world has also heard of his scholar, who, unawares, raised the foul fiend during his master's absence, and was destroyed by him. The report, true or false, of this accident, was attended with many inconveniences to the renowned philosopher. All his scholars at once deserted him—his servants disappeared. He had no one near him to put coals on his ever-burning fires while he slept, or to attend to the changeful colours of his medicines while he studied. Experiment after experiment failed, because one pair of hands was insufficient to complete them: the dark spirits laughed at him for not being able to retain a single mortal in his service.

I was then very young—very poor—and very much in love. I had been for about a year the pupil of Cornelius, though I was absent when this accident took place. On my return, my friends implored me not to return to the alchemist's abode. I trembled as I listened to the dire tale they told; I required no second warning; and when Cornelius came and offered me a purse of gold if I would remain under his roof, I felt as if Satan himself tempted me. My teeth chattered—my hair stood on end:—I ran off as fast as my trembling knees would permit.

My failing steps were directed whither for two years they had every evening been attracted,—a gently bubbling spring of pure living waters, beside which lingered a dark-haired girl, whose beaming eyes were fixed on the path I was accustomed each night to tread. I cannot remember the hour when I did not love Bertha; we had been neighbours and playmates from infancy—her parents, like mine, were of humble life, yet respectable—our attachment had been a source of pleasure to them. In an evil hour, a malignant fever carried off both her father and mother, and Bertha became an orphan. She would have found a home beneath my paternal roof, but, unfortunately, the old lady of the near castle, rich, childless, and solitary, declared her intention to adopt her. Henceforth Bertha was clad in silk—inhabited a marble palace—and was looked on as being highly favoured by fortune. But in her new situation among her new associates, Bertha remained true to the friend of her humbler days; she often visited the cottage of my father, and when forbidden to go thither, she would stray towards the neighbouring wood, and meet me beside its shady fountain.

She often declared that she owed no duty to her new protectress equal in sanctity to that which bound us. Yet still I was too poor to marry, and she grew weary of being tormented on my account. She had a haughty but an impatient spirit, and grew angry at the obstacles that prevented our union. We met now after an absence, and she had been sorely beset while I was away: she complained bitterly, and almost reproached me for being poor. I replied hastily,—

'I am honest, if I am poor!—were I not, I might soon become rich!'

This exclamation produced a thousand questions. I feared to shock her by owning the truth, but she drew it from me; and then, casting a look of disdain on me, she said—

'You pretend to love, and you fear to face the Devil for my sake!'

I protested that I had only dreaded to offend her; while she dwelt on the magnitude of the reward that I should receive. Thus encouraged—shamed by her—led on by love and hope, laughing at my late fears, with quick steps and a light heart, I returned to accept the offers of the alchemist, and was instantly installed in my office.

A year passed away. I became possessed of no insignificant sum of money. Custom had banished my fears. In spite of the most painful vigilance, I had never detected the trace of a cloven foot; nor was the studious silence of our abode ever disturbed by demoniac howls. I still continued my stolen interviews with Bertha, and Hope dawned on me—Hope—but not perfect joy; for Bertha fancied that love and security were enemies, and her pleasure was to divide them in my bosom. Though true of heart, she was somewhat of a coquette in manner; and I was jealous as a Turk. She slighted me in a thousand ways, yet would never acknowledge herself to be in the wrong. She would drive me mad with anger, and then force me to beg her pardon. Sometimes she fancied that I was not sufficiently submissive, and then she had some story of a rival, favoured by her protectress. She was surrounded by silk-clad youths—the rich and gay—What chance had the sad-robed scholar of Cornelius compared with these?

On one occasion, the philosopher made such large demands upon my time, that I was unable to meet her as I was wont. He was engaged in some mighty work, and I was forced to remain, day and night, feeding his furnaces and watching his chemical preparations. Bertha waited for me in vain at the fountain. Her haughty spirit fired at this neglect; and when at last I stole out during the few short minutes allotted to me for slumber, and hoped to be consoled by her, she received me with disdain, dismissed me in scorn, and vowed that any man should possess her hand rather than he who could not be in two places at once for her sake. She would be revenged!—And truly she was. In my dingy retreat I heard that she had been hunting, attended by Albert Hoffer. Albert Hoffer was favoured by her protectress, and the three passed in cavalcade before my smoky window. Methought that they mentioned my name—it was followed by a laugh of derision, as her dark eyes glanced contemptuously towards my abode.

Jealousy, with all its venom, and all its misery, entered my breast. Now I shed a torrent of tears, to think that I should never call her mine; and, anon, I imprecated a thousand curses on her inconstancy. Yet, still I must stir the fires of alchemist, still attend on the changes of his unintelligible medicines.

Cornelius had watched for three days and nights, nor closed his eyes. The progress of his alembics was slower than he expected: in spite of his anxiety, sleep weighed upon his eyelids. Again and again he threw off drowsiness with more than human energy; again and again it stole away his senses. He eyed his crucibles wistfully. 'Not ready yet,' he murmured; 'will another night pass before the work is accomplished? Winzy, you are vigilant—you are faithful—you have slept, my boy—you slept last night. Look at that glass vessel. The liquid it contains is of a soft rose-colour: the moment it begins to change its hue, awaken me—till then I may close my eyes. First, it will turn white, and then emit golden flashes; but wait not till then; when the rose-colour fades, rouse me.' I scarcely heard the last words, muttered, as they were, in sleep. Even then he did not quite yield to nature. 'Winzy, my boy,' he again said, 'do not touch the vessel—do not put it to your lips; it is a philter—a philter to cure love; you would not cease to love your Bertha—beware to drink!'

And he slept. His venerable head sunk on his breast, and I scarce heard his regular breathing. For a few minutes I watched the vessel—the rosy hue of the liquid remained unchanged. Then my thoughts wandered—they visited the fountain, and dwelt on a thousand charming scenes never to be renewed—never! Serpents and adders were in my heart as the word 'Never!' half formed itself on my lips. False girl!—false and cruel! Never more would she smile on me as that evening she smiled on Albert. Worthless, detested woman! I would not remain unrevenged—she should see Albert expire at her feet—she should die beneath my vengeance. She had smiled in disdain and triumph—she knew my wretchedness and her power. Yet what power had she!—the power of exciting my hate—my utter scorn—my—oh, all but indifference! Could I attain that—could I regard her with careless eyes, transferring my rejected love to one fairer and more true, that were indeed a victory!

A bright flash darted before my eyes. I had forgotten the medicine of the adept; I gazed on it with wonder: flashes of admirable beauty, more bright than those which the diamond emits when the sun's rays are on it, glanced from the surface of the liquid; an odour the most fragrant and grateful stole over my sense; the vessel seemed one globe of living radiance, lovely to the eye, and most inviting to the taste. The first thought, instinctively inspired by the grosser sense, was, I will—I must drink. I raised the vessel to my lips. 'It will cure me of love—of torture!' Already I had quaffed half of the most delicious liquor ever tasted by the palate of man, when the philosopher stirred. I started—I dropped the glass—the fluid flamed and glanced along the floor, while I felt Cornelius's gripe at my throat, as he shrieked aloud, 'Wretch! you have destroyed the labour of my life!'

The philosopher was totally unaware that I had drunk any portion of his drug. His idea was, and I gave a tacit assent to it, that I had raised the vessel from curiosity, and that, frighted at its brightness, and the flashes of intense light it gave forth, I had let it fall. I never undeceived him. The fire of the medicine was quenched—the fragrance died away—he grew calm, as a philosopher should under the heaviest trials, and dismissed me to rest.

I will not attempt to describe the sleep of glory and bliss which bathed my soul in paradise during the remaining hours of that memorable night. Words would be faint and shallow types of my enjoyment, or of the gladness that possessed my bosom when I woke. I trod air—my thoughts were in heaven. Earth appeared heaven, and my inheritance upon it was to be one trance of delight. 'This it is to be cured of love,' I thought; 'I will see Bertha this day, and she will find her lover cold and regardless; too happy to be disdainful, yet how utterly indifferent to her!'

The hours danced away. The philosopher, secure that he had once succeeded, and believing that he might again, began to concoct the same medicine once more. He was shut up with his books and drugs, and I had a holiday. I dressed myself with care; I looked in an old but polished shield, which served me for a mirror; methought my good looks had wonderfully improved. I hurried beyond the precincts of the town, joy in my soul, the beauty of heaven and earth around me. I turned my steps towards the castle—I could look on its lofty turrets with lightness of heart, for I was cured of love. My Bertha saw me afar off, as I came up the avenue. I know not what sudden impulse animated her bosom, but at the sight, she sprung with a light fawn-like bound down the marble steps, and was hastening towards me. But I had been perceived by another person. The old high-born hag, who called herself her protectress, and was her tyrant, had seen me, also; she hobbled, panting, up the terrace; a page, as ugly as herself, held up her train, and fanned her as she hurried along, and stopped my fair girl with a 'How, now, my bold mistress? whither so fast? Back to your cage—hawks are abroad!'

Bertha clasped her hands—her eyes were still bent on my approaching figure. I saw the contest. How I abhorred the old crone who checked the kind impulses of my Bertha's softening heart. Hitherto, respect for her rank had caused me to avoid the lady of the castle; now I disdained such trivial considerations. I was cured of love, and lifted above all human fears; I hastened forwards, and soon reached the terrace. How lovely Bertha looked! her eyes flashing fire, her cheeks glowing with impatience and anger, she was a thousand times more graceful and charming than ever—I no longer loved—Oh! no, I adored—worshipped—idolized her!

She had that morning been persecuted, with more than usual vehemence, to consent to an immediate marriage with my rival. She was reproached with the encouragement that she had shown him—she was threatened with being turned out of doors with disgrace and shame. Her proud spirit rose in arms at the threat; but when she remembered the scorn that she had heaped upon me, and how, perhaps, she had thus lost one whom she now regarded as her only friend, she wept with remorse and rage. At that moment I appeared. 'O, Winzy!' she exclaimed, 'take me to your mother's cot; swiftly let me leave the detested luxuries and wretchedness of this noble dwelling—take me to poverty and happiness.'

I clasped her in my arms with transport. The old lady was speechless with fury, and broke forth into invective only when we were far on our road to my natal cottage. My mother received the fair fugitive, escaped from a gilt cage to nature and liberty, with tenderness and joy; my father, who loved her, welcomed her heartily; it was a day of rejoicing, which did not need the addition of the celestial potion of the alchemist to steep me in delight.

Soon after this eventful day, I became the husband of Bertha. I ceased to be the scholar of Cornelius, but I continued his friend. I always felt grateful to him for having, unawares, procured me that delicious draught of a divine elixir, which, instead of curing me of love (sad cure! solitary and joyless remedy for evils which seem blessings to the memory), had inspired me with courage and resolution, thus winning for me an inestimable treasure in my Bertha.

I often called to mind that period of trance-like inebriation with wonder. The drink of Cornelius had not fulfilled the task for which he affirmed that it had been prepared, but its effects were more potent and blissful than words can express. They had faded by degrees, yet they lingered long—and painted life in hues of splendour. Bertha often wondered at my lightness of heart and unaccustomed gaity; for, before, I had been rather serious, or even sad, in my disposition. She loved me the better for my cheerful temper, and our days were winged by joy.

Five years afterwards I was suddenly summoned to the bedside of the dying Cornelius. He had sent for me in haste, conjuring my instant presence. I found him stretched on his pallet, enfeebled even to death; all of life that yet remained animated his piercing eyes, and they were fixed on a glass vessel, full of a roseate liquid.

'Behold,' he said, in a broken and inward voice, 'the vanity of human wishes! a second time my hopes are about to be crowned, a second time they are destroyed. Look at that liquor—you remember five years ago I had prepared the same, with the same success;—then, as now, my thirsting lips expected to taste the immortal elixir—you dashed it from me! and at present it is too late.'

He spoke with difficulty, and fell back on his pillow. I could not help saying,—

'How, revered master, can a cure for love restore you to life?'

A faint smile gleamed across his face as I listened earnestly to his scarcely intelligible answer.

'A cure for love and for all things—the Elixir of Immortality. Ah! if now I might drink, I should live for ever!'

As he spoke, a golden flash gleamed from the fluid; a well-remembered fragrance stole over the air; he raised himself, all weak as he was—strength seemed miraculously to re-enter his frame—he stretched forth his hand—a loud explosion startled me—a ray of fire shot up from the elixir, and the glass vessel which contained it was shivered to atoms! I turned my eyes towards the philosopher; he had fallen back—his eyes were glassy—his features rigid—he was dead!

But I lived, and was to live for ever! So said the unfortunate alchemist, and for a few days I believed his words. I remembered the glorious drunkeness that had followed my stolen draught. I reflected on the change I had felt in my frame—in my soul. The bounding elasticity of the one—the buoyant lightness of the other. I surveyed myself in a mirror, and could perceive no change in my features during the space of the five years which had elapsed. I remembered the radiant hues and grateful scent of that delicious beverage—worthy the gift it was capable of bestowing—I was, then, IMMORTAL!

A few days after I laughed at my credulity. The old proverb, that 'a prophet is least regarded in his own country,' was true with respect to me and my defunct master. I loved him as a man—I respected him as a sage—but I derided the notion that he could comma ˑd the powers of darkness, and laughed at the superstitious fears with which he was regarded by the vulgar. He was a wise philosopher, but had no acquaintance with any spirits but those clad in flesh and blood. His science was simply human; and human science, I soon persuaded myself, could never conquer nature's laws so far as to imprison the soul for ever within its carnal habitation. Cornelius had brewed a soul-refreshing drink—more inebriating than wine—sweeter and more fragrant than any fruit: it possessed probably strong medicinal powers, imparting gladness to the heart and vigor to the limbs; but its effects would wear out; already were they diminished in my frame. I was a lucky fellow to have quaffed health and joyous spirits, and perhaps long life, at my master's hands; but my good fortune ended there: longevity was far different from immortality.

I continued to entertain this belief for many years. Sometimes a thought stole across me—Was the alchemist indeed deceived? But my habitual credence was, that I should meet the fate of all the children of Adam at my appointed time—a little late, but still at a natural age. Yet it was certain that I retained a wonderfully youthful look. I was laughed at for my vanity in consulting the mirror so often, but I consulted it in vain—my brow was untrenched—my cheeks—my eyes—my whole person continued as untarnished as in my twentieth year.

I was troubled. I looked at the faded beauty of Bertha—I seemed more like her son. By degrees our neighbours began to make similar observations, and I found at last that I went by the name of the Scholar bewitched. Bertha herself grew uneasy. She became jealous and peevish, and at length she began to question me. We had no children; we were all in all to each other; and though, as she grew older, her vivacious spirit became a little allied to ill-temper, and her beauty sadly diminished, I cherished her in my heart as the mistress I had idolized, the wife I had sought and won with such perfect love.

At last our situation became intolerable: Bertha was fifty—I twenty years of age. I had, in very shame, in some measure adopted the habits of a more advanced age; I no longer mingled in the dance among the young and gay, but my heart bounded along with them while I restrained my feet; and a sorry figure I cut among the Nestors of our village. But before the time I mention, things were altered—we were universally shunned; we were—at least, I was—reported to have kept up an iniquitous acquaintance with some of my former master's supposed friends. Poor Bertha was pitied, but deserted, I was regarded with horror and detestation.

What was to be done? we sat by our winter fire—poverty had made itself felt, for none would buy the produce of my farm; and often I had been forced to journey twenty miles, to some place where I was not known, to dispose of our property. It is true we had saved something for an evil day—that day was come.

We sat by our lone fireside—the old-hearted youth and his antiquated wife. Again Bertha insisted on knowing the truth; she recapitulated all she had ever heard said about me, and added her own observations. She conjured me to cast off the spell; she described how much more comely gray hairs were than my chestnut locks; she descanted on the reverence and respect due to age—how preferable to the slight regard paid to mere children: could I imagine that the despicable gifts of youth and good looks outweighed disgrace, hatred, and scorn? Nay, in the end I should be burnt as a dealer in the black art, while she, to whom I had not deigned to communicate any portion of my good fortune, might be stoned as my accomplice. At length she insinuated that I must share my secret with her, and bestow on her like benefits to those I myself enjoyed, or she would denounce me—and then she burst into tears.

Thus beset, methought it was the best way to tell the truth. I revealed it as tenderly as I could, and spoke only of a *very long life*, not of immortality—which representation, indeed, coincided best with my own ideas. When I ended, I rose and said,

'And now, my Bertha, will you denounce the lover of your youth?—You will not, I know. But it is too hard, my poor wife, that you should suffer from my ill-luck and the accursed arts of Cornelius. I will leave you—you have wealth enough, and friends will return in my absence. I will go; young as I seem, and strong as I am, I can work and gain my bread among strangers, unsuspected and unknown. I loved you in youth; God is my witness that I would not desert you in age, but that your safety and happiness require it.'

I took my cap and moved towards the door; in a moment Bertha's arms were round my neck, and her lips were pressed to mine. 'No, my husband, my Winzy,' she said, 'you shall not go alone—take me with you; we will remove from this place, and, as you say, among strangers we shall be unsuspected and safe. I am not so very old as quite to shame you, my Winzy; and I dare say the charm will soon wear off, and, with the blessing of God, you will become more elderly-looking, as is fitting; you shall not leave me.'

I returned the good soul's embrace heartily. 'I will not, my Bertha; but for your sake I had not thought of such a thing. I will be your true, faithful husband while you are spared to me, and do my duty by you to the last.'

The next day we prepared secretly for our emigration. We were obliged to make great pecuniary sacrifices—it could not be helped. We realised a sum sufficient, at least, to maintain us while Bertha lived; and, without saying adieu to any one, quitted our native country to take refuge in a remote part of western France.

It was a cruel thing to transport poor Bertha from her native village, and the friends of her youth, to a new country, new language, new customs. The strange secret of my destiny rendered this removal immaterial to me; but I compassionated her deeply, and was glad to perceive that she found compensation for her misfortunes in a variety of little ridiculous circumstances. Away from all tell-tale chroniclers, she sought to decrease the apparent disparity of our ages by a thousand feminine arts—rouge, youthful dress, and assumed juvenility of manner. I could not be angry—Did not I myself wear a mask? Why quarrel with hers, because it was less successful? I grieved deeply when I remembered that this was my Bertha, whom I had loved so fondly, and won with such transport—the dark-eyed, dark-haired girl, with smiles of enchanting archness and a step like a fawn—this mincing, simpering, jealous old woman. I should have revered her gray locks and withered cheeks; but thus!—It was my work, I knew; but I did not the less deplore this type of human weakness.

Her jealousy never slept. Her chief occupation was to discover that, in spite of outward appearances, I was myself growing old. I verily believe that the poor soul loved me truly in her heart, but never had woman so tormenting a mode of displaying fondness. She would discern wrinkles in my face and decrepitude in my walk, while I bounded along in youthful vigour, the youngest looking of twenty youths. I never dared address another woman: on one occasion, fancying that the belle of the village regarded me with favouring eyes, she bought me a gray wig. Her constant discourse among her acquaintances was, that though I looked so young, there was ruin at work within my frame; and she affirmed that the worst symptom about me was my apparent health. My youth was a disease, she said, and I ought at all times to prepare, if not for a sudden and awful death, at least to awake some morning white-headed, and bowed down with all the marks of advanced years. I let her talk—I often joined in her conjectures. Her warnings chimed in with my never-ceasing speculations concerning my state, and I took an earnest, though painful, interest in listening to all that her quick wit and excited imagination could say on the subject.

Why dwell on these minute circumstances? We lived on for many long years. Bertha became bed-rid and paralytic: I nursed her as a mother might a child. She grew peevish, and still harped upon one string—of how long I should survive her. It has ever been a source of consolation to me, that I performed my duty scrupulously towards her. She had been mine in youth, she was mine in age, and at last, when I heaped the sod over her corpse, I wept to feel that I had lost all that really bound me to humanity.

Since then how many have been my cares and woes, how few and empty my enjoyments! I pause here in my history—I will pursue it no further. A sailor without rudder or compass, tossed on a stormy sea—a traveller lost on a wide-spread heath, without landmark or star to guide him—such have I been: more lost, more hopeless than either. A nearing ship, a gleam from some far cot, may save them; but I have no beacon except the hope of death.

Death! mysterious, ill-visaged friend of weak humanity! Why alone of all mortals have you cast me from your sheltering fold? O, for the peace of the grave! the deep silence of the iron-bound tomb! that thought would cease to work in my brain, and my heart beat no more with emotions varied only by new forms of sadness!

Am I immortal? I return to my first question. In the first place, is it not more probable that the beverage of the alchemist was fraught rather with longevity than eternal life? Such is my hope. And then be it remembered, that I only drank *half* of the potion prepared by him. Was not the whole necessary to complete the charm? To have drained half the Elixir of Immortality is but to be half immortal—my For-ever is thus truncated and null.

But again, who shall number the years of the half of eternity? I often try to imagine by what rule the infinite may be divided. Sometimes I fancy age advancing upon me. One gray hair I have found. Fool! do I lament? Yes, the fear of age and death often creeps coldly into my heart; and the more I live, the more I dread death, even while I abhor life. Such an enigma is man—born to perish—when he wars, as I do, against the established laws of his nature.

But for this anomaly of feeling surely I might die: the medicine of the alchemist would not be proof against fire—sword—and the strangling waters. I have gazed upon the blue depths of many a placid lake, and the tumultuous rushing of many a mighty river, and have said, peace inhabits those waters; yet I have turned my steps away, to live yet another day. I have asked myself, whether suicide would be a crime in one to whom thus only the portals of the other world could be opened. I have done all, except presenting myself as a soldier or duellist, an object of destruction to my—no, *not* my fellow-mortals, and therefore I have shrunk away. They are not my fellows. The inextinguishable power of the life in my frame, and their ephemeral existence, place us wide as the poles asunder. I could not raise a hand against the meanest or the most powerful among them.

Thus I have lived on for many a year—alone, and weary of myself—desirous of death, yet never dying—a mortal immortal. Neither ambition nor avarice can enter my mind, and the ardent love that gnaws at my heart, never to be returned—never to find an equal on which to expend itself—lives there only to torment me.

This very day I conceived a design by which I may end all—without self-slaughter, without making another man a Cain—an expedition, which mortal frame can never survive, even endured with the youth and strength that inhabits mine. Thus I shall put my immortality to the test, and rest for ever—or return, the wonder and benefactor of the human species.

Before I go, a miserable vanity has caused me to pen these pages. I would not die, and leave no name behind. Three centuries have passed since I quaffed the fatal beverage: another year shall not elapse before, encountering gigantic dangers—warring with the powers of frost in their home—beset by famine, toil, and tempest—I yield this body, too tenacious a cage for a soul which thirsts for freedom, to the destructive elements of air and water—or, if I survive, my name shall be recorded as one of the most famous among the sons of men; and, my task achieved, I shall adopt more resolute means, and, by scattering and annihilating the atoms that compose my frame, set at liberty the life imprisoned within, and so cruelly prevented from soaring from this dim earth to a sphere more congenial to its immortal essence.

1833 *

Napoleon and the Spectre

CHARLOTTE BRONTE

W ell, as I was saying, the Emperor got into bed.

'Chevalier,' says he to his valet, 'let down those window-curtains, and shut the casement before you leave the room.'

Chevalier did as he was told, and then, taking up his candlestick, departed.

In a few minutes the Emperor felt his pillow becoming rather hard, and he got up to shake it. As he did so a slight rustling noise was heard near the bed-head. His Majesty listened, but all was silent as he lay down again.

Scarcely had he settled into a peaceful attitude of repose, when he was disturbed by a sensation of thirst. Lifting himself on his elbow, he took a glass of lemonade from the small stand which was placed beside him. He refreshed himself by a deep draught. As he returned the goblet to its station a deep groan burst from a kind of closet in one corner of the apartment.

'Who's there?' cried the Emperor, seizing his pistols. 'Speak, or I'll blow your brains out.'

This threat produced no other effect than a short, sharp laugh, and a dead silence followed.

The Emperor started from his couch, and, hastily throwing on a *robe-de-chambre* which hung over the back of a chair, stepped courageously to the haunted closet. As he opened the door something rustled. He sprang forward sword in hand. No soul or even substance appeared, and the rustling, it was evident, proceeded from the falling of a cloak, which had been suspended by a peg from the door.

Half ashamed of himself he returned to bed.

*completed 1833; published 1919

Just as he was about once more to close his eyes, the light of the three wax tapers, which burned in a silver branch over the mantelpiece, was suddenly darkened. He looked up. A black, opaque shadow obscured it. Sweating with terror, the Emperor put out his hand to seize the bell-rope, but some invisible being snatched it rudely from his grasp, and at the same instant the ominous shade vanished.

'Pooh!' exclaimed Napoleon, 'it was but an ocular delusion.'

'Was it?' whispered a hollow voice, in deep mysterious tones, close to his ear. 'Was it a delusion, Emperor of France? No! all thou hast heard and seen is sad forewarning reality. Rise, lifter of the Eagle Standard! Awake, swayer of the Lily Sceptre! Follow me, Napoleon, and thou shalt see more.'

As the voice ceased, a form dawned on his astonished sight. It was that of a tall, thin man, dressed in a blue surtout edged with gold lace. It wore a black cravat very tightly round its neck, and confined by two little sticks placed behind each ear. The countenance was livid; the tongue protruded from between the teeth, and the eyes all glazed and bloodshot started with frightful prominence from their sockets.

'Mon Dieu!' exclaimed the Emperor, 'what do I see? Spectre, whence cometh thou?'

The apparition spoke not, but gliding forward beckoned Napoleon with uplifted finger to follow.

Controlled by a mysterious influence, which deprived him of the capability of either thinking or acting for himself, he obeyed in silence.

The solid wall of the apartment fell open as they approached, and, when both had passed through, it closed behind them with a noise like thunder.

They would now have been in total darkness had it not been for a dim light which shone round the ghost and revealed the damp walls of a long, vaulted passage. Down this they proceeded with mute rapidity. Ere long a cool, refreshing breeze, which rushed wailing up the vault and caused the Emperor to wrap his loose nightdress closer round, announced their approach to the open air.

This they soon reached, and Napoleon found himself in one of the principal streets of Paris.

'Worthy Spirit,' said he, shivering in the chill night air, 'permit me to return and put on some additional clothing. I will be with you again presently.'

'Forward,' replied his companion sternly.

He felt compelled, in spite of the rising indignation which almost choked him, to obey.

On they went through the deserted streets till they arrived at a lofty house built on the banks of the Seine. Here the Spectre stopped, the gates rolled back to receive them, and they entered a large marble hall which was partly concealed by a curtain drawn across, through the half transparent folds of which a bright light might be seen burning with dazzling lustre. A row of fine female figures, richly attired, stood before this screen. They wore on their heads garlands of the most beautiful flowers, but their faces were concealed by ghastly masks representing death's-heads.

'What is all this mummery?' cried the Emperor, making an effort to shake off the mental shackles by which he was so unwillingly restrained, 'Where am I, and why have I been brought here?'

'Silence,' said the guide, lolling out still further his black and bloody tongue. 'Silence, if thou wouldst escape instant death.'

The Emperor would have replied, his natural courage overcoming the temporary awe to which he had at first been subjected, but just then a strain of wild, supernatural music swelled behind the huge curtain, which waved to and fro, and bellied slowly out as if agitated by some internal commotion or battle of waving winds. At the same moment an overpowering mixture of the scents of mortal corruption, blent with the richest Eastern odours, stole through the haunted hall.

A murmur of many voices was now heard at a distance, and something grasped his arm eagerly from behind.

He turned hastily round. His eyes met the well-known countenance of Marie Louise.

'What! are you in this infernal place, too?' said he. 'What has brought you here?'

'Will your Majesty permit me to ask the same question of yourself?' said the Empress, smiling.

He made no reply; astonishment prevented him.

No curtain now intervened between him and the light. It had been removed as if by magic, and a splendid chandelier appeared suspended over his head. Throngs of ladies, richly dressed, but without death's-head masks, stood round, and a due proportion of gay cavaliers was mingled with them. Music was still sounding, but it was seen to proceed from a band of mortal musicians stationed in an orchestra near at hand. The air was yet redolent of incense, but it was incense unblended with stench.

'Mon Dieu!' cried the Emperor, 'how is all this come about? Where in the world is Piche?'

'Piche?' replied the Empress. 'What does your Majesty mean? Had you not better leave the apartment and retire to rest?'

'Leave the apartment? Why, where am I?'

'In my private drawing-room, surrounded by a few particular persons of the Court whom I had invited this evening to a ball. You entered a few minutes since in your nightdress with your eyes fixed and wide open. I suppose from the astonishment you now testify that you were walking in your sleep.'

The Emperor immediately fell into a fit of catalepsy, in which he continued during the whole of that night and the greater part of next day.

1852

The Old Nurse's Story

ELIZABETH GASKELL

You know, my dears, that your mother was an orphan, and an only child; and I dare say you have heard that your grandfather was a clergyman up in Westmorland, where I come from. I was just a girl in the village school, when, one day, your grandmother came in to ask the mistress if there was any scholar there who would do for a nurse maid; and mighty proud I was, I can tell ye, when the mistress called me up, and spoke to my being a good girl at my needle, and a steady, honest girl, and one whose parents were very respectable, though they might be poor. I thought I should like nothing better than to serve the pretty young lady, who was blushing as deep as I was as she spoke of the coming baby, and what I should have to do with it. However, I see you don't care so much for this part of my story as for what you think is to come, so I'll tell you at once. I was engaged and settled at the parsonage before Miss Rosamond (that was the baby, who is now your mother) was born. To be sure, I had little enough to do with her when she came, for she was never out of her mother's arms, and slept by her all night long; and proud enough was I sometimes when missis trusted her to me.

There never was such a baby before or since, though you've all of you been fine enough in your turns; but for sweet, winning ways, you've none of you come up to your mother. She took after her mother, who was a real lady born; a Miss Furnivall, a granddaughter of Lord Furnivall's, in Northumberland. I believe she had neither brother nor sister, and had been brought up in my lord's family till she had married your grandfather, who was just a curate, son to a shopkeeper in Carlisle—but a clever, fine gentleman as ever was—and one who was a right-down hard worker in his parish, which was very wide, and scattered all abroad over the Westmorland Fells. When your mother, little Miss Rosamond, was about four or five years old, both her parents died in a fortnight—one after the other. Ah! that was a sad time. My pretty young mistress and me was looking for another baby, when my master came home from one of his long rides, wet and tired, and took the fever he died of; and then she never held up her head again, but just lived to see her dead baby, and have it laid on her breast before she sighed away her life. My mistress had asked me, on her death-bed, never to leave Miss Rosamond; but if she had never spoken a word, I would have gone with the little child to the end of the world.

The next thing, and before we had well stilled our sobs, the executors and guardians came to settle the affairs. They were my poor young mistress's own cousin, Lord Furnivall, and Mr. Esthwaite, my master's brother, a shopkeeper in Manchester; not so well-to-do then as he was afterwards, and with a large family rising about him. Well! I don't know if it were their settling, or because of a letter my mistresss wrote on her death-bed to her cousin, my lord; but somehow it was settled that Miss Rosamond and me were to go to Furnivall Manor House, in Northumberland, and my lord spoke as if it had been her mother's wish that she should live with his family, and as if he had no objections, for that one or two more or less could make no difference in so grand a household. So though that was not the way in which I should have wished the coming of my bright and pretty pet to have been looked at—who was like a sun-beam to any family, be it ever so grand—I was well pleased that all the folks in the Dale should stare and admire when they heard I was going to be young lady's maid at my Lord Furnivall's at Furnivall Manor.

But I made a mistake in thinking we were to go and live where my lord did. It turned out that the family had left Furnivall Manor House fifty years or more. I could not hear that my poor young mistress had ever been there, though she had been brought up in the family; and I was sorry for that, for I should have liked Miss Rosamond's youth to have passed where her mother's had been.

My lord's gentlemen, from whom I asked so many questions as I durst, said that the Manor House was at the foot of the Cumberland Fells, and a very grand place; that an old Miss Furnivall, a great-aunt of my lord's, lived there, with only a few servants; but that it was a very healthy place, and my lord had thought that it would suit Miss

Rosamond very well for a few years, and that her being there might perhaps amuse his old aunt.

I was bidden by my lord to have Miss Rosamond's things ready by a certain day. He was a stern, proud man, as they say all the Lords Furnivall were; and he never spoke a word more than was necessary. Folk did say he had loved my young mistress; but that, because she knew that his father would object, she would never listen to him, and married Mr. Esthwaite, but I don't know. He never married, at any rate. But he never took much notice of Miss Rosamond; which I thought he might have done if he had cared for her dead mother. He sent his gentleman with us to Manor House, telling him to join him at Newcastle that same evening; so there was no great length of time for him to make us known to all the strangers before he, too, shook us off; and we were left, two lonely young things (I was not eighteen), in the great, old Manor House.

It seems like yesterday that we drove there. We had left our own dear parsonage very early, and we had both cried as if our hearts would break, though we were travelling in my lord's carriage, which I thought so much of once. And now it was long past noon on a September day, and we stopped to change horses for the last time at a little town all full of colliers and miners. Miss Rosamond had fallen asleep, but Mr. Henry told me to waken her, that she might see the park and the Manor House as we drove up. I thought it rather a pity; but I did what he bade me, for fear he should complain of me to my lord. We had left all signs of a town, or even a village, and were then inside the gates of a large wild park—not like the parks here in the north, but with rocks, and the noise of running water, and gnarled thorn-trees, and old oaks all white and peeled with age.

The road went up about two miles, and then we saw a great and stately house, with many trees close around it, so close that in some places their branches dragged against the walls when the wind blew; and some huge broken down; for no one seemed to take much charge of the place; to lop the wood, or to keep the moss-covered carriage-way in order. Only in front of the house all was clear. The great oval drive was without a weed; and neither tree nor creeper was allowed to grow over the long, many-windowed front; at both sides of which a wing projected, which were each the ends of other side fronts. for the house, although it was so desolate, was even grander than I expected. Behind it rose the fells, which seemed unenclosed and bare enough; and on the left-hand of the house, as you stood facing it, was a little, old-fashioned flower garden, as I found out afterwards. A door opened out upon it from the west front; it had been scooped out of the thick dark wood for some old Lady Furnivall; but the branches of the great forest trees had grown and over-shadowed it again, and there were very few flowers that would live there at that time.

When we drove up to the great front entrance, and went into the hall I thought we should be lost—it was so large, and vast, and grand. There was a chandelier, all of bronze, hung down from the middle of the ceiling; and I had never seen one before, and looked at it all in amaze. Then, at one end of the hall, was a great fire-place, as large as the sides of the houses in my country, with massy andirons and dogs to hold the wood; and by it were heavy, old-fashioned sofas. At the opposite end of the hall, to the left as you went in—on the western side—was an organ built into the wall, and so large that it filled up the best part of that end. Beyond it, on the same side, was a door; and opposite, on each side of the fire-place, were also doors leading to the east front; but those I never went through as long as I stayed in the house, so I can't tell you what lay beyond.

The afternoon was closing in, and the hall, which had no fire lighted in it, looked dark and gloomy, but we did not stay there a moment. The old servant, who had opened the door for us, bowed to Mr. Henry, and took us to through the door at the farther side of the great organ, and led us through several smaller halls and passages into the west drawing-room, where he said that Miss Furnivall was sitting. Poor little Miss Rosamond held very tight to me, as if she were scared and lost in that great place, and as for myself, I was not much better. The west drawing-room was very cheerful-looking, with a warm fire in it, and plenty of wood, comfortable furniture about. Miss Furnivall was an old lady not far from eighty, I should think, but I do not know. She was thin and tall, and had a face as full of fine wrinkles as if they had been drawn all over it with a needle's point. Her eyes were very watchful, to make up, I suppose, for her being so deaf as to be obliged to use a trumpet.

Sitting with her, working at the same great piece of tapestry, was Mrs. Stark, her maid and companion, and almost as old as she was. She had lived with Miss Furnivall ever since they were both young, and now she seemed more like a friend than a servant; she looked so cold and grey and stony—as if she had never loved or cared for anyone; and I don't suppose she did for anyone except her mistress; and, owing to the great deafness of the latter, Mrs. Stark treated her very much as if she were a child. Mr. Henry gave some message from my lord, and then he bowed good-bye to us all—taking no notice of my sweet little Miss Rosamond's outstretched hand—and left us standing there, being looked at by the two ladies through their spectacles.

I was right glad when they rang for the old footman who had shown us in at first, and told him to take us to our rooms. So we went out of that great drawing-room, and into another sitting-room, and out of that, and then up a great flight of stairs, and along a broad gallery—which was something like a library, having books all down one side and windows and writing-tables all down the other—till we came to our rooms, which I was not sorry to hear were just over the kitchens; for I began to think I should be lost in that wilderness of a house. There was an old nursery that had been used for all the little lords and ladies long ago, with a pleasant fire burning in the grate, and the kettle boiling on the hob, and tea-things spread out on the table; and out of that room was the night-nursery, with a little crib for Miss Rosamond close to my bed. And old James called up Dorothy, his wife, to bid us welcome; and both he and she were so hospitable and kind that by and by Miss Rosamond and me felt quite at home; and by the time tea was over, she was sitting on Dorothy's knee, and chattering away as fast as her little tongue could go.

I soon found out that Dorothy was from Westmorland, and that bound her and me together, as it were; and I would never wish to meet with kinder people than were old James and his wife. James had lived pretty nearly all his life in my lord's family, and thought there was no one so grand as they. He even looked down a little on his wife; because, till he had married her, she had never lived in any but a farmer's household. But he was very fond of her, as well he might be. They had one servant under them, to do all the rough work. Agnes, they called her; and she and me and James and Dorothy, with Miss Furnivall and Mrs. Stark, made up the family; always remembering my sweet Miss Rosamond. I used to wonder what they had done before she came, they thought so much of her now. Kitchen and drawing-room, it was all the same. The hard, sad Miss Furnivall, and the cold Mrs. Stark, looked pleased when she came fluttering in like a bird, playing and pranking hither and thither, with a continual murmur, and pretty prattle of gladness. I am sure, they were sorry many a time when she flitted away into the kitchen, though they were too proud to ask her to stay with them, and were a little surprised at her taste; though to be sure, as Mrs. Stark said, it was not to be wondered at, remembering what stock her father had come of.

The great, old rambling house was a famous place for little Miss Rosamond. She made expeditions all over it, with me at her heels; all except the east wing, which was never opened, and whither we never thought of going. But in the western and northern part was many a pleasant room; full of things that were curiosities to us, though they might not have been to people who had seen more. The windows were darkened by the sweeping boughs of the trees, and the ivy which had overgrown them: but, in the green gloom, we could manage to see old China jars and carved ivory boxes, and great heavy books, and, above all, the old pictures.

Once, I remember, my darling would have Dorothy go with us to tell us who they all were; for they were all portraits of some of my lord's family, though Dorothy could not tell us the names of every one. We had gone through most of the rooms, when we came to the old state drawing-room over the hall, and there was a picture of Miss Furnivall; or, as she was called in those days, Miss Grace, for she was the younger sister. Such a beauty she must have been! but with such a set, proud look, and such scorn looking out of her handsome eyes, with her eyebrows just a little raised, as if she were wondering how anyone could have the impertinence to look at her; and her lip curled at us, as we stood there gazing. She had a dress on, the like of which I had never seen before, but it was all the fashion when she was young: a hat of some soft white stuff like beaver, pulled a little over her brows, and a beautiful plume of feathers sweeping round it on one side; and her gown of blue satin was open in front to a quilted white stomacher.

'Well, to be sure!' said I, when I had gazed my fill. 'Flesh is grass, they do say; but who would have thought that Miss Furnivall had been such an out-and-out beauty, to see her now?'

'Yes,' said Dorothy. 'Folks change sadly. But if what my master's father used to say was true, Miss Furnivall, the elder sister, was handsomer than Miss Grace. Her picture is here somewhere; but, if I show it you, you must never let on, even to James, that you have seen it. Can the little lady hold her tongue, think you?' asked she.

I was not so sure, for she was such a little sweet, bold, open-spoken child, so I set her to hide herself; and then I helped Dorothy to turn a great picture, that leaned with its face towards the wall, and was not hung up as the others were. To be sure, it beat Miss Grace for beauty; and, I think, for scornful pride too, though in that matter it might be hard to choose. I could have looked at it an hour, but Dorothy seemed half frightened at having shown it to me and hurried it back again, and bade me run and find Miss Rosamond, for that there were some ugly places about the house, where she should like ill for the child to go. I was a brave, high-spirited girl, and thought little of what the old woman said, for I liked hide-and-seek as well as any child in the parish; so off I ran to find my little one.

As winter drew on, and the days grew shorter, I was sometimes almost certain that I heard a noise as if someone was playing on the great organ in the hall. I did not hear it every evening; but, certainly, I did very often; usually when I was sitting with Miss Rosamond, after I had put her to bed, and keeping quite still and silent in the bedroom. Then I used to hear it booming and swelling away in the distance. The first night, when I went down to my supper, I asked Dorothy who had been playing music, and James said very shortly that I was a gowk to take the wind soughing among the trees for music; but I saw Dorothy look at him very fearfully, and Bessy, the kitchen-maid, said something beneath her breath, and went quite white. I saw they did not like my question, so I held my peace till I was with Dorothy alone, when I knew I could get a good deal out of her.

So, the next day, I watched my time, and I coaxed and asked her who it was that played the organ; for I knew that it was the organ and not the wind well enough, for all I had kept silence before James. But Dorothy had had her lesson, I'll warrant, and never a word could I get from her. So then I tried Bessy, though I had always held my head rather above her, as I was evened to James and Dorothy, and she was little better than their servant. So she said I must never, never tell; and if I ever told, I was never to say *she* had told me; but it was a very strange noise, and she had heard it many a time, but most of all on winter nights, and before storms; and folks did say, it was the old lord playing on the great organ in the hall, just as he used to do when he was alive; but who the old lord was, or why he played, and why he played on stormy winter evenings in particular, she either could not or would not tell me. Well! I told you I had a brave heart; and I thought it was rather pleasant to have that grand music rolling about the house, let who would be the player; for now it rose above the great gusts of wind, and wailed and triumphed just like a living creature, and then it fell to a softness most complete; only it was always music and tunes, so it was nonsense to call it the wind.

I thought at first that it might be Miss Furnivall who played, unknown to Bessy; but one day when I was in the hall by myself, I opened the organ and peeped all above it and around it, as I had done to the organ in Crosthwaite Church once before, and I saw it was all broken and destroyed inside, though it looked so brave and fine; and then, though it was noonday, my flesh began to creep a little, and I shut it up, and ran away pretty quickly to my own bright nursery; and I did not like hearing the music for some time after that, any more than James and Dorothy did.

All this time Miss Rosamond was making herself more and more beloved. The old ladies liked her to dine with them at their early dinner; James stood behind Miss Furnivall's chair, and I behind Miss Rosamond's all in state; and, after dinner, she would play about in a corner of the great drawing-room, as still as any mouse, while Miss Furnivall slept, and I had my dinner in the kitchen. But she was glad enough to come to me in the nursery afterwards; for, as she said, Miss Furnivall was so sad, and Mrs. Stark so dull; but she and I were merry enough; and, by and by, I got not to care for that weird, rolling music, which did one no harm, if we did not know where it came from.

That winter was very cold. In the middle of October the frosts began, and lasted many, many weeks. I remember, one day at dinner, Miss Furnivall lifted up her sad, heavy eyes said to Mrs. Stark, 'I am afraid we shall have a terrible winter,' in a strange kind of meaning way. but Mrs. Stark pretended not to hear, and talked very loud of something else. My little lady and I did not care for the frost; not we! As long as it was dry we climbed up the steep brows, behind the house, and went up on the Fells, which were bleak, and bare enough, and there we ran races in the fresh, sharp air; and once we came down by a new path that took us past the two old gnarled holly trees, which grew about half way down by the east side of the house.

But the days grew shorter and shorter; and the old lord—if it was he—played more and more stormily and sadly on the great organ. One Sunday afternoon—it must have been towards the end of November—I asked Dorothy to take charge of little Missy when she came out of the drawing-room, after Miss Furnivall had had her nap; for it was too cold to take her with me to church, and yet I wanted to go. And Dorothy was glad enough to promise, and was so fond of the child that all seemed well; and Bessy and I set off briskly, though the sky hung heavy and black over the white earth, as if the night had never fully gone away; and the air, though still, was very biting and keen.

'We shall have a fall of snow,' said Bessy to me. And sure enough, even while we were in church, it came down thick, in great, large flakes, so thick it almost darkened the windows. It had stopped snowing before we came out, but it lay soft, thick and deep beneath our feet as we tramped home. Before we got to the hall the moon rose, and I think it was lighter then—what with the moon, and what with the white dazzling snow—than it had been when we went to church, between two and three o'clock. I have not told you that Miss Furnivall and Mrs. Stark never went to church; they used to read the prayers together, in their quiet, gloomy way; they seemed to feel the Sunday very long with their tapestry-work to be busy at.

So when I went to Dorothy in the kitchen, to fetch Miss Rosamond and take her upstairs with me, I did not much wonder when the old woman told me that the ladies had kept the child with them, and that she had never come to the kitchen, as I had bidden her when she was tired of behaving pretty in the drawing-room. So I took off my things and went to find her, and bring her to her supper in the nursery. But when I went into the best drawing-room there sat the two old ladies, very still and quiet, dropping out a word now and then but looking as if nothing so bright and merry as Miss Rosamond had ever been near them. Still I thought she might be hiding from me; it was one of her pretty ways; and that she had persuaded them to look as if they knew nothing about her; so I went softly peeping under this sofa, and behind that chair, making believe I was sadly frightened at not finding her.

'What's the matter, Hester?' said Mrs. Stark sharply. I don't know if Miss Furnivall had seen me, for, as I told you, she was very deaf, and she sat quite still, idly staring into the fire, with her hopeless face. 'I'm only looking for my little Rosy-Posy,' I replied, still thinking that the child was there, and near me, though I could not see her.

'Miss Rosamond is not here,' said Mrs. Stark. 'She went away more than an hour ago to find Dorothy.' And she too turned and went on looking into the fire.

My heart sank at this, and I began to wish I had never left my darling. I went back to Dorothy and told her. James was gone out for the day, but she and me and Bessy took lights and went up into the nursery first, and then we roamed over the great large house, calling and entreating Miss Rosamond to come out of her hiding-place, and not frighten us to death in that way. But there was no answer; no sound.

'Oh!' said I at last. 'Can she have got into the east wing and hidden there?'

But Dorothy said it was not possible, for that she herself had never been there; that the doors were always locked, and my lord's steward had the keys, she believed; at any rate, neither she nor James had ever seen them. So I said I would go back and see if, after all, she was not hidden in the drawing-room, unknown to the old ladies; and if I found her there I said I would whip her well for the fright she had given me; but I never meant to do it. Well, I went back to the west drawing-room, and I told Mrs. Stark we could not find her anywhere, and asked for leave to look all about the furniture there, for I thought now, that she might have fallen asleep in some warm hidden corner; but no! we looked, Miss Furnivall got up and looked, trembling all over, and she was nowhere there; then we set off again, everyone in the house, and looked in all the places we had searched before, but we could not find her. Miss Furnivall shivered and shook so much that Mrs. Stark took her back into the warm drawing-room; but not before they had made me promise to bring her to them when she was found. Welladay! I began to think she never would be found, when I bethought me to look out into the great front court, all covered with snow.

I was upstairs when I looked out; but it was such clear moonlight I could see, quite plain, two little footprints, which might be traced from the hall door and round the corner of the east wing. I don't know how I got down, but I tugged open the great, stiff hall door; and, throwing the skirt of my own gown over my head for a cloak, I ran out. I turned the east corner, and there a black shadow fell on the snow; but when I came again into the moonlight, there were the little foot-marks going up—up to the Fells. It was bitter cold; so cold that the air almost took the skin off my face as I ran, but I ran on, crying to think how my poor little darling must be perished and frightened. I was within sight of the holly trees when I saw a shepherd coming down the hill, bearing something in his arms wrapped in his maud. He shouted to me, and asked me if I had lost a bairn; and, when I could not speak for crying, he bore towards me, and I saw my wee bairnie lying still, and white, and stiff, in his arms, as if she had been dead. He told me he had been up the Fells to gather in his sheep, before the deep cold of night came on, and that under the holly trees (black marks on the hill-side, where no other bush was for miles around) he had found my little lady—my lamb—my queen—my darling—stiff and cold, in the terrible sleep which is frost-begotten.

Oh! the joy, and the tears of having her in my arms once again! for I would not let him carry her; but took her, maud and all, into my own arms, and held her near my own warm neck and heart, and felt the life stealing slowly back again into her little gentle limbs. But she was still insensible when we reached the hall, and I had no breath for speech. We went in by the kitchen door.

'Bring the warming-pan,' said I; and I carried her upstairs, and began undressing her by the nursery fire, which Bessy had kept up. I called my little lammie all the sweet and playful names I could think of—even while my eyes were blinded by my tears; and at last, oh! at length she opened her large, blue eyes. Then I put her into her warm bed, and sent Dorothy down to tell Miss Furnivall that all was well; and I made up my mind to sit by my darling's bedside the live-long night. She fell away into a soft sleep as soon as her pretty head had touched the pillow, and I watched by her until morning light; when she wakened up bright and clear—or so I thought at first—and, my dears, so I think now.

She said that she had fancied that she should like to go to Dorothy, for that both the old ladies were asleep, and it was very dull in the drawing-room; and that, as she was going through the west lobby, she saw the snow through the high widow falling—falling—soft and steady. But she wanted to see it lying pretty and white on the ground; so she made her way into the great hall; and then, going to the window, she saw it bright and soft upon the drive; but while she stood there, she saw a little girl, not so old as she was, 'but so pretty,' said my darling, 'and this little girl beckoned to me to come out; and oh, she was so pretty and so sweet, I could not choose but go.' And then this other little girl had taken her by the hand, and side by side the two had gone round the east corner.

'Now you are a naughty little girl, and telling stories,' said I. 'What would your good mamma, that is in heaven, and never told a story in her life, say to her little Rosamond, if she heard her—and I dare say she does—telling stories!'

'Indeed, Hester,' sobbed out my child, 'I'm telling you true. Indeed I am.'

'Don't tell me!' said I, very stern. 'I tracked you by your footmarks through the snow; there were only yours to be seen; and if you had had a little girl to go hand in hand with you up the hill, don't you think the footprints would have gone along with yours?'

'I can't help it, dear, dear Hester,' said she, crying, 'if they did not. I never looked at her feet, but she held my hand fast and tight in her little one, and it was very, very cold. She took me up the fell path, up to the holly trees; and there I saw a lady weeping and crying; but when she saw me, she hushed her weeping, and smiled very proud and grand, and took me on her knee, and began to lull me to sleep; and that's all, Hester—but that is true, and my dear mamma knows it is,' said she, crying. So I thought the child was in a fever, and pretended to believe her, as she went over her story—and over and over again, and always the same. At last Dorothy knocked at the door with Miss Rosamond's breakfast; and she told me the old ladies were down in the eating-parlour, and that they wanted to speak to me. They had both been into the night-nursery the evening before, but it was after Miss Rosamond was asleep; so they had only looked at her—not asked me any questions.

'I shall catch it,' thought I to myself, as I went along the north gallery. 'And yet,' I thought, taking courage, 'it was in their charge I left her; and it's they that's to blame for letting her steal away unknown and unwatched.' So I went in boldly and told my story. I told it all to Miss Furnivall, shouting it close to her ear; but when I came to the mention of the other little girl out in the snow, coaxing and tempting her out, and willing her up to the grand and beautiful lady by the holly tree, she threw her arms up—her old and withered arms—and cried aloud, 'Oh! Heaven, forgive! Have mercy!'

Mrs. Stark took hold of her; roughly enough, I thought; but she was past Mrs. Stark's management, and spoke to me, in a kind of wild warning and authority.

'Hester, keep her from that child! It will lure her to her death! That evil child! Tell her it is a wicked, naughty child.' Then Mrs. Stark hurried me out of the room; where, indeed, I was glad enough to go; but Miss Furnivall kept shrieking out, 'Oh! have mercy! Wilt Thou never forgive! It is many a long year ago—'

I was very uneasy in my mind after that. I durst never leave Miss Rosamond, night or day, for fear lest she might slip off again, after some fancy or other; and all the more because I thought I could make out that Miss Furnivall was crazy, from their odd ways about her; and I was afraid lest something of the same kind (which might be in the family, you know) hung over my darling. And the great frost never ceased all this time; and whenever it was a more stormy night than usual, between the gusts, and through the wind, we heard the old lord playing on the great organ. But, old lord or not, wherever Miss Rosamond went, there I followed; for my love for her, pretty, helpless orphan, was stronger than fear for the grand and terrible sound. Besides, it rested with me to keep her cheerful and merry, as beseemed her age. So we played together, and wandered together, here and there, and everywhere; for I never dared to lose sight of her again in that large and rambling house. And so it happened, that one afternoon, not long before Christmas Day, we were playing together on the billiard-table in the great hall (not that we knew the way of playing, but she liked to roll the smooth, ivory balls with her pretty hands, and I liked to do whatever she did); and, by and by, without our noticing it, it grew dusk indoors, though it was still light in the open air, and I was thinking of taking her back into the nursery, when, all of a sudden, she cried out:

'Look! Hester, look! there is my poor little girl out in the snow!'

I turned towards the long narrow windows, and there, sure enough, I saw a little girl, less than my Miss Rosamond—dressed all unfit to be out of doors such a bitter night—crying, and beating against the window-panes, as if she wanted to be let in. She seemed to sob and wail, till Miss Rosamond could bear it no longer, and was flying to the door to open it, when, all of a sudden, and close up upon us, the great organ pealed out so loud and thundering, it fairly made me tremble; and all the more, when I remembered me that, even in the stillness of that dead-cold weather, I had heard no sound of little battering hands upon the window glass, although the Phantom Child had seemed to put forth all its force; and, although I had seen it wail and cry, no faintest touch of sound had fallen upon my ears. Whether I remembered all this at the very moment, I do not know; the great organ sound had so stunned me into terror; but this I know: I caught up Miss Rosamond before she got the hall door opened, and clutched her, and carried her away, kicking and screaming, into the large bright kitchen, where Dorothy and Agnes were busy with their mince pies.

'What is the matter with my sweet one?' cried Dorothy, as I bore in Miss Rosamond, who was sobbing as if her heart would break.

'She won't let me open the door for my little girl to come in; and she'll die if she is out on the Fells all night. Cruel, naughty Hester,' she said, slapping me; but she might have struck harder, for I had seen a look of ghastly terror on Dorothy's face, which made my very blood run cold.

'Shut the back-kitchen door fast, and bolt it well,' said she to Agnes. She said no more; she gave me raisins and almonds to quiet Miss Rosamond: but she sobbed about the little girl in the snow, and would not touch any of the good things. I was thankful when she cried herself to sleep in bed. Then I stole down to the kitchen and told Dorothy I had made up my mind. I would carry my darling back to my father's house in Applethwaite; where, if we lived humbly, we lived at peace. I said I had been frightened enough with the old lord's organ-playing; but now that I had seen for myself this little moaning child, all decked out as no child in the neighbourhood could be, beating and battering to get in, yet always without any sound or noise—with the dark wound on her right shoulder; and that Miss Rosamond had known it again for the phantom that had nearly lured her to her death (which Dorothy knew was true); I would stand it no longer.

I saw Dorothy change colour once or twice. When I had done she told me she did not think I could take Miss Rosamond with me, for that she was my lord's ward, and I had no right over her; and she asked me, would I leave the child that I was so fond of just for sounds and sights that could do me no harm; and that they had all had to get used to in their turns? I was all in a hot, trembling passion; and I said it was very well for her to talk, that knew what these sights and noises betokened, and that had, perhaps, had something to do with the Spectre-Child while it was alive. And I taunted her so, that she told me all she knew, at last, and then I wished I had never been told, for it only made me afraid more than ever.

She said she had heard the tale from old neighbours, that were alive when she was first married; when folks used to come to the hall sometimes, before it had got such a bad name on the country-side: it might not be true, or it might, what she had been told.

The old lord was Miss Furnivall's father—Miss Grace as Dorothy called her, for Miss Maude was the elder, and Miss Furnivall by rights. The old lord was eaten up with pride. Such a proud man was never seen or heard of; and his daughters were like him. No one was good enough to wed them, although they had choice enough; for they were the great beauties of their day, as I had seen by their portraits where they hung in the state drawing-room. But, as the old saying is, 'Pride will have a fall'; and these two haughty beauties fell in love with the same man, and he no better than a foreign musician whom their father had down from London to play music with him at the Manor House. For above all things, next to his pride, the old lord loved music. He could play on nearly every instrument that ever was heard of: and it was a strange thing it did not soften him; but he was a fierce, dour old man, and had broken his poor wife's heart with his cruelty, they said. He was mad after music, and would pay any money for it. So he got this foreigner to come; who made such beautiful music, that they said the very birds on the trees stopped their singing to listen. And, by degrees, this foreign gentleman got such a hold over the old lord that nothing would serve him but that he must come every year; and it was he that had the great organ brought from Holland and built up in the hall, where it stood now. He taught the old lord to play on it; but many and many a time, when Lord Furnivall was thinking of nothing but his fine organ, and his finer music, the dark foreigner was walking abroad in the woods with one of the young ladies; now Miss Maude, and then Miss Grace.

Miss Maude won the day and carried off the prize—such as it was; and he and she were married, all unknown to anyone; and before he made his next yearly visit, she had been confined of a little girl at a farm-house on the Moors, while her father and Miss Grace thought she was away at Doncaster Races. But though she was a wife and a mother she was not a bit softened, but as haughty and as passionate as ever; and perhaps more so, for she was jealous of Miss Grace, to whom her foreign husband paid a deal of court—by way of blinding her—as he told his wife. But Miss Grace triumphed over Miss Maude, and Miss Maude grew fiercer and fiercer, both with her husband and with her sister; and the former—who could easily shake off what was disagreeable, and hide himself in foreign countries—went away a month before his usual time that summer, and half threatened that he would never come back again.

Meanwhile, the little girl was left at the farm-house, and her mother used to have her horse saddled and gallop wildly over the hills to see her once every week at the very least—for where she loved, she loved; and where she hated, she hated. And the old lord went on playing—playing on his organ; and the servants thought the sweet music he made had soothed down his awful temper, of which (Dorothy said) some terrible tales could be told. He grew infirm too, and had to walk with a crutch; and his son—that was the present Lord Furnivall's father—was with the army in America, and the other son at sea; so Miss Maude had it pretty much her own way, and she and Miss Grace grew colder and bitterer to each other every day; till at last they hardly ever spoke, except when the old lord was by. The foreign musician came again the next summer, but it was for the last time; for they led him such a life with their jealousy and their passions that he grew weary, and went away, and never was heard of again. And Miss Maude, who had always meant to have her marriage acknowledged when her father should be dead, was left now a deserted wife—whom nobody knew to have been married—with a child that she dared not own, although she loved it to distraction; living with a father whom she feared, and a sister whom she hated.

When the next summer passed over and the dark foreigner never came, both Miss Maude and Miss Grace grew gloomy and sad; they had a haggard look about them, though they looked handsome as ever. But by and by Miss Maude brightened; for her father grew more and more infirm, and more than ever carried away by his music; and she and Miss Grace lived almost entirely apart, having separate rooms, the one on the west side, Miss Maude on the east—those very rooms which were now shut up. So she thought she might have her little girl with her, and no one need ever know except those who dared not speak about it, and were bound to believe that it was, as she said, a cottager's child she had taken a fancy to. All this, Dorothy said, was pretty well known; but what came afterwards no one knew, except Miss Grace and Mrs. Stark, who was even then her maid, and much more of a friend to her than ever her sister had been. But the servants supposed, from words that were dropped, that Miss Maude had triumphed over Miss Grace, and told her that all the time the dark foreigner had been mocking her with pretended love he was her own husband; the colour left Miss Grace's cheek and lips that very day for ever, and she was heard to say many a time that sooner or later she would have her revenge; and Mrs. Stark was for every spying about the east rooms.

One fearful night, just after the New Year had come in, when the snow was lying thick and deep, and the flakes were still falling—fast enough to blind any one who might be out and abroad—there was a great and violent noise heard, and the old lord's voice above all, cursing and swearing awfully; and the cries of a little child; and the proud defiance of a fierce woman; and the sound of a blow; and a dead stillness; and moans and wailings dying away on the hillside! Then the old lord summoned all his servants, and told them, with terrible oaths, and words more terrible, that his daughter had disgraced herself, and that he had turned her out of doors—her, and her child—and that if ever they gave her help, or food, or shelter, he prayed that they might never enter heaven. And, all the while, Miss Grace stood by him, white and still as any stone; and when he had ended she heaved a great sigh, as much as to say her work was done, and her end was accomplished. But the old lord never touched his organ again, and died within the year; and no wonder! for, on the morrow of that wild and fearful night, the shepherds coming down the Fell side, found Miss Maude sitting all crazy and smiling, under the holly trees, nursing a dead child—with a terrible mark on its right shoulder. 'But that was not what killed it,' said Dorothy; 'it was the frost and the cold. Every wild creature was in its hole, and every beast in its fold—while the child and its mother were turned out to wander on the Fells! And now you know all, and I wonder if you are less frightened now?'

I was more frightened than ever; but I said I was not. I wished Miss Rosamond and myself well out of that dreadful house for ever; but I would not leave her, and I dared not take her away. But oh! how I watched her, and guarded her! We bolted the doors and shut the window-shutters fast, and an hour or more before dark rather than leave them open five minutes too late. But my little lady still heard the weird child crying and mourning; and not all we could do or say could keep her from wanting to go to her, and let her in from the cruel wind and the snow. All this time, I kept away from Miss Furnivall and Mrs. Stark as much as ever I could; for I feared them—I knew no good could be about them, with their grey, hard faces, and their dreamy eyes looking back into the ghastly years that were gone. But, even in my fear, I had a kind of pity—for Miss Furnivall, at least. Those gone down to the pit can hardly have a more hopeless look than that which was ever on her face. At last I even got so sorry for her—who never said a word but what was quite forced from her—that I prayed for her; and I taught Miss Rosamond to pray for one who had done a deadly sin; but often, when she came to those words, she would listen, and start up from her knees, and say, 'I hear my little girl plaining and crying very sad—Oh! let her in, or she will die!'

One night—just after New Year's Day had come at last, and the long winter had taken a turn, as I hoped—I heard the west drawing-room bell ring three times, which was a signal for me. I would not leave Miss Rosamond alone, for all she was asleep—for the old lord had been playing wilder than ever—and I feared lest my darling should waken to hear the Spectre-Child; see her I knew she could not— I had fastened the windows too well for that. So I took her out of her bed and wrapped her up in such outer clothes as were most handy, and carried her down to the drawing-room, where the old ladies sat at their tapestry-work as usual. They looked up when I came in, and Mrs. Stark asked, quite astounded, 'Why did I bring Miss Rosamond there, out of her warm bed?' I had begun to whisper, 'Because I was afraid of her being tempted out while I was away, by the wild child in the snow,' when she stopped me short (with a glance at Miss Furnivall), and said Miss Furnivall wanted me to undo some work she had done wrong, and which neither of them could see to unpick. So I laid my pretty dear on the sofa, and sat down on a stool by them, and hardened my heart against them, as I heard the wind rising and howling.

Miss Rosamond slept on sound, for all the wind blew so; and Miss Furnivall said never a word, nor looked round when the gusts shook the windows. All at once she started up to her full height, and put up one hand, as if to bid us listen.

'I hear voices!' said she, 'I hear terrible screams—I hear my father's voice!'

Just at that moment my darling wakened with a sudden start: 'My little girl is crying, oh, how she is crying!' and she tried to get up and go to her, but she got her feet entangled in the blanket, and I caught her up; for my flesh had begun to creep at these noises, which they heard while we could catch no sound. In a minute or two the noises came, gathered fast, and filled our ears; we, too, heard voices and screams, and no longer heard the winter's wind that raged abroad. Mrs. Stark looked at me, and I at her, but we dared not speak. Suddenly Miss Furnivall went towards the door, out into the ante-room, through the west lobby, and opened the door into the great hall. Mrs. Stark followed, and I durst not be left, though my heart almost stopped beating for fear. I wrapped my darling tight in my arms and went out with them. In the hall the screams were louder than ever; they sounded to come from the east wing—nearer and nearer—close on the other side of the locked-up doors—close behind them. Then I noticed that the great bronze chandelier seemed all alight, though the hall was dim, and that a fire was blazing in the vast hearth-place, though it gave no heat; and I shuddered up with terror, and folded my darling closer to me. But as I did so, the east door shook, and she, suddenly struggling to get free from me, cried, 'Hester, I must go! My little girl is there; I hear her; she is coming! Hester, I must go!'

I held her tight with all my strength; with a set will, I held her. If I had died my hands would have grasped her still, I was so resolved in my mind. Miss Furnivall stood listening, and paid no regard to my darling, who had got down to the ground and whom I, upon my knees now, was holding with both my arms clasped round her neck; she still striving and crying to get free.

All at once the east door gave way with a thundering crash, as if torn open in a violent passion, and there came into that broad and mysterious light, the figure of a tall old man, with grey hair and gleaming eyes. He drove before him, with many a relentless gesture of abhorrence, a stern and beautiful woman, with a little child clinging to her dress.

'Oh, Hester! Hester!' cried Miss Rosamond. 'It's the lady! the lady below the holly trees; and my little girl is with her. Hester! Hester! let me go to her; they are drawing me to them, I feel them, I feel them, I must go!'

Again she was almost convulsed by her efforts to get away; but I held her tighter and tighter, till I feared I should do her a hurt; but rather that than let her go towards those terrible phantoms. They passed along towards the great hall door, where the winds howled and ravened for their prey; but before they reached that, the lady turned; and I could see that she defied the old man with a fierce and proud defiance; but then she quailed—and then she threw up her arms wildly and piteously to save her child—her little child—from a blow from his uplifted crutch.

And Miss Rosamond was torn as by a power stronger than mine, and writhed in my arms, and sobbed (for by this time the poor darling was growing faint).

'They want me to go with them on to the Fells—they are drawing me to them. Oh, my little girl! I would come, but cruel, wicked Hester holds me very tight.' But when she saw the uplifted crutch she swooned away, and I thanked God for it. Just at this moment— when the tall old man, his hair streaming as in the blast of a furnace, was going to strike the little shrinking child—Miss Furnivall, the old woman by my side cried out, 'Oh Father! Father! spare the little innocent child!' But just then I saw—we all saw—another phantom shape itself, and grow clear out of the blue and misty light that filled the hall; we had not seen her till now, for it was another lady who stood by the old man, with a look of relentless hate and triumphant scorn. That figure was very beautiful to look upon, with a soft white hat drawn down over the proud brows and a red and curling lip. It was dressed in an open robe of blue satin. I had seen that figure before. It was the likeness of Miss Furnivall in her youth; and the terrible phantoms moved on, regardless of old Miss Furnivall's wild entreaty—and the uplifted crutch fell on the right shoulder of the little child, and the younger sister looked on, stony and deadly serene. But at that moment the dim lights and the fire that gave no heat went out of themselves, and Miss Furnivall lay at our feet stricken down by the palsy—death stricken.

Yes, she was carried to her bed that night never to rise again. She lay with her face to the wall muttering low but muttering always: 'Alas! alas! what is done in youth can never be undone in age! What is done in youth can never be undone in age!'

1859

The Lifted Veil

GEORGE ELIOT

I

The time of my end approaches. I have lately been subject to
attacks of *angina pectoris*; and in the ordinary course of things, my
physician tells me, I may fairly hope that my life will not be protracted
many months. Unless, then, I am cursed with an exceptional physical
constitution, as I am cursed with an exceptional mental character,
I shall not much longer groan under the wearisome burden of this
earthly existence. If it were to be otherwise—if I were to live on
to the age most men desire and provide for—I should for once have
known whether the miseries of delusive expectation can out-weigh
the miseries of true prevision. For I foresee when I shall die, and
everything that will happen in my last moments.

Just a month from this day, on 20th September, 1850, I shall be
sitting in this chair, in this study, at ten o'clock at night, longing
to die, weary of incessant insight and foresight, without delusions and
without hope. Just as I am watching a tongue of blue flame rising in
the fire, and my lamp is burning low, the horrible contraction will
begin in my chest. I shall only have time to reach the bell, and pull
it violently, before the sense of suffocation will come. No one will
answer my bell. I know why. My two servants are lovers, and will
have quarrelled. My housekeeper will have rushed out of the house
in a fury, two hours before, hoping that Perry will believe she has
gone to drown herself. Pery is alarmed at last, and is gone out after
her. The little scullery-maid is asleep on a bench: she never answers
the bell; it does not wake her. The sense of suffocation increases: my
lamp goes out with a horrible stench: I make a great effort, and
snatch at the bell again. I long for life, and there is no help. I

thirsted for the unknown: the thirst is gone. O God, let me stay
with the known, and be weary of it. I am content. Agony of
pain and suffocation—and all the while the earth, the fields, the
pebbly brook at the bottom of the rookery, the fresh scent after
the rain, the light of the morning through my chamber window,
the warmth of the hearth after a frosty air—will darkness close over
them for ever?

Darkness—darkness—no pain—nothing but darkness: but I am
passing on and on through the darkness: my thought stays in the
darkness, but always with a sense of moving onward . . .

Before that time comes, I wish to use my last hours of ease and
strength in telling the strange story of my experience. I have never
fully unbosomed myself to any human being; I have never been
encouraged to trust much in the sympathy of my fellow men. But
we have all a chance of meeting with some pity, some tenderness,
some charity, when we are dead: it is the living only who cannot be
forgiven—the living only from whom men's indulgence and reverence
are held off, like the rain by the hard east wind. While the heart
beats, bruise it—it is your only opportunity; while the eye can still
turn towards you with moist, timid entreaty, freeze it with an icy
unanswering gaze; while the ear, that delicate messenger to the inmost
sanctuary of the soul, can still take in the tones of kindness, put it
off with hard civility, or sneering compliment, or envious affectation
of indifference; while the creative brain can still throb with the
sense of injustice, with the yearning for brotherly recognition—make
haste—oppress it with your ill-considered judgements, your trivial
comparisons, your careless misrepresentations. The heart will by and
by be still—*ubi saeva indignatio ulterius cor lacerare nequit*; the eye will
cease to entreat; the ear will be deaf; the brain will have ceased from
all wants as well as from all work. Then your charitable speeches
may find vent; then you may remember and pity the toil and the
struggle and the failure; then you may give due honour to the work
achieved; then you may find extenuation for errors, and may consent
to bury them.

That is a trivial schoolboy text; why do I dwell on it? It has little
reference to me, for I shall leave no works behind me for men to
honour. I have no near relatives who will make up, by weeping over
my grave, for the wounds they inflicted on me when I was among
them. It is only the story of my life that will perhaps win a little

more sympathy from strangers when I am dead, than I ever believed it would obtain from my friends while I was living.

My childhood perhaps seems happier to me than it really was, by contrast with all the after-years. For then the curtain of the future was as impenetratable to me as to other children: I had all their delight in the present hour, their sweet indefinite hopes for the morrow; and I had a tender mother: even now, after the dreary lapse of long years, a slight trace of sensation accompanies the remembrance of her caress as she held me on her knee—her arms round my little body, her cheek pressed on mine. I had a complaint of the eyes that made me blind for a little while, and she kept me on her knee from morning till night. That unequalled love soon vanished out of my life, and even to my childish consciousness it was as if that life had become more chill. I rode my little white pony with the groom by my side as before, but there were no loving eyes looking at me as I mounted, no glad arms opened to me when I came back. Perhaps I missed my mother's love more than most children of seven or eight would have done, to whom the other pleasures of life remained as before; for I was certainly a very sensitive child. I remember still the mingled trepidation and delicious excitement with which I was affected by the tramping of the horses on the pavement in the echoing stables, by the loud resonance of the grooms' voices, by the booming bark of the dogs as my father's carriage thundered under the archway of the courtyard, by the din of the gong as it gave notice of luncheon and dinner. The measured tramp of soldiery which I sometimes heard—for my father's house lay near a county town where there were large barracks—made me sob and tremble; and yet when they were gone past, I longed for them to come back again.

I fancy my father thought me an odd child, and had little fondness for me; though he was very careful in fulfilling what he regarded as a parent's duties. But he was already past the middle of life, and I was not his only son. My mother had been his second wife, and he was five-and-forty when he married her. He was firm, unbending, intensely orderly man, in root and stem a banker, but with a flourishing graft of the active landholder, aspiring to county influence: one of those people who are always like themselves from day to day, who are uninfluenced by the weather, and neither know melancholy nor high spirits. I held him in great awe, and appeared more timid and sensitive in his presence than at other times; a circumstance

which, perhaps, helped to confirm him in the intention to educate
me on a different plan from the prescriptive one with which he
had complied in the case of my elder brother, already a tall youth
at Eton. My brother was to be his representative and successor; he
must go to Eton and Oxford, for the sake of making connexions, of
course: my father was not a man to underrate the bearing of Latin
satirists or Greek dramatists on the attainment of an aristocratic
position. But intrinsically, he had slight esteem for 'those dead but
sceptred spirits'; having qualified himself for forming an independent
opinion by reading Potter's *Aeschylus*, and dipping into Francis's
Horace. To this negative view he added a positive one, derived
from a recent connexion with mining speculations; namely, that
a scientific education was the really useful training for a younger
son. Moreover, it was clear that a shy, sensitive boy like me was
not fit to encounter the rough experience of a public school. Mr.
Letherall had said so very decidedly. Mr. Letherall was a large man
in spectacles, who one day took my small head between his large
hands, and pressed it here and there in an exploratory, suspicious
manner—then placed each of his great thumbs on my temples, and
pushed me a little way from him, and stared at me with glittering
spectacles. The contemplation appeared to displease him, for he
frowned sternly, and said to my father, drawing his thumbs across
my eyebrows—

'The deficiency is there, sir—there; and here,' he added, touching
the upper sides of my head, 'here is the excess. That must be brought
out, sir, and this must be laid to sleep.'

I was in a state of tremor, partly at the vague idea that I was the
object of reprobation, partly in the agitation of my first hatred—hatred
of this big, spectacled man, who pulled my head about as if he wanted
to buy and cheapen it.

I am not aware how much Mr. Letherall had to do with the system
afterwards adopted towards me, but it was presently clear that private
tutors, natural history, science, and the modern languages, were
the appliances by which the defects of my organisation were to
be remedied. I was very stupid about machines, so I was to be
greatly occupied with them: I had no memory for classification, so
it was particularly necessary that I should study systematic zoology and
botany; I was hungry for human deeds and humane motions, so I was
to be plentifully crammed with the mechanical powers, the elementary

bodies, and the phenomena of electricity and magnetism. A better-constituted boy would certainly have profited under my intelligent tutors, with their scientific apparatus; and would, doubtless, have found the phenomena of electricity and magnetism as fascinating as I was, every Thursday, assured they were. As it was, I could have paired off, for ignorance of whatever was taught me, with the worst Latin scholar that was ever turned out of a classical academy. I read Plutarch, and Shakespeare, and Don Quixote by the sly, and supplied myself in that way with wandering thoughts, while my tutor was assuring me that 'an improved man, as distinguished from an ignorant one, was a man who knew the reason why water ran downhill.' I had no desire to be this improved man; I was glad of the running water; I could watch it and listen to it gurgling among the pebbles and bathing the bright green water-plants, by the hour together. I did not want to know *why* it ran; I had perfect confidence that there were good reasons for what was so very beautiful.

There is no need to dwell on this part of my life. I have said enough to indicate that my nature was of the sensitive, unpractical order, and that it grew up in an uncongenial medium, which could never foster it into happy, healthy development. When I was sixteen I was sent to Geneva to complete my course of education; and the change was a very happy one to me, for the first sight of the Alps, with the setting sun on them, as we descended the Jura, seemed to me like an entrance into heaven; and the three years of my life there were spent in a perpetual sense of exaltation, as if from a draught of delicious wine, at the presence of Nature in all her awful loveliness. You will think, perhaps, that I must have been a poet, from this early sensibility to Nature. But my lot was not so happy as that. A poet pours forth his song and *believes* in the listening ear and answering soul, to which his song will be floated sooner or later. But the poet's sensibility without his voice—the poet's sensibility that finds no vent but in silent tears on the sunny bank, when the noonday light sparkles on the water, or in an inward shudder at the sound of harsh human tones, the sight of a cold human eye—this dumb passion brings with it a fatal solitude of soul in the society of one's fellowmen. My least solitary moments were those in which I pushed off in my boat, at evening, towards the centre of the lake; it seemed to me that the sky, and the glowing mountain-tops, and the wide blue water, surrounded me with a cherishing love such as no human face had shed on me since my mother's love had vanished out of my life. I used to do as Jean Jacques did—lie down in my boat and let it glide where it would, while I looked up at the departing glow leaving one mountain-top after the other, as if the prophet's chariot of fire were passing over them on its way to the home of light. Then, when the white summits were all sad and corpse-like, I had to push homeward, for I was under careful surveillance, and was allowed no late wanderings. This disposition of mine was not favourable to the formation of intimate friendships among the numerous youths of my own age who are always to be found studying at Geneva. Yet I made *one* such friendship; and, singularly enough, it was with a youth whose intellectual tendencies were the very reverse of my own. I shall call him Charles Meunier; his real surname—an English one, for he was of English extraction—having since become celebrated. He was an orphan, who lived on a miserable pittance while he pursued the medical studies for which he had a special genius. Strange! that with my vague mind, susceptible and unobservant, hating inquiry and given up to contemplation, I should have been drawn towards a youth whose strongest passion was science. But the bond was not an intellectual one; it came from a source that can happily blend the stupid with the brilliant, the dreamy with the practical: it came from community of feeling. Charles was poor and ugly, derided by Genevese *gamins*, and not acceptable in drawing-rooms. I saw that he was isolated, as I was, though from a different cause, and stimulated by a sympathetic resentment, I made timid advances towards him. It is enough to say that there sprang up as much comradeship between us as our different habits would allow; and in Charles's rare holidays we went up to the Saleve together, or took the boat to Vevey, while I listened dreamily to the monologues in which he unfolded his bold conceptions of future experiment and discovery. I mingled them confusedly in my thought with glimpses of blue water and delicate floating cloud, with the notes of birds and the distant glitter of the glacier. He knew quite well that my mind was half absent, yet he liked to talk to me in this way; for don't we talk of our hopes and our projects even to dogs and birds when they love us? I have mentioned this one friendship because of its connexion with a strange and terrible scene which I shall have to narrate in my subsequent life.

This happier life at Geneva was put an end to by a severe illness, which is partly a blank to me, partly a time of dimly-remembered suffering, with the presence of my father by my bed from time to time. Then came the languid monotony of convalescence, the days gradually breaking into variety and distinctness as my strength enabled me to take long and longer drives. On one of these more vividly remembered days, my father said to me, as he sat beside my sofa—

'When you are quite well enough to travel, Latimer, I shall take you home with me. The journey will amuse you and do you good, for I shall go through the Tyrol and Austria, and you will see many new places. Our neighbours, the Filmores, are come; Alfred will join us at Basle, and we shall all go together to Vienna, and back by Prague . . .'

My father was called away before he had finished his sentence, and he left my mind resting on the word *Prague*, with a strange sense that a new and wondrous scene was breaking upon me: a city under the broad sunshine, that seemed to me as if it were summer sunshine of a long-past century arrested in its course—unrefreshed for ages by dews of night, or the rushing rain-cloud; scorching the dusty, weary, time-eaten grandeur of a people doomed to live on in the stale repetition of memories, like deposed and superannuated kings in their regal gold inwoven tatters. The city looked so thirsty that the broad river seemed to me a sheet of metal; and the blackened statues, as I passed under their blank gaze, along the unending bridge, with their ancient garments and their saintly crowns, seemed to me the real inhabitants and owners of this place, while the busy, trivial men and women, hurrying to an fro, were a swarm of ephemeral visitants infesting it for a day. It is such grim, stony beings as these, I thought, who are the fathers of ancient faded children, in those tanned time-fretted dwellings that crowd the steep before me; who pay their court in the worn and crumbling pomp of the palace which stretches its monotonous length on the height; who worship wearily in the stifling air of the churches, urged by no fear or hope, but compelled by their doom to be ever old and undying, to live on in the rigidity of habit, as they live on in perpetual midday, without the repose of night or the new birth of morning.

A stunning clang of metal suddenly thrilled through me, and I became conscious of the objects in my room again: one of the fire-irons had fallen as Pierre opened the door to bring me my draught. My heart was palpitating violently, and I begged Pierre to leave my draught beside me; I would take it presently.

As soon as I was alone again, I began to ask myself whether I had been sleeping. Was this a dream—this wonderfully distinct vision—minute in its distinctness down to a patch of rainbow light on the pavement, transmitted through a coloured lamp in the shape of a star—of a strange city, quite unfamiliar to my imagination! I had seen no picture of Prague: it lay in my mind as a mere name, with vaguely-remembered historical associations—ill-defined memories of imperial grandeur and religious wars.

Nothing of this sort had ever occurred in my dreaming experience before, for I had often been humiliated because my dreams were only saved from being utterly disjointed and commonplace by the frequent terrors of nightmare. But I could not believe that I had been asleep, for I remembered distinctly the gradual breaking-in of the vision upon me, like the new images in a dissolving view, or the growing distinctness of the landscape as the sun lifts up the veil of the morning mist. And while I was conscious of this incipient vision, I was also conscious that Pierre came to tell my father Mr. Filmore was waiting for him, and that my father hurried out of the room. No, it was not a dream; was it—the thought was full of tremulous exultation—was it the poet's nature in me, hitherto only a troubled yearning sensibility, now manifesting itself suddenly as spontaneous creation? Surely it was in this way that Homer saw the plain of Troy, that Dante saw the abodes of the departed, that Milton saw the earthward flight of the Tempter. Was it that my illness had wrought some happy change in my organisation—given a firmer tension to my nerves—carried off some dull obstruction? I had often read of such effects—in works of fiction at least. Nay; in genuine biographies I had read of the subtilising or exalting influence of some diseases on the mental powers. Did not Novalis feel his inspiration intensified under the progress of consumption?

When my mind had dwelt for some time on this blissful idea, it seemed to me that I might perhaps test it by an exertion of my will. The vision had begun when my father was speaking of our going to Prague. I did not for a moment believe it was really a representation of that city; I believed—I hoped it was a picture that my newly liberated genius had painted in fiery haste, with the colours snatched from lazy memory. Suppose I were to fix my mind on some other place—Venice, for example, which was far more familiar to my imagination than Prague: perhaps the same sort of result would follow.

I concentrated my thoughts on Venice; I stimulated my imagination with poetic memories, and strove to feel myself present in Venice, as I had felt myself in Prague. But in vain. I was only colouring the Canaletto engravings that hung in my old bedroom at home; the picture was a shifting one, my mind wandering uncertainly in search of more vivid images; I could see no accident of form or shadow without conscious labour after the necessary conditions. It was all prosaic effort, not rapt passivity, such as I had experienced half an hour before. I was discouraged; but I remembered that inspiration was fitful.

For several days I was in a state of excited expectation, watching for a recurrence of my new gift. I sent my thoughts ranging over my world of knowledge, in the hope that they would find some object which would send a re-awakening vibration through my slumbering genius. But no; my world remained as dim as ever, and that flash of strange light refused to come again, though I watched for it with palpitating eagerness.

My father accompanied me every day in a drive and a gradually lengthening walk as my powers of walking increased; and one evening he had agreed to come and fetch me at twelve the next day, that we might go together to select a musical box, and other purchases rigorously demanded of a rich Englishman visiting Geneva. He was one of the most punctual of men and bankers, and I was always nervously anxious to be quite ready for him at the appointed time. But, to my surprise, at a quarter past twelve he had not appeared. I felt all the impatience of a convalescent who has nothing particular to do, and who has just taken a tonic in the prospect of immediate exercise that would carry off the stimulus.

Unable to sit still and reserve my strength, I walked up and down the room, looking out on the current of the Rhone, just where it leaves the dark-blue lake; but thinking all the while of the possible causes that could detain my father.

Suddenly I was conscious that my father was in the room, but not alone: there were two persons with him. Strange! I had heard no footsteps, I had not seen the door open; but I saw my father, and at his right hand our neighbour Mrs. Filmore, whom I remembered very well, though I had not seen her for five years. She was a commonplace middle aged woman, in silk and cashmere; but the lady on the left of my father was not more than twenty, a tall, slim, willowy figure with luxuriant blond hair, arranged in cunning braids and folds that looked almost too massive for the slight figure and the small-featured, thin-lipped face they crowned. But the face had not a girlish expression: the features were sharp, the pale grey eyes at once acute, restless, and sarcastic. They were fixed on me in half-smiling curiosity, and I felt a painful sensation as if a sharp wind were cutting me. The pale-green dress, and the green leaves that seemed to form a border about her pale blond hair, made me think of a Water-Nixie—for my mind was full of German lyrics, and this pale, fatal-eyed woman, with the green weeds, looked like a birth from some cold sedgy stream, the daughter of an aged river.

'Well, Latimer, you thought me long,' my father said . . .

But while the last word was in my ears, the whole group vanished, and there was nothing between me and the Chinese painted folding-screen that stood before the door. I was cold and trembling; I could only totter forward and throw myself on the sofa. This strange new power had manifested itself again . . . But *was* it a power? Might it not rather be a disease—a sort of intermittent delirium, concentrating my energy of brain into moments of unhealthy activity, and leaving my saner hours all the more barren? I felt a dizzy sense of unreality in what my eye rested on; I grasped the bell convulsively, like one trying to free himself from nightmare, and rang it twice. Pierre came with a look of alarm in his face.

'*Monsieur ne se trouve pas bien?*' he said anxiously.

'I'm tired of waiting, Pierre,' I said, as distinctly and emphatically as I could, like a man determined to be sober in spite of wine; 'I'm afraid something has happened to my father—he's usually so punctual. Run to the Hôtel des Bergues and see if he is there.'

Pierre left the room at once, with a soothing '*Bien, Monsieur*'; and I felt the better for this scene of simple, walking prose. Seeking to calm myself still further, I went into my bedroom, adjoining the *salon*, and opened a case of *eau-de-Cologne*; took out a bottle; went through the process of taking out the cork very neatly, and then rubbed the reviving spirit over my hands and forehead, and under my nostrils, drawing a new delight from the scent because I had procured it by slow details of labour, and by no strange sudden madness. Already I had begun to taste something of the horror that belongs to the lot of a human being whose nature is not adjusted to simple human conditions.

Still enjoying the scent, I returned to the *salon*, but it was not unoccupied, as it had been before I left it. In front of the Chinese folding-screen there was my father, with Mrs. Filmore on his right hand, and on his left—the slim, blond-haired girl, with the keen face and the keen eyes fixed on me in half-smiling curiosity.

'Well Latimer, you thought me long,' my father said . . .

I heard no more, felt no more, till I became conscious that I was lying with my head low on the sofa, Pierre and my father by my side. As soon as I was thoroughly revived, my father left the room, and presently returned, saying—

'I've been to tell the ladies how you are, Latimer. They were waiting in the next room. We shall put off our shopping expedition today.'

Presently he said, 'That young lady is Bertha Grant, Mrs. Filmore's orphan niece. Filmore has adopted her, and she lives with them, so you will have her for a neighbour, when we go home—perhaps for a near relation; for there is a tenderness between her and Alfred, I suspect, and I should be gratified by the match, since Filmore means to provide for her in every way as if she were his daughter. It had not occurred to me that you knew about her living with the Filmores.'

He made no further allusion to the fact of my having fainted at the moment of seeing her, and I would not for the world have told him the reason: I shrank from the idea of disclosing to any one what might be regarded as a pitiable peculiarity, most of all from betraying it to my father, who would have suspected my sanity ever after.

I do not mean to dwell with particularity on the details of my experience. I have described these two cases at length, because they had definite, clearly traceable results in my after-lot.

Shortly after this last occurrence—I think the very next day—I began to be aware of the phase in my abnormal sensibility, to which, from the languid and slight nature of my intercourse with others since my illness, I had not been alive before. This was the obtrusion on my mind of the mental process going forward in first one person, and then another, with whom I happened to be in contact: the vagrant, frivolous ideas and emotions of some uninteresting acquaintance—Mrs. Filmore, for example—would force themselves on my consciousness like an importunate, ill-played musical instrument, or the loud activity of an imprisoned insect. But this unpleasant sensibility was fitful, and left me moments of rest, when the souls of my companions were once more shut out from me, and I felt a relief such as silence brings to wearied nerves. I might have believed this importunate insight to be merely a diseased activity of the imagination, but that my prevision of incalculable words and actions proved it to have a fixed relation to the mental process in other minds. But this superadded consciousness, wearying and annoying enough when it urged on me the trivial experience of indifferent people, became an intense pain and grief when it seemed to be opening to me the souls of those who were in a close relation to me—when the rational talk, the graceful attentions, the wittily-turned phrases, and the kindly deeds, which used to make the web of their characters, were seen as if thrust asunder by a microscope vision, that showed all the intermediate frivolities, all the suppressed egoism, all the struggling chaos of puerilities, meanness, vague capricious memories, and indolent make-shift thoughts, from which human words and deeds emerge like leaflets covering a fermenting heap.

At Basle we were joined by my brother Alfred, now a handsome, self-confident man of six-and-twenty—a thorough contrast to my fragile, nervous, ineffectual self. I believe I was held to have a sort of half-womanish, half-ghostly beauty; for the portrait-painters, who are thick as weeds at Geneva, had often asked me to sit to them, and I had been the model of a dying minstrel in a fancy picture. But I thoroughly disliked my own physique and nothing but the belief that it was a condition of poetic genius would have reconciled me to it. That brief hope was quite fled, and I saw in my face now nothing but the stamp of a morbid organisation, framed for passive suffering—too feeble for the sublime resistance of poetic production. Alfred, from whom I had been almost constantly separated, and who, in his present stage of character and appearance, came before me as a perfect stranger, was bent on being extremely friendly and brother-like to me. He had the superficial kindness of a good-humoured, self-satisfied nature, that fears no rivalry, and has encountered no contrarieties. I am not sure that my disposition was good enough for me to have been quite free from envy towards him, even if our desires had not clashed, and if I had been in the healthy human condition which admits of generous confidence and charitable construction. There must always have been an antipathy between our natures. As it was, he became in a few weeks an object of intense hatred to me; and when he entered the room, still more when he spoke, it was as if a sensation of grating metal had set my teeth on edge. My diseased consciousness was more intensely and continually occupied with his thoughts and emotions, than with those of any other person who came in my way. I was perpetually exasperated with the petty promptings of his conceit, with his love of patronage, with his self-complacent belief in Bertha Grant's passion for him, with his half-pitying contempt for me—seen not in the ordinary indications of intonation and phrase and slight action, which an acute and suspicious mind is on the watch for, but in all their naked skinless complication.

For we were rivals, and our desires clashed, though he was not aware of it. I have said nothing yet of the effect Bertha Grant produced in me on a nearer acquaintance. That effect was chiefly determined by the fact that she made the only exemption, among all the human beings about me, to my unhappy gift of insight. About Bertha I was always in a state of uncertainty: I could watch the expression of her face, and speculate on its meaning; I could ask for her opinion with the real interest of ignorance; I could listen for her words and watch for her smile with hope and fear: she had for me the fascination of an unravelled destiny. I say it was this fact that chiefly determined the strong effect she produced on me: for, in the abstract, no womanly character could seem to have less affinity for that of a shrinking, romantic, passionate youth than Bertha's. She was keen, sarcastic, unimaginative, prematurely cynical, remaining critical and unmoved in the most impressive scenes, inclined to dissect all my favourite poems, and especially contemptuous towards the German lyrics which were my pet literature at that time. To this moment I am unable to define my feeling towards her: it was not ordinary boyish admiration, for she was the very opposite, even to the colour of her hair, of the ideal woman who still remained to me the type of loveliness; and she was without that enthusiasm for the great and good, which, even at the moment of her strongest dominion over me, I should have declared to be the highest element of character. But there is no tyranny more complete than that which a self-centered negative nature exercises over a morbidly sensitive nature perpetually craving sympathy and support. The most independent people feel the effect of a man's silence in heightening their value for his opinion—feel an additional triumph in conquering the reverence of a critic habitually captious and satirical: no wonder, then, that an enthusiastic self-distrusting youth should watch and wait before the closed secret of a sarcastic woman's face, as if it were the shrine of the doubtfully benignant deity who ruled his destiny. For a young enthusiast is unable to imagine the total negation in another mind of the emotions which are stirring his own; they may be feeble, latent, inactive, he thinks, but they are there—they may be called forth; sometimes, in moments of happy hallucination, he believes that they may be there in all the greater strength because he sees no outward sign of them. And this effect, as I have intimated, was heightened to its utmost intensity in me, because Bertha was the only being who remained for me in the mysterious seclusion of soul that renders such youthful delusion possible. Doubtless there was another sort of fascination at work—that subtle physical attraction which delights in cheating our psychological predictions, and in compelling the men who paint sylphs, to fall in love with some *bonne et brave femme*, heavy-heeled and freckled.

Bertha's behaviour towards me was such as to encourage all my illusions, to heighten my boyish passion, and make me more and more dependent on her smiles. Looking back with my present wretched knowledge, I conclude that her vanity and love of power were intensely gratified by the belief that I had fainted on first seeing her purely from the strong impression her person had produced on me. The most prosaic woman likes to believe herself the object of a violent, a poetic passion; and without a grain of romance in her Bertha had that spirit of intrigue which gave piquancy to the idea that the brother of the man she meant to marry was dying with love and jealousy for her sake. That she meant to marry my brother, was what at that time I did not believe; for though he was assiduous in his attentions to her, and I knew well enough that both he and my father had made up their minds to this result, there was not yet an understood engagement—there had been no explicit declaration; and Bertha habitually, while she flirted with my brother, and accepted his homage in a way that implied to him a thorough recognition of its intention, made me believe, by the subtlest looks and phrases—feminine nothings which could never be quoted against her—that he was really the object of her secret ridicule; that she thought him, as I did, a coxcomb, whom she would have pleasure in disappointing. Me she openly petted in my brother's presence, as if I were too young and sickly ever to be thought of as a lover; and that was the view he took of me. But I believe she must inwardly have delighted in the tremors into which she threw me by the coaxing way in which she patted my curls, while she laughed at my quotations. Such caresses were always given in the presence of our friends; for when we were alone together, she affected a much greater distance towards me, and now and then took the opportunity, by words or slight actions, to stimulate my foolish timid hope that she really preferred me. And why should she not follow her inclination? I was not a year younger than she was, and she was an heiress, who would soon be of age to decide for herself.

The fluctuations of hope and fear, confined to this one channel, made each day in her presence a delicious torment. There was one deliberate act of hers which especially helped to intoxicate me. When we were at Vienna her twentieth birthday occurred, and as she was very fond of ornaments, we all took the opportunity of the splendid jeweller's shops in that Teutonic Paris to purchase her a birthday present of jewellery. Mine, naturally, was the least expensive; it was an opal ring—the opal was my favourite stone, because it seems to blush and turn pale as if it had a soul. I told Bertha so when I gave it her, and said that it was an emblem of the poetic nature, changing with the changing light of heaven and of woman's eyes. In the evening she appeared elegantly dressed and wearing conspicuously all the birthday presents except mine. I looked eagerly at her fingers, but saw no opal. I had no opportunity of noticing this to her during the evening; but the next day, when I found her seated near the window alone, after breakfast, I said, 'You scorn to wear my poor opal. I should have remembered that you despised poetic natures, and should have given you coral, or turquoise, or some other opaque unresponsive stone.' 'Do I despise it?' she answered, taking hold of a delicate gold chain which she always wore round her neck and drawing out of the end from her bosom with my ring hanging to it; 'it hurts me a little, I can tell you,' she said, with her usual dubious smile, 'to wear it in that secret place; and since your poetical nature is so stupid as to prefer a more public position, I shall not endure the pain any longer.'

She took off the ring from the chain and put it on her finger, smiling still, while the blood rushed to my cheeks, and I could not trust myself to say a word of entreaty that she would keep the ring where it was before.

I was completely fooled by this, and for two days shut myself up in my room whenever Bertha was absent, that I might intoxicate myself afresh with the thought of this scene and all it implied.

I should mention that during these two months—which seemed a long life to me from the novelty and intensity of the pleasures and pains I underwent—my diseased participation in other peoples' consciousness continued to torment me; now it was my father, and now my brother, now Mrs. Filmore or her husband, and now our German courier, whose stream of thought rushed upon me like a ringing in the ears not to be got rid of, though it allowed my own impulses and ideas to continue their uninterrupted course. It was like a preternaturally heightened sense of hearing, making audible to one a roar of sound where others find perfect stillness. The weariness and disgust of this involuntary intrusion into other souls was counteracted only by my ignorance of Bertha, and my growing passion for her; a passion enormously stimulated, if not produced, by that ignorance. She was my oasis of mystery in the dreary desert of knowledge. I had never allowed my diseased condition to betray itself, or to drive me into any unusual speech or action, except once, when, in a moment of peculiar bitterness against my brother, I had forestalled some words which I knew he was going to utter—a clever observation, which he had prepared beforehand. He had occasionally a slightly-affected hesitation in his speech, and when he paused an instant after the second word, my impatience and jealousy impelled me to continue the speech for him, as if it were something we had both learned by rote. He coloured and looked astonished, as well as annoyed; and the words had no sooner escaped my lips than I felt a shock of alarm lest such an anticipation of words—very far from being words, of course, easy to divine—should have betrayed me as an exceptional being, a sort of quiet energumen, whom every one, Bertha above all, would shudder at and avoid. But I magnified, as usual, the impression any word or deed of mine could produce on others; for no one gave any sign of having noticed my interruption as more than a rudeness, to be forgiven me on the score of my feeble nervous condition.

While this superadded consciousness of the actual was almost constant with me, I had never had a recurrence of that distinct prevision which I have described in relation to my interview with Bertha; and I was waiting with eager curiosity to know whether or not my vision of Prague would prove to have been an instance of the same kind. A few days after the incident of the opal ring, we were paying one of our frequent visits to the Lichtenberg Palace. I could never look at many pictures in succession; for pictures, when they are at all powerful, affect me so strongly that one or two exhaust all my capability of contemplation. This morning I had been looking at Giorgione's picture of the cruel-eyed woman, said to be a likeness of Lucrezia Borgia. I had stood long alone before it, fascinated by the terrible reality of that cunning, relentless face, till I felt a strange poisoned sensation, as if I had long been inhaling a fatal odour, and was just beginning to be conscious of its effects. Perhaps even then I should not have moved away, if the rest of the party had not returned to this room, and announced that they were going to the Belvedere Gallery to settle a bet which had arisen between my brother and Mr. Filmore about a portrait. I followed them dreamily, and was hardly alive to what occurred till they had all gone up to the gallery, leaving me below; for I refused to come within sight of another picture that day. I made my way to the Grand Terrace, since it was agreed that we should saunter in the gardens when the dispute had been decided. I had been sitting here a short space, vaguely conscious of trim gardens, with a city and green hills in the distance, when, wishing to avoid the proximity of the sentinel, I rose and walked down the broad stone steps, intending to seat myself farther on in the gardens. Just as I reached the gravel-walk, I felt an arm slipped within mine, and a light hand gently pressing my wrist. In the same instant a strange intoxicating numbness passed over me, like the continuance or climax of the sensation I was still feeling from the gaze of Lucrezia Borgia. The gardens, the summer sky, the consciousness of Bertha's arm being within mine, all vanished, and I seemed to be suddenly in darkness, out of which there gradually broke a dim firelight, and I felt myself sitting in my father's leather chair in the library at home. I knew the fireplace—the dogs for the wood-fire—the black marble chimney-piece with the white marble medallion of the dying Cleopatra in the centre. Intense and hopeless misery was pressing on my soul; the light became stronger, for Bertha was entering with a candle in her hand—Bertha, my wife—with cruel eyes, with green jewels and green leaves on her white ball-dress; every hateful thought within her present to me . . . 'Madman, idiot! why don't you kill yourself, then?' It was a moment of hell. I saw into her pitiless soul—saw its barren worldliness, its scorching hate—and felt it clothe me round like an air I was obliged to breathe. She came with her candle and stood over me with a bitter smile of contempt; I saw the great emerald brooch on her bosom, a studded serpent with diamond eyes. I shuddered—I despised this woman with the barren soul and mean thoughts; but I felt helpless before her, as if she clutched my bleeding heart, and would clutch it till the last drop of life-blood ebbed away. She was my wife, and we hated each other. Gradually the hearth, the dim library, the candle-light disappeared—seemed to melt away into a background of light, the green serpent with the diamond eyes remaining a dark image on the retina. Then I had a sense of my eyelids quivering, and the living daylight broke in upon me; I saw gardens, and heard voices; I was seated on the steps of the Belvedere Terrace, and my friends were round me.

The tumult of mind into which I was thrown by this hideous vision made me ill for several days, and prolonged our stay in Vienna. I shuddered with horror as the scene recurred to me; and it recurred constantly, with all its minutiae, as if they had been burnt into my memory; and yet, such is the madness of the human heart under the influence of its immediate desires, I felt a wild hell-braving joy that Bertha was to be mine; for the fulfilment of my former prevision concerning her first appearance before me, left me little hope that this last hideous glimpse of the future was the mere diseased play of my own mind, and had no relation to external realities. One thing alone I looked towards as a possible means of casting doubt on my terrible conviction—the discovery that my vision of Prague had been false—and Prague was the next city on our route.

Meanwhile, I was no sooner in Bertha's society again, than I was as completely under her sway as before. What if I saw into the heart of Bertha, the matured woman—Bertha, my wife? Bertha, the *girl*, was a fascinating secret to me still: I trembled under her touch; I felt the witchery of her presence; I yearned to be assured of her love. The fear of poison is feeble against the sense of thirst. Nay, I was just as jealous of my brother as before—just as much irritated by his small patronising ways; for my pride, my diseased sensibility, were there as they had always been, and winced as inevitably under every offence as my eye winced from an intruding mote. The future, even when brought within the compass of feeling by a vision that made me shudder, had still no more than the force of an idea, compared with the force of present emotion—of my love for Bertha, of my dislike and jealousy towards my brother.

It is an old story, that men sell themselves to the tempter, and sign a bond with their blood, because it is only to take effect at a distant day; then rush on to snatch the cup their souls thirst after with an impulse not the less savage because there is a dark shadow beside them for evermore. There is no short cut, no patent tram-road, to wisdom: after all the centuries of invention, the soul's path lies through the thorny wilderness which must be still trodden in solitude, with bleeding feet, with sobs for help, as it was trodden by them of old time.

My mind speculated eagerly on the means by which I should become my brother's successful rival, for I was still too timid, in my ignorance of Bertha's actual feeling, to venture on any step that would urge from her an avowal of it. I thought I should gain confidence even for this, if my vision of Prague proved to have been veracious; and yet, the horror of that certitude! Behind the slim girl Bertha, whose words and looks I watched for, whose touch was bliss, there stood continually that Bertha with the fuller form, the harder eyes, the more rigid mouth—with the barren, selfish soul laid bare; no longer a fascinating secret, but a measured fact, urging itself perpetually on my unwilling sight. Are you unable to give me your sympathy—you who read this? Are you unable to imagine this double consciousness at work within me, flowing on like two parallel streams which never mingle their waters and blend into a common hue? Yet you must have known something of the presentiments that spring from an insight at war with passion; and my visions were only like presentiments intensified to horror. You have known the powerlessness of ideas before the might of impulse; and my visions, when once they had passed into memory, were mere ideas—pale shadows that beckoned in vain, while my hand was grasped by the living and the loved.

In after-days I thought with bitter regret that if I had foreseen something more or something different—if instead of that hideous vision which poisoned the passion it could not destroy, or if even along with it I could have had a foreshadowing of that moment when I looked on my brother's face for the last time, some softening influence would have been shed over my feeling towards him: pride and hatred would surely have been subdued into pity, and the record of those hidden sins would have been shortened. But this is one of the vain thoughts with which we men flatter ourselves. We try to believe that the egoism within us would have easily been melted, and that it was only the narrowness of our knowledge which hemmed in our generosity, our awe, our human piety, and hindered them from submerging our hard indifference to the sensations and emotions of our fellows. Our tenderness and self-renunciation seem strong when our egoism has had its day—when, after our mean striving for a triumph that is to be another's loss, the triumph comes suddenly, and we shudder at it, because it is held out by the chill hand of death.

Our arrival in Prague happened at night, and I was glad of this, for it seemed like a deferring of a terrible decisive moment, to be in the city for hours without seeing it. As we were not to remain long in Prague, but to go on speedily to Dresden, it was proposed that we should drive out the next morning and take a general view of the place, as well as visit some of its specially interesting spots, before the heat became oppressive—for we were in August, and the season was hot and dry. But it happened that the ladies were rather late at their morning toilet, and to my father's politely-repressed but perceptible annoyance, we were not in the carriage till the morning was far advanced. I thought with a sense of relief, as we entered the Jews' quarter, where we were to visit the old synagogue, that we should be kept in this flat, shut-up part of the city, until we should all be too tired and too warm to go farther, and so we should return without seeing more than the streets through which we had already passed. That would give me another day's suspense—suspense, the only form in which a fearful spirit knows the solace of hope. But, as I stood under the blackened, groined arches of that old synagogue, made dimly visible by the seven thin candles in the sacred lamp, while our Jewish cicerone reached down the Book of the Law, and read to us in its ancient tongue—I felt a shuddering impression that this strange building, with its shrunken lights, this surviving withered remnant of medieval Judaism, was of a piece with my vision. Those darkened dusty Christian saints, with their loftier arches and their larger candles, needed the consolatory scorn with which they might point to a more shrivelled death-in-life than their own.

As I expected, when we left the Jews' quarter the elders of our party wished to return to the hotel. But now, instead of rejoicing in this, as I had done beforehand, I felt a sudden overpowering impulse to go on at once to the bridge, and put an end to the suspense I had been wishing to protract. I declared, with unusual decision, that I would get out of the carriage and walk on alone; they might return without me. My father, thinking this merely a sample of my usual 'poetic nonsense,' objected that I should only do myself harm by walking in the heat; but when I persisted, he said angrily that I might follow my own absurd devices, but that Schmidt (our courier) must go with me. I assented to this, and set off with Schmidt towards the bridge. I had no sooner passed from under the archway of the grand old gate leading on to the bridge, than a trembling seized me, and I turned cold under the midday sun; yet I went on; I was in search of something—a small detail which I remembered with special intensity as part of my vision. There it was—the patch of rainbow light on the pavement transmitted through a lamp in the shape of a star.

II

Before the autumn was at an end, and while the brown leaves still stood thick on the beeches in our park, my brother and Bertha were engaged to each other, and it was understood that their marriage was to take place early in the next spring. In spite of the certainty I had felt from that moment on the bridge at Prague, that Bertha would one day be my wife, my constitutional timidity and distrust had continued to be-numb me, and the words in which I had sometimes premediated a confession of my love, had died away unuttered. The same conflict had gone on within me as before—the longing for an assurance of love from Bertha's lips, the dread lest a word of contempt and denial should fall upon me like a corrosive acid. What was the conviction of a distant necessity to me? I trembled under a present glance, I hungered after a present joy, I was clogged and chilled by a present fear. And so the days passed on: I witnessed Bertha's engagement and heard her marriage discussed as if I were under a conscious nightmare—knowing it was a dream that would vanish, but feeling stifled under the grasp of hard-clutching fingers.

When I was not in Bertha's presence—and I was with her very often, for she continued to treat me with a playful patronage that wakened no jealousy in my brother—I spent my time chiefly in wandering, in strolling, or taking long rides while the daylight lasted, and then shutting myself up with my unread books; for books had lost the power of chaining my attention. My self-consciousness was heightened to that pitch of intensity in which our own emotions take the form of a drama which urges itself imperatively on our contemplation, and we begin to weep, less under the sense of our suffering than at the thought of it. I felt a sort of pitying anguish over the pathos of my own lot: the lot of a being finely organized for pain, but with hardly any fibres that responded to pleasure—to whom the idea of future evil robbed the present of its joy, and for whom the idea of future good did not still the uneasiness of a present yearning or a present dread. I went dumbly through that stage of the poet's suffering, in which he feels the delicious pang of utterance, and makes an image of his sorrows.

I was left entirely without remonstrance concerning this dreamy wayward life: I knew my father's thought about me: 'That lad will never be good for anything in life: he may waste his years in an insignificant way on the income that falls to him: I shall not trouble myself about a career for him.'

One mild morning in the beginning of November, it happened that I was standing outside the portico patting lazy old Caesar, a Newfoundland almost blind with age, the only dog that ever took any notice of me—for the very dogs shunned me, and fawned on the happier people about me—when the groom brought up my brother's horse which was to carry him to the hunt, and my brother himself appeared at the door, florid, broad-chested, and self-complacent, feeling what a good-natured fellow he was not to behave insolently to us all on the strength of his great advantages.

'Latimer, old boy,' he said to me in a tone of compassionate cordiality, 'what a pity it is you don't have a run with the hounds now and then! The finest thing in the world for low spirits!'

'Low spirits!' I thought bitterly, as he rode away; 'that is the sort of phrase with which coarse, narrow natures like yours think to describe experience of which you can know no more than your horse knows. It is to such as you that the good of this world falls: ready dullness, healthy selfishness, good-tempered conceit—these are the keys to happiness.'

The quick thought came, that my selfishness was even stronger than his—it was only a suffering selfishness instead of an enjoying one. But then, again, by exasperating insight into Alfred's self-complacent soul, his freedom from all the doubts and fears, the unsatisfied yearnings, the exquisite tortures of sensitiveness, that had made the web of my life, seemed to absolve me from all bonds towards him. This man needed no pity, no love; those fine influences would have been as little felt by him as the delicate white mist is felt by the rock it caresses. There was no evil in store for *him*: if he was not to marry Bertha, it would be because he had found a lot pleasanter to himself.

Mr. Filmore's house lay not more than half a mile beyond our own gates, and whenever I knew my brother was gone in another direction, I went there for the chance of finding Bertha at home. Later on in the day I walked thither. By a rare accident was she alone, and we walked out in the grounds together, for she seldom went on foot beyond the trimly-kept gravel walks. I remember what a beautiful sylph she looked to me as the low November sun shone on her blond hair, and she tripped along teasing me with her usual light banter, to which I listened half-fondly, half-moodily; it was all the sign Bertha's mysterious inner self ever made to me. Today perhaps the moodiness predominated, for I had not yet shaken off the access of jealous hate which my brother had raised in me by his parting patronage. Suddenly I interrupted and startled her by saying, almost fiercely, 'Bertha, how can you love Alfred?'

She looked at me with surprise for a moment, but soon her light smile came again, and she answered sarcastically, 'Why do you suppose I love him?'

'How can you ask that, Bertha?'

'What! your wisdom thinks I must love the man I'm going to marry? The most unpleasant thing in the world. I should quarrel with him; I should be jealous of him; our *ménage* would be conducted in a very ill-bred manner. A little quiet contempt contributes greatly to the elegance of life.'

'Bertha, that is not your real feeling. Why do you delight in trying to deceive me by inventing such cynical speeches?'

'I need never take the trouble of invention in order to deceive you, my small Tasso'—(that was the mocking name she usually gave me).

'The easiest way to deceive a poet is to tell him the truth.'

She was testing the validity of her epigram in a daring way, and for a moment the shadow of my vision—the Bertha whose soul was no secret to me—passed between me and the radiant girl, the playful sylph whose feelings were a fascinating mystery. I suppose I must have shuddered, or betrayed in some other way my momentary chill of horror.

'Tasso!' she said, seizing my wrist, and peeping round into my face, 'are you really beginning to discern what a heartless girl I am? Why, you are not half the poet I thought you were; you were actually capable of believing the truth about me.'

The shadow passed from between us, and was no longer the object nearest to me. The girl whose light fingers grasped me, whose elfish charming face looked into mine—who, I thought, was betraying an interest in my feelings that she would not have directly avowed—this warm breathing presence again possessed my senses and imagination like a returning siren melody which had been overpowered for an instant by the roar of threatening waves. It was a moment as delicious to me as the waking up to a consciousness of youth after a dream of middle age. I forgot everything but my passion, and said with swimming eyes:

'Bertha, shall you love me when we are first married? I wouldn't mind if you really loved me only for a little while.'

Her look of astonishment, as she loosed my hand and started away from me, recalled me to a sense of my strange, my criminal indiscretion.

'Forgive me,' I said, hurriedly, as soon as I could speak again; 'I did not know what I was saying.'

'Ah, Tasso's mad fit has come on, I see,' she answered quietly, for she had recovered herself sooner than I had. 'Let him go home and keep his head cool. I must go in, for the sun is setting.'

I left her—full of indignation against myself. I had let slip words which, if she reflected on them, might rouse in her a suspicion of my abnormal mental condition—a suspicion which of all things I dreaded. And besides that, I was ashamed of the apparent baseness I had committed in uttering them to my brother's betrothed wife. I wandered home slowly, entering our park through a private gate instead of by the lodges. As I approached the house, I saw a man dashing off at full speed from the stable-yard across the park. Had any accident happened at home? No; perhaps it was only one of my father's peremptory business errands that required this headlong haste.

Nevertheless I quickened my pace without any distinct motive, and was soon at the house. I will not dwell on the scene I found there. My brother was dead—had been pitched from his horse, and killed on the spot by a concussion of the brain.

I went up to the room where he lay, and where my father was seated beside him with a look of rigid despair. I had shunned my father more than anyone since our return home, for the radical antipathy between our natures made my insight into his inner self a constant affliction to me. But now, as I went up to him, and stood beside him in sad silence, I felt the presence of a new element that blended us as we had never been blent before. My father had been one of the most successful men in the money-getting world: he had had no sentimental sufferings, no illness. The heaviest trouble that had befallen him was the death of his first wife. But he married my mother soon after; and I remembered he seemed exactly the same, to my keen childish observation, the week after her death as before. But now, at last, a sorrow had come—the sorrow of old age, which suffers the more from the crushing of its pride and its hopes, in proportion as the pride and hope are narrow prosaic. His son was to have been married soon—would probably have stood for the borough at the next election. That son's existence was the best motive that could be alleged for making new purchases of land every year to round off the estate. It is a dreary thing to live on doing the same things year after year, without knowing why we do them. Perhaps the tragedy of disappointed youth and passion is less piteous than the tragedy of disappointed age and worldliness.

As I saw into the desolation of my father's heart, I felt a movement of deep pity towards him, which was the beginning of a new affection—an affection that grew and strengthened in spite of the strange bitterness with which he regarded me in the first month or two after my brother's death. If it had not been for the softening influence of my compassion for him—the first deep compassion I had ever felt—I should have been stung by the perception that my father transferred the inheritance of an eldest son to me with a mortified sense that fate had compelled him to the unwelcome course of caring for me as an important being. It was only in spite of himself that he began to think of me with anxious regard. There is hardly any neglected child for whom death has made vacant a more favoured place, who will not understand what I mean.

Gradually, however, my new deference to his wishes, the effect of that patience which was born of my pity for him, won upon his affection, and he began to please himself with the endeavour to make me fill my brother's place as fully as my feebler personality would admit. I saw that the prospect which by and by presented itself of my becoming Bertha's husband was welcome to him, and he even contemplated in my case what he had not intended in my brother's—that his son and daughter-in-law should make one household with him. My softened feeling towards my father made this the happiest time I had known since childhood—these last months in which I retained the delicious illusion of loving Bertha, of longing and doubting and hoping that she might love me. She behaved with a certain new consciousness and distance towards me after my brother's death; and I too was under a double constraint—that of delicacy towards my brother's memory, and of anxiety as to the impression my abrupt words had left on her mind. But the additional screen this mutual reserve erected between us only brought me more completely under her power: no matter how empty the adytum, so that the veil be thick enough. So absolute is our soul's need of something hidden and uncertain for the maintenance of that doubt and hope and effort which are the breath of its life, that if the whole future were laid bare to us beyond today, the interest of all mankind would be bent on the hours that lie between; we should pant after the uncertainties of our one morning and our one afternoon; we should rush fiercely to the Exchange of our last possibility of speculatio, of success, of disappointment: we should have a glut of political prophets foretelling a crisis or a no-crisis within the only twenty-four hours left open to prophecy. Conceive the condition of the human mind of all propositions whatsoever were self-evident except one, which was to become self-evident at the close of a summer's day, but in the meantime might be the subject of question, of hypothesis, of debate. Art and philosophy, literature and science, would fasten like bees on that one proposition which had the honey of probability in it, and be the more eager because their enjoyment would end with sunset. Our impulses, our spiritual activities, no more adjust themselves to the idea of their future nullity, than the beating of our heart, or the irritability of our muscles.

Bertha, the slim, fair-haired girl, whose present thoughts and emotions were an enigma to me amidst the fatiguing obviousness of the other minds around me, was as absorbing to me as a single unknown today—as a single hypothetic proposition to remain problematic till sunset; and all the cramped, hemmed-in belief and disbelief, trust and distrust, of my nature, welled out in this one narrow channel.

And she made me believe that she loved me. Without ever quitting her tone of *badinage* and playful superiority, she intoxicated me with the sense that I was necessary to her, that she was never at ease unless I was near her, submitting to her playful tyranny. It costs a woman so little effort to besot us in this way! A half-repressed word, a moment's unexpected silence, even an easy fit of petulance on our account, will serve us as *hashish* for a long while. Out of the subtlest web of scarcely perceptible signs, she set me weaving the fancy that she had always unconsciously loved me better than Alfred, but that, with the ignorant fluttered sensibility of a young girl, she had been imposed on by the charm that lay for her in the distinction of being admired and chosen by a man who made so brilliant a figure in the world as my brother. She satirised herself in a very graceful way for her vanity and ambition. What was it to me that I had the light of my wretched prevision on the fact that now it was I who possessed at least all but the personal part of my brother's advantages? Our sweet illusions are half of them conscious illusions like effects of colour that we know to be made up of tinsel, broken glass, and rags.

We were married eighteen months after Alfred's death, one cold, clear morning in April, when there came hail and sunshine both together; and Bertha, in her white silk and pale-green leaves, and the pale hues of her hair and face, looked like the spirit of the morning. My father was happier than he had thought of being again: my marriage, he felt sure, would complete the desirable modification of my character, and make me practical and worldly enough to take my place in society among sane men. For he delighted in Bertha's tact and acuteness, and felt sure she would be mistress of me, and make me what she chose: I was only twenty-one, and madly in love with her. Poor father! He kept that hope a little while after our first year of marriage, and it was not quite extinct when paralysis came and saved him from utter disappointment.

I shall hurry through the rest of my story, not dwelling so much as I have hitherto done on my inward experience. When people are well known to each other, they talk rather of what befalls them externally, leaving their feelings and sentiments to be inferred.

We lived in a round of visits for some time after our return home, giving splendid dinner-parties, and making a sensation in our neighbourhood by the new lustre of our equipage, for my father had reserved this display of his increased wealth for the period of his son's marriage; and we gave our acquaintances liberal opportunity of remarking that it was a pity I made so poor a figure as an heir and a bridegroom. The nervous fatigue of this existence, the insincerities and platitudes which I had to live through twice over—through my inner and outward sense—would have been maddening to me, if I had not had that sort of intoxicated callousness which came from the delights of a first passion. A bride and bridegroom surrounded by all the appliances of wealth, hurried through the day by the whirl of society, filling their solitary moments with hastily-snatched caresses, are prepared for their future life together as the novice is prepared for the cloister—by experiencing its utmost contrast.

Through all these crowded, excited months, Bertha's inward self remained shrouded from me, and I still read her thoughts only through the language of her lips and demeanour: I had still the human interest of wondering whether what I did and said pleased her, of longing to hear a word of affection, of giving a delicious exaggeration of meaning to her smile. But I was conscious of a growing difference in her manner towards me; sometimes strong enough to be called haughty coldness, cutting and chilling me as the hail had done that came across the sunshine on our marriage morning; sometimes only perceptible in the dexterous avoidance of a *tête-à-tête* walk or dinner to which I had been looking forward. I had been deeply pained by this—had even felt a sort of crushing of the heart, from the sense that my brief day of happiness was near its setting; but still I remained dependent on Bertha, eager for the last rays of a bliss that would soon be gone for ever, hoping and watching for some after-glow more beautiful from the impending light.

I remember—how should I not remember?—the time when that dependence and hope utterly left me, when the sadness I had felt in Bertha's growing estrangement became a joy that I looked back upon with longing as a man might look back on the last pains in a paralysed limb. It was just after the close of my father's last illness, which had necessarily withdrawn us from society and thrown us more upon each other. It was the evening of my father's death. On that evening the veil which had shrouded Bertha's soul from me—had made me find in her alone among my fellow-beings the blessed possibility of mystery, and doubt, and expectations—was first withdrawn. Perhaps it was the first day since the beginning of my passion for her, in which that passion was completely neutralized by the presence of an absorbing feeling of another kind. I had been watching by my father's death-bed: I had been witnessing the last fitful yearning glance his soul had cast back on the spent inheritance of life—the last faint consciousness of love he had gathered from the pressure of my hand. What are all our personal loves when we have been sharing in that supreme agony? In the first moments when we come away from the presence of death, every other relation to the living is merged, to our feeling, in the great relation of a common nature and a common destiny.

In that state of mind I joined Bertha in her private sitting-room. She was seated in a leaning posture on a settee, with her back towards the door; the great rich coils of her pale blond hair surmounting her small neck, visible above the back of the settee. I remember, as I closed the door behind me, a cold tremulousness seizing me, and a vague sense of being hated and lonely—vague and strong, like a presentiment. I know how I looked at that moment, for I saw myself in Bertha's thought as she lifted her cutting grey eyes, and looked at me: a miserable ghost-seer, surrounded by phantoms in the noonday, trembling under a breeze when the leaves were still, without appetite for the common objects of human desires, but pining after the moonbeams. We were front to front with each other, and judged each other. The terrible moment of complete illumination had come to me, and I saw that the darkness had hidden no landscape from me, but only a blank prosaic wall: from that evening forth, through the sickening years which followed, I saw all round the narrow room of this woman's soul—saw petty artifice and mere negation where I had delighted to believe in coy sensibilities and in wit at war with latent feeling—saw the light floating vanities of the girl defining themselves into the systematic coquetry, the scheming selfishness, of the woman—saw repulsion and antipathy harden into cruel hatred, giving pain only for the sake of wreaking itself.

For Bertha too, after her kind, felt the bitterness of disillusion. She had believed that my wild poet's passion for her would make me her slave; and that, being her slave, I should execute her will in all things. With the essential shallowness of a negative, unimaginative nature, she was unable to conceive the fact that sensibilities were anything else than weaknesses. She had thought my weaknesses would put me in her power, and she found them unmanageable forces. Our positions were reversed. Before marriage she had completely mastered my imagination, for she was a secret to me; and I created the unknown thought before which I trembled as if it were hers. But now that her soul was laid open to me, now that I was compelled to share the privacy of her motives, to follow all the petty devices that preceded her words and acts, she found herself powerless with me, except to produce in me the chill shudder of repulsion—powerless, because I could be acted on by no lever within her reach. I was dead to worldly ambitions, to social vanities, to all the incentives within the compass of her narrow imagination, and I lived under influences utterly invisible to her.

She was really pitiable to have such a husband, and so all the world thought. A graceful, brilliant woman, like Bertha, who smiled on morning callers, made a figure in ballrooms, and was capable of that light repartee which, from such a woman, is accepted as wit, was secure of carrying off all sympathy from a husband who was sickly, abstracted and, as some suspected, crack-brained. Even the servants in our house gave her the balance of their regard and pity. For there were no audible quarrels between us; our alienation, our repulsion from each other, lay within the silence of our own hearts; and if the mistress went out a great deal, and seemed to dislike the master's society, was it not natural, poor thing? The master was odd. I was kind and just to my dependants, but I excited in them a shrinking, half-contemptuous pity; for this class of men and women are but slightly determined in their estimate of others by general considerations, or even experience, of character. They judge of persons as they judge of coins, and value those who pass current at a high rate.

After a time I interfered so little with Bertha's habits that it might seem wonderful how her hatred towards me could grow so intense and active as it did. But she had begun to suspect, by some involuntary betrayal of mind, that there was an abnormal power of penetration in me—that fitfully, at least, I was strangely cognizant of her thoughts and intentions, and she began to be haunted by a terror of me, which alternated every now and then with defiance. She meditated continually how the incubus could be shaken off her life—how she could be freed from this hateful bond to a being whom she at once despised as an imbecile, and dreaded as an inquisitor. For a long while she lived in the hope that my evident wretchedness would drive me to the commission of suicide; but suicide was not in my nature. I was too completely swayed by the sense that I was in the grasp of unknown forces, to believe in my power of self-release. Towards my own destiny I had become entirely passive; for my one ardent desire had spent itself, and impulse no longer predominated over knowledge. For this reason I never thought of taking any steps towards a complete separation, which would have made our alienation evident to the world. Why should I rush for help to a new course, when I was only suffering from the consequences of a deed which had been the act of my intensest will? That would have been the logic of one who had desires to gratify, and I had no desires. But Bertha and I lived more and more aloof from each other. The rich find it easy to live married and apart.

That course of our life which I have indicated in a few sentences filled the space of years. So much misery—so slow and hideous a growth of hatred and sin, may be compressed into a sentence! And men judge of each other's lives through this summary medium. They epitomize the experience of their fellow-mortal, and pronounce judgement on him in neat syntax, and feel themselves wise and virtuous—conquerors over the temptations they define in well-selected predicates. Seven years of wretchedness glide over the lips of the man who has never counted them out in moments of chill disappointment, of head and heart throbbings, of dread and vain wrestling, of remorse and despair. We learn *words* by rote, but not their meaning; *that* must be paid for with our life-blood, and printed in the subtle fibres of our nerves.

But I will hasten to finish my story. Brevity is justified at once to those who readily understand, and to those who will never understand.

Some years after my father's death, I was sitting by the dim firelight in my library one January evening—sitting in the leather chair that used to be my father's—when Bertha appeared at the door, with a candle in her hand, and advanced towards me. I knew the ball-dress she had on—the white ball-dress, with the green jewels, shone upon by the light of the wax candle which lit up the medallion of the dying Cleopatra on the mantelpiece. Why did she come to me before going out? I had not seen her in the library, which was my habitual place, for months. Why did she stand before me with the candle in her hand, with her cruel contemptuous eyes fixed on me, and the glittering serpent, like a familiar demon, on her breast? For a moment I thought this fulfilment of my vision at Vienna marked some dreadful crisis in my fate, but I saw nothing in Bertha's mind, as she stood before me except scorn for the look of overwhelming misery with which I sat before her . . . 'Fool, idiot, why don't you kill yourself, then?'—that was her thought. But at length her thoughts reverted to her errand, and she spoke aloud. The apparently indifferent nature of the errand seemed to make a ridiculous anticlimax to my prevision and agitation.

'I have had to hire a new maid. Fletcher is going to be married, and she wants me to ask you to let her husband have the public-house and farm at Molton. I wish him to have it. You must give the promise now, because Fletcher is going tomorrow morning—and quickly, because I'm in a hurry.'

'Very well; you may promise her,' I said, indifferently, and Bertha swept out of the library again.

I always shrank from the sight of a new person, and all the more when it was a person whose mental life was likely to weary my reluctant insight with worldly ignorant trivialities. But I shrank especially from the sight of this new maid, because her advent had been announced to me at a moment to which I could not cease to attach some fatality: I had a vague dread that I should find her mixed up with the dreary drama of my life—that some new sickening vision would reveal her to me as an evil genius. When at last I did unavoidably meet her, the vague dread was changed into definite disgust. She was a tall, wiry, dark-eyed woman, this Mrs. Archer, with a face handsome enough to give her coarse hard nature the odious finish of bold, self-confident coquetry. That was enough to make me avoid her, quite apart from the contemptuous feeling with which she contemplated me. I seldom saw her; but I perceived that she rapidly became a favourite with her mistress, and, after the lapse of eight or nine months, I began to be aware that there had arisen in Bertha's mind towards this woman a mingled feeling of fear and dependence, and that this feeling was associated with ill-defined images of candle-light scenes in her dressing-room, and the locking-up of something in Bertha's cabinet. My interviews with my wife had become as brief and so rarely solitary, that I had no opportunity of perceiving these images in her mind with more definiteness. The recollections of the past become contracted in the rapidity of thought till they sometimes bear hardly a more distinct resemblance to the external reality than the forms of an oriental alphabet to the objects that suggested them.

Besides, for the last year or more a modification had been going forward in my mental condition, and was growing more and more marked. My insight into the minds of those around me was becoming dimmer and more fitful, and the ideas that crowded my double consciousness became less and less dependent on any personal contact. All that was personal in me seemed to be suffering a gradual death, so that I was losing the organ through which the personal agitations and projects of others could affect me. But along with this relief from wearisome insight, there was a new development of what I concluded—as I have since found rightly—to be a prevision of external scenes. It was as if the relation between me and my fellow-men was more and more deadened, and my relation to what we call the inanimate was quickened into new life. The more I lived apart from society, and in proportion as my wretchedness subsided from the violent throb of agonised passion into the dullness of habitual pain, the more frequent and vivid became such visions as that I had had of Prague—of strange cities, of sandy plains, of gigantic ruins, of midnight skies with strange bright constellations, of mountain-passes, of grassy nooks flecked with the afternoon sunshine through the boughs: I was in the midst of such scenes, and in all of them one presence seemed to weigh on me in all these mighty shapes—the presence of something unknown and pitiless. For continual suffering had annihilated religious faith within me: to the utterly miserable—the unloving and the unloved—there is no religion possible, no worship but a worship of devils. And beyond all these, and continually recurring, was the vision of my death—the pangs, the suffocation, the last struggle, when life would be grasped at in vain.

Things were in this state near the end of the seventh year. I had become entirely free from insight, from my abnormal cognizance of any other consciousness than my own, and instead of intruding involuntarily into the world of other minds, was living continually in my own solitary future. Bertha was aware that I was greatly changed. To my surprise she had of late seemed to seek opportunities of remaining in my society, and had cultivated that kind of distant yet familiar talk which is customary between a husband and wife who live in polite and irrevocable alienation. I bore this with languid submission, and without feeling enough interest in her motives to be roused into keen observation; yet I could not help perceiving something triumphant and excited in her carriage and the expression of her face—something too subtle to express itself in words or tones, but giving one the idea that she lived in a state of expectation or hopeful suspense. My chief feeling was satisfaction that her inner self was once more shut from me; and I almost revelled for the moment in the absent melancholy that made me answer her at cross purposes, and betray utter ignorance of what she had been saying. I remember well the look and the smile with which she one day said, after a mistake of this kind on my part: 'I used to think you were a clairvoyant and that was the reason why you were so bitter against other clairvoyants, wanting to keep your monopoly; but I see now you have become rather duller than the rest of the world.'

I said nothing in reply. It occurred to me that her recent obtrusion of herself upon me might have been prompted by the wish to test my power of detecting some of her secrets; but I let the thought drop again at once: her motives and her deeds had no interest for me, and whatever pleasures she might be seeking, I had no wish to baulk her. There was still pity in my soul for every living thing, and Bertha was living—was surrounded with possibilities of misery.

Just at this time there occurred an event which roused me somewhat from my inertia, and gave me an interest in the passing moment that I had thought impossible for me. It was a visit from Charles Meunier, who had written me word that he was coming to England for relaxation from too strenuous labour, and would like to see me. Meunier had now a European reputation; but his letter to me expressed that keen remembrance of an early regard, an early debt of sympathy, which is inseparable from nobility of character: and I too felt as if his presence would be to me like a transient resurrection into a happier pre-existence.

He came, and as far as possible, I renewed our old pleasure of making *tête-à-tête* excursions, though, instead of mountains and glaciers and the wide blue lake, we had to content ourselves with mere slopes and ponds and artificial plantations. The years had changed us both, but with what different result! Meunier was now a brilliant figure in society, to whom elegant women pretended to listen, and whose acquaintance was boasted of by noblemen ambitious of brains. He repressed with the utmost delicacy any betrayal of the shock which I am sure he must have received from our meeting, or of a desire to penetrate into my condition and circumstances, and sought by the utmost exertion of his charming social powers to make our reunion agreeable. Bertha was much struck by the unexpected fascinations of a visitor whom she had expected to find presentable only on the score of his celebrity, and put forth all her coquetries and accomplishments.

Apparently she succeeded in attracting his admiration, for his manner towards her was attentive and flattering. The effect of his presence on me was so benignant, especially in those renewals of our old *tête-à-tête* wanderings, when he poured forth to me wonderful narratives of his professional experience, that more than once, when his talk turned on the psychological relations of disease, the thought crossed my mind that, if his stay with me were long enough, I might possibly bring myself to tell this man the secrets of my lot. Might there not lie some comprehension and sympathy ready for me in his large susceptible mind? But the thought only flickered feebly now and then, and died out before it could become a wish. The horror I had of again breaking in on the privacy of another soul, made me, by an irrational instinct, draw the shroud of concealment more closely around my own, as we automatically perform the gesture we feel to be wanting in another.

When Meunier's visit was approaching its conclusion, there happened an event which caused some excitement in our household, owing to the surprisingly strong effect it appeared to produce on Bertha—on Bertha, the self-possessed, who usually seemed inaccessible to feminine agitations, and did even hate in a self-restrained hygienic manner. This event was the sudden severe illness of her maid, Mrs. Archer. I have reserved to this moment the mention of a circumstance which had forced itself on my notice shortly before Meunier's arrival, namely, that there had been some quarrel between Bertha and this maid, apparently during a visit to a distant family, in which she had accompanied her mistress. I had overheard Archer speaking in a tone of bitter insolence, which I should have thought an adequate reason for immediate dismissal. No dismissal followed; on the contrary, Bertha seemed to be silently putting up with personal inconveniences from the exhibitions of this woman's temper. I was the more astonished to observe that her illness seemed a cause of strong solicitude to Bertha; that she was at the bedside night and day, and would allow no one else to officiate as head-nurse. It happened that our family doctor was out on a holiday, an accident which made Meunier's presence in the house doubly welcome, and he apparently entered into the case with an interest which seemed so much stronger than the ordinary professional feeling, that one day when he had fallen into a long fit of silence, after visiting her, I said to him:

'Is this a very peculiar case of disease, Meunier?'

'No,' he answered, 'it is an attack of peritonitis, which will be fatal, but which does not differ physically from many other cases that have come under my observation. But I'll tell you what I have on my mind. I want to make an experiment on this woman, if you will give me permission. It can do her no harm—will give her no pain—for I shall not make it until life is extinct to all purposes of sensation. I want to try the effect of transfusing blood into her arteries after the heart has ceased to beat for some minutes. I have tried the experiment again and again with animals that have died of the disease, with astounding results, and I want to try it on a human subject. I have the small tubes necessary, in a case I have with me, and the rest of the apparatus could be prepared readily. I should use my own blood—take it from my own arm. This woman won't live through the night, I'm convinced, and I want you to promise me your assistance in making the experiment. I can't do without another hand, but it would perhaps not be well to call in a medical assistant from among your provincial doctors. A disagreeable foolish version of the thing might get abroad.'

'Have you spoken to my wife on the subject?' I said, 'because she appears to be peculiarly sensitive about this woman: she has been a favourite maid.'

'To tell you the truth,' said Meunier, 'I don't want her to know about it. There are always insuperable difficulties with women in these matters, and the effect on the supposed dead body may be startling. You and I will sit up together, and be in readiness. When certain symptoms appear I shall take you in, and at the right moment we must arrange to get every one else out of the room.'

I need not give you further conversation on the subject. He entered very fully into the details, and overcame my repulsion from them, by exciting in me a mingled awe and curiosity concerning the possible results of his experiment.

We prepared everything, and he instructed me in my part as assistant. He had not told Bertha of his absolute conviction that Archer would not survive through the night, and endeavoured to persuade her to leave the patient and take a night's rest. But she was obstinate, suspecting the fact that death was at hand, and supposing that he wished merely to save her nerves. She refused to leave the sick-room. Meunier and I sat up together in the library, he making frequent visits to the sick-room, and returning with the information that the case was taking precisely the course he expected. Once he said to me, 'Can you imagine any cause of ill-feeling this woman has against her mistress, who is so devoted to her?'

'I think there was some misunderstanding between them before her illness. Why do you ask?'

'Because I have observed for the last five or six hours—since, I fancy, she has lost all hope of recovery—there seems a strange prompting in her to say something which pain and failing strength forbid her to utter; and there is a look of hideous meaning in her eyes, which she turns continually towards her mistress. In this disease the mind often remains singularly clear to the last.'

'I am not surprised at an indication of malevolent feeling in her,' I said. 'She is a woman who has always inspired me with distrust and dislike, but she managed to insinuate herself into her mistress's favour.' He was silent after this, looking at the fire with an air of absorption, till he went upstairs again. He stayed away longer than usual, and on returning, said to me quietly, 'Come now.'

I followed him to the chamber where death was hovering. The dark hangings of the large bed made a background that gave a strong relief to Bertha's pale face as I entered. She started forward as she saw me enter, and then looked at Meunier with an expression of angry inquiry: but he lifted up his hand as if to impose silence, while he fixed his glance on the dying woman and felt her pulse. The face was pinched and ghastly, a cold perspiration was on the forehead, and the eyelids were lowered so as to conceal the large dark eyes. After a minute or two, Meunier walked round to the other side of the bed where Bertha stood, and with his usual air of gentle politeness towards her begged her to leave the patient under our care—everything should be done for her—she was no longer in a state to be conscious of an affectionate presence. Bertha was hesitating, apparently almost willing to believe his assurance and to comply. She looked round at the ghastly dying face, as if to read the confirmation of that assurance, when for a moment the lowered eyelids were raised again, and it seemed as if the eyes were looking towards Bertha, but blankly. A shudder passed through Bertha's frame, and she returned to her station near the pillow, tacitly implying that she would not leave the room.

The eyelids were lifted no more. Once I looked at Bertha as she watched the face of the dying one. She wore a rich *peignoir*, and her blond hair was half covered by a lace cap: in her attire she was, as always, an elegant woman, fit to figure in a picture of modern aristocratic life: but I asked myself how that face of hers could ever have seemed to me the face of a woman born of woman, with memories of childhood, capable of pain, needing to be fondled? The features at that moment seemed to be preternaturally sharp, the eyes were so hard and eager—she looked like a cruel immortal, finding her spiritual feast in the agonies of a dying race. For across those hard features there came something like a flash when the last hour had been breathed out, and we all felt that the dark veil had completely fallen. What secret was there between Bertha and this woman? I turned my eyes from her with a horrible dread lest my insight should return, and I should be obliged to see what had been breeding about two unloving women's hearts. I felt that Bertha had been watching for the moment of death as the sealing of her secret: I thanked Heaven it could remain sealed for me.

Meunier said quietly, 'She is gone.' He then gave his arm to Bertha, and she submitted to be led out of the room.

I suppose it was at her order that two female attendants came into the room, and dismissed the younger one who had been present before. When they entered, Meunier had already opened the artery in the long thin neck that lay rigid on the pillow, and I dismissed them ordering them to remain at a distance till we rang: the doctor, I said, had an operation to perform—he was not sure about the death. For the next twenty minutes I forgot everything but Meunier and the experiment in which he was so absorbed that I think his senses would have been closed against all sounds or sights which had no relation to it. It was my task at first to keep up the artificial respiration in the body after the transfusion had been effected, but presently Meunier relieved me, and I could see the wondrous slow return of life; the breast began to heave, the inspirations became stronger, the eyelids quivered, and the soul seemed to have returned beneath them. The artificial respiration was withdrawn: still the breathing continued, and there was a movement of the lips.

Just then I heard the handle of the door moving: I suppose Bertha had heard from the women that they had been dismissed: probably a vague fear had arisen in her mind, for she entered with a look of alarm. She came to the foot of the bed and gave a stifled cry.

The dead woman's eyes were wide open, and met hers in a full recognition of hate. With a sudden strong effort, the hand that Bertha had thought for ever still was pointed towards her, and the haggard face moved. The gasping eager voice said:

'You mean to poison your husband . . . the poison is in the black cabinet . . . I got it for you . . . you laughed at me, and told lies about me behind my back, to make me disgusting . . . because you were jealous . . . are you sorry . . . now?'

The lips continued to murmur, but the sounds were no longer distinct. Soon there was no sound—only a slight movement: the flame had leaped out, and was being extinguished the faster. The wretched woman's heart-strings had been set to hatred and vengeance; the spirit of life had swept the chords for an instant, and was gone again for ever. Great God! Is this what it is to live again . . . to wake up with our unstilled thirst upon us, with our unuttered curses rising to our lips, with our muscles ready to act out their half-committed sins?

Bertha stood pale at the foot of the bed, quivering and helpless, despairing of devices, like a cunning animal whose hiding-places are surrounded by swift-advancing flame. Even Meunier looked paralysed; life for that moment ceased to be a scientific problem to him. As for me, this scene seemed of one texture with the rest of my existence: horror was my familiar, and this new revelation was only like an old pain recurring with new circumstances.

Since then Bertha and I have lived apart—she in her own neighbourhood, the mistress of half our wealth, I as a wanderer in foreign countries, until I came to this Devonshire nest to die. Bertha lives pitied and admired; for what had I against that charming woman, whom everyone but myself could have been happy with? There had been no witness of the scene in the dying room except Meunier, and while Meunier lived his lips were sealed by a promise to me.

Once or twice, weary of wandering, I rested in a favourite spot, and my heart went out towards the men and women and children whose faces were becoming familiar to me; But I was driven away again in terror at the approach of my old insight—driven away to live continually with the one Unknown Presence revealed and yet hidden by the moving curtain of the earth and sky. Till at last disease took hold of me and forced me to rest here—forced me to live in dependence on my servants. And then the curse of insight—of my double consciousness, came again, and has never left me. I knew all their narrow thoughts, their feeble regard, their half-wearied pity.

It is the 20th September, 1850. I know these figures I have just written, as if they were a long familiar inscription. I have seen them on this page in my desk unnumbered times, when the scene of my dying struggle has opened upon me . . .

1863

Circumstance

HARRIET PRESCOTT SPOFFORD

S he had remained, during all that day, with a sick neighbor,—those eastern wilds of Maine in that epoch frequently making neighbors and miles synonymous,—and so busy had she been with care and sympathy that she did not at first observe the approaching night. But finally the level rays, reddening the snow, threw their gleam upon the wall, and, hastily donning cloak and hood, she bade her friends farewell and sallied forth on her return. Home lay some three miles distant, across a copse, a meadow, and a piece of woods,—the woods being a fringe on the skirts of the great forests that stretch far away into the North. That home was one of a dozen log-houses lying a few furlongs apart from each other, with their half-cleared demesnes separating them at the rear from a wilderness untrodden save by stealthy native or deadly panther tribes.

She was in a nowise exalted frame of spirit,—on the contrary, rather depressed by the pain she had witnessed and the fatigue she had endured; but in certain temperaments such a condition throws open the mental pores, so to speak, and renders one receptive of every influence. Through the little copse she walked slowly, with her cloak folded about her, lingering to imbibe the sense of shelter, the sunset filtered in purple through the mist of woven spray and twig, the companionship of growth not sufficiently dense to band against her, the sweet home-feeling of a young and tender wintry wood. It was therefore just on the edge of the evening that she emerged from the place and began to cross the meadow-land. At one hand lay the forest to which her path wound; at the other the evening star hung over a tide of failing orange that slowly slipped down the earth's broad side to sadden other hemispheres with sweet regret. Walking rapidly now, and with her eyes wide-open, she distinctly saw in the air before her what was not there a moment ago, a winding-sheet,—cold, white, and ghastly, waved by the likeness of four wan hands,—that rose with a long inflation, and fell in rigid folds, while a voice, shaping itself from the hollowness above, spectral and melancholy, sighed,—'The Lord have mercy on the people! The Lord have mercy on the people!' Three times the sheet with its corpse-covering outline waved beneath the pale hands, and the voice, awful in its solemn and mysterious depth, sighed, 'The Lord have mercy on the people!' Then all was gone, the place was clear again, the gray sky was obstructed by no deathly blot; she looked about her, shook her shoulders decidedly, and, pulling on her hood, went forward once more.

She might have been a little frightened by such an apparition, if she had led a life of less reality than frontier settlers are apt to lead; but dealing with hard fact does not engender a flimsy habit of mind, and this woman was too sincere and earnest in her character, and too happy in her situation, to be thrown by antagonism, merely, upon superstitious fancies and chimeras of the second-sight. She did not even believe herself subject to an hallucination, but smiled simply, a little vexed that her thought could have framed such a glamour from the day's occurrences, and not sorry to lift the bough of the warder of the woods and enter and disappear in their sombre path. If she had been imaginative, she would have hesitated at her first step into a region whose dangers were not visionary; but I suppose that the thought of a little child at home would conquer that propensity in the most habituated. So, biting a bit of spicy birch, she went along. Now and then she came to a gap where the trees had been partially felled, and here she found that the lingering twilight was explained by that peculiar and perhaps electric film which sometimes sheathes the sky in diffused light for many hours before a brilliant aurora. Suddenly, a swift shadow, like the fabulous flying-dragon, writhed through the air before her, and she felt herself instantly seized and borne aloft. It was that wild beast—the most savage and serpentine and subtle and fearless of our latitudes—known by hunters as the Indian Devil, and he held her in his clutches on the broad floor of a swinging fir-bough. His long sharp claws were caught in her clothing, he worried them sagaciously a little, then, finding that ineffectual to free them, he commenced licking her bare arm with his rasping tongue and pouring over her the wide streams of his hot, foetid breath. So quick had this flashing action been that the woman had had no time for alarm; moreover, she was not of the screaming kind: but now, as she felt him endeavoring to disentangle his claws, and the horrid sense of her fate smote her, and she saw instinctively the fierce plunge of those weapons, the long strips of living flesh torn from her bones, the agony, the quivering disgust, itself a worse agony,—while by her side, and holding her in his great lithe embrace, the monster crouched, his white tusks whetting and gnashing, his eyes glaring through all the darkness like balls of red fire,—a shriek, that rang in every forest hollow, that startled every winter-housed thing, that stirred and woke the least needle of the tasselled pines, tore through her lips. A moment afterward, the beast left the arm, once white, now crimson, and looked up alertly.

She did not think at this instant to call upon God. She called upon her husband. It seemed to her that she had but one friend in the world; that was he; and again the cry, loud, clear, prolonged, echoed through the woods. It was not the shriek that disturbed the creature at his relish; he was not born in the woods to be scared of an owl, you know; what then? It must have been the echo, most musical, most resonant, repeated and yet repeated, dying with long sighs of sweet sound, vibrated from rock to river and back again from depth to depth of cave and cliff. Her thought flew after it: she knew, that, even if her husband heard it, he yet could not reach her in time; she saw that while the beast listened he would not gnaw,—and this she *felt* directly, when the rough, sharp, and multiplied stings of his tongue retouched her arm. Again her lips opened by instinct, but the sound that issued thence came by reason. She had heard that music charmed wild beasts,—just this point between life and death intensified every faculty,—and when she opened her lips the third time, it was not for shrieking, but for singing.

A little thread of melody stole out, a rill of tremulous motion; it was the cradle-song with which she rocked her baby;—how could she sing that? And then she remembered the baby sleeping rosily on the long settee before the fire,—the father cleaning his gun, with one foot on the green wooden rundle,—the merry light from the chimney dancing out and through the room, on the rafters of the ceiling with their tassels of onions and herbs, on the log walls painted with lichens and festooned with apples, on the king's-arm slung across the shelf with the old pirate's-cutlass, on the snow-pile of the bed, and on the great brass clock,—dancing, too, and lingering on the baby, with his fringed-gentian eyes, his chubby fists clenched on the pillow, and his fine breezy hair fanning with the motion of his father's foot. All this struck her in one, and made a sob of her breath, and she ceased.

Immediately the long red tongue thrust forth again. Before it touched, a song sprang to her lips, a wild sea-song, such as some sailor might be singing far out on trackless blue water that night, the shrouds whistling with frost and the sheets glued in ice,—a song with the wind in its burden and the spray in its chorus. The monster raised his head and flared the fiery eyeballs upon her, then fretted the imprisoned claws a moment and was quiet; only the breath like the vapor from some hell-pit still swathed her. Her voice, at first faint and fearful, gradually lost its quaver, grew under her control and subject to her modulation; it rose on long swells, it fell in subtle cadences, now and then its tones pealed out like bells from distant belfries on fresh sonorous mornings. She sung the song through, and, wondering lest his name of Indian Devil were not his true name, and if he would not detect her, she repeated it. Once or twice now, indeed, the beast stirred uneasily, turned, and made the bough sway at his movement. As she ended, he snapped his jaws together, and tore away the fettered member, curling it under him with a snarl,—when she burst into the gayest reel that ever answered a fiddle-bow. How many a time she had heard her husband play it on the homely fiddle made by himself from birch and cherry-wood! How many a time she had seen it danced on the floor of their one room, to the patter of wooden clogs and the rustle of homespun petticoat! How many a time she had danced it herself!—and did she not remember once, as they joined clasps for eight-hands-round, how it had lent its gay, bright measure to her life? And here she was singing it alone, in the forest, at midnight, to a wild beast! As she sent her voice trilling up and down its quick oscillations between joy and pain, the creature who grasped her uncurled his paw and scratched the bark from the bough; she must vary the spell; and her voice spun leaping along the projecting points of tune of a hornpipe. Still singing, she felt herself twisted about with a low growl and a lifting of the red lip from the glittering teeth; she broke the hornpipe's thread, and commenced unravelling a lighter, livelier thing, an Irish jig. Up and down and round about her voice flew, the beast threw back his head so that the diabolical face fronted hers, and the torrent of his breath prepared her for his feast as the anaconda slimes his prey. Frantically she darted from tune to tune; his restless movements followed her. She tired herself with dancing and vivid national airs, growing feverish and singing spasmodically as she felt her horrid tomb yawning wider. Touching in this manner all the slogan and keen clan cries, the beast moved again, but only to lay the disengaged paw across her with heavy satisfaction. She did not dare to pause; through the clear cold air, the frosty starlight, she sang. If there were yet any tremor in the tone, it was not fear,—she had learned the secret of sound at last; nor could it be chill,—for too high a fever throbbed her pulses; it was nothing but the thought of the log-house and of what might be passing within it. She fancied the baby stirring in his sleep and moving his pretty lips,—her husband rising and opening the door, looking out after her, and wondering at her absence. She fancied the light pouring through the chink and then shut in again with all the safety and comfort and joy, her husband taking down the fiddle and playing lightly with his head inclined, playing while she sang, while she sang for her life to an Indian Devil. Then she knew he was fumbling for and finding some shining fragment and scoring it down the yellowing hair, and unconsciously her voice forsook the wild wartunes and drifted into the half-gay, half-melancholy Rosin the Bow.

Suddenly she woke pierced with a pang, and the daggered tooth penetrating her flesh;—dreaming of safety, she had ceased singing and lost it. The beast had regained the use of all his limbs, and now, standing and raising his back, bristling and foaming, with sounds that would have been like hisses but for their deep and fearful sonority, he withdrew step by step toward the trunk of the tree, still with his flaming balls upon her. She was all at once free, on one end of the bough, twenty feet from the ground. She did not measure the distance, but rose to drop herself down, careless of any death, so that it were not this. Instantly, as if he scanned her thoughts, the creature bounded forward with a yell and caught her again in his dreadful hold. It might be that he was not greatly famished;

for, as she suddenly flung up her voice again, he settled himself composedly on the bough, still clasping her with invincible pressure to his rough, ravenous breast, and listening in a fascination to the sad, strange U-la-lu that now moaned forth in loud, hollow tones above him. He half closed his eyes, and sleepily reopened and shut them again.

What rending pains were close at hand! Death! and what a death! worse than any other that is to be named! Water, be it cold or warm, that which buoys up blue ice-fields, or which bathes tropical coasts with currents of balmy bliss, is yet a gentle conqueror, kisses as it kills, and draws you down gently through darkening fathoms to its heart. Death at the sword is the festival of trumpet and bugle and banner, with glory ringing out around you and distant hearts thrilling through yours. No gnawing disease can bring such hideous end as this; for that is a fiend bred of your own flesh, and this—is it a fiend, this living lump of appetites? What dread comes with the thought of perishing in flames! but fire, let it leap and hiss never so hotly, is something too remote, too alien, to inspire us with such loathly horror as a wild beast; if it has a life, that life is too utterly beyond our comprehension. Fire is not half ourselves; as it devours, arouses neither hatred nor disgust; is not to be known by the strength of our lower natures let loose; does not drip our blood into our faces from foaming chaps, nor mouth nor slaver above us with vitality. Let us be ended by fire, and we are ashes, for the winds to bear, the leaves to cover; let us be ended by wild beasts, and the base, cursed thing howls with us forever through the forest. All this she felt as she charmed him, and what force it lent to her song God knows. If her voice should fail! If the damp and cold should give her any fatal hoarseness! If all the silent powers of the forest did not conspire to help her! The dark, hollow night rose indifferently over her; the wide, cold air breathed rudely past her, lifted her wet hair and blew it down again; the great boughs swung with a ponderous strength, now and then clashed their iron lengths together and shook off a sparkle of icy spears or some long-lain weight of snow from their heavy shadows. The green depths were utterly cold and silent and stern. These beautiful haunts that all the summer were hers and rejoiced to share with her their bounty, these heavens that had yielded their largesse, these stems that had thrust their blossoms into her hands, all these friends of three moons ago forgot her now and knew her no longer.

Feeling her desolation, wild, melancholy, forsaken songs, rose thereon from that frightful aerie,—weeping, wailing tunes, that sob among the people from age to age, and overflow with otherwise unexpressed sadness,—all rude, mournful ballads,—old tearful strains, that Shakespeare heard the vagrants sing, and that rise and fall like the wind and tide,—sailor-songs, to be heard only in lone mid-watches beneath the moon and stars,—ghastly rhyming romances, such as that famous one of the Lady Margaret, when

> 'She slipped on her gown of green
> A piece below the knee,—
> And 'twas all a long cold winter's night.
> A dead corse followed she.'

Still the beast lay with closed eyes, yet never relaxing his grasp. Once a half-whine of enjoyment escaped him,—he fawned his fearful head upon her; once he scored her cheek with his tongue: savage caresses that hurt like wounds. How weary she was! and yet how terribly awake! How fuller and fuller of dismay grew the knowledge that she was only prolonging her anguish and playing with death! How appalling the thought that with her voice ceased her existence! Yet she could not sing forever; her throat was dry and hard; her very breath was a pain; her mouth was hotter than any desert-worn pilgrim's;—if she could but drop upon her burning tongue one atom of the ice that glittered about her!—but both of her arms were pinioned in the giant's vice. She remembered the winding-sheet, and for the first time in her life shivered with spiritual fear. Was it hers? She asked herself, as she sang, what sins she had committed, what life she had led, to find her punishment so soon and in these pangs,—and then she sought eagerly for some reason why her husband was not up and abroad to find her. He failed her,—her one sole hope in life; and without being aware of it, her voice forsook the songs of suffering and sorrow for old Covenanting hymns,—hymns with which her mother had lulled her, which the class-leader pitched in the chimney-corners,—grand and sweet Methodist hymns, brimming with melody and with all fantastic involutions of tune to suit that ecstatic worship,—hymns full of the beauty of holiness, steadfast, relying, sanctified by the salvation they had lent to those in worse extremity than hers,—for they had found themselves in the grasp of hell, while she was but in the jaws of death. Out of this strange music, peculiar to one character of faith, and than which there is none more beautiful in its degree nor owning a more potent sway of sound, her voice soared into the glorified chants of churches. What to her was death by cold or famine or wild beasts? 'Though He slay me, yet will I trust in him,' she sang. High and clear through the frore fair night, the level moonbeams splintering in the wood, the scarce glints of stars in the shadowy roof of branches, these sacred anthems rose,—rose as a hope from despair, as some snowy spray of flower-bells from blackest mould. Was she not in God's hands? Did not the world swing at his will? If this were in the great plan of providence, was it not best, and should she not accept it?

'He is the Lord our God; his judgments are in all the earth.'

Oh, sublime faith of our fathers, where utter self-sacrifice alone was true love, the fragrance of whose unrequired subjection was pleasanter than that of golden censers swung in purple-vapored chancels!

Never ceasing in the rhythm of her thoughts, articulated in music as they thronged, the memory of her first communion flashed over her. Again she was in that distant place on that sweet spring morning. Again the congregation rustled out, and the few remained, and she trembled to find herself among them. How well she remembered the devout, quiet faces, too accustomed to the sacred feast to glow with their inner joy! how well the snowy linen at the altar, the silver vessels slowly and silently shifting! and as the cup approached and passed, how the sense of delicious perfume stole in and heightened the transport of her prayer, and she had seemed, looking up through the windows where the sky soared blue in constant freshness, to feel all heaven's balms dripping from the portals, and to scent the lilies of eternal peace! Perhaps another would not have felt so much ecstasy as satisfaction on that occasion; but it is a true, if a later disciple, who has said, 'The Lord bestoweth his blessings there, where he findeth the vessels empty.'

'And does it need the walls of a church to renew my communion?' she asked. 'Does not every moment stand a temple four-square to God? And in that morning, with its buoyant sunlight, was I any dearer to the Heart of the World than now?—"My beloved is mine, and I am his," ' she sang over and over again, with all varied inflection and profuse tune. How gently all the winter-wrapt things bent toward her then! into what relation with her had they grown! how this common dependence was the spell of their intimacy! how at one with Nature had she become! how all the night and the silence and the forest seemed to hold its breath, and to send its soul up to God in her singing! It was no longer despondency, that singing. It was neither prayer nor petition. She had left imploring, 'How long wilt thou forget me, O Lord? Lighten mine eyes, lest I sleep the sleep of death! For in death there is no remembrance of thee,'—with countless other such fragments of supplication. She cried rather, 'Yea, though I walk through the valley of the shadow of death, I will fear no evil: for thou art with me; thy rod and thy staff, they comfort me,'—and lingered, and repeated, and sang again, 'I shall be satisfied, when I awake, with thy likeness.'

Then she thought of the Great Deliverance, when he drew her up out of many waters, and the flashing old psalm pealed forth triumphantly:—

> 'The Lord descended from above,
>   and bow'd the heavens hie:
> And underneath his fleet he cast
>   the darkness of the skie.
> On cherubs and on cherubins
>   full royally he road:
> And on the wings of all the winds
>   came flying all abroad.'

She forgot how recently, and with what a strange pity for her own shapeless form that was to be, she had quaintly sung,—

> 'O lovely appearance of death!
>   What sight upon earth is so fair?
> Not all the gay pageants that breathe
>   Can with a dead body compare!'

She remembered instead,—'In thy presence is fulness of joy; at thy right hand there are pleasures forever-more. God will redeem my soul from the power of the grave: for he shall receive me. He will swallow up death in victory.' Not once now did she say, 'Lord, how long wilt thou look on; rescue my soul from their destructions, my darling from the lions,'—for she knew that the young lions roar after their prey and seek their meat from God. 'O Lord, thou preservest man and beast!' she said.

She had no comfort or consolation in this season, such as sustained the Christian martyrs in the amphitheatre. She was not dying for her faith; there were no palms in heaven for her to wave; but how many a time had she declared,—'I had rather be a doorkeeper in the house of my God, than to dwell in the tents of wickedness!' And as the broad rays here and there broke through the dense covert of shade and lay in rivers of lustre on crystal sheathing and frozen fretting of trunk and limb and on the great spaces of refraction, they builded up visibly that house, the shining city on the hill, and singing, 'Beautiful for situation, the joy of the whole earth, is Mount Zion, on the sides of the North, the city of the Great King,' her vision climbed to that higher picture where the angel shows the dazzling thing, the holy Jerusalem descending out of heaven from God, with its splendid battlements and gates of pearls, and its foundations, the eleventh a jacinth, the twelfth an amethyst,—with its great white throne, and the rainbow round about it, in sight like unto an emerald: 'And there shall be no night there,—for the Lord God giveth them light,' she sang.

What whisper of dawn now rustled through the wilderness? How the night was passing! And still the beast crouched upon the bough, changing only the posture of his head, that again he might command her with those charmed eyes;—half their fire was gone; she could almost have released herself from his custody; yet, had she stirred, no one knows what malevolent instinct might have dominated anew. But of that she did not dream; long ago stripped of any expectation, she was experiencing in her divine rapture how mystically true it is that 'he that dwelleth in the secret place of the Most High shall abide under the shadow of the Almighty.'

Slow clarion cries now wound from the distance as the cocks caught the intelligence of day and re-echoed it faintly from farm to farm,—sleepy sentinels of night, sounding the foe's invasion, and translating that dim intuition to ringing notes of warning. Still she chanted on. A remote crash of brushwood told of some other beast on his depredations, or some night-belated traveller groping his way through the narrow path. Still she chanted on. The far, faint echoes of the chanticleers died into distance, the crashing of the branches grew nearer. No wild beast that, but a man's step,—a man's form in the moonlight, stalwart and strong,—on one arm slept a little child, in the other hand he held his gun. Still she chanted on.

Perhaps, when her husband last looked forth, he was half ashamed to find what a fear he felt for her. He knew she would never leave the child so long but for some direst need,—and yet he may have laughed at himself, as he lifted and wrapped it with awkward care, and, loading his gun and strapping on his horn, opened the door again and closed it behind him, going out and plunging into the darkness and dangers of the forest. He was more singularly alarmed than he would have been willing to acknowledge; as he had sat with his bow hovering over the strings, he had half believed to hear her voice mingling gayly with the instrument, till he paused and listened if she were not about to lift the latch and enter. As he grew nearer the heart of the forest, that intimation of melody seemed to grow more actual, to take body and breath, to come and go on long swells and ebbs of the night-breeze, to increase with tune and words, till a strange shrill singing grew ever clearer, and, as he stepped into an open space of moonbeams, far up in the branches, rocked by the wind, and singing, 'How beautiful upon the mountains are the feet of him that bringeth good tidings, that publisheth peace,' he saw his wife,—his wife,—but, great God in heaven! how? Some mad exclamation escaped him, but without diverting her. The child knew the singing voice, though never heard before in that unearthly key, and turned toward it through the veiling dreams. With a celerity almost instantaneous, it lay, in the twinkling of an eye, on the ground at the father's feet, while his gun was raised to his shoulder and levelled at the monster covering his wife with shaggy form and flaming gaze,—his wife so ghastly white, so rigid, so stained with blood, her eyes so fixedly bent above, and her lips, that had indurated into the chiselled pallor of marble, parted only with that flood of solemn song.

I do not know if it were the mother-instinct that for a moment lowered her eyes,—those eyes, so lately riveted on heaven, now suddenly seeing all life-long bliss possible. A thrill of joy pierced and shivered through her like a weapon, her voice trembled in its course, her glance lost its steady strength, fever-flushes chased each other over her face, yet she never once ceased chanting. She was quite aware, that, if her husband shot now, the ball must pierce her body before reaching any vital part of the beast,—and yet better that death, by his hand, than the other. But this her husband also knew, and he remained motionless, just covering the creature with the sight. He dared not fire, lest some wound not mortal should break the spell exercised by her voice, and the beast, enraged with pain, should rend her in atoms; moreover, the light was too uncertain for his aim. So he waited. Now and then he examined his gun to see if the damp were injuring its charge, now and then he wiped the great drops from his forehead. Again the cocks crowed with the passing hour,—the last time they were heard on that night. Cheerful home sound then, how full of safety and all comfort and rest it seemed! what sweet morning incidents of sparkling fire and sunshine, of gay household bustle, shining dresser, and cooing baby, of steaming cattle in the yard, and brimming milk-pails at the door! what pleasant voices! what laughter! what security! and here—

Now, as she sang on in the slow, endless, infinite moments, the fervent vision of God's peace was gone. Just as the grave had lost its sting, she was snatched back again into the arms of earthly hope. In vain she tried to sing, 'There remaineth a rest for the people of God,'—her eyes trembled on her husband's and she could only think of him, and of the child, and of happiness that yet might be, but with what a dreadful gulf of doubt between! She shuddered now in the suspense; all calm forsook her; she was tortured with dissolving heats or frozen with icy blasts; her face contracted, growing small and pinched; her voice was hoarse and sharp,—every tone cut like a knife,—the notes became heavy to lift,—withheld by some hostile pressure,—impossible. One gasp, a convulsive effort, and there was silence,—she had lost her voice.

The beast made a sluggish movement,—stretched and fawned like one awaking,—then, as if he would have yet more of the enchantment, stirred her slightly with his muzzle. As he did so, a sidelong hint of the man standing below with the raised gun smote him; he sprung round furiously, and, seizing his prey, was about to leap into some unknown airy den of the topmost branches now waving to the slow dawn. The late moon had rounded through the sky so that her gleam at last fell full upon the bough with fairy frosting; the wintry morning light did not yet penetrate the gloom. The woman, suspended in mid-air an instant, cast only one agonized glance beneath,—but across and through it, ere the lids could fall, shot a withering sheet of flame,—a rifle-crack, half-heard, was lost in the terrible yell of desperation that bounded after it and filled her ears with savage echoes, and in the wide arc of some eternal descent she was falling;—but the beast fell under her.

I think that the moment following must have been too sacred for us, and perhaps the three have no special interest again till they issue from the shadows of the wilderness upon the white hills that skirt their home. The father carries the child hushed again into slumber, the mother follows with no such feeble step as might be anticipated. It is not time for reaction,—the tension not yet relaxed, the nerves still vibrant, she seems to herself like some one newly made; the night was a dream; the present stamped upon her in deep satisfaction, neither weighed nor compared with the past; if she has the careful tricks of former habit, it is as an automaton; and as they slowly climb the steep under the clear gray vault and the paling morning star, and as she stops to gather a spray of the red-rose berries or a feathery tuft of dead grasses for the chimney-piece of the log-house, or a handful of brown cones for the child's play,—of these quiet, happy folk you would scarcely dream how lately they had stolen from under the banner and encampment of the great King Death. The husband proceeds a step or two in advance; the wife lingers over a singular foot-print in the snow, stoops and examines it, then looks up with a hurried word. Her husband stands alone on the hill, his arms folded across the babe, his gun fallen,—stands defined as a silhouette against the pallid sky. What is there in their home, lying below and yellowing in the light, to fix him with such a stare? She springs to his side. There is no home there. The log-house, the barns, the neighbouring farms, the fences, are all blotted out and mingled in one smoking ruin. Desolation and death were indeed there, and beneficence and life in the forest. Tomahawk and scalping-knife, descending during that night, had left behind them only this work of their accomplished hatred and one subtle foot-print in the snow.

For the rest,—the world was all before them, where to choose.

1864

The Phantom Coach

AMELIA B. EDWARDS

The circumstances I am about to relate to you have truth to recommend them. They happened to myself, and my recollection of them is as vivid as if they had taken place only yesterday. Twenty years, however, have gone by since that night. During those twenty years I have told the story to but one other person. I tell it now with a reluctance which I find it difficult to overcome. All I entreat, meanwhile, is that you will abstain from forcing your own conclusions upon me. I want nothing explained away. I desire no arguments. My mind on this subject is quite made up, and, having the testimony of my own senses to rely upon, I prefer to abide by it.

Well! It was just twenty years ago, and within a day or two of the end of the grouse season. I had been out all day with my gun, and had had no sport to speak of. The wind was due east; the month, December; the place, a bleak wide moor in the far north of England. And I had lost my way. It was not a pleasant place in which to lose one's way, with the first feathery flakes of a coming snowstorm just fluttering down upon the heather, and the leaden evening closing in all around. I shaded my eyes with my hand, and stared anxiously into the gathering darkness, where the purple moorland melted into a range of low hills, some ten or twelve miles distant. Not the faintest smoke-wreath, not the tiniest cultivated patch, or fence, or sheep-track, met my eyes in any direction. There was nothing for it but to walk on, and take my chance of finding what shelter I could, by the way. So I shouldered my gun again, and pushed wearily forward; for I had been on foot since an hour after daybreak, and had eaten nothing since breakfast.

Meanwhile, the snow began to come down with ominous steadiness, and the wind fell. After this, the cold became more intense, and the night came rapidly up. As for me, my prospects darkened with the darkening sky, and my heart grew heavy as I thought how my young wife was already watching for me through the window of our little inn parlour, and thought of all the suffering in store for her throughout this weary night. We had been married four months, and, having spent our autumn in the Highlands, were now lodging in a remote little village situated just on the verge of the great English moorlands. We were very much in love, and, of course, very happy. This morning, when we parted, she had implored me to return before dusk, and I had promised her that I would. What would I not have given to have kept my word!

Even now, weary as I was, I felt that with a supper, an hour's rest, and a guide, I might still get back to her before midnight, if only guide and shelter could be found.

And all this time, the snow fell and the night thickened. I stopped and shouted every now and then, but my shouts seemed only to make the silence deeper. Then a vague sense of uneasiness came upon me, and I began to remember stories of travellers who had walked on and on in the falling snow until, wearied out, they were fain to lie down and sleep their lives away. Would it be possible, I asked myself, to keep on thus through all the long dark night? Would there not come a time when my limbs must fail, and my resolution give way? When I, too, must sleep the sleep of death. Death! I shuddered. How hard to die just now, when life lay all so bright before me! How hard for my darling, whose whole loving heart—but that thought was not to be borne! To banish it, I shouted again, louder and longer, and then listened eagerly. Was my shout answered, or did I only fancy that I heard a far-off cry? I hallooed again, and again the echo followed. Then a wavering speck of light came suddenly out of the dark, shifting, disappearing, growing momentarily nearer and brighter. Running towards it at full speed, I found myself, to my great joy, face to face with an old man and a lantern.

'Thank God!' was the exclamation that burst involuntarily from my lips.

Blinking and frowning, he lifted his lantern and peered into my face.

'What for?' growled he, sulkily.

'Well—for you. I began to fear I should be lost in the snow.'

'Eh, then, folks do get cast away hereabout fra' time to time, an' what's to hinder you from bein' cast away likewise, if the Lord's so minded?'

'If the Lord is so minded that you and I shall be lost together, friend, we must submit,' I replied; 'but I don't mean to be lost without you. How far am I now from Dwolding?'

'A gude twenty mile, more or less.'

'And the nearest village?'

'The nearest village is Wyke, an' that's twelve mile t'other side.'

'Where do you live, then?'

'Out yonder,' said he, with a vague jerk of the lantern.

'You're going home, I presume?'

'Maybe I am.'

'Then I'm going with you.'

The old man shook his head, and rubbed his nose reflectively with the handle of the lantern.

'It ain't o' no use,' growled he. 'He 'ont let you in—not he.'

'We'll see about that,' I replied, briskly. 'Who is He?'

'The master.'

'Who is the master?'

'That's nowt to you,' was the unceremonious reply.

'Well, well; you lead the way, and I'll engage that the master shall give me shelter and a supper tonight.'

'Eh, you can try him!' muttered my reluctant guide; and, still shaking his head, he hobbled, gnome-like, away through the falling snow. A large mass loomed up presently out of the darkness, and a huge dog rushed out, barking furiously.

'Is this the house?' I asked.

'Ay, it's the house. Down, Bey!' And he fumbled in his pocket for the key.

I drew up close behind him, prepared to lose no chance of entrance, and saw in the little circle of light shed by the lantern that the door was heavily studded with iron nails, like the door of a prison. In another minute he had turned the key and I had pushed past him into the house.

Once inside, I looked round with curiosity, and found myself in a great raftered hall, which served, apparently, a variety of uses. One end was piled to the roof with corn, like a barn. The other was stored with flour-sacks, agricultural implements, casks, and all kinds of miscellaneous lumber; while from the beams overhead hung rows of hams, flitches, and bunches of dried herbs for winter use. In the centre of the floor stood some huge object gauntly dressed in a dingy wrapping-cloth, and reaching half way to the rafters. Lifting a corner of this cloth, I saw, to my surprise, a telescope of very considerable size, mounted on a rude movable platform, with four small wheels. The tube was made of painted wood, bound round with bands of metal rudely fashioned; the speculum, so far as I could estimate its size in the dim light, measured at least fifteen inches in diameter. While I was yet examining the instrument, and asking myself whether it was not the work of some self-taught optician, a bell rang sharply.

'That's for you,' said my guide, with a malicious grin. 'Yonder's his room.'

He pointed to a low black door at the opposite side of the hall. I crossed over, rapped somewhat loudly, and went in, without waiting for an invitation. A huge, white-haired old man rose from a table covered with books and papers, and confronted me sternly.

'Who are you?' said he. 'How came you here? What do you want?'

'James Murray, barrister-at-law. On foot across the moor. Meat, drink, and sleep.'

He bent his bushy brows into a portentous frown.

'Mine is not a house of entertainment,' he said, haughtily. 'Jacob, how dared you admit this stranger?'

'I didn't admit him,' grumbled the old man. 'He followed me over the muir, and shouldered his way in before me. I'm no match for six foot two.'

'And pray, sir, by what right have you forced an entrance into my house?'

'The same by which I should have clung to your boat, if I were drowning. The right of self-preservation.'

'Self-preservation?'

'There's an inch of snow on the ground already,' I replied, briefly; 'and it would be deep enough to cover my body before daybreak.'

He strode to the window, pulled aside a heavy black curtain, and looked out.

'It is true,' he said. 'You can stay, if you choose, till morning. Jacob, serve the supper.'

With this he waved me to a seat, resumed his own, and became at once absorbed in the studies from which I had disturbed him.

I placed my gun in a corner, drew a chair to the hearth, and examined my quarters at leisure. Smaller and less incongruous in its arrangements than the hall, this room contained, nevertheless, much to awaken my curiosity. The floor was carpetless. The whitewashed walls were in parts scrawled over with strange diagrams, and in others covered with shelves crowded with philosophical instruments, the uses of many of which were unknown to me. On one side of the fireplace, stood a bookcase filled with dingy folios; on the other, a small organ, fantastically decorated with painted carvings of medieval saints and devils. Through the half-opened door of a cupboard at the further end of the room, I saw a long array of geological specimens, surgical preparations, crucibles, retorts, and jars of chemicals; while on the mantelshelf beside me, amid a number of small objects, stood a model of the solar system, a small galvanic battery, and a microscope. Every chair had its burden. Every corner was heaped high with books. The very floor was littered over with maps, casts, papers, tracings, and learned lumber of all conceivable kinds.

I stared about me with an amazement increased by every fresh object upon which my eyes chanced to rest. So strange a room I had never seen; yet seemed it stranger still, to find such a room in a lone farmhouse amid those wild and solitary moors! Over and over again, I looked from my host to his surroundings, and from his surroundings back to my host, asking myself who and what he could be? His head was singularly fine; but it was more the head of a poet than of a philosopher. Broad in the temples, prominent over the eyes, and clothed with a rough profusion of perfectly white hair, it had all the ideality and much of the ruggedness that characterises the head of Ludwig van Beethoven. There were the same deep lines about the mouth, and the same stern furrows in the brow. There was the same concentration of expression. While I was yet observing him, the door opened, and Jacob brought in the supper. His master then closed his book, rose, and with more courtesy of manner than he had yet shown, invited me to the table.

A dish of ham and eggs, a loaf of brown bread, and a bottle of admirable sherry, were placed before me.

'I have but the homeliest farmhouse fare to offer you, sir,' said my entertainer. 'Your appetite, I trust, will make up for the deficiencies of our larder.'

I had already fallen upon the viands, and now protested, with the enthusiasm of a starving sportsman, that I had never eaten anything so delicious.

He bowed stiffly, and sat down to his own supper, which consisted, primitively, of a jug of milk and a basin of porridge. We ate in silence, and, when we had done, Jacob removed the tray. I then drew my chair back to the fireside. My host, somewhat to my surprise, did the same, and turning abruptly towards me, said:

'Sir, I have lived here in strict retirement for three-and-twenty years. During that time, I have not seen as many strange faces, and I have not read a single newspaper. You are the first stranger who has crossed my threshold for more than four years. Will you favour me with a few words of information respecting that outer world from which I have parted company so long?'

'Pray interrogate me,' I replied. 'I am heartily at your service.'

He bent his head in acknowledgement; leaned forward, with his elbows resting on his knees and his chin supported in the palms of his hands; stared fixedly into the fire; and proceeded to question me.

His inquiries related chiefly to scientific matters, with the later progress of which, as applied to the practical purposes of life, he was almost wholly unacquainted. No student of science myself, I replied as well as my slight information permitted; but the task was far from easy, and I was much relieved when, passing from interrogation to discussion, he began pouring forth his own conclusions upon the facts which I had been attempting to place before him. He talked, and I listened spellbound. He talked till I believe he almost forgot my presence, and only thought aloud. I had never heard anything like it then; I have never heard anything like it since. Familiar with all systems of all philosophies, subtle in analysis, bold in generalisation, he poured forth his thoughts in an uninterrupted stream, and, still leaning forward in the same moody attitude with his eyes fixed upon the fire, wandered from topic to topic, from speculation to speculation, like an inspired dreamer. From practical science to mental philosophy; from electricity in the wire to electricity in the nerve; from Watts to Mesmer, from Mesmer to Reichenbach, from Reichenbach to Swedenborg, Spinoza, Condillac, Descartes, Berkeley, Aristotle, Plato, and the Magi and mystics of the East, were transitions which, however bewildering in their variety and scope, seemed easy and harmonious upon his lips as sequences in music. By-and-by—I forget now by what link of conjecture or illustration—he passed on to that field which lies beyond the boundary line of even conjectural philosophy, and reaches no man knows whither. He spoke of the soul and its aspirations; of the spirit and its powers; of second sight; of prophecy; of those phenomena which, under the names of ghosts, spectres, and supernatural appearances, have been denied by the sceptics and attested by the credulous, of all ages.

'The world,' he said, 'grows hourly more and more sceptical of all that lies beyond its own narrow radius; and our men of science foster the fatal tendency. They condemn as fable all that resists experiment. They reject as false all that cannot be brought to the test of the laboratory or the dissecting-room. Against what superstition have they waged so long and obstinate a war, as against the belief in apparitions? And yet what superstition has maintained its hold upon the minds of men so long and so firmly? Show me any fact in physics, in history, in archæology, which is supported by testimony so wide and so various. Attested by all races of men, in all ages, and in all climates, by the soberest sages of antiquity, by the rudest savage of today, by the Christian, the Pagan, the Pantheist, the Materialist, this phenomenon is treated as a nursery tale by the philosophers of our century. Circumstantial evidence weighs with them as a feather in the balance. The comparison of causes with effects, however valuable in physical science, is put aside as worthless and unreliable. The evidence of competent witnesses, however conclusive in a court of justice, counts for nothing. He who pauses before he pronounces, is condemned as a trifler. He who believes, is a dreamer or a fool.'

He spoke with bitterness, and, having said thus, relapsed for some minutes into silence. Presently he raised his head from his hands, and added, with an altered voice and manner,

'I, sir, paused, investigated, believed, and was not ashamed to state my convictions to the world. I, too, was branded as a visionary, held up to ridicule by my contemporaries, and hooted from that field of science in which I had laboured with honour during all the best years of my life. These things happened just three-and-twenty years ago. Since then, I have lived as you see me living now, and the world has forgotten me, as I have forgotten the world. You have my history.'

'It is a very sad one,' I murmured, scarcely knowing what to answer.

'It is a very common one,' he replied. 'I have only suffered for the truth, as many a better and wiser man has suffered before me.'

He rose, as if desirous of ending the conversation, and went over to the window.

'It has ceased snowing,' he observed, as he dropped the curtain, and came back to the fireside.

'Ceased!' I exclaimed, starting eagerly to my feet. 'Oh, if it were only possible—but no! it is hopeless. Even if I could find my way across the moor, I could not walk twenty miles tonight.'

'Walk twenty miles tonight!' repeated my host. 'What are you thinking of?'

'Of my wife,' I replied, impatiently. 'Of my young wife, who does not know that I have lost my way, and who is at this momer.t breaking her heart with suspense and terror.'

'Where is she?'

'At Dwolding, twenty miles away.'

'At Dwolding,' he echoed, thoughtfully. 'Yes, the distance, it is true, is twenty miles; but—are you so very anxious to save the next six or eight hours?'

'So very, very anxious, that I would give ten guineas at this moment for a guide and a horse.'

'Your wish can be gratified at a less costly rate,' said he, smiling. 'The night mail from the north, which changes horses at Dwolding, passes within five miles of this spot, and will be due at a certain cross-road in about an hour and a quarter. If Jacob were to go with you across the moor, and put you into the old coach-road, you could find your way, I suppose, to where it joins the new one?'

'Easily—gladly.'

He smiled again, rang the bell, gave the old servant his directions, and, taking a bottle of whisky and a wineglass from the cupboard in which he kept his chemicals, said:

'The snow lies deep, and it will be difficult walking tonight on the moor. A glass of usquebaugh before you start?'

I would have declined the spirit, but he pressed it on me, and I drank it. It went down my throat like liquid flame, and almost took my breath away.

'It is strong,' he said; 'but it will help to keep out the cold. And now you have no moments to spare. Good night!'

I thanked him for his hospitality, and would have shaken hands, but that he had turned away before I could finish my sentence. In another minute I had traversed the hall, Jacob had locked the outer door behind me, and we were out on the wide white moor.

Although the wind had fallen, it was still bitterly cold. Not a star glimmered in the black vault overhead. Not a sound, save the rapid crunching of the snow beneath our feet, disturbed the heavy stillness of the night. Jacob, not too well pleased with his mission, shambled on before in sullen silence, his lantern in his hand, and his shadow at his feet. I followed, with my gun over my shoulder, as little inclined for conversation as himself. My thoughts were full of my late host. His voice yet rang in my ears. His eloquence yet held my imagination captive. I remember to this day, with surprise, how my over-excited brain retained whole sentences and parts of sentences, troops of brilliant images, and fragments of splendid reasoning, in the very words in which he had uttered them. Musing thus over what I had heard, and striving to recall a lost link here and there, I strode on at the heels of my guide, absorbed and unobservant. Presently—at the end, as it seemed to me, of only a few minutes—he came to a sudden halt, and said:

'Yon's your road. Keep the stone fence to your right hand, and you can't fail of the way.'

'This, then, is the old coach-road?'

'Ay, 'tis the old coach-road.'

'And how far do I go, before I reach the cross-roads?'

'Nigh upon three mile.'

I pulled out my purse, and he became more communicative.

'The road's a fair road enough,' said he, 'for foot passengers; but 'twas over steep and narrow for the northern traffic. You'll mind where the parapet's broken away, close again the sign-post. It's never been mended since the accident.

'What accident?'

'Eh, the night mail pitched right over into the valley below—a gude fifty feet an' more—just at the worst bit o'road in the whole county.'

'Horrible! Were many lives lost?'

'All. Four were found dead, and t'other two died next morning.'

'How long is it since this happened?'

'Just nine year.'

'Near the sign-post, you say? I will bear it in mind. Good night.'

'Gude night, sir, and thankee.' Jacob pocketed his half-crown, made a faint pretence of touching his hat, and trudged back by the way he had come.

I watched the light of his lantern till it quite disappeared, and then turned to pursue my way alone. This was no longer matter of the slightest difficulty, for, despite the dead darkness overhead, the line of stone fence showed distinctly enough against the pale gleam of the snow. How silent it seemed now, with only my footsteps to listen to; how silent and how solitary! A strange disagreeable sense of loneliness stole over me. I walked faster. I hummed a fragment of a tune. I cast up enormous sums in my head, and accumulated them at compound interest. I did my best, in short, to forget the startling speculations to which I had but just been listening, and, to some extent, I succeeded.

Meanwhile the night air seemed to become colder and colder, and though I walked fast I found it impossible to keep myself warm. My feet were like ice. I lost sensation in my hands, and grasped my gun mechanically. I even breathed with difficulty, as though, instead of traversing a quiet north country highway, I were scaling the uppermost heights of some gigantic Alp. This last symptom became presently so distressing, that I was forced to stop for a few minutes, and lean against the stone fence. As I did so, I chanced to look back up the road, and there, to my infinite relief, I saw a distant point of light, like the gleam of an approaching lantern. I at first concluded that Jacob and retraced his steps and followed me; but even as the conjecture presented itself, a second light flashed into sight—a light evidently parallel with the first, and approaching at the same rate of motion. It needed no second thought to show me that these must be the carriage-lamps of some private vehicle, though it seemed strange that any private vehicle should take a road professedly disused and dangerous.

There could be no doubt, however, of the fact, for the lamps grew larger and brighter every moment, an I even fancied I could already see the dark outline of the carriage between them. It was coming up very fast, and quite noiselessly, the snow being nearly a foot deep under the wheels.

And now the body of the vehicle became distinctly visible behind the lamps. It looked strangely lofty. A sudden suspicion flashed upon me. Was it possible that I had passed the cross-roads in the dark without observing the sign-post, and could this be the very coach which I had come to meet?

No need to ask myself that question a second time, for here it came round the bend of the road, guard and driver, one outside passenger, and four steaming greys, all wrapped in a soft haze of light, through which the lamps blazed out, like a pair of fiery meteors.

I jumped forward, waved my hat, and shouted. The mail came down at full speed, and passed me. For a moment I feared that I had not been seen or heard, but it was only for a moment. The coachman pulled up; the guard, muffled to the eyes in capes and comforters, and apparently sound asleep in the rumble, neither answered my hail nor made the slightest effort to dismount; the outside passenger did not even turn his head. I opened the door for myself, and looked in. There were but three travellers inside, so I stepped in, shut the door, slipped into the vacant corner, and congratulated myself on my good fortune.

The atmosphere of the coach seemed, if possible, colder than that of the outer air, and was pervaded by a singularly damp and disagreeable smell. I looked round at my fellow-passengers. They were all three, men, and all silent. They did not seem to be asleep, but each leaned back in his corner of the vehicle, as if absorbed in his own reflections. I attempted to open a conversation.

'How intensely cold it is tonight,' I said, addressing my opposite neighbour.

He lifted his head, looked at me, but made no reply.

'The winter,' I added, 'seems to have begun in earnest.'

Although the corner in which he sat was so dim that I could distinguish none of his features very clearly, I saw that his eyes were still turned full upon me. And yet he answered never a word.

At any other time I should have felt, and perhaps expressed, some annoyance, but at the moment I felt too ill to do either. The icy coldness of the night air had struck a chill to my very marrow, and the strange smell inside the coach was affecting me with an intolerable nausea. I shivered from head to foot, and, turning to my left-hand neighbour, asked if he had any objection to an open window?

He neither spoke nor stirred.

I repeated the question somewhat more loudly, but with the same result. Then I lost patience, and let the sash down. As I did so the leather strap broke in my hand, and I observed that the glass was covered with a thick coat of mildew, the accumulation, apparently, of years. My attention being thus drawn to the condition of the coach,

I examined it more narrowly, and saw by the uncertain light of the outer lamps that it was in the last stage of dilapidation. Every part of it was not only out of repair, but in a condition of decay. The sashes splintered at a touch. The leather fittings were crusted over with mould, and literally rotting from the woodwork. The floor was almost breaking away beneath my feet. The whole machine, in short, was foul with damp, and had evidently been dragged from some outhouse in which it had been mouldering away for years, to do another day or two of duty on the road.

I turned to the third passenger, whom I had not yet addressed, and hazarded one more remark.

'This coach,' I said, 'is in a deplorable condition. The regular mail, I suppose, is under repair?'

He moved his head slowly, and looked me in the face, without speaking a word. I shall never forget that look while I live. I turned cold at heart under it. I turn cold at heart even now when I recall it. His eyes glowed with a fiery unnatural lustre. His face was livid as the face of a corpse. His bloodless lips were drawn back as if in the agony of death, and showed the gleaming teeth between.

The words that I was about to utter died upon my lips, and a strange horror—a dreadful horror—came upon me. My sight had by this time become used to the gloom of the coach, and I could see with tolerable distinctness. I turned to my opposite neighbour. He, too, was looking at me, with the same startling pallor in his face, and the same stony glitter in his eyes. I passed my hand across my brow. I turned to the passenger on the seat beside my own, and saw—oh Heaven! how shall I describe what I saw? I saw that he was no living man—that none of them were living men, like myself! A pale phosphorescent light—the light of putrefaction—played upon their awful faces; upon their hair, dank with the dews of the grave; upon their clothes, earth-stained and dropping to pieces; upon their hands, which were the hands of corpses long buried. Only their eyes, their terrible eyes, were living; and those eyes were all turned menacingly upon me!

A shriek of terror, a wild unintelligible cry for help and mercy, burst from my lips as I flung myself against the door, and strove in vain to open it.

In that single instant, brief and vivid as a landscape beheld in the flash of summer lightning, I saw the moon shining down through a rift of stormy cloud—the ghastly sign-post rearing its warning finger by the wayside—the broken parapet—the plunging horses—the black gulf below. Then, the coach reeled like a ship at sea. Then, came a mighty crash—a sense of crushing pain—and then, darkness.

It seemed as if years had gone by when I awoke one morning from a deep sleep, and found my wife watching by my bedside. I will pass over the scene that ensued, and give you, in half a dozen words, the tale she told me with tears of thanksgiving. I had fallen over a precipice, close against the junction of the old coach-road and the new, and had only been saved from certain death by lighting upon a deep snowdrift that had accumulated at the foot of the rock beneath. In this snowdrift I was discovered at daybreak, by a couple of shepherds, who carried me to the nearest shelter, and brought a surgeon to my aid. The surgeon found me in a state of raving delirium, with a broken arm and a compound fracture of the skull. The letters in my pocket-book showed my name and address; my wife was summoned to nurse me; and, thanks to youth and a fine constitution, I came out of danger at last. The place of my fall, I need scarcely say, was precisely that at which a frightful accident had happened to the north mail nine years before.

I never told my wife the fearful events which I have just related to you. I told the surgeon who attended me; but he treated the whole adventure as a mere dream born of the fever in my brain. We discussed the question over and over again, until we found that we could discuss it with temper no longer, and then we dropped it. Others may form what conclusions they please—I *know* that twenty years ago I was the fourth inside passenger in that Phantom Coach.

1867

The Abbot's Ghost,

or

Maurice Treherne's Temptation

'A. M. BARNARD'
[LOUISA MAY ALCOTT]

Chapter I

DRAMATIS PERSONAE

'How goes it, Frank? Down first, as usual.' 'The early bird gets the worm, Major.' 'Deuced ungallant speech, considering that the lovely Octavia is the worm,' and with a significant laugh the major assumed an Englishman's favorite attitude before the fire.

His companion shot a quick glance at him, and an expression of anxiety passed over his face as he replied, with a well-feigned air of indifference. 'You are altogether too sharp, Major. I must be on my guard while you are in the house. Any new arrivals? I thought I heard a carriage drive up not long ago.'

'It was General Snowdon and his charming wife. Maurice Treherne came while we were out, and I've not seen him yet, poor fellow!'

'Aye, you may well say that; his is a hard case, if what I heard is true. I'm not booked up in the matter, and I should be, lest I make some blunder here, so tell me how things stand, Major. We've a good half hour before dinner. Sir Jasper is never punctual.'

'Yes, you've a right to know, if you are going to try your fortune with Octavia.'

The major marched through the three drawing rooms to see that no inquisitive servant was eavesdropping, and, finding all deserted, he resumed his place, while young Annon lounged on a couch as he listened with intense interest to the major's story.

'You know it was supposed that old Sir Jasper, being a bachelor, would leave his fortune to his two nephews. But he was an oddity, and as the title *must* go to young Jasper by right, the old man said Maurice should have the money. He was poor, young Jasper rich, and it seemed but just, though Madame Mère was very angry when she learned how the will was made.'

'But Maurice didn't get the fortune. How was that?'

'There was some mystery there which I shall discover in time. All went smoothly till that unlucky yachting trip, when the cousins were wrecked. Maurice saved Jasper's life, and almost lost his own in so doing. I fancy he wishes he had, rather than remain the poor cripple he is. Exposure, exertion, and neglect afterward brought on paralysis of the lower limbs, and there he is—a fine, talented, spirited fellow tied to that cursed chair like a decrepit old man.'

'How does he bear it?' asked Annon, as the major shook his gray head, with a traitorous huskiness in his last words.

'Like a philosopher or a hero. He is too proud to show his despair at such a sudden end to all his hopes, too generous to complain, for Jasper is desperately cut up about it, and too brave to be daunted by a misfortune which would drive many a man mad.'

'Is it true that Sir Jasper, knowing all this, made a new will and left every cent to his namesake?'

'Yes, and there lies the mystery. Not only did he leave it away from poor Maurice, but so tied it up that Jasper cannot transfer it, and at his death it goes to Octavia.'

'The old man must have been demented. What in heaven's name did he mean by leaving Maurice helpless and penniless after all his devotion to Jasper? Had he done anything to offend the old party?'

'No one knows; Maurice hasn't the least idea of the cause of this sudden whim, and the old man would give no reason for it. He died soon after, and the instant Jasper came to the title and estate he brought his cousin home, and treats him like a brother. Jasper is a noble fellow, with all his faults, and this act of justice increases my respect for him,' said the major heartily.

'What will Maurice do, now that he can't enter the army as he intended?' asked Annon, who now sat erect, so full of interest was he.

'Marry Octavia, and come to his own, I hope.'

'An excellent little arrangement, but Miss Treherne may object,' said Annon, rising with sudden kindling of the eye.

'I think not, if no one interferes. Pity, with women, is akin to love, and she pities her cousin in the tenderest fashion. No sister could be more devoted, and as Maurice is a handsome, talented fellow, one can easily foresee the end, if, as I said before, no one interferes to disappoint the poor lad again.'

'You espouse his cause, I see, and tell me this that I may stand aside. Thanks for the warning, Major; but as Maurice Treherne is a man of unusual power in many ways, I think we are equally matched, in spite of his misfortune. Nay, if anything, he has the advantage of me, for Miss Treherne pities him, and that is a strong ally for my rival. I'll be as generous as I can, but I'll *not* stand aside and relinquish the woman I love without a trial first.'

With an air of determination Annon faced the major, whose keen eyes had read the truth which he had but newly confessed to himself. Major Royston smiled as he listened, and said briefly, as steps approached, 'Do your best. Maurice will win.'

'We shall see,' returned Annon between his teeth.

Here their host entered, and the subject of course was dropped. But the major's words rankled in the young man's mind, and would have been doubly bitter had he known that their confidential conversation had been overheard. On either side of the great fireplace was a door leading to a suite of rooms which had been old Sir Jasper's. These apartments had been given to Maurice Treherne, and he had just returned from London, whither he had been to consult a certain famous physician. Enetering quietly, he had taken possession of his rooms, and having rested and dressed for dinner, rolled himself into the library, to which led the curtained door on the right. Sitting idly in his light, wheeled chair, ready to enter when his cousin appeared, he had heard the chat of Annon and the major. As he listened, over his usually impassive face passed varying expressions of anger, pain, bitterness, and defiance, and when the young man uttered his almost fierce 'We shall see,' Treherne smiled a scornful smile and clenched his pale hand with a gesture which proved that a year of suffering had not conquered the man's spirit, though it had crippled his strong body.

A singular face was Maurice Treherne's; well-cut and somewhat haughty features; a fine brow under the dark locks that carelessly streaked it; and remarkably piercing eyes. Slight in figure and wasted by pain, he still retained the grace as native to him as the stern fortitude which enabled him to hide the deep despair of an ambitious nature from every eye, and bear his affliction with a cheerful philosophy more pathetic than the most entire abandonment to grief. Carefully dressed, and with no hint at invalidism but the chair, he bore himself as easily and calmly as if the doom of lifelong helplessness did not hang over him. A single motion of the hand sent him rolling noiselessly to the curtained door, but as he did so, a voice exclaimed behind him, 'Wait for me, cousin.' And as he turned, a young girl approached, smiling a glad welcome as she took his hand, adding in a tone of sof* reproach, 'Home again, and not let me know it, till I heard the good news by accident.'

'Was it good news, Octavia?' and Maurice looked up at the frank face with a new expression in those penetrating eyes of his. His cousin's open glance never changed as she stroked the hair off his forehead with the caress one often gives a child, and answered eagerly, 'The best to me; the house is dull when you are away, for Jasper always becomes absorbed in horses and hounds, and leaves Mamma and me to mope by ourselves. But tell me, Maurice, what they said to you, since you would not write.'

'A little hope, with time and patience. Help me to wait, dear, help me to wait.'

His tone was infinitely sad, and as he spoke, he leaned his cheek against the kind hand he held, as if to find support and comfort there. The girl's face brightened beautifully, though her eyes filled, for to her alone did he betray his pain, and in her alone did he seek consolation.

'I will, I will with heart and hand! Thank heaven for the hope, and trust me it shall be fulfilled. You look very tired, Maurice. Why go in to dinner with all those people? Let me make you cozy here,' she added anxiously.

'Thanks, I'd rather go in, it does me good; and if I stay away, Jasper feels that he must stay with me. I dressed in haste, am I right, little nurse?'

She gave him a comprehensive glance, daintily settled his cravat, brushed back a truant lock, and, with a maternal air that was charming, said, 'My boy is always elegant, and I'm proud of him. Now we'll go in.' But with her hand on the curtain she paused, saying quickly, as a voice reached her, 'Who is that?'

'Frank Annon. Didn't you know he was coming?' Maurice eyed her keenly.

'No, Jasper never told me. Why did he ask him?'

'To please you.'

'Me! When he knows I detest the man. No matter, I've got on the color he hates, so he won't annoy me, and Mrs. Snowdon can amuse herself with him. The general has come, you know?'

Treherne smiled, well pleased, for no sign of maiden shame or pleasure did the girl's face betray, and as he watched her while she peeped, he thought with satisfaction, Annon is right, I have the advantage, and I'll keep it at all costs.

'Here is Mamma. We must go in,' said Octavia, as a stately old lady made her appearance in the drawing room.

The cousins entered together and Annon watched them covertly, while seemingly intent on paying his respects to Madame Mère, as his hostess was called by her family.

'Handsomer than ever,' he muttered, as his eye rested on the blooming girl, looking more like a rose than ever in the peach-colored silk which he had once condemned because a rival admired it. She turned to reply to the major, and Annon glanced at Treherne with an irrepressible frown, for sickness had not marred the charm of that peculiar face, so colorless and thin that it seemed cut in marble; but the keen eyes shone with a wonderful brilliancy, and the whole countenance was alive with a power of intellect and will which made the observer involuntarily exclaim, 'That man must suffer a daily martyrdom, so crippled and confined; if it lasts long he will go mad or die.'

'General and Mrs. Snowdon,' announced the servant, and a sudden pause ensued as everyone looked up to greet the newcomers.

A feeble, white-haired old man entered, leaning on the arm of an indescribably beautiful woman. Not thirty yet, tall and nobly molded, with straight black brows over magnificent eyes; rippling dark hair gathered up in a great knot, and ornamented with a single band of gold. A sweeping dress of wine-colored velvet, set off with a dazzling neck and arms decorated like her stately head with ornaments of Roman gold. At the first glance she seemed a cold, haughty creature, born to dazzle but not to win. A deeper scrutiny detected lines of suffering in that lovely face, and behind the veil of reserve, which pride forced her to wear, appeared the anguish of a strong-willed

woman burdened by a heavy cross. No one would dare express pity
or offer sympathy, for her whole air repelled it, and in her gloomy
eyes sat scorn of herself mingled with defiance of the scorn of others.
A strange, almost tragical-looking woman, in spite of beauty, grace,
and the cold sweetness of her manner. A faint smile parted her lips as
she greeted those about her, and as her husband seated himself beside
Lady Treherne, she lifted her head with a long breath, and a singular
expression of relief, as if a burden was removed, and for the time being
she was free. Sir Jasper was at her side, and as she listened, her eye
glanced from face to face.

'Who is with you now?' she asked, in a low, mellow voice that was
full of music.

'My sister and my cousin are yonder. You may remember Tavia as
a child, she is little more now. Maurice is an invalid, but the finest
fellow breathing.'

'I understand,' and Mrs. Snowdon's eyes softened with a sudden
glance of pity for one cousin and admiration for the other, for she
knew the facts.

'Major Royston, my father's friend, and Frank Annon, my own. Do
you know him?' asked Sir Jasper.

'No.'

'Then allow me to make him happy by presenting him, may
I?'

'Not now. I'd rather see your cousin.'

'Thanks, you are very kind. I'll bring him over.'

'Stay, let me go to him,' began the lady, with more feeling in face
and voice than one would believe her capable of showing.

'Pardon, it will offend him, he will not be pitied, or relinquish
any of the duties or privileges of a gentleman which he can possibly
perform. He is proud, we can understand the feeling, so let us humor
the poor fellow.'

Mrs. Snowdon bowed silently, and Sir Jasper called out in his
hearty, blunt way, as if nothing was amiss with his cousin, 'Maurice,
I've an honor for you. Come and receive it.'

Divining what it was, Treherne noiselessly crossed the room, and
with no sign of self-consciousness or embarrassment, was presented to
the handsome woman. Thinking his presence might be a restraint,
Sir Jasper went away. The instant his back was turned, a change
came over both: an almost grim expression replaced the suavity of

Treherne's face, and Mrs. Snowdon's smile faded suddenly, while a deep flush rose to her brow, as her eyes questioned his beseechingly.

'How dared you come?' he asked below his breath.

'The general insisted.'

'And you could not change his purpose; poor woman!'

'You will not be pitied, neither will I,' and her eyes flashed; then the fire was quenched in tears, and her voice lost all its pride in a pleading tone.

'Forgive me, I longed to see you since your illness, and so I "dared" to come.'

'You shall be gratified; look, quite helpless, crippled for life, perhaps.'

The chair was turned from the groups about the fire, and as he spoke, with a bitter laugh Treherne threw back the skin which covered his knees, and showed her the useless limbs once so strong and fleet. She shrank and paled, put out her hand to arrest him, and cried in an indignant whisper, 'No, no, not that! You know I never meant such cruel curiosity, such useless pain to both—'

'Be still, someone is coming,' he returned inaudibly; adding aloud, as he adjusted the skin and smoothed the rich fur as if speaking of it, 'Yes, it is a very fine one, Jasper gave it to me. He spoils me, like a dear, generous-hearted fellow as he is. Ah, Octavia, what can I do for you?'

'Nothing, thank you. I want to recall myself to Mrs. Snowdon's memory, if she will let me.'

'No need of that; I never forget happy faces and pretty pictures. Two years ago I saw you at your first ball, and longed to be a girl again.'

As she spoke, Mrs. Snowdon pressed the hand shyly offered, and smiled at the spirited face before her, though the shadow in her own eyes deepened as she met the bright glance of the girl.

'How kind you were that night! I remember you let me chatter away about my family, my cousin, and my foolish little affairs with the sweetest patience, and made me very happy by your interest. I was homesick, and Aunt could never bear to hear of those things. It was before your marriage, and all the kinder, for you were the queen of the night, yet had a word for poor little me.'

Mrs. Snowdon was pale to the lips, and Maurice impatiently tapped the arm of his chair, while the girl innocently chatted on.

'I am sorry the general is such an invalid; yet I dare say you find great happiness in taking care of him. It is so pleasant to be of use to those we love.' And as she spoke, Octavia leaned over her cousin to hand him the glove he had dropped.

The affectionate smile that accompanied the act made the color deepen again in Mrs. Snowdon's cheek, and lit a spark in her softened eyes. Her lips curled and her voice was sweetly sarcastic as she answered, 'Yes, it is charming to devote one's life to these dear invalids, and find one's reward in their gratitude. Youth, beauty, health, and happiness are small sacrifices if one wins a little comfort for the poor sufferers.'

The girl felt the sarcasm under the soft words and drew back with a troubled face.

Maurice smiled, and glanced from one to the other, saying significantly, 'Well for me that my little nurse loves her labor, and finds no sacrifice in it. I am fortunate in my choice.'

'I trust it may prove so—' Mrs. Snowdon got no further, for at that moment dinner was announced, and Sir Jasper took her away. Annon approached with him and offered his arm to Miss Treherne, but with an air of surprise, and a little gesture of refusal, she said coldly:

'My cousin always takes me in to dinner. Be good enough to escort the major.' And with her hand on the arm of the chair, she walked away with a mischievous glitter in her eyes.

Annon frowned and fell back, saying sharply, 'Come, Major, what are you doing there?'

'Making discoveries.'

Chapter II

BYPLAY

A right splendid old dowager was Lady Treherne, in her black velvet and point lace, as she sat erect and stately on a couch by the drawing-room fire, a couch which no one dare occupy in her absence, or share uninvited. The gentlemen were still over their wine, and the three ladies were alone. My lady never dozed in public, Mrs. Snowdon never gossiped, and Octavia never troubled herself to entertain any guests but those of her own age, so long pauses fell, and conversation languished, till Mrs. Snowdon roamed away into the library. As she disappeared, Lady Treherne beckoned to her daughter, who was idly making chords at the grand piano. Seating herself on the ottoman at her mother's feet, the girl took the still handsome hand in her own and amused herself with examining the old-fashioned jewels that covered it, a pretext for occupying her telltale eyes, as she suspected what was coming.

'My dear, I'm not pleased with you, and I tell you so at once, that you may amend your fault,' began Madame Mère in a tender tone, for though a haughty, imperious woman, she idolized her children.

'What have I done, Mamma?' asked the girl.

'Say rather, what have you left undone. You have been very rude to Mr. Annon. It must not occur again; not only because he is a guest, but because he is your—brother's friend.'

My lady hesitated over the word 'lover,' and changed it, for to her Octavia still seemed a child, and though anxious for the alliance, she forbore to speak openly, lest the girl should turn wilful, as she inherited her mother's high spirit.

'I'm sorry, Mamma. But how can I help it, when he teases me so that I detest him?' said Octavia, petulantly.

'How tease, my love?'

'Why, he follows me about like a dog, puts on a sentimental look when I appear; blushes, and beams, and bows at everything I say, if I am polite; frowns and sighs if I'm not; and glowers tragically at every man I speak to, even poor Maurice. Oh, Mamma, what foolish creatures men are!' And the girl laughed blithely, as she looked up for the first time into her mother's face.

My mother smiled, as she stroked the bright head at her knee, but asked quickly, 'Why say "even poor Maurice," as if it were impossible for anyone to be jealous of him?'

'But isn't it, Mamma? I thought strong, well men regarded him as one set apart and done with, since his sad misfortune.'

'Not entirely; while women pity and pet the poor fellow, his comrades will be jealous, absurd as it is.'

'No one pets him but me, and I have a right to do it, for he is my cousin,' said the girl, feeling a touch of jealousy herself.

'Rose and Blanche Talbot outdo you, my dear, and there is no cousinship to excuse them.'

'Then let Frank Annon be jealous of them, and leave me in peace. They promised to come today; I'm afraid something has happened to prevent them.' And Octavia gladly seized upon the new subject. But my lady was not to be eluded.

'They said they could not come till after dinner. They will soon arrive. Before they do so, I must say a few words, Tavia, and I beg you to give heed to them. I desire you to be courteous and amiable to Mr. Annon, and before strangers to be less attentive and affectionate to Maurice. You mean it kindly, but it looks ill, and causes disagreeable remarks.'

'Who blames me for being devoted to my cousin? Can I ever do enough to repay him for his devotion? Mamma, you forget he saved your son's life.'

Indignant tears filled the girl's eyes, and she spoke passionately, forgetting that Mrs. Snowdon was within earshot of her raised voice. With a frown my lady laid her hand on her daughter's lips, saying coldly, 'I do not forget, and I religiously discharge my every obligation by every care and comfort it is in my power to bestow. You are young, romantic, and tender-hearted. You think you must give your time and health, must sacrifice your future happiness to this duty. You are wrong, and unless you learn wisdom in season, you will find that you have done harm, not good.'

'God forbid! How can I do that? Tell me, and I will be wise in time.'

Turning the earnest face up to her own, Lady Treherne whispered anxiously, 'Has Maurice ever looked or hinted anything of love during this year he has been with us, and you his constant companion?'

'Never, Mamma; he is too honorable and too unhappy to speak or think of that. I am his little nurse, sister, and friend, no more, nor ever shall be. Do not suspect us, or put such fears into my mind, else all our comfort will be spoiled.'

Flushed and eager was the girl, but her clear eyes betrayed no tender confusion as she spoke, and all her thought seemed to be to clear her cousin from the charge of loving her too well. Lady Treherne looked relieved, paused a moment, then said, seriously but gently, 'This is well, but, child, I charge you tell me at once, if ever he forgets himself, for this thing cannot be. Once I hoped it might, now it is impossible; remember that he continue a friend and cousin, nothing more. I warn you in time, but if you neglect the warning, Maurice must go. No more of this; recollect my wish regarding Mr. Annon, and let your cousin amuse himself without you in public.'

'Mamma, do you wish me to like Frank Annon?'

The abrupt question rather disturbed my lady, but knowing her daughter's frank, impetuous nature, she felt somewhat relieved by this candor, and answered decidedly, 'I do. He is your equal in all respects; he loves you, Jasper desires it, I approve, and you, being heartwhole, can have no just objection to the alliance.'

'Has he spoken to you?'

'No, to your brother.'

'You wish this much, Mamma?'

'Very much, my child.'

'I will try to please you, then.' And stifling a sigh, the girl kissed her mother with unwonted meekness in tone and manner.

'Now I am well pleased. Be happy, my love. No one will urge or distress you. Let matters take their course, and if this hope of ours can be fulfilled, I shall be relieved of the chief care of my life.'

A sound of girlish voices here broke on their ears, and springing up, Octavia hurried to meet her friends, exclaiming joyfully, 'They have come! they have come!'

Two smiling, blooming girls met her at the door, and, being at an enthusiastic age, they gushed in girlish fashion for several minutes, making a pretty group as they stood in each other's arms, all talking at once, with frequent kisses and little bursts of laughter, as vents for their emotion. Madame Mère welcomed them and then went to join Mrs. Snowdon, leaving the trio to gossip unrestrained.

'My dearest creature, I thought we never should get here, for Papa had a tiresome dinner party, and we were obliged to stay, you know,' cried Rose, the lively sister, shaking out the pretty dress and glancing at herself in the mirror as she fluttered about the room like a butterfly.

'We were dying to come, and so charmed when you asked us, for we haven't seen you this age, darling,' added Blanche, the pensive one, smoothing her blond curls after a fresh embrace.

'I'm sorry the Ulsters couldn't come to keep Christmas with us, for we have no gentlemen but Jasper, Frank Annon, and the major. Sad, isn't it?' said Octavia, with a look of despair, which caused a fresh peal of laughter.

'One apiece, my dear, it might be worse.' And Rose privately decided to appropriate Sir Jasper.

'Where is your cousin?' asked Blanche, with a sigh of sentimental interest.

'He is here, of course, I forget him, but he is not on the flirting list, you know. We must amuse him, and not expect him to amuse us, though really, all the capital suggestions and plans for merrymaking always come from him.'

'He is better, I hope?' asked both sisters with real sympathy, making their young faces womanly and sweet.

'Yes, and has hopes of entire recovery. At least, they tell him so, though Dr. Ashley said there was no chance of it.'

'Dear, dear, how sad! Shall we see him, Tavia?'

'Certainly; he is able to be with us now in the evening, and enjoys society as much as ever. But please take no notice of his infirmity, and make no inquiries beyond the usual "How do you do." He is sensitive, and hates to be considered an invalid more than ever.'

'How charming it must be to take care of him, he is so accomplished and delightful. I quite envy you,' said Blanche pensively.

'Sir Jasper told us that the General and Mrs. Snowdon were coming. I hope they will, for I've a most intense curiosity to see her—' began Rose.

'Hush, she is here with Mamma! Why curious? What is the mystery? For you look as if there was one,' questioned Octavia under her breath.

The three charming heads bent toward one another as Rose replied in a whisper, 'If I knew, I shouldn't be inquisitive. There was a rumor that she married the old general in a fit of pique, and now repents. I asked Mamma once, but she said such matters were not for young girls to hear, and not a word more would she say. *N'importe*, I have wits of my own, and I can satisfy myself. The gentlemen are coming! Am I all right, dear?' And the three glanced at one another with a swift scrutiny that nothing could escape, then grouped themselves prettily, and waited, with a little flutter of expectation in each young heart.

In came the gentlemen, and instantly a new atmosphere seemed to pervade the drawing room, for with the first words uttered, several romances began. Sir Jasper was taken possession of by Rose, Blanche intended to devote herself to Maurice Treherne, but Annon intercepted her, and Octavia was spared any effort at politeness by this unexpected move on the part of her lover.

'He is angry, and wishes to pique me by devoting himself to

Blanche, I wish he would, with all my heart, and leave me in peace. Poor Maurice, he expects me, and I long to go to him, but must obey Mamma.' And Octavia went to join the group formed by my lady, Mrs. Snowdon, the general, and the major.

The two young couples flirted in different parts of the room, and Treherne sat alone, watching them all with eyes that pierced below the surface, reading the hidden wishes, hopes, and fears that ruled them. A singular expression sat on his face as he turned from Octavia's clear countenance to Mrs. Snowdon's gloomy one. He leaned his head upon his hand and fell into deep thought, for he was passing through one of those fateful moments which come to us all, and which may make or mar a life. Such moments come when least looked for: an unexpected meeting, a peculiar mood, some trivial circumstance, or careless word produces it, and often it is gone before we realize its presence, leaving after-effects to show us what we have gained or lost. Treherne was conscious that the present hour, and the acts that filled it, possessed unusual interest, and would exert an unusual influence on his life. Before him was the good and evil genius of his nature in the guise of those two women. Edith Snowdon had already tried her power, and accident only had saved him. Octavia, all unconscious as she was, never failed to rouse and stimulate the noblest attributes of mind and heart. A year spent in her society had done much for him, and he loved her with a strange mingling of passion, reverence, and gratitude. He knew why Edith Snowdon came, he felt that the old fascination had not lost its charm, and though fear was unknown to him, he was ill pleased at the sight of the beautiful, dangerous woman. On the other hand, he saw that Lady Treherne desired her daughter to shun him and smile on Annon; he acknowledged that he had no right to win the young creature, crippled and poor as he was, and a pang of jealous pain wrung his heart as he watched her.

Then a sense of power came to him, for helpless, poor, and seemingly an object of pity, he yet felt that he held the honor, peace, and happiness of nearly every person present in his hands. It was a strong temptation to this man, so full of repressed passion and power, so set apart and shut out from the more stirring duties and pleasures of life. A few words from his lips, and the pity all felt for him would be turned to fear, respect, and admiration. Why not utter them, and enjoy all that was possible? He owed the Trehernes nothing; why suffer injustice, dependence, and the compassion that wounds a proud man deepest? Wealth, love, pleasure might be his with a breath. Why not secure them now?

His pale face flushed, his eye kindled, and his thin hand lay clenched like a vice as these thoughts passed rapidly through his mind. A look, a word at that moment would sway him; he felt it, and leaned forward, waiting in secret suspense for the glance, the speech which should decide him for good or ill. Who shall say what subtle instinct caused Octavia to turn and smile at him with a wistful, friendly look that warmed his heart? He met it with an answering glance, which thrilled her strangely, for love, gratitude, and some mysterious intelligence met and mingled in the brilliant yet soft expression which swiftly shone and faded in her face. What it was she could not tell; she only felt that it filled her with an indescribable emotion never experienced before. In an instant it all passed, Lady Treherne spoke to her, and Blanche Talbot addressed Maurice, wondering, as she did so, if the enchanting smile he wore was meant for her.

'Mr. Annon having mercifully set me free, I came to try to cheer your solitude; but you look as if solitude made you happier than society does the rest of us,' she said without her usual affectation, for his manner impressed her.

'You are very kind and very welcome. I do find pleasures to beguile my loneliness, which gayer people would not enjoy, and it is well that I can, else I should turn morose and tyrannical, and doom some unfortunate to entertain me all day long.' He answered with a gentle courtesy which was his chief attraction to womankind.

'Pray tell me some of your devices. I'm often alone in spirit, if not so in the flesh, for Rose, though a dear girl, is not congenial, and I find no kindred soul.'

A humorous glimmer came to Treherne's eyes, as the sentimental damsel beamed a soft sigh and drooped her long lashes effectively. Ignoring the topic of 'kindred souls,' he answered coldly, 'My favorite amusement is studying the people around me. It may be rude, but tied to my corner, I cannot help watching the figures around me, and discovering their little plots and plans. I'm getting very expert, and really surprise myself sometimes by the depth of my researches.'

'I can believe it; your eyes look as if they possessed that gift. Pray don't study *me*.' And the girl shrank away with an air of genuine alarm.

Treherne smiled involuntarily, for he had read the secret of that shallow heart long ago, and was too generous to use the knowledge, however flattering it might be to him. In a reassuring tone he said, turning away the keen eyes she feared, 'I give you my word I never will, charming as it might be to study the white pages of a maidenly heart. I find plenty of others to read, so rest tranquil, Miss Blanche.'

'Who interests you most just now?' asked the girl, coloring with pleasure at his words. 'Mrs. Snowdon looks like one who has a romance to be read, if you have the skill.'

'I have read it. My lady is my study just now. I thought I knew her well, but of late she puzzles me. Human minds are more full of mysteries than any written book and more changeable than the cloud shapes in the air.'

'A fine old lady, but I fear her so intensely I should never dare to try to read her, as you say.' Blanche looked toward the object of discussion as she spoke, and added, 'Poor Tavia, how forlorn she seems. Let me ask her to join us, may I?'

'With all my heart' was the quick reply.

Blanche glided away but did not return, for my lady kept her as well as her daughter.

'That test satisfies me; well, I submit for a time, but I think I can conquer my aunt yet.' And with a patient sigh Treherne turned to observe Mrs. Snowdon.

She now stood by the fire, talking with Sir Jasper, a handsome, reckless, generous-hearted young gentleman, who very plainly showed his great admiration for the lady. When he came, she suddenly woke up from her listless mood and became as brilliantly gay as she had been unmistakably melancholy before. As she chatted, she absently pushed to and fro a small antique urn of bronze on the chimneypiece, and in doing so she more than once gave Treherne a quick, significant glance, which he answered at last by a somewhat haughty nod. Then, as if satisfied, she ceased toying with the ornament and became absorbed in Sir Jasper's gallant badinage.

The instant her son approached Mrs. Snowdon, Madame Mère grew anxious, and leaving Octavia to her friends and lover, she watched Jasper. But her surveillance availed little, for she could neither see nor hear anything amiss, yet could not rid herself of the feeling that some mutual understanding existed between them. When the party broke up for the night, she lingered till all were gone but her son and nephew.

'Well, Madame Mère, what troubles you?' asked Sir Jasper, as she looked anxiously into his face before bestowing her good-night kiss.

'I cannot tell, yet I feel ill at ease. Remember, my son, that you are the pride of my heart, and any sin or shame of yours would kill me. Good night, Maurice.' And with a stately bow she swept away.

Lounging with both elbows on the low chimneypiece, Sir Jasper smiled at his mother's fears, and said to his cousin, the instant they were alone, 'She is worried about E. S. Odd, isn't it, what instinctive antipathies women take to one another?'

'Why did you ask E. S. here?' demanded Treherne.

'My dear fellow, how could I help it? My mother wanted the general, my father's friend, and of course his wife must be asked also. I couldn't tell my mother that the lady had been a most arrant coquette, to put it mildly, and had married the old man in a pet, because my cousin and I declined to be ruined by her.'

'You *could* have told her what mischief she makes wherever she goes, and for Octavia's sake have deferred the general's visit for a time. I warn you, Jasper, harm will come of it.'

'To whom, you or me?'

'To both, perhaps, certainly to you. She was disappointed once when she lost us both by wavering between your title and my supposed fortune. She is miserable with the old man, and her only hope is in his death, for he is very feeble. You are free, and doubly attractive now, so beware, or she will entangle you before you know it.'

'Thanks, Mentor. I've no fear, and shall merely amuse myself for a week—they stay no longer.' And with a careless laugh, Sir Jasper strolled away.

'Much mischief may be done in a week, and this is the beginning of it,' muttered Treherne, as he raised himself to look under the bronze vase for the note. It was gone!

Chapter III

WHO WAS IT?

W ho had taken it? This question tormented Treherne all that
sleepless night. He suspected three persons, for only these had
approached the fire after the note was hidden. He had kept his eye
on it, he thought, till the stir of breaking up. In that moment it
must have been removed by the major, Frank Annon, or my lady;
Sir Jasper was out of the question, for he never touched an ornament
in the drawing room since he had awkwardly demolished a whole
étagère of costly trifles, to his mother's and sister's great grief.
The major evidently suspected something, Annon was jealous,
and my lady would be glad of a pretext to remove her daughter
from his reach. Trusting to his skill in reading faces, he waited
impatiently for morning, resolving to say nothing to anyone but
Mrs. Snowdon, and from her merely to inquire what the note
contained.

Treherne usually was invisible till lunch, often till dinner; therefore,
fearing to excite suspicion by unwonted activity, he did not appear
till noon. The mailbag had just been opened, and everyone was
busy over their letters, but all looked up to exchange a word
with the newcomer, and Octavia impulsively turned to meet him,
then checked herself and hid her suddenly crimsoned face behind a
newspaper. Treherne's eye took in everything, and saw at once in the
unusually late arrival of the mail a pretext for discovering the pilferer
of the note.

'All have letters but me, yet I expected one last night. Major,
have you got it among yours?' And as he spoke, Treherne fixed his
penetrating eyes full on the person he addressed.

With no sign of consciousness, no trace of confusion, the major
carefully turned over his pile, and replied in the most natural manner,
'Not a trace of it; I wish there was, for nothing annoys me more than
any delay or mistake about my letters.'

He knows nothing of it, thought Treherne, and turned to Annon,
who was deep in a long epistle from some intimate friend, with a
talent for imparting news, to judge from the reader's interest.

'Annon, I appeal to you, for I *must* discover who has robbed me of
my letter.'

'I have but one, read it, if you will, and satisfy yourself' was the brief reply.

'No, thank you. I merely asked in joke; it is doubtless among my lady's. Jasper's letters and mine often get mixed, and my lady takes care of his for him. I think you must have it, Aunt.'

Lady Treherne looked up impatiently. 'My dear Maurice, what a coil about a letter! We none of us have it, so do not punish us for the sins of your correspondent or the carelessness of the post.'

She was not the thief, for she is always intensely polite when she intends to thwart me, thought Treherne, and, apologizing for his rudeness in disturbing the, he rolled himself to his nook in a sunny window and became apparently absorbed in a new magazine.

Mrs. Snowdon was opening the general's letters for him, and, having finished her little task, she roamed away into the library, as if in search of a book. Presently returning with one, she approached Treherne, and, putting it into his hand, said, in her musically distinct voice, 'Be so kind as to find for me the passage you spoke of last night. I am curious to see it.'

Instantly comprehending her stratagem, he opened it with apparent carelessness, secured the tiny note laid among the leaves, and, selecting a passage at hazard, returned her book and resumed his own. Behind the cover of it he unfolded and read these words:

> I understand, but do not be anxious; the line I left was merely this—'I must see you alone, tell me when and where.' No one can make much of it, and I will discover the thief before dinner. Do nothing, but watch to whom I speak first on entering, when we meet in the evening, and beware of that person.

Quietly transferring the note to the fire with the wrapper of the magazine, he dismissed the matter from his mind and left Mrs. Snowdon to play detective as she pleased, while he busied himself about his own affairs.

It was a clear, bright December day, and when the young people separated to prepare for a ride, while the general and the major sunned themselves on the terrace, Lady Treherne said to her nephew, 'I am going for an airing in the pony carriage. Will you be my escort, Maurice?'

'With pleasure,' replied the young man, well knowing what was in store for him.

My lady was unusually taciturn and grave, yet seemed anxious to say something which she found difficult to utter. Treherne saw this, and ended an awkward pause by dashing boldly into the subject which occupied both.

'I think you want to say something to me about Tavie, Aunt. Am I right?'

'Yes.'

'Then let me spare you the pain of beginning, and prove my sincerity by openly stating the truth, as far as I am concerned. I love her very dearly, but I am not mad enough to dream of telling her so. I know that it is impossible, and I relinquish my hopes. Trust me. I will keep silent and see her marry Annon without a word of complaint, if you will it. I see by her altered manner that you have spoken to her, and that my little friend and nurse is to be mine no longer. Perhaps you are wise, but if you do this on my account, it is in vain—the mischief is done, and while I live I shall love my cousin. If you do it to spare her, I am dumb, and will go away rather than cause her a care or pain.'

'Do you really mean this, Maurice?' And Lady Treherne looked at him with a changed and softened face.

Turning upon her. Treherne showed her a countenance full of suffering and sincerity, of resignation and resolve, as he said earnestly, 'I do mean it; prove me in any way you please. I am not a bad fellow, Aunt, and I desire to be better. Since my misfortune I've had time to test many things, myself among others, and in spite of many faults, I do cherish the wish to keep my soul honest and true, even though my body be a wreck. It is easy to say these things, but in spite of temptation, I think I can stand firm, if you trust me.'

'My dear boy, I do trust you, and thank you gratefully for this frankness. I never forget that I owe Jasper's life to you, and never expect to repay that debt. Remember this when I seem cold or unkind, and remember also that I say now, had you been spared this affliction, I would gladly have given you my girl. But—'

'But, Aunt, hear one thing,' broke in Treherne. 'They tell me that any sudden and violent shock of surprise, joy, or sorrow may do for me what they hope time will achieve. I said nothing of this, for it is but a chance; yet while there is any hope, need I utterly renounce Octavia?'

'It is hard to refuse, and yet I cannot think it wise to build upon a chance so slight. Once let her have you, and both are made unhappy, if the hope fail. No, Maurice, it is better to be generous, and leave her free to make her own happiness elsewhere. Annon loves her, she is heart-whole, and will soon learn to love him, if you are silent. My poor boy, it seems cruel, but I must say it.'

'Shall I go away, Aunt?' was all his answer, very firmly uttered, though is lips were white.

'Not yet, only leave them to themselves, and hide your trouble if you can. Yet, if you prefer, you shall go to town, and Benson shall see that you are comfortable. Your health will be a reason, and I will come, or write often, if you are homesick. It shall depend on you, for I want to be just and kind in this hard case. You shall decide.'

'Then I will stay. I can hide my love; and to see them together will soon cease to wound me, if Octavia is happy.'

'So let it rest then, for a time. You shall miss your companion as little as possible, for I will try to fill her place. Forgive me, Maurice, and pity a mother's solicitude, for these two are the last of many children, and I am a widow now.'

Lady Treherne's voice faltered, and if any selfish hope or plan lingered in her nephew's mind, that appeal banished it and touched his better nature. Pressing her hand he said gently, 'Dear Aunt, do not lament over me. I am one set apart for afflictions, yet I will not be conquered by them. Let us forget my youth and be friendly counsellors together for the good of the two whom we both love. I must say a word about Jasper, and you will not press me to explain more than I can without breaking my promise.'

'Thank you, thank you! It is regarding that woman, I know. Tell me all you can; I will not be importunate, but I disliked her the instant I saw her, beautiful and charming as she seems.'

'When my cousin and I were in Paris, just before my illness, we met her. She was with her father then, a gay old man who led a life of pleasure, and was no fit guardian for a lovely daughter. She knew our story and, having fascinated both, paused to decide which she would accept; Jasper, for his title, or me, for my fortune. This was before my uncle changed his will, and I believed myself his heir; but, before she made her choice, something (don't ask me what, if you please) occurred to send us from Paris. On our return voyage we were wrecked, and then came my illness, disinheritance, and helplessness. Edith Dubarry heard the story, but rumour reported it falsely, and she believed both of us had lost the fortune. Her father died penniless, and in a moment of despair she married the general, whose wealth surrounds her with the luxury she loves, and whose failing health will soon restore her liberty—'

'And then, Maurice?' interrupted my lady.

'She hopes to win Jasper, I think.'

'Never! We must prevent that at all costs. I had rather see him dead before me, than the husband of such a woman. Why is she permitted to visit homes like mine? I should have been told this sooner,' exclaimed my lady angrily.

'I should have told you had I known it, and I reproved Jasper for his neglect. Do not be needlessly troubled, Aunt. There is no blemish on Mrs. Snowdon's name, and, as the wife of a brave and honorable man, she is received without question; for beauty, grace, or tact like hers can make their way anywhere. She stays but a week, and I will devote myself to her; this will save Jasper, and, if necessary, convince Tavie of my indifference—' Then he paused to stifle a sigh.

'But yourself, have you no fears for your own peace, Maurice? You must not sacrifice happiness or honor, for me or mine.'

'I am safe; I love my cousin, and that is my shield. Whatever happens remember that I tried to serve you, and sincerely endeavored to forget myself.'

'God bless you, my son! Let me call you so, and feel that, though I deny you my daughter, I give you heartily a mother's care and affection.'

Lady Treherne was as generous as she was proud, and her nephew had conquered her by confidence and submission. He acted no part, yet, even in relinquishing all, he cherished a hope that he might yet win the heart he coveted. Silently they parted, but from that hour a new and closer bond existed between the two, and exerted an unsuspected influence over the whole household.

Maurice waited with some impatience for Mrs. Snowdon's entrance, not only because of his curiosity to see if she had discovered the thief, but because of the part he had taken upon himself to play. He was equal to it, and felt a certain pleasure in it for a threefold reason. It would serve his aunt and cousin, would divert his mind from his own cares, and, perhaps by making Octavia jealous, waken love; for, though he had chosen the right, he was but a man, and moreover a lover.

Mrs. Snowdon was late. She always was, for her toilet was elaborate, and she liked to enjoy its effects upon others. The moment she entered Treherne's eye was on her, and to his intense surprise and annoyance she addressed Octavia, saying blandly, 'My dear Miss Treherne, I've been admiring your peacocks. Pray let me see you feed them tomorrow. Miss Talbot says it is a charming sight.'

'If you are on the terrace just after lunch, you will find them there, and may feed them yourself, if you like,' was the cool, civil reply.

'She looks like a peacock herself in that splendid green and gold dress, doesn't she?' whispered Rose to Sir Jasper, with a wicked laugh.

'Faith, so she does. I wish Tavie's birds had voices like Mrs. Snowdon's; their squalling annoys me intensely.'

'I rather like it, for it is honest, and no malice or mischief is hidden behind it. I always distrust those smooth, sweet voices; they are insincere. I like a full, clear tone; sharp, if you please, but decided and true.'

'Well said, Octavia. I agree with you, and your own is a perfect sample of the kind you describe.' And Treherne smiled as he rolled by to join Mrs. Snowdon, who evidently waited for him, while Octavia turned to her brother to defend her pets.

'Are you sure? How did you discover?' said Maurice, affecting to admire the lady's bouquet, as he paused beside her.

'I suspected it is the moment I saw her this morning. She is no actress; and dislike, distrust, and contempt were visible in her face when we met. Till you so cleverly told me my note was lost, I fancied she was disturbed about her brother—or you.'

A sudden pause and a keen glance followed the last softly uttered word, but Treherne met it with an inscrutable smile and a quiet 'Well, what next?'

'The moment I learned that you did not get the note I was sure she had it, and, knowing that she must have seen me put it there, in spite of her apparent innocence, I quietly asked her for it. This surprised her, this robbed the affair of any mystery, and I finished her perplexity by sending it to the major the moment she returned it to me, as if it had been intended for him. She begged pardon, said her brother was thoughtless, and she watched over him lest he should get into mischief; professed to think I meant the line for him, and behaved like a charming simpleton, as she is.'

'Quite a tumult about nothing. Poor little Tavie! you doubtlessly frightened her so that we may safely correspond hereafter.'

'You may give me an answer, now and here.'

'Very well, meet me on the terrace tomorrow morning; the peacocks will make the meeting natural enough. I usually loiter away an hour or two there, in the sunny part of the day.'

'But the girl?'

'I'll send her away.'

'You speak as if it would be an easy thing to do.'

'It will, both easy and pleasant.'

'Now you are mysterious or uncomplimentary. You either care nothing for a *tête-à-tête* with her, or you will gladly send her out of my way. Which is it?'

'You shall decide. Can I have this?'

She looked at him as he touched a rose with a warning glance, for the flower was both an emblem of love and of silence. Did he mean to hint that he recalled the past, or to warn her that someone was near? She leaned from the shadow of the curtain where she sat, and caught a glimpse of a shadow gliding away.

'Who was it?' she asked, below her breath.

'A Rose,' he answered, laughing. Then, as if the danger was over, he said, 'How will you account to the major for the message you sent him?'

'Easily, by fabricating some interesting perplexity in which I want sage counsel. He will be flattered, and by seeming to take him into my confidence, I can hoodwink the excellent man to my heart's content, for he annoys me by his odd way of mounting guard over me at all times. Now take me in to dinner, and be your former delightful self.'

'That is impossible,' he said, yet proved that it was not.

Chapter IV

FEEDING THE PEACOCKS

It was indeed a charming sight, the twelve stately birds perched on the broad stone balustrade, or prancing slowly along the terrace, with the sun gleaming on their green and golden necks and the glories of their gorgeous plumes, widespread, or sweeping like rich trains behind them. In pretty contrast to the splendid creatures was their young mistress, in her simple morning dress and fur-trimmed hood and mantle, as she stood feeding the tame pets from her hand, calling their fanciful names, laughing at their pranks, and heartily enjoying the winter sunshine, the fresh wind, and the girlish pastime. As Treherne slowly approached, he watched her with lover's eyes, and found her very sweet and blithe, and dearer in his sight than ever. She had shunned him carefully all the day before, had parted at night with a hasty handshake, and had not come as usual to bid him good-morning in the library. He had taken no notice of the change as yet, but now, remembering his promise to his aunt, he resolved to let the girl know that he fully understood the relation which henceforth was to exist between them.

'Good morning, cousin. Shall I drive you away, if I take a turn or two here?' he said, in a cheerful tone, but with a half-reproachful glance.

She looked at him an instant, then went to him with extended hand and cheeks rosier than before, while her frank eyes filled, and her voice had a traitorous tremor in it, as she said, impetuously: 'I *will* be myself for a moment, in spite of everything. Maurice, don't think me unkind, don't reproach me, or ask my leave to come where I am. There is a reason for the change you see in me; it's not caprice, it is obedience.'

'My dear girl, I know it. I meant to speak of it, and show you that I understand. Annon is a good fellow, as worthy of you as any man can be, and I wish you all the happiness you deserve.'

'Do you?' And her eyes searched his face keenly.

'Yes; do you doubt it?' And so well did he conceal his love, that neither face, voice, nor manner betrayed a hint of it.

Her eyes fell, a cloud passed over her clear countenance, and she withdrew her hand, as if to caress the hungry bird that gently pecked at the basket she held. As if to change the conversation, she said playfully, 'Poor Argus, you have lost your fine feathers, and so all desert you, except kind little Juno, who never forgets her friends. There, take it all, and share between you.'

Treherne smiled, and said quickly, 'I am a human Argus, and you have been a kind little Juno to me since I lost my plumes. Continue to be so, and you will find me a very faithful friend.'

'I will.' And as she answered, her old smile came back and her eyes met his again.

'Thanks! Now we shall get on happily. I don't ask or expect the old life—that is impossible. I knew that when lovers came, the friend would fall into the background; and I am content to be second, where I have so long been first. Do not think you neglect me; be happy with your lover, dear, and when you have no pleasanter amusement, come and see old Maurice.'

She turned her head away, that he might not see the angry color in her cheeks, the trouble in her eyes, and when she spoke, it was to say petulantly, 'I wish Jasper and Mamma would leave me in peace. I have lovers and want none. If Frank teases, I'll go into a convent and so be rid of him.'

Maurice laughed, and turned her face toward himself, saying, in his persuasive voice, 'Give him a trial first, to please your mother. It can do no harm and may amuse you. Frank is already lost, and, as you are heart-whole, why not see what you can do for him? I shall have a new study, then, and not miss you so much.'

'You are very kind; I'll do my best. I wish Mrs. Snowdon would come, if she is coming; I've an engagement at two, and Frank will look tragical if I'm not ready. He is teaching me billiards, and I really like the game, though I never thought I should.'

'That looks well. I hope you'll learn a double lesson, and Annon find a docile pupil in both.'

'You are very pale this morning; are you in pain, Maurice?' suddenly asked Octavia, dropping the tone of assumed ease and gaiety under which she had tried to hide her trouble.

'Yes, but it will soon pass. Mrs. Snowdon is coming, I saw her at the hall door a moment ago. I will show her the peacocks, if you want to go. She won't mind the change, I dare say, as you don't like her, and I do.'

'No, I am sure of that. It was an arrangement, perhaps? I understand. I will not play Mademoiselle De Trop.'

Sudden fire shone in the girl's eyes, sudden contempt curled her lip, and a glance full of meaning went from her cousin to the door, where Mrs. Snowdon appeared, waiting for her maid to bring her some additional wrappings.

'You allude to the note you stole. How came you to play that prank, Tavie?' asked Treherne tranquilly.

'I saw her put it under the urn. I thought it was for Jasper, and I took it,' she said boldly.

'Why for Jasper?'

'I remembered his speaking of meeting her long ago, and describing her beauty enthusiastically—and so did you.'

'You have a good memory.'

'I have for everything concerning those I love. I observed her manner of meeting my brother, his devotion to her, and, when they stood laughing together before the fire, I felt sure that she wished to charm him again.'

'Again? Then she did charm him once?' asked Treherne, anxious to know how much Jasper had told his sister.

'He always denied it, and declared that you were the favorite.'

Then why not think the note for me?' he asked.

'I do now' was the sharp answer.

'But she told you it was for the major, and sent it.'

'She deceived me; I am not surprised. I am glad Jasper is safe, and I wish you a pleasant *tête-à-tête*.'

Bowing with unwonted dignity, Octavia set down her basket and walked away in one direction as Mrs. Snowdon approached in another.

'I have done it now,' sighed Treherne, turning from the girlish figure to watch the stately creature who came sweeping toward him with noiseless grace.

Brilliancy and splendor became Mrs. Snowdon; she enjoyed luxury, and her beauty made many things becoming which in a plainer woman would have been out of taste, and absurd. She had wrapped herself in a genuine Eastern burnous of scarlet, blue, and gold; the hood drawn over her head framed her fine face in rich hues, and the great gilt tassels shone against her rippling black hair. She wore it with grace, and the barbaric splendor of the garment became her well. The fresh air touched her cheeks with a delicate color; her usually gloomy eyes were brilliant now, and the smile that parted her lips was full of happiness.

'Welcome, Cleopatra!' cried Treherne, with difficulty repressing a laugh, as the peacocks screamed and fled before the rustling amplitude of her drapery.

'I might reply by calling you Thaddeus of Warsaw, for you look very romantic and Polish with your pale, pensive face, and your splendid furs,' she answered, as she paused beside him with admiration very visibly expressed in her eyes.

Treherne disliked the look, and rather abruptly said, as he offered her the basket of bread, 'I have disposed of my cousin, and offered to do the honors of the peacocks. Here they are—will you feed them?'

'No, thank you—I care nothing for the fowls, as you know; I came to speak to you,' she said impatiently.

'I am at your service.'

'I wish to ask you a question or two—is it permitted?'

'What man ever refused Mrs. Snowdon a request?'

'Nay, no compliments; from you they are only satirical evasions. I was deceived when abroad, and rashly married that old man. Tell me truly how things stand.'

'Jasper has all. I have nothing.'

'I am glad of it.'

'Many thanks for the hearty speech. You at least speak sincerely,' he said bitterly.

'I do, Maurice—I do; let me prove it.'

Treherne's chair was close beside the balustrade. Mrs. Snowdon leaned on the carved railing, with her back to the house and her face screened by a tall urn. Looking steadily at him, she said rapidly and low, 'You thought I wavered between you and Jasper, when we parted two years ago. I did; but it was not between title and fortune that I hesitated. It was between duty and love. My father, a fond, foolish old man, had set his heart on seeing me a lady. I was his all; my beauty was his delight, and no untitled man was deemed worthy of me. I loved him tenderly. You may doubt this, knowing how selfish, reckless, and vain I am, but I have a heart, and with better training had been a better woman. No matter, it is too late now. Next my father, I loved you. Nay, hear me—I *will* clear myself in your eyes. I mean no wrong in the general. He is kind, indulgent, generous; I respect him—I am grateful, and while he lives, I shall be true to him.'

'Then be silent now. Do not recall the past, Edith; let it sleep, for both our sakes,' began Treherne; but she checked him imperiously.

'It shall, when I am done. I loved you, Maurice; for, of all the gay, idle, pleasure-seeking men I saw about me, you were the only one who seemed to have a thought beyond the folly of the hour. Under the seeming frivolity of your life lay something noble, heroic, and true. I felt that you had a purpose, that your present mood was but transitory—a young man's holiday, before the real work of his life began. This attracted, this won me; for even in the brief regard you then gave me, there was an earnestness no other man had shown. I wanted your respect; I longed to earn your love, to share your life, and prove that even in my neglected nature slept the power of cancelling a frivolous past by a noble future. Oh, Maurice, had you lingered one week more, I never should have been the miserable thing I am!'

There her voice faltered and failed, for all the bitterness of lost love, peace, and happiness sounded in the pathetic passion of that exclamation. She did not weep, for tears seldom dimmed those tragical eyes of hers; but she wrung her hands in mute despair, and looked down into the frost-blighted gardens below, as if she saw there a true symbol of her own ruined life. Treherne uttered not a word, but set his teeth with an almost fierce glance towards the distant figure of Sir Jasper, who was riding gaily away, like one unburdened by a memory or a care.

Hurriedly Mrs. Snowdon went on, 'My father begged and commanded me to choose your cousin. I could not break his heart, and asked for time, hoping to soften him. While I waited, that mysterious affair hurried you from Paris, and then came the wreck, the illness, and the rumour that old Sir Jasper had disinherited both nephews. They told me you were dying, and I became a passive instrument in my father's hands. I promised to recall and accept your cousin, but the old man died before it was done, and then I cared not what became of me.

'General Snowdon was my father's friend; he pitied me; he saw my desolate, destitute state, my despair and helplessness. He comforted, sustained, and saved me. I was grateful; and when he offered me his heart and home, I accepted them. He knew I had no love to give; but as a friend, a daughter, I would gladly serve him, and make his declining years as happy as I could. It was all over, when I heard that you were alive, afflicted, and poor. I longed to come and live for you. My new bonds became heavy fetters then, my wealth oppressed me, and I was doubly wretched—for I dared not tell my trouble, and it nearly drove me mad. I have seen you now; I know that you are happy; I read your cousin's love and see a peaceful life in store for you. This must content me, and I must learn to bear it as I can.'

She paused, breathless and pale, and walked rapidly along the terrace, as if to hide or control the agitation that possessed her.

Treherne still sat silent, bu this heart leaped with him, as he thought, 'She sees that Octavia loves me! A woman's eye is quick to detect love in another, and she asserts what I begin to hope. My cousin's manner just now, her dislike of Annon, her new shyness with me; it may be true, and if it is—Heaven help me—what am I saying! I must not hope, nor wish, nor dream; I must renounce and forget.'

He leaned his head upon his hand, and sat so till Mrs. Snowdon rejoined him, pale, but calm and self-possessed. As she drew near, she marked his attitude, the bitter sadness of his face, and hope sprang up within her. Perhaps she was mistaken; perhaps he did not love his cousin; perhaps he still remembered the past, and still regretted the loss of the heart she had just laid bare before him. Her husband was failing, and might die any day. And then, free, rich, beautiful, and young, what might she not become to Treherne, helpless, poor, and ambitious? With all her faults, she was generous, and this picture charmed her fancy, warmed her heart, and comforted her pain.

'Maurice,' she said softly, pausing again beside him, 'If I mistake you and your hopes, it is because I dare ask nothing for myself; but if ever a time shall come when I have liberty to give or help, ask of me *anything*, and it is gladly yours.'

He understood her, pitied her, and, seeing that she found consolation in a distant hope, he let her enjoy it while she might. Gravely, yet gratefully, he spoke, and pressed the hand extended to him with an impulsive gesture.

'Generous as ever, Edith, and impetuously frank. Thank you for your sincerity, your kindness, and the affection you once gave me. I say "once," for now duty, truth, and honor bar us from each other. My life must be solitary, yet I shall find work to do, and learn to be content. You owe all devotion to the good old man who loves you, and will not fail him, I am sure. Leave the future and the past, but let us make the present what it may be—a time to forgive and forget, to take heart and begin anew. Christmas is a fitting time for such resolves, and the birth of friendship such as ours may be.'

Something in his tone and manner struck her, and, eyeing him with soft wonder, she exclaimed, 'How changed you are!'

'Need you tell me that?' And he glanced at his helpless limbs with a bitter yet pathetic look of patience.

'No, no—not so! I mean in mind, not body. Once you were gay and careless, eager and fiery, like Jasper; now you are grave and quiet, or cheerful, and so very kind. Yet, in spite of illness and loss, you seem twice the man you were, and something wins respect, as well as admiration—and love.'

Her dark eyes filled as the last word left her lips, and the beauty of a touched heart shone in her face. Maurice looked up quickly, asking with sudden earnestness, 'Do you see it? Then it is true. Yes, I *am* changed, thank God! And she has done it.'

'Who?' demanded his companion jealously.

'Octavia. Unconsciously, yet surely, she has done much for me, and this year of seeming loss and misery has been the happiest, most profitable of my life. I have often heard that afflictions were the best teachers, and I believe it now.'

Mrs. Snowdon shook her head sadly.

'Not always; they are tormentors to some. But don't preach, Maurice. I am still a sinner, though you incline to sainthood, and I have one question more to ask. What was it that took you and Jasper so suddenly away from Paris?'

'That I can never tell you.'

'I shall discover it for myself, then.'

'It is impossible.'

'Nothing is impossible to a determined woman.'

'You can neither wring, surprise, nor bribe this secret from the two persons who hold it. I beg of you to let it rest,' said Treherne earnestly.

'I have a clue, and I shall follow it; for I am convinced that something is wrong, and you are—'

'Dear Mrs. Snowdon, are you so charmed with the birds that you forget your fellow-beings, or so charmed with one fellow-being that you forget the birds?'

As the sudden question startled both, Rose Talbot came along the terrace, with hands full of holly and a face full of merry mischief, adding as she vanished, 'I shall tell Tavie that feeding the peacocks is such congenial amusement for lovers, she and Mr. Annon had better try it.'

'Saucy gypsy!' muttered Treherne.

But Mrs. Snowdon said, with a smile of double meaning, 'Many a true word is spoken in jest.'

Chapter V

UNDER THE MISTLETOE

U nusually gay and charming the three young friends looked, dressed alike in fleecy white and holly wreaths in their hair, as they slowly descended the wide oaken stairway arm in arm. A footman was lighting the hall lamps, for the winter dusk gathered early, and the girls were merrily chatting about the evening's festivity when suddenly a loud, long shriek echoed through the hall. A heavy glass shade fell from the man's hand with a crash, and the young ladies clung to one another aghast, for mortal terror was in the cry, and a dead silence followed it.

'What was it, John?' demanded Octavia, very pale, but steady in a moment.

'I'll go and see, miss.' And the man hurried away.

'Where did the dreadful scream come from?' asked Rose, collecting her wits as rapidly as possible.

'Above us somewhere. Oh, let us go down among people; I am frightened to death,' whispered Blanche, trembling and faint.

Hurrying into the parlor, they found only Annon and the major, both looking startled, and both staring out of the windows.

'Did you hear it? What could it be? Don't go and leave us!' cried the girls in a breath, as they rushed in.

The gentlemen had heard, couldn't explain the cry, and were quite ready to protect the pretty creatures who clustered about them like frightened fawns. John speedily appeared, looking rather wild, and as eager to tell his tale as they to listen.

'It's Patty, one of the maids, miss, in a fit. She went up to the north gallery to see that the fires was right, for it takes a power of wood to warm the gallery even enough for dancing, as you know, miss. Well, it was dark, for the fires was low and her candle went out as she whisked open the door, being flurried, as the maids always is when they go in there. Halfway down the gallery she says she heard a rustling, and stopped. She's the pluckiest of 'em all, and she called out, "I see you!" thinking it was some of us trying to fright her. Nothing answered, and she went on a bit, when suddenly the fire flared up one flash, and there right before her was the ghost.'

'Don't be foolish, John. Tell us what it was,' said Octavia sharply, though her face whitened and her heart sank as the last word passed the man's lips.

'It was a tall, black figger, miss, with a dead-white face and a black hood. She see it plain, and turned to go away, but she hadn't gone a dozen steps when there it was again before her, the same tall, dark thing with the dead-white face looking out from the black hood. It lifted its arm as if to hold her, but she gave a spring and dreadful screech, and ran to Mrs. Benson's room, where she dropped in a fit.'

'How absurd to be frightened by the shadows of the figures in armor that stand along the gallery!' said Rose, boldly enough, though she would have declined entering the gallery without a light.

'Nay, I don't wonder, it's a ghostly place at night. How is the poor thing?' asked Blanche, still hanging on the major's arm in her best attitude.

'If Mamma knows nothing of it, tell Mrs. Benson to keep it from her, please. She is not well, and such things annoy her very much,' said Octavia, adding as the man turned away, 'Did anyone look in the gallery after Patty told her tale?'

'No, miss. I'll go and do it myself; I'm not afraid of man, ghost, or devil, saving your presence, ladies,' replied John.

'Where is Sir Jasper?' suddenly asked the major.

'Here I am. What a deuce of a noise someone has been making. It disturbed a capital dream. Why, Tavie, what is it?' And Sir Jasper came out of the library with a sleepy face and tumbled hair.

They told him the story, whereat he laughed heartily, and said the maids were a foolish set to be scared by a shadow. While he still laughed and joked, Mrs. Snowdon entered, looking alarmed, and anxious to know the cause of the confusion.

'How interesting! I never knew you kept a ghost. Tell me all about it, Sir Jasper, and soothe our nerves by satisfying our curiosity,' she said in her half-persuasive, half-commanding way, as she seated herself on Lady Treherne's sacred sofa.

'There's not much to tell, except that this place used to be an abbey, in fact as well as in name. An ancestor founded it, and for years the monks led a jolly life here, as one may see, for the cellar is twice as large as the chapel, and much better preserved. But another ancestor, a gay and gallant baron, took a fancy to the site for his castle, and, in spite of prayers, anathemas, and excommunication, he turned the poor fellows out, pulled down the abbey, and built this fine old place. Abbot Boniface, as he left his abbey, uttered a heavy curse on all who should live here, and vowed to haunt us till the last Treherne vanished from the face of the earth. With this amiable threat the old party left Baron Roland to his doom, and died as soon as he could in order to begin his cheerful mission.'

'Did he haunt the place?' asked Blanche eagerly.

'Yes, most faithfully from that time to this. Some say many of the monks still glide about the older parts of the abbey, for Roland spared the chapel and the north gallery which joined it to the modern building. Poor fellows, they are welcome, and once a year they shall have a chance to warm their ghostly selves by the great fires always kindled at Christmas in the gallery.'

'Mrs. Benson once told me that when the ghost walked, it was a sure sign of a coming death in the family. Is that true?' asked Rose, whose curiosity was excited by the expression of Octavia's face, and a certain uneasiness in Sir Jasper's manner in spite of his merry mood.

'There is a stupid superstition of that sort in the family, but no one except the servants believes it, of course. In times of illness some silly maid or croaking old woman can easily fancy they see a phantom, and, if death comes, they are sure of the ghostly warning. Benson saw it before my father died, and old Roger, the night my uncle was seized with apoplexy. Patty will never be made to believe that this warning does not forebode the death of Maurice or myself, for the gallant spirit leaves the ladies of our house to depart in peace. How does it strike you, cousin?'

Turning as he spoke, Sir Jasper glanced at Treherne, who had entered while he spoke.

'I am quite skeptical and indifferent to the whole affair, but I agree with Octavia that it is best to say nothing to my aunt if she is ignorant of the matter. Her rooms are a long way off, and perhaps she did not hear the confusion.'

'You seem to hear everything; you were not with us when I said that.' And Octavia looked up with an air of surprise.

Smiling significantly, Treherne answered, 'I hear, see, and understand many things that escape others. Jasper, allow me to advise you to smooth the hair which your sleep has disarranged. Mrs. Snowdon, permit me. This rich velvet catches the least speck.' And with his handkerchief he delicately brushed away several streaks of white dust which clung to the lady's skirt.

Sir Jasper turned hastily on his heel and went to remake his toilet; Mrs. Snowdon bit her lip, but thanked Treherne sweetly and begged him to fasten her glove. As he did so, she said softly, 'Be more careful next time. Octavia has keen eyes, and the major may prove inconvenient.'

'I have no fear that *you* will,' he whispered back, with a malicious glance.

Here the entrance of my lady put an end to the ghostly episode, for it was evident that she knew nothing of it. Octavia slipped away to question John, and learn that no sign of a phantom was to be seen. Treherne devoted himself to Mrs. Snowdon, and the major entertained my lady, while Sir Jasper and the girls chatted apart.

It was Christmas Eve, and a dance in the great gallery was the yearly festival at the abbey. All had been eager for it, but the maid's story seemed to have lessened their enthusiasm, though no one would own it. This annoyed Sir Jasper, and he exerted himself to clear the atmosphere by affecting gaiety he did not feel. The moment the gentlemen came in after dinner he whispered to his mother, who rose, asked the general for his arm, and led the way to the north gallery, whence the sound of music now proceeded. The rest followed in a merry procession, even Treherne, for two footmen carried him up the great stairway, chair and all.

Nothing could look less ghostly now than the haunted gallery. Fires roared up a wide chimney at either end, long rows of figures clad in armor stood on each side, one mailed hand grasping a lance, the other bearing a lighted candle, a device of Sir Jasper's. Narrow windows pierced in the thick walls let in gleams of wintry moonlight; ivy, holly, and evergreen glistened in the ruddy glow of mingled firelight and candle shine. From the arched stone roof hung tattered banners, and in the midst depended a great bunch of mistletoe. Red-cushioned seats stood in recessed window nooks, and from behind a high-covered screen of oak sounded the blithe air of Sir Roger de Coverley.

With the utmost gravity and stateliness my lady and the general led off the dance, for, according to the good old fashion, the men and maids in their best array joined the gentlefolk and danced with their betters in a high state of pride and bashfulness. Sir Jasper twirled the old housekeeper till her head spun around and around

and her decorous skirts rustled stormily; Mrs. Snowdon captivated the
gray-haired butler by her condescension; and John was made a proud
man by the hand of his young mistress. The major came out strong
among the pretty maids, and Rose danced the footmen out of breath
long before the music paused.

The merriment increased from that moment, and when the general
surprised my lady by gallantly saluting her as she unconsciously stood
under the mistletoe, the applause was immense. Everyone followed
the old gentleman's example as fast as opportunities occurred, and
the young ladies soon had as fine a color as the housemaids. More
dancing, games, songs, and all manner of festival devices filled the
evening, yet under cover of the gaiety more than one little scene was
enacted that night, and in an hour of seeming frivolity the current of
several lives was changed.

By a skilful manoeuvre Annon led Octavia to an isolated recess, as
if to rest after a brisk game, and, taking advantage of the auspicious
hour, pleaded his suit. She heard him patiently and, when he paused,
said slowly, yet decidedly, and with no sign of maiden hesitation,
'Thanks for the honor you do me, but I cannot accept it, for I do
not love you. I think I never can.'

'Have you tried?' he asked eagerly.

'Yes, indeed I have. I like you as a friend, but no more. I know
Mamma desires it, that Jasper hopes for it, and I try to please them,
but love will not be forced, so what can I do?' And she smiled in spite
of herself at her own blunt simplicity.

'No, but it can be cherished, strengthened, and in time won, with
patience and devotion. Let me try, Octavia; it is but fair, unless you
have already learned from another the lesson I hope to teach. Is it
so?'

'No, I think not. I do not understand myself as yet, I am so young,
and this so sudden. Give me time, Frank.'

She blushed and fluttered now, looked half angry, half beseeching,
and altogether lovely.

'How much time shall I give? It cannot take long to read a heart like
yours, dear.' And fancying her emotion a propitious omen, he assumed
the lover in good earnest.

'Give me time till the New Year. I will answer then, and, meantime,
leave me free to study both myself and you. We have known each other
long, I own, but, still, this changes everything, and makes you seem

another person. Be patient, Frank, and I will try to make my duty a pleasure.'

I will. God bless you for the kind hope, Octavia. It has been mine for years, and if I lose it, it will go hardly with me.'

Later in the evening General Snowdon stood examining the antique screen. In many places carved oak was pierced quite through, so that voices were audible from behind it. The musicians had gone down to supper, the young folk were quietly busy at the other end of the hall, and as the old gentleman admired the quaint carving, the sound of his own name caught his ear. The housekeeper and butler still remained, though the other servants had gone, and sitting cosily behind the screen chatted in low tones believing themselves secure.

'It *was* Mrs. Snowdon, Adam, as I'm a living woman, though I wouldn't say it to anyone but you. She and Sir Jasper were here wrapped in cloaks, and up to mischief, I'll be bound. She is a beauty, but I don't envy her, and there'll be trouble in the house if she stays long.'

'But how do you know, Mrs. Benson, she was here? Where's your proof, mum?' asked the pompous butler.

'Look at this, and then look at the outlandish trimming of the lady's dress. You men are so dull about such matters you'd never observe these little points. Well, I was here first after Patty, and my light shone on this jet ornament lying near where she saw the spirit. No one has any such tasty trifles but Mrs. Snowdon, and these are all over her gown. If that ain't proof, what is?'

'Well, admitting it, I then say what on earth should she and master be up here for, at such a time?' asked the slow-witted butler.

'Adam, we are old servants of the family, and to you I'll say what torture shouldn't draw from to another. Master has been wild, as you know, and it's my belief that he loved this lady abroad. There was a talk of some mystery, or misdeed, or misfortune, more than a year ago, and she was in it. I'm loath to say it, but I think Master loved her still, and she him. The general is an old man, she is but young, and so spirited and winsome she can't in reason care for him as for a fine, gallant gentleman like Sir Jasper. There's trouble brewing, Adam, mark my words. There's trouble brewing for the Trehernes.'

So low had the voices fallen that the listener could not have caught the words had not his ear been strained to the utmost. He did hear all, and his wasted face flashed with the wrath of a young man, then grew pale and stern as he turned to watch his wife. She stood apart from the others talking to Sir Jasper, who looked unusually handsome and debonair as he fanned her with a devoted air.

Perhaps it is true, thought the old man bitterly. They are well matched, were lovers once, no doubt, and long to be so again. Poor Edith, I was very blind. And with his gray head bowed upon his breast the general stole away, carrying an arrow in his brave old heart.

'Blanche, come here and rest, you will be ill tomorrow; and I promised Mamma to take care of you.' With which elder-sisterly command Rose led the girl to an immense old chair, which held them both. 'Now listen to me and follow my advice, for I am wise in my generation, though not yet gray. They are all busy, so leave them alone and let me show you what is to be done.'

Rose spoke softly, but with great resolution, and nodded her pretty head so energetically that the holly berries came rolling over her white shoulders.

'We are not as rich as we might be, and must establish ourselves as soon and as well as possible. I intend to be Lady Treherne. You can be the Honorable Mrs. Annon, if you give your mind to it.'

'My dear child, are you mad?' whispered Blanche.

'Far from it, but you will be if you waste your time on Maurice. He is poor, and a cripple, though very charming, I admit. He loves Tavie, and she will marry him, I am sure. She can't endure Frank, but tries to because my lady commands it. Nothing will come of it, so try your fascinations and comfort the poor man; sympathy now will foster love hereafter.'

'Don't talk so here, Rose, someone will hear us,' began her sister, but the other broke in briskly.

'No fear, a crowd is the best place for secrets. Now remember what I say, and make your game while the ball is rolling. Other people are careful not to put their plans into words, but I'm no hypocrite, and say plainly what I mean. Bear my sage counsel in mind and act wisely. Now come and begin.'

Treherne was sitting alone by one of the great fires, regarding the gay scene with serious air. For him there was neither dancing nor games; he could only roam about catching glimpses of forbidden pleasures, impossible delights, and youthful hopes forever lost to him. Sad but not morose was his face, and to Octavia it was a mute reproach which she could not long resist. Coming up as if to warm herself, she spoke to him in her usually frank and friendly way, and felt her heart beat fast when she saw how swift a change her cordial manner wrought in him.

'How pretty your holly is! Do you remember how we used to go and gather it for festivals like this, when we were happy children?' he asked, looking up at her with eyes full of tender admiration.

'Yes, I remember. Everyone wears it tonight as a badge, but you have none. Let me get you a bit, I like to have you one of us in all things.'

She leaned forward to break a green sprig from the branch over the chimneypiece; the strong draft drew in her fleecy skirt, and in an instant she was enveloped in flames.

'Maurice, save me, Help me!' cried a voice of fear and agony, and before anyone could reach her, before he himself knew how the deed was done, Treherne had thrown himself from his chair, wrapped the tiger skin tightly about her, and knelt there clasping her in his arms heedless of fire, pain, or the incoherent expressions of love that broke from his lips.

Chapter VI

MIRACLES

Great was the confusion and alarm which reigned for many minutes, but when the panic subsided two miracles appeared. Octavia was entirely uninjured, and Treherne was standing on his feet, a thing which for months he had not done without crutches. In the excitement of the moment, no one observed the wonder; all were crowding about the girl, who, pale and breathless but now self-possessed, was the first to exclaim, pointing to her cousin, who had drawn himself up, with the help of his chair, and leaned there smiling, with a face full of intense delight.

'Look at Maurice! Oh, Jasper, help him or he'll fall!'

Sir Jasper sprung to his side and put a strong arm about him, while a chorus of wonder, sympathy, and congratulations rose about them.

'Why, lad, what does it mean? Have you been deceiving us all this time?' cried Jasper, as Treherne leaned on him, looking exhausted but truly happy.

'It means that I am not to be crippled all my life; that they did not deceive me when they said a sudden shock might electrify me with a more potent magnetism than any they could apply. It *has*, and if I am cured I owe it all to you, Octavia.'

He stretched his hands to her with a gesture of such passionate gratitude that the girl covered her face to hide its traitorous tenderness, and my lady went to him, saying brokenly, as she embraced him with maternal warmth, 'God bless you for this act, Maurice, and reward you with a perfect cure. To you I owe the lives of both my children; how can I thank you as I ought?'

'I dare not tell you yet,' he whispered eagerly, then added, 'I am growing faint, Aunt. Get me away before I make a scene.'

This hint recalled my lady to her usual state of dignified self-possession. Bidding Jasper and the major help Treherne to his room without delay, she begged Rose to comfort her sister, who was sobbing hysterically, and as they all obeyed her, she led her daughter away to her own apartment, for the festivities of the evening were at an end.

At the same time Mrs. Snowdon and Annon bade my lady good-night, as if they also were about to retire, but as they reached the door of the gallery Mrs. Snowdon paused and beckoned Annon back. They were alone now, and, standing before the fire which had so nearly made that Christmas Eve a tragical one, she turned to him with a face full of interest and sympathy as she said, nodding toward the blackened shreds of Octavia's dress, and the scorched tiger skin which still lay at their feet, 'That was both a fortunate and an unfortunate little affair, but I fear Maurice's gain will be your loss. Pardon my frankness for Octavia's sake; she is a fine creature, and I long to see her given to one worthy of her. I am a woman to read faces quickly; I know that your suit does not prosper as you would have it, and I desire to help you. May I?'

'Indeed you may, and command any service of me in return. But to what do I owe this unexpected friendliness?' cried Annon, both grateful and surprised.

'To my regard for the young lady, my wish to save her from an unworthy man.'

'Do you mean Treherne?' asked Annon, more and more amazed.

'I do. Octavia must not marry a gambler!'

'My dear lady, you labor under some mistake; Treherne is by no means a gambler. I owe him no goodwill, but I cannot hear him slandered.'

'You are generous, but I am not mistaken. Can you, on your honor, assured me that Maurice never played?'

Mrs. Snowdon's keen eyes were on him, and he looked embarrassed for a moment, but answered with some hesitation, 'Why, no, I cannot say that, but I can assure you that he is not an habitual gambler. All young men of his rank play more or less, especially abroad. It is merely an amusement with most, and among men is not considered dishonorable or dangerous. Ladies think differently, I believe, at least in England.'

At the word 'abroad,' Mrs. Snowdon's face brightened, and she suddenly dropped her eyes, as if afraid of betraying some secret purpose.

'Indeed we do, and well we may, many of us having suffered from this pernicious habit. I have had special cause to dread and condemn it, and the fear that Octavia should in time suffer what I have suffered as a girl urges me to interfere where otherwise I should be dumb. Mr. Annon, there was a rumor that Maurice was forced to quit Paris, owing to some dishonorable practices at the gaming table. Is this true?'

'Nay, don't ask me; upon my soul I cannot tell you. I only know that something was amiss, but what I never learned. Various tales were whispered at the clubs, and Sir Jasper indignantly denied them all. The bravery with which Maurice saved his cousin, and the sad affliction which fell upon him, silenced the gossip, and it was soon forgotten.'

Mrs. Snowdon remained silent for a moment, with brows knit in deep thought, while Annon uneasily watched her. Suddenly she glanced over her shoulder, drew nearer, and whispered cautiously, 'Did the rumors of which you speak charge him with—' and the last word was breathed into Annon's ear almost inaudibly.

He started, as if some new light broke on him, and stared at the speaker with a troubled face for an instant, saying hastily, 'No, but now you remind me that when an affair of that sort was discussed the other day Treherne looked very odd, and rolled himself away, as if it didn't interest him. I can't believe it, and yet it may be something of the kind. That would account for old Sir Jasper's whim, and Treherne's steady denial of any knowledge of the cause. How in heaven's name did you learn this?'

'My woman's wit suggested it, and my woman's will shall confirm or destroy the suspicion. My lady and Octavia evidently know nothing, but they shall if there is any danger of the girl's being won by him.'

'You would not tell her!' exclaimed Annon.

'I will, unless you do it' was the firm answer.

'Never! To betray a friend, even to gain the woman I love, is a thing I cannot do; my honor forbids it.'

Mrs. Snowdon smiled scornfully.

'Men's code of honor is a strong one, and we poor women suffer from it. Leave this to me; do your best, and if all other means fail, you may be glad to try my device to prevent Maurice from marrying his cousin. Gratitude and pity are strong allies, and if he recovers, his strong will will move heaven and earth to gain her. Good night.' And leaving her last words to rankle in Annon's mind, Mrs. Snowdon departed to endure sleepless hours full of tormenting memories, newborn hopes, and alterations of determination and despair.

Treherne's prospect of recovery filled the whole house with delight, for his patient courage and unfailing cheerfulness had endeared him to all. It was no transient amendment, for day by day he steadily gained strength and power, passing rapidly from chair to crutches, from crutches to a cane and a friend's arm, which was always ready for him. Pain returned with returning vitality, but he bore it with a fortitude that touched all who witnessed it. At times motion was torture, yet motion was necessary lest the torpidity should return, and Treherne took his daily exercise with unfailing perseverance, saying with a smile, though great drops stood upon his forehead, 'I have something dearer even than health to win. Hold me up, Jasper, and let me stagger on, in spite of everything, till my twelve turns are made.'

He remembered Lady Treherne's words, 'If you were well, I'd gladly give my girl to you.' This inspired him with strength, endurance, and a happiness which could not be concealed. It overflowed in looks, words, and acts; it infected everyone, and made these holidays the blithest the old abbey had seen for many a day.

Annon devoted himself to Octavia, and in spite of her command to be left in peace till the New Year, she was very kind—so kind that hope flamed up in his heart, though he saw that something

like compassion often shone on him from her frank eyes, and her
compliance had no touch of the tender docility which lovers long
to see. She still avoided Treherne, but so skillfully that few observed
the change but Annon and himself. In public Sir Jasper appeared to
worship at the sprightly Rose's shrine, and she fancied her game was
prospering well.

But had any one peeped behind the scenes it would have been
discovered that during the half hour before dinner, when everyone
was in their dressing rooms and the general taking his nap, a pair
of ghostly black figures flitted about the haunted gallery, where
no servant ventured without orders. The major fancied himself the
only one who had made this discovery, for Mrs. Snowdon affected
Treherne's society in public, and was assiduous in serving and amusing
the 'dear convalescent,' as she called him. But the general did not
sleep; he too watched and waited, longing yet dreading to speak, and
hoping that this was but a harmless freak of Edith's, for her caprices
were many, and till now he had indulged them freely. This hesitation
disgusted the major, who, being a bachelor, knew little of women's
ways, and less of their powers of persuasion. The day before New Year
he took a sudden resolution, and demanded a private interview with
the general.

'I have come on an unpleasant errand, sir,' he abruptly began, as
the old man received him with an expression which rather daunted
the major. 'My friendship for Lady Treherne, and my guardianship of
her children, makes me jealous of the honor of the family. I fear it is
in danger, sir; pardon me for saying it, but your wife is the cause.'

'May I trouble you to explain, Major Royston', was all the general's
reply, as his old face grew stern and haughty.

'I will, sir, briefly. I happen to know from Jasper that there were
love passages between Miss Dubarry and himself a year or more go
in Paris. A whim parted them, and she married. So far no reproach
rests upon either, but since she came here it has been evident to
others as well as myself that Jasper's affection has revived, and that
Mrs. Snowdon does not reject and reprove it as she should. They
often meet, and from Jasper's manner I am convinced that mischief is
afloat. He is ardent, headstrong, and utterly regardless of the world's
opinion in some case. I have watched them, and what I tell you
is true.'

'Prove it.'

'I will. They meet in the north gallery, wrapped in dark cloaks, and play ghost if anyone comes. I concealed myself behind the screen last evening at dusk, and satisfied myself that my suspicions were correct. I heard little of their conversation, but that little was enough.'

'Repeat it, if you please.'

'Sir Jasper seemed pleading for some promise which she reluctantly gave, saying, 'While you live I will be true to my word with everyone but him. He will suspect, and it will be useless to keep it from him.'

'He will shoot me for this if he knows I am the traitor,' expostulated Jasper.

'He shall not know that; I can hoodwink him easily, and serve my purpose also.'

'You are mysterious, but I leave all to you and wait for my reward. When shall I have it, Edith?' She laughed, and answered so low I could not hear, for they left the gallery as they spoke. Forgive me, General, for the pain I inflict. You are the only person to whom I have spoken, and you are the only person who can properly and promptly prevent this affair from bringing open shame and scandal on an honorable house. To you I leave it, and will do my part with this infatuated young man if you will withdraw the temptation which will ruin him.'

'I will. Thank you, Major. Trust to me, and by tomorrow I will prove that I can act as becomes me.'

The grief and misery in the general's face touched the major; he silently wrung his hand and went away, thanking heaven more fervently than ever that no cursed coquette of a woman had it in her power to break his heart.

While this scene was going on above, another was taking place in the library. Treherne sat there alone, thinking happy thoughts evidently, for his eyes shone and his lips smiled as he mused, while watching the splendors of a winter sunset. A soft rustle and the faint scent of violets warned him of Mrs. Snowdon's approach, and a sudden foreboding told him that danger was near. The instant he saw her face his fear was confirmed, for exultation, resolve, and love met and mingled in the expression it wore. Leaning in the window recess, where the red light shone full on her lovely face and queenly figure, she said, softly yet with a ruthless accent below the softness, 'Dreaming dreams, Maurice, which will never come to pass, unless I will it. I know your secret, and I shall use it to prevent the fulfillment of the foolish hope you cherish.'

'Who told you?' he demanded, with an almost fierce flash of the eye
and an angry flush.

'I discovered it, as I warned you I should. My memory is good,
I recall the gossip of long ago, I observe the faces, words, and acts
of those whom I suspect, and unconscious hints from them give me
the truth.'

'I doubt it,' and Treherne smiled securely.

She stooped and whispered one short sentence into his ear.
Whatever it was it caused him to start up with a pale, panic-stricken
face, and eye her as if she had pronounced his doom.

'Do you doubt it now?' she asked coldly.

'He told you! Even your skill and craft could not discover it alone,'
be muttered.

'Nay, I told you nothing was impossible to a determined woman. I
needed no help, for I knew more than you think.'

He sank down again in a despairing attitude and hid his face,
saying mournfully, 'I might have known you would hunt me down
and dash my hopes when they were surest. How will you use this
unhappy secret?'

'I will tell Octavia, and make her duty less hard. It will be kind to
both of you, for even with her this memory would mar your happiness;
and it saves her from the shame and grief of discovering, when too
late, that she has given herself to a—'

'Stop!' he cried, in a tone that made her start and pale, as he rose
out of his chair white with a stern indignation which awed her for a
moment. 'You shall not utter that word—you know but half the truth,
and if you wrong me or trouble the girl I will turn traitor also, and
tell the general the game you are playing with my cousin. You feign
to love me as you feigned before, but his title is the bait now as then,
and you fancy that by threatening to mar my hopes you will secure my
silence, and gain your end.'

'Wrong, quite wrong. Jasper is nothing to me; I use *him* as a tool,
not you. If I threaten, it is to keep you from Octavia, who cannot
forgive the past and love you for yourself, as I have done all these
miserable months. You say I know but half the truth. Tell me the
whole and I will spare you.'

If ever a man was tempted to betray a trust it was Treherne then.
A word, and Octavia might be his; silence, and she might be lost; for

this woman was in earnest, and possessed the power to ruin his good name forever. The truth leaped to his lips and would have passed them, had not his eye fallen on the portrait of Jasper's father. This man had loved and sheltered the orphan all his life, had made of him a son, and, dying, urged him to guard and serve and save the rebellious youth he left, when most needing a father's care.

'I promised, and I will keep my promise at all costs,' sighed Treherne, and with a gesture full of pathetic patience he waved the fair tempter from him, saying steadily, 'I will never tell you, though you rob me of that which is dearer than my life. Go and work your will, but remember that when you might have won the deepest gratitude of the man you profess to love, you chose instead to earn his hatred and contempt.'

Waiting for no word of hers, he took refuge in his room, and Edith Snowdon sank down upon the couch, struggling with contending emotions of love and jealousy, remorse and despair. How long she sat there she could not tell; and approaching step recalled her to herself, and looking up she saw Octavia. As the girl approached down the long vista of the drawing rooms, her youth and beauty, innocence and candor touched that fairer and more gifted woman with an envy she had never known before. Something in the girl's face struck her instantly: a look of peace and purity, a sweet serenity more winning than loveliness, more impressive than dignity or grace. With a smile on her lips, yet a half-sad, half-tender light in her eyes, and a cluster of pale winter roses in her hand, she came on till she stood before her rival and, offering the flowers, said, in words as simple as sincere, 'Dear Mrs. Snowdon, I cannot let the last sun of the old year set on any misdeeds of mine for which I may atone. I have disliked, distrusted, and misjudged you, and now I come to you in all humility to say forgive me.'

With the girlish abandon of her impulsive nature Octavia knelt down before the woman who was plotting to destroy her happiness, laid the roses like a little peace offering on her lap, and with eloquently pleading eyes waited for pardon. For a moment Mrs. Snowdon watched her, fancying it a well-acted ruse to disarm a dangerous rival; but in that sweet face there was no art; one glance showed her that. The words smote her to the heart and won her in spite of pride or passion, as she suddenly took the girl into her arms, weeping repentant tears. Neither spoke, but in the silence each felt the barrier which had stood between them vanishing, and each learned to know the other better in that moment than in a year of common life. Octavia rejoiced that the instinct which has prompted her to make this appeal had not misled her, but assured her that behind the veil of coldness, pride, and levity which this woman wore there was a heart aching for sympathy and help and love. Mrs. Snowdon felt her worse self slip from her, leaving all that was true and noble to make her worthy of the test applied. Art she could meet with equal art, but nature conquered her. For spite of her misspent life and faulty character, the germ of virtue, which lives in the worst, was there, only waiting for the fostering sun and dew of love to strengthen it, even though the harvest be a late one.

'Forgive you!' she cried, brokenly. 'It is I who should ask forgiveness of you—I who should atone, confess, and repent. Pardon *me*, pity me, love me, for I am more wretched than you know.'

'Dear, I do with heart and soul. Believe it, and let me be your friend,' was the soft answer.

'God knows I need one!' sighed the poor woman, still holding fast the only creature who had wholly won her. 'Child, I am not good, but not so bad that I dare not look in your innocent face and call you friend. I never had one of my own sex. I never knew my mother; and no one ever saw in me the possibility of goodness, truth, and justice but you. Trust and love and help me, Octavia, and I will reward you with a better life, if I can do no more.'

'I will, and the new year shall be happier than the old.'

'God bless you for that prophecy; may I be worthy of it.'

Then as a bell warned them away, the rivals kissed each other tenderly, and parted friends. As Mrs. Snowdon entered her room, she saw her husband sitting with his gray head in his hands, and heard him murmur despairingly to himself, 'My life makes her miserable. But for the sin of it I'd die to free her.'

'No, live for me, and teach me to be happy in your love.' The clear voice startled him, but not so much as the beautiful changed face of the wife who laid the gray head on her bosom, saying tenderly, 'My kind and patient husband, you have been deceived. From me you shall know all the truth, and when you have forgiven my faulty past, you shall see how happy I will try to make your future.'

Chapter VII

A GHOSTLY REVEL

'Bless me, how dull we all are tonight!' exclaimed Rose, as the younger portion of the party wandered listlessly about the drawing rooms that evening, while my lady and the major played an absorbing game of piquet, and the general dozed peacefully at last.

'It is because Maurice is not here; he always keeps us going, for he is a fellow of infinite resources,' replied Sir Jasper, suppressing a yawn.

'Have him out then,' said Annon.

'He won't come. The poor lad is blue tonight, in spite of his improvement. Something is amiss, and there is no getting a word from him.'

'Sad memories afflict him, perhaps,' sighed Blanche.

'Don't be absurd, dear, sad memories are all nonsense; melancholy is always indigestion, and nothing is so sure a cure as fun,' said Rose briskly. 'I'm going to send a polite invitation begging him to come and amuse us. He'll accept, I haven't a doubt.'

The message was sent, but to Rose's chagrin a polite refusal was returned.

'He *shall* come. Sir Jasper, do you and Mr. Annon go as a deputation from us, and return without him at your peril' was her command.

They went, and while waiting their reappearance the sisters spoke of what all had observed.

'How lovely Mrs. Snowdon looks tonight. I always thought she owed half her charms to her skill in dress, but she never looked so beautiful as in that plain black silk, with those roses in her hair,' said Rose.

'What has she done to herself?' replied Blanche. 'I see a change, but can't account for it. She and Tavie have made some beautifying discovery, for both look altogether uplifted and angelic all of a sudden.'

'Here come the gentlemen, and, as I'm a Talbot, they haven't got him!' cried Rose as the deputation appeared, looking very crest-fallen. 'Don't come near me,' she added, irefully, 'you are disloyal cowards, and I doom you to exile till I want you. *I am* infinite in resources as well as this recreant man, and come he shall. Mrs. Snowdon, would you mind asking Mrs. Treherne to suggest something to wile away the rest of this evening? We are in despair, and can think of nothing, and you are all-powerful with him.'

'I must decline, since he refuses you' was the decided answer, as Mrs. Snowdon moved away.

'Tavie, dear, do go; we *must* have him; he always obeys you, and you would be such a public benefactor, you know.'

Without a word Octavia wrote a line and sent it by a servant. Several minutes passed, and the gentlemen began to lay wagers on the success of her trial. 'He will not come for me, you may be sure,' said Octavia. As the words passed her lips he appeared.

A general laugh greeted him, but, taking no notice of the jests at his expense, he turned to Octavia, saying quietly, 'What can I do for you, cousin?'

His colorless face and weary eyes reproached her for disturbing him, but it was too late for regret, and she answered hastily, 'We are in want of some new and amusing occupation to wile away the evening. Can you suggest something appropriate?'

'Why not sit round the hall fire and tell stories, while we wait to see the old year out, as we used to do long ago?' he asked, after a moment's thought.

'I told you so! There it is, just what we want.' And Sir Jasper looked triumphant.

'It's capital—let us begin at once. It is after ten now, so we shall not have long to wait,' cried Rose, and, taking Sir Jasper's arm, she led the way to the hall.

A great fire always burned there, and in wintertime thick carpets and curtains covered the stone floor and draped the tall windows. Plants blossomed in the warm atmosphere, and chairs and lounges stood about invitingly. The party was soon seated, and Treherne was desired to begin.

'We must have ghost stories, and in order to be properly thrilling and effective, the lights must be put out,' said Rose, who sat next him, and spoke first, as usual.

This was soon done, and only a ruddy circle of firelight was left to oppose the rapt gloom that filled the hall, where shadows now seemed to lurk in every corner.

'Don't be very dreadful, or I shall faint away,' pleaded Blanche, drawing nearer to Annon, for she had taken her sister's advice, and laid close siege to that gentleman's heart.

'I think your nerves will bear my little tale,' replied Treherne. 'When I was in India, four years ago, I had a very dear friend in my regiment—a Scotchman; I'm half Scotch myself, you know, and clannish, of course. Gordon was sent up the country on a scouting expedition, and never returned. His men reported that he left them one evening to take a survey, and his horse came home bloody and riderless. We searched, but could not find a trace of him, and I was desperate to discover and avenge his murder. About a month after his disappearance, as I sat in my tent one fearfully hot day, suddenly the canvas door flap was raised and there stood Gordon. I saw him as plainly as I see you, Jasper, and should have sprung to meet him, but something held me back. He was deathly pale, dripping with water, and in his bonny blue eyes was a wild, woeful look that made my blood run cold. I stared dumbly, for it was awful to see my friend so changed and so unearthly. Stretching his arm to me he took my hand, saying solemnly, "Come!" The touch was like ice; an ominous thrill ran through me; I started up to obey, and he was gone.'

'A horrid dream, of course. Is that all?' asked Rose.

'With his eyes on the fire and his left hand half extended, Treherne went on as if he had not heard her.

'I thought it was a fancy, and soon recovered myself, for no one had seen or heard anything of Gordon, and my native servant lay just outside my tent. A strange sensation remained in the hand the phantom touched. It was cold, damp, and white. I found it vain to try to forget this apparition; it took strong hold of me; I told Yermid, my man, and he bade me consider it a sign that I was to seek my friend. That night I dreamed I was riding up the country in hot haste; what led me I know not, but I pressed on and on, longing to reach the end. A half-dried river crossed my path, and, riding down the steep bank to ford it, I saw Gordon's body lying in the shallow water looking exactly as the vision looked. I woke in a strange mood, told the story to my commanding officer, and, as nothing was doing just then, easily got leave of absence for a week. Taking Yermid, I set out on my sad quest. I thought it folly, but I could not resist the impulse that drew me on. For seven days I searched, and the strangest part of the story is that all that time I went on exactly as in the dream, seeing what I saw there, and led by the touch of a cold hand on mine. On the seventh day I reached the river, and found my friend's body.'

'How horrible! Is it really true?' cried Mrs. Snowdon.

'As true as I am a living man. Nor is that all: this left hand of mine never has been warm since that time. See and feel for yourselves.'

He opened both hands, and all satisfied themselves that the left was smaller, paler, and colder than the right.

'Pray someone tell another story to put this out of my mind; it makes me nervous,' said Blanche.

'I'll tell one, and you may laugh to quiet your nerves. I want to have mine done with, so that I can enjoy the rest with a free mind.' With these words Rose began her tale in the good old fashion.

'Once upon a time, when we were paying a visit to my blessed grandmamma, I saw a ghost in this wise: The dear old lady was ill with a cold and kept her room, leaving us to mope, for it was very dull in the great lonely house. Blanche and I were both homesick, but didn't like to leave till she was better, so we ransacked the library and solaced ourselves with all manner of queer books. One day I found Grandmamma very low and nervous, and evidently with something on her mind. She would say nothing, but the next day was worse, and I insisted on knowing the cause, for the trouble was evidently mental. Charging me to keep it from Blanche, who was, and is, a sad coward, she told me that a spirit had appeared to her two successive nights. "If it comes a third time, I shall prepare to die," said the foolish old lady.

' "No, you won't for I'll come and stay with you and lay your ghost," I said. With some difficulty I made her yield, and after Blanche was asleep I slipped away to Grandmamma, with a book and candle for a long watch, as the spirit didn't appear till after midnight. She usually slept with her door unlocked, in case of fire or fright, and her maid was close by. That night I locked the door, telling her that spirits could come through the oak if they chose, and I preferred to have a fair trial. Well, I read and chatted and dozed till dawn and nothing appeared, so I laughed at the whole affair, and the old lady pretended to be convinced that it was all a fancy.

'Next night I slept in my own room, and in the morning was told that not only Grandmamma but Janet had seen the spirit. All in white, with streaming hair, a pale face, and a red streak at the throat. It came and parted the bed-curtains, looking in a moment, and then vanished. Janet had slept with Grandmamma and kept a lamp burning on the chimney, so both saw it.

'I was puzzled, but not frightened; I never am, and I insisted on trying again. The door was left unlocked, as on the previous night, and I lay with Grandmamma, a light burning as before. About two she clutched me as I was dropping off. I looked, and there, peeping in between the dark curtains, was a pale face with long hair all about it, and a red streak at the throat. It was very dim, the light being low, but I saw it, and after one breathless minute sprang up, caught my foot, fell down with a crash, and by the time I was around the bed, not a vestige of the thing appeared. I was angry, and vowed I'd succeed at all hazards, though I'll confess I was just a bit daunted.

'Next time Janet and I sat up in easy chairs, with bright lights burning, and both wide awake with the strongest coffee we could make. As the hour drew near we got nervous, and when the white shape came gliding in Janet hid her face. I didn't, and after one look was on the point of laughing, for the spirit was Blanche walking in her sleep. She wore a coral necklace in those days, and never took it off, and her long hair half hid her face, which had the unnatural, uncanny look somnambulists always wear. I had the sense to keep still and tell Janet what to do, so the poor child went back unwaked, and Grandmamma's spirit never walked again for I took care of that.'

'Why did you haunt the old lady?' asked Annon, as the laughter ceased.

'I don't know, unless it was that I wanted to ask leave to go home, and was afraid to do it awake, so tried when asleep. I shall not tell any story, as I was the heroine of this, but will give my turn to you, Mr. Annon,' said Blanche, with a soft glance, which was quite thrown away, for the gentleman's eyes were fixed on Octavia, who sat on a low ottoman at Mrs. Snowdon's feet in the full glow of the firelight.

'I've had very small experience in ghosts, and can only recall a little fright I once had when a boy at college. I'd been out to a party, got home tired, couldn't find my matches, and retired in the dark. Toward morning I woke, and glancing up to see if the dim light was dawn or moonshine I was horrified to see a coffin standing at the bed's foot. I rubbed my eyes to be sure I was awake, and looked with all my might. There it was, a long black coffin, and I saw the white plate in the dusk, for the moon was setting and my curtain was not drawn. "It's some trick of the fellows," I thought; "I'll not betray myself, but keep cool." Easy to say but hard to do, for it suddenly flashed into my mind that I might be in the wrong room. I glanced about, but there were the familiar objects as usual, as far as the indistinct light allowed me to see, and I made sure by feeling on the wall at the bed's head for my watchcase. It was there, and mine beyond a doubt, being peculiar in shape and fabric. Had I been to a college wine party I could have accounted for a vision, but a quiet evening in a grave professor's well-conducted family could produce no ill effects. "It's an optical illusion, or a prank of my mates. I'll sleep and forget it," I said, and for a time endeavored to do so, but curiosity overcame my resolve, and soon I peeped again. Judge of my horror when I saw the sharp white outline of a dead face, which seemed to be peeping up from the coffin. It gave me a terrible shock for I was but a lad and had been ill. I hid my face and quaked like a nervous girl, still thinking it some joke and too proud to betray fear lest I should be laughed at. How long I lay there I don't know, but when I looked again the face was farther out and the whole figure seemed rising slowly. The moon was nearly down, I had no lamp, and to be left in the dark with that awesome thing was more than I could bear. Joke or earnest, I must end the panic, and bolting out of my room I roused my neighbor. He told me I was mad or drunk, but lit a lamp and returned with me, to find my horror only a heap of clothes thrown on the table in such a way that, as the moon's pale light shot it, it struck upon my black student's gown, with a white card lying on it, and produced the effect of a coffin and plate. The face was a crumpled handkerchief, and what seemed hair a brown muffler. As the moon sank, these outlines changed and, incredible as it may seem, grew like a face. My friend not having had the fright enjoyed the joke, and "Coffins" was my sobriquet for a long while.'

'You get worse and worse. Sir Jasper, do vary the horrors by a touch of fun, or I shall run away,' said Blanche, glancing over her shoulder nervously.

'I'll do my best, and tell a story my uncle used to relate of his young days. I forget the name of the place, but it was some little country town famous among anglers. My uncle often went to fish, and always regretted that a deserted house near the trout stream was not occupied, for the inn was inconveniently distant. Speaking of this one evening as he lounged in the landlady's parlor, he asked why no one took it and let the rooms to strangers in the fishing season. "For fear of the ghostisses, your honor," replied the woman, and proceeded to tell him that three distinct spirits haunted the house. In the garret was heard the hum of a wheel and the tap of high-heeled shoes, as the ghostly spinner went to and fro. In a chamber sounded the sharpening of a knife, followed by groans and the drip of blood. The cellar was made awful by a skeleton sitting on a half-buried box and chuckling fiendishly. It seems a miser lived there once, and was believed to have starved his daughter in the garret, keeping her at work till she died. The second spirit was that of the girl's rejected lover, who cut his throat in the chamber, and the third of the miser who was found dead on the money chest he was too feeble to conceal. My uncle laughed at all this, and offered to lay the ghosts if anyone would take the house.

'This offer got abroad, and a crusty old fellow accepted it, hoping to turn a penny. He had a pretty girl, whose love had been thwarted by the old man, and whose lover was going to sea in despair. My uncle knew this and pitied the young people. He had made acquaintance with a wandering artist, and the two agreed to conquer the prejudices against the house by taking rooms there. They did so, and after satisfying themselves regarding the noises, consulted a wise old woman as to the best means of laying the ghosts. She told them if any young girl would pass a night in each haunted room, praying piously the while, that all would be well. Peggy was asked if she would do it, and being a stouthearted lass she consented, for a round sum, to try it. The first night was in the garret, and Peggy, in spite of the prophecies of the village gossips, came out alive, though listeners at the door heard the weird humming and tapping all night long. The next night all went well, and from that time no more sharpening, groaning, or dripping was heard. The third time she bade her friends good-bye and, wrapped in her red cloak, with a lamp and prayer book, went down into the cellar. Alas for pretty Peggy! When day came she was gone, and with her the miser's empty box, though his bones remained to prove how well she had done her work.

'The town was in an uproar, and the old man furious. Some said the devil had flown away with her, others that the bones were hers, and all agreed that henceforth another ghost would haunt the house. My uncle and the artist did their best to comfort the father, who sorely reproached himself for thwarting the girl's love, and declared that if Jack would find her he should have her. But Jack had sailed, and the old man "was left lamenting." The house was freed from its unearthly visitors, however, for no ghost appeared; and when my uncle left, old Martin found money and letter informing him that Peggy had spent her first two nights preparing for flight, and on the third had gone away to marry and sail with Jack. The noises had been produced by the artist, who was a ventriloquist, the skeleton had been smuggled from the surgeons, and the whole thing was a conspiracy to help Peggy and accommodate the fishermen.'

'It is evident that roguery is hereditary,' laughed Rose as the narrator paused.

'I strongly suspect that Sir Jasper the second was the true hero of that story,' added Mrs. Snowdon.

'Think what you like. I've done my part, and leave the stage for you, madam.'

'I will come last. It is your turn, dear.'

As Mrs. Snowdon softly uttered the last word, and Octavia leaned upon her knee with an affectionate glance, Treherne leaned forward to catch a glimpse of the two changed faces, and looked as if bewildered when both smiled at him, as they sat hand in hand while the girl told her story.

'Long ago a famous actress suddenly dropped dead at the close of a splendidly played tragedy. She was carried home, and preparations were made to bury her. The play had been gotten up with great care and expense, and a fine actor was the hero. The public demanded a repetition, and an inferior person was engaged to take the dead lady's part. A day's delay had been necessary, but when the night came the house was crowded. They waited both before and behind the curtain for the debut of the new actress, with much curiosity. She stood waiting for her cue, but as it was given, to the amazement of all, the great tragedienne glided upon the stage. Pale as marble, and with a strange fire in her eyes, strange pathos in her voice, strange power in her acting, she went through her part, and at the close vanished as mysteriously as she came. Great was the excitement that night, and intense the astonishment and horror next day when it was whispered abroad that the dead woman never had revived, but had lain in her coffin before the eyes of watchers all the evening, when hundreds fancied they were applauding her at the theater. The mystery never was cleared up, and Paris was divided by two opinions; one that some person marvellously like Madame Z. had personated her for the sake of a sensation; the other that the ghost of the dead actress, unable to free itself from the old duties so full of fascination to an ambitious and successful woman, had played for the last time the part which had made her famous.'

'Where did you find that, Tavie? It's very French, and not bad if you invented it,' said Sir Jasper.

'I read it in an old book, where it was much better told. Now, Edith, there is just time for your tale.'

As the word 'Edith' passed her lips, again Treherne started and eyed them both, and again they smiled, as Mrs. Snowdon caressed the smooth cheek leaning on her knee, and looking full at him began the last recital.

'You have been recounting the pranks of imaginary ghosts; let me show you the workings of some real spirits, evil and good, that haunt every heart and home, making its misery or joy. At Christmastime, in a country house, a party of friends met to keep the holidays, and very happily they might have done so had not one person marred the peace of several. Love, jealousy, deceit, and nobleness were the spirits that played their freaks with these people. The person of whom I speak was more haunted than the rest, and much tormented, being willful, proud, and jealous. Heaven help her, she had had no one to exorcise these ghosts for her, and they goaded her to do much harm. Among these friends there were more than one pair of lovers, and much tangling of plots and plans, for hearts are wayward and mysterious things, and cannot love as duty bids or prudence counsels. This woman held the key to all the secrets of the house, and, having a purpose to gain, she used her power selfishly, for a time. To satisfy a doubt, she feigned a fancy for a gentleman who once did her the honor of admiring her, and, to the great scandal of certain sage persons, permitted him to show his regard for her, knowing that it was but a transient amusement on his part as well as upon hers. In the hands of this woman lay a secret which could make or mar the happiness of the best and dearest of the party. The evil spirits which haunted her urged her to mar their peace and gratify a sinful hope. On the other side, honor, justice, and generosity prompted her to make them happy, and while she wavered there came to her a sweet enchantress who, with a word, banished the tormenting ghosts forever, and gave the haunted woman a talisman to keep her free henceforth.'

There the earnest voice faltered, and with a sudden impulse Mrs. Snowdon bent her head and kissed the fair forehead which had bent lower and lower as she went on. Each listener understood the truth, lightly veiled in that hasty fable, and each found in it a different meaning. Sir Jasper frowned and bit his lips, Annon glanced anxiously from face to face, Octavia hid hers, and Treherne's flashed with sudden intelligence, while Rose laughed low to herself, enjoying the scene. Blanche, who was getting sleepy, said, with a stifled gape, 'That is a very nice, moral little story, but I wish there had been some real ghosts in it.'

'There was. Will you come and see them?'

As she put the question, Mrs. Snowdon rose abruptly, wishing to end the séance, and beckoning them to follow glided up the great stairway. All obeyed, wondering what whim possessed her, and quite ready for any jest in store for them.

Chapter VIII

JASPER

She led them to the north gallery and, pausing at the door, said merrily, 'The ghost—or ghosts rather, for there were two—which frightened Patty were Sir Jasper and myself, meeting to discuss certain important matters which concerned Mr. Treherne. If you want to see spirits we will play phantom for you, and convince you of our power.'

'Good, let us go and have a ghostly dance, as a proper finale of our revel,' answered Rose as they flocked into the long hall.

At that moment the great clock struck twelve, and all paused to bid the old year adieu. Sir Jasper was the first to speak, for, angry with Mrs. Snowdon, yet thankful to her for making a jest to others of what had been earnest to him, he desired to hide his chagrin under a gay manner; and taking Rose around the waist was about to waltz away as she proposed, saying cheerily, 'Come one and all, and dance the new year in,' when a cry from Octavia arrested him, and turning he saw her stand, pale and trembling, pointing to the far end of the hall.

Eight narrow Gothic windows pierced either wall of the north gallery. A full moon sent her silvery light strongly in upon the eastern side, making broad bars of brightness across the floor. No fires burned there now, and wherever the moonlight did not fall deep shadows lay. As Octavia cried out, all looked, and all distinctly saw a tall, dark figure moving noiselessly across the second bar of light far down the hall.

'Is it some jest of yours?' asked Sir Jasper of Mrs. Snowdon, as the form vanished in the shadow.

'No, upon my honor, I know nothing of it! I only meant to relieve Octavia's superstitious fears by showing her our pranks', was the whispered reply as Mrs. Snowdon's cheek paled, and she drew nearer to Jasper.

'Who is there?' called Treherne in a commanding tone.

No answer, but a faint, cold breath of air seemed to sigh along the arched roof and die away as the dark figure crossed the third streak of moonlight. A strange awe fell upon them all, and no one spoke, but stood watching for the appearance of the shape. Nearer and nearer it came, and soundless steps, and as it reached the sixth window its outlines were distinctly visible. A tall, wasted figure, all in black, with a rosary hanging from the girdle, and a dark beard half concealing the face.

'The Abbot's ghost, and very well got up,' said Annon, trying to laugh but failing decidedly, for again the cold breath swept over them, causing a general shudder.

'Hush!' whispered Treherne, drawing Octavia to his side with a protecting gesture.

Once more the phantom appeared and disappeared, and as they waited for it to cross the last bar of light that lay between it and them, Mrs. Snowdon stepped forward to the edge of the shadow in which they stood, as if to confront the apparition alone. Out of the darkness it came, and in the full radiance of the light it paused. Mrs. Snowdon, being nearest, saw the face first, and uttering a faint cry dropped down upon the stone floor, covering up her eyes. Nothing human ever wore a look like that of the ghastly, hollow-eyed, pale-lipped countenance below the hood. All saw it and held their breath as it slowly raised a shadowy arm and pointed a shriveled finger at Sir Jasper.

'Speak, whatever you are, or I'll quickly prove whether you are man or spirit!' cried Jasper fiercely, stepping forward as if to grasp the extended arm that seemed to menace him alone.

An icy gust swept through the hall, and the phantom slowly receded into the shadow. Jasper sprang after it, but nothing crossed the second stream of light, and nothing remained in the shade. Like one possessed by a sudden fancy he rushed down the gallery to find all fast and empty, and to return looking very strangely. Blanche had fainted away and Annon was bearing her out of the hall. Rose was clinging to Mrs. Snowdon, and Octavia leaned against her cousin, saying in a fervent whisper, 'Thank God it did not point at you!'

'Am I then dearer than your brother?' he whispered back.

There was no audible reply, but one little hand involuntarily pressed his, though the other was outstretched toward Jasper, who came up white and startled but firm and quiet. Affecting to make light of it, he said, forcing a smile as he raised Mrs. Snowdon, 'It is some stupid joke of the servants. Let us think no more of it. Come, Edith, this is not like your usual self.'

'It was nothing human, Jasper; you know it as well as I. Oh, why did I bring you here to meet the warning phantom that haunts your house!'

'Nay, if my time is near the spirit would have found me out wherever I might be. I have no faith in that absurd superstition—I laugh at and defy it. Come down and drink my health in wine from the Abbot's own cellar.'

But no one had heart for further gaiety, and finding Lady Treherne already alarmed by Annon, they were forced to tell her all, and find their own bewilderment deepened by her unalterable belief in the evil omen.

At her command the house was searched, the servants cross-questioned, and every effort made to discover the identity of the apparition. All in vain; the house was as usual, and not a man or maid but turned pale at the idea of entering the gallery at midnight. At my lady's request, all promised to say no more upon the mystery, and separated at last to such sleep as they could enjoy.

Very grave were the faces gathered about the breakfast table next morning, and very anxious the glances cast on Sir Jasper as he came in, late as usual, looking uncommonly blithe and well. Nothing serious ever made a deep impression on his mercurial nature. Treherne had more the air of a doomed man, being very pale and worn, in spite of an occasional gleam of happiness as he looked at Octavia. He haunted Jasper like a shadow all the morning, much to that young gentleman's annoyance, for both his mother and sister hung about him with faces of ill-dissembled anxiety. By afternoon his patience gave out, and he openly rebelled against the tender guard kept over him. Ringing for his horse he said decidedly, 'I'm bored to death with the solemnity which pervades the house today, so I'm off for a brisk gallop, before I lose my temper and spirits altogether.'

'Come with me in the pony carriage, Jasper. I've not had a drive with you for a long while, and should enjoy it so much,' said my lady, detaining him.

'Mrs. Snowdon looks as if she needed air to revive her roses, and the pony carriage is just the thing for her, so I will cheerfully resign my seat to her,' he answered laughing, as he forced himself from his mother's hand.

'Take the girls in the clarence. We all want a breath of air, and you are the best whip we know. Be gallant and say yes, dear.'

'No, thank you, Tavie, that won't do. Rose and Blanche are both asleep, and you are dying to go and do likewise, after your vigils last night. As a man and a brother I beg you'll do so, and let me ride as I like.'

'Suppose you ask Annon to join you—' began Treherne with well-assumed indifference; but Sir Jasper frowned and turned sharply on him, saying, half-petulantly, half-jocosely:

'Upon my life I should think I was a boy or a baby, by the manner in which you mount guard over me today. If you think I'm going to live in daily fear of some mishap, you are all much mistaken. Ghost or no ghost, I shall make merry while I can; a short life and a jolly one has always been my motto, you know, so fare you well till dinner-time.'

They watched him gallop down the avenue, and then went their different ways, still burdened with a nameless foreboding. Octavia strolled into the conservatory, thinking to refresh herself with the balmy silence which pervaded the place, but Annon soon joined her, full of a lover's hopes and fears.

'Miss Treherne, I have ventured to come for my answer. Is my New Year to be a blissful or a sad one?' he asked eagerly.

'Forgive me if I give you an unwelcome reply, but I must be true, and so regretfully refuse the honor you do me,' she said sorrowfully.

'May I ask why?'

'Because I do not love you.'

'And you do love your cousin,' he cried angrily, pausing to watch her half-averted face.

She turned it fully toward him and answered, with her native sincerity, 'Yes I do, with all my heart, and now my mother will not thwart me, for Maurice has saved my life, and I am free to devote it all to him.'

'Happy man, I wish I had been a cripple!' sighed Annon. Then with a manful effort to be just and generous, he added heartily, 'Say no more, he deserves you; I want no sacrifice to duty; I yield, and go away, praying heaven to bless you now and always.'

He kissed her hand and left her to seek my lady and make his adieus, for no persuasion could keep him. Leaving a note for Sir Jasper, he hurried away, to the great relief of Treherne and the deep regret of Blanche, who, however, lived in hopes of another trial later in the season.

'Here comes Jasper, Mamma, safe and well,' cried Octavia an hour or two later, as she joined her mother on the terrace, where my lady had been pacing restlessly to and fro nearly ever since her son rode away.

With a smile of intense relief she waved her handkerchief as he came clattering up the drive, and seeing her he answered with hat and hand. He usually dismounted at the great hall door, but a sudden whim made him ride along the wall that lay below the terrace, for he was a fine horseman, and Mrs. Snowdon was looking from her window. As he approached, the peacocks fled screaming, and one flew up just before the horse's eyes as his master was in the act of dismounting. The spirited creature was startled, sprang partway up the low, broad steps of the terrace, and, being sharply checked, slipped, fell, and man and horse rolled down together.

Never did those who heard it forget the cry that left Lady Treherne's lips as she saw the fall. It brought out both guests and servants, to find Octavia recklessly struggling with the frightened horse, and my lady down upon the stones with her son's bleeding head in her arms.

They bore in the senseless, shattered body, and for hours tried everything that skill and science could devise to save the young man's life. But every effort was in vain, and as the sun set Sir Jasper lay dying. Conscious at last, and able to speak, he looked about him with a troubled glance, and seemed struggling with some desire that over-mastered pain and held death at bay.

'I want Maurice,' he feebly said, at length.

'Dear lad, I'm here,' answered his cousin's voice from a seat in the shadow of the half-drawn curtains.

'Always near when I need you. Many a scrape have you helped me out of, but this is beyond your power,' and a faint smile passed over Jasper's lips as the past flitted before his mind. But the smile died, and a groan of pain escaped him as he cried suddenly, 'Quick! Let me tell it before it is too late! Maurice never will, but bear the shame all his life that my dead name may be untarnished. Bring Edith; she must hear the truth.'

She was soon there, and, lying in his mother's arms, one hand in his cousin's, and one on his sister's bent head, Jasper rapidly told the secret which had burdened him for a year.

'I did it; I forged my uncle's name when I had lost so heavily at play that I dared not tell my mother, or squander more of my own fortune. I deceived Maurice, and let him think the check a genuine one; I made him present it and get the money, and when all went well I fancied I was safe. But my uncle discovered it secretly, said nothing, and, believing Maurice the forger, disinherited him. I never knew this till the old man died, and then it was too late. I confessed to Maurice, and he forgave me. He said, "I am helpless now, shut out from the world, with nothing to lose or gain, and soon to be forgotten by those who once knew me, so let the suspicion of shame, if any such there be, still cling to me, and do you go your way, rich, happy, honorable, and untouched by any shadow on your fame." Mother, I let him do it, unconscious as he was that many knew the secret sin and fancied him the doer of it.'

'Hush, Jasper, let it pass. I can bear it; I promised your dear father to be your staunch friend through life, and I have only kept my word.'

'God knows you have, but now my life ends, and I cannot die till you are cleared. Edith, I told you half the truth, and you would have used it against him had not some angel sent this girl to touch your heart. You have done your part to atone for the past, now let me do mine. Mother, Tavie loves him, he has risked life and honor for me. Repay him generously and give him this.'

With feeble touch Sir Jasper tried to lay his sister's hand in Treherne's as he spoke; Mrs. Snowdon helped him, and as my lady bowed her head in silent acquiescence, a joyful smile shone on the dying man's face.

'One more confession, and then I am ready,' he said, looking up into the face of the woman whom he had loved with all the power of a shallow nature. 'It was a jest to you, Edith, but it was bitter earnest to me, for I loved you, sinful as it was. Ask your husband to forgive me, and tell him it was better I should die than live to mar a good man's peace. Kiss me once, and make him happy for my sake.'

She touched his cold lips with remorseful tenderness, and in the same breath registered a vow to obey that dying prayer.

'Tavie dear, Maurice, my brother, God bless you both. Good-bye, Mother. He will be a better son than I have been to you.' Then, the reckless spirit of the man surviving to the last, Sir Jasper laughed faintly, as he seemed to beckon some invisible shape, and died saying gaily, 'Now, Father Abbot, lead on, I'll follow you.'

A year later three weddings were celebrated on the same day and in the same church, Maurice Treherne, a well man, led up his cousin. Frank Annon rewarded Blanche's patient siege by an unconditional surrender, and, to the infinite amusement of Mrs. Grundy, Major Royston publicly confessed himself outgeneraled by merry Rose. The triple wedding feast was celebrated at Treherne Abbey, and no uncanny visitor marred its festivities, for never again was the north gallery haunted by the ghostly Abbot.

1869

Kentucky's Ghost

ELIZABETH STUART PHELPS

True? Every syllable.

That was a very fair yarn of yours, Tom Brown, very fair for a landsman, but I'll bet you a doughnut I can beat it; and all on the square, too, as I say,—which is more, if I don't mistake, than you could take oath to. Not to say that I never stretched my yarn a little on the fo'castle in my younger days, like the rest of 'em; but what with living under roofs so long past, and a call from the parson regular in strawberry time, and having to do the flogging consequent on the inakkeracies of statement follering on the growing up of six boys, a man learns to trim his words a little, Tom, and no mistake. It's very much as it is with the talk of the sea growing strange to you from hearing nothing but lubbers who don't know a mizzen-mast from a church-steeple.

It was somewhere about twenty years ago last October, if I recollect fair, that we were laying in for that particular trip to Madagascar. I've done that little voyage to Madagascar when the sea was like so much burning oil, and the sky like so much burning brass, and the fo'castle as nigh as hell as every fo'castle was in a calm; I've done it when we came sneaking into port with nigh about every spar gone and pumps going night and day; and I've done it with a drunken captain on starvation rations,—duff that a dog on land wouldn't have touched and two teaspoonfuls of water to the day,—but someways or other, of all the times we headed for the East Shore I don't seem to remember any quite as distinct as this.

We cleared from Long Wharf in the ship Madonna,—which they tell me means, My Lady, and a pretty name it was; it was apt to give me that gentle kind of feeling when I spoke it, which is surprising when you consider what a dull old hull she was, never logging over ten knots, and uncertain at that. It may have been because of Moll's coming down once in a while in a days that we lay at dock, bringing the boy with her, and sitting up on deck in a little white apron, knitting. She was a very good-looking woman, was my wife, in those days, and I felt proud of her,—natural, with the lads looking on.

'Molly,' I used to say, sometimes,—'Molly Madonna!'

'Nonsense!' says she, giving a clack to her needles,—pleased enough though, I warrant you, and turning a very pretty pink about the cheeks for a four-years' wife. Seeing as how she was always a lady to me, and a true one, and a gentle, though she wasn't much at manners or book-learning, and though I never gave her a silk gown in her life, she was quite content, you see, and so was I.

I used to speak my thought about the name sometimes, when the lads weren't particularly noisy, but they laughed at me mostly. I was rough enough and bad enough in those days; as rough as the rest, and as bad as the rest, I suppose, but yet I seemed to have my notions a little different from the others. 'Jake's poetry,' they called 'em.

We were loading for the East Short trade, as I said, didn't I? There isn't much of the genuine, old-fashioned trade left in these days, except the whiskey branch, which will be brisk, I take it, till the Malagasy carry the prohibitory law by a large majority in both houses. We had a little whiskey in the hold, I remember, that trip, with a good stock of knives, red flannel, handsaws, nails and cotton. We were hoping to be at home again within the year. We were well provisioned, and Dodd,—he was the cook,—Dodd made about as fair coffee as you're likely to find in the galley of a trader. As for our officers, when I say the less said of them the better, it ain't so much that I mean to be disrespectful as that I mean to put it tenderly. Officers in the merchant service, especially if it happens to be the African service, are brutal men quite as often as they ain't (at least, that's my experience; and when some of your great ship-owners argue the case with me,—as I'm free to say they have done before now,—I say, 'That's my experience, sir,' which is all I've got to say);—brutal men, and about as fit for their positions as if they'd been imported for the purpose a little indirect from Davy Jones's Locker. Though they do say that the flogging is pretty much done away with in these days, which makes a difference.

Sometimes on a sunshiny afternoon, when the muddy water showed a little muddier than usual, on account of the clouds being the color of silver, and all the air the color of gold, when the oily barrels were knocking about on the wharves, and the smells were strong from the fish-houses, and the men shouted and the mates swore, and our baby ran about deck a-play with everybody (he was a cunning little chap with red stockings and bare knees, and the lads took quite a shine to him), 'Jake,' his mother would say, with a little sigh,—low, so that the captain never heard,—'think if it was *him* gone away for a year in company the like of that!'

Then she would drop her shining needles, and call the little fellow back sharp, and catch him up into her arms.

Go into the keeping-room there, Tom, and ask her all about it. Bless you! she remembers those days at dock better than I do. She could tell you to this hour the color of my shirt, and how long my hair was, and what I ate, and how I looked, and what I said. I didn't generally swear so thick when she was about.

Well; we weighed, along the last of the month, in pretty good spirits. The Madonna was as staunch and seaworthy as any eight-hundred-tonner in the harbor, if she was clumsy; we turned in, some sixteen of us or thereabouts, into the fo'castle,—a jolly set, mostly old messmates, and well content with one another; and the breeze was stiff from the west, with a fair sky.

The night before we were off, Molly and I took a walk upon the wharves after supper. I carried the baby. A boy, sitting on some boxes, pulled my sleeve as we went by, and asked me, pointing to the Madonna, if I would tell him the name of the ship.

'Find out for yourself,' said I, not over-pleased to be interrupted.

'Don't be cross to him,' says Molly. The baby threw a kiss at the boy, and Molly smiled at him through the dark. I don't suppose I should ever have remembered the lubber from that day to this, except that I liked the looks of Molly smiling at him through the dark.

My wife and I said good-bye the next morning in a little sheltered place among the lumber on the wharf; she was one of your women who never liked to do their crying before folks.

She climbed on the pile of lumber and sat down, a little flushed and quivery, to watch us off. I remember seeing her there with the baby till we were well down the channel. I remember noticing the bay as it grew cleaner, and thinking that I would break off swearing; and I remember cursing Bob Smart like a pirate within an hour.

The breeze held steadier than we'd looked for, and we'd made a good offing and discharged the pilot by nightfall. Mr. Whitmarsh—he was the mate—was aft with the captain. The boys were singing a little; the smell of the coffee was coming up, hot and homelike, from the galley. I was up in the maintop, I forget what for, when all at once there came a cry and a shout; and, when I touched deck, I saw a crowd around the fore-hatch.

'What's all this noise for?' says Mr. Whitmarsh, coming up and scowling.

'A stow-away, sir! A boy stowed away!' said Bob, catching the officer's tone quick enough. Bob always tested the wind well, when a storm was brewing. He jerked the poor fellow out of the hold, and pushed him along to the mate's feet.

I say 'poor fellow,' and you'd never wonder why if you'd seen as much of stowing away as I have.

I'd as lief see a son of mine in a Carolina slavegang as to see him lead the life of a stow-away. What with the officers from feeling that they've been taken in, and the men, who catch their cue from their superiors, and the spite of the lawful boy who hired in the proper way, he don't have what you call a tender time.

This chap was a little fellow, slight for his years, which might have been fifteen, I take it. He was palish, with a jerk of thin hair on his forehead. He was hungry, and homesick, and frightened. He looked about on all our faces, and then he cowered a little, and lay still just as Bob had thrown him.

'We—ell,' says Whitmarsh, very slow, 'if you don't repent your bargain before you go ashore, my fine fellow,—me, if I'm mate of the Madonna! and take that for your pains!'

Upon that he kicks the poor little lubber from quarter-deck to bowsprit, or nearly, and goes down to his supper. The men laugh a little, then they whistle a little, then they finish their song quite gay and well acquainted, with the coffee steaming away in the galley. Nobody has a word for the boy,—bless you, no!

I'll venture he wouldn't have had a mouthful that night if it had not been for me; and I can't say as I should have bothered myself about him, if it had not come across me sudden, while he sat there rubbing his eyes quite violent, with his face to the west'ard (the sun was setting reddish), that I had seen the lad before; then I remembered walking on the wharves, and him on the box, and Molly saying softly that I was cross to him.

Seeing that my wife had smiled at him, and my baby thrown a kiss at him, it went against me, you see, not to look after the little rascal a bit that night.

'But you've got no business here, you know,' said I 'Nobody wants you.'

'I wish I was ashore!' said he,—'I wish I was ashore!'

With that he begins to rub his eyes so very violent that I stopped. There was good stuff in him too; for he choked and winked at me, and did it all up, about the sun on the water and a cold in the head, and well as I could myself just about.

I don't know whether it was on account of being taken a little notice of that night, but the lad always kind of hung about me afterwards; chased me round with his eyes in a way he had, and did odd jobs for me without the asking.

One night before the first week was out, he hauled alongside of me on the windlass. I was trying a new pipe (and a very good one, too), so I didn't give him much notice for a while.

'You did this job up shrewd, Kent,' said I, by and by; 'how did you steer in?'—for it did not often happen that the Madonna got fairly out of port with a boy unbeknown in her hold.

'Watch was drunk; I crawled down ahind the whiskey. It was hot, you bet, and dark, I lay and thought how hungry I was,' says he.

'Friends at home?' says I.

Upon that he gives me a nod, very short, and gets up and walks off whistling.

The first Sunday out that chap didn't know any more what to do with himself than a lobster just put on to boil. Sunday's cleaning day at sea, you know. The lads washed up, and sat round, little knots of them, mending their trousers. Bob got out his cards. Me and a few mates took it comfortable under the to'gallant fo'castle (I being on watch below), reeling off the stiffest yarns we had in tow. Kent looked on at euchre awhile, then listened to us awhile, then walked about uneasy.

By and by says Bob, 'Look over there,—spry!' and there was Kent, sitting curled away in a heap under the stern of the long-boat. He had a book. Bob crawls behind and snatches it up, unbeknown, out of his hands; then he falls to laughing as if he would strangle, and gives the book a toss to me. It was a bit of Testament, black and old. There was writing on the yellow leaf, this way:—

'Kentucky Hodge.
  'from his Affecshunate mother
'who prays, For you evry day, Amen.'

The boy turned fust red, then white, and straightened up quite sudden, but he never said a word, only sat down again and let us laugh it out. I've lost my reckoning if he ever heard the last of it. He told me one day how he came by the name, but I forget exactly. Something about an old fellow—uncle, I believe—as died in Kentuck,, and the name was moniment-like, you see. He used to seem cut up a bit about it at first, for the lads took to it famously; but he got used to it in a week or two, and, seeing as they meant him no unkindness, took it quite cheery.

One other thing I noticed was that he never had the book about after that. He fell into our ways next Sunday more easy.

They don't take the Bible just the way you would, Tom,—as a general thing, sailors don't; though I will say that I never saw the man at sea who didn't give it the credit of being an uncommon good yarn.

But I tell you, Tom Brown, I felt sorry for that boy. It's punishment bad enough for a little scamp like him leaving the honest shore, and folks to home that were a bit tender of him maybe, to rough it on a trader, learning how to slush down a back-stay, or tie reef-points with frozen fingers in a snow-squall.

But that's not the worst of it, by no means. If ever there was a cold-blooded, cruel man, with a wicked eye and a fist like a mallet, it was Job Whitmarsh, taken at his best. And I believe, of all the trips I've taken, him being mate of the Madonna, Kentucky found him at his worst. Bradley—that's the second mate—was none too gentle in his ways, you may be sure; but he never held a candle to Mr. Whitmarsh. He took a spite to the boy from the first, and he kept it on a steady strain to the last, right along, just about so.

I've seen him beat that boy till the blood ran down in little pools on deck; then send him up, all wet and red, to clear the to'sail halliards; and when, what, what with the pain and faintness, he dizzied a little, and clung to the ratlines, half blind, he would have him down and

flog him till the cap'n interfered,—which would happen occasionally
on a fair day when he had taken just enough to be good-natured. He
used to rack his brains for the words he slung at the boy working quiet
enough beside him. It was odd, now, the talk he would get off. Bob
Smart couldn't any more come up to it than I could: we used to
try sometimes, but we had to give in always. If curses had been a
marketable article, Whitmarsh would have taken out his patent and
made his fortune by inventing of them, new and ingenious. Then
he used to kick the lad down the fo'castle ladder; he used to work
him, sick or well, as he wouldn't have worked a dray-horse; he used
to chase him all about deck at the rope's end; he used to mast-head
him for hours on the stretch; he used to starve him out in the hold.
It didn't come in my line to be over-tender, but I turned sick at
heart, Tom, more times than one, looking on helpless, and me a great
stout fellow.

I remember now—don't know as I've thought of it for twenty
years—a thing McCallum said one night; McCallum was Scotch,—an
old fellow with gray hair; told the best yarns on the fo'castle always.

'Mark my words, shipmates,' says he, 'when Job Whitmarsh's time
comes to go as straight to hell as Judas, that boy will bring his
summons. Dead or alive, that boy will bring his summons.'

One day I recollect especial that the lad was sick with fever on
him, and took to his hammock. Whitmarsh drove him on deck, and
ordered him aloft. I was standing near by, trimming the spanker.
Kentucky staggered for'ard a little and sat down. There was a rope's-
end there, knotted three times. The mate struck him.

'I'm very weak, sir,' says he.

He struck him again. He struck him twice more. The boy fell over
a little, and lay where he fell.

I don't know what ailed me, but all of a sudden I seemed to be lying
off Long Wharf, with the clouds the color of silver, and the air the
color of gold, and Molly in a white apron with her shining needles,
and the baby a-play in his red stockings about the deck.

'Think if it was him!' says she, or she seems to say,—'think of it
was *him*!'

And the next I knew I'd let slip my tongue in a jiffy, and given it to
the mate that furious and unrespectful as I'll wager Whitmarsh never
got before. And the next I knew after that they had the irons on me.

'Sorry about that, eh?' said he, the day before they took 'em off.

'*No*, sir,' says I. And I never was. Kentucky never forgot that. I had helped him occasional in the beginning,—learned him how to veer and haul a brace, let go or belay a sheet,—but let him alone general speaking, and went about my own business. That week in irons I really believe that lad never forgot.

One time—it was on a Saturday night, and the mate had been uncommon furious that week—Kentucky turned on him, very pale and slow (I was up in the mizzen-top, and heard him quite distinct).

'Mr. Whitmarsh,' says he,—'Mr. Whitmarsh,'—he draws his breath in,—'Mr. Whitmarsh,'—three times,—'you've got the power and you know it, and so do the gentlemen who put you here; and I'm only a stow-away boy, and things are all in a tangle, but *you'll be sorry yet for every time you've laid your hands on me!*'

He hadn't a pleasant look about the eyes either, when he said it.

Fact was, that first month on the Madonna had done the lad no good. He had a surly, sullen way with him, some'at like what I've seen about a chained dog. At the first, his talk had been clean as my baby's, and he would blush like any girl at Bob Smart's stories; but he got used to Bob, and pretty good, in time, at small swearing.

I don't think I should have noticed it so much if it had not been for seeming to see Molly, and the sun, and the knitting-needles, and the child upon the deck, and hearing of it over, 'Think if it was *him!*' Sometimes on a Sunday night I used to think it was a pity. Not that I was any better than the rest, except so far as the married men are always steadier. Go through any crew the sea over, and it is the lads who have homes of their own and little children in 'em as keep the straightest.

Sometimes, too, I used to take a fancy that I could have listened to a word from a parson, or a good brisk psalm-tune, and taken it in vary good part. A year is a long pull for twenty-five men to be becalmed with each other and the devil. I don't set up to be pious myself, but I'm not a fool, and I know that if we'd had so much as one officer abroad who feared God and kept his commandments, we should have been the better men for it. It's very much with religion as it is with cayenne pepper,—if it's there, you know it.

If you had your ships on the sea by the dozen, you'd bethink you of that? Bless you, Tom! if you were in Rome you'd do as the Romans do. You'd have your ledgers, and your children, and your churches and Sunday schools, and freed niggers, and 'lections, and what not, and never stop to think whether the lads that sailed your ships across the world had souls, or not,—and be a good sort of man too. That's the way of the world. Take it easy, Tom,—take it easy.

Well, things went along just about so with us till we neared the Cape. It's not a pretty place, the Cape, on a winter's voyage. I can't say as I ever was what you may call scar't after the first time rounding it, but it's not a pretty place.

I don't seem to remember much about Kent along there till there come a Friday at the first of December. It was a still day, with a little haze, like white sand sifted across the sunbeam on a kitchen table. The lad was quiet-like all day, chasing me about with his eyes.

'Sick?' says I.

'No,' says he.

'Whitmarsh drunk?' says I.

'No,' says he.

A little after dark I was lying on a coil of ropes, napping it. The boys were having the Bay of Biscay quite lively, and I waked up on the jump in the choruses. Kent came up while they were telling

> 'How she lay
> On that day
> In the *Bay* of BISCAY O!'

He was not singing. He sat down beside me, and first I thought I wouldn't trouble myself about him, and then I thought I would.

So I opens one eye at him encouraging. He crawls up a little closer to me. It was rather dark where we sat, with a great greenish shadow dropping from the mainsail. The wind was up a little, and the light at helm looked flickery and red.

'Jake,' says he all at once, 'where's your mother?'

'In—heaven!' says I, all taken aback; and if ever I came nigh what you might call a little disrespect to your mother, it was on that occasion, from being taken so aback.

'Oh!' said he. 'Got any women-folks to home that miss you?' asks he, by and by.

Said I, 'Shouldn't wonder.'

After that he sits still a little with his elbows on his knees; then he speers at me sidewise awhile; then said he, 'I s'pose *I've* got a mother to home. I ran away from her.'

This, mind you, is the first time he has ever spoke about his folks since he came aboard.

'She was asleep down in the south chamber,' says he. 'I got out the window. There was one white shirt she'd made for meetin' and such. I've never worn it out here. I hadn't the heart. It has a collar and some cuffs, you know. She had a headache making of it. She's been follering me round all day, a sewing on that shirt. When I come in she would look up bright-like and smiling. Father's dead. There ain't anybody but me. All day long she's been follering of me round.'

So then he gets up, and joins the lads, and tries to sing a little; but he comes back very still and sits down. We could see the flickery light upon the boys' faces, and on the rigging, and on the cap'n, who was damning to bo'sen a little aft.

'Jake,' says he, quite low, 'look here. I've been thinking. Do you reckon there's a chap here—just one, perhaps—who's said his prayers since he came aboard?'

'*No!*' said I, quite short: for I'd have bet my head on it.

I can remember, as if it was this morning, just how the question sounded, and the answer. I can't seem to put it into words how it came all over me. The wind was turning brisk, and we'd just eased her with a few reefs; Bob Smart, out furling the flying jib, got soaked; me and the boy sitting silent, were spattered. I remember watching the curve of the great swells, mahogany color, with the tip of the white, and thinking how like it was to a big creature hissing and foaming at the mouth, and thinking all at once something about Him holding of the sea in a balance, and not a word bespoke to beg his favor respectful since we weighed our anchor, and the cap'n yonder calling on Him just that minute to sent the Madonna to the bottom, if the bo'sen hadn't disobeyed his orders about the squaring of the after-yards.

'From his Affecshunate mother who prays, For you evry day, Amen,' whispers Kentucky, presently, very soft. 'The book's tore up. Mr. Whitmarsh wadded his old gun with it. But I remember.'

Then said he: 'It's 'most bedtime to home. She's setting in a little rocking-chair,—a green one. There's a fire, and the dog. She sets all by herself.'

Then he begins again: 'She has to bring in her own wood now. There's a gray ribbon on her cap. When she goes to meetin' she wears a gray bunnet. She's drawed the curtains and the door is locked. But she thinks I'll be coming home sorry some day,—I'm sure she thinks I'll be coming home sorry.'

Just then there comes the order, 'Port watch ahoy! Tumble up there lively!' so I turns out, and the lad turns in, and the night settles down a little black, and my hands and head are full. Next day it blows a clean, all but a bank of gray, very thin and still,—about the size of that cloud you see through the side window, Tom,—which lay just abeam of us.

The sea, I thought, looked like a great purple pin-cushion, with a mast or two stuck in on the horizon for the pins. 'Jake's poetry,' the boys said that was.

By noon that little gray bank had grown up thick, like a wall. By sundown the cap'n let his liquor alone, and kept the deck. By night we were in chop-seas, with a very ugly wind.

'Steer small, there!' cries Whitmarsh, growing hot about the face,—for we made a terribly crooked wake, with a broad sheer, and the old hull strained heavily,—'steer small there, I tell you! Mind your eye now, McCallum, with your foresail! Furl the royals! Send down the royals! Cheerily, men! Where's that lubber Kent? Up with you, lively now!'

Kentucky sprang for'ard at the order, then stopped short. Anybody as knows a royal from an anchor wouldn't have blamed the lad. I'll take oath to 't it's no play for an old tar, stout and full in size, sending down the royals in a gale like that; let alone a boy of fifteen year on his first voyage.

But the mate takes to swearing (it would have turned a parson faint to hear him), and Kent shoots away up,—the great mast swinging like a pendulum to and fro, and the reef-points snapping, and the blocks creaking, and the sails flapping to that extent as you wouldn't consider possible unless you'd been before the mast yourself. It reminded me of evil birds I've read of, that stun a man with their wings; strike *you* to the bottom, Tom, before you could say Jack Robinson.

Kent stuck bravely as far as the cross-trees. There he slipped and struggled and clung in the dark and noise awhile, then comes sliding down the back-stay.

'I'm not afraid, sir,' says he; 'but I cannot do it.'

For answer Whitmarsh takes to the rope's-end. So Kentucky is up again, and slips and struggles and clings again, and then lays down again.

At this the men begin to grumble a little low.

'Will you kill the lad?' said I. I get a blow for my pains, that sends me off my feet none too easy; and when I rub the stars out of my eyes the boy is up again, and the mate behind him with the rope. Whitmarsh stopped when he'd gone far enough. The lad climbed on. Once he looked back. He never opened his lips; he just looked back. If I've seen him once since, in my thinking, I've seen him twenty times,—up in the shadow of the great gray wings, a looking back.

After that there was only a cry, and a splash, and the Madonna racing along with the gale twelve knots. If it had been the whole crew overboard, she could never have stopped for them that night.

'Well,' said the cap'n, 'you've done it now.'

Whitmarsh turns his back.

By and by, when the wind fell, and the hurry was over, and I had the time to think a steady thought, being in the morning watch, I seemed to see the old lady in the gray bunnet setting by the fire. And the dog. And the green rocking-chair. And the front door, with the boy walking in on a sunny afternoon to take her by surprise.

Then I remember leaning over to look down, and wondering if the lad were thinking of it too, and what had happened to him now, these two hours back, and just about where he was, and how he liked his new quarters, and many other strange and curious things.

And while I sat there thinking, the Sunday-morning stars cut through the clouds, and the solemn Sunday-morning light began to break upon the sea.

We had a quiet run of it, after that, into port, where we lay about a couple of months or so, trading off for a fair stock of palm-oil, ivory, and hides. The days were hot and purple and still. We hadn't what you might call a blow, if I recollect accurate, till we rounded the Cape again, heading for home.

We were rounding that Cape again, heading for home, when that happened which you may believe me or not, as you take the notion, Tom; though why a man who can swallow Daniel and the lion's den, or take down t'other chap who lived three days comfortable into the inside of a whale, should make faces at what I've got to tell I can't see.

It was just about the spot that we lost the boy that we fell upon the worst gale of the trip. It struck us quite sudden. Whitmarsh was a little high. He wasn't apt to be drunk in a gale, if it gave him warning sufficient.

Well, you see, there must be somebody to furl the main-royal again, and he pitched onto McCallum. McCallum hadn't his beat for fighting out the royal in a blow.

So he piled away lively, up to the to'-sail yard. There, all of a sudden, he stopped. Next we knew he was down like heat-lightning.

His face had gone very white.

'What's to pay with *you?*' roared Whitmarsh.

Said McCallum, *'There's somebody up there, sir.'*

Screamed Whitmarsh, 'You're gone an idiot!'

Said McCallum, very quiet and distinct: 'There's somebody up there, sir. I saw him quite plain. He saw me. I called up. He called down. Says he, *'Don't you come up!'* and hang me if I'll stir a step for you or any other man to-night!'

I never saw the face of any man alive go the turn that mate's face went. If he wouldn't have relished knocking the Scotchman dead before his eyes, I've lost my guess. Can't say what he would have done to the old fellow, if there'd been any time to lose.

He'd the sense left to see there wasn't overmuch, so he orders out Bob Smart direct.

Bob goes up steady, with a quid in his cheek and a cool eye. Half-way amid to'-sail and to'-gallant he stops, and down he comes, spinning.

'Be drowned if there ain't!' said he. 'He's sitting square upon the yard. I never see the boy Kentucky, if he isn't sitting on that yard. *"Don't you come up!"* he cries out,—*"don't you come up!"'*

'Bob's drunk, and McCallum's a fool!' said Jim Welch, standing by. So Welch volunteers up, and takes Jaloffe with him. They were a couple of the coolest hands aboard,—Welch and Jaloffe. So up they goes, and down they comes like the rest, by the back-stays, by the run.

'He beckoned of me back!' says Welch. 'He hollered not to come up! not to come up!'

After that there wasn't a man of us would stir aloft, not for love nor money.

Well, Whitmarsh he stamped, and he swore, and he knocked us about furious; but we sat and looked at one another's eyes, and never stirred. Something cold, like a frost-bite, seemed to crawl along from man to man, looking into one another's eyes.

'I'll shame ye all, then, for a set of cowardly lubbers!' cries the mate; and what with the anger and the drink he was as good as his word, and up the rat-lines in a twinkle.

In a flash we were after him,—he was our officer, you see, and we felt ashamed,—me at the head, and the lads following after.

I got to the futtock shrouds, and there I stopped, for I saw him myself,—a palish boy, with a jerk of thin hair on his forehead; I'd have known him anywhere in this world or t'other. I saw him just as distinct as I see you, Tom Brown, sitting on that yard quite steady with the royal flapping like to flap him off.

I reckon I've had as much experience fore and aft, in the course of fifteen years aboard, as any man that ever tied a reef-point in a nor'easter; but I never saw a sight like that, not before nor since.

I won't say that I didn't wish myself well on deck; but I will say that I stuck to the shrouds, and looked on steady.

Whitmarsh, swearing that that royal should be furled, went on and went up.

It was after that I heard the voice. It came straight from the figure of the boy upon the upper yard.

But this time it says, 'Come up! Come up!' And then, a little louder, 'Come up! Come up! Come up! Come up!' So he goes up, and next I knew there was a cry,—and next a splash,—and then I saw the royal flapping from the empty yard, and the mate was gone, and the boy.

Job Whitmarsh was never seen again, alow or aloft, that night or ever after.

I was telling the tale to our parson this summer,—he's a fair-minded chap, the parson, in spite of a little natural leaning to strawberries, which I always take in very good part,—and he turned it about in his mind some time.

'If it was the boy,' says he,—' and I can't say as I see any reason especial why it shouldn't have been,—I've been wondering what his spiritooal condition was. A soul in hell,'—the parson believes in hell, I take it, because he can't help himself; but he has that solemn, tender way of preaching it as makes you feel he wouldn't have so much as a chicken get there if he could help it,—'a lost soul,' says the parson (I don't know as I get the words exact),—'a soul that has gone and been and got there of its own free will and choosing would be as like as not to haul another soul alongside if he could. Then again, if the mate's time had come, you see, and his chances were over, why, that's the will of the Lord, and it's hell for him whichever side of death he is, and nobody's fault but hisn; and the boy might be in the good place, and do the errand all the same. That's just about it, Brown,' says he. 'A man goes his own gait, and, if he won't go to heaven, he *won't*, and the good God himself can't help it. He throws the shining gates all open wide, and he never shut them on any poor fellow as would have entered in, and he never, never will.'

Which I thought was sensible of the parson, and very prettily put.

There's Molly frying flapjacks now, and flapjacks won't wait for no man, you know, no more than time and tide, else I should have talked till midnight, very like. to tell the time we made on that trip home, and how green the harbor looked a sailing up, and of Molly and the baby coming down to meet me in a little boat that danced about (for we cast a little down the channel), and how she climbed up a laughing and a crying all to once, about my neck, and how the boy had grown, and how when he ran about the deck (the little shaver had his first pair of boots on that very afternoon) I bethought me of the other time, and of Molly's words, and of the lad we'd left behind us in the purple days.

Just as we were hauling up, I says to my wife: 'Who's that old lady setting there upon the lumber, with a gray bunnet, and a gray ribbon on her cap?'

For there was an old lady there, and I saw the sun all about her, and all on the blazing yellow boards, and I grew a little dazed and dazzled.

'I don't know,' said Molly, catching onto me a little close. 'She comes there every day. They say she sits and watches for her lad as ran away.'

So then I seemed to know, as well as every I knew afterwards, who it was. And I thought of the dog. And the green rocking-chair. And the book that Whitmarsh wadded his old gun with. And the front-door, with the boy a walking in.

So we three went up the wharf,—Molly and the baby and me,—and sat down beside her on the yellow boards. I can't remember rightly what I said, but I remember her sitting silent in the sunshine till I had told her all there was to tell.

'*Don't cry!*' says Molly, when I got through,—which it was the more surprising of Molly, considering as she was doing the crying all to herself. The old lady never cried, you see. She sat with her eyes wide open under her gray bunnet, and her lips a moving. After a while I made it out what it was she said: 'The only son—of his mother—and she—'

By and by she gets up, and goes her ways, and Molly and I walk home together, with our little boy between us.

1871

The Ghost in the Cap'n Brown House

HARRIET BEECHER STOWE

N ow, Sam, tell us certain true, is there any such things as
ghosts?'

'Be there ghosts?' said Sam, immediately translating into his
vernacular grammar: 'wal, now that are's jest the question, ye see.'

'Well, grandma thinks there are, and Aunt Lois thinks it's all
nonsense. Why, Aunt Lois don't even believe the stories in Cotton
Mather's "Magnalia." '

'Wanter know?' said Sam, with a tone of slow, languid meditation.

We were sitting on a bank of the Charles River, fishing. The soft
melancholy red of evening was fading off in streaks on the glassy
water, and the houses of Oldtown were beginning to loom through
the gloom, solemn and ghostly. There are times and tones and moods
of nature that make all the vulgar, daily real seem shadowy, vague,
and supernatural, as if the outlines of this hard material present
were fading into the invisible and unknown. So Oldtown, with its
elm-trees, its great square white houses, its meeting-house and tavern
and blacksmith's shop and mill, which at high noon seem as real and
as commonplace as possible, at this hour of the evening were dreamy
and solemn. They rose up blurred, indistinct, dark; here and there
winking candles sent long lines of light through the shadows, and little
drops of unforeseen rain rippled the sheeny darkness of the water.

'Wal, you see, boys, in them things it's jest as well to mind your
granny. There's a consid'able sight o' gumption in grandmas. You look
at the folks that's allus tellin' you what they don't believe,—they don't
believe this, and they don't believe that,—and what sort o' folks is

they? Why, like yer Aunt Lois, sort o' stringy and dry. There ain't no 'sorption got out o' not believin' nothin'.

'Lord a massy! we don't know nothin' 'bout them things. We hain't ben there, and can't say that there ain't no ghosts and sich; can we, now?'

We agreed to that fact, and sat a little closer to Sam in the gathering gloom.

'Tell us about the Cap'n Brown house, Sam.'

'Ye didn't never go over the Cap'n Brown house?'

No, we had not that advantage.

'Wal, yer see, Cap'n Brown he made all his money to sea, in furrin parts, and then come here to Oldtown to settle down.

'Now, there ain't now knowin' 'bout these 'ere old shipmasters, where they's ben, or what they's ben a doin', or how they got their money. Ask me no questions, and I'll tell ye no lies, is 'bout the best philosophy for them. Wal, it didn't do no good to ask Cap'n Brown questions too close, 'cause you didn't git no satisfaction. Nobody rightly knew 'bout who his folks was, or where they come from, and, ef a body asked him, he used to say that the very fust he know'd 'bout himself he was a young man walkin' the streets in London.

'But, yer see, boys, he hed money, and that is about all folks wanter know when a man comes to settle down. And he bought that 'are place, and built that 'are house. He built it all sea-cap'n fashion, so's to feel as much at home as he could. The parlor was like a ship's cabin. The table and chairs was fastened down to the floor, and the closets was made with holes to set the casters and the decanters and bottles in, jest's they be at sea; and there was stanchions to hold on by; and they say that blowy nights the cap'n used to fire up pretty well with his grog, till he hed about all he could carry, and then he'd set and hold on, and hear the wind blow, and kind o' feel out to sea right there to hum. There wasn't no Mis' Cap'n Brown, and there didn't seem likely to be none. And whether there ever hed been one, nobody know'd. He hed an old black Guinea nigger-woman, named Quassia, that did his work. She was shaped pretty much like one o' these 'ere great crooknecked-squashes. She wa'n't no gret beauty, I can tell you; and she used to wear a gret red turban and a yaller short gown and red petticoat, and a gret string o' gold beads round her neck, and gret big gold hoops in her ears, made right in the middle o' Africa among the heathen there. For all she was black, she thought a heap o' herself, and was consid'able sort o predominative over the cap'n. Lord massy! boys, it's allus so. Get a man and a woman together,—any sort o' woman you're a mind to, don't care who 'tis,—and one way or another she gets the rule over him, and he jest has to train to her fife. Some does it one way, and some does it another; some does it by jawin', and some does it by kissin', and some does it by faculty and contrivance; but one way or another they allers does it. Old Cap'n Brown was a good stout, stocky kind o' John Bull sort o' fellow, and a good judge o' sperits, and allers kep' the best in them are cupboards o' his'n; but, fust and last, things in his house went pretty much as old Quassia said.

'Folks got to kind o' respectin' Quassia. She come to meetin' Sunday regular, and sot all fixed up in red and yaller and green, with glass beads and what not, lookin' for all the world like one o' them ugly Indian idols; but she was well-behaved as any Christian. She was a master hand at cookin'. Her bread and biscuits couldn't be beat, and no couldn't her pies, and there wa'n't no such pound-cake as she made nowhere. Wal, this 'ere story I'm a goin' to tell you was told me by Cinthy Pendleton. There ain't a more respectable gal, old or young, than Cinthy nowheres. She lives over to Sherburne now, and I hear tell she's sot up a manty-makin' business; but then she used to do tailorin' in Oldtown. She was a member o' the church, and a good Christian as ever was. Wal, ye see, Quassia she got Cinthy to come up and spend a week to the Cap'n Brown house, a doin' tailorin' and a fixin' over his close: 'twas along toward the fust o' March. Cinthy she sot by the fire in the front parlor with her goose and her press-board and her work: for there wa'n't no company callin', and the snow was drifted four feet deep right across the front door; so there wa'n't much danger o' any body comin' in. And the cap'n he was a perlite man to wimmen; and Cinthy she liked it jest as well not to have company, 'cause the cap'n he'd make himself entertainin' tellin' on her sea-stories, and all about this adventures among the Ammonites, and Perresites, and Jebusites, and all sorts o' heathen people he'd been among.

'Wal, that 'are week there come on the master snow-storm. Of all the snow-storms that hed ben, that 'are was the beater; and I tell you the wind blew as if 'twas the last chance it was ever goin' to hev. Wal, it's kind o' scary like to be shet up in a lone house with all natur' a kind o' breakin' out, and goin' on so, and the snow a comin' down so thick ye can't see 'cross the street, and the wind a pipin' and a squeelin' and a rumblin' and a tumblin' fust down this chimney and then down that. I tell you, it sort o' sets a feller thinkin' o' the three great things,—death, judgment, and etarnaty; and I don't care who the folks is, nor how good they be, there's times when they must be feelin' putty consid'able solemn.

'Wal, Cinthy she said she kind o' felt so along, and she hed a sort o' queer feelin' come over her as if there was somebody or somethin' round the house more'n appeared. She said she sort o' felt it in the air; but it seemed to her silly, and she tried to get over it. But two or three times, she said, when it got to be dusk, she felt somebody go by her up the stairs. The front entry wa'n't very light in the day time, and in the storm, come five o'clock, it was so dark that all you could see was jest a gleam o' somethin', and two or three times when she started to go up stairs she see a soft white suthin' that seemed goin' up before her, and she stopped with her heart a beatin' like a trip-hammer, and she sort o' saw it go up and along the entry to the cap'n's door, and then it seemed to go right through, 'cause the door didn't open.

'Wal, Cinthy says she to old Quassia, says she, "Is there anybody lives in this house but us?"

' "Anybody lives here?" says Quassia: "What you mean?" says she.

'Says Cinthy, "I thought somebody went past me on the stairs last night and to-night."

'Lord massy! how old Quassia did screech and laugh. "Good Lord!" says she, "how foolish white folks is! Somebody went past you? Was't the capt'in?"

' "No, it wa'n't the cap'n," says she: "it was somethin' soft and white, and moved very still; it was like somethin' in the air," says she.

'Then Quassia she haw-hawed louder. Says she, "It's hysterikes, Miss Cinthy; that's all it is."

'Wal, Cinthy she was kind o' 'shamed, but for all that she couldn't help herself. Sometimes evenin's she'd be a settin' with the cap'n, and she'd think she'd hear somebody a movin' in his room overhead; and she knowed it wa'n't Quassia, 'cause Quassia was ironin' in the kitchen. She took pains once or twice to find out that 'are.

'Wal, ye see, the cap'n's room was the gret front upper chamber over the parlor, and then right opposite to it was the gret spae chamber where Cinthy slept. It was jest as grand as could be, with a gret four-post mahogany bedstead and damask curtains brought over from England; but it was cold enough to freeze a white bear solid,—the way spare chambers allers is. Then there was the entry between, run straight through the house: one side was old Quassia's room, and the other was a sort o' storeroom, where the old cap'n kep' all sorts o' traps.

'Wal, Cinthy she kep' a hevin' things happen and a seein' thins, till she didn't railly know what was in it. Once when she come into the parlor jest at sundown, she was sure she see a white figure a vanishin' out o' the door that went towards the side entry. She said it was so dusk, that all she could see was jest this white figure, and it jest went out still as a cat as she come in.

'Wal, Cinthy didn't like to speak to the cap'n about it. She was a close woman, putty prudent, Cinthy was.

'But one night, 'bout the middle o' the week, this 'ere thing kind o' come to a crisis.

'Cinthy said she'd ben up putty late a sewin' and a finishin' off down in the parlor; and the cap'n he sot up with her, and was consid'able cheerful and entertainin', tellin' her all about things over the Bermudys, and off to Chiny and Japan, and round the world ginerally. The storm that hed been a blowin' all the week was about as furious as ever; and the cap'n he stirred up a mess o' flip, and hed it for her hot to go to bed on. He was a good-natured critter, and allers had feelin's for lone women; and I s'pose he knew 'twas sort o' desolate for Cinthy.

'Wal, takin' the flip so right the last think afore goin' to bed, she went right off to sleep as sound as a nut, and slep' on till somewhere about mornin', when she said somethin' waked her broad awake in a minute. Her eyes flew wide open like a spring, and the storm hed gone down and the moon come out: and there, standin' right in the moonlight by her bed, was a woman jest as white as a sheet, with black hair hangin' down to her waist, and the brightest, mourn-fullest black eyes you ever see. She stood there lookin' right at Cinthy; and Cinthy thinks that was what waked her up; 'cause, you know, ef anybody stands and looks steady at folks asleep it's apt to wake 'em.

'Any way, Cinthy said she felt jest as ef she was turnin' to stone. She couldn't move nor speak. She lay a minute, and then she shut her eyes, and begun to say her prayers; and a minute after she opened 'em, and it was gone.

'Cinthy was a sensible gal, and one that allers hed her thoughts about her; and she jest got up and put a shawl round her shoulders, and went first and looked at the doors, and they was both on 'em locked jest as she left 'em when she went to bed. Then she looked under the bed and in the closet, and felt all round the room; where she couldn't see she felt her way, and there wa'n't nothin' there.

'Wal, next mornin' Cinthy got up and went home, and she kep' it to herself a good while. Finally, one day when she was workin' to our house she told Hepsy about it, and Hepsy she told me.'

'Well, Sam,' we said, after a pause, in which we heard only the rustle of leaves and the ticking of branches against each other, 'what do you suppose it was?'

'Wal, there 'tis: you know jest as much about it as I do. Hepsy told Cinthy it might 'a' ben a dream; so it might, but Cinthy she was sure it wa'n't a dream, 'cause she remembers plain hearin' the old clock on the stairs strike four while she had her eyes open lookin' at the woman; and then she only shet 'em a minute, jest to say 'Now I lay me,' and opened 'em and she was gone.

'Wal, Cinthy told Hepsy, and Hepsy she kep' it putty close. She didn't tell it to nobody except Aunt Sally Dickerson and the Widder Bije Smith and your Grandma Badger and the minister's wife and they every one o' 'em 'greed it ought to be kep close, 'cause it would make talk. Wal, come spring somehow or other it seemed to 'a' got all over Oldtown. I heard on 't to the store and up to the tavern; and Jake Marshall he says to me one day, "What's this 'ere about the cap'n's house?" And the Widder Loker she says to me, "There's ben a ghost seen in the cap'n's house;" and I heard on 't clear over to Needham and Sherburne.

'Some o' the women they drew themselves up putty stiff and proper. Your Aunt Lois was one on 'em.

'"Ghost," says she; "don't tell me! Perhaps it would be best ef 'twas a ghost," says she. She didn't think there ought to be no sich doin's in nobody's house; and your grandma she shet her up, and told her she didn't oughter talk so.'

'Talk how?' said I, interrupting Sam with wonder. 'What did Aunt Lois mean?'

'Why, you see,' said Sam mysteriously, 'there allers is folks in every town that's jest like the Sadducees in old times: they won't believe in angel nor sperit, no way you can fix it; and ef things is seen and done in a house, why, they say, it's 'cause there's somebody there; there's some sort o' deviltry or trick about it.

'So the story got round that there was a woman kep' private in Cap'n Brown's house, and that he brought her from furrin parts; and it growed and growed, till there was all sorts o' ways o' tellin on 't.

'Some said they'd seen her a settin at an open winder. Some said that moonlight nights they'd seen her a walkin' out in the back garden kind o' in and out 'mong the bean-poles and squash-vines.

'You see, it come on spring and summer; and the winders o' the Cap'n Brown house stood open, and folks was all a watchin' on 'em day and night. Aunt Sally Dickerson told the minister's wife that she'd seen a plain daylight a woman a settin' at the chamber winder atween four and five o'clock in the mornin',—jist a settin' a lookin' out and a doin' nothin', like anybody else. She was very white and pale, and had black eyes.

'Some said that it was a nun the cap'n had brought away from a Roman Catholic convent in Spain, and some said he'd got her out o' the Inquisition.

'Aunt Sally said she thought the minister ought to call and inquire why she didn't come to meetin', and who she was, and all about her: 'cause, you see, she said it might be all right enough ef folks only know'd jest how things was; but ef they didn't, why, folks will talk.'

'Well, did the minister do it?'

'What, Parson Lothrop? Wal, no, he didn't. He made a call on the cap'n in a regular way, and asked arter his health and all his family. But the cap'n he seemed jest as jolly and chipper as a spring robin, and he gin the minister some o' his old Jamaiky; and the minister he come away and said he didn't see nothin'; and no he didn't. Folks never does see nothin' when they aint' lookin' where 'tis. Fact is, Parson Lothrop wa'n't fond o' interferin'; he was a master hand to slick things over. Your grandma she used to mourn about it, 'cause she said he never gin no p'int to the doctrines; but 'twas all of a piece, he kind o' took every thing the smooth way.

'But your grandma she believed in the ghost, and so did Lady Lothrop. I was up to her house t'other day fixin' a door-knob, and says she, "Sam your wife told me a strange story about the Cap'n Brown house."

'"Yes, ma'am, she did," says I.

'"Well, what do you think of it?" says she.

' "Wal, sometimes I think, and then agin I don't know," says I. "There's Cinthy she's a member o' the church and a good pious gal,' says I.

' "Yes, Sam," says Lady Lothrop, says she; "and Sam," says she, "it is jest like something that happened once to my grandmother when she was livin' in the old Province House in Bostin." Says she, "These 'ere things is the mysteries of Providence, and it's jest as well not to have 'em too much talked about."

' "Jest so," says I,—"jest so." That 'are's what every woman I've talked with says; and I guess, fust and last, I've talked with twenty,—good, safe church-members,—and they's every one o' opinion that this 'ere oughtn't to be talked about. Why, over to the deakin's t'other night we went it all over as much as two or three hours, and we concluded that the best way was to keep quite still about it; and that's jest what they say over to Needham and Sherburne. I've been all round a hushin' this 'ere up, and I hain't found but a few people that hedn't the particulars one way or another." There 'ere what I says to Lady Lothrop. The fact was, I never did see no report so, nor make sich sort o' sarchin's o' heart, as this 'ere. It railly did beat all; 'cause, ef 'twas a ghost, why there was the p'int proved, ye see. Cinthy's a church-member, and she see it, and got right up and sarched the room: but then agin, ef 'twas a woman, why that 'are was kind o' awful; it gives cause, ye see, for thinkin' all sorts o' things. There was Cap'n Brown, to be sure, he wa'n't a church-member; but yet he was as honest and regular a man as any goin', as fur as any on us could see. To be sure, nobody know'd where he come from but that wa'n't no reason agin' him: this 'ere might a ben a crazy sister, or some poor critter that he took out o' the best o' motives; and the Scriptur' says, "Charity hopeth all things." But then, ye see, folks will talk,—that 'are's the pester o' all these things,—and they did some on 'em talk consid'able strong about the cap'n; but somehow or other, there didn't nobody come to the p'int o' facin' on him down, and sayin' square out, "Cap'n Brown, have you got a woman in your house, or hain't you? or is it a ghost, or what is it?" Folks somehow never does come to that. Ye see, there was the cap'n so respectable, a settin' up every Sunday there in his pew, with his ruffles round his hands and his red broadcloth cloak and his cocked hat. Why, folks' hearts sort o' failed 'em when it come to sayin' any thing right to him. They thought and kind o' whispered round that the minister or the deakins oughter do it: but Lord massy! ministers, I s'pose, has feelin's like the rest on us; they don't want to eat all the hard cheeses that nobody else won't eat. Anyhow, there wasn't nothin' said direct to the cap'n; and jest for want o' that all the folks in Oldtown kep' a bilin' and a bilin' like a kettle o' soap, till it seemed all the time as if they'd bile over.

'Some o' the wimmen tried to get somethin' out o' Quassy. Lord massy! you might as well 'a' tried to get it out an old tom-turkey, that'll strut and gobble and quitter, and drag his wings on the ground, and fly at you, but won't say nothin'. Quassy she screeched her queer sort o' laugh; and she told 'em that they was a makin' fools o' themselves, and that the cap'n's matters wa'n't none o' their bisness; and that was true enough. As to goin' into Quassia's room, or into any o' the store-rooms or closets she kep' the keys of, you might as well hev gone into a lion's den. She kep' all her places locked up tight; and there was no gettin' at nothin' in the Cap'n Brown house, else I believe some o' the wimmen would 'a' sent a sarch-warrant.'

'Well,' said I, 'what came of it? Didn't anybody ever find out?'

'Wal,' said Sam, 'it come to an end sort o', and didn't come to an end. It was jest this 'ere way. You see, along in October, jest in the cider-makin' time, Abel Flint he was took down with dysentery and died. You 'member the Flint house: it stood on a little rise o' ground jest lookin' over towards the Brown house. Wal, there was Aunt Sally Dickerson and the Widder Bije Smith, they set up with the corpse. He was laid out in the back chamber, you see, over the milk-room and kitchen; but there was cold victuals and sich in the front chamber where the watchers sot. Wal, now, Aunt Sally she told me that between three and four o'clock she heard wheels a rumblin', and she went to the winder, and it was clear starlight; and she see a coach come up to the Cap'n Brown house; and she see the cap'n come out bringin' a woman all wrapped in a cloak, and old Quassy came arter with her arms full o' bundles; and he put her into the kerridge, and shet her in, and it driv off; and she see old Quassy stand lookin' over the fence arter it. She tried to wake up the widder, but 'twas towards mornin', and the widder allers was a hard sleeper; so there wa'n't no witness but her.'

'Well, then, it wasn't a ghost,' said I, 'after all, and it *was* a woman.'

'Wal, there 'tis, you see. Folks don't know that 'are yit, 'cause there it's jest as broad as 'tis long. Now, look at it. There's Cinthy, she's a

good, pious gal: she locks her chamber doors, both on 'em, and goes
to bed, and wakes up in the night, and there's a woman there. She
jest shets her eyes, and the woman's gone. She gits up and looks, and
both doors is locked jest as she left 'em. That 'ere woman wa'n't flesh
and blood now, now way,—not such flesh and blood as we knows on;
but then they say Cinthy might hev dreamed it!

'Wal, now, look at it t'other way. there's Aunt Sally Dickerson;
she's a good woman and a church-member: wal, she sees a woman
in a cloak with all her bundles brought out o' Cap'n Brown's house,
and put into a kerridge, and driv off, atween three and four o'clock in
the mornin'. Wal, that 'ere shows there must 'a' ben a real live woman
kep' there privately, and so what Cinthy saw wasn't a ghost.

'Wal, now, Cinthy says Aunt Sally might 'a' dreamed it,—that
she got her head so full o' stories about the Cap'n Brown house,
and watched it till she got asleep, and hed this 'ere dream; and, as
there didn't nobody else see it, it might 'a' ben, you know. Aunt
Sally's clear she didn't dream, and then agin Cinthy's clear *she* didn't
dream; but which on 'em was awake, or which on 'em was asleep, is
what ain't settled on Oldtown yet.'

1873

Behold It Was a Dream

RHODA BROUGHTON

Chapter I

Yesterday morning I received the following letter:

'Weston House, Caulfield,—shire.

'MY DEAR DINAH,—You *must* come: I scorn all your excuses, and see through their flimsiness. I have no doubt that you are much better amused in Dublin, frolicking round ball-rooms with a succession of horse-soldiers, and watching her Majesty's household troops play Polo in the Phoenix Park, but no matter—you *must* come. We have no particular inducements to hold out. We lead an exclusively bucolic, cow-milking, pig-fattening, roast-mutton-eating, and to-bed-at-ten-o'clock-going life; but no matter—you *must* come. I want you to see how happy two dull elderly people may be, with no special brightness in their lot to make them so. My old man—he is surprisingly ugly at the first glance, but grows upon one afterwards—sends you his respects, and bids me say that he will meet you at *any* station on *any* day at *any* hour of the day or night. If you succeed in evading our persistence this time, you will be a cleverer woman than I take you for.

'Ever yours affectionately,

'*August 15th.* 'JANE WATSON.

'P.S.—We will invite our little scarlet-headed curate to dinner to meet you, so as to soften your fall from the society of the Plungers.'

This is my answer:

'MY DEAR JANE,—Kill the fat calf in all haste, and put the bake-meats into the over, for I will come. Do not, however, imagine that I am moved thereunto by the prospect of the bright-headed curate. Believe me, my dear, I am as yet at a distance of ten long good years from an addiction to the minor clergy. If I survive the crossing of that seething, heaving, tumbling abomination, St. George's Channel, you may expect me on Tuesday next. I have been groping for hours in "Bradshaw's" darkness that I may be felt, and I have arrived at length at this twilight result, that I may arrive at your station at 6.55 P.M. But the ways of "Bradshaw" are not our ways, and I *may* either rush violently past or never attain it. If I do, and if, on my arrival, I see some rustic vehicle, guided by a startling ugly gentleman, awaiting me, I shall know, from your wifely description, that it is your "old man." Till Tuesday, then,

'Affectionately yours,

'DINAH BELLAIRS.

'*August 17th.*'

I am as good as my word; on Tuesday I set off. For four mortal hours and a half I am disastrously, hideously, diabolically sick. For four hours and a half I curse the day on which I was born, the day on which Jane Watson was born, the day on which her old man was born, and lastly—but oh! not, *not* leastly—the day and the dock on which and in which the *Leinster's* plunging, curtsying, throbbing body was born. On arriving at Holyhead, feeling convinced from my sensations that, as the French say, I touch my last hour, I indistinctly request to be allowed to stay on board and *die*, then and there; but as the stewardess and my maid take a different view of my situation, and insist upon forcing my cloak and bonnet on my dying body and limp head, I at length succeed in staggering on deck and off the accursed boat. I am then well shaken up for two or three hours in the Irish mail, and, after crawling along a slow bye-line for two or three hours more, am at length at 6.55, landed, battered, tired, dust-blacked, and qualmish, at the little roadside station of Caulfield. My maid and I are the only passengers who descend. The train snorts its slow way onwards, and I am left gazing at the calm, crimson death of the August sun, and smelling the sweet-peas in the station-master's garden border. I look round in search of Jane's promised tax-cart, and steel my nerves for the contemplation of her old man's unlovely features. But the only vehicle which I see is a tiny two-wheeled pony carriage, drawn by a small and tub-shaped bay pony, and driven by a lady in a hat, whose face is turned expectantly towards me. I go up and recognise my friend, whom I have not seen for two years—not since before she fell in with her old man and espoused him.

'I thought it safest, after all, to come myself,' she says, with a bright laugh, 'My old man looked so handsome this morning, that I thought you would never recognise him from my description. Get in, dear, and let us trot home as quickly as we can.'

I comply, and for the next half-hour sit (while the cool evening wind is blowing the dust off my hot and jaded face) stealing amazed glances at my companion's cheery features. *Cheery!* That is the very last word that, excepting in an ironical sense, any one would have applied to my friend Jane two years ago. Two years ago Jane was thirty-five, the elderly eldest daughter of a large family, hustled into obscurity, jostled, shelved, by half-a-dozen younger, fresher sisters; an elderly girl, addicted to lachrymose verse about the gone, and the dead, and the for-ever-lost. Apparently the gone has come back, the dead resuscitated, the for-ever-lost been found again. The peaky, sour virgin is transformed into a gracious matron, with a kindly, comely face, pleasure making and pleasure feeling. Oh, Happiness! what powder or paste, or milk of roses, can make old cheeks young again in the cunning way that you do? If you would but bide steadily with us, we might live for ever, always young and always handsome.

My musings on Jane's metamorphosis, combined with a tired headache, make me somewhat silent, and indeed there is mostly a slackness of conversation between the two dearest allies on first meeting after absence—a sort of hesitating shiver before plunging into the sea of talk that both know lies in readiness for them.

'Have you got your harvest in yet?' I ask, more for the sake of not utterly holding my tongue than from any profound interest in the subject, as we jog briskly along between the yellow cornfields, where the dry bound sheaves are standing in golden rows in the red sunset light.

'Not yet,' answers Jane; 'we have only just begun to cut some of it. However, thank God, the weather looks as settled as possible; there is not a streak of watery lilac in the west.'

My headache is almost gone, and I am beginning to think kindly of dinner—a subject from which all day until now my mind has hastily

turned with a sensation of hideous inward revolt—by the time that the
fat pony pulls up before the old-world dark porch of a modest little
house, which has bashfully hidden its original face under a veil of
crowded clematis flowers and stalwart ivy. Set as in a picture-frame by
the large drooped ivy-leaves, I see a tall and moderately hard-featured
gentleman of middle age, perhaps, of the two, rather inclining towards
elderly, smiling at us a little shyly.

'This is my old man,' cries Jane, stepping gaily out, and giving him
a friendly introductory pat on the shoulder. 'Old man, this is Dinah.'

Having thus been made known to each other we shake hands, but
neither of us can arrive at anything pretty to say. Then I follow
Jane into her little house, the little house for which she has so
happily exchanged her tenth part of the large and noisy paternal
mansion. It is an old house, and everything about it has the moderate
shabbiness of old age and long and careful wear. Little thick-walled
rooms, dark and cool, with flowers and flower scents lying in wait
for you everywhere—a silent, fragrant, childless house. To me, who
have had oily locomotives snorting and racing through my head all
day, its dumb sweetness seems like heaven.

'And now that we have secured you, we do not mean to let you go
in a hurry,' says Jane hospitably that night at bedtime, lighting the
candles on my dressing-table.

'You are determined to make my mouth water, I see,' say I,
interrupting a yawn to laugh. 'Lone lorn me, who have neither old
man nor dear little house, nor any prospect of ultimately attaining
either.'

'But if you honestly are not bored you will stay with us a good
bit?' she says, laying her hand with kind entreaty on my sleeve. 'St.
George's Channel is not lightly to be faced again.'

'Perhaps I shall stay until you are obliged to go away yourselves
to get rid of me,' return I, smiling. 'Such things have happened.
Yes, without joking, I will stay a month. Then, by the end of a
month, if you have not found me out thoroughly, I think I may
pass among men for a more amiable woman than I have ever yet had
the reputation of.'

A quarter of an hour later I am laying down my head among
soft and snow-white pillows, and saying to myself that this delicious
sensation of utter drowsy repose, of soft darkness and odorous quiet,
is cheaply purchased, even by the ridiculous anguish which my own

sufferings, and—hardly less than my own sufferings—the demoniac sights and sounds afforded by my fellow passengers, caused me on board the accursed *Leinster*—

'Built in the eclipse, and rigged with curses dark.'

Chapter II

'Well, I cannot say that you look much rested, says Jane, next morning, coming in to greet me, smiling and fresh—(yes, sceptic of eighteen, even a woman of thirty-seven may look fresh in a print gown on an August morning, when she has a well of lasting quiet happiness inside her)—coming in with a bunch of creamy *gloire de Dijons* in her hand for the breakfast table. 'You look infinitely more fagged than you did when I left you last night!'

'Do I?' say I, rather faintly.

'I am afraid you did not sleep much?' suggests Jane, a little crestfallen at the insult to her feather beds implied by my wakefulness. 'Some people never can sleep the first night in a strange bed, and I stupidly forgot to ask you whether you liked the feather bed or mattress at the top.'

'Yes, I did sleep,' I answered gloomily. 'I wish to heaven I had not!'

'Wish—to—heaven—you—had—not?' repeats Jane slowly, with a slight astonished pause between each word. 'My dear child, for what other purpose did you go to bed?'

'I—I—had bad dreams,' say I, shuddering a little; and then, taking her hand, roses and all, in mine: 'Dear Jane, do not think me quite run mad, but—but—have you got a "Bradshaw" in the house?'

'A "Bradshaw?" What on earth do you want with "Bradshaw?"' says my hostess, her face lengthening considerably, and a slight tincture of natural coldness coming into her tone.

'I know it seems rude—insultingly rude,' say I, still holding her hand and speaking almost lachrymosely: 'but do you know, my dear, I really am afraid that—that—I shall have to leave you—to-day?'

'To leave us?' repeats she, withdrawing her hand and growing angrily red. What! when not twenty-four hours ago you settled to stay *a month* with us? What have we done between then and now to disgust you with us?'

'Nothing—nothing,' cry I eagerly; 'how can you suggest such a thing? I never had a kinder welcome or ever saw a place that charmed me more; but—but—'

'But what?' asked Jane, her colour subsiding and looking a little mollified.

'It is best to tell the truth, I suppose,' say I, sighing, 'even though I know that you will laugh at me—will call me vapourish-sottishly superstitious; but I had an awful and hideous dream last night.'

'Is that all?' she says, looking relieved, and beginning to arrange her roses in an old china bowl. 'And do you think that all dreams are confined to this house? I never heard before of their affecting any one special place more than another. Perhaps no sooner are you back in Dublin, in your own room and your own bed, than you will have a still worse and uglier one.'

I shake my head. 'But it was about this house—about *you*.'

'About *me*?' she says, with an accent of a little aroused interest.

'About you and your husband,' I answer earnestly. 'Shall I tell it you? Whether you say "Yes" or "No" I must. Perhaps it came as a warning; such things have happened. Yes; say what you will, I cannot believe that any vision so consistent—so tangibly real and utterly free from the jumbled incongruities and unlikenesses of ordinary dreams—could have meant nothing, Shall I begin?'

'By all means,' answers Mrs. Watson, sitting down in an arm-chair and smiling easily. 'I am quite prepared to listen—and *dis*believe.'

'You know,' say I, narratively, coming and standing close before her, 'how utterly tired out I was when you left me last night. I could hardly answer your questions for yawning. I do not think that I was ten minutes in getting into bed, and it seemed like heaven when I laid my head down on the pillow. I felt as if I should sleep till the Day of Judgment. Well, you know, when one is asleep one has, of course, no measure of time, and I have no idea what hour it was *really*; but at some time, in the blackest and darkest of the night, I seemed to wake. It appeared as if a noise had woke me—a noise which at first neither frightened nor surprised me in the least, but which seemed quite natural, and which I accounted for in the muddled drowsy way in which one does account for things when half asleep. But as I gradually grew to a fuller consciousness I found out, with a cold shudder, that the noise I heard was not one that belonged to the night; nothing that one could lay on wind in the chimney, or mice behind the wainscot, or ill-fitting boards. It was a sound of muffled struggling, and once I heard a sort of choked, strangled cry. I sat up in bed, perfectly numbed with fright, and for a moment could hear nothing for the singing of the blood in my head, and the loud battering of my heart against my side. Then I thought that if it were anything bad—if I were going to be murdered—I had at least rather be in the light than the dark, and see in what sort of shape my fate was coming, so I slid out of bed and threw my dressing-gown over my shoulders. I had stupidly forgotten, in my weariness, over night, to put the matches by the bedside, and could not for the life of me recollect where they were. Also, my knowledge of the geography of the room was so small, that in the utter blackness, without even the palest, greyest ray from the window to help me I was by no means sure in which direction the door lay. I can feel *now* the pain of the blow I gave this right side against the sharp corner of the table in passing; I was quite surprised this morning not to find the mark of a bruise there. At last, in my groping, I came upon the handle and turned the key in the lock. It gave a little squeak, and again I stopped for a moment, overcome by ungovernable fear. Then I silently opened the door and looked out. You know that your door is exactly opposite mine. By the line of red light underneath it, I could see that, at all events, some one was awake and astir within, for the light was brighter than that given by a nightlight. By the broader band of red light on the right side of it I could also perceive that the door was ajar. I stood stock still and listened. The two sounds of struggling and chokedly crying had both ceased. All the noise that remained was that of some person quietly moving about on unbooted feet. "Perhaps Jane's dog Smut is ill and she is sitting up with it; she was saying last night, I remember, that she was afraid it was beginning with the distemper. Perhaps either she or her old man have been taken with some trifling temporary sickness. Perhaps the noise of crying out that I certainly heard was one of them fighting with a nightmare." Trying, by such like suggestions, to hearten myself up, I stole across the passage and peeped in—'

I paused in my narrative.

'Well?' says Jane, a little impatiently.

She has dropped her flowers. They lie in odorous dewy confusion in her lap. She is listening rather eagerly. I cover my face with my hands.

'Oh! my dear,' I cry, 'I do not think I can go on. It was *too* dreadful! Now that I am telling it I seem to be doing and hearing it over again—'

'I do not call it very kind to keep me on the rack,' she says, with a rather forced laugh. 'Probably I am imagining something much worse than the reality. For heaven's sake speak up! What *did* you see?'

I take hold of her hand and continue. 'You know that in your room the bed exactly faces the door. Well, when I looked in, looked in with eyes blinking at first, and dazzled by the long darkness they had been in, it seemed to me as if that bed were only one horrible sheet of crimson; but as my sight grew clearer I saw what it was that caused that frightful impression of universal red—' Again I pause with a gasp and feeling of oppressed breathing.

'Go on! go on!' cries my companion, leaning forward, and speaking with some petulance. 'Are you never going to get to the point?'

'Jane,' say I solemnly, 'do not laugh at me, nor pooh pooh me, for it is God's truth—as clearly and vividly as I see you now, strong, flourishing, and alive, so clearly, so vividly, with no more of dream haziness nor of contradiction in details than there is in the view I now have of this room and of you—I saw you *both*—you and your husband, lying *dead—murdered*—drowned in your own blood!'

'What, both of us?' she says, trying to laugh, but her healthy cheek was rather paled.

'Both of you,' I answer, with growing excitement. 'You, Jane, had evidently been the one first attacked—taken off in your sleep—for you were lying just as you would have lain in slumber, only that across your throat from there to there' (touching first one ear and then the other), 'there was a huge and yawning gash.'

'Pleasant,' replies she, with a slight shiver.

'I never saw anyone dead,' continue I earnestly, 'never until last night. I had not the faintest idea how dead people looked, even people who died, quietly, nor has any picture ever given me at all a clear conception of death's dread look. How then could I have *imagined* the hideous contraction and distortion of feature, and staring starting open eyes—glazed yet agonised—the tightly clenched teeth that go to make up the picture, that is *now, this very minute,* standing out in ugly vividness before my mind's eye?' I stop, but she does not avail herself of the pause to make any remark, neither does she look any longer at all laughingly inclined.

'And yet,' continue I, with a voice shaken by emotion, 'it was *you,* *very* you, not partly you and partly someone else, as is mostly the case in dreams, but as much *you* as the *you* I am touching now' (laying my finger on her arm as I speak).

'And my old man, Robin,' says poor Jane, rather tearfully, after a moment's silence, 'what about him? Did you see him? Was he dead too?'

'It was evidently he whom I had heard struggling and crying,' I answer, with a strong shudder, which I cannot keep down, 'for it was clear that he had fought for his life. He was lying half on the bed and half on the floor, and one clenched hand was grasping a great piece of the sheet; he was lying head downwards, as if, after his last struggle, he had fallen forwards. All his grey hair was reddened and stained, and I could see that the rift in his throat was as deep as that in yours.'

'I wish you would stop,' cries Jane, pale as ashes, and speaking with an accent of unwilling terror; 'you are making me quite sick!'

'I *must* finish,' I answer earnestly, 'since it has come in time I am sure it has come for some purpose. Listen to me till the end; it is very near.' She does not speak, and I take her silence for assent. 'I was staring at you both in a stony way,' I go on, 'feeling—if I felt at all—that I was turning idiotic with horror—standing in exactly the same spot, with my neck craned to look round the door, and my eyes unable to stir from that hideous scarlet bed, when a slight noise, as of someone cautiously stepping on the carpet, turned my stony terror into a living quivering agony. I looked and saw a man with his back towards me walking across the room from the bed to the dressing-table. He was dressed in the dirty fustian of an ordinary workman, and in his hand he held a red wet sickle. When he reached the dressing-table he laid it down on the floor beside him, and began to collect all the rings, open the cases of the bracelets, and hurry the trinkets of all sorts into his pockets. While he was thus busy I caught a full view of the reflection of the face in the glass—' I stop for breath, my heart is panting almost as hardly as it seemed to pant during the awful moments I am describing.

'What was he like—what was he like?' cries Jane, greatly excited. 'Did you see him distinctly enough to recollect his features again? Would you know him again if you saw him?'

'Should I know my own face if I saw it in the glass?' I ask scornfully.

'I see every line of it *now* more clearly than I do yours, though that is before my eyes, and the other only before my memory—'

'Well, what was he like?—be quick, for heaven's sake.

'The first moment that I caught sight of him,' continue I, speaking quickly, 'I felt certain that he was Irish; to no other nationality could such a type of face have belonged. His wild rough hair fell down over his forehead, reaching his shagged and overhanging brows. He had the wide grinning slit of a mouth—the long nose, the cunningly twinkling eyes—that one so often sees, in combination with a shambling gait and ragged tailcoat, at the railway stations or in the harvest fields at this time of year.' A pause. 'I do not know how it came to me,' I go on presently; 'but I felt as convinced as if I had been told—as if I had known it for a positive fact—that he was one of your own labourers—one of your own harvest men. Have you any Irishmen working for you?'

'Of course we have,' answers Jane, rather sharply, 'but that proves nothing. Do not they, as you observed just now, come over in droves at this time of the year for the harvest?'

'I am sorry,' say I, sighing. 'I wish you had not. Well, let me finish; I have just done—I had been holding the door-handle mechanically in my hand; I suppose I pulled it unconsciously towards me, for the door-hinge creaked a little, but quite audibly. To my unspeakable horror the man turned round and saw me. Good God! he would cut my throat too with that red, *red* reaping-hook! I tried to get into my passage and lock the door, but the key was in the inside. I tried to scream, I tried to run; but voice and legs disobeyed me. The bed and room and man began to dance before me; a black earthquake seemed to swallow me up, and I suppose I fell down in a swoon. When I awoke *really* the blessed morning had come, and a robin was singing outside my window on an apple bough. There—you have it all, and now let me look for a "Bradshaw," for I am so frightened and unhinged that go I must.'

Chapter III

'I must own that it has taken away my appetite,' I say, with rather a sickly smile, as we sit round the breakfast table.

'I assure you that I meant no insult to your fresh eggs and bread-and-butter, but I simply *cannot* eat.'

'It certainly was an exceptionally dreadful dream,' says Jane, whose colour has returned, and who is a good deal fortified and reassured by the influences of breakfast and of her husband's scepticism; for a condensed and shortened version of my dream has been told to him, and he has easily laughed it to scorn. 'Exceptionally dreadful, chiefly from its extreme consistency and precision of detail. But still, you know, dear, one has had hideous dreams one's self times out of mind and they never came to anything. I remember once I dreamt that all my teeth came out in my mouth at once—double ones and all; but that was ten years ago, and they still keep their situations, nor did I about that time lose any friend, which they say such a dream is a sign of.'

'You say that some unaccountable instinct told you that the hero of your dream was one of my own men,' says Robin, turning towards me with a covert smile of benevolent contempt for my superstitiousness; 'did not I understand you to say so?'

'Yes,' reply I, not in the least shaken by his hardly-veiled disbelief, 'I do not know how it came to me, but I was as much persuaded of that, and am so still, as I am of my own identity.'

'I will tell you of a plan then to prove the truth of your vision,' returns he, smiling. 'I will take you through the fields this morning and you shall see all my men at work, both the ordinary staff and the harvest casuals, Irish and all. If amongst them you find the counterpart of Jane's and my murderer' (a smile) 'I will promise *then*—no, not even *then* can I promise to believe you, for there is such a family likeness between all Irishmen, at all events, between all the Irishmen that one sees *out* of Ireland.'

'Take me,' I say, eagerly, jumping up; 'now, this *minute*! You cannot be more anxious nor half so anxious to prove me a false prophet as I am to be proved one.'

'I am quite at your service,' he answers, 'as soon as you please. Jenny, get your hat and come too.'

'And if we do *not* find him,' says Jane, smiling playfully—'I think I am growing pretty easy on that head—you will promise to eat a great deal of luncheon and never *mention* "Bradshaw" again?'

'I promise,' reply I, gravely. 'And if, on the other hand, we *do* find him, you will promise to put no more obstacles in the way of my going, but will let me depart in peace without taking any offence thereat?'

'It is a bargain,' she says gaily. 'Witness, Robin.'

So we set off in the bright dewiness of the morning on our walk over Robin's farm. It is a grand harvest day, and the whitened sheaves are everywhere drying, drying in the genial sun. We have been walking for an hour, and both Jane and I are rather tired. The sun beats with all his late-summer strength on our heads and takes the force and spring out of our hot limbs.

'The hour of triumph is approaching,' says Robin, with a quiet smile, as we drew near an open gate through which a loaded wain, shedding ripe wheat ears from its abundance as it crawls along, is passing. 'And time for it too; it is a quarter past twelve, and you have been on your legs for fully an hour. Miss Bellairs, you must make haste and find the murderer, for there is only one more field to do it in.'

'Is not there?' I cry eagerly. 'Oh, I *am* glad! Thank God, I begin to breathe again.'

We pass through the open gate and begin to tread across the stubble, for almost the last load has gone.

'We must get nearer the hedge,' says Robin, 'or you will not see their faces; they are all at dinner.'

We do as he suggests. In the shadow of the hedge we walk close in front of the row of heated labourers, who, sitting or lying on the hedge bank, are eating unattractive-looking dinners. I scan one face after another—honest bovine English faces. I have seen a hundred thousand faces *like* each one of the faces now before me—very like, but the exact counterpart of none. We are getting to the end of the row, I beginning to feel rather ashamed, though infinitely relieved, and to smile at my own expense. I look again and my heart suddenly stands still and turns to stone within me. He is *there!*—not a hand-breadth from me! Great God! how well I have remembered his face, even to the unsightly smallpox seams, the shagged locks, the grinning, slit mouth, the little sly, base eyes. He is employed in no murderous occupation *now*; he is harmlessly cutting hunks of coarse bread and fat cold bacon with a clasp knife, but yet I have no more doubt that it is *he*—he whom I saw with the crimsoned sickle in his stained hand—than I have that it is I who am stonily, shiveringly stared at him.

'Well, Miss Bellairs, who is right?' asks Robin's cheery voice at my elbow. 'Perish "Bradshaw" and all his labyrinths! Are you satisfied now? Good heavens!' (catching a sudden sight of my face) 'how white you are! Do you mean to say that you have found him at last? Impossible!'

'Yes, I have found him,' I answer, in a low and unsteady tone. 'I knew I should. Look there he is!—close to us, the third from the end.'

I turn away my head, unable to bear the hideous recollections and associations that the sight of the man calls up, and I suppose that they both look.

'Are you sure that you are not letting your imagination carry you away?' asks he presently, in a tone of gentle, kindly remonstrance. 'As I said before, these fellows are all so much alike; they have all the same look of debased, squalid cunning. Oblige me by looking once again, so as to be quite sure.'

I obey. Reluctantly I look at him once again. Apparently becoming aware that he is the object of our notice, he lifts his small dull eyes, and looks back at me. It is the same face—they are the same eyes that turned from the plundered dressing-table to catch sight of me last night. 'There is no mistake,' I answer, shuddering from head to foot. 'Take me away, please—as quick as you can—out of the field—home!'

They comply, and over the hot fields and through the hot noon air we step silently homewards. As we reach the cool and ivied porch of the house, I speak for the first time. 'You believe me *now*?'

He hesitates.

'I was staggered for a moment, I will own,' he answers, with candid gravity; 'but I have been thinking it over, and, on reflection, I have come to the conclusion that the highly excited state of your imagination is answerable for the heightening of the resemblance which exists between all the Irish of that class into an identity with the particular Irishman you dreamed of, and whose face (by your own showing) you only saw dimly reflected in the glass.'

'*Not* dimly,' repeat I emphatically, 'unless I now see that sun dimly' (pointing to him, as he gloriously, blindingly blazes from the sky). 'You will not be warned by me then?' I continue passionately, after an interval. 'You will run the risk of my dream coming true—you will stay on here in spite of it? Oh, if I could persuade you to go from home—anywhere—anywhere—for a time, until the danger was past!'

'And leave the harvest to itself?' answers he, with a smile of quiet sarcasm; 'be a loser of two hundred or three hundred pounds, probably,

and a laughing-stock to my acquaintance into the bargain, and all
for—what? A dream—a fancy—a nightmare!'

'But do you know anything of the man?—of his antecedents?—of
his character?' I persist eagerly.

He shrugs his shoulders.

'None whatever; nothing to his disadvantage, certainly. He came
over with a lot of others a fortnight ago, and I engaged him for
harvesting. For anything I have heard to the contrary, he is simple,
inoffensive fellow enough.'

I am silenced, but not convinced. I turn to Jane.

'You remember your promise; you will now put no more hindrances
in the way of my going?'

'You do not mean to say that you are going, really?' says Jane, who
is looking rather awed by what she calls the surprising coincidence,
but is still a good deal heartened up by her husband's want of faith.

'I do,' reply I, emphatically. 'I should go stark staring mad if I were
to sleep another night in that room. I shall go to Chester to-night and
cross to-morrow from Holyhead.'

I do as I say. I make my maid, to her extreme surprise, repack my
just unpacked wardrobe, and take an afternoon train to Chester. As
I drive away with bag and baggage down the leafy lane, I look back
and see my two friends standing at their gate, Jane is leaning her
head on her old man's shoulder, and looking rather wistfully after
me; an expression of mingled regret for my departure and vexation at
my folly clouding their kind and happy faces. At least my last living
recollection of them is a pleasant one.

Chapter IV

The joy with which my family welcomed my return is largely mingled
with surprise, but still more largely with curiosity, as to the cause of
my so sudden reappearance. But I keep my own counsel. I have a
reluctance to give the real reason, and possess no inventive faculty in
the way of lying, so I give none. I say, 'I *am* back: is not that enough
for you? Set your minds at rest, for that is as much as you will ever
know about the matter.'

For one thing, I am occasionally rather ashamed of my conduct.
It is not that the impression produced by my dream is *effaced*, but
that absence and distance from the scene and the persons of it have

produced their natural weakening effect. Once or twice during the voyage, when writhing in laughable torments in the ladies' cabin of the steamboat, I said to myself, 'Most likely you are a fool!' I therefore continually ward off the cross-questionings of my family with what defensive armour of silence and evasion I may.

'I feel convinced it was the husband,' says one of my sisters, after a long catechism, which, as usual, has resulted in nothing. 'You are too loyal to your friend to own it, but I always felt sure that any man who could take compassion on that poor peevish old Jane must be some wonderful freak of nature. Come, confess. Is not he a cross between an ourang-outang and a Methodist parson?'

'He is nothing of the kind,' reply I, in some heat, recalling the libelled Robin's clean fresh-coloured *human* face. 'You will be very lucky if you ever secure anyone half so kind, pleasant and gentleman-like.'

Three days after my return, I received a letter from Jane:

'Weston House, Caulfield,—shire.

'MY DEAR DINAH,

'I hope you are safe home again, and that you have made up your mind that two crossings of St. George's Channel within forty-eight hours are almost as bad as having your throat cut, according to the programme you laid out for *us*. I have good news for you. Our murderer elect is *gone*. After hearing of the connection that there was to be between us, Robin naturally was rather interested in him, and found out his name, which is the melodious one of Watty Doolan. After asking his name, he asked other things about him, and finding that he never did a stroke of work and was inclined to be tipsy and quarrelsome, he paid and packed him off at once. He is now, I hope, on his way back to his native shores, and if he murders anybody it will be *you*, my dear. Goodbye, Dinah. Hardly yet have I forgiven you for the way in which you frightened me with your graphic description of poor Robin and me, with our heads loose and waggling.

'Ever yours affectionately,

'JANE WATSON.'

I fold up this note with a feeling of exceeding relief, and a thorough faith that I have been a superstitious hysterical fool. More resolved than ever am I to keep the reason for my return profoundly secret from my family. The next morning but one we are all in the breakfast-room after breakfast, hanging about, and looking at the papers. My sister has just thrown down the *Times*, with a pettish exclamation that there is nothing in it, and that it really is not worth while paying threepence a day to see nothing but advertisements and police-reports. I pick it up as she throws it down, and look listlessly over its tall columns from top to bottom. Suddenly my listlessness vanishes. What is this that I am reading?—this in staring capitals?

'Shocking Tragedy at Caulfield.'
'Double Murder.'

I am in the middle of the paragraph before I realise what it is.

'From an early hour of the morning this village has been the scene of deep and painful excitement in consequence of the discovery of the atrocious murder of Mr. and Mrs. Watson, of Weston House, two of its most respected habitants. It appears that the deceased had retired to rest on Tuesday night at their usual hour, and in their usual health and spirits. The housemaid, on going to call them at the accustomed hour on Wednesday morning, received no answer, in spite of repeated knocking. She therefore at length opened the door and entered. The rest of the servants, attracted by her cries, rushed to the spot, and found the unfortunate gentleman and lady lying on the bed with their throats cut from ear to ear. Life must have been extinct for some hours, as they were both perfectly cold. The room presented a hideous spectacle, being literally swimming in blood. A reaping hook, evidently the instrument with which the crime was perpetrated, was picked up near the door. An Irish labourer of the name of Watty Doolan, discharged by the lamented gentleman a few days ago on account of misconduct, has already been arrested on strong suspicion, as at an early hour on Wednesday morning, he was seen by a farm labourer, who was going to his work, washing his waistcoat at a retired spot in the stream which flows through the meadows below the scene of the murder. On being apprehended and searched, several small articles of jewelry, identified as having belonged to Mrs. Watson, were discovered in his possession.

I drop the paper and sink into a chair, feeling deadly sick.

So you see that my dream came true, after all.

The facts narrated in the above story occurred in Ireland. The only liberty I have taken with them is in transplanting them to England.

1876

The Secret Chamber

MARGARET OLIPHANT

I

Castle Gowrie is one of the most famous and interesting in all
Scotland. It is a beautiful old house, to start with,—perfect
in old feudal grandeur, with its clustered turrets and walls that
could withstand an army,—its labyrinths, its hidden stairs, its long
mysterious passages—passages that seem in many cases to lead to
nothing, but of which no one can be too sure what they lead to. The
front, with its fine gateway and flanking towers, is approached now
by velvet lawns, and a peaceful, beautiful old avenue, with double
rows of trees, like a cathedral; and the woods out of which these grey
towers rise, look as soft and rich in foliage, if not so lofty in growth,
as the groves of the South. But this softness of aspect is all new to the
place,—that is, new within the century or two which count for but
little in the history of a dwelling-place, some part of which, at least,
has been standing since the days when the Saxon Athelings brought
such share of the arts as belonged to them to solidify and regulate the
original Celtic art which reared incised stones upon rude burial-places,
and twined mystic knots on its crosses, before historic days. Even
of this primitive decoration there are relics at Gowrie, where the
twistings and twinings of Runic cords appear still on some bits of
ancient wall, solid as rocks, and almost as everlasting. From these to
the graceful French turrets, which recall many a grey chateau, what
a long interval of years! But these are filled with stirring chronicles
enough, besides the dim, not always decipherable records, which
different developments of architecture have left on the old house.
The Earls of Gowrie had been in the heat of every commotion that

took place on or about the Highland line for more generations than any but a Celtic pen could record. Rebellions, revenges, insurrections, conspiracies, nothing in which blood was shed and lands lost, took place in Scotland, in which they had not had a share; and the annals of the house are very full, and not without many a stain. They had been a bold and vigorous race—with much evil in them, and some good; never insignificant, whatever else they might be. It could not be said, however, that they are remarkable nowadays. Since the first Stuart rising, known in Scotland as 'the Fifteen,' they have not done much that has been worth recording; but yet their family history has always been of an unusual kind. The Randolphs could not be called eccentric in themselves: on the contrary, when you know them, they were at bottom a respectable race, full of all the country-gentleman virtues; and yet their public career, such as it was, had been marked by the strangest leaps and jerks of vicissitude. You would have said an impulsive, fanciful family—now making a grasp at some visionary advantage, now rushing into some wild speculation, now making a sudden sally into public life—but soon falling back into mediocrity, not able apparently, even when the impulse was purely selfish and mercenary, to keep it up. But this would not have been at all a true conception of the family character; their actual virtues were not of the imaginative order, and their freaks were a mystery to their friends. Nevertheless these freaks were what the general world was most aware of in the Randolph race. The late Earl had been a representative peer of Scotland (they had no English title), and had made quite a wonderful start, and for a year or two had seemed about to attain a very eminent place in Scotch affairs; but his ambition was found to have made use of some very equivocal modes of gaining influence, and he dropped accordingly at once and for ever from the political firmament. This was quite a common circumstance in the family. An apparently brilliant beginning, a discovery of evil means adopted for ambitious ends, a sudden subsidence, and the curious conclusion at the end of everything that this schemer, this unscrupulous speculator or politician, was a dull, good man after all—unambitious, contented, full of domestic kindness and benevolence. This family peculiarity made the history of the Randolphs a very strange one, broken by the oddest interruptions, and with no consistency in it. There was another circumstance, however, which attracted still more the wonder and observation of the public. For one who can appreciate

such a recondite matter as family character, there are hundreds who
are interested in a family secret, and this the house of Randolph
possessed in perfection. It was a mystery which piqued the imagination
and excited the interest of the entire country. The story went, that
somewhere hid amid the massive walls and tortuous passages there was
a secret chamber in Gowrie Castle. Everybody knew of its existence;
but save the Earl, his heir, and one other person, not of the family,
but filling a confidential post in their service, no mortal knew where
this mysterious hiding-place was. There had been countless guesses
made at it, and expedients of all kinds invented to find it out. Every
visitor who ever entered the old gateway, nay, even passing travellers
who saw the turrets from the road, searched keenly for some trace of
this mysterious chamber. But all guesses and researches were equally
in vain.

I was about to say that no ghost-story I ever heard of has been so
steadily and long believed. But this would be a mistake, for nobody
knew even with any certainty that there was a ghost connected with
it. A secret chamber was nothing wonderful in so old a house. No
doubt they exist in many such old houses, and are always curious
and interesting—strange relics, more moving than any history, of
the time when a man was not safe in his own house, and when
it might be necessary to secure a refuge beyond the reach of spies
or traitors at a moment's notice. Such a refuge was a necessity of
life to a great medieval noble. The peculiarity about this secret
chamber, however, was that some secret connected with the very
existence of the family was always understood to be involved in it.
It was not only the secret hiding-place for an emergency, a kind
of historical possession presupposing the importance of his race, of
which a man might be honestly proud; but there was something
hidden in it of which assuredly the race could not be proud. It
is wonderful how easily a family learns to pique itself upon any
distinctive possession. A ghost is a sign of importance not to be
despised; a haunted room is worth as much as a small farm to
the complacency of the family that owns it. And no doubt the
younger branches of the Gowrie family—the light-minded portion of
the race—felt this, and were proud of their unfathomable secret, and
felt a thrill of agreeable awe and piquant suggestion go through them,
when they remembered the mysterious something which they did not
know in their familiar home. That thrill ran through the entire circle

of visitors, and children, and servants, when the Earl peremptorily forbade a projected improvement, or stopped a reckless exploration. They looked at each other with a pleasurable shiver. 'Did you hear?' they said. 'He will not let Lady Gowrie have that closet she wants so much in that bit of wall. He sent the workmen about their business before they could touch it, though the wall is twenty feet thick if it is an inch; ah!' said the visitors, looking at each other; and this lively suggestion sent tinglings of excitement to their very finger-points; but even to his wife, mourning the commodious closet she had intended, the Earl made no explanations. For anything she knew, it might be there, next to her room, this mysterious lurking-place; and it may be supposed that this suggestion conveyed to Lady Gowrie's veins a thrill more keen and strange, perhaps too vivid to be pleasant. But she was not in the favoured or unfortunate number of those to whom the truth could be revealed.

I need not say what the different theories on the subject were. Some thought there had been a treacherous massacre there, and that the secret chamber was blocked by the skeletons of murdered guests,—a treachery no doubt covering the family with shame in its day, but so condoned by long softening of years as to have all the shame taken out of it. The Randolphs could not have felt their character affected by any such interesting historical record. They were not so morbidly sensitive. Some said, on the other hand, that Earl Robert, the wicked Earl, was shut up there in everlasting penance, playing cards with the devil for his soul. But it would have been too great a feather in the family cap to have thus got the devil, or even one of his angels, bottled up, as it were, and safely in hand, to make it possible that any lasting stigma could be connected with such a fact as this. What a thing it would be to know where to lay one's hand upon the Prince of Darkness, and prove him once for all, cloven foot and everything else, to the confusion of gainsayers!

So this was not to be received as a satisfactory solution, nor could any other be suggested which was more to the purpose. The popular mind gave it up, and yet never gave it up; and still everybody who visits Gowrie, be it as a guest, be it as a tourist, be it only as a gazer from a passing carriage, or from the flying railway train which just glimpses its turrets in the distance, daily and yearly spends a certain amount of curiosity, wonderment, and conjecture about the Secret Chamber—the most piquant and undiscoverable wonder which has endured unguessed and undeciphered to modern times.

This was how the matter stood when young John Randolph, Lord Lindores, came of age. He was a young man of great character and energy, not like the usual Randolph strain—for, as we have said, the type of character common in this romantically-situated family, notwithstanding the erratic incidents common to them, was that of dullness and honesty, especially in their early days. But young Lindores was not so. He was honest and honourable, but not dull. He had gone through almost a remarkable course at school and at the university—not perhaps in quite the ordinary way of scholarship, but enough to attract men's eyes to him. He had made more than one great speech at the Union. He was full of ambition, and force, and life, intending all sorts of great things, and meaning to make his position a stepping-stone to all that was excellent in public life. Not for him the country-gentleman existence which was congenial to his father. The idea of succeeding to the family honours and becoming a Scotch peer, either represented or representative, filled him with horror; and filial piety in his case was made warm by all the energy of personal hopes when he prayed that his father might live, if not for ever, yet longer than any Lord Gowrie had lived for the last century or two. He was as sure of his election for the county the next time there was a chance, as anybody can be certain of anything; and in the meantime he meant to travel, to go to America, to go no-one could tell where, seeking for instruction and experience, as is the manner of high-spirited young men with parliamentary tendencies in the present day. In former times he would have gone 'to the wars in the Hie Germanie,' or on a crusade to the Holy Land; but the days of the crusaders and of the soldiers of fortune being over, Lindores followed the fashion of his time. He had made all his arrangements for his tour, which his father did not oppose. On the contrary, Lord Gowrie encouraged all those plans, though with an air of melancholy indulgence which his son could not understand. 'It will do you good,' he said, with a sigh. 'Yes, yes, my boy; the best thing for you.' This, no doubt, was true enough; but there was an implied feeling that the young man would require something to do him good—that he would want the soothing of change and the gratification of his wishes, as one might speak of a convalescent or the victim of some calamity. This tone puzzled Lindores, who, though he thought it a fine thing to travel and acquire information, was as scornful of the idea of being done good to as is natural to any fine young fellow fresh from Oxford and the triumphs of the Union. But he reflected that the old school had its own way of treating things, and was satisfied. All was settled accordingly for this journey, before he came home to go through the ceremonial performances of the coming of age, the dinner of the tenantry, the speeches, the congratulations, his father's banquet, his mother's ball. It was in summer, and the country was as gay as all the entertainments that were to be given in his honour. His friend who was going to accompany him on his tour, as he had accompanied him through a considerable portion of his life—Almeric Ffarrington, a young man of the same aspirations—came up to Scotland with him for these festivities. And as they rushed through their night on the Great Northern Railway, in the intervals of two naps, they had a scrap of conversation as to these birthday glories. 'It will be a bore, but it will not last long,' said Lindores. They were both of the opinion that anything that did not produce information or promote culture was a bore.

'But is there not a revelation to be made to you, among all the other things you have to go through?' said Ffarrington. 'Have not you to be introduced to the secret chamber, and all that sort of thing? I should like to be of the party there, Lindores.'

'Ah,' said the heir, 'I had forgotten that part of it,' which, however, was not the case. 'Indeed I don't know if I am to be told. Even family dogmas are shaken nowadays.'

'Oh, I should insist on that,' said Ffarrington, lightly. 'It is not many who have the chance of paying such a visit—better than Home and all the mediums. I should insist upon that.'

'I have no reason to suppose that it has any connection with Home or the mediums,' said Lindores, slightly nettled. He was himself an *esprit fort*; but a mystery in one's own family is not like vulgar mysteries. He liked it to be respected.

'Oh, no offence,' said his companion. 'I have always thought that a railway train would be a great chance for the spirits. If one was to show suddenly in that vacant seat beside you, what a triumphant proof of their existence that would be! but they don't take advantage of their opportunities.'

Lindores could not tell what it was that made him think at that moment of a portrait he had seen in a back room at the castle of old

Earl Robert, the wicked Earl. It was a bad portrait—a daub—a copy made by an amateur of the genuine portrait, which, out of horror of Earl Robert and his wicked ways, had been removed by some intermediate lord from its place in the gallery. Lindores had never seen the original—nothing but this daub of a copy. Yet somehow this face occurred to him by some strange link of association—seemed to come into his eyes as his friend spoke. A slight shiver ran over him. It was strange. He made no reply to Ffarrington, but he set himself to think how it could be that the latent presence in his mind of some anticipation of this approaching disclosure, touched into life by his friend's suggestion, should have called out of his memory a momentary realisation of the acknowledged magician of the family. This sentence is full of long words; but unfortunately long words are required in such a case. And the process was very simple when you traced it out. It was the clearest case of unconscious cerebration. He shut his eyes by way of securing privacy while he thought it out; and being tired, and not at all alarmed by his unconscious cerebration, before he opened them again fell fast asleep.

And his birthday, which was the day following his arrival at Glenlyon, was a very busy day. He had not time to think of anything but the immediate occupations of the moment. Public and private greetings, congratulations, offerings, poured upon him. The Gowries were popular in this generation, which was far from being usual in the family. Lady Gowrie was kind and generous, with that kindness which comes from the heart, and which is the only kindness likely to impress the keen-sighted popular judgment; and Lord Gowrie had but little of the equivocal reputation of his predecessors. They could be splendid now and then on great occasions, though in general they were homely enough; all which the public likes. It was a bore, Lindores said; but yet the young man did not dislike the honours, and the adulation, and all the hearty speeches and good wishes. It is sweet to a young man to feel himself the centre of all hopes. It seemed very reasonable to him—very natural—that he should be so, and that the farmers should feel a pride of anticipation in thinking of his future speeches in Parliament. He promised to them with the sincerest good faith that he would not disappoint their expectations—that he would feel their interest in him an additional spur. What was so natural as that interest and these expectations? He was almost solemnised by his own position—so young, looked up to by so many people—so many hopes depending on him; and yet it was quite natural. His father, however, was still more solemnised that Lindores—and this was strange, to say the least. His face grew graver and graver as the day went on, till it almost seemed as if he were dissatisfied with his son's popularity, or had some painful thought weighing on his mind. He was restless and eager for the termination of the dinner, and to get rid of his guests; and as soon as they were gone, showed an equal anxiety that his son should retire too. 'Go to bed at once, as a favour to me.' Lord Gowrie said. 'You will have a great deal of fatigue—to-morrow.' 'You need not be afraid for me, sir,' said Lindores, half affronted; but he obeyed, being tired. He had not once thought of the secret to be disclosed to him, through all that long day. But when he woke suddenly with a start in the middle of the night, to find the candles all lighted in his room, and his father standing by his bedside, Lindores instantly thought of it, and in a moment felt that the leading event—the chief incident of all that had happened—was going to take place now.

II

Lord Gowrie was very grave, and very pale. He was standing with his hand on his son's shoulder to wake him; his dress was unchanged from the moment they had parted. And the sight of this formal costume was very bewildering to the young man as he started up in his bed. But next moment he seemed to know exactly how it was, and, more than that, to have known it all his life. Explanation seemed unnecessary. At any other moment, in any other place, a man would be startled to be suddenly woke up in the middle of the night. But Lindores had no such feeling: he did not even ask a question, but sprang up, and fixed his eyes, taking in all the strange circumstances, on his father's face.

'Get up, my boy,' said Lord Gowrie, 'and dress as quickly as you can; it is full time. I have lighted your candles, and your things are all ready. You have had a good long sleep.'

Even now he did not ask, What is it? as under any other circumstances he would have done. He got up without a word, with an impulse of nervous speed and rapidity of movement such as only excitement can give, and dressed himself, his father helping him silently. It was a curious scene: the room gleaming with lights, the silence, the hurried toilet, the stillness of deep night all around. The house, though so full, and with the echoes of festivity but just over, was quiet as if there was not a creature within it—more quiet, indeed, for the stillness of vacancy is not half so impressive as the stillness of hushed and slumbering life.

Lord Gowrie went to the table when this first step was over, and poured out a glass of wine from a bottle which stood there,—a rich, golden-coloured, perfumy wine, which sent its scent through the room. 'You will want all your strength,' he said; 'take this before you go. It is the famous Imperial Tokay; there is only a little left, and you will want all your strength.'

Lindores took the wine; he had never drunk any like it before, and the peculiar fragrance remained in his mind, as perfumes so often do, with a whole world of association in them. His father's eyes dwelt upon him with a melancholy sympathy. 'You are going to encounter the greatest trial of your life,' he said; and taking the young man's hand into his, felt his pulse. 'It is quick, but it is quite firm, and you have had a good long sleep.' Then he did what it needs a great deal of pressure to induce an Englishman to do,—he kissed his son on the cheek. 'God bless you!' he said, faltering, 'Come, now, everything is ready, Lindores.'

He took up in his hand a small lamp, which he had apparently brought with him, and led the way. By this time Lindores began to feel himself again, and to wake to the consciousness of all his own superiorities and enlightenments. The simple sense that he was one of the members of a family with a mystery, and that the moment of his personal encounter with this special power of darkness had come, had been the first thrilling, overwhelming thought. But now as he followed his father, Lindores began to remember that he himself was not altogether like other men; that there was that in him which would make it natural that he should throw some light, hitherto unthought of, upon this carefully-preserved darkness. What secret even there might be in it—secret of hereditary tendency, of psychic force, of mental conformation, or of some curious combination of circumstances at once more and less potent than these—it was for him to find out. He gathered all his forces about him, reminded himself of modern enlightenment, and bade his nerves be steel to all vulgar horrors. He, too, felt his own pulse as he followed his father. To spend the night perhaps amongst the skeletons of that old-world massacre, and to repent the sins of his ancestors—to be brought within the range of some optical illusion believed in hitherto by all the generations, and

which, no doubt, was of a startling kind, or his father would not look
so serious,—any of these he felt himself quite strong to encounter. His
heart and spirit rose. A young man has but seldom the opportunity
of distinguishing himself so early in his career; and his was such a
chance as occurs to very few. No doubt it was something that would
be extremely trying to the nerves and imagination. He called up all
his powers to vanquish both. And along with this call upon himself
to exertion, there was the less serious impulse of curiosity: he would
see at last what the Secret Chamber was, where it was, how it fitted
into the labyrinths of the old house. This he tried to put in its due
place as a moment interesting object. He said to himself that he would
willingly have gone a long journey at any time to be present at such
an exploration; and there is no doubt that in other circumstances a
secret chamber, with probably some unthought-of historical interest in
it, would have been a very fascinating discovery. He tried very hard to
excite himself about this; but it was curious how fictitious he felt the
interest, and how conscious he was that it was an effort to feel any
curiosity at all on the subject. The fact was, that the Secret Chamber
was entirely secondary—thrown back, as all accessories are, by a more
pressing interest. The overpowering thought of what was in it drove
aside all healthy, natural curiosity about itself.

It must not be supposed, however, that the father and son had a
long way to go to have time for all these thoughts. Thoughts travel
at lightning speed, and there was abundant leisure for this between
the time they had left the door of Lindores' room and gone down the
corridor, no further off than to Lord Gowrie's own chamber, naturally
one of the chief rooms of the house. Nearly opposite this, a few steps
further on, was a little neglected room devoted to lumber, with which
Lindores had been familiar all his life. Why this nest of old rubbish,
dust, and cob-webs should be so near the bedroom of the head of the
house had been a matter of surprise to many people—to the guests
who saw it while exploring, and to each new servant in succession
who planned an attack upon its ancient stores, scandalised by finding
it to have been neglected by their predecessors. All their attempts to
clear it out had, however, been resisted, nobody could tell how, or
indeed thought it worth while to inquire. As for Lindores, he had
been used to the place from his childhood, and therefore accepted
it as the most natural thing in the world. He had been in and
out a hundred times in his play. And it was here, he remembered

suddenly, that he had seen the bad picture of Earl Robert which had so curiously come into his eyes on his journeying here, by a mental movement which he had identified at once as unconscious cerebration. The first feeling in his mind, as his father went to the open door of this lumber-room, was a mixture of amusement and surprise. What was he going to pick up there? some old pentacle, some amulet or scrap of antiquated magic to act as armour against the evil one? But Lord Gowrie, going on and setting down the lamp on the table, turned round upon his son with a face of agitation and pain which barred all further amusement: he grasped him by the hand, crushing it between his own. 'Now my boy, my dear son,' he said, in tones that were scarcely audible. His countenance was full of the dreary pain of a looker-on—one who has no share in the excitement of personal danger, but has the more terrible part of watching those who are in deadliest peril. He was a powerful man, and his large form shook with emotion; great beads of moisture stood upon his forehead. An old sword with a cross handle lay upon a dusty chair among other dusty and battered relics. 'Take this with you,' he said, in the same inaudible, breathless way—whether as a weapon, whether as a religious symbol, Lindores could not guess. The young man took it mechanically. His father pushed open a door which it seemed to him he had never seen before, and led him into another vaulted chamber. Here even the limited powers of speech Lord Gowrie had retained seemed to forsake him, and his voice became a mere hoarse murmur in his throat. For want of speech he pointed to another door in the further corner of this small vacant room, gave him to understand by a gesture that he was to knock there, and then went back into the lumber-room. The door into this was left open, and a faint glimmer of the lamp shed light into this little intermediate place—this debatable land between the seen and the unseen. In spite of himself, Lindores' heart began to beat. He made a breathless pause, feeling his head go round. He held the old sword in his hand, not knowing what it was. Then, summoning all his courage, he went forward and knocked at the closed door. His knock was not loud, but it seemed to echo all over the silent house. Would everybody hear and wake, and rush to see what had happened? This caprice of imagination seized upon him, ousting all the firmer thoughts, the steadfast calm of mind with which he ought to have encountered the mystery. Would they all rush in, in wild *déshabille*, in terror and dismay, before the door opened?

How long it was of opening! He touched the panel with his hand
again.—This time there was no delay. In a moment, as if thrown
suddenly open by someone within, the door moved. It opened just
wide enough to let him enter, stopping half-way as if someone
invisible held it, wide enough for welcome, but no more. Lindores
stepped across the threshold with a beating heart. What was he about
to see? the skeletons of the murdered victims? a ghostly charnel-house
full of bloody traces of crime? He seemed to be hurried and pushed in
as he made that step. What was this world of mystery into which he
was plunged—what was it he saw?

He saw—nothing—except what was agreeable enough to behold,—
an antiquated room hung with tapestry, very old tapestry of rude
design, its colours faded into softness and harmony; between its folds
here and there a panel of carved wood, rude too in design, with
traces of half-worn gilding: a table covered with strange instruments,
parchments, chemical tubes, and curious machinery, all with a
quaintness of form and dimness of material that spoke of age. A
heavy old velvet cover, thick with embroidery faded almost out of
all colour, was on the table; on the wall above it, something that
looked like a very old Venetian mirror, the glass so dim and crusted
that it scarcely reflected at all; on the floor an old soft Persian
carpet, worn into a vague blending of all colours. This was all that
he thought he saw. His heart, which had been thumping so loud as
almost to choke him, stopped that tremendous upward and downward
motion like a steam piston; and he grew calm. Perfectly still, dim,
unoccupied: yet not so dim either; there was no apparent source of
light, no windows, curtains of tapestry drawn everywhere—no lamp
visible, no fire—and yet a kind of strange light which made everything
quite clear. He looked round, trying to smile at his terrors, trying
to say to himself that it was the most curious place he had ever
seen—that he must show Ffarrington some of that tapestry—that he
must really bring away a panel of that carving,—when he suddenly
saw that the door was shut by which he had entered—nay, more
than shut, undiscernible, covered like all the rest of the walls by
that strange tapestry. At this his heart began to beat again in
spite of him. He looked round once more, and woke up to more
vivid being with a sudden start. Had his eyes been incapable of
vision on his first entrance? Unoccupied? Who was that in the
great chair?

It seemed to Lindores that he had seen neither the chair nor the man when he came in. There they were, however, solid and unmistakable; the chair carved like the panels, the man seated in front of the table. He looked at Lindores with a calm and open gaze, inspecting him. The young man's heart seemed in his throat fluttering like a bird, but he was brave, and his mind made one final effort to break this spell. He tried to speak, labouring with a voice that would not sound, and with lips too parched to form a word. 'I see how it is,' was what he wanted to say. It was Earl Robert's face that was looking at him; and startled as he was, he dragged forth his philosophy to support him. What could it be but optical delusions, unconscious cerebration, occult seizure by the impressed and struggling mind of this one countenance? But he could not hear himself speak any word as he stood convulsed, struggling with dry lips and choking voice.

The Appearance smiled, as if knowing his thoughts—not unkindly, not malignly—with a certain amusement mingled with scorn. Then he spoke, and the sound seemed to breathe through the room not like any voice that Lindores had ever heard, a kind ot utterance of the place, like the rustle of the air or the ripple of the sea. 'You will learn better tonight: this is no phantom of your brain; it is I.'

'In God's name,' cried the young man in his soul; he did not know whether the words ever got into the air or not, if there was any air;—'in God's name, who are you?'

The figure rose as if coming to him to reply; and Lindores, overcome by the apparent approach, struggled into utterance. A cry came from him—he heard it this time—and even in his extremity felt a pang the more to hear the terror in his own voice. But he did not flinch, he stood desperate, all his strength concentrated in the act; he neither turned nor recoiled. Vaguely gleaming through his mind came the thought that to be thus brought in contact with the unseen was the experiment to be most desired on earth, the final settlement of a hundred questions; but his faculties were not sufficiently under command to entertain it. He only stood firm, that was all.

And the figure did not approach him; after a moment it subsided back again into the chair—subsided, for no sound, not the faintest, accompanied its movements. It was the form of a man of middle age, the hair white, but the beard only crisped with grey, the features those of the picture—a familiar face, more or less like all the Randolphs, but with an air of domination and power altogether unlike that of

the race. He was dressed in a long robe of dark colour, embroidered
with strange lines and angles. There was nothing repellent or terrible
in his air—nothing except the noiselessness, the calm, the absolute
stillness, which was as much in the place as in him, to keep up
the involuntary trembling of the beholder. His expression was full
of dignity and thoughtfulness, and not malignant or unkind. He
might have been the kindly patriarch of the house, watching over
its fortunes in a seclusion that he had chosen. The pulses that had
been beating in Lindores were stilled. What was his panic for? a
gleam even of self-ridicule took possession of him, to be standing
there like an absurd hero of antiquated romance with the rusty, dusty
sword—good for nothing, surely not adapted for use against this noble
old magician—in his hand—

'You are right,' said the voice, once more answering his thoughts;
'what could you do with that sword against me, young Lindores? Put
it by. Why should my children meet me like an enemy? You are my
flesh and blood. Give me your hand.'

A shiver ran through the young man's frame. The hand that was
held out to him was large and shapely and white, with a straight line
across the palm—a family token upon which the Randolphs prided
themselves—a friendly hand; and the face smiled upon him, fixing
him with those calm, profound, blue eyes. 'Come,' said the voice.
The word seemed to fill the place, melting upon him from every
corner, whispering round him with softest persuasion. He was lulled
and calmed in spite of himself. Spirit or no spirit, why should not
he accept this proferred courtesy? What harm could come of it? The
chief thing that retained him was the dragging of the old sword, heavy
and useless, which he held mechanically, but which some internal
feeling—he could not tell what—prevented him from putting down.
Superstition, was it?

'Yes, that is superstition,' said his ancestor, serenely, 'put it down
and come?'

'You know my thoughts,' said Lindores; 'I did not speak.'

'Your mind spoke, and spoke justly. Put down that emblem of
brute force and superstition together. Here it is the intelligence that
is supreme. Come.'

Lindores stood doubtful. He was calm; the power of thought was
restored to him. If this benevolent venerable patriarch was all he
seemed, why his father's terror? why the secrecy in which his being

was involved? His own mind, though calm, did not seem to act in the usual way. Thoughts seemed to be driven across it as by a wind. One of these came to him suddenly now—

> 'How there looked him in the face,
> An angel beautiful and bright,
> And how he knew it was a fiend.'

The words were not ended, when Earl Robert replied suddenly with impatience in his voice, 'Fiends are of the fancy of men; like angels and other follies. I am your father. You know me; and you are mine, Lindores. I have power beyond what you can understand; but I want flesh and blood to reign and to enjoy. Come, Lindores!'

He put out his other hand. The action, the look, were those of kindness, almost of longing, and the face was familiar, the voice was that of the race. Supernatural! was it supernatural that this man should live here shut up for ages? and why? and how? Was there any explanation of it? The young man's brain began to reel. He could not tell which was real—the life he had left half and hour ago, or this. He tried to look round him, but could not; his eyes were caught by those other kindred eyes, which seemed to dilate and deepen as he looked at them, and drew him with a strange compulsion. He felt himself yielding, swaying towards the strange being who thus invited him What might happen if he yielded? And he could not turn away, he could not tear himself from the fascination of those eyes. With a sudden strange impulse which was half despair and half a bewildering half-conscious desire to try one potency against another, he thrust forward the cross of the old sword between him and those appealing hands. 'In the name of God!' he said.

Lindores never could tell whether it was that he himself grew faint, and that the dimness of swooning came into his eyes after this violence and strange of emotion, or if it was his spell that worked. But there was an instantaneous change. Everything swam around him for the moment, a giddiness and blindness seized him, and he saw nothing but the vague outlines of the room, empty as when he entered it. But gradually his consciousness came back, and he found himself standing on the same spot as before, clutching the old sword, and gradually, as though a dream, recognised the same figure emerging out of the mist which—was it solely in his own eyes?—had enveloped everything. But it was no longer in the same attitude. The hands which had been stretched out to him were busy now with some of the strange instruments on the table, moving about, now in the action of writing, now as if managing the keys of a telegraph. Lindores felt that his brain was all atwist and set wrong; but he was still a human being of this century. He thought of the telegraph with a keen thrill of curiosity in the midst of his reviving sensations. What communication was this which was going on before his eyes? The magician worked on. He had his face turned towards his victim, but his hands moved with unceasing activity. And Lindores, as he grew accustomed to the position, began to weary—to feel like a neglected suitor waiting for an audience. To be wound up to such a strain of feeling, then left to wait, was intolerable; impatience seized upon him. What circumstances can exist, however horrible, in which a human being will not feel impatience? He made a great many efforts to speak before he could succeed. It seemed to him that his body felt more fear than he did—that his muscles were contracted, his throat parched, his tongue refusing its office, although his mind was unaffected and undismayed. At last he found an utterance in spite of all resistance of his flesh and blood.

'Who are you?' he said hoarsely. 'You that live here and oppress this house?'

The vision raised its eyes full upon him, with again that strange shadow of a smile, mocking yet not unkind. 'Do you remember me,' he said, 'on your journey here?'

'That was—a delusion.' The young man gasped for breath.

'More like that you are a delusion. You have lasted but one-and-twenty years, and I—for centuries.'

'How? For centuries—and why? Answer me—are you man or demon?' cried Lindores, tearing the words as he felt out of his own throat. 'Are you living or dead?'

The magician looked at him with the same intense gaze as before. 'Be on my side, and you shall know everything, Lindores. I want one of my own race. Others I could have in plenty; but I want *you*. A Randolph, a Randolph! and *you*. Dead! do I seem dead? You shall have everything—more than dreams can give—if you will be on my side.'

Can he give what he has not? was the thought that ran through the mind of Lindores. But he could not speak it. Something that choked and stifled him was in his throat.

'Can I give what I have not? I have everything—power, the one thing worth having; and you shall have more than power, for you are young—my son! Lindores!'

To argue was natural, and gave the young man strength. 'Is this life,' he said, 'here? What is all your power worth—here? To sit for ages, and make a race unhappy?'

A momentary convulsion came across the still face. 'You scorn me', he cried, with an appearance of emotion, 'because you do not understand how I move the world. Power! 'Tis more than fancy can grasp. And you shall have it!' said the wizard, with what looked like a show of enthusiasm. He seemed to come nearer, to grow larger. He put forth his hand again, this time so close that it seemed impossible to escape. And a crowd of wishes seemed to rush upon the mind of Lindores. What harm to try if this might be true? To try what it meant—perhaps nothing, delusions, vain show, and then there could be no harm; or perhaps there was knowledge to be had, which was power. Try, try, try! the air buzzed about him. The room seemed full of voices urging him. His bodily frame rose into a tremendous whirl of excitement, his veins seemed to swell to bursting, his lips seemed to force a yes, in spite of him, quivering as they came apart. The hiss of the s seemed in his ears. He changed it into the name which was a spell too, and cried, 'Help me, God!' not knowing why.

Then there came another pause—he felt as if he had been dropped from something that had held him, and had fallen, and was faint. The excitement had been more than he could bear. Once more everything swam around him, and he did not know where he was. Had he escaped altogether? was the first waking wonder of consciousness in his mind. But when he could think and see again, he was still in the same spot, surrounded by the old curtains and the carved panels—but alone. He felt, too, that he was able to move, but the strangest dual consciousness was in him throughout all the rest of his trial. His body felt to him as a frightened horse feels to a traveller at night—a thing separate from him, more frightened than he was—starting aside at every step, seeing more than its master. His limbs shook with fear and weakness, almost refusing to obey the action of his will, trembling under him with jerks aside when he compelled himself to move. The hair stood upright on his head—every finger trembled as with palsy—his lips, his eyelids, quivered with nervous agitation. But his mind was strong, stimulated to a desperate calm. He dragged himself round the room, he crossed the very spot where the magician had been—all was vacant, silent, clear. Had he vanquished the enemy? This thought came into his mind with an involuntary triumph. The old strain of feeling came back. Such efforts might be produced, perhaps, only by imagination, by excitement, by delusion—

Lindores looked up, by a sudden attraction he could not tell what: and the blood suddenly froze in his veins that had been so boiling and fermenting. Some one was looking at him from the old mirror on the wall. A face not human and life-like, like that of the inhabitant of this place, but ghostly and terrible, like one of the dead; and while he looked, a crowd of other faces came behind, all looking at him, some mournfully, some with a menace in their terrible eyes. The mirror did not change, but within its small dim space seemed to contain an innumerable company, crowded above and below, all with one gaze at him. His lips dropped apart with a gasp of horror. More and more and more! He was standing close by the table when this crowd came. Then all at once there was laid upon him a cold hand. He turned; close to his side, brushing him with his robe, holding him fast by the arm, sat Earl Robert in his great chair. A shriek came from the young man's lips. He seemed to hear it echoing away into unfathomable distance. The cold touch penetrated to his very soul.

'Do you try spells upon me, Lindores? That is a tool of the past. You shall have something better to work with. And are you so sure of whom you call upon? If there is such a one, why should He help you who never called on Him before?'

Lindores could not tell if these words were spoken; it was a communication rapid as the thoughts in his mind. And he felt as if something answered that was not all himself. He seemed to stand passive and hear the argument. 'Does God reckon with a man in trouble, whether he has ever called to Him before? I call now' (now he felt it was himself that said): 'go evil spirit!—go, dead and cursed!—go, in the name of God!'

He felt himself flung violently against the wall. A faint laugh, stifled in the throat, and followed by a groan, rolled round the room; the old curtains seemed to open here and there, and flutter, as if with comings and goings. Lindores leaned with his back against the wall, and all his senses restored to him. He felt blood trickle down his neck; and in this contact once more with the physical, his body, in its madness of fright, grew manageable. For the first time he felt wholly master of himself. Though the magician was standing in his place, a great, majestic, appalling figure, he did not shrink. 'Liar!' he cried, in a voice that rang and echoed as in natural air—'clinging to miserable life like a worm—like a reptile; promising all things, having nothing, but this den, unvisited by the light of day. Is this your power—your superiority to men who die? is it for this that you oppress a race, and make a house unhappy? I vow, in God's name, your reign is over! You and your secret shall last no more.'

There was no reply. But Lindores felt his terrible ancestor's eyes getting once more that mesmeric mastery over him which had already almost overcome his powers. He must withdraw his own, or perish. He had a human horror of turning his back upon that watchful adversary: to face him seemed the only safety; but to face him was to be conquered. Slowly, with a pang indescribable, he tore himself from that gaze: it seemed to drag his eyes out of their sockets, his heart out of his bosom. Resolutely, with the daring of desperation, he turned round to the spot where he entered—the spot where no door was,—hearing already in anticipation the step after him—feeling the grip that would crush and smother his exhausted life—but too desperate to care.

III

How wonderful is the blue dawning of the new day before the sun! not rosy-fingered, like that Aurora of the Greeks who comes later with all her wealth; but still, dreamy, wonderful, stealing out of the unseen, abashed by the solemnity of the new birth. When anxious watchers see that first brightness come stealing upon the waiting skies, what mingled relief and renewal of misery is in it! another long day to toil through—yet another sad night over! Lord Gowrie sat among the dust and cobwebs, his lamp flaring idly into the blue morning. He had heard his son's human voice, though nothing more; and he expected to have him brought out by invisible hands, as had happened to himself, and left lying in long deathly swoon outside that mystic door. This was how it had happend to heir after heir, as told from father to son, one after another, as the secret came down. One or two bearers of the name Lindores, had never recovered; most of them had been saddened and subdued for life. He remembered sadly the freshness of existence which had never come back to himself; the hopes that had never blossomed again; the assurance with which never more he had been able to go about the world. And now his son would be as himself—the glory gone out of his living—his ambitions, his aspirations wrecked. He had not been endowed as his boy was—he had been a plain, honest man, and nothing more; but experience and life had given him wisdom enough to smile by times at the coquetries of mind in which Lindores indulged. Were they all over now, those freaks of young intelligence, those enthusiasms of the soul? The curse of the house had come upon him—the magnetism of that strange presence, ever living, ever watchful, present in all the family history. His heart was sore for his son; and yet along with this there was a certain consolation to him in having henceforward a partner in the secret—someone to whom he could talk of it as he had not been able to talk since his own father died. Almost all the mental struggles which Gowrie had known had been connected with this mystery; and he had been obliged to hide them in his bosom—to conceal them even when they rent him in two. Now he had a partner in his trouble. This was what he was thinking as he sat through the night. How slowly the moments passed! He was not aware of the daylight coming in. After a while even thought got suspended in listening. Was not the time nearly over? He rose and began to pace about the encumbered space, which was but a step or two in extent. There was an old cupboard in the wall, in which there were restoratives—pungent essences and cordials, and fresh water which he had himself brought—everything was ready; presently the ghastly body of his boy, half dead, would be thrust forth into his care.

But this was not how it happened. While he waited, so intent that his whole frame seemed to be capable of hearing, he heard the closing of the door, boldly shut with a sound that rose in muffled echoes through the house and Lindores himself appeared, ghastly indeed as a dead man, but walking upright and firmly, the lines of his face drawn, and his eyes staring. Lord Gowrie uttered a cry. He was more alarmed by this unexpected return than by the helpless prostration of the swoon which he had expected. He recoiled from his son as if he too had been a spirit. 'Lindores!' he cried; was it Lindores, or someone else in his place? The boy seemed as if he did not see him. He went straight forward to where the water stood on the dusty table, and took a great draught, then turned to the door. 'Lindores!' said his father, in a miserable anxiety; 'don't you know me?' Even then the young man only half looked at him, and put out a hand almost as cold as the hand that had clutched himself in the Secret Chamber; a faint smile came upon his face. 'Don't stay here,' he whispered; 'come! come!'

Lord Gowrie drew his son's arm within his own, and felt the thrill through and through him of nerves strained beyond mortal strength. He could scarcely keep up with him as he stalked along the corridor to his room, stumbling as if he could not see, yet swift as an arrow. When they reached his room he turned and closed and locked the door, then laughed as he staggered to the bed. 'That will not keep him out, will it?' he said.

'Lindores,' said his father, 'I expected to find you unconscious. I am almost more frightened to find you like this. I need not ask if you have seen him—'

'Oh, I have seen him. The old liar! Father, promise to expose him, to turn him out—promise to clear out that accursed old nest! It is our own fault. Why have we left such a place shut out from the eye of day? Isn't there something in the Bible about those who do evil hating the light?'

'Lindores! you don't often quote the Bible.'

'No, I suppose not; but there is more truth in—many things than we thought.'

'Lie down,' said the anxious father. 'Take some of this wine—try to sleep.'

'Take it away; give me no more of that devil's drink. Talk to me—that's better. Did you go through it all the same, poor papa?—and hold me fast. You are warm—you are honest!' he cried. He put forth his hands over his father's, warming them with the contact. He put his cheek like a child against his father's arm. He gave a faint laugh, with the tears in his eyes. 'Warm and honest,' he repeated. 'Kind flesh and blood! and did you go through it all the same?'

'My boy!' cried the father, feeling his heart glow and swell over the son who had been parted from him for years by that development of young manhood and ripening intellect which so often severs and loosens the ties of home. Lord Gowrie had felt that Lindores half despised his simple mind and duller imagination; but this childlike clinging overcame him, and tears stood in his eyes. 'I fainted, I suppose. I never knew how it ended. They made what they liked of me. But you, my brave boy, you came out of your own will.'

Lindores shivered. 'I fled!' he said. 'No honour in that. I had not courage to face him longer. I will tell you by-and-by. But I want to know about you.'

What an ease it was to the father to speak! For years and years this had been shut up in his breast. It had made him lonely in the midst of his friends.

'Thank God,' he said, 'that I can speak to you, Lindores. Often and often I have been tempted to tell your mother. But why should I make her miserable? She knows there is something; she knows when I see him, but she knows no more.'

'When you see him?' Lindores raised himself, with a return of his first ghastly look, in his bed. Then he raised his clenched fist wildly, and shook it in the air. 'Vile devil, coward, deceiver!'

'Oh hush, hush, hush, Lindores! God help us! what troubles you may bring!'

'And God help me, whatever troubles I bring,' said the young man. 'I defy him, father. An accursed being like that must be less, not more powerful, than we are—with God to back us. Only stand by me: stand by me—'

'Hush, Lindores! You don't feel it yet—never to get out of hearing of him all your life! He will make you pay for it—if not now, after; when you remember he is there; whatever happens, knowing everything! But I hope it will not be so bad with you as with me, my poor boy. God help you indeed if it is, for you have more imagination and more mind. I am able to forget him sometimes when I am occupied—when in the hunting-field, going across country. But you are not a hunting man, my poor boy,' said Lord Gowrie, with a curious mixture of a regret, which was less serious than the other. Then he lowered his voice. 'Lindores, this is what has happened to me since the moment I gave him my hand.'

'I did not give him my hand.'

'You did not give him your hand? God bless you, my boy! You stood out?' he cried, with tears again rushing to his eyes, 'and they say—they say—but I don't know if there is any truth in it.' Lord Gowrie got up from his son's side, and walked up and down with excited steps. 'If there should be truth in it! Many people think the whole thing is a fancy. If there should be truth in it, Lindores!'

'In what, father?'

'They say, if he is once resisted his power is broken—once refused. *You* could stand against him—you! Forgive me, my boy, as I hope God will forgive me, to have thought so little of His best gifts,' cried Lord Gowrie, coming back with wet eyes; and stooping, he kissed his son's hand. 'I thought you would be more shaken by being more mind than body,' he said, humbly. 'I thought if I could but have saved you from the trial; and *you* are the conqueror!'

'Am I the conqueror? I think all my bones are broken, father—out of their sockets,' said the young man, in a low voice. 'I think I shall go to sleep.'

'Yes, rest, my boy. It is the best thing for you,' said the father, though with a pang of momentary disappointment. Lindores fell back upon the pillow. He was so pale that there were moments when the anxious watcher thought him not sleeping but dead. He put his hand out feebly, and grasped his father's hand. 'Warm— honest,' he said, with a feeble smile about his lips, and fell asleep.

The daylight was full in the room, breaking through shutters and curtains and mocking at the lamp that still flared on the table. It seemed an emblem of the disorders, mental and material, of this strange night; and, as such, it affected the plain imagination of Lord Gowrie, who would have fain got up to extinguish it, and whose mind returned again and again, in spite of him, to this symptom of disturbance. By-and-by, when Lindores' grasp relaxed, and he got his hand free, he got up from his son's bedside, and put out the lamp, putting it carefully out of the way. With equal care he put away the wine from the table, and gave the room its ordinary aspect, softly opening a window to let in the fresh air of the morning. The park lay fresh in the early sunshine, still, except for the twittering of the birds, refreshed with dews, and shining in that soft radiance of the morning which is over before mortal cares are stirring. Never, perhaps, had Gowrie looked out upon the beautiful world around his house without a thought of the weird existence which was going on so near to him, which had gone on for centuries, shut up out of sight of the sunshine. The Secret Chamber had been present with him since ever he saw it. He had never been able to get free of the spell of it. He had felt himself watched, surrounded, spied upon, day after day, since he was of the age of Lindores, and that was thirty years ago. He turned it all over in his mind, as he stood there and his son slept. It had been on his lips to tell it all to his boy, who had now come to inherit the enlightenment of his race. And it was a disappointment to him to have it all forced back again, and silence imposed upon him once more. Would he care to hear it when he woke? would he not rather, as Lord Gowrie remembered to have done himself, thrust the thought as far as he could away from him, and endeavour to forget for the moment—until the time came when he would not be permitted to forget? He had been like that himself, he recollected now. He had not wished to hear his own father's tale. 'I remember,' he said to himself; 'I remember'—turning over everything in his mind—if Lindores might only be willing to hear the story when he woke! But then he himself had not been willing when he was Lindores, and he could understand his son, and could not blame him; but it would be a disappointment. He was thinking this when he heard Lindores' voice calling him. He went back hastily to his bedside. It was strange to see him in his evening dress with his worn face, in the fresh light of the morning, which poured in at every crevice. 'Does my mother know?' said Lindores; 'what will she think?'

'She knows something; she knows you have some trial to go through. Most likely she will be praying for us both; that's the way of women,' said Lord Gowrie, with the tremulous tenderness which comes into a man's voice sometimes when he speaks of a good wife. 'I'll go and ease her mind, and tell her all is well over—'

'Not yet. Tell me first,' said the young man, putting his hand upon his father's arm.

What an ease it was! 'I was not so good to my father,' he thought to himself, with sudden penitence for the long-past, long-forgotten fault, which, indeed, he had never realised as a fault before. And then he told his son what had been the story of his life—how he had scarcely ever sat alone without feeling, from some corner of the room, from behind some curtain, those eyes upon him; and how, in the difficulties of his life, that secret inhabitant of the house had been present, sitting by him and advising him. 'Whenever there has been anything to do; when there has been a question between two ways, all in a moment I have seen him by me: I feel when he is coming. It does not matter where I am—here or anywhere—as soon as ever there is a question of family business; and always he persuades me to the wrong way, Lindores. Sometimes I yield to him, how can I help it? He makes everything so clear; he makes wrong seem right. If I have done unjust things in my day—'

'You have not, father.'

'I have: there were these Highland people I turned out. I did not mean to do it, Lindores; but he showed me that it would be better for the family. And my poor sister that married Tweedside and was wretched all her life. It was his doing, that marriage; he said she would be rich, and so she was, poor thing, poor thing! and died of it. And old Macalister's lease—Lindores, Lindores! when there is any business it makes my heart sick. I know he will come, and advise wrong, and tell me—something I will repent after.'

'The thing to do is to decide beforehand, that, good or bad, you will not take his advice.'

Lord Gowrie shivered. 'I am not strong like you, or clever; I cannot resist. Sometimes I repent in time and don't do it; and then! But for your mother and you children, there is many a day I would not have given a farthing for my life.'

'Father,' said Lindores, springing from his bed, 'two of us together can do many things. Give me your word to clear out this cursed den of darkness this very day.'

'Lindores, hush, hush, for the sake of heaven!'

'I will not, for the sake of heaven! Throw it open—let everybody who likes see it—make and end of the secret—pull down everything, curtains, walls. What do you say?—sprinkle holy water? Are you laughing at me?'

'I did not speak,' said Earl Gowrie, growing very pale, and grasping his son's arm with both his hands. 'Hush, boy; do you think he does not hear?'

And then there was a low laugh close to them—so close that both shrank; a laugh no louder than a breath.

'Did you laugh—father?'

'No, Lindores.' Lord Gowrie had his eyes fixed. He was as pale as the dead. He held his son tight for a moment; then his gaze and his grasp relaxed, and he fell back feebly in a chair.

'You see!' he said; 'whatever we do it will be the same; we are under his power.'

And then there ensued the blank pause with which baffled men confront a hopeless situation. But at that moment the first faint stirrings of the house—a window being opened, a bar undone, a movement of feet, and subdued voices—became audible in the stillness of the morning. Lord Gowrie roused himself at once. 'We must not be

found like this,' he said; 'we must not show how we have spent the
night. It is over, thank God! and oh, my boy, forgive me! I am thankful
there are two of us to bear it; it makes the burden lighter—though I ask
your pardon humbly for saying so. I would have saved you if I could,
Lindores.'

'I don't wish to have been saved; but *I* will not bear it. I will end
it,' the young man said, with an oath out of which his emotion took
all profanity. His father said, 'Hush, hush.' With a look of terror and
pain, he left him; and yet there was a thrill of tender pride in his
mind. How brave the boy was! even after he had been *there*. Could
it be that this would all come to nothing, as every other attempt to
resist had done before?

'I suppose you know all about it now, Lindores,' said his friend
Ffarrington, after breakfast; 'luckily for us who are going over the
house. What a glorious old place it is!'

'I don't think that Lindores enjoys the glorious old place today,' said
another of the guests under his breath. 'How pale he is! He doesn't
look as if he had slept.'

'I will take you over every nook where I have ever been,' said
Lindores. He looked at his father with almost command in his eyes.
'Come with me, all of you. We shall have no more secrets here.'

'Are you mad?' said his father in his ear.

'Never mind,' cried the young man. 'Oh, trust me; I will do it with
judgment. Is everybody ready?' There was an excitement about him
that half frightened, half roused the party. They all rose, eager, yet
doubtful. His mother came to him and took his arm.

'Lindores! you will do nothing to vex your father; don't make him
unhappy. I don't know your secrets, you two; but look, he has enough
to bear.'

'I want you to know our secrets, mother. Why should we have
secrets from you?'

'Why, indeed?' she said, with tears in her eyes. 'But, Lindores, my
dearest boy, don't make it worse for *him*.'

'I give you my word, I will be wary,' he said; and she left him to
go to his father, who followed the party, with an anxious look upon
his face.

'Are you coming, too?' he asked.

'I? No; I will not go: but trust him—trust the boy, John.'

'He can do nothing; he will not be able to do anything,' he said.

And thus the guests set out on their round—the son in advance, excited and tremulous, the father anxious and watchful behind. They began in the usual way, with the old state-rooms and picture-gallery; and in a short time the party had half forgotten that there was anything unusual in the inspection. When, however, they were half-way down the gallery, Lindores stopped short with an air of wonder. 'You have had it put back then?' he said. He was standing in front of the vacant space where Earl Robert's portrait ought to have been. 'What is it?' they all cried, crowding upon him, ready for any marvel. But as there was nothing to be seen, the strangers smiled among themselves. 'Yes, to be sure, there is nothing so suggestive as a vacant place,' said a lady who was of the party. 'Whose portrait ought to be there, Lord Lindores?'

He looked at his father, who made a slight assenting gesture, then shook his head drearily.

'Who put it there?' Lindores said, in a whisper.

'It is not there; but you and I see it,' said Lord Gowrie, with a sigh.

Then the strangers perceived that something had moved the father and the son, and, notwithstanding their eager curiosity, obeyed the dictates of politeness, and dispersed into groups looking at the other pictures. Lindores set his teeth and clenched his hands. Fury was growing upon him—not the awe that filled his father's mind. 'We will leave the rest of this to another time,' he cried, turning to the others, almost fiercely. 'Come, I will show you something more striking now.' He made no further pretence of going systematically over the house. He turned and went straight upstairs, and along the corridor. 'Are we going over the bedrooms?' some one said. Lindores led the way straight to the old lumber-room, a strange place for such a gay party. The ladies drew their dresses about them. There was not room for half of them. Those who could get in began to handle the strange things that lay about, touching them with dainty fingers, exclaiming how dusty they were. The window was half blocked up by old armour and rusty weapons; but this did not hinder the full summer daylight from penetrating in a flood of light. Lindores went in with fiery determination on his face. He went straight to the wall, as if he would go through, then paused with a blank gaze. 'Where is the door?' he said.

'You are forgetting yourself,' said Lord Gowrie, speaking over the heads of the others. 'Lindores! you know very well there never was any door there; the wall is very thick; you can see by the depth of the window. There is no door there.'

The young man felt it over with his hand. The wall was smooth, and covered with the dust of ages. With a groan he turned away. At this moment a suppressed laugh, low, yet distinct, sounded close by him. 'You laughed?' he said, fiercely, to Ffarrington, striking his hand upon his shoulder.

'I—laughed! Nothing was farther from my thoughts,' said his friend, who was curiously examining something that lay upon an old carved chair. 'Look here! what a wonderful sword, cross-hilted! Is it an Andrea? What's the matter, Lindores?'

Lindores had seized it from his hands; he dashed it against the wall with a suppressed oath. The two or three people in the room stood aghast.

'Lindores!' his father said, in a tone of warning. The young man dropped the useless weapon with a groan. 'Then God help us!' he said; 'but I will find another way.'

'There is a very interesting room close by,' said Lord Gowrie, hastily—'this way! Lindores has been put out by—some changes that have been made without his knowledge,' he said, calmly. 'You must not mind him. He is disappointed. He is perhaps too much accustomed to have his own way.'

But Lord Gowrie knew that no one believed him. He took them to the adjoining room, and told them some easy story of an apparition that was supposed to haunt it. 'Have you ever seen it?' the guests said, pretending interest. 'Not I; but we don't mind ghosts in this house,' he answered, with a smile. And then they resumed their round of the old noble mystic house.

I cannot tell the reader what young Lindores has done to carry out his pledged word and redeem his family. It may not be known, perhaps, for another generation, and it will not be for me to write that concluding chapter: but when, in the ripeness of time, it can be narrated, no one will say that the mystery of Gowrie Castle has been a vulgar horror, though there are some who are disposed to think so now.

1883

The Ghost of
Charlotte Cray

FLORENCE MARRYAT

M r Sigismund Braggett was sitting in the little room he called his
study, wrapped in a profound—not to say a mournful—reverie.
Now, there was nothing in the present life nor surroundings of Mr
Braggett to account for such a demonstration. He was a publisher and
bookseller; a man well to do, with a thriving business in the city,
and the prettiest of all pretty villas at Streatham. And he was only
just turned forty; had not a grey hair in his head nor a false tooth
in his mouth; and had been married but three short months to one
of the fairest and most affectionate specimens of English womanhood
that ever transformed a bachelor's quarters into Paradise.

What more could Mr Sigismund Braggett possibly want? Nothing!
His trouble lay in the fact that he had got rather more than he
wanted. Most of us have our little peccadilloes in this world—awkward
reminiscences that we would like to bury five fathoms deep, and
never hear mentioned again, but that have an uncomfortable habit
of cropping up at the most inconvenient moments; and no mortal is
more likely to be troubled with them than a middle-aged bachelor who
has taken to matrimony.

Mr Sigismund Braggett had no idea what he was going in for when
he led the blushing Emily Primrose up to the altar, and swore to
be hers, and hers only, until death should them part. He had no
conception a woman's curiosity could be so keen, her tongue so
long, and her inventive faculties so correct. He had spent whole days
before the fatal moment of marriage in burning letters, erasing initials,
destroying locks of hair, and making offerings of affection look as if

he had purchased them with his own money. But it had been of little avail. Mrs Braggett had swooped down upon him like a beautiful bird of prey, and wheedled, coaxed, or kissed him out of half his secrets before he knew what he was about. But he had never told her about Charlotte Cray. And now he almost wished that he had done so, for Charlotte Cray was the cause of his present dejected mood.

Now, there are ladies *and* ladies in this world. Some are very shy, and will only permit themselves to be wooed by stealth. Others, again, are the pursuers rather than the pursued, and chase the wounded or the flying even to the very doors of their stronghold, or lie in wait for them like an octopus, stretching out their tentacles on every side in search of victims.

And to the latter class Miss Charlotte Cray decidedly belonged. Not a person worth mourning over, you will naturally say. But, then, Mr Sigismund Braggett had not behaved well to her. She was one of the 'peccadilloes.' She was an authoress—not an author, mind you, which term smacks more of the profession than the sex—but an 'authoress,' with lots of the 'ladylike' about the plots of her stories and the metre of her rhymes. They had come together in the sweet connection of publisher and writer—had met first in a dingy, dusty little office at the back of his house of business, and laid the foundation of their friendship with the average amount of chaffering and prevarication that usually attend such proceedings.

Mr Braggett ran a risk in publishing Miss Cray's tales or verses, but he found her useful in so many other ways that he used occasionally to hold forth a sop to Cerberus in the shape of publicity for the sake of keeping her in his employ. For Miss Charlotte Cray—who was as old as himself, and had arrived at the period of life when women are said to pray 'Any, good Lord, any!'—was really a clever woman, and could turn her hand to most things required of her, or upon which she had set her mind; and she had most decidedly set her mind upon marrying Mr Braggett, and he—to serve his own purposes—had permitted her to cherish the idea, and this was the Nemesis that was weighing him down in the study at the present moment. He had complimented Miss Cray, and given her presents, and taken her out a-pleasuring, all because she was useful to him, and did odd jobs that no one else would undertake, and for less than any one else would have accepted; and he had known the while that she was in love with him, and that she believed he was in love with her.

He had not thought much of it at the time. He had not then made up his mind to marry Emily Primrose, and considered that what pleased Miss Cray, and harmed no one else, was fair play for all sides. But he had come to see things differently now. He had been married three months and the first two weeks had been very bitter ones to him. Miss Cray had written him torrents of reproaches during that unhappy period, besides calling day after day at his office to deliver them in person. This and her threats had frightened him out of his life. He had lived in hourly terror lest the clerks should overhear what passed at their interviews, or that his wife should be made acquainted with them.

He had implored Miss Cray, both by word of mouth and letter, to cease her persecution of him; but all the reply he received was that he was a base and perjured man, and that she should continue to call at his office, and write to him through the penny post, until he had introduced her to his wife. For therein lay the height and depth of his offending. He had been afraid to bring Emily and Miss Cray together, and the latter resented the omission as an insult. It was bad enough to find that Sigismund Braggett, whose hair she wore next her heart, and whose photograph stood as in a shrine upon her bedroom mantelpiece, had married another woman, without giving her even the chance of a refusal, but it was worse still to come to the conclusion that he did not intend her to have a glimpse into the garden of Eden he had created for himself.

Miss Cray was a lady of vivid imagination and strong aspirations. All was not lost in her ideas, although Mr Braggett *had* proved false to the hopes he had raised. Wives did not live for ever; and the chances and changes of this life were so numerous, that stranger things had happened than that Mr Braggett might think fit to make better use of the second opportunity afforded him than he had done of the first. But if she were not to continue even his friend, it was too hard. But the perjured publisher had continued resolute, notwithstanding all Miss Cray's persecution, and now he had neither seen nor heard from her for a month; and, man-like, he was beginning to wonder what had become of her, and whether she had found anybody to console her for his untruth. Mr Braggett did not wish to comfort Miss Cray himself; but he did not quite like the notion of her being comforted.

After all—so he soliloquised—he had been very cruel to her; for the poor thing was devoted to him. How her eyes used to sparkle and her cheek to flush when she entered his office, and how eagerly she would undertake any work for him, however disagreeable to perform! He knew well that she had expected to be Mrs Braggett, and it must have been a terrible disappointment to her when he married Emily Primrose.

Why had he not asked her out to Violet Villa since? What harm could she do as a visitor there? particularly if he cautioned her first as to the peculiarity of Mrs Braggett's disposition, and the quickness with which her jealousy was excited. It was close upon Christmas-time, the period when all old friends meet together and patch up, if they cannot entirely forget, everything that has annoyed them in the past. Mr Braggett pictured to himself the poor old maid sitting solitary in her small rooms at Hammersmith, no longer able to live in the expectation of seeing his manly form at the wicket-gate, about to enter and cheer her solitude. The thought smote him as a two-edged sword, and he sat down at once and penned Miss Charlotte a note, in which he inquired after her health, and hoped that they should soon see her at Violet Villa.

He felt much better after this note was written and despatched. He came out of the little study and entered the cheerful drawing-room, and sat with his pretty wife by the light of the fire, telling her of the lonely lady to whom he had just proposed to introduce her.

'An old friend of mine, Emily. A clever, agreeable woman, though rather eccentric. You will be polite to her, I know, for my sake.'

'An *old* woman, is she?' said Mrs Braggett, elevating her eyebrows. 'And what do you call "old," Siggy, I should like to know?'

'Twice as old as yourself, my dear—five-and-forty at the very least, and not personable-looking, even for that age. Yet I think you will find her a pleasant companion, and I am sure she will be enchanted with you.'

'I don't know that: clever women don't like me, as a rule, though I don't know why.'

'They are jealous of your beauty, my darling; but Miss Cray is above such meanness, and will value you for your own sake.'

'She'd better not let me catch her valuing me for *yours*,' responded Mrs Braggett, with a flash of the eye that made her husband ready to regret the dangerous experiment he was about to make of bringing together two women who had each, in her own way, a claim upon him, and each the will to maintain it.

So he dropped the subject of Miss Charlotte Cray, and took to admiring his wife's complexion instead, so that the evening passed harmoniously, and both parties were satisfied.

For two days Mr Braggett received no answer from Miss Cray, which rather surprised him. He had quite expected that on the reception of his invitation she would rush down to his office and into his arms, behind the shelter of the ground-glass door that enclosed his chair of authority. For Miss Charlotte had been used on occasions to indulge in rapturous demonstrations of the sort, and the remembrance of Mrs Braggett located in Violet Villa would have been no obstacle whatever to her. She believed she had a prior claim to Mr Braggett. However, nothing of the kind happened, and the perjured publisher was becoming strongly imbued with the idea that he must go out to Hammersmith and see if he could not make his peace with her in person, particularly as he had several odd jobs for Christmas-tide, which no one could undertake so well as herself, when a letter with a black-edged border was put into his hand. He opened it mechanically, not knowing the writing; but its contents shocked him beyond measure.

> 'HONOURED SIR,—I am sorry to tell you that Miss Cray died at my house a week ago, and was buried yesterday. She spoke of you several times during her last illness, and if you would like to hear any further particulars, and will call on me at the old address, I shall be most happy to furnish you with them.—Yours respectfully,
>
> 'MARY THOMPSON.'

When Mr Braggett read this news, you might have knocked him over with a feather. It is not always true that a living dog is better than a dead lion. Some people gain considerably in the estimation of their friends by leaving this world, and Miss Charlotte Cray was one of them. Her persecution had ceased for ever, and her amiable weaknesses were alone held in remembrance. Mr Braggett felt a positive relief in the knowledge that his dead friend and his wife would never now be brought in contact with each other; but at the same time he blamed himself more than was needful, perhaps, for not having seen nor communicated with Miss Cray for so long before her death. He came down to breakfast with a portentously grave face that morning, and imparted the sad intelligence to Mrs Braggett with the air of an undertaker. Emily wondered, pitied, and sympathised, but the dead lady was no more to her than any other stranger; and she was surprised her husband looked so solemn over it all. Mr Braggett, however, could not dismiss the subject easily from his mind. It haunted him during the business hours of the morning, and as soon as he could conveniently leave his office, he posted away to Hammersmith. The little house in which Miss Cray used to live looked just the same, both inside and outside: how strange it seemed that *she* should have flown away from it for ever! And here was her landlady, Mrs Thompson, bobbing and curtseying to him in the same old black net cap with artificial flowers in it, and the same stuff gown she had worn since he first saw her, with her apron in her hand, it is true, ready to go to her eyes as soon as a reasonable opportunity occurred, but otherwise the same Mrs Thompson as before. And yet she would never wait upon *her* again.

'It was all so sudden, sir,' she said, in answer to Mr Braggett's inquiries, 'that there was no time to send for nobody.'

'But Miss Cray had my address.'

'Ah! perhaps so; but she was off her head, poor dear, and couldn't think of nothing. But she remembered you, sir, to the last; for the very morning she died, she sprung up in bed and called out, "Sigismund! Sigismund!" as loud as ever she could, and she never spoke to anybody afterwards, not one word.'

'She left no message for me?'

'None, sir. I asked her the day before she went if I was to say nothing to you for her (knowing you was such friends), and all her answer was, "I wrote to him. He's got my letter." So I thought, perhaps, you had heard, sir.'

'Not for some time past. It seems terribly sudden to me, not having heard even of her illness. Where is she buried?'

'Close by in the churchyard, sir. My little girl will go with you and show you the place, if you'd like to see it.'

Mr Braggett accepted her offer and left.

When he was standing by a heap of clods they called a grave, and had dismissed the child, he drew out Miss Cray's last letter, which he carried in his pocket, and read it over.

'You tell me that I am not to call at your office again, except on business' (so it ran), 'nor to send letters to your private address, lest it should come to the knowledge of your wife, and create unpleasantness between you; but I *shall* call, and I *shall* write, until I have seen Mrs Braggett, and, if you don't take care, I will introduce myself to her and tell her the reason you have been afraid to do so.'

This letter had made Mr Braggett terribly angry at the time of reception. He had puffed and fumed, and cursed Miss Charlotte by all his gods for daring to threaten him. But he read it with different feelings now Miss Charlotte was down there, six feet beneath the ground he stood on, and he could feel only compassion for her frenzy, and resentment against himself for having excited it. As he travelled home from Hammersmith to Streatham, he was a very dejected publisher indeed.

He did not tell Mrs Braggett the reason of his melancholy, but it affected him to that degree that he could not go to office on the following day, but stayed at home instead, to be petted and waited upon by his pretty wife, which treatment resulted in a complete cure. The next morning, therefore, he started for London as briskly as ever, and arrived at office before his usual time. A clerk, deputed to receive all messages for his master, followed him behind the ground-glass doors, with a packet of letters.

'Mr Van Ower was here yesterday, sir. He will let you have the copy before the end of the week, and Messrs. Hanleys' foreman called on particular business, and will look in to-day at eleven. And Mr Ellis came to ask if there was any answer to his letter yet; and Miss Cray called, sir; and that's all.'

'*Who* did you say?' cried Braggett.

'Miss Cray, sir. She waited for you above an hour, but I told her I thought you couldn't mean to come into town at all, so she went.'

'Do you know what you're talking about, Hewetson? You said *Miss Cray!*'

'And I meant it, sir—Miss Charlotte Cray. Burns spoke to her as well as I.'

'Good heavens!' exclaimed Mr Braggett, turning as white as a sheet. 'Go at once and send Burns to me.' Burns came.

'Burns, who was the lady that called to see me yesterday?'

'Miss Cray, sir. She had a very thick veil on, and she looked so pale that I asked her if she had been ill, and she said "Yes." She sat in the office for over an hour, hoping you'd come in, but as you didn't, she went away again.'

'Did she lift her veil?'

'Not whilst I spoke to her, sir.'

'How do you know it was Miss Cray, then?'

The clerk stared. 'Well, sir, we all know her pretty well by this time.'

'Did you ask her name?'

'No, sir; there was no need to do it.'

'You're mistaken, that's all, both you and Hewetson. It couldn't have been Miss Cray! I know for certain that she is—is—is—not in London at present. It must have been a stranger.'

'It was not, indeed, sir, begging your pardon. I could tell Miss Cray anywhere, by her figure and her voice, without seeing her face. But I *did* see her face, and remarked how awfully pale she was—just like death, sir!'

'There! there! that will do! It's of no consequence, and you can go back to your work.'

But any one who had seen Mr Braggett, when left alone in his office, would not have said he thought the matter of no consequence. The perspiration broke out upon his forehead, although it was December, and he rocked himself backward and forward in his chair with agitation.

At last he rose hurriedly, upset his throne, and dashed through the outer premises in the face of twenty people waiting to speak to him. As soon as he could find his voice, he hailed a hansom, and drove to Hammersmith. Good Mrs Thompson opening the door to him, thought he looked as if he had just come out of a fever.

'Lor' bless me, sir! whatever's the matter?'

'Mrs Thompson, have you told me the truth about Miss Cray? Is she really dead?'

'*Really dead*, sir! Why, I closed her eyes, and put her in the coffin with my own hands! If she ain't dead, I don't know who is! But if you doubt my word, you'd better ask the doctor that gave the certificate for her.'

'What is the doctor's name?'

'Dodson; he lives opposite.'

'You must forgive my strange questions, Mrs Thompson, but I have had a terrible dream about my poor friend, and I think I should like to talk to the doctor about her.'

'Oh, very good, sir,' cried the landlady, much offended. 'I'm not afraid of what the doctor will tell you. She had excellent nursing and everything as she could desire, and there's nothing on my conscience on that score, so I'll wish you good morning.' And with that Mrs Thompson slammed the door in Mr Braggett's face.

He found Dr Dodson at home.

'If I understand you rightly,' said the practitioner, looking rather steadfastly in the scared face of his visitor, 'you wish, as a friend of the late Miss Cray's, to see a copy of the certificate of her death? Very good, sir; here it is. She died, as you will perceive, on the twenty-fifth of November, of peritonitis. She had, I can assure you, every attention and care, but nothing could have saved her.'

'You are quite sure, then, she is dead?' demanded Mr Braggett, in a vague manner.

The doctor looked at him as if he were not quite sure if he were sane.

'If seeing a patient die, and her corpse coffined and buried, is being sure she is dead, *I* am in no doubt whatever about Miss Cray.'

'It is very strange—most strange and unaccountable,' murmured poor Mr Braggett, in reply, as he shuffled out of the doctor's passage, and took his way back to the office.

Here, however, after an interval of rest and a strong brandy and soda, he managed to pull himself together, and to come to the conclusion that the doctor and Mrs Thompson *could* not be mistaken, and that, consequently, the clerks *must*. He did not mention the subject again to them, however; and as the days went on, and nothing more was heard of the mysterious stranger's visit, Mr Braggett put it altogether out of his mind.

At the end of a fortnight, however, when he was thinking of something totally different, young Hewetson remarked to him, carelessly,—

'Miss Cray was here again yesterday, sir. She walked in just as your cab had left the door.'

All the horror of his first suspicions returned with double force upon the unhappy man's mind.

'Don't talk nonsense!' he gasped, angrily, as soon as he could speak. 'Don't attempt to play any of your tricks on me, young man, or it will be the worse for you, I can tell you.'

'Tricks, sir!' stammered the clerk. 'I don't know what you are alluding to. I am only telling you the truth. You have always desired me to be most particular in letting you know the names of the people who call in your absence, and I thought I was only doing my duty in making a point of ascertaining them—'

'Yes, yes! Hewetson, of course,' replied Mr Braggett, passing his handkerchief over his brow, 'and you are quite right in following my directions as closely as possible; only—in this case you are completely mistaken, and it is the second time you have committed the error.'

'Mistaken!'

'Yes!—as mistaken as it is possible for a man to be! Miss Cray *could* not have called at this office yesterday.'

'But she did, sir.'

'Am I labouring under some horrible nightmare?' exclaimed the publisher, 'or are we playing at cross purposes? Can you mean the Miss Cray I mean?'

'I am speaking of Miss Charlotte Cray, sir, the author of "Sweet Gwendoline,"—the lady who has undertaken so much of our compilation the last two years, and who has a long nose, and wears her hair in curls. I never knew there was another Miss Cray; but if there are two, that is the one I mean.'

'Still I *cannot* believe it, Hewetson, for the Miss Cray who has been associated with our firm died on the twenty-fifth of last month.'

'*Died*, sir! Is Miss Cray dead? Oh, it can't be! It's some humbugging trick that's been played upon you, for I'd swear she was in this room yesterday afternoon, as full of life as she's ever been since I knew her. She didn't talk much, it's true, for she seemed in a hurry to be off again, but she had got on the same dress and bonnet she was in here last, and she made herself as much at home in the office as she ever did. Besides,' continued Hewetson, as though suddenly remembering something, 'she left a note for you, sir.'

'A note! Why did you not say so before?'

'It slipped my memory when you began to doubt my word in that way, sir. But you'll find it in the bronze vase. She told me to tell you she had placed it there.'

Mr Braggett made a dash at the vase, and found the three-cornered note as he had been told. Yes! it was Charlotte's handwriting, or the facsimile of it, there was no doubt of that; and his hands shook so he could hardly open the paper. It contained these words:

'You tell me that I am not to call at your office again, except on business, nor to send letters to your private address, lest it should come to the knowledge of your wife, and create unpleasantness between you;

but I *shall* call, and I *shall* write until I have seen Mrs Braggett, and if you don't take care I will introduce myself to her, and tell her the reason you have been afraid to do so.'

Precisely the same words, in the same writing of the letter he still carried in his breast-pocket, and which no mortal eyes but his and hers had ever seen. As the unhappy man sat gazing at the opened note, his whole body shook as if he were attacked by ague.

'It is Miss Cray's handwriting, isn't it, sir?'

'It looks like it, Hewetson, but it cannot be. I tell you it is an impossibility! Miss Cray died last month, and I have seen not only her grave, but the doctor and nurse who attended her in her last illness. It is folly, then, to suppose either that she called here or wrote that letter.'

'Then *who could it have been*, sir?' said Hewetson, attacked with a sudden terror in his turn.

'That is impossible for me to say; but should the lady call again, you had better ask her boldly for her name and address.'

'I'd rather you'd depute the office to anybody but me, sir,' replied the clerk, as he hastily backed out of the room.

Mr Braggett, dying with suspense and conjecture, went through his business as best he could, and hurried home to Violet Villa.

There he found that his wife had been spending the day with a friend, and only entered the house a few minutes before himself.

'Siggy, dear!' she commenced, as soon as he joined her in the drawing-room after dinner; 'I really think we should have the fastenings and bolts of this house looked to. Such a funny thing happened whilst I was out this afternoon. Ellen has just been telling me about it.'

'What sort of a thing, dear?'

'Well, I left home as early as twelve, you know, and told the servants I shouldn't be back until dinner-time; so they were all enjoying themselves in the kitchen, I suppose, when cook told Ellen she heard a footstep in the drawing-room. Ellen thought at first it must be cook's fancy, because she was sure the front door was fastened; but when they listened, they all heard the noise together, so she ran upstairs, and what on earth do you think she saw?'

'How can I guess, my dear?'

'Why, a lady, seated in this very room, as if she was waiting for somebody. She was oldish, Ellen says, and had a very white face, with

long curls hanging down each side of it; and she wore a blue bonnet
with white feathers, and a long black cloak, and—'

'Emily, Emily! Stop! You don't know what you're talking about.
That girl is a fool; you must send her away. That is, how could the
lady have got in if the door was closed? Good heavens! you'll all drive
me mad between you with your folly!' exclaimed Mr Braggett, as he
threw himself back in his chair, with an exclamation that sounded
very like a groan.

Pretty Mrs Braggett was offended. What had she said or done
that her husband should doubt her word? She tossed her head in
indignation, and remained silent. If Mr Braggett wanted any further
information, he would have to apologise.

'Forgive me, darling,' he said, after a long pause. 'I don't think I'm
very well this evening, but your story seemed to upset me.'

'I don't see why it should upset you,' returned Mrs Braggett. 'If
strangers are allowed to come prowling about the house in this way,
we shall be robbed some day, and then you'll say I should have told
you of it.'

'Wouldn't she—this person—give her name?'

'Oh! I'd rather say no more about it. You had better ask Ellen.'

'No, Emily! I'd rather hear it from you.'

'Well, don't interrupt me again, then. When Ellen saw the woman
seated here, she asked her her name and business at once, but she
gave no answer, and only sat and stared at her. And so Ellen, feeling
very uncomfortable, had just turned round to call up cook, when the
woman got up, and dashed past her like a flash of lightning, and they
saw nothing more of her!'

'Which way did she leave the house?'

'Nobody knows any more than how she came in. The servants
declare the hall-door was neither opened nor shut—but, of course,
it must have been. She was a tall gaunt woman, Ellen says, about
fifty, and she's sure her hair was dyed. She must have come to steal
something, and that's why I say we ought to have the house made
more secure. Why, Siggy! Siggy! what's the matter? Here, Ellen! Jane!
come, quick, some of you! Your master's fainted!'

And, sure enough, the repeated shocks and horrors of the day had
had such an effect upon poor Mr Braggett, that for a moment he
did lose all consciousness of what surrounded him. He was thankful
to take advantage of the Christmas holidays, to run over to Paris

with his wife, and try to forget, in the many marvels of that city, the awful fear that fastened upon him at the mention of anything connected with home. He might be enjoying himself to the top of his bent; but directly the remembrance of Charlotte Cray crossed his mind, all sense of enjoyment vanished, and he trembled at the mere thought of returning to his business, as a child does when sent to bed in the dark.

He tried to hide the state of his feelings from Mrs Braggett, but she was too sharp for him. The simple, blushing Emily Primrose had developed, under the influence of the matrimonial forcing-frame, into a good watch-dog, and nothing escaped her notice.

Left to her own conjecture, she attributed his frequent moods of dejection to the existence of some other woman, and became jealous accordingly. If Siggy did not love her, why had he married her? She felt certain there was some other horrid creature who had engaged his affections and would not leave him alone, even now that he was her own lawful property. And to find out who the 'horrid creature' was became Mrs Emily's constant idea. When she had found out, she meant to give her a piece of her mind, never fear! Meanwhile Mr Braggett's evident distaste to returning to business only served to increase his wife's suspicions. A clear conscience, she argued, would know no fear. So they were not a happy couple, as they set their faces once more towards England. Mr Braggett's dread of re-entering his office amounted almost to terror, and Mrs Braggett, putting this and that together, resolved that she would fathom the mystery, if it lay in feminine *finesse* to do so. She did not whisper a word of her intentions to dear Siggy, you may be sure of that! She worked after the manner of her amiable sex, like a cat in the dark, or a worm boring through the earth, and appearing on the surface when least expected.

So poor Mr Braggett brought her home again, heavy at heart indeed, but quite ignorant that any designs were being made against him. I think he would have given a thousand pounds to be spared the duty of attending office the day after his arrival. But it was necessary, and he went, like a publisher and a Briton. But Mrs Emily had noted his trepidation and his fears, and laid her plans accordingly. She had never been asked to enter those mysterious precincts, the house of business. Mr Braggett had not thought it necessary that her blooming loveliness should be made acquainted with its dingy, dusty accessories, but she meant to see them for herself to-day. So she waited till he had left Violet Villa ten minutes, and then she dressed and followed him by the next train to London.

Mr Sigismund Braggett meanwhile had gone on his way, as people go to a dentist, determined to do what was right, but with an indefinite sort of idea that he might never come out of it alive. He dreaded to hear what might have happened in his absence, and he delayed his arrival at the office for half-an-hour, by walking there instead of taking a cab as usual, in order to put off the evil moment. As he entered the place, however, he saw at a glance that his efforts were vain, and that something had occurred. The customary formality and precision of the office were upset, and the clerks, instead of bending over their ledgers, or attending to the demands of business, were all huddled together at one end whispering and gesticulating to each other. But as soon as the publisher appeared, a dead silence fell upon the group, and they only stared at him with an air of horrid mystery.

'What is the matter now?' he demanded, angrily, for like most men when in a fright which they are ashamed to exhibit, Mr Sigismund Braggett tried to cover his want of courage by bounce.

The young man called Hewetson advanced towards him, with a face the colour of ashes, and pointed towards the ground-glass doors dumbly.

'What do you mean? Can't you speak? What's come to the lot of you, that you are neglecting my business in this fashion to make fools of yourselves?'

'If you please, sir, she's in there.'

Mr Braggett started back as if he'd been shot. But still he tried to have it out.

'She! Who's she?'

'Miss Cray, sir.'

'Haven't I told you already that's a lie.'

'Will you judge for yourself, Mr Braggett?' said a grey-haired man, stepping forward. 'I was on the stairs myself just now when Miss Cray passed me, and I have no doubt whatever but that you will find her in your private room, however much the reports that have lately reached you may seem against the probability of such a thing.'

Mr Braggett's teeth chattered in his head as he advanced to the ground-glass doors, through the panes of one of which there was a little peephole to ascertain if the room were occupied or not. He stooped and looked in. At the table, with her back towards him, was seated the well-known figure of Charlotte Cray. He recognised at once the long black mantle in which she was wont to drape her gaunt figure—the blue bonnet, with its dejected-looking, uncurled feather—the lank curls which rested on her shoulders—and the black-leather bag, with a steel clasp, which she always carried in her hand. It was the embodiment of Charlotte Cray, he had no doubt of that; but how could he reconcile the fact of her being there with the damp clods he had seen piled upon her grave, with the certificate of death, and the doctor's and landlady's assertion that they had watched her last moments?

At last he prepared, with desperate energy, to turn the handle of the door. At that moment the attention of the more frivolous of the clerks was directed from his actions by the entrance of an uncommonly pretty woman at the other end of the outer office. Such a lovely creature as this seldom brightened the gloom of their dusty abiding-place. Lilies, roses, and carnations vied with each other in her complexion, whilst the sunniest of locks, and the brightest of blue eyes, lent her face a girlish charm not easily described. What could this fashionably-attired Venus want in their house of business?

'Is Mr Braggett here? I am Mrs Braggett. Please show me in to him immediately.'

They glanced at the ground-glass doors of the inner office. They had already closed behind the manly form of their employer.

'This way, madam,' one said, deferentially, as he escorted her to the presence of Mr Braggett.

Meanwhile, Sigismund had opened the portals of the Temple of Mystery, and with trembling knees entered it. The figure in the chair did not stir at his approach. He stood at the door irresolute. What should he do or say?

'Charlotte,' he whispered.

Still she did not move.

At that moment his wife entered.

'Oh, Sigismund!' cried Mrs Emily, reproachfully, 'I knew you were keeping something from me, and now I've caught you in the very act. Who is this lady, and what is her name? I shall refuse to leave the room until I know it.'

At the sound of her rival's voice, the woman in the chair rose quickly to her feet and confronted them. Yes! there was Charlotte

Cray, precisely similar to what she had appeared in life, only with an uncertainty and vagueness about the lines of the familiar features that made them ghastly.

She stood there, looking Mrs Emily full in the face, but only for a moment, for, even as she gazed, the lineaments grew less and less distinct, with the shape of the figure that supported them, until, with a crash, the apparition seemed to fall in and disappear, and the place that had known her was filled with empty air.

'Where is she gone?' exclaimed Mrs Braggett, in a tone of utter amazement.

'Where is *who* gone?' repeated Mr Braggett, hardly able to articulate from fear.

'The lady in the chair!'

'There was no one there except in your own imagination. It was my great-coat that you mistook for a figure,' returned her husband hastily, as he threw the article in question over the back of the arm-chair.

'But how could that have been?' said his pretty wife, rubbing her eyes. 'How could I think a coat had eyes, and hair, and features? I am *sure* I saw a woman seated there, and that she rose and stared at me. Siggy! tell me it was true. It seems so incomprehensible that I should have been mistaken.'

'You must question your own sense. You see that the room is empty now, except for ourselves, and you know that no one has left it. If you like to search under the table, you can.'

'Ah! now, Siggy, you are laughing at me, because you know that would be folly. But there was certainly some one here—only, where can she have disappeared to?'

'Suppose we discuss the matter at a more convenient season,' replied Mr Braggett, as he drew his wife's arm through his arm. 'Hewetson! you will be able to tell Mr Hume that he was mistaken. Say, also, that I shall not be back in the office to-day. I am not so strong as I thought I was, and feel quite unequal to business. Tell him to come out to Streatham this evening with my letters, and I will talk with him there.'

What passed at that interview was never disclosed; but pretty Mrs Braggett was much rejoiced, a short time afterwards, by her husband telling her that he had resolved to resign his active share of the business, and devote the rest of his life to her and Violet Villa. He would have no more occasion, therefore, to visit the office, and be exposed to the temptation of spending four or five hours out of every twelve away from her side. For, though Mrs Emily had arrived at the conclusion that the momentary glimpse she caught of a lady in Siggy's office must have been a delusion, she was not quite satisfied by his assertions that she would never have found a more tangible cause for her jealousy.

But Sigismund Braggett knew more than he chose to tell Mrs Emily. He knew that what she had witnessed was no delusion, but a reality; and that Charlotte Cray had carried out her dying determination to call at his office and his private residence, *until she had seen his wife!*

1888

Lady Farquhar's Old Lady, A True Ghost Story

MRS MOLESWORTH

'One that was a woman, sir; but, rest her soul, she's dead.'

I myself have never seen a ghost (I am by no means sure that I wish ever to do so), but I have a friend whose experience in this respect has been less limited than mine. Till lately, however, I had never heard the details of Lady Farquhar's adventure, though the fact of there being a ghost story which she could, if she chose, relate with the authority of an eye-witness, had been more than once alluded to before me. Living at extreme ends of the country, it is but seldom my friend and I are able to meet; but a few months ago I had the good fortune to spend some days in her house, and one evening our conversation happening to fall on the subject of the possibility of so-called 'supernatural' visitations or communications, suddenly what I had heard returned to my memory.

'By the bye,' I exclaimed, 'we need not go far for an authority on the question. You have seen a ghost yourself, Margaret. I remember once hearing it alluded to before you, and you did not contradict it. I have so often meant to ask you for the whole story. Do tell it to us now.'

Lady Farquhar hesitated for a moment, and her usually bright expression grew somewhat graver. When she spoke, it seemed to be with a slight effort.

'You mean what they all call the story of "my old lady," I suppose,' she said at last. 'Oh yes, if you care to hear it, I will tell it you. But there is not much to tell, remember.'

'There seldom is in *true* stories of the kind,' I replied. 'Genuine ghost stories are generally abrupt and inconsequent in the extreme, but on this very account all the more impressive. Don't you think so?'

'I don't know that I am a fair judge,' she answered. 'Indeed,' she went on rather gravely, 'my own opinion is that what you call *true* ghost stories are very seldom told at all.'

'How do you mean? I don't quite understand you,' I said, a little perplexed by her words and tone.

'I mean,' she replied, 'that people who really believe they have come in contact with—with anything of that kind, seldom care to speak about it.'

'Do you really think so? do you mean that you feel so yourself?' I exclaimed with considerable surprise. 'I had no idea you did, or I would not have mentioned the subject. Of course you know I would not ask you to tell it if it is the least painful or disagreeable to you to talk about it.'

'But it isn't. Oh no, it is not nearly so bad as that,' she replied, with a smile. 'I cannot really say that it is either painful or disagreeable to me to recall it, for I cannot exactly apply either of those words to the thing itself. All that I feel is a sort of shrinking from the subject, strong enough to prevent my ever alluding to it lightly or carelessly. Of all things, I should dislike to have a joke made of it. But with you I have no fear of that. And you trust me, don't you? I don't mean as to truthfulness only; but you don't think me deficient in common sense and self-control—not morbid, or very apt to be run away with by my imagination?'

'Not the sort of person one would pick out as likely to see ghosts?' I replied. 'Certainly not. You are far too sensible and healthy and vigorous. I can't, very readily, fancy you the victim of delusion of any kind. But as to ghosts—are they or are they not delusions? There lies the question! Tell us your experience of them, any way.'

So she told the story I had asked for—told it in the simplest language, and with no exaggeration of tone or manner, as we sat there in her pretty drawing-room, our chairs drawn close to the fire, for it was Christmas time, and the weather was 'seasonable.' Two or three of Margaret's children were in the room, though not within hearing of us; all looked bright and cheerful, nothing mysterious. Yet notwithstanding the total deficiency of ghostly accessories, the story impressed me vividly.

'It was early in the spring of '55 that it happened,' began Lady Farquhar; 'I never forget the year, for a reason I will tell you afterwards. It is fully fifteen years ago now—a long time—but I am still quite able to recall the *feeling* this strange adventure of mine left on me, though a few details and particulars have grown confused and misty. I think it often happens so when one tries, as it were *too* hard, to be accurate and unexaggerated in telling over anything. One's very honesty is against one. I have not told it over many times, but each time it seems more difficult to tell it quite exactly; the impression left at the time was so powerful that I have always dreaded incorrectness or exaggeration creeping in. It reminds me, too, of the curious way in which a familiar word or name grows distorted, and then cloudy and strange, if one looks at it too long or thinks about it too much. But I must get on with my story.

'Well, to begin again. In the winter of '54–'55 we were living—my mother, my sisters, and I, that is, and from time to time my brother—in, or rather near, a quiet little village on the south coast of Ireland. We had gone there, before the worst of the winter began at home, for the sake of my health. I had not been as well as usual for some time (this was greatly owing, I believe, to my having lately endured unusual anxiety of mind), and my dear mother dreaded the cold weather for me, and determined to avoid it. I say that I had had unusual anxiety to bear, still it was not of a kind to render me morbid or fanciful. And what is even more to the point, my mind was perfectly free from prepossession or association in connection with the place we were living in, or the people who had lived there before us. I simply knew nothing whatever of these people, and I had no sort of fancy about the house—that it was haunted, or anything of that kind; and indeed I never heard that it *was* thought to be haunted. It did not look like it; it was just a moderate-sized, somewhat old-fashioned country, or rather sea-side, house, furnished, with the exception of one room, in an ordinary enough modern style. The exception was a small room on the bedroom floor, which, though not locked off (that is to say, the key was left in the lock outside), was not given up for our use, as it was crowded with musty old furniture, packed closely together, and all of a fashion many, many years older than that of the contents of the rest of the house. I remember some of the pieces of furniture still, though I think I was only once or twice in the room all the time we were there. There were two or three old-fashioned cabinets or bureaux; there was a regular four-post bedstead, with the gloomy curtains still hanging round it; and ever so many spider-legged chairs and rickety tables; and I rather think in one corner there was a spinet. But there was nothing particularly curious or attractive, and we never thought of meddling with the things or "poking about," as girls sometimes do; for we always thought it was by mistake that this room had not been locked off altogether, so that no one should meddle with anything in it.

'We had rented the house for six months from a Captain Marchmont, a half-pay officer, naval or military, I don't know which, for we never saw him, and all the negotiations were managed by an agent. Captain Marchmont and his family, as a rule, lived at Ballyreina all the year round—they found it cheap and healthy, I suppose—but this year they had preferred to pass the winter in some livelier neighbourhood, and they were very glad to let the house. It never occurred to us to doubt our landlord's being the owner of it: it was not till some time after we left that we learned that he himself was only a tenant, though a tenant of long standing. There were no people about to make friends with, or to hear local gossip from. There were no gentry within visiting distance, and if there had been, we should hardly have cared to make friends for so short a time as we were to be there. The people of the village were mostly fishermen and their families; there were so many of them, we never got to know any specially. The doctor and the priest and the Protestant clergyman were all newcomers, and all three very uninteresting. The clergyman used to dine with us sometimes, as my brother had had some sort of introduction to him when we came to Ballyreina; but we never heard anything about the place from him. He was a great talker, too; I am sure he would have told us anything he knew. In short, there was nothing romantic or suggestive either about our house or the village. But we didn't care. You see we had gone there simply for rest and quiet and pure air, and we got what we wanted.

'Well, one evening about the middle of March I was up in my room dressing for dinner, and just as I had about finished dressing, my sister Helen came in. I remember her saying as she came in, "Aren't you ready yet, Maggie? Are you making yourself extra smart for Mr. Conroy?" Mr. Conroy was the clergyman; he was dining with us that night. And then Helen looked at me and found fault with me, half in fun of course, for not having put on a prettier dress. I remember I said it was good enough for Mr. Conroy, who was no favourite of mine; but Helen wasn't satisfied till I agreed to wear a bright scarlet neck-ribbon of hers, and she ran off to her room to fetch it. I followed her almost immediately. Her room and mine, I must, by the bye, explain, were at extreme ends of a passage several yards in length. There was a wall on one side of this passage, and a balustrade overlooking the staircase on the other. My room was at the end nearest the top of the staircase. There were no doors along the passage leading to Helen's room, but just beside her door, at the end, was that of the unused room I told you of, filled with the old furniture.

The passage was lighted from above by a skylight—I mean, it was by no means dark or shadowy—and on the evening I am speaking of, it was still clear daylight. We dined early at Ballyreina; I don't think it could have been more than a quarter to five when Helen came into my room. Well, as I was saying, I followed her almost immediately, so quickly that as I came out of my room I was in time to catch sight of her as she ran along the passage, and to see her go into her own room.

Just as I lost sight of her—I was coming along more deliberately, you understand—suddenly, how or when exactly I cannot tell, I perceived *another* figure walking along the passage in front of me. It was a woman, a little thin woman, but though she had her back to me, something in her gait told me she was not young. She seemed a little bent, and walked feebly. I can remember her dress even now with the most perfect distinctness. She had a gown of gray clinging stuff, rather scanty in the skirt, and one of those funny little old-fashioned black shawls with a sewed-on border, that you seldom see nowadays. Do you know the kind I mean? It was a narrow, shawl-pattern border, and there was a short tufty black fringe below the border. And she had a gray poke bonnet, a bonnet made of silk "gathered" on to a large stiff frame; "drawn" bonnets they used to be called. I took in all these details of her dress in a moment, and even in that moment I noticed too that the materials of her clothes looked *good*, though so plain and old-fashioned. But somehow my first impulse when I saw her was to call out, "Fraser, is that you?" Fraser was my mother's maid: she was a young woman, and not the least like the person in front of me, but I think a vague idea rushed across my mind that it might be Fraser dressed up to trick the other servants. But the figure took no notice of my exclamation; it, or she, walked on quietly, not even turning her head round in the least; she walked slowly down the passage, seemingly quite unconscious of my presence, and, to my extreme amazement, disappeared into the unused room. The key, as I think I told you, was always turned in the lock—that is to say, the door was locked, but the key was left in it; but the old woman did not seem to me to unlock the door, or even to turn the handle. There seemed no obstacle in her way: she just quietly, as it were, walked *through* the door. Even by this time I hardly think I felt *frightened*. What I had seen had passed too quickly for me as yet to realise its strangeness. Still I felt perplexed and vaguely uneasy, and I hurried on to my sister's room. She was standing by the toilet-table, searching for the ribbon. I think I must have looked startled, for before I could speak she called out, "Maggie, whatever is the matter with you? You look as if you were going to faint." I asked her if she had heard anything, though it was an inconsistent question, for to *my* ears there had been no sound at all. Helen answered, "Yes:" a moment before I came into the room she had heard the lock of the lumber-room (so we called it) door click, and had wondered what I could be going in there for. Then I told her what I had seen. She looked a little startled, but declared it must have been one of the servants.

'"If it is a trick of the servants," I answered, "it should be exposed;" and when Helen offered to search through the lumber-room with me at once, I was very ready to agree to it. I was so satisfied of the reality of what I had seen, that I declared to Helen that the old woman, whoever she was, *must* be in the room; it stood to reason that, having gone in, she must still be there, as she could not possibly have come out again without our knowledge.

'So, plucking up our courage, we went to the lumber-room door. I felt so certain that but a moment before, some one had opened it, that I took hold of the knob quite confidently and turned it, just as one always does to open a door. The handle turned, but the door did not yield. I stooped down to see why; the reason was plain enough: the door was still locked, locked as usual, and the key in the lock! Then Helen and I stared at each other: *her* mind was evidently recurring to the sound she had heard; what *I* began to think I can hardly put in words.

'But when we got over this new start a little, we set to work to search the room as we had intended. And we searched it thoroughly, I assure you. We dragged the old tables and chairs out of their corners, and peeped behind the cabinets and chests of drawers where no one *could* have been hidden. Then we climbed upon the old bedstead, and shook the curtains till we were covered with dust; and then we crawled under the valances, and came out looking like sweeps; but there was nothing to be found. There was certainly *no-one* in the room, and by all appearances no one could have been there for weeks. We had hardly time to make ourselves fit to be seen when the dinner-bell rang, and we had to hurry downstairs. As we ran down we agreed to say nothing of what had happened before the servants, but after dinner in the drawing-room we told our story. My mother and brother listened to it attentively, said it was very strange, and owned themselves as puzzled as we. Mr. Conroy of course laughed uproariously, and made us dislike him more than ever.

After he had gone we talked it over again among ourselves, and my mother, who hated mysteries, did her utmost to explain what I had seen in a matter-of-fact, natural way. Was I sure it was not only Helen herself I had seen, after fancying she had reached her own room? Was I quite certain it was not Fraser after all, carrying a shawl perhaps, which made her look different? Might it not have been this, that, or the other? It was no use. Nothing could convince me that I had *not* seen what I had seen; and though, to satisfy my mother, we cross-questioned Fraser, it was with no result in the way of explanation. Fraser evidently knew nothing that could throw light on it, and she was quite certain that at the time I had seen the figure, both the other servants were downstairs in the kitchen. Fraser was perfectly trustworthy; we warned her not to frighten the others by speaking about the affair at all, but we could not leave off speaking about it among ourselves. We spoke about it so much for the next few days, that at last my mother lost patience, and forbade us to mention it again. At least she *pretended* to lose patience; in reality I believe she put a stop to the discussion because she thought it might have a bad effect on our nerves, on mine especially; for I found out afterwards that in her anxiety she even went the length of writing about it to our old doctor at home, and that it was by his advice she acted in forbidding us to talk about it any more. Poor dear mother! I don't know that it was very sound advice. One's mind often runs all the more on things one is forbidden to mention. It certainly was so with me, for I thought over my strange adventure almost incessantly for some days after we left off talking about it.'

Here Margaret paused.

'And is that all?' I asked, feeling a little disappointed, I think, at the unsatisfactory ending to the 'true ghost story.'

'All!' repeated Lady Farquhar, rousing herself as if from a reverie, 'all! oh, dear no. I have sometimes wished it had been, for I don't think what I have told you would have left any long-lasting impression on me. All! oh, dear no. I am only at the beginning of my story.'

So we resettled ourselves again to listen, and Lady Farquhar continued:—

'For some days, as I said, I could not help thinking a good deal of the mysterious old woman I had seen. Still, I assure you, I was not exactly frightened. I was more puzzled—puzzled and annoyed at not being able in any way to explain the mystery. But by ten days or so from the time of my first adventure the impression was beginning to fade. Indeed, the day before the evening I am now going to tell you of, I don't think my old lady had been in my head at all. It was filled with other things. So, don't you see, the explaining away what I saw as entirely a delusion, a fancy of my own brain, has a weak point here; for *had* it been all my fancy, it would surely have happened *sooner*—at the time my mind really was full of the subject. Though even if it had been so, it would not have explained the curious coincidence of my "fancy" with facts, actual facts of which at the time I was in complete ignorance. It must have been just about ten days after my first adventure that I happened one evening, between eight and nine o'clock, to be alone upstairs in my own room. We had dined at half-past five as usual, and had been sitting together in the drawing-room since dinner, but I had made some little excuse for coming upstairs; the truth being that I wanted to be alone to read over a letter which the evening post (there actually was an evening post at Ballyreina) had brought me, and which I had only had time to glance at. It was a very welcome and dearly-prized letter, and the reading of it made me very happy. I don't think I had felt so happy all the months we had been in Ireland as I was feeling that evening. Do you remember my saying I never forget the year all this happened? It was the year '55 and the month of March, the spring following that first dreadful "Crimean winter," and news had just come to England of the Czar's death, and everyone was wondering and hoping and fearing what would be the results of it. I had no very near friends in the Crimea, but of course, like everyone else, I was intensely interested in all that was going on, and in this letter of mine there was told the news of the Czar's death, and there was a good deal of comment upon it. I had read my letter—more than once, I daresay—and was beginning to think I must go down to the others in the drawing-room. But the fire in my bedroom was very tempting; it was burning so brightly, that though I had got up from my chair by the fireside to leave the room, and had blown out the candle I had read my letter by, I yielded to the inclination to sit down again for a minute or two to dream pleasant dreams and think pleasant thoughts.

At last I rose and turned towards the door—it was standing wide open, by the bye. But I had hardly made a step from the fireplace when I was stopped short by what I saw. Again the same strange indefinable feeling of not knowing how or when it had come there, again the same painful sensation of perplexity (not yet amounting to fear) as to whom or what it was I saw before me. The room, you must understand, was perfectly flooded with the firelight; except in the corners, perhaps, every object was as distinct as possible. And the object I was staring at was not in a corner, but standing there right before me—between me and the open door, alas!—in the middle of the room. It was the old woman again, but this time with her face towards me, with a look upon it, it seemed to me, as if she were conscious of my presence. It is very difficult to tell over thoughts and feelings that can hardly have taken any time to pass, or that passed almost simultaneously. My *very* first impulse this time was, as it had been the first time I saw her, to explain in some natural way the presence before me. I think this says something for my common sense, does it not? My mind did not readily desert matters of fact, you see. I did not think of Fraser this time, but the thought went through my mind, "She must be some friend of the servants who comes in to see them of an evening. Perhaps they have sent her up to look at my fire." So at first I looked up at her with simple inquiry. But as I looked my feelings changed. I realised that this was the same being who had appeared so mysteriously once before; I recognised every detail of her dress; I even noticed it more acutely than the first time—for instance, I recollect observing that here and there the short tufty fringe of her shawl was stuck together, instead of hanging smoothly and evenly all round. I looked up at her face. I cannot now describe the features beyond saying that the whole face was refined and pleasing, and that in the expression there was certainly nothing to alarm or repel. It was rather wistful and beseeching, the look in the eyes anxious, the lips slightly parted, as if she were on the point of speaking. I have since thought that if *I* had spoken, if I *could* have spoken—for I did make one effort to do so, but no audible words would come at my bidding—the spell that bound the poor soul, this mysterious wanderer from some shadowy borderland between life and death, might have been broken, and the message that I now believe burdened her delivered. Sometimes I wish I could have done it; but then, again—oh no! a *voice* from those unreal lips would have been too awful—flesh and blood could not have stood it.

For another instant I kept my eyes fixed upon her without moving; then there came over me at last with an awful thrill, a sort of suffocating gasp of horror, the consciousness, the actual realisation of the fact that this before me, this *presence,* was no living human being, no dweller in our familiar world, not a woman, but a ghost! Oh, it was an awful moment! I pray that I may never again endure another like it. There is something so indescribably frightful in the feeling that we are on the verge of being tried *beyond* what we can bear, that ordinary conditions are slipping away from under us, that in another moment reason or life itself must snap with the strain; and all these feelings I then underwent.

At last I moved, moved backwards from the figure. I dared not attempt to *pass* her. Yet I could not at first turn away from her. I stepped backwards, facing her still as I did so, till I was close to the fireplace. Then I turned sharply from her, sat down again on the low chair still standing by the hearth, resolutely forcing myself to gaze into the fire, which was blazing cheerfully, though conscious all the time of a terrible fascination urging me to look round again to the middle of the room. Gradually, however, now that I no longer *saw* her, I began a little to recover myself. I tried to bring my sense and reason to bear on the matter. "This being," I said to myself, "whoever and whatever she is, *cannot harm* me. I am under God's protection as much at this moment as at any moment of my life. All creatures, even disembodied spirits, if there be such, and this among them, if it be one, are under His control. *Why* should I be afraid? I am being tried; my courage and trust are being tried to the utmost: let me prove them, let me keep my own self-respect, by mastering this cowardly, unreasonable terror." And after a time I began to feel stronger and surer of myself. Then I rose from my seat and turned towards the door again; and oh, the relief of seeing that the way was clear; my terrible visitor had disappeared! I hastened across the room, I passed the few steps of passage that lay between my door and the staircase, and hurried down the first flight in a sort of suppressed agony of eagerness to find myself again safe in the living human companionship of my mother and sisters in the cheerful drawing-room below. But my trial was not yet over, indeed it seemed to me afterwards that it had only now reached its height; perhaps the strain on my nervous system was now beginning to tell, and my powers of endurance were all but exhausted. I cannot say if it was so or not. I can only say that my agony of terror, of horror, of absolute *fear,* was far past describing in words, when, just as I reached the little landing at the foot of the first short staircase, and was on the point of running down the longer flight still before me, I saw *again,* coming slowly *up* the steps, as if to meet me, the ghostly figure of the old woman. It was too much. I was reckless by this time; I could not stop. I rushed down the staircase, brushing past the figure as I went: I use the word intentionally—I did *brush* past her, I *felt* her. This part of my experience was, I believe, quite at variance with the sensations of orthodox ghost-seers; but I am really telling you all I was conscious of. Then I hardly remember anything more; my agony broke out at last in a loud shrill cry, and I suppose I fainted. I only know that when I recovered my senses I was in the drawing-room, on the sofa, surrounded by my terrified mother and sisters. But it was not for some time that I could find voice or courage to tell them what had happened to me; for several days I was on the brink of a serious illness, and for long afterwards I could not endure to be left alone, even in the broadest daylight.'

Lady Farquhar stopped. I fancied, however, from her manner that there was more to tell, so I said nothing; and in a minute or two she went on speaking.

'We did not stay long at Ballyreina after this. I was not sorry to leave it; but still, before the time came for us to do so, I had begun to recover from the most painful part of the impression left upon me by my strange adventure. And when I was at home again, far from the place where it had happened, I gradually lost the feeling of horror altogether, and remembered it only as a very curious and inexplicable experience. Now and then even, I did not shrink from talking about it, generally, I think, with a vague hope that somehow, some time or other, light might be thrown upon it. Not that I ever expected, or could have believed it possible, that the supernatural character of the adventure could be explained away; but I always had a misty fancy that sooner or later I should find out *something* about my old lady, as we came to call her; who she had been and what her history was.'

'And did you?' I asked eagerly.

'Yes, I did,' Margaret answered. 'To some extent, at least, I learnt the explanation of what I had seen. This was how it was: nearly a year after we had left Ireland I was staying with one of my aunts, and one evening some young people who were also visiting her began to talk about ghosts, and my aunt, who had heard something of the story from my mother, begged me to tell it. I did so, just as I have now told it to you. When I had finished, an elderly lady who was present, and who had listened very attentively, surprised me a little by asking the name of the house where it happened. "Was it Ballyreina?" she said. I answered "Yes," wondering how she knew it, for I had not mentioned it.

'"Then I can tell you whom you saw," she exclaimed; "it must have been one of the old Miss Fitzgeralds—the eldest one. The description suits her exactly."

'I was quite puzzled. We had never heard of any Fitzgeralds at Ballyreina. I said so to the lady, and asked her to explain what she meant. She told me all she knew. It appeared there had been a family of that name for many generations at Ballyreina. Once upon a time—a long-ago once upon a time—the Fitzgeralds had been great and rich; but gradually one misfortune after another had brought them down in the world, and at the time my informant heard about them the only representatives of the old family were three maiden ladies already elderly. Mrs. Gordon, the lady who told me all this, had met them once, and had been much impressed by what she heard of them. They had got poorer and poorer, till at last they had to give up the struggle, and sell, or let on a long lease, their dear old home, Ballyreina. They were too proud to remain in their own country after this, and spent the rest of their lives on the Continent, wandering about from place to place. The most curious part of it was that nearly all their wandering was actually *on foot*. They were too poor to afford to travel much in the usual way, and yet, once torn from their old associations, the travelling mania seized them; they seemed absolutely unable to rest. So on foot, and speaking not a word of any language but their own, these three desolate sisters journeyed over a great part of the Continent. They visited most of the principal towns, and were well known in several. I daresay they are still remembered at some of the places they used to stay at, though never for more than a short time together. Mrs. Gordon had met them somewhere, I forget where, but it was many years ago. Since then she had never heard of them; she did not know if they were alive or dead; she was only certain that the description of my old lady was exactly like that of the eldest of the sisters, and that the name of their old home was Ballyreina. And I remember her saying, "If ever a heart was buried in a house, it was that of poor old Miss Fitzgerald."

'That was all Mrs. Gordon could tell me,' continued Lady Farquhar; 'but it led to my learning a little more. I told my brother what I had heard. He used often at that time to be in Ireland on business; and to satisfy me, the next time he went he visited the village of Ballyreina again, and in one way and another he found out a few particulars. The house, you remember, had been let to us by a Captain Marchmont. He, my brother discovered, was not the owner of the place, as we had naturally imagined, but only rented it on a very long lease from some ladies of the name of Fitzgerald. It had been in Captain Marchmont's possession for a great many years at the time he let it to us, and the Fitzgeralds, never returning there even to visit it, had come to be almost forgotten. The room with the old-fashioned furniture had been reserved by the owners of the place to leave some of their poor old treasures in—relics too cumbersome to be carried about with them in their strange wanderings, but too precious, evidently, to be parted with. We, of course, never could know what may not have been hidden away in some of the queer old bureaux I told you of. Family papers of importance, perhaps; possibly some ancient love-letters, forgotten in the confusion of their leave-taking; a lock of hair, or a withered flower, perhaps, that she, my poor old lady, would fain have clasped in her hand when dying, or have had buried with her. Ah, yes; there must be many a pitiful old story that is never told.'

Lady Farquhar stopped and gazed dreamily and half sadly into the fire.

'Then Miss Fitzgerald *was* dead when you were at Ballyreina?' I asked.

Margaret looked up with some surprise.

'Did I not say so?' she exclaimed. 'That was the point of most interest in what my brother discovered. He could not hear the exact date of her death, but he learnt with certainty that she was dead—had died, at Geneva I think, some time in the month of March in the previous year; *the same month, March '55, in which I had twice seen the apparition at Ballyreina.'*

This was my friend's ghost story.

1891

In a Far-Off World

OLIVE SCHREINER

There is a world in one of the far-off stars, and things do not happen here as they happen there.

In that world were a man and woman; they had one work, and they walked together side by side on many days, and were friends—and that is a thing that happens now and then in this world also.

But there was something in that star-world that there is not here. There was a thick wood: where the trees grew closest, and the stems were interlocked, and the summer sun never shone, there stood a shrine. In the day all was quiet, but at night, when the stars shone or the moon glinted on the tree-tops, and all was quiet below, if one crept here quite alone and knelt on the steps of the stone altar, and uncovering one's breast, so wounded it that the blood fell down on the altar steps, then whatever he who knelt there wished for was granted him. And all this happens, as I said, because it is a far-off world, and things often happen there as they do not happen here.

Now, the man and woman walked together; and the woman wished well to the man. One night when the moon was shining so that the leaves of all the trees glinted, and the waves of the sea were silvery, the woman walked alone to the forest. It was dark there; the moonlight fell only in little flecks on the dead leaves under her feet, and the branches were knotted tight overhead. Farther in it got darker, not even a fleck of moonlight shone. Then she came to the shrine; she knelt down before it and prayed; there came no answer. Then she uncovered her breast; with a sharp two-edged stone that lay there she wounded it. The drops dripped slowly down on to the stone, and a voice cried, 'What do you seek?'

She answered, 'There is a man; I hold him nearer than anything. I would give him the best of all blessings.'

The voice said, 'What is it?'

The girl said, 'I know not, but that which is most good for him I wish him to have.'

The voice said, 'Your prayer is answered; he shall have it.'

Then she stood up. She covered her breast and held the garment tight upon it with her hand, and ran out of the forest, and the dead leaves fluttered under her feet. Out in the moonlight the soft air was blowing, and the sand glittered on the beach. She ran along the smooth shore, then suddenly she stood still. Out across the water there was something moving. She shaded her eyes and looked. It was a boat; it was sliding swiftly over the moonlit water out to sea. One stood upright in it; the face the moonlight did not show, but the figure she knew. It was passing swiftly; it seemed as if no one propelled it; the moonlight's shimmer did not let her see clearly, and the boat was far from shore, but it seemed almost as if there was another figure sitting in the stern. Faster and faster it glided over the water away, away. She ran along the shore; she came no nearer it. The garment she had held closed fluttered open; she stretched out her arms, and the moonlight shone on her long loose hair.

Then a voice beside her whispered, 'What is it?'

She cried, 'With my blood I bought the best of all gifts for him. I have come to bring it him! He is going from me!'

The voice whispered softly, 'Your prayer was answered. It has been given him.'

She cried, 'What is it?'

The voice answered, 'It is that he might leave you.'

The girl stood still.

Far out at sea the boat was lost to sight beyond the moonlight sheen.

The voice spoke softly, 'Art thou contented?'

She said, 'I am contented.'

At her feet the waves broke in long ripples softly on the shore.

1892

Death and the Woman

GERTRUDE ATHERTON

Her husband was dying, and she was alone with him. Nothing could exceed the desolation of her surroundings. She and the man who was going from her were in the third-floor-back of a New York boarding-house. It was summer, and the other boarders were in the country; all the servants except the cook had been dismissed, and she, when not working, slept profoundly on the fifth floor. The landlady also was out of town on a brief holiday.

The window was open to admit the thick unstirring air; no sound rose from the row of long narrow yards, nor from the tall deep houses annexed. The latter deadened the rattle of the streets. At intervals the distant Elevated lumbered protestingly along, its grunts and screams muffled by the hot suspended ocean.

She sat there plunged in the profoundest grief that can come to the human soul, for in all other agony hope flickers, however forlornly. She gazed dully at the unconscious breathing form of the man who had been friend, and companion, and lover, during five years of youth too vigorous and hopeful to be warped by uneven fortune. It was wasted by disease; the face was shrunken; the night garment hung loosely about a body which had never been disfigured by flesh, but had been muscular with exercise and full-blooded with health. She was glad that the body was changed; glad that its beauty, too, had gone some otherwhere than into the coffin. She had loved his hands as apart from himself; loved their strong warm magnetism. They lay limp and yellow on the quilt: she knew that they were already cold, and that moisture was gathering on them. For a moment something convulsed within her. *They* had gone too. She repeated the words twice, and, after them, '*for ever*.' And the while the sweetness of their pressure came back to her.

She leaned suddenly over him. He was in there still, somewhere. *Where?* If he had not ceased to breathe, the Ego, the Soul, the Personality, was still in the sodden clay which had shaped to give it speech. Why could it not manifest itself to her? Was it still conscious in there, unable to project itself through the disintegrating matter which was the only medium its Creator had vouchsafed it? Did it struggle there, seeing her agony, sharing it, longing for the complete disintegration which should put an end to its torment? She called his name, she even shook him slightly, mad to tear the body apart and find her mate, yet even in that tortured moment realising that violence would hasten his going.

The dying man took no notice of her, and she opened his gown and put her cheek to his heart, calling him again. There had never been more perfect union; how could the bond still be so strong if he were not at the other end of it? He was there, her other part; until dead he must be living. There was no intermediate state. Why should he be as entombed and unresponding as if the screws were in the lid? But the faintly beating heart did not quicken beneath her lips. She extended her arms suddenly, describing eccentric lines, above, about him, rapidly opening and closing her hands as if to clutch some escaping object; then sprang to her feet, and went to the window. She feared insanity. She had asked to be left alone with her dying husband, and she did not wish to lose her reason and shriek a crowd of people about her.

The green plots in the yards were not apparent, she noticed. Something heavy, like a pall, rested upon them. Then she understood that the day was over and that night was coming.

She returned swiftly to the bedside, wondering if she had remained away hours or seconds, and if he were dead. His face was still discernible, and Death had not relaxed it. She laid her own against it, then withdrew it with shuddering flesh, her teeth smiting each other as if an icy wind had passed.

She let herself fall back in the chair, clasping her hands against her heart, watching with expanding eyes the white sculptured face which, in the gathering dark, was becoming less defined of outline. Did she light the gas it would draw mosquitoes, and she could not shut from him the little air he must be mechanically grateful for. And she did not want to see the opening eye—the falling jaw.

Her vision became so fixed that at length she saw nothing, and closed her eyes and waited for the moisture to rise and relieve the strain. When she opened them his face had disappeared; the humid waves above the house-tops put out even the light of the stars, and night was come.

Fearfully, she approached her ear to his lips; he still breathed. She made a motion to kiss him, then threw herself back in a quiver of agony—they were not the lips she had known, and she would have nothing less.

His breathing was so faint that in her half-reclining position she could not hear it, could not be aware of the moment of his death. She extended her arm resolutely and laid her hand on his heart. Not only must she feel his going, but, so strong had been the comradeship between them, it was a matter of loving honour to stand by him to the last.

She sat there in the hot heavy night, pressing her hand hard against the ebbing heart of the unseen, and awaited Death. Suddenly an odd fancy possessed her. Where was Death? Why was he tarrying? Who was detaining him? From what quarter would he come? He was taking his leisure, drawing near with footsteps as measured as those of men keeping time to a funeral march. By a wayward deflection she thought of the slow music that was always turned on in the theatre when the heroine was about to appear, or something eventful to happen. She had always thought that sort of thing ridiculous and inartistic. So had He.

She drew her brows together angrily, wondering at her levity, and pressed her relaxed palm against the heart it kept guard over. For a moment the sweat stood on her face; then the pent-up breath burst from her lungs. He still lived.

Once more the fancy wantoned above the stunned heart. Death— *where* was he? What a curious experience: to be sitting alone in a big house—she knew that the cook had stolen out—waiting for Death to come and snatch her husband from her. No; he would not snatch, he would steal upon his prey as noiselessly as the approach of Sin to Innocence—an invisible, unfair, sneaking enemy, with whom no man's strength could grapple. If he would only come like a man, and take his chances like a man! Women had been known to reach the hearts of giants with the dagger's point. But he would creep upon her.

She gave an exclamation of horror. Something was creeping over the window-sill. Her limbs palsied, but she struggled to her feet and looked back, her eyes dragged about against her own volition. Two small green stars glared menacingly at her just above the sill; then the cat possessing them leaped downward, and the stars disappeared.

She realised that she was horribly frightened. 'Is it possible?' she thought. 'Am I afraid of Death, and of Death that has not yet come? I have always been rather a brave woman; *He* used to call me heroic; but then with him it was impossible to fear anything. And I begged them to leave me alone with him as the last of earthly boons. Oh, shame!'

But she was still quaking as she resumed her seat, and laid her hand again on his heart. She wished that she had asked Mary to sit outside the door; there was no bell in the room. To call would be worse than desecrating the house of God, and she would not leave him for one moment. To return and find him dead—gone alone!

Her knees smote each other. It was idle to deny it; she was in a state of unreasoning terror. Her eyes rolled apprehensively about; she wondered if she should see It when It came; wondered how far off It was now. Not very far; the heart was barely pulsing. She had heard of the power of the corpse to drive brave men to frenzy, and had wondered, having no morbid horror of the dead. But this! To wait—and wait—and wait—perhaps for hours—past the midnight—on to the small hours—while that awful, determined, leisurely Something stole nearer and nearer.

She bent to him who had been her protector, with a spasm of anger. Where was the indomitable spirit that had held her all these years with such strong and loving clasp? How could he leave her? How could he desert her? Her head fell back and moved restlessly against the cushion; moaning with the agony of loss, she recalled him as he had been. Then fear once more took possession of her, and she sat erect, rigid, breathless, awaiting the approach of Death.

Suddenly, far down in the house, on the first-floor, her strained hearing took note of a sound—a wary, muffled sound, as if some one were creeping up the stair, fearful of being heard. Slowly! It seemed to count a hundred between the laying down of each foot. She gave a hysterical gasp. Where was the slow music?

Her face, her body, were wet—as if a wave of death-sweat had broken over them. There was a stiff feeling at the roots of her hair; she wondered if it were really standing erect. But she could not raise her hand to ascertain. Possibly it was only the colouring matter freezing and bleaching. Her muscles were flabby, her nerves twitched helplessly.

She knew that it was Death who was coming to her through the silent deserted house; knew that it was the sensitive ear of her intelligence that heard him, not the dull coarse-grained ear of the body.

He toiled up the stair painfully, as if he were old and tired with much work. But *how* could he afford to loiter, with all the work he had to do? Every minute, every second, he must be in demand to hook his cold hard finger about a soul struggling to escape from its putrefying tenement. But probably he had his emissaries, his minions: for only those worthy of the honour did he come in person.

He reached the first landing and crept like a cat down the hall to the next stair, then crawled slowly up as before. Light as the footfalls were, they were squarely planted, unfaltering; slow, they never halted.

Mechanically she pressed her jerking hand closer against the heart; its beats were almost done. They would finish, she calculated, just as those footfalls paused beside the bed.

She was no longer a human being; she was an Intelligence and an Ear. Not a sound came from without, even the Elevated appeared to be temporarily off duty; but inside the big quiet house that footfall was waxing louder, louder, until iron feet crashed on iron stairs and echo thundered.

She had counted the steps—one—two—three—irritated beyond endurance at the long deliberate pauses between. As they climbed and clanged with slow precision she continued to count, audibly and with equal precision, noting their hollow reverberation. How many steps had the stair? She wished she knew. No need! The colossal trampling announced the lessening distance in an increasing volume of sound not to be misunderstood. It turned the curve; it reached the landing; it advanced—slowly—down the hall; it paused before her door. Then knuckles of iron shook the frail panels. Her nerveless tongue gave no invitation. The knocking became more imperious; the very walls vibrated. The handle turned, swiftly and firmly. With a wild instinctive movement she flung herself into the arms of her husband.

When Mary opened the door and entered the room she found a dead woman lying across a dead man.

1893

Man-Size in Marble

EDITH NESBIT

Although every word of this tale is true, I do not expect people to believe it. Nowadays a 'rational explanation' is required before belief is possible. Let me, at once, offer the 'rational explanation' which finds most favour among those who have heard the tale of my life's tragedy. It is held that we were 'under a delusion', she and I, on that 31st of October; and that this supposition places the whole matter on a satisfactory and believable basis. The reader can judge, when he, too, has heard my story, how far this is an 'explanation', and in what sense it is 'rational'. There were three who took part in this; Laura and I and another man. The other man lives still, and can speak to the truth of the least credible part of my story.

I never knew in my life what it was to have as much money as would supply the most ordinary needs of life—good colours, canvasses, brushes, books and cab-fares—and when we were married we knew quite well that we should only be able to live at all by 'strict punctuality and attention to business'. I used to paint in those days, and Laura used to write, and we felt sure we could keep the pot at least simmering. Living in London was out of the question, so we went to look for a cottage in the country, which should be at once sanitary and picturesque. So rarely do these two qualities meet in one cottage that our search was for some time quite fruitless. We tried advertisements, but most of the desirable rural residences which we did look at, proved to be lacking in both essentials, and when a cottage chanced to have drains, it always had stucco as well and was shaped like a tea-caddy. And if we found a vine or a rose-covered porch, corruption invariably lurked within. Our minds got so befogged by the eloquence of house-agents, and the rival disadvantages of the fever-traps and outrages to beauty which we had seen and scorned, that I very much doubt whether either of us, on our wedding morning, knew the difference between a house and a haystack. But when we got away from friends and house-agents on our honeymoon, our wits grew clear again, and we knew a pretty cottage when at last we saw one. It was at Brenzett—a little village set on a hill, over against the southern marshes. We had gone there from the little fishing village, where we were staying, to see the church, and two fields from the church we found this cottage. It stood quite by itself about two miles from Brenzett village. It was a low building with rooms sticking out in unexpected places. There was a bit of stonework—ivy-covered and moss-grown, just two old rooms, all that was left of a big house that once stood there—and round this stonework the house had grown up. Stripped of its roses and jasmine, it would have been hideous. As it stood it was charming, and after a brief examination, enthusiasm usurped the place of discretion and we took it. It was absurdly cheap. The rest of our honeymoon we spent in grubbing about in second-hand shops in Ashford, picking up bits of old oak and Chippendale chairs for our furnishing. We wound up with a run up to town and a visit to Liberty's, and soon the low, oak-beamed, lattice-windowed rooms began to be home. There was a jolly old-fashioned garden, with grass paths and no end of hollyhocks, and sunflowers, and big lilies, and roses with thousands of small sweet flowers. From the window you could see the marsh-pastures, and beyond them the blue, thin line of the sea. We were as happy as the summer was glorious, and settled down into work sooner than we ourselves expected. I was never tired of sketching the view and the wonderful cloud effects from the open lattice, and Laura would sit at the table and write verses about them, in which I mostly played the part of foreground.

We got a tall, old, peasant woman to do for us. Her face and figure were good, though her cooking was of the homeliest; but she understood all about gardening, and told us all the old names of the coppices and cornfields, and the stories of the smugglers and the highwaymen, and, better still, of the 'things that walked', and of the 'sights' which met one in lonely lanes of a starlight night. She was a great comfort to us, because Laura hated housekeeping as much as I loved folk-lore, and we soon came to leave all the domestic business to Mrs Dorman, and to use her legends in little magazine stories which brought in guineas.

We had three months of married happiness. We did not have a single quarrel. And then it happened. One October evening I had been down to smoke a pipe with the doctor—our only neighbour—a pleasant young Irishman. Laura had stayed at home to finish a comic sketch of a village episode for the *Monthly Marplot*. I left her laughing over her own jokes, and came in to see her a crumpled heap of pale muslin, weeping on the window seat.

'Good heavens, my darling, what's the matter?' I cried, taking her in my arms. She leaned her head against my shoulder, and went on crying. I had never seen her cry before—we had always been so happy, you see—and I felt sure some frightful misfortune had happened.

'What *is* the matter? Do speak!'

'It's Mrs Dorman,' she sobbed.

'What has she done?' I inquired, immensely relieved.

'She says she must go before the end of the month, and she says her niece is ill; she's gone down to see her now, but I don't believe that's the reason, because her niece is always ill. I believe someone has been setting her against us. Her manner was so queer—'

'Never mind, Pussy,' I said. 'Whatever you do, don't cry, or I shall have to cry, too, to keep you in countenance, and then you'll never respect your man again.'

She dried her eyes obediently on my handkerchief, and even smiled faintly.

'But, you see,' she went on, 'it is really serious, because these village people are so sheepy; and if one won't do a thing, you may be sure none of the others will. And I shall have to cook the dinners and wash up all the hateful, greasy plates; and you'll have to carry cans of water about, and clean the boots and knives—and we shall never have any time for work, or earn any money or anything. We shall have to work all day, and only be able to rest when we are waiting for the kettle to boil!'

I represented to her that, even if we had to perform these duties, the day would still present some margin for other toils and recreations. But she refused to see the matter in any but the greyest light. She was very unreasonable, and I told her so, but in my heart . . . well, who wants a woman to be reasonable?

'I'll speak to Mrs Dorman when she comes back, and see if I can't come to terms with her,' I said. 'Perhaps she wants a rise in her screw. It will be all right. Let's walk up to the church.'

The church was a large and lonely one, and we loved to go there, especially upon bright nights. The path skirted a wood, cut through it once, and ran along the crest of the hill through two meadows and round the churchyard wall, over which the old yews loomed in black masses of shadow. This path, which was partly paved, was called the 'bier-balk', for it had long been the way by which the corpses had been carried to burial. The churchyard was richly treed, and was shaded by great elms, which stood just outside and stretched their kind arms out over the dead. A large, low porch let one into the building by a Norman doorway and a heavy oak door studded with iron. Inside, the arches rose into darkness, and between them shone the reticulated windows, which stood out white in the moonlight. In the chancel, the windows were of rich glass, which showed in faint light their noble colouring and made the black oak of the choir pews hardly more solid than the shadows. But on each side of the altar lay a grey marble figure of a knight in full armour, lying upon a low slab, with hands held up in everlasting prayer, and these figures, oddly enough, were always to be seen if there was any glimmer of light in the church. Their names were lost, but the peasants told of them that they had been fierce and wicked men, marauders by land and sea, who had been the scourge of their time, and had been guilty of deeds so foul that the house they had lived in—the big house, by the way, that had stood on the site of our cottage—had been stricken by lightning and the vengeance of Heaven. But for all that, the gold of their heirs had bought them a place in the church. Looking at the bad, hard faces reproduced in the marble, this story was easily believed.

The church looked at its best on that night, for the shadows of the yew trees fell through the windows upon the floor of the nave, and touched the pillars with tattered shadow. We sat down together without speaking, and watched the solemn beauty of the old church with some of that awe which inspired its early builders. We walked to the chancel and looked at the sleeping warriors. Then we rested on the stone seat in the porch, looking out over the stretch of quiet moonlit meadows, feeling in every fibre of our being the peace of the

night and of our happy love; and came away at last with a sense
that even scrubbing and black-leading were, at their worst, but small
troubles.

Mrs Dorman had come back from the village, and I at once invited
her to a *tête-à-tête*.

'Now, Mrs Dorman,' I said, when I had got her into my painting-
room, 'what's all this about your not staying with us?'

'I should be glad to get away, sir, before the end of the month,' she
answered, with her usual placid dignity.

'Have you any fault to find, Mrs Dorman?'

'None at all, sir; you and your lady have always been most kind,
I'm sure—'

'Well, what is it? Are your wages not high enough?'

'No, sir, I gets quite enough.'

'Then why not stay?'

'I'd rather not,' with some hesitation. 'My niece is ill.'

'But your niece has been ill ever since we came.'

No answer. There was a long and awkward silence. I broke it.

'Can't you stay for another month?' I asked.

'No, sir. I'm bound to go on Thursday.'

And this was Monday.

'Well, I must say, I think you might have let us know before.
There's no time now to get anyone else, and your mistress is not fit
to do heavy housework. Can't you stay till next week?'

'I might be able to come back next week.'

I was now convinced that all she wanted was a brief holiday, which
we should have been willing enough to let her have as soon as we
could get a substitute.

'But why must you go this week?' I persisted. 'Come, out with
it.'

Mrs Dorman drew the little shawl, which she always wore, tightly
across her bosom, as though she were cold. Then she said, with a sort
of effort:

'They say, sir, as this was a big house in Catholic times, and there
was a many deeds done here.'

The nature of the 'deeds' might be vaguely inferred from the
inflection of Mrs Dorman's voice, which was enough to make one's
blood run cold. I was glad that Laura was not in the room. She was
always nervous, as highly strung natures are, and I felt that these tales

about our house, told by this old peasant woman with her impressive manner and contagious credulity, might have made our home less dear to my wife.

'Tell me all about it, Mrs Dorman,' I said. 'You needn't mind about telling me. I'm not like the young people, who make fun of such things.'

Which was partly true.

'Well, sir,' she sank her voice, 'you may have seen in the church, beside the altar, two shapes—'

'You mean the effigies of the knights in armour?' I said cheerfully.

'I mean them two bodies drawed out man-size in marble,' she returned; and I had to admit that her description was a thousand times more graphic than mine.

'They do say as on All Saints' Eve them two bodies sits up on their slabs and gets off of them, and then walks down the aisle *in their marble*'—(another good phrase, Mrs Dorman)—'and as the church clock strikes eleven, they walks out of the church door, and over the graves, and along the bier-balk, and if it's a wet night there's the marks of their feet in the morning.'

'And where do they go?' I asked, rather fascinated.

'They comes back to their old home, sir, and if anyone meets them—'

'Well, what then?' I asked.

But no, not another word could I get from her, save that her niece was ill, and that she must go. After what I had heard I scorned to discuss the niece, and tried to get from Mrs Dorman more details of the legend. I could get nothing but warnings.

'Whatever you do, sir, lock the door early on All Saints' Eve, and make the blessed cross-sign over the doorstep and on the windows.'

'But has anyone ever seen these things?' I persisted.

'That's not for me to say. I know what I know.'

'Well, who was here last year?'

'No one, sir. The lady as owned the house only stayed here in the summer, and she always went to London a full month afore *the* night. And I'm sorry to inconvenience you and your lady, but my niece is ill, and I must go on Thursday.'

I could have shaken her for her reiteration of that obvious fiction.

She was determined to go, nor could our united entreaties move her in the least.

I did not tell Laura the legend of the shapes that 'walked in their marble', partly because a legend concerning our house might trouble my wife, and partly, I think, for some more occult reason. This was not quite the same to me as any other story, and I did not want to talk about it till the day was over. I had very soon almost ceased to think of the legend, however. I was painting a portrait of Laura, against the lattice window, and I could not think of much else. I had got a splendid background of yellow and grey sunset, and was working away with enthusiasm at her face. On Thursday Mrs Dorman went. She relented, at parting, so far as to say:

'Don't you put yourselves about too much, ma'am, and if there's any little thing I can do next week, I'm sure I shan't mind.'

From which I inferred that she wished to come back to us after Hallowe'en. Up to the last she adhered to the fiction of the niece.

Thursday passed off pretty well. Laura showed marked ability in the matter of steak and potatoes, and I confess that my knives, and the plates, which I insisted upon washing, were better done than I had dared to expect. It was all so good, so simple, so pleasant. As I write of it, I almost forget what came after. But now I must remember, and tell.

Friday came. It is about what happened on that Friday that this is written. I wonder if I should have believed it if anyone had told it to me. I will write the story of it as quickly and plainly as I can. Everything that happened on that day is burnt into my brain. I shall not forget anything, nor leave anything out.

I got up early, I remember, and lighted the kitchen fire, and had just achieved a smoky success, when my wife came running down, as sunny and sweet as the clear October morning itself. We prepared breakfast together, and found it very good fun. The housework was soon done, and when brushes and brooms and pails were quiet again, the house was still indeed. It is wonderful what a difference *one* makes in a house. We really missed Mrs Dorman, quite apart from considerations of pots and pans. We spent the day in dusting our books and putting them straight, and dined gaily on cold steak and coffee. Laura was, if possible, brighter and gayer and sweeter than usual, and I began to think that a little domestic toil was really good for her. We had never been so merry since we were married, and the walk we had that afternoon was, I think, the happiest time of all my life. When we had watched the deep scarlet clouds slowly pale into leaden gray against a pale-green sky, and saw the white mists curl up along the hedgerows in the distant marsh, we came back to the house, silently, hand in hand.

'You are sad, Pussy,' I said half-jestingly, as we sat down together in our little parlour. I expected a disclaimer, for my own silence had been the silence of complete happiness. To my surprise, she said:

'Yes, I think I am sad, or rather I am uneasy. I hope I am not going to be ill. I have shivered three or four times since we came in, and it's not really cold, is it?'

'No,' I said, and hoped it was not a chill caught from the treacherous marsh mists that roll up from the marshes in the dying light. No, she said, she did not think so. Then, after a silence, she spoke suddenly:

'Do you ever have presentiments of evil?'

'No,' I said, smiling; 'and I shouldn't believe in them if I had.'

'I do,' she went on; 'the night my father died I knew it, though he was right away in the north of Scotland.' I did not answer in words.

She sat looking at the fire in silence for some time, gently stroking my hand. At last she sprang up, came behind me, and drawing my head back, kissed me.

'There, it's over now,' she said. 'What a baby I am. Come, light the candles, and we'll have some of these new Rubinstein duets.'

And we spent a happy hour or two at the piano.

At about half-past ten, I began to fill the good-night pipe, but Laura looked so white that I felt that it would be brutal of me to fill our sitting-room with the fumes of strong cavendish.

'I'll take my pipe outside,' I said.

'Let me come too.'

'No, sweetheart, not tonight; you're much too tired. I shan't be long. Get to bed, or I shall have an invalid to nurse tomorrow, as well as the boots to clean.'

I kissed her and was turning to go, when she flung her arms round my neck and held me very closely. I stroked her hair.

'Come, Pussy, you're over-tired. The housework has been too much for you.'

She loosened her clasp a little and drew a deep breath.

'No. We've been very happy today, Jack, haven't we? Don't stay out too long.'

'I won't, Puss cat,' I said.

I strolled out of the front door, leaving it unlatched. What a night it was! The jagged masses of heavy, dark cloud were rolling at intervals from horizon to horizon, and thin, white wreaths covered the stars. Through all the rush of the cloud river, the moon swam, breasting the waves and disappearing again in the darkness. When, now and again, her light reached the woodlands, they seemed to be slowly and noiselessly waving in time to the clouds above them. There was a strange, grey light over all the earth; the fields had that shadowy bloom over them which only comes from the marriage of dew and moonshine, or frost and starlight.

I walked up and down, drinking in the beauty of the quiet earth and changing sky. The night was absolutely silent. Nothing seemed to be abroad. There was no scurrying of rabbits, or twitter of half-asleep birds. And though the clouds went sailing across the sky, the wind that drove them never came low enough to rustle the dead leaves in the woodland paths. Across the meadow, I could see the church tower standing out black and grey against the sky. I walked there, thinking over our three months of happiness, and of my wife—her dear eyes, her pretty ways. Oh, my girl! my own little girl; what a vision came to me then of a long, glad life for you and me together!

I heard a bell-beat from the church. Eleven already! I turned to go in, but the night held me. I could not go back into our little warm rooms yet. I would go right on up to the church. I felt vaguely that it would be good to carry my love and thankfulness to the sanctuary, whither so many loads of sorrow and gladness had been borne by men and women dead long since.

I looked in at the low window as I went by. Laura was half lying on her chair in front of the fire. I could not see her face, only her head showed dark against the pale blue wall. She was quite still. Asleep no doubt. My heart reached out to her, as I went on. There must be a God, I thought, and a God that was good. How otherwise could anything so sweet and dear as she ever have been imagined?

I walked slowly along the edge of the wood. A sound broke the stillness of the night. I stopped and listened. The sound stopped too. I went on, and now distinctly I heard another step than mine answer mine like an echo. It was a poacher or a wood-stealer, most likely, for these were not unknown in our Arcadia. But, whoever it was, he was a fool not to step more lightly. I turned into the wood, and now the footstep seemed to come from the path I had

just left. It must be an echo, I thought. The wood lay lovely in
the moonlight. The large, dying ferns and the brushwood showed
where, through thinning foliage, the pale light came down. The tree
trunks stood up like Gothic columns all around me. They reminded
me of the church, and I turned into the bier-balk and passed through
the corpse-gate between the graves to the low porch. I paused for a
moment on the stone seat where Laura and I had last night watched
the fading landscape. Then I noticed that the door of the church was
open, and I blamed myself for having left it unlatched the other night.
We were the only people who ever cared to come to the church except
on Sundays, and I was vexed to think that through our carelessness
the damp autumn airs had had a chance of getting in and injuring
the old fabric. I went in. It will seem strange perhaps that I should
have gone half-way up the aisle before I remembered—with a sudden
chill, followed by as sudden a rush of self-contempt—that this was the
very day and hour when, according to tradition, the 'shapes drawed
out man-size in marble', began to walk.

Having thus remembered the legend, and remembered it with a
shiver of which I was ashamed, I could not do otherwise than walk
up towards the altar, just to look at the figures—as I said to myself;
really what I wanted was to assure myself, first, that I did not believe
the legend, and, secondly, that it was not true. I was rather glad that
I had come. I thought that now I could tell Mrs Dorman how vain
her fancies were, and how peacefully the marble figures slept on
through the ghostly hour. With my hands in my pockets, I passed
up the aisle. In the grey, dim light, the eastern end of the church
looked larger than usual, and the arches above the tombs looked larger
too. The moon came out and showed me the reason. I stopped short,
my heart gave a great leap that nearly choked me, and then sank
sickeningly.

The 'bodies drawed out man-size' *were gone,* and their marble slabs
lay wide and bare in the vague moonlight that slanted through the
west window.

Were they really gone? or was I mad? Clenching my nerves, I
stooped and passed my hand over the smooth slabs and felt their
flat unbroken surface. Had someone taken the things away? Was it
some vile practical joke? I would make sure, anyway. In an instant I
had made a torch of a newspaper which happened to be in my pocket,
and lighting it held it high above my head. Its yellow glare illumined

the dark arches and those slabs. The figures *were* gone. And I was alone in the church; or was I alone?

And then a horror seized me, a horror indefinable and indescribable—an overwhelming certainty of supreme and accomplished calamity. I flung down the torch and tore along the aisle and out through the door, biting my lips as I ran to keep myself from shrieking aloud. Was I mad—or what was this that possessed me? I leaped the churchyard wall and took the straight cut across the fields, led by the light from our windows. Just as I got over the first stile, a dark figure seemed to spring out of the ground. Mad still with the certainty of misfortune, I made for the thing that stood in my path, shouting 'Get out of the way, can't you?'

But my push met with a very vigorous resistance. My arms were caught just above the elbow and held as in a vice, and the raw-boned Irish doctor actually shook me.

'Would ye?' he cried in his own unmistakable accents—'would ye, then?'

'Let me go, you fool,' I gasped. 'The marble figures have gone from the church; I tell you they've gone.'

He broke into a ringing laugh. 'I'll have to give ye a draught tomorrow, I see. Ye've been smoking too much and listening to old wives' tales.'

'I'll tell you I've seen the bare slabs.'

'Well, come back with me. I'm going up to old Palmer's—his daughter's ill—it's only hysteria, but it's as bad as it can be; we'll look in at the church and let *me* see the bare slabs.'

'You go if you like,' I said, a little less frantic for his laughter, 'I'm going home to my wife.'

'Rubbish, man,' said he; 'D'ye think I'll permit of that? Are ye to go saying all yer life that ye've seen solid marble endowed with vitality, and me to go all my life saying ye were a coward? No, sir—ye shan't do ut!'

The quiet night—a human voice—and I think also the physical contact with this six feet of solid common sense, brought me back a little to my ordinary self, and the word 'coward' was a shower-bath.

'Come on, then,' I said sullenly, 'perhaps you're right.'

He still held my arm tightly. We got over the stile and back to the church. All was still as death. The place smelt very damp and earthy. We walked up the aisle. I am not ashamed to confess I shut my eyes; I knew the figures would not be there, I heard Kelly strike a match.

'Here they are, ye see, right enough; ye've been dreaming or drinking, asking yer pardon for the imputation.'

I opened my eyes. By Kelly's expiring vesta I saw two shapes lying 'in their marble' on their slabs. I drew a deep breath and caught his hand.

'I'm awfully indebted to you,' I said. 'It must have been some trick of the light, or I have been working rather hard, perhaps that's it. Do you know, I was quite convinced they were gone.'

'I'm aware of that,' he answered rather grimly; 'ye'll have to be careful of that brain of yours, my friend, I assure you.'

He was leaning over and looking at the righthand figure, whose stone face was the most villainous and deadly in expression. He struck another match.

'By Jove!' he said, 'something has been going on here—this hand is broken.'

And so it was. I was certain that it had been perfect the last time Laura and I had been there.

'Perhaps someone had *tried* to remove them,' said the young doctor.

'That won't account for my impression,' I objected.

'Too much painting and tobacco will account for what you call your impression,' he said.

'Come along,' I said, 'or my wife will be getting anxious. You'll come in and have a drop of whisky, and drink confusion to ghosts and better sense to me.'

'I ought to go up to Palmer's, but it's so late now, I'd best leave it till the morning,' he replied. 'I was kept late at the Union, and I've had to see a lot of people since. All right, I'll come back with ye.'

I think he fancied I needed him more than did Palmer's girl, so, discussing how such an illusion could have been possible, and deducing from this experience large generalities concerning ghostly apparitions, we saw, as we walked up the garden path, that bright light streamed out of the front door, and presently saw that the parlour door was open too. Had she gone out?

'Come in,' I said, and Dr Kelly followed me into the parlour. It was all ablaze with candles, not only the wax ones, but at least a dozen guttering, glaring, tallow dips, stuck in vases and ornaments in unlikely places. Light, I knew, was Laura's remedy for nervousness. Poor child! Why had I left her? Brute that I was.

We glanced round the room, and at first we did not see her. The window was open and the draught set all the candles flaring one way. Her chair was empty, and her handkerchief and book lay on the floor. I turned to the window. There, in the recess of the window, I saw her. Oh, my child, my love, had she gone to that window to watch for me? To what had she turned with that look of frantic fear and horror? Had she thought that it was my step she heard and turned to meet—what?

She had fallen back against a table in the window, and her body lay half on it and half on the window-seat, and her head hung down over the table, the brown hair loosened and fallen to the carpet. Her lips were drawn back and her eyes wide, wide open. They saw nothing now. What had they last seen?

The doctor moved towards her. But I pushed him aside and sprang to her; caught her in my arms, and cried—

'It's all right, Laura! I've got you safe, dear!'

She fell into my arms in a heap. I clasped her and kissed her, and called her by all her pet names, but I think I knew all the time that she was dead. Her hands were tightly clenched. In one of them she held something fast. When I was quite sure that she was dead, and that nothing mattered at all any more, I let him open her hand to see what she held.

It was a grey marble finger.

1894

The Banshee's Warning

MRS. J. H. RIDDELL

Many a year, before chloroform was thought of, there lived in an old rambling house, in Gerrard Street, Soho, a clever Irishman called Hertford O'Donnell.

After Hertford O'Donnell he was entitled to write, M.R.C.S., for he had studied hard to gain this distinction, and the older surgeons at Guy's (his hospital) considered him one of the most rising operators of the day.

Having said chloroform was unknown at the time this story opens, it will strike my readers that, if Hertford O'Donnell were a rising and successful operator in those days, of necessity he combined within himself a larger number of striking qualities than are by any means necessary to form a successful operator in these.

There was more than mere hand skill, more than even thorough knowledge of his profession, then needful for the man, who, dealing with conscious subjects, essayed to rid them of some of the diseases to which flesh is heir. There was greater courage required in the manipulator of old than is altogether essential at present. Then, as now, a thorough mastery of his instruments, a steady hand, a keen eye, a quick dexterity were indispensable to a good operator; but, added to all these things, there formerly required a pulse which knew no quickening, a mental strength which never faltered, a ready power of adaptation in unexpected circumstances, fertility of resource in difficult cases, and a brave front under all emergencies.

If I refrain from adding that a hard as well as a courageous heart was an important item in the programme, it is only out of deference to general opinion, which, amongst other strange delusions, clings to the belief that courage and hardness are antagonistic qualities.

Hertford O'Donnell, however, was hard as steel. He understood his work, and he did it thoroughly; but he cared no more for quivering nerves and shrinking muscles, for screams of agony, for faces white with pain, and teeth clenched in the extremity of anguish, than he did for the stony countenances of the dead, which so often in the dissecting room appalled younger and less experienced men.

He had no sentiment, and he had no sympathy. The human body was to him, merely an ingenious piece of mechanism, which it was at once a pleasure and a profit to understand. Precisely as Brunel loved the Thames Tunnel, or any other singular engineering feat, so O'Donnell loved a patient on whom he had operated successfully, more especially if the ailment possessed by the patient were of a rare and difficult character.

And for this reason he was much liked by all who came under his hands, since patients are apt to mistake a surgeon's interest in their cases for interest in themselves; and it was gratifying to John Dicks, plasterer, and Timothy Regan, labourer, to be the happy possessors of remarkable diseases, which produced a cordial understanding between them and the handsome Irishman.

If he had been hard and cool at the moment of hacking them to pieces, that was all forgotten or remembered only as a virtue, when, after being discharged from hospital like soldiers who have served in a severe campaign, they met Mr. O'Donnell in the street, and were accosted by that rising individual just as though he considered himself nobody.

He had a royal memory, this stranger in a strange land, both for faces and cases; and like the rest of his countrymen, he never felt it beneath his dignity to talk cordially to corduroy and fustian.

In London, as at Calgillan, he never held back his tongue from speaking a cheery or a kindly word. His manners were pliable enough, if his heart were not; and the porters, and the patients, and the nurses, and the students at Guy's were all pleased to see Hertford O'Donnell.

Rain, hail, sunshine, it was all the same; there was a life and a brightness about the man which communicated itself to those with whom he came in contact. Let the mud in the Borough be a foot deep or the London fog as thick as pea-soup, Mr. O'Donnell never lost his temper, never muttered a surly reply to the gate-keeper's salutation, but spoke out blithely and cheerfully to his pupils and his patients, to the sick and to the well, to those below and to those above him.

And yet, spite of all these good qualities, spite of his handsome face, his fine figure, his easy address, and his unquestionable skill as an operator, the dons, who acknowledged his talent, shook their heads gravely when two or three of them in private and solemn conclave, talked confidentially of their younger brother.

If there were many things in his favour, there were more in his disfavour. He was Irish—not merely by the accident of birth, which might have been forgiven, since a man cannot be held accountable for such caprices of Nature, but by every other accident and design which is objectionable to the orthodox and respectable and representative English mind.

In speech, appearance, manner, taste, modes of expression, habits of life, Hertford O'Donnell was Irish. To the core of his heart he loved the island which he declared he never meant to re-visit; and amongst the English he moved to all intents and purposes a foreigner, who was resolved, so said the great prophets at Guy's, to rush to destruction as fast as he could, and let no man hinder him.

'He means to go the whole length of his tether,' observed one of the ancient wiseacres to another; which speech implied a conviction that Hertford O'Donnell having sold himself to the Evil One, had determined to dive the full length of his rope into wickedness before being pulled to that shore where even wickedness is negative—where there are no mad carouses, no wild, sinful excitements, nothing but impotent wailing and gnashing of teeth.

A reckless, graceless, clever, wicked devil—going to his natural home as fast as in London any one can possibly speed thither; this was the opinion his superiors, held of the man who lived all alone with a house-keeper and her husband (who acted as butler) in his big house near Soho.

Gerrard Street—made famous by De Quincey, was not then an utterly shady and forgotten locality; carriage-patients found their way to the rising young surgeon—some great personages thought it not beneath them to fee an individual whose consulting rooms were situated on what was even then considered the wrong side of Regent Street. He was making money, and he was spending it; he was over head and ears in debt—useless, vulgar debt—senselessly contracted, never bravely faced. He had lived at an awful pace ever since he came to London, a pace which only a man who hopes and expects to die young can ever travel.

Life, what good was it? Death, was he a child, or a woman, or a coward, to be afraid of that hereafter? God knew all about the trifle which had upset his coach, better than the dons at Guy's.

Hertford O'Donnell understood the world pretty thoroughly, and the ways thereof were to him as roads often traversed; therefore, when he said that at the Day of Judgment he felt certain he should come off as well as many of those who censured him, it may be assumed, that, although his views of post-mortem punishment were vague, unsatisfactory and infidel, still his information as to the peccadilloes of his neighbours was such as consoled himself.

And yet, living all alone in the old house near Soho Square, grave thoughts would intrude into the surgeon's mind—thoughts which were, so to say, italicized by peremptory letters, and still more peremptory visits from people who wanted money.

Although he had many acquaintances he had no single friend, and accordingly these thoughts were received and brooded over in solitude—in those hours when, after returning from dinner, or supper, or congenial carouse, he sat in his dreary rooms, smoking his pipe and considering means and ways, chances and certainties.

In good truth he had started in London with some vague idea that as his life in it would not be of long continuance, the pace at which he elected to travel could be of little consequence; but the years since his first entry into the Metropolis were now piled one on the top of another, his youth was behind him, his chances of longevity, spite of the way he had striven to injure his constitution, quite as good as ever. He had come to that period in existence, to that narrow strip of tableland, whence the ascent of youth and the descent of age are equally discernible—when, simply because he has lived for so many years, it strikes a man as possible he may have to live for just as many more, with the ability for hard work gone, with the boon companions scattered, with the capacity for enjoying convivial meetings a mere memory, with small means perhaps, with no bright hopes, with the pomp and the circumstance and the fairy carriages, and the glamour which youth flings over earthly objects, faded away like the pageant of yesterday, while the dreary ceremony of living has to be gone through to-day and to-morrow and the morrow after, as

though the gay cavalcade and the martial music, and the glittering
helmets and the prancing steeds were still accompanying the wayfarer
to his journey's end.

Ah! my friends, there comes a moment when we must all leave the
coach, with its four bright bays, its pleasant outside freight, its cheery
company, its guard who blows the horn so merrily through villages and
along lonely country roads.

Long before we reach that final stage, where the black business
claims us for its own especial property, we have to bid goodbye to
all easy, thoughtless journeying, and betake ourselves, with what zest
we may, to traversing the common of reality. There is no royal road
across it that ever I heard of. From the King on his throne to the
labourer who vaguely imagines what manner of being a king is, we
have all to tramp across that desert at one period of our lives, at
all events; and that period usually is when, as I have said, a man
starts to find the hopes, and the strength, and the buoyancy of
youth left behind, while years and years of life lie stretching out
before him.

The coach he has travelled by drops him here. There is no appeal,
there is no help; therefore, let him take off his hat and wish the new
passengers good speed, without either envy or repining.

Behold, he has had his turn, and let whosoever will, mount on
the box-seat of life again, and tip the coachman and handle the
ribbons—he shall take that pleasant journey no more, no more for
ever.

Even supposing a man's Spring-time to have been a cold and
ungenial one, with bitter easterly winds and nipping frosts, biting
the buds and retarding the blossoms, still it was Spring for all
that—Spring with the young green leaves sprouting forth, with the
flowers unfolding tenderly, with the songs of the birds and the rush
of waters, with the Summer before and the Autumn afar off, and
Winter remote as death and eternity, but when once the trees have
donned their Summer foliage, when the pure white blossoms have
disappeared, and the gorgeous red and orange and purple blaze of
many-coloured flowers fills the gardens, then if there come a wet,
dreary day, the idea of Autumn and Winter is not so difficult
to realise. When once twelve o'clock is reached, the evening and
night become facts, not possibilities; and it was of the afternoon,
and the evening, and the night, Hertford O'Donnell sat thinking

on the Christmas Eve, when I crave permission to introduce him to my readers.

A good-looking man ladies considered him. A tall, dark-complexioned, black-haired, straight-limbed, deeply divinely blue-eyed fellow, with a soft voice, with a pleasant brogue, who had ridden like a centaur over the loose stone walls in Connemara, who had danced all night at the Dublin balls, who had walked across the Bennebeola Mountains, gun in hand, day after day, without weariness, who had fished in every one of the hundred lakes you can behold from the top of that mountain near the Recess Hotel, who had led a mad, wild life in Trinity College, and a wilder, perhaps, while 'studying for a doctor'—as the Irish phrase goes—in Edinburgh, and who, after the death of his eldest brother left him free to return to Calgillan, and pursue the usual utterly useless, utterly purposeless, utterly pleasant life of an Irish gentleman possessed of health, birth, and expectations, suddenly kicked over the paternal traces, bade adieu to Calgillan Castle and the blandishments of a certain beautiful Miss Clifden, beloved of his mother, and laid out to be his wife, walked down the avenue without even so much company as a Gossoon to carry his carpet-bag, shook the dust from his feet at the lodge gates, and took his seat on the coach, never once looking back at Calgillan, where his favourite mare was standing in the stable, his greyhounds chasing one another round the home paddock, his gun at half-cock in his dressing-room and his fishing-tackle all in order and ready for use.

He had not kissed his mother, or asked for his father's blessing; he left Miss Clifden, arrayed in her brand-new riding-habit, without a word of affection or regret; he had spoken no syllable of farewell to any servant about the place; only when the old woman at the lodge bade him good morning and God-blessed his handsome face, he recommended her bitterly to look at it well for she would never see it more.

Twelve years and a half had passed since then, without either Nancy Blake or any other one of the Calgillan people having set eyes on Master Hertford's handsome face.

He had kept his vow to himself; he had not written home; he had not been indebted to mother or father for even a tenpenny-piece during the whole of that time; he had lived without friends; and he had lived without God—so far as God ever lets a man live without him.

One thing only he felt to be needful—money; money to keep him when the evil days of sickness, or age, or loss of practice came upon him. Though a spendthrift, he was not a simpleton; around him he saw men, who, having started with fairer prospects than his own, were, nevertheless, reduced to indigence; and he knew that what had happened to others might happen to himself.

An unlucky cut, slipping on a piece of orange-peel in the street, the merest accident imaginable, is sufficient to change opulence to beggary in the life's programme of an individual, whose income depends on eye, on nerve, on hand; and, besides the consciousness of this fact, Hertford O'Donnell knew that beyond a certain point in his profession, progress was not easy.

It did not depend quite on the strength of his own bow and shield whether he counted his earnings by hundreds or thousands. Work may achieve competence; but mere work cannot, in a profession, at all events, compass fortune.

He looked around him, and he perceived that the majority of great men—great and wealthy—had been indebted for their elevation, more to the accident of birth, patronage, connection, or marriage, than to personal ability.

Personal ability, no doubt, they possessed; but then, little Jones, who lived in Frith Street, and who could barely keep himself and his wife and family, had ability, too, only he lacked the concomitants of success.

He wanted something or someone to puff him into notoriety—a brother at Court—a lord's leg to mend—a rich wife to give him prestige in Society; and in the absence of this something or someone, he had grown grey-haired and faint-hearted while labouring for a world which utterly despises its most obsequious servants.

'Clatter along the streets with a pair of fine horses, snub the middle classes, and drive over the commonalty—that is the way to compass wealth and popularity in England,' said Hertford O'Donnell, bitterly; and as the man desired wealth and popularity, he sat before his fire, with a foot on each hob, and a short pipe in his mouth, considering how he might best obtain the means to clatter along the streets in his carriage, and splash plebeians with mud from his wheels like the best.

In Dublin he could, by means of his name and connection, have done well; but then he was not in Dublin, neither did he want to be.

The bitterest memories of his life were inseparable from the very name of the Green Island, and he had no desire to return to it.

Besides, in Dublin, heiresses are not quite so plentiful as in London; and an heiress, Hertford O'Donnell had decided, would do more for him than years of steady work.

A rich wife could clear him of debt, introduce him to fashionable practice, afford him that measure of social respectability which a medical bachelor invariably lacks, deliver him from the loneliness of Gerrard Street, and the domination of Mr. and Mrs. Coles.

To most men, deliberately bartering away their independence for money seems so prosaic a business that they strive to gloss it over even to themselves, and to assign every reason for their choice, save that which is really the influencing one.

Not so, however, with Hertford O'Donnell. He sat beside the fire scoffing over his proposed bargain—thinking of the lady's age, her money bags, her desirable house in town, her seat in the country, her snobbishness, her folly.

'It would be a fitting ending,' he sneered, 'and why I did not settle the matter to-night passes my comprehension. I am not a fool, to be frightened with old women's tales; and yet I must have turned white. I felt I did, and she asked me whether I were ill. And then to think of my being such an idiot as to ask her if she had heard anything like a cry, as though she would be likely to hear *that*, she with her poor parvenu blood, which I often imagine must have been mixed with some of her father's strong pickling vinegar. What the deuce could I have been dreaming about? I wonder what it really was.' And Hertford O'Donnell pushed his hair back off his forehead, and took another draught from the too familiar tumbler, which was placed conveniently on the chimney-piece.

'After expressly making up my mind to propose, too!' he mentally continued. 'Could it have been conscience—that myth, which somebody, who knew nothing about the matter, said, "Makes cowards of us all?" I don't believe in conscience; and even if there be such a thing capable of being developed by sentiment and cultivation, why should it trouble me? I have no intention of wronging Miss Janet Price Ingot, not the least. Honestly and fairly I shall marry her; honestly and fairly I shall act by her. An old wife is not exactly an ornamental article of furniture in a man's house; and I do not know that the fact of her being well gilded makes her look any handsomer. But she shall have no cause for complaint; and I will go and dine with her to-morrow, and settle the matter.'

Having arrived at which resolution, Mr. O'Donnell arose, kicked down the fire—burning hollow—with the heel of his boot, knocked the ashes out of his pipe, emptied his tumbler, and bethought him it was time to go to bed. He was not in the habit of taking his rest so early as a quarter to twelve o'clock; but he felt unusually weary—tired mentally and bodily—and lonely beyond all power of expression.

'The fair Janet would be better than this,' he said, half aloud; and then, with a start and a shiver, and a blanched face, he turned sharply round, whilst a low, sobbing, wailing cry echoed mournfully through the room. No form of words could give an idea of the sound. The plaintiveness of the Æolian harp—that plaintiveness which so soon affects and lowers the highest spirits—would have seemed wildly gay in comparison with the sadness of the cry which seemed floating in the air. As the Summer wind comes and goes amongst the trees, so that mournful wail came and went—came and went. It came in a rush of sound, like a gradual crescendo managed by a skilful musician, and died away in a lingering note, so gently that the listener could scarcely tell the exact moment when it faded into utter silence.

I say faded, for it disappeared as the coast line disappears in the twilight, and there was total stillness in the apartment.

Then, for the first time, Hertford O'Donnell looked at his dog, and beholding the creature crouched into a corner beside the fireplace, called upon him to come out.

His voice sounded strange even to himself, and apparently the dog thought so too, for he made no effort to obey the summons.

'Come here, sir,' his master repeated, and then the animal came crawling reluctantly forward with his hair on end, his eyes almost starting from his head, trembling violently, as the surgeon, who caressed him, felt.

'So you heard it, Brian?' he said to the dog. 'And so your ears are sharper than Miss Ingot's, old fellow. It's a mighty queer thing to think of, being favoured with a visit from a Banshee in Gerrard Street; and as the lady has travelled so far, I only wish I knew whether there is any sort of refreshment she would like to take after her long journey.'

He spoke loudly, and with a certain mocking defiance, seeming to think the phantom he addressed would reply; but when he stopped at the end of his sentence, no sound came through the stillness. There was a dead silence in the room—a silence broken only by the falling of the cinders on the hearth and the breathing of his dog.

'If my visitor would tell me,' he proceeded, 'for whom this lamentation is being made, whether for myself, or for some member of my illustrious family, I should feel immensely obliged. It seems too much honour for a poor surgeon to have such attention paid him. Good Heavens! What is that?' he exclaimed, as a ring, loud and peremptory, woke all the echoes in the house, and brought his house-keeper, in a state of distressing *déshabillé*, 'out of her warm bed,' as she subsequently stated, to the head of the staircase.

Across the hall Hertford O'Donnell strode, relieved at the prospect of speaking to any living being. He took no precaution of putting up the chain, but flung the door wide. A dozen burglars would have proved welcome in comparison with that ghostly intruder he had been interviewing; therefore, as has been said, he threw the door wide, admitting a rush of wet, cold air, which made poor Mrs. Coles' few remaining teeth chatter in her head.

'Who is there? What do you want?' asked the surgeon, seeing no person, and hearing no voice. 'Who is there? Why the devil can't you speak?'

When even this polite exhortation failed to elicit an answer, he passed out into the night and looked up the street and down the street, to see nothing but the driving rain and the blinking lights.

'If this goes on much longer I shall soon think I must be either mad or drunk,' he muttered, as he re-entered the house and locked and bolted the door once more.

'Lord's sake! What is the matter, sir?' asked Mrs. Coles, from the upper flight, careful only to reveal the borders of her night-cap to Mr. O'Donnell's admiring gaze. 'Is anybody killed? Have you to go out, sir?'

'It was only a run-away ring,' he answered, trying to reassure himself with an explanation he did not in his heart believe.

'Run-away—I'd run away them!' murmured Mrs. Coles, as she retired to the conjugal couch, where Coles was, to quote her own expression, 'snoring like a pig through it all.'

Almost immediately afterwards she heard her master ascend the stairs and close his bedroom door.

'Madam will surely be too much of a gentlewoman to intrude here,' thought the surgeon, scoffing even at his own fears; but when he lay down he did not put out his light, and made Brian leap up and crouch on the coverlet beside him.

The man was fairly frightened, and would have thought it no discredit to his manhood to acknowledge as much. He was not afraid of death, he was not afraid of trouble, he was not afraid of danger; but he was afraid of the Banshee; and as he laid with his hand on the dog's head, he recalled the many stories he had been told concerning this family retainer in the days of his youth.

He had not thought about her for years and years. Never before had he heard her voice himself. When his brother died she had not thought it necessary to travel up to Dublin and give him notice of the impending catastrophe. 'If she had, I would have gone down to Calgillan, and perhaps saved his life,' considered the surgeon. 'I wonder who this is for? If for me, that will settle my debts and my marriage. If I could be quite certain it was either of the old people, I would start to-morrow.'

Then vaguely his mind wandered on to think of every Banshee story he had ever heard in his life. About the beautiful lady with the wreath of flowers, who sat on the rocks below Red Castle, in the County Antrim, crying till one of the sons died for love of her; about the Round Chamber at Dunluce, which was swept clean by the Banshee every night; about the bed in a certain great house in Ireland, which was slept in constantly, although no human being ever passed in or out after dark; about that General Officer who, the night before Waterloo, said to a friend, 'I have heard the Banshee, and shall not come off the field alive to-morrow; break the news gently to poor Carry;' and who, nevertheless, coming safe off the field, had subsequently news about poor Carry broken tenderly and pitifully to him; about the lad, who, aloft in the rigging, hearing through the night a sobbing and wailing coming over the waters, went down to the captain and told him he was afraid they were somehow out of their reckoning, just in time to save the ship, which, when morning broke, they found but for his warning would have been on the rocks. It was blowing great guns, and the sea was all in a fret and turmoil, and they could sometimes see in the trough of the waves, as down a valley, the cruel black reefs they had escaped.

On deck the captain stood speaking to the boy who had saved them, and asking how he knew of their danger; and when the lad told him, the captain laughed, and said her ladyship had been outwitted that time.

But the boy answered, with a grave shake of his head, that the warning was either for him or his, and that if he got safe to port there would be bad tidings waiting for him from home; whereupon the captain bade him go below, and get some brandy and lie down.

He got the brandy, and he lay down, but he never rose again; and when the storm abated—when a great calm succeeded to the previous tempest—there was a very solemn funeral at sea; and on their arrival at Liverpool the captain took a journey to Ireland to tell a widowed mother how her only son died, and to bear his few effects to the poor desolate soul.

And Hertford O'Donnell thought again about his own father riding full-chase across country, and hearing, as he galloped by a clump of plantation, something like a sobbing and wailing. The hounds were in full cry, but he still felt, as he afterwards expressed it, that there was something among those trees he could not pass; and so he jumped off his horse, and hung the reins over the branch of a Scotch fir, and beat the cover well, but not a thing could he find in it.

Then, for the first time in his life, Miles O'Donnell turned his horse's head *from* the hunt, and, within a mile of Calgillan, met a man running to tell him his brother's gun had burst, and injured him mortally.

And he remembered the story also, of how Mary O'Donnell, his great aunt, being married to a young Englishman, heard the Banshee as she sat one evening waiting for his return; and of how she, thinking the bridge by which he often came home unsafe for horse and man, went out in a great panic, to meet and entreat him to go round by the main road for her sake. Sir Everard was riding along in the moonlight, making straight for the bridge, when he beheld a figure dressed all in white crossing it. Then there was a crash, and the figure disappeared.

The lady was rescued and brought back to the hall; but next morning there were two dead bodies within its walls—those of Lady Eyreton and her still-born son.

Quicker than I write them, these memories chased one another through Hertford O'Donnell's brain; and there was one more terrible memory than any, which would recur to him, concerning an Irish nobleman who, seated alone in his great town-house in London, heard the Banshee, and rushed out to get rid of the phantom, which wailed in his ear, nevertheless, as he strode down Piccadilly. And then the surgeon remembered how that nobleman went with a friend to the Opera, feeling sure that there no Banshee, unless she had a box, could find admittance, until suddenly he heard her singing up amongst the highest part of the scenery, with a terrible mournfulness, and a pathos which made the prima donna's tenderest notes seem harsh by comparison.

As he came out, some quarrel arose between him and a famous fire-eater, against whom he stumbled; and the result was that the next afternoon there was a new Lord —— vice Lord ——, killed in a duel with Captain Bravo.

Memories like these are not the most enlivening possible; they are apt to make a man fanciful, and nervous, and wakeful; but as time ran on, Hertford O'Donnell fell asleep, with his candle still burning, and Brian's cold nose pressed against his hand.

He dreamt of his mother's family—the Hertfords of Artingbury, Yorkshire, far-off relatives of Lord Hertford—so far off that even Mrs. O'Donnell held no clue to the genealogical maze.

He thought he was at Artingbury, fishing; that it was a misty Summer morning, and the fish rising beautifully. In his dreams he hooked one after another, and the boy who was with him threw them into the basket.

At last there was one more difficult to land than the others; and the boy, in his eagerness to watch the sport, drew nearer and nearer to the brink, while the fisher, intent on his prey, failed to notice his companion's danger.

Suddenly there was a cry, a splash, and the boy disappeared from sight.

Next instant he rose again, however, and then, for the first time, Hertford O'Donnell saw his face.

It was one he knew well.

In a moment he plunged into the water, and struck out for the lad. He had him by the hair, he was turning to bring him back to land, when the stream suddenly changed into a wide, wild, shoreless sea, where the billows were chasing one another with a mad demoniac mirth.

For a while O'Donnell kept the lad and himself afloat. They were swept under the waves, and came up again, only to see larger waves rushing towards them; but through all, the surgeon never loosened his hold, until a tremendous billow, engulphing them both, tore the boy from his grasp.

With the horror of his dream upon him he awoke, to hear a voice saying quite distinctly:

'Go to the hospital—go at once!'

The surgeon started up in bed, rubbed his eyes, and looked around. The candle was flickering faintly in its socket. Brian, with his ears pricked forward, had raised his head at his master's sudden movement.

Everything was quiet, but still those words were ringing in his ear:

'Go to the hospital—go at once!'

The tremendous peal of the bell over night, and this sentence, seemed to be simultaneous.

That he was wanted at Guy's—wanted imperatively—came to O'Donnell like an inspiration. Neither sense nor reason had anything to do with the conviction that roused him out of bed, and made him dress as speedily as possible, and grope his way down the staircase, Brian following.

He opened the front door, and passed out into the darkness. The rain was over, and the stars were shining as he pursued his way down Newport Market, and thence, winding in and out in a south-easterly direction, through Lincoln's Inn Fields and Old Square to Chancery Lane, whence he proceeded to St. Paul's.

Along the deserted streets he resolutely continued his walk. He did not know what he was going to Guy's for. Some instinct was urging him on, and he neither strove to combat nor control it. Only once did the thought of turning back cross his mind, and that was at the archway leading into Old Square. There he had paused for a moment, asking himself whether he were not gone stark, staring mad; but Guy's seemed preferable to the haunted house in Gerrard Street, and he walked resolutely on, determined to say, if any surprise were expressed at his appearance, that he had been sent for.

Sent for?—yea, truly; but by whom?

On through Cannon Street; on over London Bridge, where the lights flickered in the river, and the sullen plash of the water flowing beneath the arches, washing the stone piers, could be heard, now the human din was hushed and lulled to sleep. On, thinking of many things: of the days of his youth; of his dead brother; of his father's heavily-encumbered estate; of the fortune his mother had vowed she would leave to some charity rather than to him, if he refused to marry according to her choice; of his wild life in London; of the terrible cry he had heard over-night—that unearthly wail which he could not drive from his memory even when he entered Guy's, and confronted the porter, who said:

'You have been sent for, sir; did you meet the messenger?'

Like one in a dream, Hertford O'Donnell heard him; like one in a dream, also, he asked what was the matter.

'Bad accident, sir; fire; fell off a balcony—unsafe—old building. Mother and child—a son; child with compound fracture of thigh.'

This, the joint information of porter and house-surgeon, mingled together, and made a boom in Mr. O'Donnell's ears like the sound of the sea breaking on a shingly shore.

Only one sentence he understood properly—'Immediate amputation necessary.' At this point he grew cool; he was the careful, cautious, successful surgeon in a moment.

'The child you say?' he answered. 'Let me see him.'

The Guy's Hospital of to-day may be different to the Guy's Hertford O'Donnell knew so well. Railways have, I believe, swept away the old operating room; railways may have changed the position of the former accident ward, to reach which, in the days of which I am writing, the two surgeons had to pass a staircase leading to the upper stories.

On the lower step of this staircase, partially in shadow, Hertford O'Donnell beheld, as he came forward, an old woman seated.

An old woman with streaming grey hair, with attenuated arms, with head bowed forward, with scanty clothing, with bare feet; who never looked up at their approach, but sat unnoticing, shaking her head and wringing her hands in an extremity of despair.

'Who is that?' asked Mr. O'Donnell, almost involuntarily.

'Who is what?' demanded his companion.

'That—that woman,' was the reply.

'What woman?'

'There—are you blind?—seated on the bottom step of the staircase. What is she doing?' persisted Mr. O'Donnell.

'There is no woman near us,' his companion answered, looking at the rising surgeon very much as though he suspected him of seeing double.

'No woman!' scoffed Hertford. 'Do you expect me to disbelieve the evidence of my own eyes?' and he walked up to the figure, meaning to touch it.

But as he essayed to do so, the woman seemed to rise in the air and float away, with her arms stretched high up over her head, uttering such a wail of pain, and agony, and distress, as caused the Irishman's blood to curdle.

'My God! Did you hear that?' he said to his companion.

'What?' was the reply.

Then, although he knew the sound had fallen on deaf ears, he answered:

'The wail of the Banshee! Some of my people are doomed!'

'I trust not,' answered the house-surgeon, who had an idea, nevertheless, that Hertford O'Donnell's Banshee lived in a whisky bottle, and would at some not remote day make an end of the rising and clever operator.

With nerves utterly shaken, Mr. O'Donnell walked forward to the accident ward. There with his face shaded from the light, lay his patient—a young boy, with a compound fracture of the thigh.

In that ward, in the face of actual danger or pain capable of relief the surgeon had never known faltering or fear; and now he carefully examined the injury, felt the pulse, inquired as to the treatment pursued, and ordered the sufferer to be carried to the operating room.

While he was looking out his instruments he heard the boy lying on the table murmur faintly:

'Tell her not to cry so—tell her not to cry.'

'What is he talking about?' Hertford O'Donnell inquired.

'The nurse says he has been speaking about some woman crying ever since he came in—his mother, most likely,' answered one of the attendants.

'He is delirious then?' observed the surgeon.

'No, sir,' pleaded the boy, excitedly, 'no; it is that woman—that woman with the grey hair. I saw her looking from the upper window before the balcony gave way. She has never left me since, and she won't be quiet, wringing her hands and crying.'

'Can you see her now?' Hertford O'Donnell inquired, stepping to the side of the table. 'Point out where she is.'

Then the lad stretched forth a feeble finger in the direction of the door, where clearly, as he had seen her seated on the stairs, the surgeon saw a woman standing—a woman with grey hair and scanty clothing, and upstretched arms and bare feet.

'A word with you, sir,' O'Donnell said to the house-surgeon, drawing him back from the table. 'I cannot perform this operation: send for some other person. I am ill; I am incapable.'

'But,' pleaded the other, 'there is no time to get anyone else. We sent for Mr. West, before we troubled you, but he was out of town, and all the rest of the surgeons live so far away. Mortification may set in at any moment, and—'

'Do you think you require to teach me my business?' was the reply. 'I know the boy's life hangs on a thread, and that is the very reason I cannot operate. I am not fit for it. I tell you I have seen to-night that which unnerves me utterly. My hand is not steady. Send for someone else without delay. Say I am ill—dead!—what you please. Heavens! There she is again, right over the boy! Do you hear her?' and Hertford O'Donnell fell fainting on the floor.

How long he lay in that death-like swoon I cannot say; but when he returned to consciousness, the principal physician of Guy's was standing beside him in the cold grey light of the Christmas morning.

'The boy?' murmured O'Donnell, faintly.

'Now, my dear fellow, keep yourself quiet,' was the reply.

'The boy?' he repeated, irritably. 'Who operated?'

'No one,' Dr. Lanson answered. 'It would have been useless cruelty. Mortification had set in, and—'

Hertford O'Donnell turned his face to the wall, and his friend could not see it.

'Do not distress yourself,' went on the physician, kindly. 'Allington says he could not have survived the operation in any case. He was quite delirious from the first, raving about a woman with grey hair and—'

'I know,' Hertford O'Donnell interrupted; 'and the boy had a mother, they told me, or I dreamt it.'

'Yes, she was bruised and shaken, but not seriously injured.'

'Has she blue eyes and fair hair—fair hair all rippling and wavy? Is she white as a lily, with just a faint flush of colour in her cheek? Is she young and trusting and innocent? No; I am wandering. She must be nearly thirty now. Go, for God's sake, and tell me if you can find a woman you could imagine having once been as a girl such as I describe.'

'Irish?' asked the doctor; and O'Donnell made a gesture of assent.

'It is she then,' was the reply; 'a woman with the face of an angel.'

'A woman who should have been my wife,' the surgeon answered; 'whose child was my son.'

'Lord help you!' ejaculated the doctor. Then Hertford O'Donnell raised himself from the sofa where they had laid him, and told his companion the story of his life—how there had been bitter feud between his people and her people—how they were divided by old animosities and by difference of religion—how they had met by stealth, and exchanged rings and vows, all for naught—how his family had insulted hers, so that her father, wishful for her to marry a kinsman of his own, bore her off to a far-away land, and made her write him a letter of eternal farewell—how his own parents had kept all knowledge of the quarrel from him till she was utterly beyond his reach—how they had vowed to discard him unless he agreed to marry according to their wishes—how he left his home, and came to London, and pushed his fortune. All this Hertford O'Donnell repeated; and when he had finished, the bells were ringing for morning service—ringing loudly, ringing joyfully, 'Peace on earth, goodwill towards men.'

But there was little peace that morning for Hertford O'Donnell. He had to look on the face of his dead son, wherein he beheld, as though reflected, the face of the boy in his dream.

Afterwards, stealthily he followed his friend, and beheld, with her eyes closed, her cheeks pale and pinched, her hair thinner but still falling like a veil over her, the love of his youth, the only woman he had ever loved devotedly and unselfishly.

There is little space left here to tell of how the two met at last—of how the stone of the years seemed suddenly rolled away from the tomb of their past, and their youth arose and returned to them, even amid their tears.

She had been true to him, through persecution, through contumely, through kindness, which was more trying; through shame, and grief, and poverty, she had been loyal to the lover of her youth; and before the New Year dawned there came a letter from Calgillan, saying that the Banshee's wail had been heard there, and praying Hertford, if he were still alive, to let bygones be bygones, in consideration of the long years of estrangement—the anguish and remorse of his afflicted parents.

More than that. Hertford O'Donnell, if a reckless man, was an honourable; and so, on the Christmas Day when he was to have proposed for Miss Ingot, he went to that lady, and told her how he had wooed and won, in the years of his youth, one who after many days was miraculously restored to him; and from the hour in which he took her into his confidence, he never thought her either vulgar or foolish, but rather he paid homage to the woman who, when she had heard the whole tale repeated, said, simply, 'Ask her to come to me till you can claim her—and God bless you both!'

1901

Caulfield's Crime

ALICE PERRIN

Caulfield was a sulky, bad-tempered individual who made no friends and was deservedly unpopular, but he had the reputation of being the finest shot in the Punjab, and of possessing a knowledge of sporting matters that was almost superhuman. He was an extremely jealous shot, and hardly ever invited a companion to join him on his shooting trips, so it may be understood that I was keenly alive to the honour conferred on me when he suddenly asked me to go out for three days' small game shooting with him.

'I know a string of *jheels*,' he said, 'about thirty miles from here, where the duck and snipe must swarm. I marked the place down when I was out last month, and I've made arrangements to go there next Friday morning. You can come, too, if you like.'

I readily accepted the ungracious invitation, though I could hardly account for it, knowing his solitary ways, except that he probably thought I was unlikely to assert myself, being but a youngster, and also he knew me better than he did most people, for our houses were next door, and I often strolled over to examine his enormous collection of skins and horns and other sporting trophies.

I bragged about the coming expedition in the Club that evening, and was well snubbed by two or three men who would have given anything to know the whereabouts of Caulfield's string of *jheels*, and who spitefully warned me to be careful that Caulfield did not end by shooting *me*.

'I believe he'd kill any chap who annoyed him,' said one of them, looking round to make sure that Caulfield was not at hand. 'I never met such a nasty-tempered fellow, I believe he's mad. But he can shoot, and what he doesn't know about game isn't worth knowing.'

Caulfield and I rode out the thirty miles early on the Friday morning, having sent our camp on ahead the previous night. We found our tents pitched in the scanty shade of some stunted *dâk* jungle trees with thick, dry bark, flat, shapeless leaves, that clattered together when stirred by the wind, and wicked-looking red blossoms. It was not a cheerful spot, and the soil was largely mixed with salt which had worked its way in white patches to the surface, and only encouraged the growth of the rankest of grass.

Before us stretched a dreary outlook of shallow lake and swampy ground, broken by dark patches of reeds and little bushy islands, while on the left a miserable mud village overlooked the water. The sun had barely cleared away the thick, heavy mist, which was still slowly rising here and there, and the *jheel* birds were wading majestically in search of their breakfast of small fish, and uttering harsh, discordant cries.

To my astonishment, Caulfield seemed a changed man. He was in excellent spirits, his eyes were bright, and the sullen frown had gone from his forehead.

'Isn't it a lovely spot?' he said, laughing and rubbing his hands. 'Beyond that village the snipe ought to rise in thousands from the rice fields. We shan't be able to shoot it all in three days, worse luck, but we'll keep it dark, and come again. Let's have breakfast. I don't want to lose any time.'

Half an hour later we started, our guns over our shoulders, and a couple of servants behind us carrying the luncheon and cartridge bags. My spirits rose with Caulfield's, for I felt we had the certainty of an excellent day's sport before us.

But the birds were unaccountably wild and few and far between, and luck seemed dead against us. 'Some brutes' had evidently been there before us and harried the birds, was Caulfield's opinion, delivered with disappointed rage, and after tramping and wading all day, we returned, weary and crestfallen, with only a few couple of snipe and half-a-dozen teal between us. Caulfield was so angry he could hardly eat any dinner, and afterwards sat cursing his luck and the culprits who had forestalled us, till we could neither of us keep awake any longer.

The next morning we took a different route from the previous day, but with no better result. On and on, and round and round we tramped, with only an occasional shot here and there, and at last, long after mid-day, we sat wearily down to eat our luncheon. I was ravenously hungry, and greedily devoured my share of the provisions, but Caulfield hardly touched a mouthful, and only sat moodily examining his gun, and taking long pulls from his whisky flask. We were seated on the roots of a large tamarind tree, close to the village, and the place had a dreary, depressing appearance. The yellow mud walls were ruined and crumbling, and the inhabitants seemed scanty and poverty-stricken. Two ragged old women were squatting a short distance off, watching us with dim, apathetic eyes, and a few naked children were playing near them, while some bigger boys were driving two or three lean buffaloes towards the water.

Presently another figure came in sight—a *fakir*, or mendicant priest, as was evident by the tawny masses of wool woven amongst his own black locks and hanging in ropes below his shoulders, the ashes smeared over the almost naked body, and the hollow gourd for alms which he held in his hand. The man's face was long and thin, and his pointed teeth glistened in the sunlight as he demanded money in a dismal monotone. Caulfield flung a pebble at him and told him roughly to be off, with the result that the man slowly disappeared behind a clump of tall, feathery grass.

'Did you notice that brute's face?' said Caulfield as we rose to start again. 'He must have been a pariah dog in a former existence. He was exactly like one!'

'Or a jackal perhaps,' I answered carelessly. 'He looked more like a wild beast.'

Then we walked on, skirting the village and plunging into the damp, soft rice fields. We put up a wisp of snipe, which we followed till we had shot them nearly all, and then, to our joy, we heard a rush of wings overhead, and a lot of duck went down into the corner of a *jheel* in front of us.

'We've got 'em!' said Caulfield, and we hurried on till we were almost within shot of the birds, and could hear them calling to each other in their fancied security. But suddenly they rose again in wild confusion, and with loud cries of alarm were out of range in a second. Caulfield swore, and so did I, and our rage was increased ten-fold when the disturber of the birds appeared in sight, and proved to be the *fakir* who had paid us a visit at luncheon-time. Caulfield shook his fist at the man and abused him freely in Hindustani, but without moving a muscle of his dog-like face the *fakir* passed us and continued on his way.

Words could not describe Caulfield's vexation.

'They were pintail, all of them,' he said, 'and the first decent chance we've had since we came out. To think of that beastly *fakir* spoiling the whole show, and I don't suppose he had the least idea what he had done.'

'Probably not,' I replied, 'unless there was some spite in it because you threw a stone at him that time.'

'Well, come along,' said Caulfield, with resignation, 'we must make haste as it will be dark soon, and I want to try a place over by those palms before we knock off. We may as well let the servants go back as they've had a hard day. Have you got some cartridges in your pocket?'

'Yes, plenty,' I answered, and after despatching the two men back to the camp with what little game we had got, we walked on in silence.

The sun was sinking in a red ball and the air was heavy with damp, as the white mist stole slowly over the still, cold *jheels*. Far overhead came the first faint cackle of the wild geese returning home for the night, and presently as we approached the clump of palms we saw more water glistening between the rough stems, and on it, to our delight, a multitude of duck and teal.

But the next moment there was a whir-r-r of wings like the rumble of thunder, and a dense mass of birds flew straight into the air and wheeled bodily away, while the sharp, cold atmosphere resounded with their startled cries. Caulfield said nothing, but he set his jaw and walked rapidly forward, while I followed. We skirted the group of palms, and on the other side we came upon our friend the *fakir*, who had again succeeded in spoiling our sport. The long, lanky figure was drawn to its full height, and white eyeballs and jagged teeth caught the red glint of the setting sun, and he waved his hand triumphantly in the direction of the vanishing cloud of birds.

Then there came the loud report of a gun, and the next thing I saw was a quivering body on the ground, the wild eyes staring open in the agony of death. Caulfield had shot the *fakir*, and now he stood looking down at what he had done, while I knelt beside the body and tried hopelessly to persuade myself that life was not extinct. When I got up we gazed at each other for a moment in silence.

'What are we to do?' I asked presently.

'Well, you know what it means,' Caulfield said in a queer, hard voice. 'Killing a native is no joke in these days, and I should come out of it pretty badly.'

I glanced at the body in horror. The face was rigid, and seemed more beastlike than ever. I looked at Caulfield again before I spoke, hesitatingly.

'Of course the whole thing was unpremeditated—an accident.'

'No, it wasn't,' he said defiantly. 'I meant to shoot the brute, and it served him right. And you can't say anything else if it comes out. But I don't see why anyone should know about it but ourselves.'

'It's a nasty business,' I said, my heart sinking at the suggestion of concealment.

'It will be nastier still if we don't keep it dark, and you won't like having to give me away, you know. Either we must bury the thing here and say nothing about it, or else we must take it back to the station and stand the devil's own fuss. Probably I shall be kicked out of the service.'

'Of course I'll stand by you,' I said with an effort, 'but we can't do anything this minute. We'd better hide it in that long grass and come back after dinner. We must have something to dig with.'

Caulfield agreed sullenly, and between us we pushed the body in amongst the thick, coarse grass, which completely concealed it, and then made our way back to the camp. We ordered dinner and pretended to eat it, after which we sat for half an hour smoking, until the plates were cleared away and the servants had left the tent. Then I put my hunting-knife into my pocket, and Caulfield picked up a kitchen chopper that his bearer had left lying on the floor, after hammering a stiff joint of a camp chair, and we quitted the tent casually as though intending to have a stroll in the moonlight, which was almost as bright as day. We walked slowly at first, gradually increasing our pace as we left the camp behind us, and Caulfield never spoke a word until we came close to the tall grass that hid the *fakir*'s body. Then he suddenly clutched my arm.

'God in heaven!' he whispered, pointing ahead, 'what is that?'

I saw the grass moving, and heard a scraping sound that made my heart stand still. We moved forward in desperation and parted the grass with our hands. A large jackal was lying on the *fakir*'s body, grinning and snarling at being disturbed over his hideous meal.

'Drive it away,' said Caulfield, hoarsely. But the brute refused to move, and as it lay there showing its teeth, its face reminded me horribly of the wretched man dead beneath its feet. I turned sick and faint, so Caulfield shouted and shook the grass and threw clods of soil at the animal, which rose at last and slunk slowly away. It was an unusually large jackal, more like a wolf, and had lost one of its ears. The coat was rough and mangy and thickly sprinkled with grey.

For more than an hour we worked desperately with the chopper and hunting-knife, being greatly aided in our task by a rift in the ground where the soil had been softened by water running from the *jheel*, and finally we stood up with the sweat pouring from our faces, and stamped down the earth which now covered all traces of Caulfield's crime. We had filled the grave with some large stones that were lying about (remnants of some ancient temple, long ago deserted and forgotten), thus feeling secure that it could not easily be disturbed by animals.

The next morning we returned to the station and Caulfield shut himself up more than ever. He entirely dropped his shooting, which before had been his one pleasure, and the only person he ever spoke to, unofficially, was myself.

The end of April came with its plague of insects and scorching winds. The hours grew long and weary with the heat, and dust storms howled and swirled over the station, bringing perhaps a few tantalizing drops of rain, or more often leaving the air thick with a copper-coloured haze.

One night when it was too hot to sleep, Caulfield suddenly appeared in my verandah and asked me to let him stay the night in my bungalow.

'I know I'm an ass,' he said in awkward apology, 'but I can't stay by myself. I get all sorts of beastly ideas.'

I asked no questions, but gave him a cheroot and tried to cheer him up, telling him scraps of gossip, and encouraging him to talk, when a sound outside made us both start. It proved to be only the weird, plaintive cry of a jackal, but Caulfield sprang to his feet, shaking all over.

'There it is again!' he exclaimed. 'It has followed me over here. Listen!' turning his haggard, sleepless eyes on me. 'Every night that brute comes and howls round my house, and I tell you, on my oath, it's the same jackal we saw eating the poor devil I shot.'

'Nonsense, my dear chap,' I said, pushing him back into the chair, 'you must have got fever. Jackals come and howl round my house all night. That's nothing.'

'Look here,' said Caulfield, very calmly, 'I have no more fever than you have, and if you imagine I am delirious you are mistaken.' He lowered his voice. 'I looked out one night and saw the brute. It had only one ear!'

In spite of my own common sense and the certainty that Caulfield was not himself, my blood ran cold, and after I had succeeded in quieting him and he had dropped off to sleep on the couch, I sat in my long chair for hours, going over in my mind every detail of that horrible night in the jungle.

Several times after this Caulfield came to me and repeated the same tale. He swore he was being haunted by the jackal we had driven away from the *fakir*'s body, and finally took it into his head that the spirit of the murdered man had entered the animal and was bent on obtaining vengeance.

Then he suddenly ceased coming over to me, and when I went to see him he would hardly speak, and only seemed anxious to get rid of me. I urged him to take leave or see a doctor, but he angrily refused to do either, and said he wished I would keep away from him altogether. So I left him alone for a couple of days, but on the third evening my conscience pricked me for having neglected him, and I was preparing to go over to his bungalow, when his bearer rushed in with a face of terror and besought me to come without delay. He said he feared his master was dying, and he had already sent for the doctor. The latter arrived in Caulfield's verandah simultaneously with myself, and together we entered the sick man's room. Caulfield was lying unconscious on his bed.

'He had a sort of fit, Sahib,' said the frightened bearer, and proceeded to explain how his master had behaved.

The doctor bent over the bed.

'Do you happen to know if he had been bitten by a dog lately?' he asked, looking up at me.

'Not to my knowledge,' I answered, while the faint wail of a jackal out across the plain struck a chill to my heart.

For twenty-four hours we stayed with Caulfield watching the terrible struggles we were powerless to relieve, and which lasted till the end came. He was never able to speak after the first paroxysm, which had occurred before we arrived, so we could not learn from him whether he had been bitten or not, neither could the doctor discover any scar on his body which might have been made by the teeth of an animal. Yet there was no shadow of doubt that Caulfield's death was due to hydrophobia.

As we stood in the next room when all was over, drinking the dead man's whisky and soda, which we badly needed, we questioned the bearer closely, but he could tell us little or nothing. His master, he said, did not keep dogs, nor had the bearer ever heard of his having been bitten by one; but there had been a mad jackal about the place nearly three weeks ago which his master had tried to shoot but failed.

'It couldn't have been that,' said the doctor; 'he would have come to me if he had been bitten by a jackal.'

'No,' I answered mechanically, 'it could not have been that.' And I went into the bedroom to take a last look at poor Caulfield's thin, white face with its ghastly, hunted expression, for there was now nothing more that I could do for him.

Then I picked up a lantern and stepped out into the dark verandah, intending to go home. As I did so, something came silently round the corner of the house and stood in my path. I raised my lantern and caught a glimpse of a mass of grey fur, two fiery yellow eyes, and bared, glistening teeth. It was only a stray jackal, and I struck at it with my stick, but instead of running away it slipped past me and entered Caulfield's room. The light fell on the animal's head, and I saw that it had only one ear.

In a frenzy I rushed back into the house calling for the doctor and servants.

'I saw a jackal come in here,' I said, searching round the bedroom, 'hunt it out at once.'

Every nook and corner was examined, but no jackal was found.

'Go home to bed, my boy, and keep quiet till I come and see you in the morning.' said the doctor, looking at me keenly. 'This business has shaken your nerves, and your imagination is beginning to play you tricks. Good-night.'

'Good-night,' I answered, and went slowly back to my bungalow, trying to persuade myself that he was right.

1902

The Wind in the Rose-Bush

MARY E. WILKINS

Ford Village has no railroad station, being on the other side of the river from Porter's Falls, and accessible only by the ford which gives it its name, and a ferry line.

The ferry-boat was waiting when Rebecca Flint got off the train with her bag and lunch basket. When she and her small trunk were safely embarked she sat stiff and straight and calm in the ferry-boat as it shot swiftly and smoothly across stream. There was a horse attached to a light country wagon on board, and he pawed the deck uneasily. His owner stood near, with a wary eye upon him, although he was chewing, with as dully reflective an expression as a cow. Beside Rebecca sat a woman of about her own age, who kept looking at her with furtive curiosity; her husband, short and stout and saturnine, stood near her. Rebecca paid no attention to either of them. She was tall and spare and pale, the type of a spinster, yet with rudimentary lines and expressions of matronhood. She all unconsciously held her shawl, rolled up in a canvas bag, on her left hip, as if it had been a child. She wore a settled frown of dissent at life, but it was the frown of a mother who regarded life as a froward child, rather than as an overwhelming fate.

The other woman continued staring at her; she was mildly stupid, except for an overdeveloped curiosity which made her at times sharp beyond belief. Her eyes glittered, red spots came on her flaccid cheeks; she kept opening her mouth to speak, making little abortive motions. Finally she could endure it no longer; she nudged Rebecca boldly.

'A pleasant day,' said she.

Rebecca looked at her and nodded coldly.

'Yes, very,' she assented.

'Have you come far?'

'I have come from Michigan.'

'Oh!' said the woman, with awe. 'It's a long way,' she remarked, presently.

'Yes, it is,' replied Rebecca, conclusively.

Still the other woman was not daunted; there was something which she determined to know, possibly roused thereto by a vague sense of incongruity in the other's appearance. 'It's a long ways to come and leave a family,' she remarked with painful slyness.

'I ain't got any family to leave,' returned Rebecca, shortly.

'Then you ain't—'

'No, I ain't.'

'Oh!' said the woman.

Rebecca looked straight ahead at the race of the river.

It was a long ferry. Finally Rebecca herself waxed unexpectedly loquacious. She turned to the older woman and inquired if she knew John Dent's widow who lived in Ford Village. 'Her husband died about three years ago,' said she, by way of detail.

The woman started violently. She turned pale, then she flushed; she cast a strange glance at her husband, who was regarding both women with a sort of stolid keenness.

'Yes, I guess I do,' faltered the woman, finally.

'Well, his first wife was my sister,' said Rebecca with the air of one imparting important intelligence.

'Was she?' responded the other woman, feebly. She glanced at her husband with an expression of doubt and terror, and he shook his head forbiddingly.

'I'm going to see her and take my niece Agnes home with me,' said Rebecca.

Then the woman gave such a violent start that she noticed it.

'What is the matter?' she asked.

'Nothin', I guess,' replied the woman, with eyes on her husband, who was slowly shaking his head, like a Chinese toy.

'Is my niece sick?' asked Rebecca with quick suspicion.

'No, she ain't sick,' replied the woman with alacrity, then she caught her breath with a gasp.

'When did you see her?'

'Let me see; I ain't seen her for some little time,' replied the woman. Then she caught her breath again.

'She ought to have grown up real pretty, if she takes after my sister. She was a real pretty woman,' Rebecca said, wistfully.

'Yes, I guess she did grow up pretty,' replied the woman in a trembling voice.

'What kind of a woman is the second wife?'

The woman glanced at her husband's warning face. She continued to gaze at him while she replied in a choking voice to Rebecca:

'I—guess she's a nice woman,' she replied. 'I—don't know, I—guess so. I—don't see much of her.'

'I felt kind of hurt that John married again so quick,' said Rebecca; 'but I suppose he wanted his house kept, and Agnes wanted care. I wasn't so situated that I could take her when her mother died. I had my own mother to care for, and I was school-teaching. Now mother has gone, and my uncle died six months ago and left me quite a little property, and I've given up my school and I've come for Agnes. I guess she'll be glad to go with me, though I suppose her stepmother is a good woman and has always done for her.'

The man's warning shake at his wife was fairly portentous.

'I guess so,' said she.

'John always wrote that she was a beautiful woman,' said Rebecca.

Then the ferry-boat grated on the shore.

John Dent's widow had sent a horse and wagon to meet her sister-in-law. When the woman and her husband went down the road, on which Rebecca in the wagon with her trunk soon passed them, she said, reproachfully:

'Seems as if I'd ought to have told her, Thomas.'

'Let her find it out herself,' replied the man. 'Don't you go to burnin' your fingers in other folks' puddin', Maria.'

'Do you s'pose she'll see anything?' asked the woman with a spasmodic shudder and a terrified roll of her eyes.

'See!' returned her husband with stolid scorn. 'Better be sure there's anything to see.'

'Oh, Thomas, they say—'

'Lord, ain't you found out that what they say is mostly lies?'

'But if it should be true, and she's a nervous woman, she might be scared enough to lose her wits,' said his wife, staring uneasily after

Rebecca's erect figure in the wagon disappearing over the crest of the hilly road.

'Wits that's so easy upset ain't worth much,' declared the man. 'You keep out of it, Maria.'

Rebecca in the meantime rode on in the wagon, beside a flaxen-headed boy, who looked, to her understanding, not very bright. She asked him a question, and he paid no attention. She repeated it, and he responded with a bewildered and incoherent grunt. Then she let him alone, after making sure that he knew how to drive straight.

They had travelled about half a mile, passed the village square, and gone a short distance beyond, when the boy drew up with a sudden Whoa! before a very prosperous-looking house. It had been one of the aboriginal cottages of the vicinity, small and white, with a roof extending on one side over a piazza, and a tiny 'L' jutting out in the rear, on the right hand. Now the cottage was transformed by dormer windows, a bay window on the piazzaless side, a carved railing down the front steps, and a modern hardwood door.

'Is this John Dent's house?' asked Rebecca.

The boy was as sparing of speech as a philosopher. His only response was in flinging the reins over the horse's back, stretching out one foot to the shaft, and leaping out of the wagon, then going around to the rear for the trunk. Rebecca got out and went toward the house. Its white paint had a new gloss; its blinds were an immaculate apple green; the lawn was trimmed as smooth as velvet, and it was dotted with scrupulous groups of hydrangeas and cannas.

'I always understood that John Dent was well-to-do,' Rebecca reflected, comfortably. 'I guess Agnes will have considerable. I've got enough, but it will come in handy for her schooling. She can have advantages.'

The boy dragged the trunk up the fine gravel walk, but before he reached the steps leading up to the piazza, for the house stood on a terrace, the front door opened and a fair, frizzled head of a very large and handsome woman appeared. She held up her black silk skirt, disclosing voluminous ruffles of starched embroidery, and waited for Rebecca. She smiled placidly, her pink, double-chinned face widened and dimpled, but her blue eyes were wary and calculating. She extended her hand as Rebecca climbed the steps.

'This is Miss Flint, I suppose,' said she.

'Yes, ma'am,' replied Rebecca, noticing with bewilderment a curious expression compounded of fear and defiance on the other's face.

'Your letter only arrived this morning,' said Mrs. Dent, in a steady voice. Her great face was a uniform pink, and her china-blue eyes were at once aggressive and veiled with secrecy.

'Yes, I hardly thought you'd get my letter,' replied Rebecca. 'I felt as if I could not wait to hear from you before I came. I supposed you would be so situated that you could have me a little while without putting you out too much, from what John used to write me about his circumstances, and when I had that money so unexpected I felt as if I must come for Agnes. I suppose you will be willing to give her up. You know she's my own blood, and of course she's no relation to you, though you must have got attached to her. I know from her picture what a sweet girl she must be, and John always said she looked like her own mother, and Grace was a beautiful woman, if she was my sister.'

Rebecca stopped and stared at the other woman in amazement and alarm. The great handsome blonde creature stood speechless, livid, gasping, with her hand to her heart, her lips parted in a horrible caricature of a smile.

'Are you sick!' cried Rebecca, drawing near. 'Don't you want me to get you some water!'

Then Mrs. Dent recovered herself with a great effort. 'It is nothing,' she said. 'I am subject to—spells. I am over it now. Won't you come in, Miss Flint?'

As she spoke, the beautiful deep-rose color suffused her face, her blue eyes met her visitor's with the opaqueness of turquoise—with a revelation of blue, but a concealment of all behind.

Rebecca followed her hostess in, and the boy, who had waited quiescently, climbed the steps with the trunk. But before they entered the door a strange thing happened. On the upper terrace, close to the piazza post, grew a great rose-bush, and on it, late in the season though it was, one small red, perfect rose.

Rebecca looked at it, and the other woman extended her hand with a quick gesture. 'Don't you pick that rose!' she brusquely cried.

Rebecca drew herself up with stiff dignity.

'I ain't in the habit of picking other folks' roses without leave,' said she.

As Rebecca spoke she started violently and lost sight of her resentment, for something singular happened. Suddenly the rosebush was agitated violently as if by a gust of wind, yet it was a remarkably still day. Not a leaf of the hydrangea standing on the terrace close to the rose trembled.

'What on earth—' began Rebecca; then she stopped with a gasp at the sight of the other woman's face. Although a face, it gave somehow the impression of a desperately clutched hand of secrecy.

'Come in!' said she in a harsh voice, which seemed to come forth from her chest with no intervention of the organs of speech. 'Come into the house. I'm getting cold out here.'

'What makes that rose-bush blow so when there isn't any wind?' asked Rebecca, trembling with vague horror, yet resolute.

'I don't see as it is blowing,' returned the woman, calmly. And as she spoke, indeed, the bush was quiet.

'It was blowing,' declared Rebecca.

'It isn't now,' said Mrs. Dent. 'I can't try to account for everything that blows out-of-doors. I have too much to do.'

She spoke scornfully and confidently, with defiant, unflinching eyes, first on the bush, then on Rebecca, and led the way into the house.

'It looked queer,' persisted Rebecca, but she followed, and also the boy with the trunk.

Rebecca entered an interior, prosperous, even elegant, according to her simple ideas. There were Brussels carpets, lace curtains, and plenty of brilliant upholstery and polished wood.

'You're real nicely situated,' remarked Rebecca after she had become a little accustomed to her new surroundings and the two women were seated at the tea-table.

Mrs. Dent stared with a hard complacency from behind her silver-plated service. 'Yes, I be,' said she.

'You got all the things new?' said Rebecca, hesitatingly, with a jealous memory of her dead sister's bridal furnishings.

'Yes,' said Mrs. Dent. 'I was never one to want dead folks' things, and I had money enough of my own, so I wasn't beholden to John. I had the old duds put up at auction. They didn't bring much.'

'I suppose you saved some for Agnes. She'll want some of her poor mother's things when she is grown up,' said Rebecca with some indignation.

The defiant stare of Mrs. Dent's blue eyes waxed more intense. 'There's a few things up garret,' said she.

'She'll be likely to value them,' remarked Rebecca. As she spoke she glanced at the window. 'Isn't it 'most time for her to be coming home?' she asked.

"Most time,' answered Mrs. Dent, carelessly; 'but when she gets over to Addie Slocum's she never knows when to come home.'

'Is Addie Slocum her intimate friend?'

'Intimate as any.'

'Maybe we can have her come out to see Agnes when she's living with me,' said Rebecca, wistfully. 'I suppose she'll be likely to be homesick at first.'

'Most likely,' answered Mrs. Dent.

'Does she call you mother?' Rebecca asked.

'No, she calls me Aunt Emeline,' replied the other woman, shortly. 'When did you say you were going home?'

'In about a week, I thought, if she can be ready to go so soon,' answered Rebecca with a surprised look.

She reflected that she would not remain a day longer than she could help after such an inhospitable look and question.

'Oh, as far as that goes,' said Mrs. Dent, 'it wouldn't make any difference about her being ready. You could go home whenever you felt that you must, and she could come afterward.'

'Alone?'

'Why not? She's a big girl now, and you don't have to change cars.'

'My niece will go home when I do, and not travel alone; and if I can't wait here for her, in the house that used to be her mother's and my sister's home, I'll go and board somewhere,' returned Rebecca with warmth.

'Oh, you can stay here as long as you want to. You're welcome,' said Mrs. Dent.

Then Rebecca started. 'There she is!' she declared in a trembling, exultant voice. Nobody knew how she longed to see the girl.

'She isn't as late as I thought she'd be,' said Mrs. Dent, and again that curious, subtle change passed over her face, and again it settled into that stony impassiveness.

Rebecca stared at the door, waiting for it to open. 'Where is she?' she asked, presently.

'I guess she's stopped to take off her hat in the entry,' suggested Mrs. Dent.

Rebecca waited. 'Why don't she come? It can't take her all this time to take off her hat.'

For answer Mrs. Dent rose with a stiff jerk and threw open the door.

'Agnes!' she called. 'Agnes!' Then she turned and eyed Rebecca. 'She ain't there.'

'I saw her pass the window,' said Rebecca in bewilderment.

'You must have been mistaken.'

'I know I did,' persisted Rebecca.

'You couldn't have.'

'I did. I saw first a shadow go over the ceiling, then I saw her in the glass there'—she pointed to a mirror over the sideboard opposite—'and then the shadow passed the window.'

'How did she look in the glass?'

'Little and light-haired, with the light hair kind of tossing over her forehead.'

'You couldn't have seen her.'

'Was that like Agnes?'

'Like enough; but of course you didn't see her. You've been thinking so much about her that you thought you did.'

'You thought *you* did.'

'I thought I saw a shadow pass the window, but I must have been mistaken. She didn't come in, or we would have seen her before now. I knew it was too early for her to get home from Addie Slocum's, anyhow.'

When Rebecca went to bed Agnes had not returned. Rebecca had resolved that she would not retire until the girl came, but she was very tired, and she reasoned with herself that she was foolish. Besides, Mrs. Dent suggested that Agnes might go to the church social with Addie Slocum. When Rebecca suggested that she be sent for and told that her aunt had come, Mrs. Dent laughed meaningly.

'I guess you'll find out that a young girl ain't so ready to leave a sociable, where there's boys, to see her aunt,' said she.

'She's too young,' said Rebecca, incredulously and indignantly.

'She's sixteen,' replied Mrs. Dent; 'and she's always been great for the boys.'

'She's going to school four years after I get her before she thinks of boys,' declared Rebecca.

'We'll see,' laughed the other woman.

After Rebecca went to bed, she lay awake a long time listening for the sound of girlish laughter and a boy's voice under her window; then she fell asleep.

The next morning she was down early. Mrs. Dent, who kept no servants, was busily preparing breakfast.

'Don't Agnes help you about breakfast?' asked Rebecca.

'No, I let her lay,' replied Mrs. Dent, shortly.

'What time did she get home last night?'

'She didn't get home.'

'What?'

'She didn't get home. She stayed with Addie. She often does.'

'Without sending you word?'

'Oh, she knew I wouldn't worry.'

'When will she be home?'

'Oh, I guess she'll be along pretty soon.'

Rebecca was uneasy, but she tried to conceal it, for she knew of no good reason for uneasiness. What was there to occasion alarm in the fact of one young girl staying overnight with another? She could not eat much breakfast. Afterward she went out on the little piazza, although her hostess strove furtively to stop her.

'Why don't you go out back of the house? It's real pretty—a view over the river,' she said.

'I guess I'll go out here,' replied Rebecca. She had a purpose—to watch for the absent girl.

Presently Rebecca came hustling into the house through the sitting room, into the kitchen where Mrs. Dent was cooking.

'That rose-bush!' she gasped.

Mrs. Dent turned and faced her.

'What of it?'

'It's a-blowing.'

'What of it?'

'There isn't a mite of wind this morning.'

Mrs. Dent turned with an inimitable toss of her fair head. 'If you think I can spend my time puzzling over such nonsense as—' she began, but Rebecca interrupted her with a cry and a rush to the door.

'There she is now!' she cried.

She flung the door wide open, and curiously enough a breeze came in and her own gray hair tossed, and a paper blew off the table to the floor with a loud rustle, but there was nobody in sight.

'There's nobody here,' Rebecca said.

She looked blankly at the other woman, who brought her rolling-pin down on a slab of pie crust with a thud.

'I didn't hear anybody,' she said, calmly.

'*I saw somebody pass that window!*'

'You were mistaken again.'

'I *know* I saw somebody.'

'You couldn't have. Please shut that door.'

Rebecca shut the door. She sat down beside the window and looked out on the autumnal yard, with its little curve of footpath to the kitchen door.

'What smells so strong of roses in this room?' she said, presently. She sniffed hard.

'I don't smell anything but these nutmegs.'

'It is not nutmeg.'

'I don't smell anything else.'

'Where do you suppose Agnes is?'

'Oh, perhaps she has gone over the ferry to Porter's Falls with Addie. She often does. Addie's got an aunt over there, and Addie's got a cousin, a real pretty boy.'

'You suppose she's gone over there?'

'Mebbe. I shouldn't wonder.'

'When should she be home?'

'Oh, not before afternoon.'

Rebecca waited with all the patience she could muster. She kept reassuring herself, telling herself that it was all natural, that the other woman could not help it, but she made up her mind that if Agnes did not return that afternoon she should be sent for.

When it was four o'clock she started up with resolution. She had been furtively watching the onyx clock on the sitting-room mantel; she had timed herself. She had said that if Agnes was not home by that time she should demand that she be sent for. She rose and stood before Mrs. Dent, who looked up coolly from her embroidery.

'I've waited just as long as I'm going to,' she said. 'I've come 'way from Michigan to see my own sister's daughter and take her home with me. I've been here ever since yesterday—twenty-four hours—and I haven't seen her. Now I'm going to. I want her sent for.'

Mrs. Dent folded her embroidery and rose.

'Well, I don't blame you,' she said. 'It is high time she came home. I'll go right over and get her myself.'

Rebecca heaved a sigh of relief. She hardly knew what she had suspected or feared, but she knew that her position had been one of antagonism if not accusation, and she was sensible of relief.

'I wish you would,' she said, gratefully, and went back to her chair, while Mrs. Dent got her shawl and her little white head-tie. 'I wouldn't trouble you, but I do feel as if I couldn't wait any longer to see her,' she remarked, apologetically.

'Oh, it ain't any trouble at all,' said Mrs. Dent as she went out. 'I don't blame you; you have waited long enough.'

Rebecca sat at the window watching breathlessly until Mrs. Dent came stepping through the yard alone. She ran to the door and saw, hardly noticing it this time, that the rose-bush was again violently agitated, yet with no wind evident elsewhere.

'Where is she?' she cried.

Mrs. Dent laughed with stiff lips as she came up the steps over the terrace. 'Girls will be girls,' said she. 'She's gone with Addie to Lincoln. Addie's got an uncle who's conductor on the train, and lives there, and he got 'em passes, and they're goin' to stay to Addie's Aunt Margaret's a few days. Mrs. Slocum said Agnes didn't have time to come over and ask me before the train went, but she took it on herself to say it would be all right, and—'

'Why hadn't she been over to tell you?' Rebecca was angry, though not suspicious. She even saw no reason for her anger.

'Oh, she was putting up grapes. She was coming over just as soon as she got the black off her hands. She heard I had company, and her hands were a sight. She was holding them over sulphur matches.'

'You say she's going to stay a few days?' repeated Rebecca, dazedly.

'Yes; till Thursday, Mrs. Slocum said.'

'How far is Lincoln from here?'

'About fifty miles. It'll be a real treat to her. Mrs. Slocum's sister is a real nice woman.'

'It is goin' to make it pretty late about my goin' home.'

'If you don't feel as if you could wait, I'll get her ready and send her on just as soon as I can,' Mrs. Dent said, sweetly.

'I'm going to wait,' said Rebecca, grimly.

The two women sat down again, and Mrs. Dent took up her embroidery.

'Is there any sewing I can do for her?' Rebecca asked, finally, in a desperate way. 'If I can get her sewing along some–'

Mrs. Dent arose with alacrity and fetched a mass of white from the closet. 'Here,' she said, 'if you want to sew the lace on this nightgown. I was going to put her to it, but she'll be glad enough to get rid of it. She ought to have this and one more before she goes. I don't like to send her away without some good underclothing.'

Rebecca snatched at the little white garment and sewed feverishly.

That night she wakened from a deep sleep a little after midnight and lay a minute trying to collect her faculties and explain to herself what she was listening to. At last she discovered that it was the then popular strains of 'The Maiden's Prayer' floating up through the floor from the piano in the sitting room below. She jumped up, threw a shawl over her nightgown, and hurried downstairs trembling. There was nobody in the sitting room; the piano was silent. She ran to Mrs. Dent's bedroom and called hysterically:

'Emeline! Emeline!'

'What is it?' asked Mrs. Dent's voice from the bed. The voice was stern, but had a note of consciousness in it.

'Who—who was that playing 'The Maiden's Prayer' in the sitting room, on the piano?'

'I didn't hear anybody.'

'There was some one.'

'I didn't hear anything.'

'I tell you there was some one. But—*there ain't anybody there.*'

'I didn't hear anything.'

'I did—somebody playing 'The Maiden's Prayer' on the piano. Has Agnes got home? I *want to know.*'

'Of course Agnes hasn't got home,' answered Mrs. Dent with rising inflection. 'Be you gone crazy over that girl? The last boat from Porter's Falls was in before we went to bed. Of course she ain't come.'

'I heard—'

'You were dreaming.'

'I wasn't; I was broad awake.'

Rebecca went back to her chamber and kept her lamp burning all night.

The next morning her eyes upon Mrs. Dent were wary and blazing with suppressed excitement. She kept opening her mouth as if to speak, then frowning, and setting her lips hard. After breakfast she went upstairs, and came down presently with her coat and bonnet.

'Now, Emeline,' she said, 'I want to know where the Slocums live.'

Mrs. Dent gave a strange, long, half-lidded glance at her. She was finishing her coffee.

'Why?' she asked.

'I'm going over there and find out if they have heard anything from her daughter and Agnes since they went away. I don't like what I heard last night.'

'You must have been dreaming.'

'It don't make any odds whether I was or not. Does she play "The Maiden's Prayer" on the piano? I want to know.'

'What if she does? She plays it a little, I believe. I don't know. She don't half play it, anyhow; she ain't got an ear.'

'That wasn't half played last night. I don't like such things happening. I ain't superstitious, but I don't like it. I'm going. Where do the Slocums live?'

'You go down the road over the bridge past the old grist mill, then you turn to the left; it's the only house for half a mile. You can't miss it. It has a barn with a ship in full sail on the cupola.'

'Well, I'm going. I don't feel easy.'

About two hours later Rebecca returned. There were red spots on her cheeks. She looked wild. 'I've been there,' she said, 'and there isn't a soul at home. Something *has* happened.'

'What has happened?'

'I don't know. Something. I had a warning last night. There wasn't a soul there. They've been sent for to Lincoln.'

'Did you see anybody to ask?' asked Mrs. Dent with thinly concealed anxiety.

'I asked the woman that lives on the turn of the road. She's stone deaf. I suppose you know. She listened while I screamed at her to know where the Slocums were, and then she said, 'Mrs. Smith don't live here.' I didn't see anybody on the road, and that's the only house. What do you suppose it means?'

'I don't suppose it means much of anything,' replied Mrs. Dent, coolly. 'Mr. Slocum is conductor on the railroad, and he'd be away, anyway, and Mrs. Slocum often goes early when he does, to spend the day with her sister in Porter's Falls. She'd be more likely to go away than Addie.'

'And you don't think anything has happened?' Rebecca asked with diminishing distrust before the reasonableness of it.

'Land, no!'

Rebecca went upstairs to lay aside her coat and bonnet. But she came hurrying back with them still on.

'Who's been in my room?' she gasped. Her face was pale as ashes.

Mrs. Dent also paled as she regarded her.

'What do you mean?' she asked, slowly.

'I found when I went upstairs that—little nightgown of—Agnes's on—the bed, laid out. It was—*laid out.* The sleeves were folded across the bosom, and there was that little red rose between them. Emeline, what is it? Emeline, what's the matter? Oh!'

Mrs. Dent was struggling for breath in great, choking gasps. She clung to the back of a chair. Rebecca, trembling herself so she could scarcely keep on her feet, got her some water.

As soon as she recovered herself Mrs. Dent regarded her with eyes full of the strangest mixture of fear and horror and hostility.

'What do you mean talking so?' she said in a hard voice.

'It *is there.*'

'Nonsense. You threw it down and it fell that way.'

'It was folded in my bureau drawer.'

'It couldn't have been.'

'Who picked that red rose?'

'Look on the bush,' Mrs. Dent replied shortly.

Rebecca looked at her; her mouth gaped. She hurried out of the room. When she came back her eyes seemed to protrude. (She had in the meantime hastened upstairs, and come down with tottering steps, clinging to the banister.)

'Now I want to know what all this means?' she demanded.

'What what means?'

'The rose is on the bush, and it's gone from the bed in my room! Is this house haunted, or what?'

'I don't know anything about a house being haunted. I don't believe in such things. Be you crazy?' Mrs. Dent spoke with gathering force. The color flashed back to her cheeks.

'No,' said Rebecca, shortly, 'I ain't crazy yet, but I shall be if this keeps on much longer. I'm going to find out where that girl is before night.'

Mrs. Dent eyed her.

'What be you going to do?'

'I'm going to Lincoln.'

A faint triumphant smile overspread Mrs. Dent's large face.

'You can't,' said she; 'there ain't any train.'

'No train?'

'No; there ain't any afternoon train from the Falls to Lincoln.'

'Then I'm going over to the Slocums' again to-night.'

However, Rebecca did not go; such a rain came up as deterred even her resolution, and she had only her best dresses with her. Then in the evening came the letter from the Michigan village which she had left nearly a week ago. It was from her cousin, a single woman, who had come to keep her house while she was away. It was a pleasant unexciting letter enough, all the first of it, and related mostly how she missed Rebecca; how she hoped she was having pleasant weather and kept her health; and how her friend, Mrs. Greenaway, had come to stay with her since she had felt lonesome the first night in the house; how she hoped Rebecca would have no objections to this, although nothing had been said about it, since she had not realized that she might be nervous alone. The cousin was painfully conscientious, hence the letter. Rebecca smiled in spite of her disturbed mind as she read it; then her eye caught the postscript. That was in a different hand, purporting to be written by the friend, Mrs. Hannah Greenaway, informing her that the cousin had fallen down the cellar stairs and broken her hip, and was in a dangerous condition, and begging Rebecca to return at once, as she herself was rheumatic and unable to nurse her properly, and no one else could be obtained.

Rebecca looked at Mrs. Dent, who had come to her room with the letter quite late; it was half-past nine, and she had gone upstairs for the night.

'Where did this come from?' she asked.

'Mr. Amblecrom brought it,' she replied.

'Who's he?'

'The postmaster. He often brings the letters that come on the late mail. He knows I ain't anybody to send. He brought yours about your coming. He said he and his wife came over on the ferry-boat with you.'

'I remember him,' Rebecca replied, shortly. 'There's bad news in this letter.'

Mrs. Dent's face took on an expression of serious inquiry.

'Yes, my Cousin Harriet has fallen down the cellar stairs—they were always dangerous—and she's broken her hip, and I've got to take the first train home to-morrow.'

'You don't say so. I'm dreadfully sorry.'

'No, you ain't sorry!' said Rebecca with a look as if she leaped. 'You're glad. I don't know why, but you're glad. You've wanted to get rid of me for some reason ever since I came. I don't know why. You're a strange woman. Now you've got your way, and I hope you're satisfied.'

'How you talk.'

Mrs. Dent spoke in a faintly injured voice, but there was a light in her eyes.

'I talk the way it is. Well, I'm going to-morrow morning, and I want you, just as soon as Agnes Dent comes home, to send her out to me. Don't you wait for anything. You pack what clothes she's got, and don't wait even to mend them, and you buy her ticket. I'll leave the money, and you send her along. She don't have to change cars. You start her off, when she gets home, on the next train!'

'Very well,' replied the other woman. She had an expression of covert amusement.

'Mind you do it.'

'Very well, Rebecca.'

Rebecca started on her journey the next morning. When she arrived, two days later, she found her cousin in perfect health. She found, moreover, that the friend had not written the postscript in the cousin's letter. Rebecca would have returned to Ford Village the next morning, but the fatigue and nervous strain had been too much for her. She was not able to move from her bed. She had a species of low fever induced by anxiety and fatigue. But she could write, and she did, to the Slocums, and she received no answer. She also wrote to Mrs. Dent; she even sent numerous telegrams, with no response. Finally she wrote to the postmaster, and an answer arrived by the first possible mail. The letter was short, curt, and to the purpose. Mr. Amblecrom, the postmaster, was a man of few words, and especially wary as to his expressions in a letter.

'Dear madam,' he wrote, 'your favour rec'ed. No Slocums in Ford's Village. All dead. Addie ten years ago, her mother two years later, her father five. House vacant. Mrs. John Dent said to have neglected stepdaughter. Girl was sick. Medicine not given. Talk of taking action. Not enough evidence. House said to be haunted. Strange sights and sounds. Your niece, Agnes Dent, died a year ago, about this time.

Yours truly,

'THOMAS AMBLECROM.'

1905

Sultana's Dream

ROKEYA SAKHAWAT HOSSAIN

One evening I was lounging in an easy chair in my bedroom and thinking lazily of the condition of Indian womanhood. I am not sure whether I dozed off or not. But, as far as I remember, I was wide awake. I saw the moonlit sky sparkling with thousands of diamondlike stars, very distinctly.

All of a sudden a lady stood before me; how she came in, I do not know. I took her for my friend, Sister Sara.

'Good morning,' said Sister Sara. I smiled inwardly as I knew it was not morning, but starry night. However, I replied to her, saying, 'How do you do?'

'I am all right, thank you. Will you please come out and have a look at our garden?'

I looked again at the moon through the open window, and thought there was no harm in going out at that time. The menservants outside were fast asleep just then, and I could have a pleasant walk with Sister Sara.

I used to have my walks with Sister Sara, when we were at Darjeeling. Many a time did we walk hand in hand and talk lightheartedly in the botanical gardens there. I fancied Sister Sara had probably come to take me to some such garden, and I readily accepted her offer and went out with her.

When walking I found to my surprise that it was a fine morning. The town was fully awake and the streets alive with bustling crowds. I was feeling very shy, thinking I was walking in the street in broad daylight, but there was not a single man visible.

Some of the passers-by made jokes at me. Though I could not understand their language, yet I felt sure they were joking. I asked my friend, 'What do they say?'

'The women say you look very mannish.'

'Mannish?' said I. 'What do they mean by that?'

'They mean that you are shy and timid like men.'

'Shy and timid like men?' It was really a joke. I became very nervous when I found that my companion was not Sister Sara, but a stranger. Oh, what a fool had I been to mistake this lady for my dear old friend Sister Sara.

She felt my fingers tremble in her hand, as we were walking hand in hand.

'What is the matter, dear, dear?' she said affectionately.

'I feel somewhat awkward,' I said, in a rather apologizing tone, 'as being a purdahnishin woman I am not accustomed to walking about unveiled.'

'You need not be afraid of coming across a man here. This is Ladyland, free from sin and harm. Virtue herself reigns here.'

By and by I was enjoying the scenery. Really it was very grand. I mistook a patch of green grass for a velvet cushion. Feeling as if I were walking on a soft carpet, I looked down and found the path covered with moss and flowers.

'How nice it is,' said I.

'Do you like it?' asked Sister Sara. (I continued calling her "Sister Sara," and she kept calling me by my name.)

'Yes, very much; but I do not like to tread on the tender and sweet flowers.'

'Never mind, dear Sultana. Your treading will not harm them; they are street flowers.'

'The whole place looks like a garden,' said I admiringly. 'You have arranged every plant so skillfully.'

'Your Calcutta could become a nicer garden than this, if only your countrymen wanted to make it so.'

'They would think it useless to give so much attention to horticulture, while they have so many other things to do.'

'They could not find a better excuse,' said she with [a] smile.

I became very curious to know where the men were. I met more than a hundred women while walking there, but not a single man.

'Where are the men?' I asked her.

'In their proper places, where they ought to be.'

'Pray let me know what you mean by "their proper places."'

'Oh, I see my mistake, you cannot know our customs, as you were never here before. We shut our men indoors.'

'Just as we are kept in the zenana?'

'Exactly so.'

'How funny.' I burst into a laugh. Sister Sara laughed too.

'But, dear Sultana, how unfair it is to shut in the harmless women and let loose the men.'

'Why? It is not safe for us to come out of the zenana, as we are naturally weak.'

'Yes, it is not safe so long as there are men about the streets, nor is it so when a wild animal enters a marketplace.'

'Of course not.'

'Suppose some lunatics escape from the asylum and begin to do all sorts of mischief to men, horses, and other creatures: in that case what will your countrymen do?'

'They will try to capture them and put them back into their asylum.'

'Thank you! And you do not think it wise to keep sane people inside an asylum and let loose the insane?'

'Of course not!' said I, laughing lightly.

'As a matter of fact, in your country this very thing is done! Men, who do or at least are capable of doing no end of mischief, are let loose and the innocent women shut up in the zenana! How can you trust those untrained men out of doors?'

'We have no hand or voice in the management of our social affairs. In India man is lord and master. He has taken to himself all powers and privileges and shut up the women in the zenana.'

'Why do you allow yourselves to be shut up?'

'Because it cannot be helped as they are stronger than women.'

'A lion is stronger than a man, but it does not enable him to dominate the human race. You have neglected the duty you owe to yourselves, and you have lost your natural rights by shutting your eyes to your own interests.'

'But my dear Sister Sara, if we do everything by ourselves, what will the men do then?'

'They should not do anything, excuse me; they are fit for nothing. Only catch them and put them into the zenana.'

'But would it be very easy to catch and put them inside the four walls?' said I. 'And even if this were done, would all their business—political and commercial—also go with them into the zenana?'

Sister Sara made no reply. She only smiled sweetly. Perhaps she thought it was useless to argue with one who was no better than a frog in a well.

By this time we reached Sister Sara's house. It was situated in a beautiful heart-shaped garden. It was a bungalow with a corrugated iron roof. It was cooler and nicer than any of our rich buildings. I cannot describe how neat and nicely furnished and how tastefully decorated it was.

We sat side by side. She brought out of the parlor a piece of embroidery work and began putting on a fresh design.

'Do you know knitting and needlework?'

'Yes: we have nothing else to do in our zenana.'

'But we do not trust our zenana members with embroidery!' she said laughing, 'as a man has not patience enough to pass thread through a needlehole even!'

'Have you done all this work yourself?' I asked her, pointing to the various pieces of embroidered teapoy cloths.

'Yes.'

'How can you find time to do all these? You have to do the office work as well? Have you not?'

'Yes. I do not stick to the laboratory all day long. I finish my work in two hours.'

'In two hours! How do you manage? In our land the officers, magistrates, for instance, work seven hours daily.'

'I have seen some of them doing their work. Do you think they work all the seven hours?'

'Certainly they do!'

'No, dear Sultana, they do not. They dawdle away their time in smoking. Some smoke two or three cheroots during the office time. They talk much about their work, but do little. Suppose one cheroot takes half an hour to burn off, and a man smokes twelve cheroots daily; then, you see, he wastes six hours every day in sheer smoking.'

We talked on various subjects; and I learned that they were not subject to any kind of epidemic disease, nor did they suffer from mosquito bites as we do. I was very much astonished to hear that in Ladyland no one died in youth except by rare accident.

'Will you care to see our kitchen?' she asked me.

'With pleasure,' said I, and we went to see it. Of course the men had been asked to clear off when I was going there. The kitchen was situated in a beautiful vegetable garden. Every creeper, every tomato plant, was itself an ornament. I found no smoke, nor any chimney either in the kitchen—it was clean and bright; the windows were decorated with flower garlands. There was no sign of coal or fire.

'How do you cook?' I asked.

'With solar heat,' she said, at the same time showing me the pipe, through which passed the concentrated sunlight and heat. And she cooked something then and there to show me the process.

'How did you manage to gather and store up the sun heat?' I asked her in amazement.

'Let me tell you a little of our past history, then. Thirty years ago, when our present Queen was thirteen years old, she inherited the throne. She was Queen in name only, the Prime Minister really ruling the country.

'Our good Queen liked science very much. She circulated an order that all the women in her country should be educated. Accordingly a number of girls' schools were founded and supported by the Government. Education was spread far and wide among women. And early marriage also was stopped. No woman was to be allowed to marry before she was twenty-one. I must tell you that, before this change, we had been kept in strict purdah.'

'How the tables are turned,' I interposed with a laugh.

'But the seclusion is the same,' she said. 'In a few years we had separate universities, where no men were admitted.

'In the capital, where our Queen lives, there are two universities. One of these invented a wonderful balloon, to which they attached a number of pipes. By means of this captive balloon, which they managed to keep afloat above the cloudland, they could draw as much water from the atmosphere as they pleased. As the water was incessantly being drawn by the university people, no cloud gathered and the ingenious Lady Principal stopped rain and storms thereby.'

'Really! Now I understand why there is no mud here!' said I. But I could not understand how it was possible to accumulate water in the pipes. She explained to me how it was done; but I was unable to understand her, as my scientific knowledge was very limited. However, she went on:

'When the other university came to know of this, they became exceedingly jealous and tried to do something more extraordinary still. They invented an instrument by which they could collect as much sun heat as they wanted. And they kept the heat stored up to be distributed among others as required.

'While the women were engaged in scientific researches, the men of this country were busy increasing their military power. When they came to know that the female universities were able to draw water from the atmosphere and collect heat from the sun, they only laughed at the members of the universities and called the whole thing "a sentimental nightmare"!'

'Your achievements are very wonderful indeed! But tell me how you managed to put the men of your country into the zenana. Did you entrap them first?'

'No.'

'It is not likely that they would surrender their free and open air life of their own accord and confine themselves within the four walls of the zenana! They must have been overpowered.'

'Yes, they have been!'

'By whom?—by some lady warriors, I suppose?'

'No, not by arms.'

'Yes, it cannot be so. Men's arms are stronger than women's. Then?'

'By brain.'

'Even their brains are bigger and heavier than women's. Are they not?'

'Yes, but what of that? An elephant also has got a bigger and heavier brain than a man has. Yet man can enchain elephants and employ them, according to his own wishes.'

'Well said, but tell me, please, how it all actually happened. I am dying to know it!'

'Women's brains are somewhat quicker than men's. Ten years ago, when the military officers called our scientific discoveries "a sentimental nightmare," some of the young ladies wanted to say something in reply to those remarks. But both the Lady Principals restrained them and said they should reply not by word but by deed, if ever they got the opportunity. And they had not long to wait for that opportunity.'

'How marvelous!' I heartily clapped my hands.

'And now the proud gentlemen are dreaming sentimental dreams themselves.

'Soon afterward certain persons came from a neighboring country and took shelter in ours. They were in trouble, having committed some political offence. The King, who cared more for power than for good government, asked our kindhearted Queen to hand them over to his officers. She refused, as it was against her principle to turn out refugees. For this refusal the King declared war against our country.

'Our military officers sprang to their feet at once and marched out to meet the enemy.

'The enemy, however, was too strong for them. Our soldiers fought bravely, no doubt. But in spite of all their bravery the foreign army advanced step by step to invade our country.

'Nearly all the men had gone out to fight; even a boy of sixteen was not left home. Most of our warriors were killed, the rest driven back, and the enemy came within twenty-five miles of the capital.

'A meeting of a number of wise ladies was held at the Queen's palace to advise [as] to what should be done to save the land.

'Some proposed to fight like soldiers; others objected and said that women were not trained to fight with swords and guns, nor were they accustomed to fighting with any weapons. A third party regretfully remarked that they were hopelessly weak of body.

'If you cannot save your country for lack of physical strength, said the Queen, try to do so by brain power.

'There was a dead silence for a few minutes. Her Royal Highness said again, "I must commit suicide if the land and my honor are lost."

'Then the Lady Principal of the second university (who had collected sun heat), who had been silently thinking during the consultation, remarked that they were all but lost; and there was little hope left for them. There was, however, one plan [that] she would like to try, and this would be her first and last effort; if she failed in this, there would be nothing left but to commit suicide. All present solemnly vowed that they would never allow themselves to be enslaved, no matter what happened.

'The Queen thanked them heartily, and asked the Lady Principal to try her plan.

'The Lady Principal rose again and said, "Before we go out the men must enter the zenanas. I make this prayer for the sake of purdah." "Yes, of course," replied Her Royal Highness.

'On the following day the Queen called upon all men to retire into zenanas for the sake of honor and liberty.

'Wounded and tired as they were, they took that order rather for a boon! They bowed low and entered the zenanas without uttering a single word of protest. They were sure that there was no hope for this country at all.

'Then the Lady Principal with her two thousand students marched to the battlefield, and arriving there directed all the rays of the concentrated sun light and heat toward the enemy.

'The heat and light were too much for them to bear. They all ran away panic-stricken, not knowing in their bewilderment how to counteract that scorching heat. When they fled away leaving their guns and other ammunitions of war, they were burned down by means of the same sun heat.

'Since then no one has tried to invade our country any more.'

'And since then your countrymen never tried to come out of the zenana?'

'Yes, they wanted to be free. Some of the Police Commissioners and District Magistrates sent word to the Queen to the effect that the Military Officers certainly deserved to be imprisoned for their failure; but they [had] never neglected their duty and therefore they should not be punished, and they prayed to be restored to their respective offices.

'Her Royal Highness sent them a circular letter, intimating to them that if their services should ever be needed they would be sent for, and that in the meanwhile they should remain where they were.

'Now that they are accustomed to the purdah system and have ceased to grumble at their seclusion, we call the system *mardana* instead of zenana.'

'But how do you manage,' I asked Sister Sara, 'to do without the police or magistrates in case of theft or murder?'

'Since the mardana system has been established, there has been no more crime or sin; therefore we do not require a policeman to find out a culprit, nor do we want a magistrate to try a criminal case.'

'That is very good, indeed. I suppose if there were any dishonest person, you could very easily chastise her. As you gained a decisive victory without shedding a single drop of blood, you could drive off crime and criminals too without much difficulty!'

'Now, dear Sultana, will you sit here or come to my parlor?' she asked me.

'Your kitchen is not inferior to a queen's boudoir!' I replied with a pleasant smile, 'but we must leave it now; for the gentlemen may be cursing me for keeping them away from their duties in the kitchen so long.' We both laughed heartily.

'How my friends at home will be amused and amazed, when I go back and tell them that in the far-off Ladyland, ladies rule over the country and control all social matters, while gentlemen are kept in the mardanas to mind babies, to cook, and to do all sorts of domestic work; and that cooking is so easy a thing that it is simply a pleasure to cook!'

'Yes, tell them about all that you see here.'

'Please let me know how you carry on land cultivation and how you plow the land and do other hard manual work.'

'Our fields are tilled by means of electricity, which supplies motive power for other hard work as well, and we employ it for our aerial conveyances too. We have no railroad nor any paved streets here.'

'Therefore neither street nor railway accidents occur here,' said I. 'Do not you ever suffer from want of rainwater?' I asked.

'Never since the "water balloon" has been set up. You see the big balloon and pipes attached thereto. By their aid we can draw as much rainwater as we require. Nor do we ever suffer from flood or thunderstorms. We are all very busy making nature yield as much as she can. We do not find time to quarrel with one another as we never sit idle. Our noble Queen is exceedingly fond of botany; it is her ambition to convert the whole country into one grand garden.'

'The idea is excellent. What is your chief food?'

'Fruits.'

'How do you keep your country cool in hot weather? We regard the rainfall in summer as a blessing from heaven.'

'When the heat becomes unbearable, we sprinkle the ground with plentiful showers drawn from the artificial fountains. And in cold weather we keep our rooms warm with sun heat.'

She showed me her bathroom, the roof of which was removable. She could enjoy a shower [or] bath whenever she liked, by simply removing the roof (which was like the lid of a box) and turning on the tap of the shower pipe.

'You are a lucky people!' ejaculated I. 'You know no want. What is your religion, may I ask?'

'Our religion is based on Love and Truth. It is our religious duty to love one another and to be absolutely truthful. If any person lies, she or he is . . .'

'Punished with death?'

'No, not with death. We do not take pleasure in killing a creature of God—especially a human being. The liar is asked to leave this land for good and never to come to it again.'

'Is an offender never forgiven?'

'Yes, if that person repents sincerely.'

'Are you not allowed to see any man, except your own relations?'

'No one except sacred relations.'

'Our circle of sacred relations is very limited, even first cousins are not sacred.'

'But ours is very large; a distant cousin is as sacred as a brother.'

'That is very good. I see Purity itself reigns over your land. I should like to see the good Queen, who is so sagacious and farsighted and who has made all these rules.'

'All right,' said Sister Sara.

Then she screwed a couple of seats on to a square piece of plank. To this plank she attached two smooth and well-polished balls. When I asked her what the balls were for, she said they were hydrogen balls and they were used to overcome the force of gravity. The balls were of different capacities, to be used according to the different weights desired to be overcome. She then fastened to the air-car two winglike blades, which, she said, were worked by electricity. After we were comfortably seated she touched a knob and the blades began to whirl, moving faster and faster every moment. At first we were raised to the height of about six or seven feet and then off we flew. And before I could realize that we had commenced moving, we reached the garden of the Queen.

My friend lowered the air-car by reversing the action of the machine, and when the car touched the ground the machine was stopped and we got out.

I had seen from the air-car the Queen walking on a garden path with her little daughter (who was four years old) and her maids of honor.

'Halloo! you here!' cried the Queen, addressing Sister Sara. I was introduced to Her Royal Highness and was received by her cordially without any ceremony.

I was very much delighted to make her acquaintance. In [the] course of the conversation I had with her, the Queen told me that she had no objection to permitting her subjects to trade with other countries. 'But,' she continued, 'no trade was possible with countries where the women were kept in the zenanas and so unable to come and trade with us. Men, we find, are rather of lower morals and so we do not like dealing with them. We do not covet other people's land, we do not fight for a piece of diamond though it may be a thousandfold brighter than the Koh-i-Noor,* nor do we grudge a ruler his Peacock Throne.** We dive deep into the ocean of knowledge and try to find out the precious gems [that] Nature has kept in store for us. We enjoy Nature's gifts as much as we can.'

After taking leave of the Queen, I visited the famous universities, and was shown over some of their factories, laboratories, and observatories.

After visiting the above places of interest, we got again into the air-car, but as soon as it began moving I somehow slipped down and the fall startled me out of my dream. And on opening my eyes, I found myself in my own bedroom still lounging in the easy chair!

*The Koh-i-Noor ('mountain of light') is the name of a large and exceptionally brilliant diamond in the possession of the Mughal rulers of India, currently part of the British Crown Jewels. To Indians, it is a symbol of great wealth.

**The Peacock Throne is a famous jewel-encrusted throne built for the Mughal Emperor Shah Jahan, also known for the Taj Mahal. It was carried away from Delhi by the Persian invader Nadir Shah. Its current location is the cause of much speculation. Many think that one of the thrones displayed in the Istanbul Museum is the Peacock Throne. It is a long-standing symbol of royal power and splendor to Indians.

1908

The Woman with
the Hood

L. T. MEADE

It was late in the October of a certain year when I was asked to
become 'locum tenens' to a country practitioner in one of the
midland counties. He was taken ill and obliged to leave home hastily.
I therefore entered on my duties without having any indication of the
sort of patients whom I was to visit. I was a young man at the time,
and a great enthusiast with regard to the medical profession. I believed
in personal influence and the magnetism of a strong personality as
being all-conducive to the furtherance of the curative art. I had no
experience, however, to guide me with regard to country patients,
my work hitherto having been amongst the large population of
a manufacturing town. On the very night of my arrival my first
experience as a country doctor began. I had just got into bed, and
was dozing off into a sound sleep, when the night bell which hung
in my room rang pretty sharply. I jumped up and went to the tube,
calling down to ask what was the matter.

'Are you the new doctor?' asked the voice.

'Yes, my name is Bruce; who wants me?'

'Mrs. Frayling of Garth Hall. The young lady is very bad. I have got
a trap here; how soon can you be ready?'

'In a couple of minutes,' I answered. I hastily got into my clothes,
and in less than five minutes had mounted beside a rough-looking
man, into a high gig. He touched his horse, who bounded off, at a
great speed, and I found myself rattling through the country in the
dead of night.

'How far off is the Hall?' I asked.

'A matter of two miles,' was the reply.

'Do you know anything of the nature of the young lady's illness?'

'Yes I do; it is the old thing.'

'Can you not enlighten me?' I asked, seeing that the man had shut up his lips and employed himself flicking his horse with the end of his long whip. The beast flew faster and faster, the man turned and fixed his eyes full upon me in the moonlight.

'They'll tell you when you get there,' he said. 'All I can say is that you will do no good, no one can, the matter ain't in our province. We are turning into the avenue now; you will soon know for yourself.'

We dashed down a long avenue, and drew up in a couple of moments at a door sheltered by a big porch. I saw a tall lady in evening dress standing in the brightly lighted hall within.

'Have you brought the doctor, Thompson?' I heard her say to the man who had driven me.

'Yes, ma'am,' was the reply. 'The new doctor, Doctor Bruce.'

'Oh! Then Dr. Mackenzie has really left?'

'He left this morning, ma'am, I told you so.'

I heard her utter a slight sigh of disappointment.

'Come this way, Dr. Bruce,' she said. 'I am sorry to have troubled you.'

She led me as she spoke across the hall and into a drawing-room of lofty dimensions, beautifully furnished in modern style. It was now between one and two in the morning, but the whole house was lit up as if the night were several hours younger. Mrs. Frayling wore a black evening dress, low to the neck and with demi sleeves. She had dark eyes and a beautiful, kindly face. It looked haggard now and alarmed.

'The fact is,' she said, 'I have sent for you on a most extraordinary mission. I do not know that I should have troubled a strange doctor, but I hoped that Dr. Mackenzie had not yet left.'

'He left this morning,' I said. 'He was very ill; a case of nervous breakdown. He could not even wait to give me instructions with regard to my patients.'

'Ah, yes,' she said averting her eyes from mine as she spoke. 'Our doctor used to be as hale a man as could be found in the country round. Nervous breakdown; I think I understand. I hope, Dr. Bruce, that you are not troubled by nerves.'

'Certainly not,' I answered. 'As far as I am concerned they don't exist. Now what can I do for you, Mrs. Frayling?'

'I want you to see my daughter. I want you to try and quiet her terrors. Dr. Mackenzie used to be able to do so, but of late—'

'Her terrors!' I said. 'I must ask you to explain further.'

'I am going to do so. My daughter, Lucy, she is my only child, is sorely troubled by the appearance of an apparition.'

I could scarcely forbear from smiling.

'Your daughter wants change,' I said, 'change of scene and air.'

'That is the queer thing,' said Mrs. Frayling; 'she will not take change, nothing will induce her to leave Garth Hall; and yet living here is slowly but surely bringing her either to her grave or to a worse fate, that of a lunatic asylum. She went to bed to-night as usual, but an hour afterwards I was awakened by her screams; I ran to her room and found her sitting up in bed, trembling violently. Her eyes were fixed on a certain part of the room; they were wide open, and had a look of the most horrified agony in them which I have never seen in the human face. She did not see me when I went into the room, but when I touched her hand she clasped it tightly.

' "Tell her to go away, mother," she said, "she won't stir for me; I cannot speak to her, I have not the courage, and she is waiting for me to speak; tell her to go away, mother—tell her to cease to trouble me—tell her to go."

'I could see nothing, Dr. Bruce, but she continued to stare just towards the foot of her bed, and described the terrible thing which was troubling her.

' "Can't you see her yourself?" she said. "She is a dead woman, and she comes here night after night—see her yellow face—oh, mother, tell her to go—tell her to go!"

'I did what I could for my poor child, but no words of mine could soothe or reassure her. The room was bright with firelight, and there were several candles burning, I could not see a soul. At last the poor girl fainted off with terror. I then sent a messenger for Dr. Mackenzie. She now lies moaning in her bed, our old nurse is sitting with her. She is terribly weak, and drops of agony are standing on her forehead. She cannot long continue this awful strain.'

'It must be a case of delusion,' I said. 'You say you saw nothing in the room?'

'Nothing; but it is only right to tell you that the house is haunted.'

I smiled, and fidgetted in my chair.

'Ah! I know,' said Mrs. Frayling, 'that you naturally do not believe in ghosts and apparitions, but perhaps you would change your mind if you lived long at Garth Hall. I have lived here for the last twelve years, and can certainly testify to the fact of having heard most unaccountable sounds, but I have never seen anything. My daughter, Lucy, has been educated abroad, and did not come to Garth Hall to live until three months ago; it was soon after this that the apparition began to appear to her. Now it is her nightly torment, and it is simply killing her, and yet she refuses to go. Every day she says to me, "I know, mother, that that awful spirit is in fearful trouble, and perhaps to-night I may have the courage to speak to it," but night after night much the same thing takes place; the poor child endures the agony until she faints right off, and each day her nerves are weaker and her whole strength more completely shattered.'

'Well, I will go up now and see the patient,' I said. 'It is of course nothing whatever but a case of strong delusion, and against her will, Mrs. Frayling, it is your duty to remove your daughter from this house immediately.'

'You will tell a different story after you have seen her,' said the mother.

She rose as she spoke and conducted me up some shallow bright-looking stairs. She then led me into a large bedroom on the first landing. The fire burned brightly in the grate, and four or five candles stood about in different directions. Their light fell full upon the form of a very young and extremely beautiful girl.

Her face was as white as the pillow on which it rested; her eyes were shut, and the dark fringe of her long eyelashes rested on her cheeks; her hair was tossed over the pillow; her hands, thin to emaciation, lay outside the coverlet; now and then her fingers worked convulsively.

Bending gently forward I took her wrist between my finger and thumb. The pulse was very faint and slow. As I was feeling it she opened her eyes.

'Who are you?' she asked, looking at me without any alarm, and with only a very languid curiosity in her tone.

'I am the new doctor who has come in Dr. Mackenzie's place,' I answered. 'My name is Bruce.'

She gave me just the ghost of a smile.

'Mine is not a case for the doctor,' she said. 'Has mother told you what troubles me?'

'Yes,' I answered. 'You are very nervous and must not be alone. I will sit with you for a little.'

'It makes no difference whether you are here or not,' she said. 'She will come back again in about an hour. You may or may not see her. She will certainly come, and then my awful terrors will begin again.'

'Well, we will wait for her together,' I said, as cheerfully as I could.

I moved a chair forward as I spoke and sat down by the bedside.

Miss Frayling shut her eyes with a little impatient gesture. I motioned to Mrs. Frayling to seat herself not far away; and going deliberately to some of the candles put them out. The light no longer fell strongly on the bed—the patient was in shadow. I hoped she might fall into really deep slumber and not awaken till the morning light had banished ghostly terrors. She certainly seemed to have sunk into gentle and calm sleep; the expression of her face seemed to smooth out, her brow was no longer corrugated with anxious wrinkles—gentle smiles played about her lips. She looked like the child she was. I guessed as I watched her that her years could not number more than seventeen or eighteen.

'She is better,' said Mrs. Frayling. 'She may not have another attack to-night.' As she spoke she rose, and telling me she would return in a few minutes, left the room. She and I were the only watchers by the sick girl, the servants having retired to bed. Mrs. Frayling went to fetch something. She had scarcely done so before I was conscious of a complete change in the aspect of the room—it had felt home-like, warm, and comfortable up to this moment; now I was distinctly conscious of a sense of chill. I could not account for my sensations, but most undoubtedly my heart began to beat more quickly than was quite agreeable; I felt a creeping sensation down my back—the cold seemed to grow greater.

I said to myself, 'The fire wants replenishing,' but I had an unaccountable aversion to stirring; I did not even want to turn my head. At the same moment Miss Frayling, who had been sleeping so peacefully, began evidently to dream; her face worked with agitation; she suddenly opened her eyes and uttered a sharp, piercing cry.

'Keep her back,' she said, flinging out her arms, as if she wanted to push something from her.

I started up instantly, and went to the bedside.

At this moment Mrs. Frayling came into the room. The moment she did so the sense of chill and unaccountable horror left me; the room became once more warm and home-like. I looked at the fire, it was piled up high in the grate and was burning merrily. Miss Frayling, however, did not share my pleasanter sensations.

'I said she would come back,' she exclaimed, pointing with her finger to the foot of the bed.

I looked in that direction but could see nothing.

'Can't you see her? Oh, I wish you could see her,' she cried. 'She stands there at the foot of the bed; she wears a hood, and her face is yellow. She has been dead a long time, and I know she wants to say something. I cannot speak to her. Oh, tell her to go away; tell her to go away.'

'Shut your eyes, Miss Frayling; do not look,' I said.

Then I turned and boldly faced the empty space where the excited girl had seen the apparition.

'Whoever you are, leave us now,' I said in an authoritative voice. 'We are not prepared for you to-night. Leave us now.'

To my surprise Miss Frayling gave a gleeful laugh.

'Why, she has gone,' she exclaimed in a voice of relief. 'She walked out of the door—I saw her go. I don't believe she will come back at present. How queer! Then you did see her, Dr. Bruce?'

'No,' I answered; 'I saw nothing.'

'But she heard you; she nodded her head once and then went. She will come back again, of course; but perhaps not to-night. I don't feel frightened any longer. I believe I shall sleep.'

She snuggled down under the bedclothes.

'Have some of this beef-tea, Lucy,' said her mother, bringing a cup up to the bedside. It was steaming hot, she had gone away to warm it.

'Yes, I feel faint and hungry,' replied the girl; she raised her pretty head and allowed her mother to feed and pet her.

'I am much better,' she said. 'I know she won't come back again to-night; you need not stay with me any longer, Dr. Bruce.'

'I will stay with her, Doctor; you must lie down in another room,' said the mother.

I consented to go as far as the ante-room. There was a comfortable sofa there, and I had scarcely laid my head upon it before I fell into a sound slumber.

When I awakened it was broad daylight and Mrs. Frayling was standing over me.

'Lucy is much better and is getting up,' she said. 'She looks almost herself. What an extraordinary effect your words had, Dr. Bruce.'

'They came as a sort of inspiration,' I said; 'I did not mean them to be anything special.'

'Then you do not believe that she really saw the apparition?'

'Certainly not; her brain is very much excited and overwrought. You ought to take her away to-day.'

'That is the queer thing,' said Mrs. Frayling. 'I told you that she would not consent to leave the house, believing, poor child, that her mission was to try and comfort this awful ghost, in case she could summon courage to speak to it. She told me this morning, however, that she was quite willing to go and suggested that we should sleep at the Metropole in town to-night.'

'The best thing possible,' I said. 'Take her away immediately. Give her plenty of occupation and variety, and let her see heaps of cheerful people. She will doubtless soon get over her terrors.'

'It is very strange,' repeated Mrs. Frayling. 'Her attitude of mind seems completely altered. She wishes to see you for a moment before you leave us. I will meet you in the breakfast-room in a quarter of an hour, Dr. Bruce.'

I made a hasty toilet and followed Mrs. Frayling downstairs. We ate breakfast almost in silence, and just before the meal was over Miss Frayling made her appearance. She was a very slightly-built girl, tall and graceful as a reed. She came straight up to me.

'I don't know how to thank you,' she said, holding out her hand.

'Why?' I asked in astonishment. 'I am glad I was able to relieve you, but I am rather puzzled to know what great thing I really did.'

'Why, don't you know?' she answered. 'Can't you guess? She will come to you now. I don't believe she will trouble me any more.'

'Well, I am stronger to receive her than you are,' I said, smiling and trying to humour the girl's fancy.

Soon afterwards I took my leave and returned to Dr. Mackenzie's house. I spent the day without anything special occurring, and in the evening, being dead tired, went to bed as usual. Dr. Mackenzie's house was an essentially modern one. Anything less ghostly than the squarely-built cheerful rooms could scarcely be imagined. I was alone in the house with the exception of his servants. I went to bed, and had scarcely laid my head on the pillow before I was sound asleep. I was suddenly awakened out of my first slumbers by someone calling to me through the speaking-tube.

'Yes, I will come immediately,' I answered.

I sprang out of bed and applied my ear to the tube.

'You are wanted at Garth Hall,' said the voice.

'But surely there is no one ill there to-night?' I said.

'You are wanted immediately; come without delay,' was the reply.

'I will be with you in a minute,' I answered.

I felt almost annoyed, but there was no help for it. I hurried into my clothes and went downstairs.

'How very silly of Mrs. Frayling not to have taken her daughter away—shall I have to go through a repetition of last night's scene over again?' I thought.

I opened the hall door, expecting to see a horse and gig, and the man who had driven me the night before. To my astonishment there was not a soul in sight.

'What can this mean?' I said to myself. 'Has the messenger been careless enough not to bring a trap—it will be very troublesome if I have to get my own horse out at this hour—where can the man be?'

I looked to right and left—the night was a moonlit one—there was not a soul in sight. Very much provoked, but never for a moment doubting that I was really summoned, I went off to the stables, saddled Dr. Mackenzie's horse, Rover, and mounting, rode off to Garth Hall. The hour was quite late, between twelve and one o'clock. When I drew up at the door the house was in total darkness.

'What can this mean?' I said to myself. I rang a bell fiercely, and after a long time a servant put her head out of an upper window.

'Who is there?' she asked.

'I—Dr. Bruce,' I cried. 'I have been sent for in a hurry to see Miss Frayling.'

'Good Lord!' I heard the woman exclaim. 'Wait a minute, sir, and I will come down to you,' she shouted.

In a couple of minutes the great hall door was unchained and unlocked, and a respectable middle-aged woman stood on the steps.

'Miss Frayling has gone to London with her mother, sir,' she said. 'You are quite certain you were sent for?'

'Quite,' I answered. 'Your man—the man who came last night—'

'Not Thompson!' she cried.

'Yes, the same man called for me through the speaking tube to come here at once—he said Miss Frayling was ill, and wanted me.'

'It must have been a hoax, sir,' said the housekeeper, but I noticed a troubled and perplexed look on her face. 'I am very sorry indeed, but Miss Frayling is not here—we do not expect the ladies back for some weeks,' she added.

'I am sorry I troubled you,' I answered; I turned my horse's head and went home again.

The next day I set enquiries on foot with regard to the hoax which had been played upon me. Whoever had done the trick, no one was ready to own to it, and I noticed that the servants looked mysterious and nodded their heads when I said it was to Garth Hall I had been summoned.

The next night the same thing occurred. My night bell was rung and a voice shouted to me through the speaking-tube to come immediately to Garth Hall. I took no notice whatever of the trick, but determined to lay a trap for the impertinent intruder on my repose for the following night. I had a very savage dog, and I tied him outside the house. My housekeeper also agreed to sit up. Between twelve and one o'clock I was called again. I flew to my window and looked out. There was not a soul in sight, but a queer sense of indescribable chill and unaccountable horror took sudden possession of me. The dog was crouching down on the ground with his face hidden in his paws; he was moaning feebly. I dressed, went downstairs, unchained him and brought him up to my room. He crept on to my bed and lay there trembling; I will own to the fact that his master shared the unaccountable horror. What was the matter? I dared not answer this question even to myself. Mrs. Marks, my housekeeper, looked very solemn and grave the next morning.

'Sir,' she said, when she brought in breakfast, 'if I were you, I would go away from here. There is something very queer at the Hall and it seems to me—but there, I cannot speak of it.'

'There are some things best not spoken of,' I said shortly; 'whoever is playing me a hoax has not chosen to reveal himself or herself. We can best tire the unlucky individual out by taking no notice.'

'Yes, sir, perhaps that is best. Now I have got some news for you.'

'What is that?' I asked.

'Mrs. and Miss Frayling returned to the Hall this morning.'

'This morning!' I exclaimed, in astonishment, 'but it is not yet nine o'clock.'

'True, sir, but early as the hour is they passed this house not half-an-hour ago in the closed brougham. Miss Frayling looked very white, and the good lady, her mother, full of anxiety. I caught a glimpse of them as I was cleaning the steps; I doubt not, sir, but you will be summoned to the Hall to-day.'

'Perhaps so,' I answered briefly.

Mrs. Marks looked at me as if she would say something further, but refrained, and to my relief soon afterwards left me alone.

I finished my breakfast and went out about my daily rounds. I do not think myself destitute of pluck but I cannot pretend that I liked the present position. What was the mystery? What horrible dark joke was being played? With my healthy bringing up I could not really ascribe the thing to supernatural agency. A trick there was, of course. I vowed that I would find it out before I was much older, but then I remembered the chill and the terror which had assailed me when sitting up with Miss Frayling. The same chill and terror had come over me when I suddenly opened my window the night before.

'The best thing I can do is not to think of this,' I commented, and then I absorbed myself with my patients.

Nothing occurred of any moment that day, nor was I summoned to attend the ladies at Garth Hall. About ten o'clock that night I had to go out to attend a farmer's wife who was suddenly taken ill. I sat with her for a little time and did not return till about half past eleven. I then went straight up to my room and went to bed. I had scarcely fallen into my first slumber when I was aroused by the sharp ringing of my night bell. I felt inclined for a moment not to pay the least attention to it, but as it rang again with a quick imperative sound, I got up, more from the force of habit than anything else, and calling through the speaking-tube, applied my ear to it.

'Dr. Bruce, will you come at once to Garth Hall?' called a voice.

'No, I will not,' I called back in reply.

There was a pause below, evidently of astonishment—and then the voice called again.

'I don't think you quite understand, sir. Mrs. Frayling wants you to visit Miss Frayling immediately; the young lady is very ill.'

I was about to put the cap on the tube and return to my bed when I distinctly heard the crunch of wheels beneath my window and the pawing of an impatient horse. I crossed the room, threw open the window and looked out. A horse and gig were now standing under the window, and the man, Thompson, who had summoned me on the first night, was staring up at me.

'For God's sake, come, sir,' he said. 'The young lady is mortal bad.'

'I will be with you in a minute,' I said. I dressed myself trembling.

In an incredibly short space of time Thompson and I arrived at the Hall. Through our entire drive the man never spoke, but when we drew up at the great porch he uttered a heavy sigh of relief and muttered the words: 'The devil is in this business. I don't pretend to understand it.'

I looked at him, but resolved to take no notice of his queer remark. Mrs. Frayling met me on the steps.

'Come in at once,' she said. She took both my hands in hers and drew me into the house. We entered her cheerful drawing-room. The poor lady's face was ghastly, her eyes full not only of trouble, but of horror.

'Now, Dr. Bruce,' she said, 'you must do your best.'

'In what way?' I said.

'I fear my poor girl is mad. Unless you can manage to relieve her mind, she certainly will be by morning.'

'Tell me what has happened since I last saw you, as briefly as possible,' I said.

'I will do so,' she replied. 'Acting on your instructions, Lucy and I went to the Metropole. She was quite happy on the first day, but in the middle of the night grew very much disturbed. She and I were sleeping together. She awakened me and told me that the apparition at Garth Hall was pulling her—that the woman in the hood was imperatively demanding her presence.

' "I know what has happened," said Lucy. "Dr. Bruce has refused to help her. She has gone to him but he won't respond to her efforts to bring him on the scene. How cruel he is!"

'I soothed the poor child as best I could, and towards morning she dropped off asleep. The next night she was in a still greater state of terror, again assuring me that the lady in the hood was drawing her, and that you, Dr. Bruce, were turning a deaf ear to her entreaties. On the third night she became almost frantic.

' "I must go back," she said. "My spirit is being torn out of my body. If I am not back at Garth Hall early in the morning I shall die."

'Her distress and horror were so extreme that I had to humour her. We took the very earliest train from London, and arrived at the Hall at nine o'clock. During the day Lucy was gentle and subdued; she seemed relieved at being back again, told me that she would go early to bed and that she hoped that she might have a good night. About an hour ago I heard her screaming violently, and, rushing to her room, found her in almost a state of collapse from horror—she kept pointing in a certain direction, but could not speak. I sent Thompson off in a hurry for you. As soon as ever I said I would do so she became a little better, and said she would dress herself. It is her intention now to ask you to spend the night with us, and, if possible, speak again to the horrible thing which is driving my child into a madhouse.'

'I will tell you something strange,' I said, when Mrs. Frayling paused, 'I was undoubtedly called during the last three nights. A voice shouted through my speaking-tube, desiring me to come to Garth Hall. On the first night I went, feeling sure that I was really summoned; since then I have believed that it was a hoax.'

'Oh, this is awful,' said Mrs. Frayling, trembling excessively; she turned and asked me to follow her upstairs. We entered the same spacious and cheerful bedroom; Lucy Frayling was now pacing up and down in front of the fireplace; she did not notice either of us when we came in; the expression on her face was almost that of an insane person. The pupils of her eyes were widely dilated.

'Lucy,' said her mother, 'Here is Dr. Bruce.'

She paused when my name was mentioned and looked at me fixedly. Her eyes grew dark with anger—she clenched her hand.

'You were faithless,' she said; 'she wanted you, and you would not accept the burden; you told me when last I saw you that you were glad she had turned to you, for you are stronger than me, but you are a coward.'

'Come, come,' I said, trying to speak cheerfully. 'I am here now, and will do anything you wish.'

'I will prove you,' said Miss Frayling, in a eager voice; 'She will come again presently; when she comes, will you speak to her?'

'Certainly,' I replied, 'but remember I may not see her.'

'I will tell you when she appears; I will point with my hand—I may not have power to utter words—but I will point to where she stands. When I do, speak to her; ask her why she troubles us—promise—you spoke once, speak again.'

'I promise,' I replied, and my voice sounded solemn and intense.

Miss Frayling heaved a deep sigh of relief, she went and stood by the mantlepiece with her back to the fire. I sat down on the nearest chair, and Mrs. Frayling followed my example. The clock ticked loudly on the mantlepiece, the candles burned with a steady gleam, the fire threw out cheerful flames, all was silent in the chamber. There was not a stir, not a sound. The minutes flew on. Miss Frayling stood as quiet as if she were turned into stone; suddenly she spoke,

'There is an adverse influence here,' she said. 'Mother, will you go into the ante-room. You can leave the door open, but will you stay in the ante-room for a little?'

Mrs. Frayling glanced at me; I nodded to her to comply. She left the room, going into a pretty little boudoir out of which the bedroom opened. I could see her from where I sat. Lucy now slightly altered her position. I saw that her eyes were fixed in the direction of another door, which opened from the outside corridor into the room. I tried to speak, to say something cheerful, but she held up her finger to stop me.

'She is coming,' she said, in a stifled voice. 'I feel the first stirring of the indescribable agony which always heralds her approach. Oh, my God, help me to endure. Was ever girl tortured as I am, before?'

She wrung her slight hands, her brows were knit, I saw the perspiration standing in great drops on her brow. I thought she would faint, and was about to rise to administer some restorative, when in the far distance I distinctly heard a sound; it was the sound of a woman's footsteps. It came along, softly tapping on the floor as it came; I heard the swish of a dress, the sound came nearer, the handle of the door was turned, I started and looked round. I did not see anybody, but immediately the room was filled with that sense of cold and chill which I had twice before experienced. My heart beat to suffocation, I felt my tongue cleave to the roof of my mouth, I was so overpowered by my own sensations that I had no time to watch Miss Frayling. Suddenly I heard her utter a low groan. I made a violent effort and turned my face in her direction. The poor girl was staring straight before her as if she were turned into stone. Her eyes were fixed in the direction of the door.

She raised her hand slowly and tremblingly, and pointed in the direction where her eyes were fixed. I looked across the room. Was it fancy, or was I conscious of a faint blue mist where no mist ought to be? I am not certain on that point, but I know at the same moment the horror which had almost overbalanced my reason suddenly left me. I found my voice.

'What do you want?' I said. 'Why do you trouble us? What is the matter?'

The words had scarcely passed my lips before Miss Frayling's face underwent a queer change; she was also relieved from the agony of terror which was overmasting her.

'She is beckoning,' she said; 'come quickly.'

She sprang across the room as she spoke, and seized a candle.

'Come at once,' she said in a breathless voice, 'she is beckoning—come.'

Miss Frayling ran out of the room; I followed her, and Mrs. Frayling who had come to the door while this strange scene was going on, accompanied us. Miss Frayling still taking the lead, we went downstairs. The whole house was full of strange unaccountable chill. We entered the upper hall, and then turning to our left, went down some steep stairs which led into a cellar.

'Where are you going now?' asked Mrs. Frayling.

'Come on, mother, come on,' called Lucy, 'she will tell us what to do.'

We turned at the foot of the stairs into a low arched room with one tiny window. There was a heavy buttress of wall here which bulged out in an unaccountable manner. The moment we entered this room, Lucy turned and faced us.

'She has gone in there,' she said—'right into the wall.'

'Well,' I said, 'now that we have followed her, let us go back—it is very cold in the cellar.'

Miss Frayling laughed hysterically.

'Do you think,' she said, 'that I will go back now. We must have this wall opened—can you do it, Dr. Bruce? Can you do it now, this moment? Mother, are there tools anywhere?'

'Not now, dear, not to-night,' said the mother.

'Yes, to-night, this moment,' exclaimed the girl. 'Let Thompson be called—we have not a moment to lose. She went in right through this wall and smiled at me as she went. Poor, poor ghost! I believe her sad wanderings are nearly over.'

'What are we to do?' said Mrs. Frayling, turning to me.

'We will open the wall at once,' I said. 'It will not be difficult to remove a few bricks. If you will kindly tell me where Thompson is I will fetch him.'

'No, I will go for him myself,' said Mrs. Frayling.

She left the cellar, returning in the space of a few minutes with the man. He brought a crowbar and other tools with him. He and I quickly removed some bricks. As soon as we had done so we found an empty space inside, into which we could thrust our hands. We made it a little larger and then were able to insert a candle. Lying on the floor within this space was a human skeleton.

I cried out at the awful discovery we had made, but Miss Frayling showed neither surprise nor terror.

'Poor ghost!' repeated the girl; 'she will rest now. It was worth all this fearful suffering to bring her rest at last.'

The discovery of the skeleton was the topic of the neighbourhood. It was given Christian burial in due course, and from that hour to this the ghost at Garth Hall has never appeared.

I cannot pretend to account for this story in any way—no one has ever found out why those human bones were built into the old wall. The whole thing is queer and uncomfortable, a phenomenon which will not be explained on this side Eternity.

1914

*If I Were a Man**

CHARLOTTE PERKINS GILMAN

'If I were a man, . . .' that was what pretty little Mollie Mathewson always said when Gerald would not do what she wanted him to—which was seldom.

That was what she said this bright morning, with a stamp of her little high-heeled slipper, just because he had made a fuss about that bill, the long one with the 'account rendered,' which she had forgotten to give him the first time and been afraid to the second—and now he had taken it from the postman himself.

Mollie was 'true to type.' She was a beautiful instance of what is reverentially called 'a true woman.' Little, of course—no true woman may be big. Pretty, of course—no true woman could possibly be plain. Whimsical, capricious, charming, changeable, devoted to pretty clothes and always 'wearing them well,' as the esoteric phrase has it. (This does not refer to the clothes—they do not wear well in the least—but to some special grace of putting them on and carrying them about, granted to but few, it appears.)

She was also a loving wife and a devoted mother possessed of 'the social gift' and the love of 'society' that goes with it, and, with all these was fond and proud of her home and managed it as capably as—well, as most women do.

If ever there was a true woman it was Mollie Mathewson, yet she was wishing heart and soul she was a man.

And all of a sudden she was!

She was Gerald, walking down the path so erect and square-shouldered, in a hurry for his morning train, as usual, and, it must be confessed, in something of a temper.

Her own words were ringing in her ears—not only the 'last word,'

*'If I Were a Man' was published in the *July 1914* issue of Physical Culture, 31–34 but several that had gone before, and she was holding her lips tight shut, not to say something she would be sorry for. But instead of acquiescence in the position taken by that angry little figure on the veranda, what she felt was a sort of superior pride, a sympathy as with weakness, a feeling that 'I must be gentle with her,' in spite of the temper.

A man! Really a man—with only enough subconscious memory of herself remaining to make her recognize the differences.

At first there was a funny sense of size and weight and extra thickness, the feet and hands seemed strangely large, and her long, straight, free legs swung forward at a gait that made her feel as if on stilts.

This presently passed, and in its place, growing all day, wherever she went, came a new and delightful feeling of being *the right size*.

Everything fitted now. Her back snugly against the seat-back, her feet comfortably on the floor. Her feet? . . . His feet! She studied them carefully. Never before, since her early school days, had she felt such freedom and comfort as to feet—they were firm and solid on the ground when she walked; quick, springy, safe—as when, moved by an unrecognizable impulse, she had run after, caught, and swung aboard the car.

Another impulse fished in a convenient pocket for change— instantly, automatically, bringing forth a nickel for the conductor and a penny for the newsboy.

These pockets came as a revelation. Of course she had known they were there, had counted them, made fun of them, mended them, even envied them; but she never had dreamed of how it *felt* to have pockets.

Behind her newspaper she let her consciousness, that odd mingled consciousness, rove from pocket to pocket, realizing the armored assurance of having all those things at hand, instantly get-at-able, ready to meet emergencies. The cigar case gave her a warm feeling of comfort—it was full; the firmly held fountain pen, safe unless she stood on her head; the keys, pencils, letters, documents, notebook, checkbook, bill folder—all at once, with a deep rushing sense of power and pride, she felt what she had never felt before in all her life—the possession of money, of her own earned money—hers to give or to withhold, not to beg for, tease for, wheedle for—hers.

That bill—why, if it had come to her—to him, that is—he would have paid it as a matter of course, and never mentioned it—to her.

Then, being he, sitting there so easily and firmly with his money in his pockets, she wakened to his life-long consciousness about money. Boyhood—its desires and dreams, ambitions. Young manhood—working tremendously for the wherewithal to make a home—for her. The present years with all their net of cares and hopes and dangers; the present moment, when he needed every cent for special plans of great importance, and this bill, long overdue and demanding payment, meant an amount of inconvenience wholly unnecessary if it had been given him when it first came; also, the man's keen dislike of that 'account rendered.'

'Women have no business sense!' she found herself saying. 'And all that money just for hats—idiotic, useless, ugly things!'

With that she began to see the hats of the women in the car as she had never seen hats before. The men's seemed normal, dignified, becoming, with enough variety for personal taste, and with distinction in style and in age, such as she had never noticed before. But the women's—

With the eyes of a man and the brain of a man; with the memory of a whole lifetime of free action wherein the hat, close-fitting on cropped hair, had been no handicap; she now perceived the hats of women.

The massed fluffed hair was at once attractive and foolish, and on that hair, at every angle, in all colors, tipped, twisted, tortured into every crooked shape, made of any substance chance might offer, perched these formless objects. Then, on their formlessness the trimmings—these squirts of stiff feathers, these violent outstanding bows of glistening ribbon, these swaying, projecting masses of plumage which tormented the faces of bystanders.

Never in all her life had she imagined that this idolized millinery could look, to those who paid for it, like the decorations of an insane monkey.

And yet, when there came into the car a little woman, as foolish as any, but pretty and sweet-looking, up rose Gerald Mathewson and gave her his seat. And, later, when there came in a handsome red-cheeked girl, whose hat was wilder, more violent in color and eccentric in shape than any other—when she stood nearby and her soft curling plumes swept his cheek once and again—he felt a sense of sudden pleasure at the intimate tickling touch—and she, deep down within, felt such a wave of shame as might well drown a thousand hats forever.

When he took his train, his seat in the smoking car, she had a new surprise. All about him were the other men, commuters too, and many of them friends of his.

To her, they would have been distinguished as 'Mary Wade's husband,' 'the man Belle Grant is engaged to,' 'that rich Mr. Shopworth,' or 'that pleasant Mr. Beale.' And they would all have lifted their hats to her, bowed, made polite conversation if near enough—especially Mr. Beale.

Now came the feeling of open-eyed acquaintance, of knowing men—as they were. The mere amount of this knowledge was a surprise to her—the whole background of talk from boyhood up, the gossip of barber-shop and club, the conversation of morning and evening hours on trains, the knowledge of political affiliation, of business standing and prospects, of character—in a light she had never known before.

The came and talked to Gerald, one and another. He seemed quite popular. And as they talked, with this new memory and new understanding, an understanding which seemed to include all these men's minds, there poured in on the submerged consciousness beneath a new, a startling knowledge—what men really think of women.

Good, average, American men were there; married men for the most part, and happy—as happiness goes in general. In the minds of each and all there seemed to be a two-story department, quite apart from the rest of their ideas, a separate place where they kept their thoughts and feelings about women.

In the upper half were the tenderest emotions, the most exquisite ideals, the sweetest memories, all lovely sentiments as to 'home' and 'mother,' all delicate admiring adjectives, a sort of sanctuary, where a veiled statue, blindly adored, shared place with beloved yet commonplace experiences.

In the lower half—here that buried consciousness woke to keen distress—they kept quite another assortment of ideas. Here, even in this clean-minded husband of hers, was the memory of stories told at men's dinners, of worse ones overheard in street or car, of base traditions, coarse epithets, gross experiences—known, though not shared.

And all these in the department 'woman,' while in the rest of the mind—here was new knowledge indeed.

The world opened before her. Not the world she had been reared in—where Home had covered all the map, almost, and the rest had been 'foreign,' or 'unexplored country,' but the world as it was—man's world, as made, lived in, and seen, by men.

It was dizzying. To see the houses that fled so fast across the car window, in terms of builders' bills, or of some technical insight into materials and methods; to see a passing village with lamentable knowledge of who 'owned it' and of how its Boss was rapidly aspiring in state power, or of how that kind of paving was a failure; to see shops, not as mere exhibitions of desirable objects, but as business ventures, many mere sinking ships, some promising a profitable voyage—this new world bewildered her.

She—as Gerald—had already forgotten about that bill, over which she—as Mollie—was still crying at home. Gerald was 'talking business' with this man, 'talking politics' with that, and now sympathizing with the carefully withheld troubles of a neighbor.

Mollie had always sympathized with the neighbor's wife before.

She began to struggle violently with this large dominant masculine consciousness. She remembered with sudden clearness things she had read, lectures she had heard, and resented with increasing intensity this serene masculine preoccupation with the male point of view.

Mr. Miles, the little fussy man who lived on the other side of the street, was talking now. He had a large complacent wife; Mollie had never liked her much, but had always thought him rather nice—he was so punctilious in small courtesies.

And here he was talking to Gerald—such talk!

'Had to come in here,' he said. 'Gave my seat to a dame who was bound to have it. There's nothing they won't get when they make up their minds to it—eh?'

'No fear!' said the big man in the next seat. 'They haven't much mind to make up, you know—and if they do, they'll change it.'

'The real danger,' began the Rev. Alfred Smythe, the new Episcopal clergyman, a thin, nervous, tall man with a face several centuries behind the times, 'is that they will overstep the limits of their God-appointed sphere.'

'Their natural limits ought to hold 'em, I think,' said cheerful Dr. Jones. 'You can't get around physiology, I tell you.'

'I've never seen any limits, myself, not to what they want, anyhow,' said Mr. Miles. 'Merely a rich husband and a fine house and no end

of bonnets and dresses, and the latest thing in motors, and a few
diamonds—and so on. Keeps us pretty busy.'

There was a tired gray man across the aisle. He had a very nice
wife, always beautifully dressed, and three unmarried daughters, also
beautifully dressed—Mollie knew them. She knew he worked hard,
too, and she looked at him now a little anxiously.

But he smiled cheerfully.

'Do you good, Miles,' he said. 'What else would a man work for? A
good woman is about the best thing on earth.'

'And a bad one's the worst, that's sure,' responded Miles.

'She's a pretty weak sister, viewed professionally,' Dr. Jones averred
with solemnity, and the Rev Alfred Smythe added, 'She brought evil
into the world.'

Gerald Mathewson sat up straight. Something was stirring in him
which he did not recognize—yet could not resist.

'Seems to me we all talk like Noah,' he suggested drily. 'Or the
ancient Hindu scriptures. Women have their limitations, but so do
we. God knows. Haven't we known girls in school and college just as
smart as we were?'

'They cannot play our games,' coldly replied the clergyman.

Gerald measured his meager proportions with a practiced eye.

'I never was particularly good at football myself,' he modestly
admitted, 'but I've known women who could outlast a man in
all-round endurance. Besides—life isn't spent in athletics!'

This was sadly true. They all looked down the aisle where a heavily
ill-dressed man with a bad complexion sat alone. He had held the top
of the columns once, with headlines and photographs. Now he earned
less than any of them.

'It's time we woke up,' pursued Gerald, still inwardly urged to
unfamiliar speech. 'Women are pretty much *people*, seems to me. I
know they dress like fools—but who's to blame for that? We invent
all those idiotic hats of theirs, and design their crazy fashions, and,
what's more, if a woman is courageous enough to wear common-sense
clothes—and shoes—which of us wants to dance with her?

'Yes, we blame them for grafting on us, but are we willing to let our
wives work? We are not. It hurts our pride, that's all. We are always
criticizing them for making mercenary marriages, but what do we call
a girl who marries a chump with no money? Just a poor fool, that's
all. And they know it.

'As for Mother Eve—I wasn't there and can't deny the story, but I will say this. If she brought evil into the world, we men have had the lion's share of keeping it going ever since—how about that?'

They drew into the city, and all day long in his business, Gerald was vaguely conscious of new views, strange feelings, and the submerged Mollie learned and learned.

1915

Consequences

WILLA CATHER

Henry Eastman, a lawyer, aged forty, was standing beside the Flatiron Building in a driving November rainstorm, signaling frantically for a taxi. It was six-thirty, and everything on wheels was engaged. The streets were in confusion about him, the sky was in turmoil above him, and the Flatiron Building, which seemed about to blow down, threw water like a mill-shoot. Suddenly, out of the brutal struggle of men and cars and machines and people tilting at each other with umbrellas, a quiet, well-mannered limousine paused before him, at the curb, and an agreeable, ruddy countenance confronted him through the open window of the car.

'Don't you want me to pick you up, Mr Eastman? I'm running directly home now.'

Eastman recognized Kier Cavenaugh, a young man of pleasure, who lived in the house on Central Park South, where he himself had an apartment.

'Don't I?' he exclaimed, bolting into the car. 'I'll risk getting your cushions wet without compunction. I came up in a taxi, but I didn't hold it. Bad economy. I thought I saw your car down on Fourteenth Street about half an hour ago.'

The owner of the car smiled. He had a pleasant, round face and round eyes, and a fringe of smooth, yellow hair showed under the brim of his soft felt hat. 'With a lot of little broilers fluttering into it? You did. I know some girls who work in the cheap shops down there. I happened to be downtown and I stopped and took a load of them home. I do sometimes. Saves their poor little clothes, you know. Their shoes are never any good.'

Eastman looked at his rescuer. 'Aren't they notoriously afraid of cars and smooth young men?' he enquired.

Cavenaugh shook his head. 'They know which cars are safe and which are chancy. They put each other wise. You have to take a bunch at a time, of course. The Italian girls can never come along; their men shoot. The girls understand, all right; but their fathers don't. One gets to see queer places, sometimes, taking them home.'

Eastman laughed drily. 'Every time I touch the circle of your acquaintance, Cavenaugh, it's a little wider. You must know New York pretty well by this time.'

'Yes, but I'm on my good behavior below Twenty-third Street,' the young man replied with simplicity. 'My little friends down there would give me a good character. They're wise little girls. They have grand ways with each other, a romantic code of loyalty. You can find a good many of the lost virtues among them.'

The car was standing still in a traffic block at Fortieth Street, when Cavenaugh suddenly drew his face away from the window and touched Eastman's arm. 'Look, please. You see that hansom with the bony gray horse—driver has a broken hat and red flannel around his throat. Can you see who is inside?'

Eastman peered out. The hansom was just cutting across the line, and the driver was making a great fuss about it, bobbing his head and waving his whip. He jerked his dripping old horse into Fortieth Street and clattered off past the Public Library grounds towards Sixth Avenue. 'No, I couldn't see the passenger. Someone you know?'

'Could you see whether there was a passenger?' Cavenaugh asked.

'Why, yes. A man, I think. I saw his elbow on the apron. No driver ever behaves like that unless he has a passenger.'

'Yes, I may have been mistaken,' Cavenaugh murmured absent-mindedly. Ten minutes or so later, after Cavenaugh's car had turned off Fifth Avenue into Fifty-eighth Street, Eastman exclaimed, 'There's your same cabby, and his cart's empty. He's headed for a drink now, I suppose.' The driver in the broken hat and the red flannel neck cloth was still brandishing the whip over his old gray. He was coming from the west now, and turned down Sixth Avenue, under the elevated.

Cavenaugh's car stopped at the bachelor apartment house between Sixth and Seventh Avenues where he and Eastman lived, and they went up in the elevator together. They were still talking when the lift stopped at Cavenaugh's floor, and Eastman stepped out with him and walked down the hall, finishing his sentence while Cavenaugh found his latch-key. When he opened the door, a wave of fresh cigarette smoke greeted them. Cavenaugh stopped short and stared into his hallway. 'Now how in the devil—!' he exclaimed angrily.

'Someone waiting for you? Oh, no, thanks. I wasn't coming in. I have to work tonight. Thank you, but I couldn't.' Eastman nodded and went up the two flights to his own rooms.

Though Eastman did not customarily keep a servant he had this winter a man who had been lent to him by a friend who was abroad. Rollins met him at the door and took his coat and hat.

'Put out my dinner clothes, Rollins, and then get out of here until ten o'clock. I've promised to go to a supper tonight. I shan't be dining. I've had a late tea and I'm going to work until ten. You may put out some kumiss and biscuit for me.'

Rollins took himself off, and Eastman settled down at the big table in his sitting-room. He had to read a lot of letters submitted as evidence in a breach of contract case, and before he got very far he found that long paragraphs in some of the letters were written in German. He had a German dictionary at his office, but none here. Rollins had gone, and anyhow, the bookstores would be closed. He remembered having seen a row of dictionaries on the lower shelf of one of Cavenaugh's bookcases. Cavenaugh had a lot of books, though he never read anything but new stuff. Eastman prudently turned down his student's lamp very low—the thing had an evil habit of smoking—and went down two flights to Cavenaugh's door.

The young man himself answered Eastman's ring. He was freshly dressed for the evening, except for a brown smoking jacket, and his yellow hair had been brushed until it shone. He hesitated as he confronted his caller, still holding the door knob, and his round eyes and smooth forehead made their best imitation of a frown. When Eastman began to apologize, Cavenaugh's manner suddenly changed. He caught his arm and jerked him into the narrow hall. 'Come in, come in. Right along!' he said excitedly. 'Right along,' he repeated as he pushed Eastman before him into his sitting-room. 'Well I'll—' he stopped short at the door and looked about his own room with an air of complete mystification. The back window was wide open and a strong wind was blowing in. Cavenaugh walked over to the window and stuck out his head, looking up and down the fire escape. When he pulled his head in, he drew down the sash.

'I had a visitor I wanted you to see,' he explained with a nervous smile.' At least I thought I had. He must have gone out that way,' nodding toward the window.

'Call him back. I only came to borrow a German dictionary, if you have one. Can't stay. Call him back.'

Cavenaugh shook his head despondently. 'No use. He's beat it. Nowhere in sight.'

'He must be active. Has he left something?' Eastman pointed to a very dirty white glove that lay on the floor under the window.

'Yes, that's his.' Cavenaugh reached for his tongs, picked up the glove, and tossed it into the grate, where it quickly shriveled on the coals. Eastman felt that he had happened in upon something disagreeable, possibly something shady, and he wanted to get away at once. Cavenaugh stood staring at the fire and seemed stupid and dazed; so he repeated his request rather sternly, 'I think I've seen a German dictionary down there among your books. May I have it?'

Cavenaugh blinked at him. 'A German dictionary? Oh, possibly! Those were my father's. I scarcely know what there is.' He put down the tongs and began to wipe his hands nervously with his handkerchief.

Eastman went over to the bookcase behind the Chesterfield, opened the door, swooped upon the book he wanted and stuck it under his arm. He felt perfectly certain now that something shady had been going on in Cavenaugh's rooms, and he saw no reason why he should come in for any hang-over. 'Thanks. I'll send it back tomorrow,' he said curtly as he made for the door.

Cavenaugh followed him. 'Wait a moment. I wanted you to see him. You did see his glove,' glancing at the grate.

Eastman laughed disagreeably. 'I saw a glove. That's not evidence. Do your friends often use that means of exit? Somewhat inconvenient.'

Cavenaugh gave him a startled glance. 'Wouldn't you think so? For an old man, a very rickety old party? The ladders are steep, you know, and rusty.' He approached the window again and put it up softly. In a moment he drew his head back with a jerk. He caught Eastman's arm and shoved him toward the window. 'Hurry, please. Look! Down there.' He pointed to the little patch of paved court four flights down.

The square of pavement was so small and the walls about it were so high, that it was a good deal like looking down a well. Four tall buildings backed upon the same court and made a kind of shaft, with flagstones at the bottom, and at the top a square of dark blue with some stars in it. At the bottom of the shaft Eastman saw a black figure, a man in a caped coat and a tall hat stealing cautiously around, not across the square of pavement, keeping close to the dark wall and avoiding the streak of light that fell on the flagstones from a window in the opposite house. Seen from that height he was of course fore-shortened and probably looked more shambling and decrepit than he was. He picked his way along with exaggerated care and looked like a silly old cat crossing a wet street. When he reached the gate that led into an alleyway between two buildings, he felt about for the latch, opened the door a mere crack, and then shot out under the feeble lamp that burned in the brick arch over the gateway. The door closed after him.

'He'll get run in,' Eastman remarked curtly, turning away from the window. 'That door shouldn't be left unlocked. Any crook could come in. I'll speak to the janitor about it, if you don't mind,' he added sarcastically.

'Wish you would.' Cavenaugh stood brushing down the front of his jacket, first with his right hand and then with his left. 'You saw him, didn't you?'

'Enough of him. Seems eccentric. I have to see a lot of buggy people. They don't take me in any more. But I'm keeping you and I'm in a hurry myself. Good night.'

Cavenaugh put out his hand detainingly and started to say something; but Eastman rudely turned his back and went down the hall and out of the door. He had never felt anything shady about Cavenaugh before, and he was sorry he had had gone down for the dictionary. In five minutes he was deep in his papers; but in the half hour when he was loafing before he dressed to go out, the young man's curious behaviour came into his mind again.

Eastman had merely a neighborly acquaintance with Cavenaugh. He had been to a supper at the young man's rooms once, but he didn't particularly like Cavenaugh's friends; so the next time he was asked, he had another engagement. He liked Cavenaugh himself, if for nothing else than because he was so cheerful and trim and ruddy. A good complexion is always at a premium in New York, especially when it shines reassuringly on a man who does everything in the world to lose it. It encourages fellow mortals as to the inherent vigor of the human organism and the amount of bad treatment it will stand for. 'Footprints that perhaps another,' etc.

Cavenaugh, he knew, had plenty of money. He was the son of a Pennsylvania preacher, who died soon after he discovered that his ancestral acres were full of petroleum, and Kier had come to New York to burn some of the oil. He was thirty-two and was still at it; spent his life, literally, among the breakers. His motor hit the Park every morning as if it were the first time ever. He took people out to supper every night. He went from restaurant to restaurant, sometimes to half-a-dozen in an evening. The head waiters were his hosts and their cordiality made him happy. They made a life-line for him up Broadway and down Fifth Avenue. Cavenaugh was still fresh and smooth, round and plump, with a lustre to his hair and white teeth and a clear look in his round eyes. He seemed absolutely unwearied and unimpaired; never bored and never carried away.

Eastman always smiled when he met Cavenaugh in the entrance hall, serenely going forth to or returning from gladiatorial combats with joy, or when he saw him rolling smoothly up to the door in his car in the morning after a restful night in one of the remarkable new roadhouses he was always finding. Eastman had seen a good many young men disappear on Cavenaugh's route, and he admired this young man's endurance.

Tonight, for the first time, he had got a whiff of something unwholesome about the fellow—bad nerves, bad company, something on hand that he was ashamed of, a visitor old and vicious, who must have had a key to Cavenaugh's apartment, for he was evidently there when Cavenaugh returned at seven o'clock. Probably it was the same man Cavenaugh had seen in the hansom. He must have been able to let himself in, for Cavenaugh kept no man but his chauffeur; or perhaps the janitor had been instructed to let him in. In either case, and whoever he was, it was clear enough that Cavenaugh was ashamed of him and was mixing up in questionable business of some kind.

Eastman sent Cavenaugh's book back by Rollins, and for the next few weeks he had no word with him beyond a casual greeting when they happened to meet in the hall or the elevator. One Sunday morning Cavenaugh telephoned up to him to ask if he could motor out to a roadhouse in Connecticut that afternoon and have support; but when Eastman found there were to be other guests he declined.

On New Year's Eve Eastman dined at the University Club at six o'clock and hurried home before the usual manifestations of insanity had begun in the streets. When Rollins brought his smoking coat, he asked him whether he wouldn't like to get off early.

'Yes, sir. But won't you be dressing, Mr Eastman?' he inquired.

'Not tonight.' Eastman handed him a bill. 'Bring some change in the morning. There'll be fees.'

Rollins lost no time in putting everything to rights for the night, and Eastman couldn't help wishing that he were in such a hurry to be off somewhere himself. When he heard the hall door close softly, he wondered if there were any place, after all, that he wanted to go. From his window he looked down at the long lines of motors and taxis waiting for a signal to cross Broadway. He thought of some of their probable destinations and decided that none of those places pulled him very hard. The night was warm and wet, the air was drizzly. Vapor hung in clouds about the Times Building, half hid the top of it, and made a luminous haze along Broadway. While he was looking down at the army of wet, black carriage-tops and their reflected headlights and tail-lights, Eastman heard a ring at his door. He deliberated. If it were a caller, the hall porter would have telephoned up. It must be the janitor. When he opened the door, there stood a rosy young man in a tuxedo, without a coat or hat.

'Pardon. Should I have telephoned? I half thought you wouldn't be in.'

Eastman laughed. 'Come in, Cavenaugh. You weren't sure whether you wanted company or not, eh, and you were trying to let chance decide it? That was exactly my state of mind. Let's accept the verdict.' When they emerged from the narrow hall into his sitting-room, he pointed out a seat by the fire to his guest. He brought a tray of decanters and soda bottles and placed it on his writing table.

Cavenaugh hesitated, standing by the fire. 'Sure you weren't starting for somewhere?'

'Do I look it? No, I was just making up my mind to stick it out alone when you rang. Have one?' he picked up a tall tumbler.

'Yes, thank you. I always do.'

Eastman chuckled. 'Lucky boy! So will I. I had a very early dinner. New York is the most arid place on holidays,' he continued as he rattled the ice in the glasses. 'When one gets too old to hit the rapids down there, and tired of gobbling food to heathenish dance music, there is absolutely no place where you can get a chop and some milk toast in peace, unless you have strong ties of blood brotherhood on upper Fifth Avenue. But you, why aren't you starting for somewhere?'

The young man sipped his soda and shook his head as he replied:

'Oh, I couldn't get a chop, either. I know only flashy people, of course.' He looked up at his host with such a grave and candid expression that Eastman decided there couldn't be anything very crooked about the fellow. His smooth cheeks were positively cherubic.

'Well, what's the matter with them? Aren't they flashing tonight?'

'Only the very new ones seem to flash on New Year's Eve. The older ones fade away. Maybe they are hunting a chop, too.'

'Well'—Eastman sat down—'holidays do dash one. I was just about to write a letter to a pair of maiden aunts in my old home town, up-state; old coasting hill, snow-covered pines, lights in the church windows. That's what you've saved me from.'

Cavenaugh shook himself. 'Oh, I'm sure that wouldn't have been good for you. Pardon me,' he rose and took a photograph from the bookcase, a handsome man in shooting clothes. 'Dudley, isn't it? Did you know him well?'

'Yes. An old friend. Terrible thing, wasn't it?' I haven't got over the jolt yet.'

'His suicide? Yes, terrible! Did you know his wife?'

'Slightly. Well enough to admire her very much. She must be terribly broken up. I wonder Dudley didn't think of that.'

Cavenaugh replaced the photograph carefully, lit a cigarette, and standing before the fire began to smoke. 'Would you mind telling me about him? I never met him, but of course, I'd read a lot about him, and I can't help feeling interested. It was a queer thing.'

Eastman took out his cigar case and leaned back in his deep chair. 'In the days when I knew him best he hadn't any story, like the happy nations. Everything was properly arranged for him before he was born. He came into the world happy, healthy, clever, straight, with the right sort of connections and the right kind of fortune, neither too large nor too small. He helped to make the world an agreeable place to live in until he was twenty-six. Then he married as he should have married. His wife was a Californian, educated abroad. Beautiful. You have seen her picture?'

Cavenaugh nodded. 'Oh, many of them.'

'She was interesting, too. Though she was distinctly a person of the world, she had retained something, just enough of the large Western manner. She had the habit of authority, of calling out a special train if she needed it, of using all our ingenious mechanical contrivances lightly and easily, without over-rating them. She and Dudley knew how to live better than most people. Their house was the most charming one I have ever known in New York. You felt freedom there, and a zest of life, and safety—absolute sanctuary—from everything sordid or petty. A whole society like that would justify the creation of man and would make our planet shine with a soft, peculiar radiance among the constellations. You think I'm putting it on thick?'

The young man sighed gently. 'Oh, no! One has always felt there must be people like that. I've never known any.'

'They had two children, beautiful ones. After they had been married for eight years, Rosina met this Spaniard. He must have amounted to something. She wasn't a flighty woman. She came home and told Dudley how matters stood. He persuaded her to stay at home for six months and try to pull up. They were both fair-minded people, and I'm sure as if I were the Almighty, that she did try. But at the end of the time, Rosina went quietly off to Spain, and Dudley went to hunt in the Canadian Rockies. I met his party out there. I didn't know his wife had left him and talked about her a good deal. I noticed that he never drank anything, and his light used to shine through the log chinks of his room until all hours, even after a hard day's hunting. When I got back to New York, rumors were creeping about. Dudley did not come back. He bought a ranch in Wyoming, built a big log house and kept splendid dogs and horses. One of his sisters went out to keep house for him, and the children were there when they were not in school. He had a great many visitors, and everyone who came back talked about how well Dudley kept things going.

'He put in two years out there. Then, last month, he had to come back on business. A trust fund had to be settled up, and he was administrator. I saw him at the club; same light, quick step, same gracious handshake. He was getting gray, and there was something softer in his manner; but he had a fine red tan on his face and said he found it delightful to be here in the season when everything is going hard. The Madison Avenue house had been closed since Rosina left it. He went there to get some things his sister wanted.

That, of course, was the mistake. He went alone, in the afternoon, and didn't go out for dinner—found some sherry and tins of biscuits in the sideboard. He shot himself sometime that night. There were pistols in his smoking-room. They found burnt out candles beside him in the morning. The gas and electricity were shut off. I suppose there, in his own house, among his own things, it was too much for him. He left no letters.'

Cavenaugh blinked and brushed the lapel of his coat. 'I suppose,' he said slowly, 'that every suicide is logical and reasonable, if one knew all the facts.'

Eastman roused himself. 'No, I don't think so. I've known too many fellows who went off like that—more than I deserve, I think—and some of them were absolutely inexplicable. I can understand Dudley; but I can't see why healthy bachelors, with money enough, like ourselves, need such a device. It reminds me of what Dr Johnson said, that the most discouraging thing about life is the number of fads and hobbies and fake religions it takes to put people through a few years of it.'

'Dr Johnson? The specialist? Oh, the old fellow!' said Cavenaugh imperturbably. 'Yes, that's interesting. Still, I fancy if one knew the facts—Did you know about Wyatt?'

'I don't think so.'

'You wouldn't, probably. He was just a fellow about town who spent money. He wasn't one of the *forestieri*, though. Had connections here and owned a fine old place over on Staten Island. He went in for botany, and had been all over, hunting things; rusts, I believe. He had a yacht and used to take a gay crowd down about the South Seas, botanizing. He really did botanize, I believe. I never knew such a spender—only not flashy. He helped a lot of fellows and he was awfully good to girls, the kind who come down here to get a little fun, who don't like to work and still aren't really tough, the kind you see talking hard for their dinner. Nobody knows what becomes of them, or what they get out of it, and there are hundreds of new ones every year. He helped dozens of 'em; it was he who got me curious about the little shop girls. Well, one afternoon when his tea was brought, he took prussic acid instead. He didn't leave any letters, either; people of any taste don't. They wouldn't leave any material reminder if they could help it. His lawyers found that he had just $314.72 above his debts when he died. He had planned to spend all his money, and then take his tea; he had worked it out carefully.'

Eastman reached for his pipe and pushed his chair away from the fire. 'That looks like a considered case, but I don't think philosophical suicides like that are common. I think they usually come from stress of feeling and are really, as the newspapers call them, desperate acts; done without a motive. You remember when Anna Karenina was under the wheels, she kept saying. "Why am I here?"'

Cavenaugh rubbed his upper lip with his pink finger and made an effort to wrinkle his brows. 'May I, please?' reaching for the whiskey. 'But have you,' he asked, blinking as the soda flew at him, 'have you ever known yourself, cases that were really inexplicable?'

'A few too many. I was in Washington just before Captain Jack Purden was married and I saw a good deal of him. Popular army man, fine record in the Philippines, married a charming girl with lots of money; mutual devotion. It was the gayest wedding of the winter, and they started for Japan. They stopped in San Francisco for a week and missed their boat because, as the bride wrote back to Washington, they were too happy to move. They took the next boat, were both good sailors, had exceptional weather. After they had been out for two weeks, Jack got up from his deck chair one afternoon, yawned, put down his book, and stood before his wife. "Stop reading for a moment and look at me." She laughed and asked him why. "Because you happen to be good to look at." He nodded to her, went back to the stern and was never seen again. Must have gone down to the lower deck and slipped overboard, behind the machinery. It was the luncheon hour, not many people about; steamer cutting through a soft green sea. That's one of the most baffling cases I know. His friends raked up his past, and it was as trim as a cottage garden. If he'd so much as dropped an ink spot on his fatigue uniform, they'd have found it. He wasn't emotional or moody; wasn't, indeed, very interesting; simply a good soldier, fond of all the pompous little formalities that make up a military man's life. What do you make of that, my boy?'

Cavenaugh stroked his chin. 'It's very puzzling, I admit. Still, if one knew everything—'

'But we do know everything. His friends wanted to find something to help them out, to help the girl out, to help the case of the human creature.'

'Oh, I don't mean things that people could unearth,' said Cavenaugh uneasily. 'But possibly there were things that couldn't be found out.'

Eastman shrugged his shoulders. 'It's my experience that when there are "things" as you call them, they're very apt to be found. There is no such thing as a secret. To make any move at all one has to employ human agencies, employ at least one human agent. Even when the pirates killed the men who buried their gold for them, the bones told the story.'

Cavenaugh rubbed his hands together and smiled his sunny smile.

'I like that idea. It's reassuring. If we can have no secrets, it means that we can't, after all, go so far afield as we might,' he hesitated, 'yes, as we might.'

Eastman looked at him sourly. 'Cavenaugh, when you've practised law in New York for twelve years, you find that people can't go far in any direction, except—' He thrust his forefinger sharply at the floor. 'Even in that direction, few people can do anything out of the ordinary. Our range is limited. Skip a few baths, and we become personally objectionable. The slightest carelessness can rot a man's integrity or give him ptomaine poisoning. We keep up only the incessant cleansing operations, of mind and body. What we call character, is held together by all sorts of tacks and strings and glue.'

Cavenaugh looked startled. 'Come now, it's not so bad as that, is it?' I've always thought that a serious man, like you, must know a lot of Launcelots.' When Eastman only laughed, the younger man squirmed about in his chair. He spoke again hastily, as if he were embarrassed. 'Your military friend may have had personal experiences, however, that his friends couldn't possibly get a line on. He may accidentally have come to a place where he saw himself in too unpleasant a light. I believe people can be chilled by a draft from outside, somewhere.'

'Outside?' Eastman echoed. 'Ah, you mean the far outside! Ghosts, delusions, eh?'

Cavenaugh winced. 'That's putting it strong. Why not say tips from the outside? Delusions belong to a diseased mind, don't they? There are some of us who have no minds to speak of, who yet have had experiences. I've had a little something in that line myself and I don't look it, do I?'

Eastman looked at the bland countenance turned toward him. 'Not exactly. What's your delusion?'

'It's not a delusion. It's a haunt.'

The lawyer chuckled. 'Soul of a lost Casino girl?'

'No; an old gentleman. A most unattractive old gentleman, who follows me about.'

'Does he want money?'

Cavenaugh sat up straight. 'No. I wish to God he wanted anything—but the pleasure of my society! I'd let him clean me out to be rid of him. He's a real article. You saw him yourself that night when you came to my rooms to borrow a dictionary, and he went down the fire escape. You saw him down in the court.'

'Well, I saw somebody down in the court, but I'm too cautious to take it for granted that I saw what you saw. Why, anyhow, should I see your haunt? If it was your friend I saw, he impressd me disagreeably. How did you pick him up?'

Cavenaugh looked gloomy. 'That was queer, too. Charley Burke and I had motored out to Long Beach, about a year ago, sometime in October, I think. We had supper and stayed until late. When we were coming home, my car broke down. We had a lot of girls along who had to get back for morning rehearsals and things; so I sent them all into town in Charley's car, and he was to send a man back to tow me home. I was driving myself, and didn't want to leave my machine. We had not taken a direct road back; so I was stuck in a lonesome, woody place, no houses about. I got chilly and made a fire, and was putting in the time comfortably enough, when this old party steps up. He was in shabby evening clothes and a top hat, and had on his usual white gloves. How he got there, at three o'clock in the morning, miles from any town or railway. I'll leave it to you to figure out. *He* surely had no car. When I saw him coming up to the fire, I disliked him. He had a silly, apologetic walk. His teeth were chattering, and I asked him to sit down. He got down like a clothes-horse folding up. I offered him a cigarette, and when he took off his gloves I couldn't help noticing how knotted and spotty his hands were. He was asthmatic, and took his breath with a wheeze. "Haven't you got anything—refreshing in there?" he asked, nodding at the car. When I told him I hadn't, he sighed. "Ah, you young fellows are greedy. You drink it all up. You drink it all up, all up—up!" he kept chewing it over.'

Cavenaugh paused and looked embarrassed again. 'The thing that was most unpleasant is difficult to explain. The old man sat there by the fire and leered at me with a silly sort of admiration that was—well, more than humiliating. "Gay boy, gay dog!" he would mutter, and when he grinned he showed his teeth, worn and yellow—shells. I remembered that it was better to talk casually to insane people; so I remarked carelessly that I had been out with a party and got stuck.

'"Oh yes, I remember," he said, "Flora and Lottie and Maybelle and Marcelline, and poor Kate."

'He had named them correctly; so I began to think I had been hitting the bright waters too hard.

'Things I drank never had seemed to make me woody; but you can never tell when trouble is going to hit you. I pulled my hat down and tried to look as uncommunicative as possible; but he kept croaking on from time to time, like this: "Poor Katie! Splendid arms, but dope got her. She took up with Eastern religions after she had her hair dyed. Got to going to a Swami's joint, and smoking opium. Temple of the Lotus, it was called, and the police raided it."

'This was nonsense, of course; the young woman was in the pink of condition. I let him rave, but I decided that if something didn't come out for me pretty soon, I'd foot it across Long Island. There wasn't room enough for the two of us. I got up and took another try at my car. He hopped right after me.

'"Good car," he wheezed, "better than the little Ford."

'I'd had a Ford before, but so has everybody; that was a safe guess.

'"Still," he went on, "that run in from Huntington Bay in the rain wasn't bad. Arrested for speeding, he—he."

'It was true I had made such a run, under rather unusual circumstances, and had been arrested. When at last I heard my life-boat snorting up the road, my visitor got up, sighed, and stepped back into the shadow of the trees. I didn't wait to see what became of him, you may believe. That was visitation number one. What do you think of it?'

Cavenaugh looked at his host defiantly. Eastman smiled.

'I think you'd better change your mode of life, Cavenaugh. Had many returns?' he enquired.

'Too many, by far.' The young man took a turn about the room and came back to the fire. Standing by the mantel he lit another cigarette before going on with his story:

'The second visitation happened in the street, early in the evening, about eight o'clock. I was held up in a traffic block before the Plaza. My chauffeur was driving. Old Nibbs steps up out of the crowd, opens the door of my car, gets in and sits down beside me. He had on wilted evening clothes, same as before, and there was some sort of heavy scent about him. Such an unpleasant old party! A thorough-going rotter; you knew it at once. This time he wasn't talkative, as he had been when I first saw him. He leaned back in the car as if he owned it, crossed his hands on his stick and looked out at the crowd—sort of hungrily.

'I own I really felt a loathing compassion for him. We got down the avenue slowly. I kept looking out at the mounted police. But what could I do? Have him pulled? I was afraid to. I was awfully afraid of getting him into the papers.

'"I'm going to the New Astor," I said at last. "Can I take you anywhere?"

' "No, thank you," says he. "I get out when you do, I'm due on West Forty-fourth. I'm dining tonight with Marcelline—all that is left of her!'

'He put his hand at his hat brim with a gruesome salute. Such a scandalous, foolish old face as he had! When we pulled up at the Astor, I stuck my hand in my pocket and asked him if he'd like a little loan.

'No, thank you, but"—he leaned over and whispered, ugh!—"but save a little, save a little. Forty years from now—a little—comes in handy. Save a little."

'His eyes fairly glittered as he made his remark. I jumped out. I'd have jumped into the North River. When he tripped off, I asked my chauffeur if he'd noticed the man who got into the car with me. He said he knew someone was with me, but he hadn't noticed just when he got in. Want to hear any more?'

Cavenaugh dropped into his chair again. His plump cheeks were a trifle more flushed than usual, but he was perfectly calm. Eastman felt that the young man believed in what he was telling him.

'Of course I do. It's very interesting. I don't see quite where you are coming out though.'

Cavenaugh sniffed. 'No more do I. I really feel that I've been put upon. I haven't deserved it any more than any other fellow of my kind. Doesn't impress you disagreeably?'

'Well, rather so. Has anyone else seen your friend?'

'You saw him.'

'We won't count that. As I said, there's no certainty that you and I saw the same person in the court that night. Has anyone else had a look in?'

'People sense him rather than see him. He usually crops up when I'm alone or in a crowd on the street. He never approaches me when I'm with people I know, though I've seen him hanging about the doors of theatres when I come out with a party; loafing around the stage exit, under a wall; or across the street, in a doorway. To be frank, I'm not anxious to introduce him. The third time, it was I who came upon him. In November my driver, Harry, had a sudden attack of appendicitis. I took him to the Presbyterian Hospital in the car, early in the evening. When I came home, I found the old villain in my rooms. I offered him a drink, and he sat down. It was the first time I had seen him in a steady light, with his hat off.

'His face is lined like a railway map, and as to color—Lord, what a liver! His scalp grows tight to his skull, and his hair is dyed until it's perfectly dead, like a piece of black cloth.'

Cavenaugh ran his fingers through his own neatly trimmed thatch, and seemed to forget where he was for a moment.

'I had a twin brother, Brian, who died when we were sixteen. I have a photograph of him on my wall, an enlargement from a Kodak of him, doing a high jump, rather good thing, full of action. It seemed to annoy the old gentleman. He kept looking at it and lifting his eyebrows, and finally he got up, tip-toed across the room, and turned the picture to the wall.

' "Poor Brian". Fine fellow, but died young," says he.

'Next morning, there was the picture, still reversed.'

'Did he stay long?' Eastman asked interestedly.

'Half an hour, by the clock.'

'Did he talk?'

'Well, he rambled.'

'What about?'

Cavenaugh rubbed his pale eyebrows before answering.

'About things that an old man ought to want to forget. His conversation is highly objectionable. Of course he knows me like a book; everything I've ever done or thought. But when he recalls them, he throws a bad light on them, somehow. Things that weren't much off color, look rotten. He doesn't leave one a shred of self-respect, he really doesn't. That's the amount of it.' The young man whipped out his handkerchief and wiped his face.

'You mean he really talks about things that none of your friends know?'

'Oh dear, yes! Recalls things that happened in school. Anything disagreeable. Funny things, he always turns Brian's picture to the wall.'

'Does he come often?'

'Yes, oftener, now. Of course I don't know how he gets in downstairs. The hall boys never see him. But he has a key to my door. I don't know how he got it, but I can hear him turn it in the lock.'

'Why don't you keep your driver with you, or telephone for me to come down?'

'He'd only grin and go down the fire escape as he did before. He's often done it when Harry's come in suddenly. Everybody has to be alone sometimes, you know. Besides, I don't want anybody to see him. He has me there.'

'But why not? Why do you feel responsible for him?'

Cavenaugh smiled wearily. 'That's rather the point, isn't it? Why do I? But I absolutely do. That identifies him, more than his knowing all about my life and my affairs.'

Eastman looked at Cavenaugh thoughtfully. 'Well, I should advise you to go in for something altogether different and new, and go in for it hard; business, engineering, metallurgy, something this old fellow wouldn't be interested in. See if you can make him remember logarithms.'

Cavenaugh sighed. 'No, he has me there, too. People never really change; they go on being themselves. But I would never made much trouble. Why can't they let me alone, damn it! I'd never hurt anybody, except perhaps—'

'Except your old gentleman, eh?' Eastman laughed. 'Seriously, Cavenaugh, if you want to shake him, I think a year on a ranch would do it. He would never be coaxed far from his favorite haunts. He would dread Montana.'

Cavenaugh pursued up his lips. 'So do I!'

'Oh, you think you do. Try it, and you'll find out. A gun and a horse beats all this sort of thing. Besides losing your haunt, you'd be putting ten years in the bank for yourself. I know a good ranch where they take people, if you want to try it.'

'Thank you. I'll consider. Do you think I'm batty?'

'No, but I think you've been doing one sort of thing too long. You need big horizons. Get out of this.'

Cavenaugh smiled meekly. He rose lazily and yawned behind his hand. 'It's late, and I've taken your whole evening.' He strolled over to the window and looked out. 'Queer place, New York; rough on the little fellows. Don't you feel sorry for them, the girls especially? I do. What a fight they put up for a little fun! Why, even that old goat is sorry for them, the only decent thing he kept.'

Eastman followed him to the door and stood in the hall, while Cavenaugh waited for the elevator. When the car came up Cavenaugh extended his pink, warm hand. 'Good night.'

The cage sank and his rosy countenance disappeared, his round-eyed smile being the last thing to go.

Weeks passed before Eastman saw Cavenaugh again. One morning, just as he was starting for Washington to argue a case before the Supreme Court, Cavenaugh telephoned him at his office to ask him about the Montana ranch he had recommended; said he meant to take his advice and go out there for the spring and summer.

When Eastman got back from Washington, he saw dusty trunks, just up from the trunk room, before Cavenaugh's door. Next morning, when he stopped to see what the young man was about, he found Cavenaugh in his shirt sleeves, packing.

'I'm really going; off tomorrow night. You didn't think it of me, did you?' he asked gaily.

'Oh, I've always had hopes of you!' Eastman declared. 'But you are in a hurry, it seems to me.'

'Yes, I am in a hurry.' Cavenaugh shot a pair of leggings into one of the open trunks. 'I telegraphed your ranch people, used your name, and they said it would be all right. By the way, some of my crowd are giving a little dinner for me at Rector's tonight. Couldn't you be persuaded, as it's a farewell occasion?' Cavenaugh looked at him hopefully.

Eastman laughed and shook his head. 'Sorry, Cavenaugh, but that's too gay a world for me. I've got too much work lined up before me. I wish I had time to stop and look at your guns, though. You seem to know something about guns. You've more than you'll need, but nobody can have too many good ones.' He put down one of the revolvers regretfully. 'I'll drop in to see you in the morning, if you're up.'

'I shall be up, all right. I've warned my crowd that I'll cut away before midnight.'

'You won't, though,' Eastman called back over his shoulder as he hurried downstairs.

The next morning, while Eastman was dressing, Rollins came in greatly excited.

'I'm a little late, sir. I was stopped by Harry, Mr Cavenaugh's driver. Mr Cavenaugh shot himself last night, sir.'

Eastman dropped his vest and sat down on his shoe-box. 'You're drunk, Rollins,' he shouted. 'He's going away today!'

'Yes, sir. Harry found him this morning. Ah, he's quite dead, sir. Harry's telephoned for the coroner. Harry don't know what to do with the ticket.'

Eastman pulled on his coat and ran down the stairway. Cavenaugh's trunks were strapped and piled before the door. Harry was walking up and down the hall with a long green railroad ticket in his hand and a look of complete stupidity on his face.

'What shall I do about the ticket, Mr Eastman?' he whispered. 'And what about his trunks? He had me tell the transfer people to come early. They may be here any minute. Yes, sir. I brought him home in the car last night, before twelve, as cheerful as could be.'

'Be quiet, Harry. Where is he?'

'In his bed, sir.'

Eastman went into Cavenaugh's sleeping-room. When he came back to the sitting-room, he looked over the writing table; railway folders, time-tables, receipted bills, nothing else. He looked up for the photograph of Cavenaugh's twin brother. There it was, turned to the wall. Eastman took it down and looked at it; a boy in track clothes, half lying in the air, going over the string shoulders first, above the heads of a crowd of lads who were running and cheering. The face was somewhat blurred by the motion and the bright sunlight. Eastman put the picture back, as he found it. Had Cavenaugh entertained his visitor last night, and had the old man been more convincing than usual? 'Well, at any rate, he's seen to it that the old man can't establish identity. What a soft lot they are, fellows like poor Cavenaugh!' Eastman thought of his office as a delightful place.

1916

Kerfol

EDITH WHARTON

I

'You ought to buy it,' said my host; 'it's just the place for a solitary-minded devil like you. And it would be rather worth while to own the most romantic house in Brittany. The present people are dead broke, and it's going for a song—you ought to buy it.'

It was not with the least idea of living up to the character my friend Lanrivain ascribed to me (as a matter of fact, under my unsociable exterior I have always had secret yearnings for domesticity) that I took his hint one autumn afternoon and went to Kerfol. My friend was motoring over to Quimper on business: he dropped me on the way, at a cross-road on a heath, and said: 'First turn to the right and second to the left. Then straight ahead till you see an avenue. If you meet any peasants, don't ask your way. They don't understand French, and they would pretend they did and mix you up. I'll be back for you here by sunset—and don't forget the tombs in the chapel.'

I followed Lanrivain's directions with the hesitation occasioned by the usual difficulty of remembering whether he had said the first turn to the right and second to the left, or the contrary. If I had met a peasant I should certainly have asked, and probably been sent astray; but I had the desert landscape to myself, and so stumbled on the right turn and walked across the heath till I came to an avenue. It was so unlike any other avenue I have ever seen that I instantly knew it must be *the* avenue. The gray-trunked trees sprang up straight to a great height and then interwove their pale-gray branches in a long tunnel through which the autumn light fell faintly. I know most trees by name, but I haven't to this day been able to decide what those trees were. They had the tall curve of elms, the tenuity of poplars, the ashen colour of olives under a rainy sky; and they stretched ahead of me for half a mile or more without a break in their arch. If ever I saw an avenue that unmistakably led to something, it was the avenue of Kerfol. My heart beat a little as I began to walk down it.

Presently the trees ended and I came to a fortified gate in a long wall. Between me and the wall was an open space of grass, with other gray avenues radiating from it. Behind the wall were tall slate roofs mossed with silver, a chapel belfry, the top of a keep. A moat filled with wild shrubs and brambles surrounded the place; the draw-bridge had been replaced by a stone arch, and the portcullis by an iron gate. I stood for a long time on the hither side of the moat, gazing about me, and letting the influence of the place sink in. I said to myself: 'If I wait long enough, the guardian will turn up and show me the tombs—' and I rather hoped he wouldn't turn up too soon.

I sat down on a stone and lit a cigarette. As soon as I had done it, it struck me as a puerile and portentous thing to do, with that great blind house looking down at me, and all the empty avenues converging on me. It may have been the depth of the silence that made me so conscious of my gesture. The squeak of my match sounded as loud as the scraping of a brake, and I almost fancied I heard it fall when I tossed it onto the grass. But there was more than that: a sense of irrelevance, of littleness, of futile bravado, in sitting there puffing my cigarette-smoke into the face of such a past.

I knew nothing of the history of Kerfol—I was new to Brittany, and Lanrivain had never mentioned the name to me till the day before—but one couldn't as much as glance at that pile without feeling in it a long accumulation of history. What kind of history I was not prepared to guess: perhaps only that sheer weight of many associated lives and deaths which gives a majesty to all old houses. But the aspect of Kerfol suggested something more—a perspective of stern and cruel memories stretching away, like its own gray avenues, into a blur of darkness.

Certainly no house had ever more completely and finally broken with the present. As it stood there, lifting its proud roofs and gables to the sky, it might have been its own funeral monument. 'Tombs in the chapel? The whole place is a tomb!' I reflected. I hoped more and more that the guardian would not come. The details of the place, however striking, would seem trivial compared with its collective

impressiveness; and I wanted only to sit there and be penetrated by
the weight of its silence.

'It's the very place for you!' Lanrivain had said; and I was overcome
by the almost blasphemous frivolity of suggesting to any living being
that Kerfol was the place for him. 'Is it possible that any one could
not see—?' I wondered. I did not finish the thought: what I meant
was undefinable. I stood up and wandered toward the gate. I was
beginning to want to know more; not to *see* more—I was by now
so sure it was not a question of seeing—but to feel more: feel all the
place had to communicate. 'But to get in one will have to rout out
the keeper,' I thought reluctantly, and hesitated. Finally, I crossed
the bridge and tried the iron gate. It yielded, and I walked through
the tunnel formed by the thickness of the *chemin de ronde*. At the
farther end, a wooden barricade had been laid across the entrance,
and beyond it was a court enclosed in noble architecture. The main
building faced me; and I now saw that one half was a mere ruined
front, with gaping windows through which the wild growths of the
moat and the trees of the park were visible. The rest of the house was
still in its robust beauty. One end abutted on the round tower, the
other on the small traceried chapel, and in an angle of the building
stood a graceful well-head crowned with mossy urns. A few roses grew
against the walls, and on an upper window-sill I remember noticing a
pot of fuchsias.

My sense of the pressure of the invisible began to yield to my
architectural interest. The building was so fine that I felt a desire to
explore it for its own sake. I looked about the court, wondering in
which corner the guardian lodged. Then I pushed open the barrier and
went in. As I did so, a dog barred my way. He was such a remarkably
beautiful little dog that for a moment he made me forget the splendid
place he was defending. I was not sure of his breed at the time, but
have since learned that it was Chinese, and that he was of a rare
variety called the 'Sleeve-dog'. He was very small and golden brown,
with large brown eyes and a ruffled throat: he looked like a large tawny
chrysanthemum. I said to myself: 'These little beasts always snap and
scream, and somebody will be out in a minute.'

The little animal stood before me, forbidding, almost menacing:
there was anger in his large brown eyes. But he made no sound, he
came no nearer. Instead, as I advanced, he gradually fell back, and I
noticed that another dog, a vague rough brindled thing, had limped

up on a lame leg. 'There'll be a hubbub now,' I thought; for at the same moment a third dog, a long-haired white mongrel, slipped out of a doorway and joined the others. All three stood looking at me with grave eyes; but not a sound came from them. As I advanced they continued to fall back on muffled paws, still watching me. 'At a given point, they'll all charge at my ankles: it's one of the jokes that dogs who live together put up on one,' I thought. I was not alarmed, for they were neither large nor formidable. But they let me wander about the court as I pleased, following me at a little distance—always the same distance—and always keeping their eyes on me. Presently I looked across at the ruined façade, and saw that in one of its empty window-frames another dog stood: a white pointer with one brown ear. He was an old grave dog, much more experienced than the others; and he seemed to be observing me with a deeper intentness.

'I'll hear from *him*,' I said to myself; but he stood in the window-frame, against the trees of the park, and continued to watch me without moving. I stared back at him for a time, to see if the sense that he was being watched would not rouse him. Half the width of the court lay between us, and we gazed at each other silently across it. But he did not stir, and at last I turned away. Behind me I found the rest of the pack, with a newcomer added: a small black greyhound with pale agate-coloured eyes. He was shivering a little, and his expression was more timid than that of the others. I noticed that he kept a little behind them. And still there was not a sound.

I stood there for fully five minutes, the circle about me—waiting, as they seemed to be waiting. At last I went up to the little golden-brown and stooped to pat him. As I did so, I heard myself give a nervous laugh. The little dog did not start, or growl, or take his eyes from me—he simply slipped back about a yard, and then paused and continued to look at me. 'Oh, hang it!' I exclaimed, and walked across the court toward the well.

As I advanced, the dogs separated and slid away into different corners of the court. I examined the urns on the well, tried a locked door or two, and looked up and down the dumb façade; then I faced about toward the chapel. When I turned I perceived that all the dogs had disappeared except the old pointer, who still watched me from the window. It was rather a relief to be rid of that cloud of witnesses; and I began to look about me for a way to the back of the house. 'Perhaps there'll be somebody in the garden,' I thought. I found a way across the moat, scrambled over a wall smothered in brambles, and got into the garden. A few lean hydrangeas and geraniums pined in the flower-beds, and the ancient house looked down on them indifferently. Its garden side was plainer and severer than the others: the long granite front, with its few windows and steep roof, looked like a fortress-prison. I walked around the farther wing, went up some disjointed steps, and entered the deep twilight of a narrow and incredibly old box-walk. The walk was just wide enough for one person to slip through, and its branches met overhead. It was like the ghost of a box-walk, its lustrous green all turning to the shadowy grayness of the avenues. I walked on and on, the branches hitting me in the face and springing back with a dry rattle; and at length I came out on the grassy top of the *chemin de ronde*. I walked along it to the gate-tower, looking down into the court, which was just below me. Not a human being was in sight; and neither were the dogs. I found a flight of steps in the thickness of the wall and went down them; and when I emerged again into the court, there stood the circle of dogs, the golden-brown one a little ahead of the others, the black greyhound shivering in the rear.

'Oh, hang it—you uncomfortable beasts, you!' I exclaimed, my voice startling me with a sudden echo. The dogs stood motionless, watching me. I knew by this time that they would not try to prevent my approaching the house, and the knowledge left me free to examine them. I had a feeling that they must be horribly cowed to be so silent and inert. Yet they did not look hungry or ill-treated. Their coats were smooth and they were not thin, except the shivering greyhound. It was more as if they had lived a long time with people who never spoke to them or looked at them: as though the silence of the place had gradually benumbed their busy inquisitive natures. And this strange passivity, this almost human lassitude, seemed to me sadder than the misery of starved and beaten animals. I should have liked to rouse them for a minute, to coax them into a game or a scamper; but the longer I looked into their fixed and weary eyes the more preposterous the idea became. With the windows of that house looking down on us, how could I have imagined such a thing? The dogs knew better: *they* knew what the house would tolerate and what it would not. I even fancied that they knew what was passing through my mind, and pitied me for my frivolity. But even that feeling probably reached them through a thick fog of listlessness. I had an idea that their distance from me was as nothing to my remoteness from them. The impression they produced was that of having in common one memory so deep and dark that nothing that had happened since was worth either a growl or a wag.

'I say,' I broke out abruptly, addressing myself to the dumb circle, 'do you know what you look like, the whole lot of you? You look as if you'd seen a ghost—that's how you look! I wonder if there is a ghost here, and nobody but you left for it to appear to?' The dogs continued to gaze at me without moving . . .

It was dark when I saw Lanrivain's motor lamps at the cross-roads—and I wasn't exactly sorry to see them. I had the sense of having escaped from the loneliest place in the whole world, and of not liking loneliness—to that degree—as much as I had imagined I should. My friend had brought his solicitor back from Quimper for the night, and seated beside a fat and affable stranger I felt no inclination to talk of Kerfol . . .

But that evening, when Lanrivain and the solicitor were closeted in the study. Madame de Lanrivain began to question me in the drawing-room.

'Well—are you going to buy Kerfol?' she asked, tilting up her gay chin from her embroidery.

'I haven't decided yet. The fact is, I couldn't get into the house,' I said, as if I had simply postponed my decision, and meant to go back for another look.

'You couldn't get in? Why, what happened? The family are mad to sell the place, and the old guardian has orders—'

'Very likely. But the old guardian wasn't there.'

'What a pity! He must have gone to market. But his daughter—?'

'There was nobody about. At least I saw no one.'

'How extraordinary! Literally nobody?'

'Nobody but a lot of dogs—a whole pack of them—who seemed to have the place to themselves.'

Madame de Lanrivain let the embroidery slip to her knee and folded her hands on it. For several minutes she looked at me thoughtfully.

'A pack of dogs—you *saw* them?'

'Saw them? I saw nothing else!'

'How many?' She dropped her voice a little. 'I've always wondered—'

I looked at her with surprise: I had supposed the place to be familiar to her. 'Have you never been to Kerfol?' I asked.

'Oh, yes: often. But never on that day.'

'What day?'

'I'd quite forgotten—and so had Hervé, I'm sure. If we'd remembered, we never should have sent you today—but then, after all, one doesn't half believe that sort of thing, does one?'

'What sort of thing?' I asked, involuntarily sinking my voice to the level of hers. Inwardly I was thinking: 'I *knew* there was something . . .'

Madame de Lanrivain cleared her throat and produced a reassuring smile. 'Didn't Hervé tell you the story of Kerfol? An ancestor of his was mixed up in it. You know every Breton house has its ghost-story; and some of them are rather unpleasant.'

'Yes—but those dogs?'

'Well, those dogs are the ghosts of Kerfol. At least, the peasants say there's one day in the year when a lot of dogs appear there; and that day the keeper and his daughter go off to Morlaix and get drunk. The women in Brittany drink dreadfully.' She stooped to match a silk; then she lifted her charming inquisitive Parisian face. 'Did you *really* see a lot of dogs? There isn't one at Kerfol,' she said.

II

Lanrivain, the next day, hunted out a shabby calf volume from the back of an upper shelf of his library.

'Yes—here it is. What does it call itself? *A History of the Assizes of the Duchy of Brittany. Quimper*, 1702. The book was written about a hundred years later than the Kerfol affair; but I believe the account is transcribed pretty literally from the judicial records. Anyhow, it's queer reading. And there's a Hervé de Lanrivian mixed up in it—not exactly *my* style, as you'll see. But then he's only a collateral. Here, take the book up to bed with you. I don't exactly remember the details; but after you've read it I'll bet anything you'll leave your light burning all night!'

I left my light burning all night, as he had predicted; but it was chiefly because, till near dawn, I was absorbed in my reading. The account of the trial of Anne de Cornault, wife of the lord of Kerfol, was long and closely printed. It was, as my friend had said, probably an almost literal transcription of what took place in the court-room; and the trial lasted nearly a month. Besides, the type of the book was very bad . . .

At first I thought of translating the old record. But it is full of wearisome repetitions, and the main lines of the story are forever straying off into side issues. So I have tried to disentangle it, and give it here in simpler form. At times, however, I have reverted to the text because no other words could have conveyed so exactly the sense of what I felt at Kerfol; and nowhere have I added anything of my own.

III

It was in the year 16—that Yves de Cornault, lord of the domain of Kerfol, went to the *pardon* of Locronan to perform his religious duties. He was a rich and powerful noble, then in his sixty-second year, but hale and sturdy, a great horseman and hunter and a pious man. So all his neighbours attested. In appearance he was short and broad, with a swarthy face, legs slightly bowed from the saddle, a hanging nose and broad hands with black hairs on them. He had married young and lost his wife and son soon after, and since then had lived alone at Kerfol. Twice a year he went to Morlaix, where he had a handsome house by the river, and spent a week or ten days there; and occasionally he rode to Rennes on business. Witnesses were found to declare that during these absences he led a life different from the one he was known to lead at Kerfol, where he busied himself with his estate, attended mass daily, and found his only amusement in hunting the wild boar and water-fowl. But these rumours are not particularly relevant, and it is certain that among people of his own class in the neighbourhood he passed for a stern and even austere man, observant of his religious obligations, and keeping strictly to himself. There was no talk of any familiarity with the women on his estate, though at that time the nobility were very free with their peasants. Some people said he had never looked at a woman since his wife's death; but such things are hard to prove, and the evidence on this point was not worth much.

Well, in his sixty-second year, Yves de Cornault went to the *pardon* at Locronan, and saw there a young lady of Douarnenez, who had ridden over pillion behind her father to do her duty to the saint. Her name was Anne de Barrigan, and she came of good old Breton stock, but much less great and powerful than that of Yves de Cornault; and her father had squandered his fortune at cards, and lived almost like a peasant in his little granite manor on the moors . . . I have said I would add nothing of my own to this bald statement of a strange case; but I must interrupt myself here to describe the young lady who rode up to the lych-gate of Locronan at the very moment when the Baron de Cornault was also dismounting there. I take my description from a faded drawing in red crayon, sober and truthful enough to be by a late pupil of the Clouets, which hangs in Lanrivain's study, and is said to be a portrait of Anne de Barrigan. It is unsigned and has no mark of identity but the initials A. B., and the date 16—, the year after her marriage. It represents a young woman with a small oval face, almost pointed, yet wide enough for a full mouth with a tender depression at the corners. The nose is small, and the eyebrows are set rather high, far apart, and as lightly pencilled as the eyebrows in a Chinese painting. The forehead is high and serious, and the hair, which one feels to be fine and thick and fair, is drawn off it and lies close like a cap. The eyes are neither large nor small, hazel probably, with a look at once shy and steady. A pair of beautiful long hands are crossed below the lady's breast . . .

The chaplain of Kerfol, and other witnesses, averred that when the Baron came back from Locronan he jumped from his horse, ordered another to be instantly saddled, called to a young page to come with him, and rode away that same evening to the south. His steward followed the next morning with coffers laden on a pair of pack mules. The following week Yves de Cornault rode back to Kerfol, sent for his vassals and tenants, and told them he was to be married at All Saints to Anne de Barrigan of Douarnenez. And on All Saints' Day the marriage took place.

As to the next few years, the evidence on both sides seems to show that they passed happily for the couple. No one was found to say that Yves de Cornault had been unkind to his wife, and it was plain to all that he was content with his bargain. Indeed, it was admitted by the chaplain and other witnesses for the prosecution that the young lady had a softening influence on her husband, and that he became less exacting with his tenants, less harsh to peasants and dependants, and less subject to the fits of gloomy silence which had darkened his widowhood. As to his wife, the only grievance her champions could call up in her behalf was that Kerfol was a lonely place, and that when her husband was away on business at Rennes or Morlaix—whither she was never taken—she was not allowed so much as to walk in the park unaccompanied. But no one asserted that she was unhappy, though one servant-woman said she had surprised her crying, and had heard her say that she was a woman accursed to have no child, and nothing in life to call her own. But that was a natural enough feeling in a wife attached to her husband; and certainly it must have been a great brief to Yves de Cornaualt that she bore no son. Yet he never made her feel her childlessness as a reproach—she admits this in her evidence—but seemed to try to make her forget it by showering gifts and favours on her. Rich though he was, he had never been openhanded; but nothing was too fine for his wife, in the way of silks or gems or linen, or whatever else she fancied. Every wandering merchant was welcome at Kerfol, and when the master was called away he never came back without bringing his wife a handsome present—something curious and particular—from Morlaix or Rennes or Quimper. One of the waiting-women gave, in cross-examination, an interesting list of one year's gifts, which I copy. From Morlaix, a carved ivory junk with Chinamen at the oars, that a strange sailor had brought back as a votive offering for Notre Dame de la Clarté, above Ploumanac'h; from Quimper, an embroidered gown, worked by the nuns of the Assumption; from Rennes, a silver rose that opened and showed an amber virgin with a crown of garnets; from Morlaix, again, a length of Damascus velvet shot with gold, bought of a Jew from Syria; and for Michaelmas that same year, from Rennes, a necklet or bracelet of round stones—emeralds and pearls and rubies—strung like beads on a fine gold chain. This was the present that pleased the lady best, the woman said. Later on, as it happened, it was produced at the trial, and appears to have struck the Judges and the public as a curious and valuable jewel.

The very same winter, the Baron absented himself again, this time as far as Bordeaux, and on his return he brought his wife something even odder and prettier than the bracelet. It was a winter evening when he rode up to Kerfol and, walking into the hall, found her sitting by the hearth, her chin on her hand, looking into the fire. He carried a velvet box in his hand and, setting it down, lifted the lid and let out a little golden-brown dog.

Anne de Cornault exclaimed with pleasure as the little creature bounded toward her. 'Oh, it looks like a bird or a butterfly!' she cried as she picked it up; and the dog put its paws on her shoulders and looked at her with eyes 'like a Christian's'. After that she would never have it out of her sight, and petted and talked to it as if it had been a child—as indeed it was the nearest thing to a child she was to know. Yves de Cornault was much pleased with his purchase. The dog had been brought to him by a sailor from an East India merchant-man, and the sailor had bought it of a pilgrim in a bazaar at Jaffa, who had stolen it from a nobleman's wife in China, a perfectly permissible thing to do, since the pilgrim was a Christian and the nobleman a heathen doomed to hellfire. Yves de Cornault had paid a long price for the dog, for they were beginning to be in demand at the French court, and the sailor knew he had got hold of a good thing; but Anne's pleasure was so great that, to see her laugh and play with the little animal, her husband would doubtless have given twice the sum.

So far, all the evidence is at one, and the narrative plain sailing; but now the steering becomes difficult. I will try to keep as nearly as possible to Anne's own statements; though toward the end, poor thing . . .

Well, to go back. The very year after the little brown dog was brought to Kerfol, Yves de Cornault, one winter night, was found dead at the head of a narrow flight of stairs leading down from his wife's rooms to a door opening on the court. It was his wife who found him and gave the alarm, so distracted, poor wretch, with fear and horror—for his blood was all over her—that at first the roused household could not make out what she was saying, and thought she had suddenly gone mad. But there, sure enough, at the top of the stairs lay her husband, stone dead, and head foremost, the blood from his wounds dripping down to the steps below him. He had been dreadfully scratched and gashed about the face and throat, as if with curious pointed weapons; and one of his legs had a deep tear in it which had cut an artery, and probably caused his death. but how did he come there, and who had murdered him?

His wife declared that she had been asleep in her bed, and hearing his cry had rushed out to find him lying on the stairs; but this was immediately questioned. In the first place, it was proved that from her room she could not have heard the struggle on the stairs, owing to the thickness of the walls and the length of the intervening passage; then it was evident that she had not been in bed and asleep, since she was dressed when she roused the house, and her bed had not been slept in. Moreover, the door at the bottom of the stairs was ajar, and it was noticed by the chaplain (an observant man) that the dress she wore was stained with blood about the knees, and that there were traces of small blood-stained hands low down on the staircase walls, so that it was conjectured that she had really been at the postern-door when her husband fell and, feeling her way up to him in the darkness on her hands and knees, had been stained by his blood dripping down on her. Of course it was argued on the other side that the blood-marks on her dress might have been caused by her kneeling down by her husband when she rushed out of her room; but there was the open door below, and the fact that the finger-marks in the staircase all pointed upward.

The accused held to her statement for the first two days, in spite of its improbability; but on the third day word was brought to her that Hervé de Lanrivain, a young nobleman of the neighbourhood, had been arrested for complicity in the crime. Two or three witnesses thereupon came forward to say that it was known throughout the country that Lanrivain had formerly been on good terms with the lady of Cornault; but that he had been absent from Brittany for over a year, and people had ceased to associate their names. The witnesses who made this statement were not of a very reputable sort. One was an old herb-gatherer suspected of witchcraft, another a drunken clerk from a neighbouring parish, the third a half-witted shepherd who could be made to say anything; and it was clear that the prosecution was not satisfied with its case, and would have liked to find more definite proof of Lanrivain's complicity than the statement of the herb-gatherer, who swore to having seen him climbing the wall of the park on the night of the murder. One way of patching out incomplete proofs in those days was to put some sort of pressure, moral or physical, on the accused person. It is not clear what pressure was put on Anne de Cornault; but on the third day, when she was brought in court, she 'appeared weak and wandering', and after being encouraged to collect herself and speak the truth, on her honour and the wounds of her Blessed Redeemer, she confessed that she had in fact gone down the stairs to speak with Hervé de Lanrivain (who denied everything), and had been surprised there by the sound of her husband's fall. That was better; and the prosecution rubbed its hands with satisfaction. The satisfaction increased when various dependants living at Kerfol were induced to say—with apparent sincerity—that during the year or two preceding his death their master had once more grown uncertain and irascible, and subject to the fits of brooding silence which his household had learned to dread before his second marriage. This seemed to show that things had not been going well at Kerfol; though no one could be found to say that there had been any signs of open disagreement between husband and wife.

Anne de Cornault, when questioned as to her reason for going down at night to open the door to Hervé de Lanrivain, made an answer which must have sent a smile around the court. She said it was because she was lonely and wanted to talk with the young man. Was this the only reason? she was asked; and replied: 'Yes, by the Cross over your Lordships' heads.' 'But why at midnight?' the court asked. 'Because I could see him in no other way.' I can see the exchange of glances across the ermine collars under the Crucifix.

Anne de Cornault, further questioned, said that her married life had been extremely lonely: 'desolate' was the word she used. It was true that her husband seldom spoke harshly to her; but there were days when he did not speak at all. It was true that he had never struck or threatened her; but he kept her like a prisoner at Kerfol, and when he rode away to Morlaix or Quimper or Rennes he set so close a watch on her that she could not pick a flower in the garden without having a waiting woman at her heels. 'I am no Queen, to need such honours,' she once said to him; and he had answered that a man who has a treasure does not leave the key in the lock when he goes out. 'Then take me with you,' she urged; but to this he said that towns were pernicious places, and young wives better off at their own firesides.

'But what did you want to say to Hervé de Lanrivain?' the court asked; and she answered: 'To ask him to take me away.'

'Ah—you confess that you went down to him with adulterous thoughts?'

'No.'

'Then why did you want him to take you away?'

'Because I was afraid for my life.'

'Of whom were you afraid?'

'Of my husband.'

'Why were you afraid of your husband?'

'Because he had strangled my little dog.'

Another smile must have passed around the courtroom: in days when any nobleman had a right to hang his peasants—and most of them exercised it—pinching a pet animal's wind-pipe was nothing to make a fuss about.

At this point one of the Judges, who appears to have had a certain sympathy for the accused, suggested that she should be allowed to explain herself in her own way; and she thereupon made the following statement.

The first years of her marriage had been lonely; but her husband had not been unkind to her. If she had had a child she would not have been unhappy; but the days were long, and it rained too much.

It was true that her husband, whenever he went away and left her, brought her a handsome present on his return; but this did not make up for the loneliness. At least nothing had, till he brought her the little brown dog from the East: after that she was much less unhappy. Her husband seemed pleased that she was so fond of the dog; he gave her leave to put her jewelled bracelet around its neck, and to keep it always with her.

One day she had fallen asleep in her room, with the dog at her feet, as his habit was. Her feet were bare and resting on his back. Suddenly she was waked by her husband: he stood beside her, smiling not unkindly.

'You look like my great-grandmother, Juliane de Cornault, lying in the chapel with her feet on a little dog,' he said.

The analogy sent a chill through her, but she laughed and answered: 'Well, when I am dead you must put me beside her, carved in marble, with my dog at my feet.'

'Oho—we'll wait and see,' he said, laughing also, but with his black brows close together. 'The dog is the emblem of fidelity.'

'And do you doubt my right to lie with mine at my feet?'

'When I'm in doubt I find out,' he answered. 'I am an old man,' he added, 'and people say I make you lead a lonely life. But I swear you shall have your monument if you earn it.'

'And I swear to be faithful,' she returned, 'if only for the sake of having my little dog at my feet.'

Not long afterward he went on business to the Quimper Assizes; and while he was away his aunt, the widow of a great nobleman of the duchy, came to spend a night at Kerfol on her way to the *pardon* of Ste. Barbe. She was a woman of piety and consequence, and much respected by Yves de Cornault, and when she proposed to Anne to go with her to Ste. Barbe no one could object, and even the chaplain declared himself in favour of the pilgrimage. So Anne set out for Ste. Barbe, and there for the first time she talked with Hervé de Lanrivain. He had come once or twice to Kerfol with his father, but she had never before exchanged a dozen words with him. They did not talk for more than five minutes now: it was under the chestnuts, as the procession was coming out of the chapel. He said: 'I pity you,' and she was surprised, for she had not supposed that any one thought her an object of pity. He added: 'Call for me when you need me,' and she smiled a little, but was glad afterward, and thought often of the meeting.

She confessed to having seem him three times afterward: not more. How or where she would not say—one had the impression that she feared to implicate some one. Their meetings had been rare and brief; and at the last he had told her that he was starting the next day for a foreign country, on a mission which was not without peril and might keep him for many months absent. He asked her for a remembrance, and she had none to give him but the collar about the little dog's neck. She was sorry afterward that she had given it, but he was so unhappy at going that she had not had the courage to refuse.

Her husband was away at the time. When he returned a few days later he picked up the animal to pet it, and noticed that its collar was missing. His wife told him that the dog had lost it in the undergrowth of the park, and that she and her maids had hunted a whole day for it. It was true, she explained to the court, that she had made the maids search for the necklet—they all believed the dog had lost it in the park . . .

Her husband made no comment, and that evening at supper he was in his usual mood, between good and bad: you could never tell which. He talked a good deal, describing what he had seen and done at Rennes; but now and then he stopped and looked hard at her, and when she went to bed she found her little dog strangled on her pillow. The little thing was dead, but still warm; she stooped to lift it, and her distress turned to horror when she discovered that it had been strangled by twisting twice round its throat the necklet she had given to Lanrivain.

The next morning at dawn she buried the dog in the garden, and hid the necklet in her breast. She said nothing to her husband, then or later, and he said nothing to her; but that day he had a peasant hanged for stealing a faggot in the park, and the next day he nearly beat to death a young horse he was breaking.

Winter set in, and the short days passed, and the long nights, one by one; and she heard nothing of Hervé de Lanrivain. It might be that her husband had killed him; or merely that he had been robbed of the necklet. Day after day by the hearth among the spinning maids, night after night alone on her bed, she wondered and trembled. Sometimes at table her husband looked across at her and smiled; and then she felt sure that Lanrivain was dead. She dared not try to get news of him, for she was sure her husband would find out if she did: she had an idea that he could find out anything. Even when a witch-woman who was a noted seer, and could show you the whole world in her crystal, came to the castle for a night's shelter, and the maids flocked to her, Anne held back.

The winter was long and black and rainy. One day, in Yves de Cornault's absence, some gypsies came to Kerfol with a troop of performing dogs. Anne bought the smallest and cleverest, a white dog with a feathery coat and one blue and one brown eye. It seemed to have been ill-treated by the gypsies, and clung to her plaintively when she took it from them. That evening her husband came back, and when she went to bed she found the dog strangled on her pillow.

After that she said to herself that she would never have another dog, but one bitter cold evening a poor lean greyhound was found whining at the castle-gate, and she took him in and forbade the maids to speak of him to her husband. She hid him in a room that no one went to, smuggled food to him from her own plate, made him a warm bed to lie on and petted him like a child.

Yves de Cornault came home, and the next day she found the greyhound strangled on her pillow. She wept in secret, but said nothing, and resolved that even if she met a dog dying of hunger she would never bring him into the castle; but one day she found a young sheep-dog, a brindled puppy with good blue eyes, lying with a broken leg in the snow of the park. Yves de Cornault was at Rennes, and she brought the dog in, warmed and fed it, tied up its leg and hid it in the castle till her husband's return. The day before, she gave it to a peasant woman who lived a long way off, and paid her handsomely to care for it and say nothing; but that night she heard a whining and scratching at her door, and when opened it the lame puppy, drenched and shivering, jumped up on her with little sobbing barks. She hid him in her bed, and the next morning was about to have him taken back to the peasant woman when she heard her husband ride into the court. She shut the dog in a chest, and went down to receive him. An hour or two later, when she returned to her room, the puppy lay strangled on her pillow . . .

After that she dared not make a pet of any other dog; and her loneliness became almost unendurable. Sometimes, when she crossed the court of the castle, and thought no one was looking, she stopped to pat the old pointer at the gate. But one day as she was caressing him her husband came out of the chapel; and the next day the old dog was gone . . .

This curious narrative was not told in one sitting of the court, or received without impatience and incredulous comment. It was plain that the Judges were surprised by its puerility, and that it did not help the accused in the eyes of the public. It was an odd tale, certainly; but what did it prove? That Yves de Cornault disliked dogs, and that his wife, to gratify her own fancy, persistently ignored this dislike. As for pleading this trivial disagreement as an excuse for her relations—whatever their nature—with her supposed accomplice, the argument was so absurd that her own lawyer manifestly regretted having let her make use of it, and tried several times to cut short her story. But she went on to the end, with a kind of hypnotized insistence, as though the scenes she evoked were so real to her that she had forgotten where she was and imagined herself to be re-living them.

At length the Judge who had previously shown a certain kindness to her said (leaning forward a little, one may suppose, from his row of dozing colleagues): 'Then you would have us believe that you murdered your husband because he would not let you keep a pet dog?'

'I did not murder my husband.'

'Who did, then? Hervé de Lanrivain?'

'No.'

'Who then? Can you tell us?'

'Yes, I can tell you. The dogs—' At that point she was carried out of the court in a swoon.

It was evident that her lawyer tried to get her to abandon this line of defence. Possibly her explanation, whatever it was, had seemed convincing when she poured it out to him in the heat of their first private colloquy; but now that was exposed to the cold daylight of judicial scrutiny, and the banter of the town, he was thoroughly ashamed of it, and would have sacrificed her without a scruple to save his professional reputation. But the obstinate Judge—who perhaps, after all, was more inquisitive than kindly—evidently wanted to hear the story out, and she was ordered, the next day, to continue her deposition.

She said that after the disappearance of the old watchdog nothing particular happened for a month or two. Her husband was much as usual: she did not remember any special incident. But one evening a pedlar woman came to the castle and was selling trinkets to the maids. She had no heart for trinkets, but she stood looking on while the women made their choice. And then, she did not know how, but the pedlar coaxed her into buying for herself a pear-shaped pomander with a strong scent in it—she had once seen something of the kind on a gypsy woman. She had no desire for the pomander, and did not know why she had bought it. The pedlar said that whoever wore it had the power to read the future; but she did not really believe that, or care much either. However, she bought the thing and took it up to her room, where she sat turning it about in her hand. Then the strange scent attracted her and she began to wonder what kind of spice was in the box. She opened it and found a gray bean rolled in a strip of paper; and on the paper she saw a sign she knew and a message from Hervé de Lanrivain, saying that he was at home again and would be at the door in the court that night after the moon had set . . .

She burned the paper and sat down to think. It was nightfall, and her husband was at home . . . She had no way of warning Lanrivain, and there was nothing to do but to wait . . .

At this point I fancy the drowsy court-room beginning to wake up. Even to the oldest hand on the bench there must have been certain relish in picturing the feelings of a woman on receiving such a message at nightfall from a man living twenty miles away, to whom she had no means of sending a warning . . .

She was not a clever woman, I imagine; and as the first result of her cogitation she appears to have made the mistake of being, that evening, too kind to her husband. She could not ply him with wine, according to the traditional expedient, for though he drank heavily at times he had a strong head; and when he drank beyond its strength it was because he chose to, and not because a woman coaxed him. Not his wife, at any rate—she was an old story by now. As I read the case, I fancy there was no feeling for her left in him but the hatred occasioned by his supposed dishonour.

At any rate, she tried to call up her old graces; but early in the evening he complained of pains and fever, and left the hall to go up to the closet where he sometimes slept. His servant carried him a cup of hot wine, and brought back word that he was sleeping and not to be disturbed; and an hour later, when Anne lifted the tapestry and listened at his door, she heard his loud regular breathing. She thought it might be a feint, and stayed a long time barefooted in the passage, her ear to the crack; but the breathing went on too steadily and naturally to be other than that of a man in a sound sleep. She crept back to her room reassured, and stood in the window watching the moon set through the trees of the park. The sky was misty and starless, and after the moon went down the night was black as pitch. She knew the time had come, and stole along the passage, past her husband's door—where she stopped again to listen to his breathing—to the top of the stairs. There she paused a moment, and assured herself that no one was following her; then she began to go down the stairs in the darkness. They were so steep and winding that she had to go very slowly, for fear of stumbling. Her one thought was to get the door unbolted, tell Lanrivain to make his escape, and hasten back to her room. She had tried the bolt earlier in the evening, and managed to put a little grease on it; but nevertheless, when she drew it, it gave a squeak . . . not loud, but it made her heart stop; and the next minute, overhead, she heard a noise . . .

'What noise?' the prosecution interposed.

'My husband's voice calling out my name and cursing me.'

'What did you hear after that?'

'A terrible scream and a fall.'

'Where was Hervé de Lanrivain at this time?'

'He was standing outside in the court. I just made him out in the darkness. I told him for God's sake to go, and then I pushed the door shut.'

'What did you do next?'

'I stood at the foot of the stairs and listened.'

'What did you hear?'

'I heard dogs snarling and panting.' (Visible discouragement of the bench, boredom of the public, and exasperation of the lawyer for the defence. Dogs again! but the inquisitive Judge insisted.)

'What dogs?'

She bent her head and spoke so low that she had to be told to repeat her answer: 'I don't know.'

'How do you mean—you don't know?'

'I don't know what dogs . . .'

The Judge again intervened: 'Try to tell us exactly what happened. How long did you remain at the foot of the stairs?'

'Only a few minutes.'

'And what was going on meanwhile overhead?'

'The dogs kept on snarling and panting. Once or twice he cried out. I think he moaned once. Then he was quiet.'

'Then what happened?'

'Then I heard a sound like the noise of a pack when the wolf is thrown to them—gulping and lapping.'

(There was a groan of disgust and repulsion through the court, and another attempted intervention by the distracted lawyer. But the inquisitive Judge was still inquisitive.)

'And all the while you did not go up?'

'Yes—I went up then—to drive them off.'

'The dogs?'

'Yes.'

'Well—?'

'When I got there it was quite dark. I found my husband's flint and steel and struck a spark. I saw him lying there. He was dead.'

'And the dogs?'

'The dogs were gone.'

'Gone—where to?'

'I don't know. There was no way out—and there were no dogs at Kerfol.'

She straightened herself to her full height, threw her arms above her head, and fell down on the stone floor with a long scream. There was a moment of confusion in the court-room. Someone on the bench was heard to say: 'This is clearly a case for the ecclesiastical authorities'—and the prisoner's lawyer doubtless jumped at the suggestion.

After this, the trial loses itself in a maze of cross-questioning and squabbling. Every witness who was called corroborated Anne de Cornault's statement that there were no dogs at Kerfol: had been none for several months. The master of the house had taken a dislike to dogs, there was no denying it. But, on the other hand, at the inquest, there had been long and bitter discussions as to the nature of the dead man's wounds. One of the surgeons called in had spoken of marks that looked like bites. The suggestion of witchcraft was revived, and the opposing lawyers hurled tomes of necromancy at each other.

At last Anne de Cornault was brought back into court—at the instance of the same Judge—and asked if she knew where the dogs she spoke of could have come from. On the body of her Redeemer she swore that she did not. Then the Judge put his final question: 'If the dogs you think you heard had been known to you, do you think you would have recognized them by their barking?'

'Yes.'

'Did you recognize them?'

'Yes.'

'What dogs do you take them to have been?'

'My dead dogs,' she said in a whisper . . . She was taken out of court, not to reappear there again. There was some kind of ecclesiastical investigation, and the end of the business was that the Judges disagreed with each other, and with the ecclesiastical committee, and that Anne de Cornault was finally handed over to the keeping of her husband's family, who shut her up in the keep of Kerfol, where she is said to have died many years later, a harmless mad-woman.

So ends her story. As for that of Hervé de Lanrivain, I had only to apply to his collateral descendant for its subsequent details. The evidence against the young man being insufficient, and his family influence in the duchy considerable, he was set free, and left soon afterwards for Paris. He was probably in no mood for a worldly life, and he appears to have come almost immediately under the influence of the famous M. Arnauld d'Andilly and the gentlemen of Port Royal. A year or two later he was received into their Order, and without achieving any particular distinction he followed its good and evil fortunes till his death some twenty years later. Lanrivain showed me a portrait of him by a pupil of Philippe de Champaigne: sad eyes, an impulsive mouth and a narrow brow. Poor Hervé de Lanrivain:

it was a gray ending. Yet as I looked at his stiff and sallow effigy, in the dark dress of the Jansenists, I almost found myself envying his fate. After all, in the course of his life two great things had happened to him: he had loved romantically, and he must have talked with Pascal . . .

1917

A Suburban Fairy
Tale

KATHERINE MANSFIELD

M r. and Mrs. B. sat at breakfast in the cosy red dining-room of
their 'snug little crib just under half-an-hour's run from the
City.'

There was a good fire in the grate—for the dining-room was the
living-room as well—the two windows overlooking the cold empty
garden patch were closed, and the air smelled agreeably of bacon
and eggs, toast and coffee. Now that this rationing business was really
over Mr. B. made a point of a throughly good tuck-in before facing
the very real perils of the day. He didn't mind who knew it—he was
a true Englishman about his breakfast—he had to have it; he'd cave
in without it, and if you told him that these Continental chaps could
get through half the morning's work he did on a roll and a cup of
coffee—you simply didn't know what you were talking about.

Mr. B. was a stout youngish man who hadn't been able—worse
luck—to chuck his job and join the Army; he'd tried for four years
to get another chap to take his place, but it was no go. He sat at
the head of the table reading the *Daily Mail*. Mrs. B. was a youngish
plump little body, rather like a pigeon. She sat opposite, preening
herself behind the coffee set and keeping an eye of warning love on
Little B. who perched between them, swathed in a napkin and tapping
the top of a soft-boiled egg.

Alas! Little B. was not at all the child that such parents had every
right to expect. He was no fat little trot, no dumpling, no firm little
pudding. He was undersized for his age, with legs like macaroni, tiny
claws, soft, soft hair that felt like mouse fur and big wide-open eyes.

For some strange reason everything in life seemed the wrong size for Little B.—too big and too violent. Everything knocked him over, took the wind out of his feeble sails and left him gasping and frightened. Mr. and Mrs. B were quite powerless to prevent this; they could only pick him up after the mischief was done—and try to set him going again. And Mrs. B. loved him as only weak children are loved—and when Mr. B. thought what a marvellous little chap he was too—thought of the spunk of the little man, he—well he—by George—he . . .

'Why aren't there two kinds of eggs?' said little B. 'Why aren't there little eggs for children and big eggs like what this one is for grown-ups?'

'Scotch hares,' said Mr. B. 'Fine Scotch hares for 5s. 3d. How about getting one, old girl?'

'It would be a nice change, wouldn't it?' said Mrs. B. 'Jugged.'

And they looked across at each other and there floated between them the Scotch hare in its rich gravy with stuffing balls and a white pot of redcurrant jelly accompanying it.

'We might have had it for the week-end,' said Mrs. B. 'But the butcher has promised me a nice little sirloin and it seems a pity' . . . Yes, it did, and yet . . . Dear me, it was very difficult to decide. The hare would have been such a change—on the other hand, could you beat a really nice little sirloin?

'There's hare soup, too,' said Mr. B. drumming his fingers on the table. 'Best soup in the world!'

'O-oh!' cried Little B. so suddenly and sharply that it gave them quite a start—'Look at the whole lot of sparrows flown on to our lawn'—he waved his spoon. 'Look at them,' he cried, 'Look!' And while he spoke, even though the windows were closed, they heard a loud shrill cheeping and chirping, from the garden.

'Get on with your breakfast like a good boy, do,' said his mother, and his father said, 'You stick to the egg, old man, and look sharp about it.'

'But look at them—look at them all hopping,' he cried. 'They don't keep still not for a minute. Do you think they're hungry, father?'

Cheek-a-cheep-cheep-cheek! cried the sparrows.

'Best postpone it perhaps till next week,' said Mr. B., 'and trust to luck they're still to be had then.'

'Yes, perhaps that would be wiser,' said Mrs. B.

Mr. B. picked another plum out of his paper.

'Have you bought any of those controlled dates yet?'

'I managed to get two pounds yesterday,' said Mrs. B.

'Well, a date pudding's a good thing,' said Mr. B. And they looked across at each other and there floated between them a dark round pudding covered with creamy sauce. 'It would be a nice change, wouldn't it?' said Mrs. B.

Outside on the grey frozen grass the funny eager sparrows hopped and fluttered. They were never for a moment still. They cried, flapped their ungainly wings. Little B., his egg finished, got down, took his bread and marmalade to eat at the window.

'Do let us give them some crumbs,' he said. 'Do open the window, father, and throw them something. Father, *please!*'

'Oh, don't nag, child,' said Mrs. B., and his father said—'Can't go opening windows, old man. You'd get your head bitten off.'

'But they're hungry,' cried Little B., and the sparrows' little voices were like ringing of little knives being sharpened. *Cheek-a-cheep-cheep-cheek!* they cried.

Little B. dropped his bread and marmalade inside the china flower-pot in front of the window. He slipped behind the thick curtains to see better, and Mr. and Mrs. B. went on reading about what you could get now without coupons—no more ration books after May—a glut of cheese—a glut of it—whole cheeses revolved in the air between them like celestial bodies.

Suddenly as Little B. watched the sparrows on the grey frozen grass, they grew, they changed, still flapping and squeaking. They turned into tiny little boys, in brown coats, dancing, jigging outside, up and down outside the window squeaking, 'Want something to eat, want something to eat!' Little B. held with both hands to the curtain. 'Father,' he whispered, 'Father! They're not sparrows. They're little boys. Listen, Father!' But Mr. and Mrs. B. would not hear. He tried again. 'Mother,' he whispered. 'Look at the little boys. They're not sparrows, Mother!' But nobody noticed his nonsense.

'All this talk about famine,' cried Mr. B., 'all a Fake, all a Blind.'

With white shining faces, their arms flapping in the big coats, the little boys danced. 'Want something to eat, want something to eat.'

'Father,' muttered Little B. 'Listen, Father! Mother, listen, please!'

'Really!' said Mrs. B. 'The noise those birds are making! I've never heard such a thing.'

'Fetch me my shoes, old man,' said Mr. B.
Cheek-a-cheep-cheep-cheek! said the sparrows.

Now where had that child got to? 'Come and finish your nice cocoa, my pet,' said Mrs. B.

Mr. B. lifted the heavy cloth and whispered, 'Come on, Rover,' but no little dog was there.

'He's behind the curtain,' said Mrs. B.

'He never went out of the room,' said Mr. B.

Mrs. B. went over to the window and Mr. B. followed. And they looked out. There on the grey frozen grass, with a white, white face, the little boy's thin arms flapping like wings, in front of them all, the smallest, tiniest was Little B. Mr. and Mrs. B. heard his voice above all the voices. 'Want something to eat, want something to eat.'

Somehow, somehow, they opened the window. 'You shall! All of you. Come in *at once*. Old man! Little man!'

But it was too late. The little boys were changed into sparrows again, and away they flew—out of sight—out of call.

1921

A Haunted House

VIRGINIA WOOLF

Whatever hour you woke there was a door shutting. From room to room they went, hand in hand, lifting here, opening there, making sure—a ghostly couple.

'Here we left it,' she said. And he added, 'Oh, but here too! 'It's upstairs,' she murmured. 'And in the garden,' he whispered. 'Quietly,' they said, 'or we shall wake them.'

But it wasn't that you woke us. Oh, no. 'They're looking for it' they're drawing the curtain,' one might say, and so read on a page or two. 'Now they've found it,' one would be certain, stopping the pencil on the margin. And then, tired of reading, one might rise and see for oneself, the house all empty, the doors standing open, only the wood pigeons bubbling with content and the hum of the threshing machine sounding from the farm. 'What did I come in here for? What did I want to find?, My hands were empty. 'Perhaps it's upstairs then?' The apples were in the loft. And so down again, the garden still as ever, only the book had slipped into the grass.

But they had found it in the drawing room. Not that one could ever see them. The window panes reflected apples, reflected roses; all the leaves were green in the glass. If they moved in the drawing-room, the apple only turned its yellow side. Yet, the moment after, if the door was opened, spread about the floor, hung upon the walls, pendant from the ceiling—what? My hands were empty. The shadow of a thrush crossed the carpet; from the deepest wells of silence the wood pigeon drew its bubble of sound. 'Safe, safe, safe,' the pulse of the house beat softly. 'The treasure buried; the room . . .' the pulse stopped short. Oh, was that the buried treasure?

A moment later the light had faded. Out in the garden then? But the trees spun darkness for a wandering beam of sun. So fine, so rare, coolly sunk beneath the surface the beam I sought always burnt behind the glass. Death was the glass; death was between us; coming to the woman first, hundreds of years ago, leaving the house, sealing all the windows; the rooms were darkened. He left it, left her, went North, went East, saw the stars turned in the Southern sky; sought the house, found it dropped beneath the Downs. 'Safe, safe, safe,' the pulse of the house beat gladly. 'The treasure yours.'

The wind roars up the avenue. Trees stoop and bend this way and that. Moonbeams splash and spill wildly in the rain. But the beam of the lamp falls straight from the window. The candle burns stiff and still. Wandering through the house, opening the windows, whispering not to wake us, the ghostly couple seek their joy.

'Here we slept,' she says. And he adds, 'Kisses without number.' 'Waking in the morning—' 'Silver between the trees—' 'Upstairs—' 'In the garden—' 'When summer came—' 'In winter snowtime—' The doors go shutting far in the distance, gently knocking like the pulse of a heart.

Nearer they come; cease at the doorway. The wind falls, the rain slides silver down the glass. Our eyes darken; we hear no steps beside us; we see no lady spread her ghostly cloak. His hands shield the lantern. 'Look,' he breathes. 'Sound asleep. Love upon their lips.'

Stooping, holding their silver lamp above us, long they look and deeply. Long they pause. The wind drives straightly; the flame stoops slightly. Wild beams of moonlight cross both floor and wall, and, meeting, stain the faces bent; the faces pondering; the faces that search the sleepers and seek their hidden joy.

'Safe, safe, safe,' the heart of the house beats proudly. 'Long years—' he sighs. 'Again you found me.' 'Here,' she murmurs, 'sleeping; in the garden reading; laughing, rolling apples in the loft. Here we left our treasure—' Stooping, their light lifts the lids upon my eyes. 'Safe! safe! safe!' the pulse of the house beats wildly. Waking, I cry 'Oh, is this *your* buried treasure? The light in the heart.'

1923

The Nature of the Evidence

MAY SINCLAIR

This is the story Marston told me. He didn't want to tell it. I had to tear it from him bit by bit. I've pieced the bits together in their time order, and explained things here and there, but the facts are the facts he gave me. There's nothing that I didn't get out of him somehow.

Out of *him*—you'll admit my source is unimpeachable. Edward Marston, the great K.C., and the author of an admirable work on 'The Logic of Evidence.' You should have read the chapters on 'What Evidence Is and What It Is Not.' You may say he lied; but if you knew Marston you'd know he wouldn't lie, for the simple reason that he's incapable of inventing anything. So that, if you ask me whether I believe this tale, all I can say is, I believe the things happened, because he said they happened and because they happened to him. As for what they *were*—well, I don't pretend to explain it, neither would he.

You know he was married twice. He adored his first wife, Rosamund, and Rosamund adored him. I suppose they were completely happy. She was fifteen years younger than he, and beautiful. I wish I could make you see how beautiful. Her eyes and mouth had the same sort of bow, full and wide-sweeping, and they stared out of her face with the same grave, contemplative innocence. Her mouth was finished off at each corner with the loveliest little moulding, rounded like the pistil of a flower. She wore her hair in a solid gold fringe over her forehead, like a child's, and a big coil at the back. When it was let down it hung in a heavy cable to her waist. Marston used to tease her about it. She had a trick of tossing back the rope in the night when it was hot under her, and it would fall smack across his face and hurt him.

There was a pathos about her that I can't describe—a curious, pure, sweet beauty, like a child's; perfect, and perfectly immature; so immature that you couldn't conceive its lasting—like that—any more than childhood lasts. Marston used to say it made him nervous. He was afraid of waking up in the morning and finding that it had changed in the night. And her beauty was so much a part of herself that you couldn't think of her without it. Somehow you felt that if it went she must go too.

Well, she went first.

For a year afterwards Marston existed dangerously, always on the edge of a break-down. If he didn't go over altogether it was because his work saved him. He had no consoling theories. He was one of those bigoted materialists of the nineteenth century type who believe that consciousness is a purely physiological function, and that when your body's dead, *you're* dead. He saw no reason to suppose the contrary. 'When you consider,' he used to say, 'the nature of the evidence!'

It's as well to bear this in mind, so as to realize that he hadn't any bias or anticipation. Rosamund survived for him only in his memory. And in his memory he was still in love with her. At the same time he used to discuss quite cynically the chances of his marrying again.

It seems that on their honeymoon they had gone into that. Rosamund said she hated to think of his being lonely and miserable, supposing she died before he did. She would like him to marry again. If, she stipulated, he married the right woman.

He had put it to her: 'And if I marry the wrong one?'

And she had said, That would be different. She couldn't bear that.

He remembered all this afterwards; but there was nothing in it to make him suppose, at the time, that she would take action.

We talked it over, he and I, one night.

'I suppose,' he said, 'I shall have to marry again. It's a physical necessity. But it won't be anything more. I shan't marry the sort of woman who'll expect anything more. I won't put another woman in Rosamund's place. There'll be no unfaithfulness about it.'

And there wasn't. Soon after that first year he married Pauline Silver.

She was a daughter of old Justice Parker, who was a friend of Marston's people. He hadn't seen the girl till she came home from India after her divorce.

Yes, there'd been a divorce. Silver had behaved very decently. He'd let her bring it against *him*, to save her. But there were some queer stories going about. They didn't get round to Marston, because he was so mixed up with her people; and if they had he wouldn't have believed them. He'd made up his mind he'd marry Pauline the first minute he'd seen her. She was handsome; the hard, black, white and vermilion kind, with a little aristocratic nose and a lascivious mouth.

It was, as he had meant it to be, nothing but physical infatuation on both sides. No question of Pauline's taking Rosamund's place.

Marston had a big case on at the time.

They were in such a hurry that they couldn't wait till it was over; and as it kept him in London they agreed to put off their honeymoon till the autumn, and he took her straight to his own house in Curzon Street.

This, he admitted afterwards, was the part he hated. The Curzon Street house was associated with Rosamund; especially their bed-room—Rosamund's bedroom—and his library. The library was the room Rosamund liked best because it was his room. She had her place in the corner by the hearth, and they were always alone there together in the evenings when his work was done, and when it wasn't done she would still sit with him, keeping quiet in her corner with a book.

Luckily for Marston, at the first sight of the library Pauline took a dislike to it.

I can hear her. 'Br-rr-rh! There's something beastly about this room, Edward. I can't think how you can sit in it.'

And Edward, a little caustic:

'*You* needn't, if you don't like it.'

'I certainly shan't.'

She stood there—I can see her—on the hearthrug by Rosamund's chair, looking uncommonly handsome and lascivious. He was going to take her in his arms and kiss her vermilion mouth, when, he said, something stopped him. Stopped him clean, as if it had risen up and stepped between them. He supposed it was the memory of Rosamund, vivid in the place that had been hers.

You see it was just that place, of silent, intimate communion, that Pauline would never take. And the rich, coarse, contented creature didn't even want to take it. He saw that he would be left alone there, all right, with his memory.

But the bedroom was another matter. That, Pauline had made it understood from the beginning, she would have to have. Indeed, there was no other he could well have offered her. The drawing-room covered the whole of the first floor. The bedrooms above were cramped, and this one had been formed by throwing the two front rooms into one. It looked south, and the bathroom opened out of it at the back. Marston's small northern room had a door on the narrow landing at right angles to his wife's door. He could hardly expect her to sleep there, still less in any of the tight boxes on the top floor. He said he wished he had sold the Curzon Street house.

But Pauline was enchanted with the wide, three-windowed piece that was to be hers. It had been exquisitely furnished for poor little Rosamund; all seventeenth century walnut wood, Bokhara rugs, thick silk curtains, deep blue with purple linings, and a big, rich bed covered with a purple counterpane embroidered in blue.

One thing Marston insisted on: that *he* should sleep on Rosamund's side of the bed, and Pauline in his own old place. He didn't want to see Pauline's body where Rosamund's had been. Of course he had to lie about it and pretend he had always slept on the side next the window.

I can see Pauline going about in that room, looking at everything; looking at herself, her black, white and vermilion, in the glass that had held Rosamund's pure rose and gold; opening the wardrobe where Rosamund's dresses used to hang, sniffing up the delicate, flower scent of Rosamund, not caring, covering it with her own thick trail.

And Marston (who cared abominably)—I can see him getting more miserable and at the same time more excited as the wedding evening went on. He took her to the play to fill up the time, or perhaps to get her out of Rosamund's rooms; God knows. I can see them sitting in the stalls, bored and restless, starting up and ⌐ ⌐ ͑t before the thing was half over, and coming back to that hoṵ ͓ in Curzon Street before eleven o'clock.

It wasn't much past eleven when he went to her room.

I told you her door was at right angles to his, and the landing was narrow, so that anybody standing by Pauline's door must have been seen the minute he opened his. He hadn't even to cross the landing to get to her.

Well, Marston swears that there was nothing there when he opened his own door; but when he came to Pauline's he saw Rosamund standing up before it; and, he said, '*She wouldn't let me in.*'

Her arms were stretched out, barring the passage. Oh yes, he saw her face, Rosamund's face; I gathered that it was utterly sweet, and utterly inexorable. He couldn't pass her.

So he turned into his own room, backing, he says, so that he could keep looking at her. And when he stood on the threshold of his own door she wasn't there.

No, he wasn't frightened. He couldn't tell me what he felt; but he left his door open all night because he couldn't bear to shut it on her. And he made no other attempt to go in to Pauline; he was so convinced that the phantasm of Rosamund would come again and stop him.

I don't know what sort of excuse he made to Pauline the next morning. He was she was very stiff and sulky all day; and no wonder. He was still infatuated with her, and I don't think that the phantasm of Rosamund had put him off Pauline in the least. In fact, he persuaded himself that the things was nothing but a hallucination, due, no doubt, to his excitement.

Anyhow, he didn't expect to see it at the door again the next night.

Yes. It was there. Only, this time, he said, it drew aside to let him pass. It smiled at him, as if it were saying, 'Go in, if you must; you'll see what'll happen.'

He had no sense that it had followed him into the room; he felt certain that, this time, it would let him be.

It was when he approached Pauline's bed, which had been Rosamund's bed, that she appeared again, standing between it and him, and stretching out her arms to keep him back.

All that Pauline could see was her bridegroom backing and backing, then standing there, fixed, and the look on his face. That in itself was enough to frighten her.

She said, 'What's the matter with you, Edward?'

He didn't move.

'What are you standing there for? Why don't you come to bed?'

Then Marston seems to have lost his head and blurted it out:

'I can't. I can't.'

'Can't what?' said Pauline from the bed.

'Can't sleep with you. She won't let me.'

'She?'

'Rosamund. My wife. She's there.'

'What on earth are you talking about?'

'She's there. I tell you. She won't let me. She's pushing me back.'

He says Pauline must have thought he was drunk or something. Remember, she *saw* nothing but Edward, his face, and his mysterious attitude. He must have looked very drunk.

She sat up in bed, with her hard, black eyes blazing away at him, and told him to leave the room that minute. Which he did.

The next day she had it out with him. I gathered that she kept on talking about the 'state' he was in.

'You came to my room, Edward, in a *disgraceful* state.'

I suppose Marston said he was sorry; but he couldn't help it; he wasn't drunk. He stuck to it that Rosamund was there. He had seen her. And Pauline said, if he wasn't drunk then he must be mad, and he said meekly, 'Perhaps I *am* mad.'

That set her off, and she broke out in a fury. He was no more mad than she was; but he didn't care for her; he was making ridiculous excuses; shamming, to put her off. There was some other woman.

Marston asked her what on earth she supposed he'd married her for. Then she burst out crying and said she didn't know.

Then he seems to have made it up with Pauline. He managed to make her believe he wasn't lying, that he really had seen something, and between them they arrived at a rational explanation of the appearance. He had been overworking. Rosamund's phantasm was nothing but a hallucination of his exhausted brain.

This theory carried him on till bed-time. Then, he says, he began to wonder what would happen, what Rosamund's phantasm would do next. Each morning his passion for Pauline had come back again, increased by frustration, and it worked itself up crescendo, towards night. Supposing he *had* seen Rosamund. He might see her again. He had become suddenly subject to hallucinations. But as long as you *knew* you were hallucinated you were all right.

So what they agreed to do that night was by way of precaution, in case the thing came again. It might even be sufficient in itself to prevent his seeing anything.

Instead of going in to Pauline he was to get into the room before she did, and she was to come to him there. That, they said, would break the spell. To make him feel even safer he meant to be in bed before Pauline came.

Well, he got into the room all right.

It was when he tried to get into bed that he saw her (I mean Rosamund).

She was lying there, in his place next the window, her own place, lying in her immature child-like beauty and sleeping, the firm full bow of her mouth softened by sleep. She was perfect in every detail, the lashes of her shut eyelids golden on her white cheeks, the solid gold of her square fringe shining, and the great braided golden rope of her hair flung back on the pillow.

He knelt down by the bed and pressed his forehead into the bedclothes, close to her side. He declared he could feel her breathe.

He stayed there for the twenty minutes Pauline took to undress and come to him. He says the minutes stretched out like hours. Pauline found him still kneeling with his face pressed into the bedclothes. When he got up he staggered.

She asked him what he was doing and why he wasn't in bed. And he said, 'It's no use. I can't I can't.'

But somehow he couldn't tell her that Rosamund was there. Rosamund was too sacred; he couldn't talk about her. He only said:

'You'd better sleep in my room to-night.'

He was staring down at the place in the bed where he still saw Rosamund. Pauline couldn't have seen anything but the bedclothes, the sheet smoothed above an invisible breast, and the hollow in the pillow. She said she'd do nothing of the sort. She wasn't going to be frightened out of her own room. He could do as he liked.

He couldn't leave them there; he couldn't leave Pauline with Rosamund, and he couldn't leave Rosamund with Pauline. So he sat up in a chair with his back turned to the bed. No. He didn't make any attempt to go back. He says he knew she was still lying there, guarding his place, which was her place. The odd thing is that he wasn't in the least disturbed or frightened or surprised. He took the whole thing as a matter of course. And presently he dozed off into a sleep.

A scream woke him and the sound of a violent body leaping out of the bed and thudding on to its feet. He switched on the light and saw the bedclothes flung back and Pauline standing on the floor with her mouth open.

He went to her and held her. She was cold to the touch and shaking with terror, and her jaws dropped as if she was palsied.

She said, 'Edward, there's something in the bed.'

He glanced again at the bed. It was empty.

'There isn't,' he said. 'Look.'

He stripped the bed to the foot-rail, so that she could see.

'There *was* something.'

'Do you see it.'

'No. I felt it.'

She told him. First something had come swinging, smack across her face. A thick, heavy rope of woman's hair. It had waked her. Then she had put out her hands and felt the body. A woman's body, soft and horrible; her fingers had sunk into the shallow breasts. Then she had screamed and jumped.

And she couldn't stay in the room. The room, she said, was 'beastly.'

She slept in Marston's room, in his small single bed, and he sat up with her all night, on a chair.

She believed now that he had really seen something, and she remembered that the library was beastly, too. Haunted by something. She supposed that was what she had felt. Very well. Two rooms in the house were haunted; their bedroom and the library. They would just have to avoid those two rooms. She had made up her mind, you see, that it was nothing but a case of an ordinary haunted house; the sort of thing you're always hearing about and never believe in till it happens to yourself. Marston didn't like to point out to her that the house hadn't been haunted till she came into it.

The following night, the fourth night, she was to sleep in the spare room on the top floor, next to the servants, and Marston in his own room.

But Marston didn't sleep. He kept on wondering whether he would or would not go up to Pauline's room. That made him horribly restless, and instead of undressing and going to bed, he sat up on a chair with a book. He wasn't nervous; but he had a queer feeling that something

was going to happen, and that he must be ready for it, and that he'd
better be dressed.

It must have been soon after midnight when he heard the door knob
turning very slowly and softly.

The door opened behind him and Pauline came in, moving without
a sound, and stood before him. It gave him a shock; for he had been
thinking of Rosamund, and when he heard the door knob turn it was
the phantasm of Rosamund that he expected to see coming in. He
says, for the first minute, it was this appearance of Pauline that struck
him as the uncanny and unnatural thing.

She had nothing, absolutely nothing on but a transparent white
chiffony sort of dressing-gown. She was trying to undo it. He could
see her hands shaking as her fingers fumbled with the fastenings.

He got up suddenly, and they just stood there before each other,
saying nothing, staring at each other. He was fascinated by her, by the
sheer glamour of her body, gleaming white through the thin stuff, and
by the movement of her fingers. I think I've said she was a beautiful
woman, and her beauty at that moment was overpowering.

And still he stared at her without saying anything. It sounds as if
their silence lasted quite a long time, but in reality it couldn't have
been more than some fraction of a second.

The she began. 'Oh, Edward, for God's sake *say* something.
Oughtn't I to have come?'

And she went on without waiting for an answer. 'Are you thinking
of *her*? Because, if—if you are, I'm not going to let her drive you away
from me . . . I'm not going to . . . She'll keep on coming as long as
we don't— Can't you see that this is the way to stop it . . .? When
you take me in your arms.'

She slipped off the loose sleeves of the chiffon thing and it fell to
her feet. Marston says he heard a queer sound, something between
a groan and a grunt, and was amazed to find that it came from
himself.

He hadn't touched her yet—mind you, it went quicker than it takes
to tell, it was still an affair of the fraction of a second—they were
holding out their arms to each other, when the door opened again
without a sound, and, without visible passage, the phantasm was
there. It came incredibly fast, and thin at first, like a shaft of light
sliding between them. It didn't do anything; there was no beating of
hands, only, as it took on its full form, its perfect likeness of flesh

and blood, it made its presence felt like a push, a force, driving them asunder.

Pauline hadn't seen it yet. She thought it was Marston who was beating her back. She cried out: 'Oh, don't, don't push me away!' She stooped below the phantasm's guard and clung to his knees, writhing and crying. For a moment it was a struggle between her moving flesh and that still, supernatural being.

And in that moment Marston realized that he hated Pauline. She was fighting Rosamund with her gross flesh and blood, taking a mean advantage of her embodied state to beat down the heavenly, discarnate thing.

He called to her to let go.

'It's not I,' he shouted. 'Can't you *see* her?'

Then, suddenly, she saw, and let go, and dropped, crouching on the floor and trying to cover herself. This time she had given no cry.

The phantasm gave way; it moved slowly towards the door, and as it went it looked back over its shoulder at Marston, it trailed a hand, signalling to him to come.

He went out after it, hardly aware of Pauline's naked body that still writhed there, clutching at his feet as they passed, and drew itself after him, like a worm, like a beast, along the floor.

She must have got up at once and followed them out on to the landing; for, as he went down the stairs behind the phantasm, he could see Pauline's face, distorted with lust and terror, peering at them above the stairhead. She saw them descend the last flight, and cross the hall at the bottom and go into the library. The door shut behind them.

Something happened in there. Marston never told me precisely what it was, and I didn't ask him. Anyhow, that finished it.

The next day Pauline ran away to her own people. She couldn't stay in Marston's house because it was haunted by Rosamund, and he wouldn't leave it for the same reason.

And she never came back; for she was not only afraid of Rosamund, she was afraid of Marston. And if she *had* come it wouldn't have been any good. Marston was convinced that, as often as he attempted to get to Pauline, something would stop him. Pauline certainly felt that, if Rosamund were pushed to it, she might show herself in some still more sinister and terrifying form. She knew when she was beaten.

And there was more in it than that. I believe he tried to explain it to her; said he had married her on the assumption that Rosamund was dead, but that now he knew she was alive; she was, as he put it, 'there.' He tried to make her see that if he had Rosamund he couldn't have *her*. Rosamund's presence in the world annulled their contract.

You see I'm convinced that something *did* happen that night in the library. I say, he never told me precisely what it was, but he once let something out. We were discussing one of Pauline's love-affairs (after the separation she gave him endless grounds for divorce).

'Poor Pauline,' he said, 'she thinks she's so passionate.'

'Well,' I said, 'wasn't she?'

Then he burst out. 'No. She doesn't know what passion is. None of you know. You haven't the faintest conception. You'd have to get rid of your bodies first. I didn't know until—'

He stopped himself. I think he was going to say, 'until Rosamund came back and showed me.' For he leaned forward and whispered: 'It isn't a localized affair at all . . . If you only knew—'

So I don't think it was just faithfulness to a revived memory. I take it there had been, behind that shut door, some experience, some terrible and exquisite contact. More penetrating than sight or touch. More—more extensive: passion at all points of being.

Perhaps the supreme moment of it, the ecstasy, only came when her phantasm had disappeared.

He couldn't go back to Pauline after *that*.

1929

The Unbolted Door

MRS BELLOC LOWNDES

'Leave that door alone, young feller; and remember once for all that it's never to be locked or bolted. Not that there's any fear of it's being locked, as the master always has the key on him.'

Mrs. Torquil heard the muffled words. Cote, their seventy-year-old butler, instructing the new footman in slow, impressive tones, as is the way of butlers when addressing their humble subordinates.

But this subordinate belonged to the new dispensation, so he answered back.

'That's a funny idea—that is.'

'It may seem funny to you, seeing you're a stranger, Henry, but 'tis only a sad one to me.'

'Sad? Why that, Mr. Cote?'

From where Anne Torquil had stayed her steps at the door of her bedchamber, she heard the now quavering, long familiar, old voice, answer— ''Twas this way it happened. Mr. John—and a rare nice young chap he was—was not just put down "killed" by his Colonel, when he didn't come back from what was then styled "a raid in the henemy lines". He was just reported "missing". Cruel I called it then, and cruel I calls it now—for 'twas bound to encourage false hopes.'

'It must 'a done, Mr. Cote,'—the young voice had become grave.

'Mrs. Torquil knew well enough what 'missing' meant. But the master, he just couldn't bring hisself to believe his son—his heir, too, mind you—had gone, so to speak, for ever. I mind well how a few days after the Armistice, Mr. Torquil came along one night just as I was locking up, and he says, says he, 'Just leave the door of the small hall as it is, Cote. Master John always came into the house that way, because of the short cut from the gate. Many soldiers are coming back now from Germany who was put down as 'missing', so my son may walk through that door hany day.' That's what he said then, poor gentleman; and that door, Henry, has never been locked or bolted, since.'

The men's footsteps died away, and something stirred in Anne Torquil's unhappy atrophied heart. How very strange that she should not have known, till to-night, of her husband's order? It was true that at all ages past babyhood, the boy had been wont to burst through the outer door of what he called 'the small hall' with a cry of 'Mother! Where are you? Upstairs?' And yet, dearly as he loved her, close as they were to one another, she had always known that John had cared most for his inarticulate father.

She was so moved, now, that something of the frightful anguish of six years ago came back, and restlessly she began to walk up and down the beautiful bedroom many of her friends envied her. How piteous that to her it should be a room of intolerable memories.

In the wide Jacobean bed, where she now spent her often wakeful nights, had been born the son whose coming had seemed inevitable. Convinced that as to this matter she would be as lucky as in all else, she had laughed at the thought that her baby could be a girl. How often, in the last six years, she had wished she had died on the glorious day her boy was born.

Her good friend then, and till her good friends, Dr. Maynard, the old village doctor, had taken it on himself, more than once, during the perfect years which had followed John's birth, to hint that it was a pity the child had no brother, no sister, to share his delightful nursery. But she, Anne Torquil, had been wilfully deaf to such advice. Always, during the whole of her happy spoilt young life, she had done what she wanted; and never had she done anything she had not definitely wished to do. She had given her Jack a splendid son, what good old Cote called an heir; that, surely, was quite enough?

Suddenly now, she stopped in her pacing opposite a carved wood mirror. She had been standing just here during her last happy moment of life. It was in the autumn of 1918; her husband was home, convalescing from what had been a severe wound; there were rumours of Peace, and they were confidently expecting their boy home on his first leave. At exactly three o'clock, on a fine early October day, there had come what had been, then, a very familiar knuckle knock on her door. Even when she was a bride of seventeen, and the two were more like a pair of happy children than a married couple, Jack had always knocked before he came into his wife's, Anne's, room.

Blithely she had called out, 'Come in!'

And he had come in, with a telegram open in his hand.

It was as if she could hear now, to-night, six years later, the sound of his hoarse voice uttering her name—and then, when she had put up her arm with an instinctive violent movement to ward off the blow, the further words, 'Thank God not killed, my darling! Only missing.'

Only missing? And John's father had gone on not only hoping against hope, but firmly convinced that, from the depths of some German prison, or even from some German mental home, the boy would come back.

She, from the first, in dry-eyed despair, had felt no hope at all. And her husband's obstinate—what to herself she more than once harshly called his idiotic—optimism, had pained, exasperated, sometimes maddened, her.

She stared now, as if hypnotized, at her own reflection in the dark glass of the mirror. Though she would be forty-five on her next birthday, it was true, as tiresome people so often told her, that she still, at times, looked like a girl. Time had scarcely touched her lovely face and slender rounded figure with his rude finger; but Jack Torquil, not yet fifty, might have been ten years older than his age. For the first time in her life, to-night, Anne asked herself, with a touch of unease, if her husband was as unhappy as she was herself.

This evening she had watched him sitting hunched up in an easychair, a book in his hand, on the other side of the fire. Suddenly he had taken up a pencil—it was a thing Jack Torquil was given to do, and it always irritated his wife—and marked a passage in the book he was reading. Looking up, he had thrown her a queer, shamed, pleading, look; and when he had risen and left the library, to go through his usual ritual of taking a turn out of doors with the three dogs, she had walked across the room to see what it was he had marked in his book. And then she had been at once annoyed, diverted, and, maybe, a little touched; for what her husband had marked had been two lines, the first ridiculously familiar, the second, till this moment, unknown to her.

> 'It is the little rift within the lute
> That by and by will make the music mute.'

And now, while slowly undressing, she remembered the two lines
Jack had marked. What he, no doubt, still thought of as 'a little rift'
between them was, in actual fact, a chasm which was ever yawning
wider and wider. Yet once, only once, in their now long joint life, had
she spoken bitter words to him.

It had been years ago, at a time when he was still full of hope,
and she, alas! starkly hopeless, as to their son's possible return.
The lover in him had awakened, and when his lips had sought
hers she had said fiercely, 'Never, Jack. Never again.' So literally
had he accepted her decree, that not once, since then, had he even
knocked on the door of the room they had shared so blissfully for
twenty-one years.

To-day, the eve of Armistice Day, had been an intolerable day,
and Anne told herself that next year they would have people here
for the first fortnight of November. They were rich, hospitable—both,
in their quite different ways, popular. But the real reason why they
were never alone, excepting for the Christmas holidays, and part of
November of each year, was that a dual solitude becomes intolerable
when shared by a man and woman who were once ardent, exulting
happy, lovers.

As Anne Torquil got into her great bed, the stable clock began to
strike twelve, ushering in another Armistice Day; and, as she lay back,
smarting, difficult tears rose to her still undimmed eyes.

The thought of her boy was very near to her to-night, so near,
indeed, that an overwhelming wish to gaze on his pictured face came
over her.

Slipping out of bed, she went over to a painted cabinet where she
kept certain sacred, secret things. Among them was her husband's
adoring letters, each beginning My *darling little love*, written during
their short engagement; also all her son's photographs from babyhood.

She had had a sketch of him done by Sargent when he was at
Sandhurst. That now hung in his father's bedroom. There was no
portrait of him in any other part of the house which knew him no
more. Some of their later friends did not know they had ever had
a child.

Unlocking the drawer in which lay all the photographs of John,
she took out the last one, taken of him just after he had received

his commission, and wearing his first uniform. While she gazed into the boyish face, he seemed to be smiling proudly, confidently, merrily, up at her.

As she put it back in the drawer, she remembered a clumsy attempt, most kindly meant, of sympathy on the part of their Vicar. He had met her during one of the long lonely walks she had taken that first year of woe, in between her still strenuous war work, for, after the Armistice, Torquilton House had gone on for a long time being a soldiers' convalescent hospital. And, 'Who being dead, yet liveth', the Vicar had said in a low voice.

Throwing her head back, she had exclaimed: 'You know my husband is still quite convinced that John was not killed? He thinks he may come back any day.'

With a startled look, and making no attempt to answer her, the would-be comforter had gone his way.

To-day, at almost the same place, oddly enough, she had had such an encounter with old Dr. Maynard which had not hurt, so much as angered her. He had retired in 1919, and she never saw him alone, now. But this time his only son—a son the war had spared—had dropped him from their car, so that he might have a little walk.

The old man had taken her hand in his, and said feelingly, 'I should like to think you happy, dear Mrs. Torquil. And, as she had shaken her head—she couldn't pretend to him—he had gone on, with a touch of real admiration in his feeble voice, 'You're wonderful! You won't mind my saying so? But how young you keep! Why this afternoon, you might be twenty-five instead of—'

'Nearly forty-five? Yes, and I do still feel young, worse luck. I'd give a good deal to feel old, Dr. Maynard.'

And then he had said a word about her husband which brought the colour rushing up into her face. The doctor had always been chary of his words, but every word had always told. 'Can't you bring yourself to be kind to him?' he had said, looking straight into her still lovely face. She had answered at once, and very coldly, 'Not in the way you mean.'

Shaking his white head sadly he had taken her hand in his again, 'You must forgive an old friend—eh?'

She had nodded quickly. But she had felt then, and she felt now, that she could not forgive that—yes, impertinent—question.

The twelfth stroke of the clock fell on the still air, and all at once she heard the electric light being turned out in the hall below, followed by the sound of her husband's footsteps coming up the stairs. There came over her an odd, unexpected impulse. Just to go out and bid him good night. But she restrained that impulse. All the same, she walked across to the door, and, turning off the light, noiselessly opened it a little way.

Jack Torquil was making his way up the easy stairs with the steps of an old man, though, as she and Dr. Maynard both knew, he was still young at heart, however deeply grief and hope deferred had scarred his face. And, still feeling moved by what their old manservant had unconsciously revealed, she waited to hear those slow footsteps make their way into the room which was no longer called 'Mr. Torquil's dressing-room.'

And then it was as if her heart stood still, for the handle of the unbolted door in the hall below turned in the darkness, and there came an upward rush of cold air, followed by her husband's startled shout, 'Who goes there?'

There was a moment's pause, and after that pause, as if from infinitely far away, there rang out two words in a voice she had never thought to hear again, even in another life, for Anne Torquil had come not to believe the promise the Vicar had repeated, thinking to comfort her.

And the words uttered in her son's voice pierced her innermost soul, for 'Poor father', was all her beloved had came back to say.

Then she heard Jack Torquil's eager, joyful—'John? My dear, dear boy!' and the sound of his feet pounding down the stairs.

As she rushed out to the circular gallery, she heard the handle turn again in the darkness. The lights below were put full on and, looking over the balustrade, she saw her husband standing in the empty hall, staring, with bewildered eyes, at the closed door.

At last he turned, and, looking up, saw her pale face and wide-open eyes gazing down.

'You heard him, too, Anne?'

Straightening herself, she ran round the gallery and so downstairs. There, with what had become a way of forgotten tenderness, she took his hand. 'Of course I heard him too! The door opened, and he came in with the wind. Having said what was in his dear mind he went back—but where, Jack, where?'

Later that night, as Anne lay in his arms, John's father muttered, 'He came back for you, my darling; to comfort you. That was quite right.'

'For me, Jack? Oh no!'

'But he did, little love. Surely you heard what he said?' And she felt the surprise in his voice.

She whispered, 'What did he say—to you?'

'Only what you heard—only the two words, Anne, "Dear mother".'

He waited a moment, and then he said humbly, for he was a very simple kind of man, 'Just to let you know, dearest, and perhaps to let me know too, that all is well with the child.'

1931

The Buick Saloon

MARY O'MALLEY

To Mrs. James St. George Bernard Bowlby it seemed almost providential that she should recover from the series of illnesses which had perforce kept her in England, at the precise moment when Bowlby was promoted from being No. 2 to being No. 1 in the Grand Oriental Bank in Peking. Her improved health and his improved circumstances made it obvious that now at last she should join him, and she wrote to suggest it. Bowlby of course agreed, and out she came. He went down to meet her in Shanghai, but business having called him further still, to Hongkong, Mrs. Bowlby proceeded to Peking alone, and took up her quarters in the big, ugly grey-brick house over the Bank in Legation Street. She tried, as many managers' wives had tried before her, to do her best with the solid mahogany and green leather furniture provided by the Bank, wondering the while how Bowlby, so dependent always on the feminine touch on his life and surroundings, had endured the lesser solidities of the sub-manager's house alone for so long. She bought silks and black-wood and scroll paintings. She also bought a car. 'You'll need a car, and you'd better have a saloon, because of the dust,' Bowlby had said.

People who come to Peking without motors of their own seldom buy new ones. There are always second-hand cars going, from many sources; the leavings of transferred diplomatists, the jetsam of financial ventures, the sediment of conferences. So one morning Mrs. Bowlby went down with Thompson, the new No. 2 in the Bank, to Maxon's garage in the Nan Shih Tzu to choose her car. After much conversation with the Canadian manager they pitched on a Buick saloon. It was a Buick of the type which is practically standard in the Far East, and had been entirely repainted outside, a respectable dark blue; the inside had been newly done up in a pleasant soft grey which appealed to Mrs. Bowlby. The manager was loud in its praises. The suspension was excellent. ('You want that on these roads, Mrs. Bowlby.') The driver and his colleague sat outside. ('Much better, Mr. Thompson. If these fellows have been eating garlic—they shouldn't, but they do—') Thompson knew they did, and agreed heartily. Mrs. Bowlby, new such transactions, wanted to know who the car had belonged to. The manager was firmly vague. This was not a commission sale—he had bought the car when the owner left. Very good people—'from the Quarter'. This fully satisfied Thompson, who knew that only Europeans live (above the rose, anyhow) in the Legation Quarter of Peking.

So the Buick saloon was bought. Thompson, having heard at the Club that the late Grand Oriental chauffeur drank petrol, did not re-engage him with the rest of the servants according to custom, but secured instead for Mrs. Bowlby the chauffeur of a departing manager of the Banque Franco-Belge. By the time Bowlby returned from Hongkong the chauffeur and his colleague had been fitted out with khaki livery for winter, with white for summer—in either case with trim gold cuff-and-hat-bands—and Mrs. Bowlby, in her blue saloon, had settled down to pay her calls.

In Peking the newcomer calls first; a curious and discouraging system. It is an ordeal even to the hardened. Mrs. Bowlby was not hardened; she was a small, shy, frail woman, who wore grey by preference, and looked grey—eyes, hair and skin. She had no idea of asserting herself; if she had things in her—subtleties, delicacies—she did not wear them outside; she did not impose herself. She hated the calls. But as she was also extremely conscientious, day after day, trying to fortify herself by the sight of the two khaki-and-gold figures in front of her, exhaling their possible garlic to the outer air beyond the glass partition, she called. She called on the diplomats' wives in the Quarter; she called on 'the Salt' (officials of the Salt Gabelle); she called on the Customs—English, Italian, American, and French; she called on the Posts—French, Italian, American, and English. The annual displacement of pasteboard in Peking must amount to many tons, and in this useful work Mrs. Bowlby, alone in the grey interior of her car, faithfully took her share. She carried with her a little list on which, with the help of her Number One boy (as much a permanent fixture in the Bank house, almost, as the doors and windows), she had written out the styles, titles, and addresses of the ladies she wished to visit. The late chauffeur of the Banque Franco-Belge spoke excellent French; so did Mrs. Bowlby—it was one of her few accomplishments; but as no Chinese can or will master European names, the European needs must learn and use the peculiar versions current among them. '*Ta Ch'in ch'ai T'ai-t'ai, Turkwo-fu*' read out Mrs. Bowlby when she wished to call on the wife of the German Minister. '*Oui, Madame!*' said Shwang. '*Pé T'ai-t'ai, Kung Hsien Hut'ung*' read out Mrs. Bowlby when visiting Mrs. Bray, the doctor's wife; but when she wished to call on Mrs. Bennett, the wife of the Commandant of the English Guard, and Mrs. Baines, the Chaplain's wife, she found that they were both *Pé T'ai-t'ai* too—which led to confusion.

It began towards the end of the first week. Possibly it was her absorption in the lists and the Chinese names that prevented her from noticing it sooner, but at the end of that week Mrs. Bowlby would have sworn that she heard French spoken beside her as she drove about. Once, a little later, as she was driving down the Rue Marco Polo to fetch her husband from the Club, a voice said: '*C'est lui!*' in an underbreath, eagerly—or so she thought. The windows were lowered, and Mrs. Bowlby put it down to the servants in front. But it persisted. More than once she thought she heard a soft sigh. 'Nerves!' thought Mrs. Bowlby—her nerves were always a menace to her, and Peking, she knew, was bad for them.

She went on saying 'nerves' for two or three more days; then, one afternoon, she changed her mind. She was driving along the Ta Chiang an Chieh, the great thoroughfare running east and west outside the Legation Quarter, where the trams ring and clang past the scarlet walls and golden roofs of the Forbidden City, and long lines of camels, coming in with coal from the country as they have come for centuries, cross the road between the Dodges and Daimlers of the new China. It was a soft, brilliant afternoon in April, and the cinder track along the Glacis of the Quarter was thronged with riders; polo had begun, and as the car neared Hatamen Street she caught a glimpse of the white and scarlet figures through the drifting dust on her right. At the corner of the Hatamen the car stopped; a string of camels was passing up to the great gateway, and she had to wait.

She sat back in the car, glad of the pause; she was unusually moved by the loveliness of the day, by the beauty and strangeness of the scene, by the whole magic of spring in Peking. She was going later to watch the polo, a terrifying game; she wished Jim didn't play. Suddenly, across her idle thoughts, a voice beside her spoke clearly. 'Au revoir!' it said, 'mon très-cher. Ne tombe pas, je t'en prie.' And as the car moved forward behind the last of the camels, soft and unmistakable there came a sigh, and the words, 'Ce polo! Quel sport affreux! Dieu, que je le déteste!' in a passionate undertone.

'That wasn't the chauffeur!' was what Mrs. Bowlby found herself saying. The front windows were up. And besides, that low, rather husky voice, the cultivated and clear accent, could not be confounded for a moment with Shwang's guttural French. And besides, what chauffeur would talk like that? The thing was ridiculous. 'And it wasn't nerves this time,' said Mrs. Bowlby, her thoughts running this way and that round the phenomenon. 'She did say it.' 'Then it was she who said: 'C'est lui!' before—' she said almost triumphantly, a moment later.

Curiously, though she was puzzled and startled, she realized presently that she was not in the least frightened. That someone with a beautiful voice should speak French in her car was absurd and impossible, but it wasn't alarming. In her timid way Mrs. Bowlby rather prided herself on her common sense, and as she shopped and called she considered this extraordinary occurrence from all the commonsense points of view that she could think of, but it remained a baffling and obstinate fact. Before her drive was over she found herself wishing simply to hear the voice again. It was ridiculous, but she did. And she had her wish. As the car turned into Legation Street an hour later she saw that it was too late to go to the polo; the last chukka was over, and the players were leaving the ground, over which dust still hung in the low brilliant light, in cars and rickshas. As she passed the gate the voice spoke again—almost in front of her, this time, as though the speaker were leaning forward to the window. 'Le viola!' it said—and then, quite loudly, 'Jacques!' Mrs. Bowlby almost leaned out of the window herself, to look for whoever was being summoned—as she sat back, conscious of her folly, she heard again beside her, quite low, 'Il ne m'a pas vue.'

There was no mistake about it. It was broad daylight; there she was in her car, bowling along Legation Street—past the Belgian Bank, past the German Legation; rickshas skimming in front of her, Madame de Réan bowing to her. And just as clear and certain as all these things had been this woman's voice, calling to 'Jacques', whoever he was—terrified lest he should fall at polo, hating the game for his sake. What a lovely voice it was! Who was she, Mrs. Bowlby wondered, and what and who was Jacques? 'Mon très'cher!' she had called him—a delicious expression. It belonged to the day and the place—it was near to her own mood as she had sat at the corner of the Hatamen and noticed the spring, and hated the polo too for Jim's sake. She would have liked to call Jim 'mon très-cher', only he would have been so surprised.

The thought of Bowlby brought her up with a round turn. What would he say to this affair? Instantly, though she prolonged the discussion with herself for form's sake, she knew that she was not going to tell him. Not yet, anyhow. Bowlby had not been very satisfied with her choice of a car as it was—he said it was too big and too expensive to run. Besides, there was the question of her nerves. If he failed to hear the voice too she would be in a terribly difficult position. But there was more to it than that. She had a faint sense that she had been eavesdropping, however involuntarily. She had no right to give away even a voice which said 'mon très-cher' in that tone.

This feeling grew upon her in the days that followed. The voice that haunted the Buick became of almost daily occurrence, furnishing a curious secret background to her social routine of calls and 'At Homes'. It spoke always in French, always to or about 'Jacques'—a person, whoever he was, greatly loved. Sometimes it was clear to Mrs. Bowlby that she was hearing only half of a conversation between the two, as one does at the telephone. The man's voice she never heard, but, as at the telephone, she could often guess at what he said. Much of the speech was trivial enough; arrangements for meetings at lunches, at the Polo; for week-end parties at Pao-ma-chang in the temple of this person or that. This was more eerie than anything else to Mrs. Bowlby—the hearing of plans concerned with people she knew. 'Alors, dimanche prochain, chez les Milne'. Meeting 'les Milne' soon after, she would stare at them uneasily, as though by looking long enough she might find about them some trace of the presence which was more familiar to her than their own. Her voice was making ghosts of the living. But whether plans, or snatches of talk about people or ponies, there came always, sooner or later, the undernote of tenderness, now hesitant, now frank—the close concern, the monopolizing happiness of a woman in love.

It puzzled Mrs. Bowlby that the car should only register, as it were, the woman's voice. But then the whole affair bristled with puzzles.

Why did Bowlby hear nothing? For he did not—she would have realized her worst fears if she *had* told him. She remembered always the first time that the voice spoke when he was with her. They were going to a *Thé Dansant* at the Peking Hotel, a farewell party for some Minister. As the car swung out of the Jade Canal Road, past the policemen who stand with fixed bayonets at the edge of the Glacis, the voice began suddenly, as it so often did, in French—'Then I leave thee now—thou wilt send back the car?' And as they lurched across the tramlines towards the huge European building and pulled up, it went on 'But to-night, one will dance, *n'est-ce pas?*'

'Goodness, what a crowd!' said Bowlby. 'This is going to be simply awful. Don't let's stay long. Will half an hour be enough, do you think?'

Mrs. Bowlby stared at him without answering. Was it possible? She nearly gave herself away in the shock of her astonishment. 'What's the matter?' said Bowlby. 'What are you looking at?'

Bowlby had not heard a word!

She noticed other things. There were certain places where the voice 'came through', so to speak, more clearly and regularly than elsewhere. Intermittent fragments, sometimes unintelligible, occurred anywhere. But she came to know where to expect to hear most. Near the polo ground, for instance, which she hardly ever passed without hearing some expression of anxiety or pride. She often went to the polo, for Jim was a keen and brilliant player; but it was a horror to hr while he played, and this feeling was a sort of link, it seemed to her, between her and her unseen companion. More and more, too, she heard it near the Hatamen and the *hu-t'ungs* or alleys to the east of it. Mrs. Bowlby liked the East City. It lies rather in a backwater, between the crowded noisy thoroughfare of Hatamen Street, with its trams, dust, cars and camels, and the silent angle of the Tartar Wall, rising above the low one-storey houses. A good many Europeans live there, and she was always glad when a call took her that way, through the narrow *hu-t'ungs* where the car lurched over heaps of rubbish or skidded in the deep dust, and rickshas pulled aside into gateways to let her pass. Many of these lanes end vaguely in big open spaces, where pigs root among the refuse and little boys wander about, singing long monotonous songs with a curious jerky rhythm in their high nasal voices. Sometimes, as she waited before a scarlet door, a flute-player out of sight would begin to play, and the thin sweet melody filled the sunny air between the blank grey walls. Flowering trees showed here and there above them; coppersmiths plied their trade on the steps of carved marble gateways; dogs and beggars sunned themselves under the white and scarlet walls of temple courtyards. Here, more than anywhere else, the voice spoke clearly, freely, continuously, the rapid rounded French syllables falling on the air from nowhere, now high, light, and merry, with teasing words and inflection, now sinking into low murmurs of rapturous happiness. At such times Mrs. Bowlby sat wholly absorbed in listening, drawn by the lovely voice into a life not her own and held fascinated by the spell of this passionate adventure. Happy as she was with Bowlby, her life with him had never known anything like this. He had never wanted, and she had never dared to use the endearments lavished by the late owner of the Buick saloon on her Jacques.

She heard enough to follow the course of the affair pretty closely. They met when they could in public, but somewhere in the Chinese City there was clearly a meeting-place of their own—'*notre petit asile*'. And gradually this haven began to take shape in Mrs. Bowlby's mind. Joyous references were made to various features of it. To-morrow they would drink tea on the stone table under 'our great white pine'. There was the fish-pond shaped like a shamrock where one of the goldfish died—'*pourtant en Irelande cela porte bonheur, le trèfle, n'est-ce pas?*' The parapet of this pond broke away and had to be repaired and 'Jacques' made some sort of inscription in the damp mortar, for the voice thrilled softly one day as it murmured: '*Maintenant il se lit là pour toujours, ton amour!*' And all through that enchanted spring, first the lilac bushes perfumed the hours spent beneath the pine, and then the acacias that stood in a square round the shamrock pond. Still more that life and hers seemed to Mrs. Bowlby strangely mingled; her own lilacs bloomed and scented the courtyard behind the grey Bank building, and one day as they drove to lunch in the British Legation she drew Jim's attention to the scent of the acacias, which drowned the whole compound in perfume. But Bowlby said, with a sort of shiver, that he hated the smell; and he swore at the chauffeur in French, which he spoke even better than his wife.

The desire grew on Mrs. Bowlby to know more of her pair, who and what they were and how their story ended. But it seemed wholly impossible to find out. Her reticences made her quite unequal to setting anyone on to question the people at the garage again. And

then one day, accidentally, the clue was given to her. She had been
calling at one of the houses in the French Legation; the two house
servants, in blue and silver gowns, stood respectfully on the steps;
her footman held open the door of the car for her. As she seated
herself the voice said in a clear tone of command, '*Deux cent trente,
Por Hua Shan Hut'ung!*' Acting on an impulse which surprised her,
Mrs. Bowlby repeated the order—'*Deux cent trente, Por Hua Shan
Hut'ung,*' she said. Shwang's colleague bowed and shut the door. But
she caught sight, as she spoke, of the faces of the two servants on the
steps. Was it imagination? Surely not. She would have sworn that a
flicker of some emotion—surprise, and recollection—had appeared for
a moment on their sealed and impassive countenances. In Peking the
servants in Legation houses are commonly handed on from employer
to employer, like the furniture, and the fact struck on her with sudden
conviction—they had heard those words before!

Her heart rose with excitement as the car swung out of the
compound into Legation Street. Where was it going? She had no
idea where the Por Hua Shan Hut'ung was. Was she about to get a
stage nearer to the solution of the mystery at last? At the Hatamen
the Buick turned south along the Glacis. So far so good. They left
the Hatamen, bumped into the Suchow Hut'ung, followed on down
the Tung Tsung Pu Hut'ung right into the heart of the East City. Her
breath came fast. It must be right. Now they were skirting the edge of
one of the rubbish-strewn open spaces, and the East Wall rose close
ahead of them. They turned left, parallel with it; turned right again
towards it; stopped. Shwang beckoned to a pancake-seller who was
rolling out his wares in a doorway, and a colloquy in Chinese ensued.
They went on slowly then, down a lane between high walls which
ended at the Wall's very foot, and pulled up some hundred yards short
of it before a high scarlet door, whose rows of golden knobs in fives
betokened the former dwelling of some Chinese of rank.

It was only when Liu came to open the door and held out his
cotton-gloved hand for her cards that Mrs. Bowlby realized that she
had no idea what she was going to do. She could not call on a voice!
She summoned Shwang, Liu's French was not his strong point. 'Ask,'
she said to Shwang, 'who lives here—the T'ai-t'ai's name.' Shwang
rang the bell. There was a long pause. Shwang rang again. There
came a sound of shuffling feet inside; creaking on its hinges the
door opened, and the head of an old Chinaman, thinly bearded and

topped with a little black cap, appeared in the crack. A conversation followed, and then Shwang returned to the car.

'The house is empty,' he said. 'Ask him who lived there last,' said Mrs. Bowlby. Another and longer conversation followed, but at last Shwang came to the window with the information that a foreign T'ai-t'ai, '*Fa-kwa T'ai-t'ai*' (French lady) he thought, had lived there, but she had gone away. With that Mrs. Bowlby had to be content. It was something. It might be much. The car had moved on towards the Wall, seeking a place to turn, when an idea struck her. Telling Shwang to wait, she got out, and glanced along the foot of the Wall in both directions. Yes! Some two hundred yards from where she stood one of those huge ramps, used in former times to ride or drive up on to the summit of the Wall, descended into the dusty strip of waste land at its foot. She hurried towards it, nervously, picking her way between the rough fallen lumps of stone and heaps of rubbish; she was afraid that the servants would regard her action as strange, and that when she reached the foot of the ramp she might not be able to get up it. Since Boxer times the top of the Tartar Wall is forbidden as a promenade, save for a short strip just above the Legation Quarter, and the ramps are stoutly closed at the foot, theoretically. But in China theory and practice do not always correspond, Mrs. Bowlby knew; and as she hurried, she hoped.

Her hope was justified. Though a solid wooden barrier closed the foot of the ramp, a few feet higher up a little bolt-hole, large enough to admit a goat or a small man, had been picked away in the masonry of the parapet. Mrs. Bowlby scrambled through and found herself on the cobbled slope of the ramp; panting a little, she walked up it on to the Wall. The great flagged top, broad enough for two motor-lorries to drive abreast, stretched away to left and right; a thick undergrowth of thorny bushes had sprung up between the flags, and through them wound a little path, manifestly used by goats and goat-herds. Below her Peking lay spread out—a city turned by the trees which grow in every courtyard into the semblance of a green wood, out of which rose the immense gold roofs of the Forbidden City; beyond it, far away, the faint mauve line of the Western Hills hung on the sky.

But Mrs. Bowlby had no eyes for the unparalleled view. Peeping cautiously through the battlements she located the Buick saloon, shining incongruously neat and modern in its squalid and deserted surroundings; by it she took her bearings, and moved with a beating heart along the little path between the thorns. Hoopoes flew out in front of her, calling their sweet note, and perched again, raising and lowering their crests; she never heeded them, nor her torn silk stockings. Now she was above the car; yes, there was the lane up which they had come, and the wall beyond it was the wall of that house! she could see the doorkeeper, doll-like below her, still standing in his scarlet doorway, watching the car curiously. The garden wall stretched up close to the foot of the City Wall itself, so that, as she came abreast of it, the whole compound—the house, with its manifold courtyards, and the formal garden—lay spread out at her feet with the minute perfection of a child's toy farm on the floor.

Mrs. Bowlby stood looking down at it. A dream-like sense of unreality came over her, greater than any yet caused even by her impossible voice. A magnificent white pine, trunk and branches gleaming as if white-washed among its dark needles, rose out of the garden, and below it stood a round stone table among groups of lilacs. Just as the voice had described it! Close by, separated from the pine garden by a wall pierced with a fan-shaped door-way, was another with a goldfish pond shaped like a shamrock, and round it stood a square pleached alley of acacias. Flowers in great tubs bloomed everywhere. Here was the very setting of her lovers' secret idyll, silent, sunny, sweet, it lay under the brooding protection of the Tartar Wall. Here she was indeed near to the heart of her mystery, Mrs. Bowlby felt, as she leaned on the stone parapet, looking down at the deserted garden. A strange fancy came to her that she would have liked to bring Jim here, and people it once again. But she and Jim, she reflected with a little sigh, were staid married people, with no need of a secret haven hidden away in the East City. And with the thought of Jim the claims of everyday life reasserted themselves. She must go—and with a last glance at the garden she hastened back to the car.

During the next day or so Mrs. Bowlby brooded over her new discovery and all that had led to it. Everything—the place where the address had been given by the voice, the flicker of recognition on the faces of the servants at the house in the French Legation, the fact of the doorkeeper in the East City having mentioned a *Fa-kwa t'ai-t'ai* as his late employer, pointed to one thing—that the former owner of the Buick saloon had lived in the house where she had first called on that momentous afternoon. More than ever, now, the thing took hold of her—having penetrated the secret of the voice so far, she felt that

she must follow it further yet. Timid or not, she must brace herself to
ask some questions.

At a dinner a few nights later she found herself seated next to
Mr. van Adam. Mr. van Adam was an elderly American, the *doyen*
of Peking society, who had seen everything and known everyone
since before Boxer days—a walking memory and a mine of social
information. Mrs. Bowlby determined to apply to him. She displayed
unwonted craft. She spoke of Legation compounds in general, and
of the French compound in particular; she praised the garden of the
house where she had called. And then, 'Who lived there before
the Vernets came?' she asked, and waited eagerly for the answer.
Mr. van Adam eyed her a little curiously, she thought, but replied
that it was a certain Count d'Ardennes. 'Was he married?' Mrs.
Bowlby next enquired. Oh yes, he was married right enough—but
the usual reminiscent flow of anecdote seemed to fail Mr. van Adam
in this case. Struggling against a vague sense of difficulty, of a hitch
somewhere, Mrs. Bowlby pushed on nevertheless to an enquiry as to
what the Comtesse d'Ardennes was like. 'A siren!' Mr. van Adam
replied briefly—adding 'lovely creature, though, as ever stepped.'

He edged away rather from the subject, or so it seemed to Mrs.
Bowlby, but she nerved herself to another question—'Had they a
car?' Mr. van Adam fairly stared, at that; then he broke into a laugh.
'Car?' Why, yes—she went everywhere in a yellow Buick—we used
to call it "the canary".' The talk drifted off on to cars in general,
and Mrs. Bowlby let it drift; she was revolving in her mind the
form of her last question. Her curiosity must look odd, she reflected
nervously; it was all more difficult, somehow, than she had expected.
Her craft was failing her—she could not think of a good excuse
for further questions that would not run the risk of betraying her
secret. There must have been a scandal—there *would* have been,
of course; but Mrs. Bowlby was not of the order of women who in
Peking ask cooly at the dinner-table: 'And what was *her* scandal?'
At dessert, in desperation, she put it hurriedly, badly—'when did the
d'Ardennes leave?'

Mr. van Adam paused before he answered: 'Oh, going on for a year
ago, now. she was ill, they said—looked it, anyway—and went back
to France. He was transferred to Bangkok soon after, but I don't know
if she's gone out to him again. The East didn't suit her.' 'Oh, poor
thing!' murmured Mrs. Bowlby, softly and sincerely, her heart full of

pity for the woman with the lovely voice and the lovely name, whose failing health had severed her from her Jacques. Not even love such as hers could control this wretched feeble body, reflected Mrs. Bowlby, whom few places suited. The ladies rose, and too absorbed in her reflections to pay any further attention to Mr. van Adam, she rose and went with them.

At this stage, Mrs. Bowlby went to Pei-t'ai-ho for the summer. Peking, with a temperature of over 100 degrees in the shade, is no place for delicate women in July and August. Cars are not allowed on the sandy roads of the pleasant straggling seaside resort, and missionaries and diplomatists alike are obliged to fall back on rickshas and donkeys as a means of locomotion. So the Buick saloon was left in Peking with Jim, who came down for long weekends as often as he could. Thus separated from her car, and in changed surroundings, Mrs. Bowlby endeavoured to take stock of the whole affair dispassionately. Get away from it she could not. Bathing, idling on the hot sunny beach, walking through the green paths bordered with maize and kaoliang, sitting out in the blessedly cool dark after dinner, she found herself as much absorbed as ever in this personality whose secret life she so strangely shared. Curiously enough, she felt no wish to ask any more questions of anyone. With her knowledge of Madame d'Ardennes' name the sense of eavesdropping had returned in full force. One thing struck her as a little odd: that if there *had* been a scandal she should not have heard of it—in Peking, where scandals were innumerable, and treated with startling openness and frank disregard. Perhaps she had been mistaken, though, in Mr. van Adam's attitude, and there had not been one. Or—the illumination came to her belated and suddenly—hadn't Mr. van Adam's son in the Customs, who went home last year, been called Jack? He had! and Mrs. Bowlby shuddered at the thought of her clumsiness. She could not have chosen a worse person for her enquiries.

Another thing, at Pei-t'ai-ho, she realized with a certain astonishment—that she had not been perceptibly shocked by this intrigue. Mrs. Bowlby had always believed herself to hold thoroughly conventional British views on marriage; the late owner of the Buick saloon clearly had not, yet Mrs. Bowlby had never thought of censuring her. She had even been a little resentful of Mr. van Adam's calling her a 'siren'. Sirens were cold-hearted creatures, who lured men frivolously to their doom; her voice was not the voice of a siren. Mrs. Bowlby was all on the side of her voice. Didn't such love justify itself, argued Mrs. Bowlby, awake at last to her own moral failure to condemn another, or very nearly? Perhaps, she caught herself thinking, if people knew as much about all love-affairs as she knew about this one, they would be less censorious.

Mrs. Bowlby stayed late at pei-t'ai-ho, well on into September, till the breezes blew chilly off the sea, the green paths had faded to a dusty yellow, and the maize and kaolaing were being cut. When she returned to Peking she was at once very busy—calling begins all over again after the seaside holiday, and she spent hours in the Buick saloon leaving cards. The voice was with her again, as before. But something had overshadowed the blissful happiness of the spring days; there was an undernote of distress, of foreboding, often, in the conversations. What exactly caused it she could not make out. But it increased, and one day half-way through October, driving in the East City, the voice dropped away into a burst of passionate sobbing. This distressed Mrs. Bowlby extraordinarily. It was a strange and terrible thing to sit in the car with those low, heart-broken sounds at her side. She almost put out her arms to take and comfort the lovely unhappy creature—but there was only empty air, and the empty seat, with her bag, her book, and her little calling list. Obeying one of those sudden impulses which the voice alone seemed to call out in her, she abandoned her calls and told Shwang to drive to the Por Hua Shan Hut'ung. As they neared it the sobs beside her ceased, and murmured apologies for being *un peu énervé* followed.

When she reached the house Mrs. Bowlby got out, and again climbed the ramp on to the Tartar Wall. The thorns and bushes between the battlements were brown and sere, and ho hoopoes flew and fluted among them. She reached the spot where she could look down into the garden. The lilacs were bare now, as her own were; the tubs of flowers were gone, and heaps of leaves had drifted round the feet of the acacias—only the white pine stood up, stately and untouched by the general decay. A deep melancholy took hold of Mrs. Bowlby; already shaken by the sobs in the car, the desolation of this deserted autumn garden weighed with an intense oppression on her spirit. She turned away, slowly, and slowly descended to the Buick. The sense of impending misfortune had seized on her too; something, she vaguely felt, had come to an end in that garden.

As she was about to get into the car another impulse moved her. She felt an overmastering desire to enter that garden and see its features from close at hand. The oppression still hung over her, and she felt that a visit to the garden might in some way resolve it. She looked in her purse and found a five-dollar note. Handing it to the startled Shwang—'Give that,' said Mrs. Bowlby, 'to the *k'ai-men-ti*, and tell him I wish to walk in the garden of that house.' Shwang bowed; rang the bell, conversed; Mrs. Bowlby waited, trembling with impatience, till the clinching argument of the note was at last produced, and the old man whom she had seen before beckoned to her to enter.

She followed him through several courtyards. It was a rambling Chinese house, little modernized; the blind paper lattices of the windows looked blankly on to the miniature lakes and rocky landscapes in the open courts. Finally they passed through a round doorway into the garden below the Tartar Wall, and bowing, the old custodian stood aside to let her walk alone.

Before her rose the white pine, and she strolled towards it, and sitting down on a marble bench beside the round stone table, gazed about her. Beautiful even in its decay, melancholy, serene, and garden lay under the battlements which cut the pale autumn sky behind her. And here the owner of the voice had sat, hidden and secure, her lover beside her! A sudden burst of tears surprised Mrs. Bowlby. Cruel Life, she thought, which parts dear lovers. Had *she* too sat here alone? A sharp unexpected sense of her own solitude drove Mrs. Bowlby up from her seat. This visit was a mistake; her oppression was not lightened; to have sat in this place seemed somehow to have involved herself in the disaster and misery of that parted pair. She wandered on, through the fan-shaped doorway, and came to a halt beside the goldfish pond. Staring at it through her tears, she noticed the repair to the coping of which the voice had spoken, where 'Jacques' had made an inscription in the damp mortar. She moved round to the place where it still showed white against the grey surface, murmuring, '*Maintenant il se lit là pour toujours, ton amour!*'—the phrase of the voice had stayed rooted in her mind. Stooping down, she read the inscription, scratched out neatly and carefully with a penknife in the fine plaster:

'Douce sépulture, mon coeur dans ton coeur,
Doux Paradis, mon âme dans ton âme.'

And below two sets of initials:

A. de A.
de
J. St. G. B. B.

The verse touched Mrs. Bowlby to fresh tears, and it was actually a moment or two before she focussed her attention on the initials. When she did, she started back as though a serpent had stung her, and shut her eyes, and stood still. Then with a curious blind movement she opened her bag and took out one of her own cards, and laid it on the coping beside the inscription, as if to compare them. Mrs. J. St. G. B. Bowlby—the fine black letters stared up at her, uncompromising and clear, from the white oblong, beside the capitals cut in the plaster. There could be no mistake. Her mystery was solved at last, but it seemed as if she could not take it in. 'Jim?' murmured Mrs. Bowlby to herself, as if puzzled—and then 'Jacques?' Slowly, while she stood there, all the connections and verifications unrolled themselves, backwards in her mind, with devastating certainty and force. Her sentiment, her intuition on the wall had been terribly right—something *had* come to an end in that garden that day. Standing by the shamrock pond, with the first waves of an engulfing desolation sweeping over her, hardly conscious of her words, she whispered: *Pourtant cela porte bonheur, le trèfle, n'est ce pas?'*

And with that second quotation from the voice she seemed at last to wake from the sort of stupor in which she had stood. Intolerable! She must hear no more. Passing back, almost running, into the pine garden, she beckoned to the old *k'ai-men-ti* take her out. He led her again, bowing, through the courtyards to the great gateway. Through the open red and gold doors she saw the Buick saloon, dark and shiny, standing as she had so often, and with what pleasure, seen it stand before how many doors? She stopped and looked round her almost wildly—behind her the garden, before her the Buick! Liu caught sight of her, and flew to hold open the door. But Mrs. Bowlby did not get in. She made Shwang call a ricksha, and when it came ordered him to direct the coolie to take her to the Bank house. Shwang, exercising the respectful supervision which Chinese servants are wont to bestow on their employers, reminded her that she was to go to the polo to pick up the *lao'yé*, Bowlby. Before his astonished eye his mistress shuddered visibly from head to foot. 'The Bank! The Bank!' she repeated, with a sort of desperate impatience.

Standing before his scarlet door, lighting his little black and silver pipe, the old *k'ai-men-ti* watched them go. First the ricksha, with a small drooping grey figure in it, lurched down the dusty *hu-t'ung*, and after it, empty, bumped the Buick saloon.

1933

Shambleau

C. L. MOORE

Man was conquered space before. You may be sure of that. Somewhere beyond the Egyptians, in that dimness out of which come echoes of half-mythical names—Atlantis, Mu—somewhere back of history's first beginnings there must have been an age when mankind, like us today, built cities of steel to house its star-roving ships, and knew the names of the planets in their own native tongues—heard Venus' people call their wet world 'Sha-ardol' in that soft, sweet slurring speech and mimicked Mar's guttural 'Lakkdiz' from the harsh tongues of Mars' dryland dwellers. You may be sure of it. Man has conquered Space before, and out of that conquest faint, faint echoes run still through a world that has forgotten the very fact of a civilization which must have been as mighty as our own. There have been too many myths and legends for us to doubt it. The myth of the Medusa, for instance, can never have had its roots in the soil of Earth. That tale of the snake-haired Gorgon whose gaze turned he gazer to stone never originated about any creature that Earth nourished. And those ancient Greeks who told the story must have remembered, dimly and half believing, a tale of antiquity about some strange being from one of the outlying planets their remotest ancestors once trod.

'Shambleau! Ha . . . Shambleau!' The wild hysteria of the mob rocketed from wall to wall of Lakkdarol's narrow streets and the storming of heavy boots over the slag-red pavement made an ominous undernote to that swelling bay, 'Shambleau! Shambleau!'

Northwest Smith heard it coming and stepped into the nearest doorway, laying a wary hand on his heat-gun's grip, and his colourless eyes narrowed. Strange sounds were common enough in the streets of Earth's latest colony on Mars—a raw, red little town where anything might happen, and very often did. But Northwest Smith, whose name is known and respected in every dive and wild outpost on a dozen wild planets, was a cautious man, despite his reputation. He set his back against the wall and gripped his pistol, and heard the rising shout come nearer and nearer.

Then into his range of vision flashed a red running figure, dodging like a hunted hare from shelter to shelter in the narrow street. It was a girl—a berry-brown girl in a single tattered garment whose scarlet burnt the eyes with its brilliance. She ran wearily, and he could hear her gasping breath from where he stood. As she came into view he saw her hesitate and lean one hand against the wall for support, and glance wildly around for shelter. She must not have seen him in the depths of the doorway, for as the bay of the mob grew louder and the pounding of feet sounded almost at the corner she gave a despairing little moan and dodged into the recess at his very side.

When she saw him standing there, tall and leather-brown, hand on his heat-gun, she sobbed once, inarticulately, and collapsed at his feet, a huddle of burning scarlet and bare, brown limbs.

Smith had not seen her face, but she was a girl, and sweetly made and in danger; and though he had not the reputation of a chivalrous man, something in her hopeless huddle at his feet touched that chord of sympathy for the underdog that stirs in every Earthman, and he pushed her gently into the corner behind him and jerked out his gun, just as the first of the running mob rounded the corner.

It was a motley crowd, Earthmen and Martians and a sprinkling of Venusian swampmen and strange, nameless denizens of unnamed planets—a typical Lakkdarol mob. When the first of them turned the corner and saw the empty street before them there was a faltering in the rush, and the foremost spread out and began to search the doorways on both sides of the street.

'Looking for something?' Smith's sardonic call sounded clear above the clamour of the mob.

The turned. The shouting died for a moment as they took in the scene before them—tall Earthman in the space-explorer's leathern garb, all one colour from the burning of savage suns save for the sinister pallor of his no-coloured eyes in a scarred and resolute face, gun in his steady hand and the scarlet girl crouched behind him, panting.

The foremost of the crowd—a burly Earthman in tattered leather from which the Patrol insignia had been ripped away—stared for a moment with a strange expression of incredulity on his face overspreading the savage exultation of the chase. Then he let loose a deep-throated bellow, 'Shambleau!' and lunged forward. Behind him the mob took up the cry again, 'Shambleau! Shambleau! Shambleau!' and surged after.

Smith, lounging negligently against the wall, arms folded and gun-hand draped over his left forearm, looked incapable of swift motion, but at the leader's first forward step the pistol swept in a practised half-circle and the dazzle of blue-white heat leaping from its muzzle seared an arc in the slag pavement at his feet. It was an old gesture, and not a man in the crowd but understood it. The foremost recoiled swiftly against the surge of those in the rear, and for a moment there was confusion as the tides met and struggled. Smith's mouth curled into a grim curve as he watched. The man in the mutilated Patrol uniform lifted a threatening fist and stepped to the very edge of the deadline, while the crowd rocked to and fro behind him.

'Are you crossing that line?' queried Smith in an ominously gentle voice.

'We want that girl!'

'Come and get her!' Recklessly Smith grinned into his face. He saw danger there, but his defiance was not the foolhardy gesture it seemed. An expert psychologist of mobs from long experience, he sensed no murder here. Not a gun had appeared in any hand in the crowd. They desired the girl with an inexplicable bloodthirstiness he was at a loss to understand, but towards himself he sensed no such fury. A mauling he might expect, but his life was in no danger. Guns would have appeared before now if they were coming out at all. So he grinned in the man's angry face and leaned lazily against the wall.

Behind their self-appointed leader the crowd milled impatiently, and threatening voices began to rise again. Smith heard the girl moan at his feet.

'What do you want with her?' he demanded.

'She's Shambleau! Shambleau, you fool! Kick her out of there—we'll take care of her!'

'I'm taking care of her,' drawled Smith.

'She's Shambleau, I tell you! Damn your hide, man, we never let those things live! Kick her out here!'

The repeated name had no meaning to him, but Smith's innate stubbornness rose defiantly as the crowd surged forward to the very edge of the arc, their clamour growing louder. 'Shambleau! Kick her out here! Give us Shambleau! Shambleau!'

Smith dropped his indolent pose like a cloak and planted both feet wide, swinging up his gun threateningly. 'Keep back!' he yelled. 'She's mine! Keep back!'

He had no intention of using that heat-beam. He knew by now that they would not kill him unless he started the gun-play himself, and he did not mean to give up his life for any girl alive. But a severe mauling he expected, and he braced himself instinctively as the mob heaved within itself.

To his astonishment a thing happened then that he had never known to happen before. At his shouted defiance the foremost of the mob—those who had heard him clearly—drew back a little, not in alarm but evidently surprised. The ex-Patrolman said, 'Yours! She's *yours?*' in a voice from which puzzlement crowded out the anger.

Smith spread his booted legs wide before the crouching figure and flourished his gun.

'Yes,' he said. 'And I'm keeping her! Stand back there!'

The man stared at him wordlessly, and horror and disgust and incredulity mingled on his weather-beaten face. The incredulity triumphed for a moment and he said again:

'*Yours!*'

Smith nodded defiance.

The man stepped back suddenly, unutterable contempt in his very pose. He waved an arm to the crowd and said loudly. 'It's—his!' and the press melted away, gone silent, too, and the look of contempt spread from face to face.

The ex-Patrolman spat on the slag-paved street and turned his back indifferently. 'Keep her, then,' he advised briefly over one shoulder. 'But don't let her out again in this town!'

Smith stared in perplexity almost open-mouthed as the suddenly scornful mob began to break up. His mind was in a whirl. That such bloodthirsty animosity should vanish in a breath he could not believe. And the curious mingling of contempt and disgust on the faces he saw baffled him even more. Lakkdarol was anything but a puritan town—it did not enter his head for a moment that his claiming the brown girl as his own had caused that strangely shocked revulsion to spread through the crowd. No, it was something deeper-rooted than that. Instinctive, instant disgust had been in the faces he saw—they would have looked less so if he had admitted cannibalism or *Pharol*-worship.

And as they were leaving his vicinity as swiftly as if whatever unknowing sin had been committed were contagious. The street was emptying as rapidly as it had filled. He saw a sleek Venusian glance back over his shoulder as he turned the corner and sneer, 'Shambleau!' and the word awoke a new line of speculation in Smith's mind. Shambleau! Vaguely of French origin it must be. And strange enough to hear it from the lips of Venusians and Martian drylanders, but it was their use of it that puzzled him more. 'We never let those things live,' the ex-Patrolman had said. It reminded him dimly of something . . . an ancient line from some writing in his own tongue . . . 'Thou shalt not suffer a witch to live.' He smiled to himself at the similarity, and simultaneously was aware of the girl at his elbow.

She had risen soundlessly. He turned to face her, sheathing his gun and stared at first with curiosity and then in the entirely frank openness with which men regard that which is not wholly human. For she was not. He knew it at a glance, though the brown, sweet body was shaped like a woman's and she wore the garment of scarlet—he saw it was leather—with an ease that few unhuman beings achieve towards clothing. He knew it from the moment he looked into her eyes, and a shiver of unrest went over him as he met them. They were frankly green as young grass, with slit-like, feline pupils that pulsed unceasingly, and there was a look of dark, animal wisdom in their depths—that look of the best which sees more than man.

There was no hair upon her face—neither brows nor lashes, and he would have sworn that the tight scarlet turban bound around her head covered baldness. She had three fingers and a thumb, and her feet had four digits apiece too, and all sixteen of them were tipped with round claws that sheathed back into the flesh like a cat's. She ran her tongue over her lips—a thin, pink, flat tongue as feline as her eyes—and spoke with difficulty. He felt that that throat and tongue had never been shaped for human speech.

'Not—afraid now,' she said softly, and her little teeth were white and pointed as a kitten's.

'What did they want you for?' he asked her curiously. 'What had you done? Shambleau . . . is that your name?'

'I—not talk your—speech,' she demurred hesitantly.

'Well, try to—I want to know. Why were they chasing you? Will you be safe on the street now, or hadn't you better get indoors somewhere? They looked dangerous.'

'I—go with you.' She brought it out with difficulty.

'Say you!' Smith grinned. 'What are you, anyhow? You look like a kitten to me.'

'Shambleau.' She said it sombrely.

'Where d'you live? Are you a Martian?'

'I come from—from far—from long ago—far country—'

'Wait!' laughed Smith. 'You're getting your wires crossed! You're not a Martian?'

She drew herself up very straight beside him, lifting the turbaned head, and there was something queenly in the poise of her.

'Martian?' she said scornfully. 'My people—are—are—you have no word. Your speech—hard for me.'

'What's yours? I might know it—try me.'

She lifted her head and met his eyes squarely, and there was in hers a subtle amusement—he could have sworn it.

'Some day I—speak to you in—my own language,' she promised, and the pink tongue flicked out over her lips, swiftly, hungrily.

Approaching footsteps on the red pavement interrupted Smith's reply. A dryland Martian came past, reeling a little and exuding an aroma of *segir*-whisky, the Venusian brand. When he caught the red flash of the girl's tatters he turned his head sharply, and as his *segir*-steeped brain took in the fact of her presence, he lurched towards the recess unsteadily, bawling, 'Shambleau, by *Pharol*! Shambleau!' and reached out a clutching hand.

Smith struck it aside contemptuously.

'On your way, drylander,' he advised.

The man drew back and stared, blear-eyed.

'Yours, eh?' he croaked. '*Zut*! You're welcome to it!' And like the ex-Patrolman before him spat on the pavement and turned away, muttering harshly in the blasphemous tongue of the drylands.

Smith watched him shuffle off, and there was a crease between his colourless eyes, a nameless unease rising within him.

'Come on,' he said abruptly to the girl. 'If this sort of thing is going to happen we'd better get indoors. Where shall I take you?'

'With—you,' she murmured.

He stared down into the flat green eyes. Those ceaselessly pulsing pupils disturbed him, but it seemed to him, vaguely, that behind the animal shallows of her gaze was a shutter—a closed barrier that might at any moment open to reveal the very deeps of that dark knowledge he sensed there.

Roughly he said again, 'Come on, then,' and stepped down into the street.

She pattered along a pace or two behind him, making no effort to keep up with his long strides, and though Smith—as men know from Venus to Jupiter's moons—walks as softly as a cat, even in spacemen's boots, the girl at his heels slid like a shadow over the rough pavement, making no sound that even the lightness of his footsteps was loud in the empty street.

Smith chose the less frequented ways of Lakkdarol, and somewhat shamefacedly thanked his nameless gods that his lodgings were not far away, for the few pedestrians he met turned and stared after the two with that by now familiar mingling of horror and contempt which he was as far as ever from understanding.

The room he had engaged was a single cubicle in a lodging-house on the edge of the city. Lakkdarol, raw camp-town that it was in those days, could have furnished little better anywhere within its limits, and Smith's errand there was not one he wished to advertise. He had slept in worse places than this before, and knew that he would do so again.

There was no one in sight when he entered, and the girl slipped up the stairs at his heels and vanished through the door, shadowy, unseen by anyone in the house. Smith closed the door and leaned his broad shoulders against the panels, regarding her speculatively.

She took in what little the room had to offer in a glance—frowsy bed, rickety table, mirror hanging unevenly and cracked against the wall, unpainted chairs—a typical camp-town room in an Earth settlement abroad. She accepted its poverty in that single glance, dismissed it, then crossed to the window and leaned out for a moment, gazing across the low roof-tops towards the barren countryside beyond, red slag under the late afternoon sun.

'You can stay here,' said Smith abruptly, 'until I leave town. I'm waiting here for a friend to come in from Venus. Have you eaten?'

'Yes,' said the girl quickly. 'I shall—need no—food for—a while.'

'Well—' Smith glanced around the room. 'I'll be in some time tonight. You can go or stay just as you please. Better lock the door behind me.'

With no more formality than that he left her. The door closed and he heard the key turn, and smiled to himself. He did not expect then, ever to see her again.

He went down the steps and out into the late-slanting sunlight with a mind so full of other matters that the brown girl receded very quickly into the background. Smith's errand in Lakkdarol, like most of his errands, is better not spoken of. Man lives as he must, and Smith's living was a perilous affair outside the law and ruled by the ray-gun only. It is enough to say that the shipping-port and its cargoes outbound interested him deeply just now, and that the friend he awaited was Yarol the Venusian, in that swift little Edsel ship the *Maid* that can flash from world to world with a derisive speed that laughs at Patrol boats and leaves pursuers floundering in the ether far behind. Smith and Yarol and the *Maid* were a trinity that had caused the Patrol leaders much worry and many grey hairs in the past, and the future looked very bright to Smith himself that evening as he left his lodging-house.

Lakkdarol roars by night, as Earthmen's camp-towns have a way of doing on every planet where Earth's outposts are, and it was beginning lustily as Smith went down among the awakening lights towards the centre of town. His business there does not concern us. He mingled with the crowds where the lights were brightest, and there was the click of ivory counters and the jingle of silver, and red *segir* gurgled invitingly from black Venusian bottles, and much later Smith strolled homeward under the moving moons of Mars, and if the street wavered a little under his feet now and then—why, that is only understandable. Not even Smith could drink red *segir* at every bar from the *Martian Lamb* to the *New Chicago* and remain entirely steady on his feet. But he found his way back with very little difficulty—considering—and spent a good five minutes hunting for his key before he remembered he had left it in the inner lock for the girl.

He knocked then, and there was no sound of footsteps from within, but in a few moments the latch clicked and the door swung open. She retreated soundlessly before him as he entered, and took up her favourite place against the window, leaning back on the sill and outlined against the starry sky beyond. The room was in darkness.

Smith flipped the switch by the door and then leaned back against the panels, steadying himself. The cool night air had sobered him a little, and his head was clear enough—liquor went to Smith's feet, not his head, or he would never have come this far along the lawless way he had chosen. He lounged against the door now and regarded the girl in the sudden glare of the bulbs, blinking a little as much at the scarlet of her clothing as at the light.

'So you stayed,' he said.

'I—waited,' she answered softly, leaning farther back against the sill and clasping the rough wood with slim, three-fingered hands, pale-brown against the darkness.

'Why?'

She did not answer that, but her mouth curved into a slow smile. On a woman it would have been reply enough—provocative, daring. On Shambleau there was something pitiful and horrible in it—so human on the face of one half-animal. And yet . . . that sweet brown body curving so softly from the tatters of scarlet leather—the velvety texture of that brownness—the white-flashing smile . . . Smith was aware of a stirring excitement within him. After all—time would be hanging heavy now until Yarol came . . . Speculatively he allowed the steel-pale eyes to wander over her, with a slow regard that missed nothing. And when he spoke he was aware that his voice had deepened a little.

'Come here,' he said.

She came forward slowly, on bare clawed feet that made no slightest sound on the floor, and stood before him with downcast eyes and mouth trembling in that pitifully human smile. He took her by the shoulders—velvety soft shoulders, of a creamy smoothness that was not the texture of human flesh. A little tremor went over her, perceptibly, at the contact of his hands. Northwest Smith caught his breath suddenly and dragged her to him . . . sweet yielding brownness in the circle of his arms . . . heard her own breath catch and quicken as her velvety arms closed about his neck. And then he was looking down into her face, very near, and the green animal eyes met his with the pulsing pupils and the flicker of—something—deep behind their shallows—and through the rising clamour of his blood even as he stooped his lips to hers, Smith felt something deep within him shudder away—inexplicable, instinctive, revolted. What it might be he had no words to tell, but the very touch of her was suddenly loathsome—so soft a velvet and unhuman—and it might have been an animal's face that lifted itself to his mouth—the dark knowledge looked hungrily from the darkness of those slit pupils—and for a mad instant he knew that same wild, feverish revulsion he had seen in the faces of the mob . . .

'God!' he gasped, a far more ancient invocation against evil than he realized, then or ever, and he gripped her arms from his neck, swung her away with such a force that she reeled half across the room. Smith fell back against the door, breathing heavily, and stared at her while the wild revolt died slowly within him.

She had fallen to the floor beneath the window, and as she lay there against the wall with bent head he saw, curiously, that her turban had slipped—the turban that he had been so sure covered baldness—and a lock of scarlet hair fell below the binding leather, hair as scarlet as her garment, as unhumanly red as her eyes were unhumanly green. He stared, and shook his head dizzily and stared again, for it seemed to him that the thick lock of crimson had moved, *squirmed* of itself against her cheek.

At the contact of it her hands flew up and she tucked it away with a very human gesture and then dropped her head again into her hands. And from the deep shadow of her fingers he thought she was staring up at him covertly.

Smith drew a deep breath and passed a hand across his forehead. The inexplicable moment had gone as quickly as it came—too swiftly for him to understand or analyze. 'Got to lay off the *segir*,' he told himself unsteadily. Had he imagined that scarlet hair? After all, she was no more than a pretty brown girl-creature from one of the many half-human races peopling the planets. No more than that, after all. A pretty little thing, but animal . . . He laughed a little shakily.

'No more of that,' he said. 'God knows I'm no angel, but there's got to be a limit somewhere. Here.' He crossed to the bed and sorted out a pair of blankets from the untidy heap, tossing them to the far corner of the room. 'You can sleep there.'

Wordlessly she rose from the floor and began to rearrange the blankets, the uncomprehending resignation of the animal eloquent in every line of her.

Smith had a strange dream that night. He thought he had awakened to a room full of darkness and moonlight and moving shadows, for the nearer moon of Mars was racing through the sky and everything on the planets below her was endued with a restless life in the dark. And something . . . some nameless, unthinkable thing . . . was coiled about his throat . . . something like a soft snake, wet and warm. It lay loose and light about his neck . . . and it was moving

gently, very gently, with a soft, caressive pressure that sent little
thrills of delight through every nerve and fibre of him, a perilous
delight—beyond physical pleasure, deeper than joy of the mind. That
warm softness was caressing the very root of his soul with a terrible
intimacy. The ecstasy of it left him weak, and yet he knew—in a
flash of knowledge born of this impossible dream—that this should not
be handled . . . And with that knowledge a horror broke upon him,
turning pleasure into a rapture of revulsion, hateful, horrible—but still
most foully sweet. He tried to lift his hands and tear the dream-
monstrosity from his throat—tried but half-heartedly; for though his
soul was revolted to its very deeps, yet the delight of his body was so
great that his hands all but refused the attempt. But when at last he
tried to lift his arms a cold shock went over him and he found that he
could not stir . . . his body lay stony as marble beneath the blankets,
a living marble that shuddered with a dreadful delight through every
rigid vein.

The revulsion grew strong upon him as he struggled against the
paralyzing dream—a struggle of soul against sluggish body—titanically,
until the moving dark was streaked with blankness that clouded and
closed about him at last and he sank back into the oblivion from
which he had awakend.

Next morning, when the bright sunlight shining through Mars' clear
thin air awakened him, Smith lay for a while trying to remember. The
dream had been more vivid than reality, but he could not now quite
recall . . . only that it had been more sweet and horrible than anything
else in life. He lay puzzling for a while, until a soft sound from the
corner aroused him from his thoughts and he sat up to see the girl
lying in a cat-like coil on her bankets, watching him with round,
grave eyes. He regarded her somewhat ruefully.

'Morning,' he said. 'I've just had the devil of a dream . . . Well,
hungry?'

She shook her head silently, and he could have sworn there was a
covert gleam of strange amusement in her eyes.

He stretched and yawned, dismissing the nightmare temporarily
from his mind.

'What am I going to do with you?' he enquired, turning to more
immediate matters. 'I'm leaving here in a day or two and I can't take
you along, you know. Where'd you come from in the first place?'

Again she shook her head.

'Not telling? Well, it's your own business. You can stay here until I give up the room. From then on you'll have to do your own worrying.'

He swung his feet to the floor and reached for his clothes.

Ten minutes later, slipping the heat-gun into its holster at his thigh, Smith turned to the girl. 'There's food-concentrate in that box on the table. It ought to hold you until I get back. And you'd better lock the door again after I've gone.'

Her wide, unwavering stare was his only answer, and he was not sure she had understood, but at any rate the lock clicked after him as before, and he went down the steps with a faint grin on his lips.

The memory of last night's extraordinary dream was slipping from him, as such memories do, and by the time he had reached the street the girl and the dream and all of yesterday's happenings were blotted out by the sharp necessities of the present.

Again the intricate business that had brought him here claimed his attention. He went about it to the exclusion of all else, and there was a good reason behind everything he did from the moment he stepped out into the street until the time when he turned back again at evening; though had one chosen to follow him during the day his apparently aimless rambling through Lakkdarol would have seemed very pointless.

He must have spent two hours at the least idling by the space-port, watching with sleepy, colourless eyes the ships that came and went, the passengers, the vessels lying at wait, the cargoes—particularly the cargoes. He made the rounds of the town's saloons once more, consuming many glasses of varied liquors in the course of the day and engaging in idle conversation with men of all races and worlds, usually in their own languages, for Smith was a linguist of repute among his contemporaries. He heard the gossip of the spaceways, news from a dozen planets of a thousand different events. He heard the latest joke about the Venusian Emperor and the latest report on the Chino-Aryan war and the latest song hot from the lips of Rose Robertson, whom every man on the civilized planets adored as 'the Georgia Rose.' He passed the day quite profitably, for his own purposes, which do not concern us now, and it was not until late evening, when he turned homeward again, that the thought of the brown girl in his room took definite shape in his mind, though it had been lurking there, formless and submerged, all day.

He had no idea what comprised her usual diet, but he bought a can of New York roast beef and one of Venusian frogbroth and a dozen fresh canal-apples and two pounds of that Earth lettuce that grows so vigorously in the fertile canal-soil of Mars. He felt that she must surely find something to her liking in this broad variety of edibles, and—for his day had been very satisfactory—he hummed *The Green Hills of Earth* to himself in a surprisingly good baritone as he climbed the stairs.

The door was locked, as before, and he was reduced to kicking the lower panels gently with his boot, for his arms were full. She opened the door with that softness that was characteristic of her and stood regarding him in the semi-darkness as he stumbled to the table with his load. The room was unlit again.

'Why don't you turn on the lights?' he demanded irritably after he had barked his shin on the chair by the table in an effort to deposit his burden there.

'Light and—dark—they are alike—to me,' she murmured.

'Cat eyes, eh? Well, you look the part. Here, I've brought you some dinner. Take your choice. Fond of roast beef? Or how about a little frog-broth?'

She shook her head and backed away a step.

'No,' she said. 'I can not—eat your food.'

Smith's brows wrinkled. 'Didn't you have any of the food-tablets?'

Again the red turban shook negatively.

'Then you haven't had anything for—why, more than twenty-four hours! You must be starved.'

'Not hungry,' she denied.

'What can I find for you to eat, then? There's time yet if I hurry. You've got to eat, child.'

'I shall—eat,' she said softly. 'Before long—I shall—feed. Have no—worry.'

She turned away then and stood at the window, looking out over the moonlit landscape as if to end the conversation. Smith cast her a puzzled glance as he opened the can of roast beef. There had been an odd undernote in that assurance that, undefinably, he did not like. And the girl had teeth and tongue and presumably a fairly human digestive system, to judge from her human form. It was nonsense for her to pretend that he could find nothing that she could eat. She must have had some of the food concentrate after all, he decided, prying up the thermos lid of the inner container to release the long-sealed savour of the hot meat inside.

'Well, if you won't eat you won't,' he observed philosophically as he poured hot broth and diced beef into the dish-like lid of the thermos can and extracted the spoon from its hiding-place between the inner and outer receptacles. She turned a little to watch him as he pulled up a rickety chair and sat down to the food, and after a while the realization that her green gaze was fixed so unwinkingly upon him made the man nervous and he said between bites of creamy canal-apple, 'Why don't you try a little of this? It's good.'

'The food—I eat is—better,' her soft voice told him in its hesitant murmur, and again he felt rather than heard a faint undernote of unpleasantness in the words. A sudden suspicion struck him as he pondered on that last remark—some vague memory of horror-tales told about campfires in the past—and he swung round in the chair to look at her, a tiny, creeping fear unaccountably arising. There had been that in her words—in her unspoken words that menaced . . .

She stood up beneath his gaze demurely, wide green eyes with their pulsing pupils meeting his without a falter. But her mouth was scarlet and her teeth were sharp . . .

'What food do you eat?' he demanded. And then, after a pause, very softly, 'Blood?'

She stared at him for a moment, uncomprehending; then something like amusement curled her lips and she said scornfully. 'You think me—vampire, eh? No—I am Shambleau!'

Unmistakably there were scorn and amusement in her voice at the suggestion, but as unmistakably she knew what he meant—accepted it as a logical suspicion—vampires! Fairy-tales—but fairy-tales this unhuman, outland creature was most familiar with. Smith was not a credulous man, nor a superstitious one, but he had seen too many strange things himself to doubt that the wildest legend might have a basis of fact. And there was something namelessly strange about her . . .

He puzzled over it for a while between deep bites of the canal-apple. And though he wanted to question her about a great many things, he did not, for he knew how futile it would be.

He said nothing more until the meat was finished and another canal-apple had followed the first, and he had cleared away the meal by the simple expedient of tossing the empty can out of the window. Then he lay back in the chair and surveyed her from half-closed eyes, colourless in a face tanned like saddle-leather. And again he was conscious of the brown, soft curves of her, velvety-subtle arcs and planes of smooth flesh under the tatters of scarlet leather. Vampire she might be, unhuman she certainly was, but desirable beyond words as she sat submissive beneath his low regard, her red-turbaned head bent, her clawed fingers lying in her lap. They sat very still for a while, and the silence throbbed between them.

She was so like a woman—an Earth woman—sweet and submissive and demure, and softer than soft fur, if he could forget the three-fingered claws and the pulsing eyes—and that deeper strangeness beyond words . . . (Had he dreamed that red lock of hair that moved? Had it been *segir* that woke the wild revulsion he knew when he held her in his arms? Why had the mob so thirsted for her?) He sat and stared, and despite the mystery of her and the half-suspicions that thronged his mind—for she was so beautifully soft and curved under those revealing tatters—he slowly realized that his pulses were mounting, became aware of a kindling within . . . brown girl-creature with downcast eyes . . . and then the lids lifted and the green flatness of a cat's gaze met his, and last night's revulsion woke swiftly again, like a warning bell that clanged as their eyes met—animal, after all, too sleek and soft for humanity, and that inner strangeness . . .

Smith shrugged and sat up. His failings were legion, but the weakness of the flesh was not among the major ones. He motioned the girl to her pallet of blankets in the corner and turned to his own bed.

From deeps of sound sleep he awoke much later. He awoke suddenly and completely, and with that inner excitement that presages something momentous. He awoke to brilliant moonlight, turning the room so bright that he could see the scarlet of the girl's rags as she sat up on her pallet. She was awake, she was sitting with her shoulder half turned to him and her head bent, and some warning instinct crawled coldly up his spine as he watched what she was doing. And yet it was a very ordinary thing for a girl to do—any girl, anywhere. She was unbinding her turban.

He watched, not breathing, a presentiment of something horrible stirring in his brain, inexplicably . . . The red folds loosened, and—he knew then that he had not dreamed—again a scarlet lock swung down against her cheek . . . a hair, was it? a lock of hair? . . . thick as a thick worm it fell, plumply, against that smooth cheek . . . more scarlet than blood and thick as a crawling worm . . . and like a worm it crawled.

Smith rose on an elbow, not realizing the motion, and fixed an unwinking stare, with a sort of sick, fascinated incredulity, on that—that lock of hair. He had not dreamed. Until now he had taken it for granted that it was the *segir* which had made it seem to move on that evening before. But now . . . it was lengthening, stretching, moving of itself. It must be hair, but it *crawled*; with a sickening life of its own it squirmed down against her cheek, caressingly, revoltingly, impossibly . . . Wet, it was, and round and thick and shining . . .

She unfastened the last fold and whipped the turban off. From what he saw then Smith would have turned his eyes away—and he had looked on dreadful things before without flinching—but he could not stir. He could only lie there on his elbow staring at the mass of scarlet, squirming— worms, hairs, what?—that writhed over her head in a dreadful mockery of ringlets. And it was lengthening, falling, somehow growing before his eyes, down over her shoulders in a spilling cascade, a mass that even at the beginning could never have been hidden under the skull-tight turban she had worn. He was beyond wondering, but he realized that. And still it squirmed and lengthened and fell, and she shook it out in a horrible travesty of a woman shaking out her unbound hair—until the unspeakable tangle of it—twisting, writhing, obscenely scarlet—hung to her waist and beyond, and still lengthened, an endless mass of crawling horror that until now, somehow, impossibly, had been hidden under the tight-bound turban. It was like a nest of blind, restless red worms . . . it was—it was like naked entrails endowed with an unnatural aliveness, terrible beyond words.

Smith lay in the shadows, frozen without and within in a sick numbness that came of utter shock and revulsion.

She shook out the obscene, unspeakable tangle over her shoulders, and somehow he knew that she going to turn in a moment and that he must meet her eyes. The thought of that meeting stopped his heart with dread, more awfully than anything else in this nightmare horror;

for nightmare it must be, surely. But he knew without trying that he could not wrench his eyes away—the sickened fascination of that sight held him motionless, and somehow there was a certain beauty . . .

Her head was turning. The crawling awfulness rippled and squirmed at the motion, writhing thick and wet and shining over the soft brown shoulders about which they fell now in obscene cascades that all but hid her body. Her head was turning. Smith lay numb. And very slowly he saw the round of her cheek foreshorten and her profile come into view, all the scarlet horrors twisting ominously, and the profile shortened in turn and her full face came slowly round towards the bed—moonlight shining brilliantly as day on the pretty girl-face, demure and sweet, framed in tangled obscenity that crawled . . .

The green eyes met his. He felt a perceptible shock, and a shudder rippled down his paralyzed spine, leaving an icy numbness in its wake. He felt the goose-flesh rising. But that numbness and cold horror he scarcely realized, for the green eyes were locked with his in a long, long look that somehow presaged nameless things—not altogether unpleasant things—the voiceless voice of her mind assailing him with little murmurous promises . . .

For a moment he went down into a blind abyss of submission; and then, somehow, the very sight of that obscenity in eyes that did not then realize they saw it, was dreadful enough to draw him out of the seductive darkness . . . the sight of her crawling and alive with unnamable horror.

She rose, and down about her in a cascade fell the squirming scarlet of—of what grew upon her head. It fell in a long, alive cloak to her bare feet on the floor, hiding her in a wave of dreadful, wet, writhing life. She put up her hands and like a swimmer she parted the waterfall of it, tossing the masses back over her shoulders to reveal her own brown body, sweetly curved. She smiled exquisitely, and in starting waves back from her forehead and down about her in a hideous back-ground writhed the snaky wetness of her living tresses. And Smith knew that he looked upon Medusa.

The knowledge of that—the realization of vast back-grounds reaching into misted history—shook him out of his frozen horror for a moment, and in that moment he met her eyes again, smiling, green as glass in the moonlight, half hooded under drooping lids. Through the twisting scarlet she held out her arms. And there was something soul-shakingly desirable about her, so that all the blood surged to his head suddenly and he stumbled to his feet like a sleeper in a dream as she swayed towards him, infinitely sweet in her cloak of living horror.

And somehow there was beauty in it, the wet scarlet writhings with moonlight sliding, and shining along the thick, worm-round tresses and losing itself in the masses only to glint again and move silvery along writhing tendrils—and awful, shuddering beauty more dreadful than any ugliness could be.

But all this, again, he but half realized, for the insidious murmur was coiling again through his brain, promising, caressing, alluring, sweeter than honey; and the green eyes that held his were clear and burning like the depths of a jewel, and behind the pulsing slits of darkness he was staring into a greater dark that held all things . . . He had known—dimly he had known when he first gazed into those flat animal shallows that behind them lay this—all beauty and terror, all horror and delight, in the infinite darkness upon which her eyes opened like windows, paned with emerald glass.

Her lips moved, and in a murmur that blended indistinguishably with the silence and the sway of her body and the dreadful sway of her—her hair—she whispered—very softly, very passionately, 'I shall—speak to you now—in my own tongue—oh, beloved!'

And in her living cloak she swayed to him, the murmur swelling seductive and caressing in his innermost brain—promising, compelling, sweeter than sweet. His flesh crawled to the horror of her, but it was a perverted revulsion that clasped what it loathed. His arms slid round her under the sliding cloak, wet, wet and warm and hideously alive—and the sweet velvet body was clinging to his, her arms locked about his neck—and with a whisper and a rush the unspeakable horror closed about them both.

In nightmares until he died he remembered that moment when the living tresses of Shambleau first folded him in their embrace. A nauseous, smothering odour as the wetness shut around him—thick, pulsing worms clasping every inch of his body, sliding, writhing, their wetness and warmth striking through his garments as if he stood naked to their embrace.

All this in a graven instant—and after that a tangled flash of conflicting sensation before oblivion closed over him. For he remembered the dream—and knew it for nightmare reality now, and the sliding, gently moving caresses of those wet, warm worms upon his flesh was an ecstasy above words—that deeper ecstasy that strikes beyond the body and beyond the mind and tickles the very roots of the soul with unnatural delight. So he stood, rigid as marble, as helplessly stony as any of Medusa's victims in ancient legends were, while the terrible pleasure of Shambleau thrilled and shuddered through every fibre of him; through every atom of his body and the intangible atoms of what men call the soul, through all that was Smith the dreadful pleasure ran. And it was truly dreadful. Dimly he knew it, even as his body answered to the root-deep ecstasy, a foul and dreadful wooing from which his very soul shuddered away—and yet in the innermost depths of that soul some grinning traitor shivered with delight. But deeply, behind all this, he knew horror and revulsion and despair beyond telling, while the intimate caresses crawled obscenely in the secret places of his soul—knew that the soul should not be handled—and shook with the perilous pleasure through it all.

And this conflict and knowledge, this mingling of rapture and revulsion all took place in the flashing of a moment while the scarlet worms coiled and crawled upon him, sending deep, obscene tremors of that infinite pleasure into every atom that made up Smith. And he could not stir in that slimy, ecstatic embrace—and a weakness was flooding that grew deeper after each succeeding wave of intense delight, and the traitor in his soul strengthened and drowned out the revulsion—and something within him ceased to struggle as he sank wholly into a blazing darkness that was oblivion to all else but that devouring rapture . . .

The young Venusian climbing the stairs to his friend's lodging-room pulled out his key absent-mindedly, a pucker forming between his fine brows. He was slim, as all Venusians are, as fair and sleek as any of them, and as with most of his countrymen the look of cherubic innocence on his face was wholly deceptive. He had the face of a fallen angel, without Lucifer's majesty to redeem it; for a black devil grinned in his eyes and there were faint lines of ruthlessness and dissipation about his mouth to tell of the long years behind him that had run the gamut of experiences and made his name, next to Smith's, the most hated and the most respected in the records of the Patrol.

He mounted the stairs now with a puzzled frown between his eyes. He had come into Lakkdarol on the noon liner—the *Maid* in her hold very skilfully disguised with paint and otherwise—to find in lamentable disorder the affairs he had expected to be settled. And cautious inquiry elicited the information that Smith had not been seen for three days. That was not like his friend, he'd never failed before, and the two stood to lose not only a large sum of money but also their personal safety by the inexplicable lapse on the part of Smith. Yarol could think of one solution only: fate had at last caught up with his friend. Nothing but physical disability could explain it.

Still puzzling, he fitted his key in the lock and swung the door open.

In that first moment, as the door opened, he sensed something very wrong . . . The room was darkened, and for a while he could see nothing, but at the first breathe he scented a strange, unnamable odour, half sickening, half sweet. And deep stirrings of ancestral memory awoke within him—ancient swamp-born memories from Venusian ancestors far away and long ago . . .

Yarol laid his hand on his gun, lightly, and opened the door wider. In the dimness all he could see at first was a curious mound in the far corner . . . Then his eyes grew accustomed to the dark, and he saw it more clearly, a mound that somehow heaved and stirred within itself . . . A mound of—he caught his breath sharply—a mound like a mass of entrails, living, moving, writhing with an unspeakable aliveness. Then a hot Venusian oath broke from his lips and he cleared the door-sill in a swift stride, slammed the door and set his back against it, gun ready in his hand, although his flesh crawled—for he knew . . .

'Smith!' he said softly, in a voice thick with horror. 'Northwest!'

The moving mass stirred—shuddered—sank back into crawling quiescence again.

'Smith! Smith!' The Venusian's voice was gentle and insistent, and it quivered a little with terror.

An impatient ripple went over the whole mass of aliveness in the corner. It stirred again, reluctantly, then tendril by writhing tendril it began to part itself and fall aside, and very slowly the brown of a spaceman's leather appeared beneath it, all slimed and shining.

'Smith! Northwest!' Yarol's persistent whisper came again, urgently, and with a dream-like slowness the leather garments moved . . . a man sat up in the midst of the writhing forms, a man who once, long ago, might have been Northwest Smith. From head to foot he was slimy from the embrace of the crawling horror about him. His face was that of some creature beyond humanity—dead-alive, fixed in a grey stare, and the look of terrible ecstasy that overspread it seemed to come from somewhere far within, a faint reflection from immeasurable distances beyond the flesh. And as there is mystery and magic in the moonlight which is after all but a reflection of the everyday sun, so in that grey face turned to the door was a terror unnamable and sweet, a reflection of ecstasy beyond the understanding of any who have known only earthly ecstasy themselves. And as he sat there turning a blank, eyeless face to Yarol the red worms writhed ceaselessly about him, very gently, with a soft, caressive motion that never slacked.

'Smith . . . come here! Smith . . . get up . . . Smith, Smith!' Yarol's whisper hissed in the silence, commanding, urgent—but he made no move to leave the door.

And with a dreadful slowness, like a dead man rising, Smith stood up in the nest of slimy scarlet. He swayed drunkenly on his feet, and two or three crimson tendrils came writhing up his legs to the knees and wound themselves there, supportingly, moving with a ceaseless caress that seemed to give him some hidden strength, for he said then, without inflection:

'Go away. Go away. Leave me alone.' And the dead ecstatic face never changed.

'Smith!' Yarol's voice was desperate. 'Smith, listen! Smith, can't you hear me?'

'Go away,' the monotonous voice said. 'Go away. Go away. Go—'

'Not unless you come too. Can't you hear? Smith! Smith! I'll—'

He hushed in mid-phrase, and once more the ancestral prickle of race-memory shivered down his back, for the scarlet mass was moving again, violently, rising . . .

Yarol pressed back against the door and gripped his gun, and the name of a god he had forgotten years ago rose to his lips unbidden. For he knew what was coming next and the knowledge was more dreadful than any ignorance could have been.

The red, writhing mass rose higher, and the tendrils parted and a human face looked out—no, half human, with green cat-eyes that shone in the dimness like lighted jewels, compellingly . . .

Yarol breathed 'Shar!' again and flung up an arm across his face, and the tingle of meeting that green gaze for even an instant went thrilling through him perilously.

'Smith!' he called in despair. 'Smith, can't you hear me?'

'Go away,' said that voice that was not Smith's. 'Go away.'

And somehow, although he dared not look, Yarol knew that the—the other—had parted those worm-thick tresses and stood there in all the human sweetness of the brown, curved woman's body, cloaked in living horror. And he felt the eyes upon him, and something was crying insistently in his brain to lower that shielding arm . . . He was lost—he knew it, and the knowledge gave him that courage which comes from despair. The voice in his brain was growing, swelling, deafening him with a roaring command that all but swept him before it—command to lower that arm—to meet the eyes that opened upon darkness—to submit—and a promise, murmurous and sweet and evil beyond words, of pleasure to come . . .

But somehow he kept his head—somehow, dizzily, he was gripping his gun in his upflung hand—somehow, incredibly, crossing the narrow room with averted face, groping for Smith's shoulder. There was a moment of blind fumbling in emptiness, and then he found it, and gripped the leather that was slimy and dreadful and wet—and simultaneously he felt something loop gently about his ankle and a shock of repulsive pleasure went through him, and then another coil, and another, wound about his feet.

Yarol set his teeth and gripped the shoulder hard, and his hand shuddered of itself, for the feel of that leather was slimy as the worms about his ankles, and a faint tingle of obscene delight went through him from the contact.

That caressive pressure on his legs was all he could feel, and the voice in his brain drowned out all other sounds, and his body obeyed him reluctantly—but somehow he gave one heave of tremendous effort and swung Smith, stumbling, out of that nest of horror. The twining tendrils ripped loose with a little sucking sound, and the whole mass quivered and reached after, and then Yarol forgot his friend utterly and turned his whole being to the hopeless task of freeing himself. For only a part of him was fighting, now—only a part of him struggled against the twining obscenities, and in his innermost brain the sweet, seductive murmur sounded, and his body clamoured to surrender . . .

'Shar! Shar y'danis . . . Shar mor'la-rol—' prayed Yarol, gasping and half unconscious that he spoke, boy's prayers that he had forgotten years ago, and with his back half turned to the central mass he kicked desperately with his heavy boots at the red, writhing worms about him. They gave back before him, quivering and curling themselves out of reach, and though he knew that more were reaching for his throat from behind, at least he could go on struggling until he was forced to meet those eyes . . .

He stamped and kicked and stamped again, and for one instant he was free of the slimy grip as the bruised worms curled back from his heavy feet, and he lurched away dizzily, sick with revulsion and despair as he fought off the coils, and then he lifted his eyes and saw the cracked mirror on the wall. Dimly in its reflection he could see the writhing scarlet horror behind him, cat face peering out with its demure girl-smile, dreadfully human, and all the red tendrils reaching after him. And remembrance of something he had read long ago swept incongruously over him, and the gasp of relief and hope that he gave shook for a moment the grip of the command in his brain.

Without pausing for a breath he swung the gun over his shoulder, the reflected barrel in line with the reflected horror in the mirror, and flicked the catch.

In the mirror he saw its blue flame leap in a dazzling spate across the dimness, full into the midst of that squirming, reaching mass behind him. There was a hiss and a blaze and a high, thin scream of inhuman malice and despair—the flame cut a wide arc and went out as the gun fell from his hand, and Yarol pitched forward to the floor.

Northwest Smith opened his eyes to Martian sunlight streaming thinly through the dingy window. Something wet and cold was slapping his face, and the familiar fiery sting of *segir*-whisky burnt his throat.

'Smith!' Yarol's voice was saying from far away. 'N.W.! Wake up, damn you! Wake up!'

'I'm—awake,' Smith managed to articulate thickly. 'Wha's matter?'

Then a cup-rim was thrust against his teeth and Yarol said irritably. 'Drink it, you fool!'

Smith swallowed obediently and more of the fire-hot *segir* flowed down his grateful throat. It spread a warmth through his body that awakened him from the numbness that had gripped him until now, and helped a little towards driving out the all-devouring weakness he was becoming aware of slowly. He lay still for a few minutes while the warmth of the whisky went through him, and memory sluggishly began to permeate his brain with the spread of the *segir*. Nightmare memories . . . sweet and terrible . . . memories of—'

'God!' gasped Smith suddenly, and tried to sit up. Weakness smote him like a blow, and for an instant the room wheeled as he fell back against something firm and warm—Yarol's shoulder. The Venusian's arm supported him while the room steadied, and after a while he twisted a little and stared into the other's black gaze.

Yarol was holding him with one arm and finishing the mug of *segir* himself, and the black eyes met his over the rim and crinkled into sudden laughter, half hysterical after that terror that was passed.

'By *Pharol*!' gasped Yarol, choking into his mug. 'By *Pharol*, N.W.! I'm never gonna let you forget this! Next time you have to drag me out of a mass I'll say—'

'Let it go,' said Smith. 'What's been going on? How—'

'Shambleau.' Yarol's laughter died. 'Shambleau! What were you doing with a thing like that?'

'What was it?' Smith asked soberly.

'Mean to say you didn't know? But where'd you find it? How—'

'Suppose you tell me first what you know,' said Smith firmly. 'And another swig of that *segir*, too, please. I need it.'

'Can you hold the mug now? Feel better?'

'Yeah—some. I can hold it—thanks. Now go on.'

'Well—I don't know just where to start. They call them Shambleau—'

'Good God, is there more than one?'

'It's a—a sort of race, I think, one of the very oldest. Where they come from nobody knows. The name sounds a little French, doesn't it? But it goes back beyond the start of history. There have always been Shambleau.'

'I never heard of 'em.'

'Not many people have. And those who know don't care to talk about it much.'

'Well, half this town knows. I hadn't any idea what they were talking about, then. And I still don't understand, but—'

'Yes, it happens like this, sometimes. They'll appear, and the news will spread and the town will get together and hunt them down, and after that—well, the story doesn't get around very far. It's too—too unbelievable.'

'But—my God, Yarol!—what was it? Where'd it come from? How—'

'Nobody knows just where they come from. Another planet—maybe some undiscovered one. Some say Venus—I know there are some rather awful legends of them handed down in our family—that's how I've heard about it. And the minute I opened that door, awhile back—I—I think I knew that smell . . .'

'But—what *are* they?'

'God knows. Not human, though they have the human form. Or that may be only an illusion . . . or maybe I'm crazy. I don't know. They're a species of the vampire—or maybe the vampire is a species of—of them. Their normal form must be that—that mass, and in that form they draw nourishment from the—I suppose the life-forces of men. And they take some form—usually a woman form, I think, and key you up to the highest pitch of emotion before they—begin. That's to work the life-force up to intensity so it'll be easier . . . And they give, always, that horrible, foul pleasure as they—feed. There are some men who, if they survive the first experience, take to it like a drug—can't give it up—keep the thing with them all their lives—which isn't long—feeding it for that ghastly satisfaction. Worse than smoking *ming* or—or praying to *Pharol*.'

Yes,' said Smith. 'I'm beginning to understand why that crowd was so surprised and—and disgusted when I said—well, never mind. Go on.'

'Did you get to talk to—to it?' asked Yarol.

'I tried to. It couldn't speak very well. I asked it where it came from and it said—"from far away and long ago"—something like that.'

'I wonder. Possibly some unknown planet—but I think not. You know there are so many wild stories with some basis of fact to start from, that I've sometimes wondered—mightn't there be a lot more of even worse and wilder superstitions we've never even heard of? Things like this blasphemous and foul, that those who know have to keep still about? Awful, fantastic things running around loose that we never hear rumours of at all!

'These things—they've been in existence for countless ages. No one knows when or where they first appeared. Those who've seen them, as we saw this one, don't talk about it. It's just one of those vague, misty rumours you find half hinted at in old books sometimes . . . I believe they are an older race than man, spawned from ancient seed in times before ours, perhaps on planets that have gone to dust, and so horrible to man that when they are discovered the discoverers keep still about it—forget them again as quickly as they can.

'And they go back to time immemorial. I suppose you recognized the legend of Medusa? There isn't any question that the ancient Greeks knew of them. Does it mean that there have been civilizations before yours that set out from Earth and explored other planets? Or did one of the Shambleau somehow make its way into Greece three thousand years ago? If you think about it long enough you'll go off your head! I wonder how many other legends are based on things like this—things we don't suspect, things we'll never know.

'The Gorgon, Medusa, a beautiful woman with—with snakes for hair, and a gaze that turned men to stone, and Perseus finally killed her—I remembered this just by accident. N.W., and it saved your life and mine—Perseus killed her by using a mirror as he fought to reflect what he dared not look at directly. I wonder what the old Greek who first started that legend would have thought if he'd know that three thousand years later his story would save the lives of two men on another planet. I wonder what that Greek's own story was, and how he met the thing, and what happened . . .

'Well, there's a lot we'll never know. Wouldn't the records of that race of—of *things*, whatever they are, be worth reading! Records of other planets and other ages and all the beginnings of mankind! But I don't suppose they've kept any records. I don't suppose they've even any place to keep them—from what little I know, or anyone knows about it, they're like the Wandering Jew, just bobbing up here and there at long intervals, and where they stay in the meantime I'd give my eyes to know! But I don't believe that terribly hypnotic power they have indicates any super-human intelligence. It's their means of getting food—just like a frog's long tongue or a carnivorous flower's odour. Those are physical because the frog and the flower eat physical food. The Shambleau uses a—a mental reach to get mental food. I don't quite know how to put it. And just as a beast that eats the bodies of other animals acquires with each meal greater power over the bodies of the rest, so the Shambleau, stoking itself up with the life-forces of men, increases it power over the minds and the souls of other men. But I'm talking about things I can't define—things I'm not sure exist.

'I only know that when I felt—when those tentacles closed around my legs—I didn't want to pull loose, I felt sensations that—that—oh, I'm fouled and filthy to the very deepest part of me by that—pleasure—and yet—'

'I know,' said Smith slowly. The effect of the *segir* was beginning to wear off, and weakness as washing back over him in waves, and when he spoke he was half meditating in a low voice, scarcely realizing that Yarol listened. 'I know it—much better than you do—and there's something so indescribably awful that the thing emanates, something so utterly at odds with everything human—there aren't any words to say it. For a while I was a part of it, literally, sharing its thoughts and memories and emotions and hungers, and—well, it's over now and I don't remember very clearly, but the only part left free was that part of me that was all but insane from the—the obscenity of the thing. And yet it was a pleasure so sweet—I think there must be some nucleus of utter evil in me—in everyone—that needs only the proper stimulus to get complete control; because even while I was sick all through from the touch of those—things—there was something in me that was—was simply gibbering with delight . . . Because of that I saw things—and knew things—horrible, wild things I can't quite remember—visited unbelievable places, looked backward through the memory of that—creature—I was with, and saw—God, I wish I could remember!'

'You ought to thank your God you can't,' said Yarol soberly.

His voice roused Smith from the half-trance he had fallen into, and he rose on his elbow, swaying a little from weakness. The room was wavering before him, and he closed his eyes, not to see it, but he asked, 'You say they—they don't turn up again? No way of finding—another?'

Yarol did not answer for a moment. He laid his hands on the other man's shoulders and pressed him back, and then sat staring down into the dark, ravaged face with a new strange, undefinable look upon it that he had never seen there before—whose meaning he knew too well.

'Smith,' he said finally, and his black eyes for once were steady and serious, and the little grinning devil had vanished from behind them, 'Smith, I've never asked your word on anything before, but I've—I've earned the right to do it now, and I'm asking you to promise me one thing.'

Smith's colourless eyes met the black gaze unsteadily. Irresolution was in them, and a little fear of what that promise might be. And for just a moment Yarol was looking, not into his friend's familiar eyes, but into a wide grey blankness that held all horror and delight—a pale sea with unspeakable pleasures sunk beneath it. Then the wide stare focused again and Smith's eyes met his squarely and Smith's voice said. 'Go ahead. I'll promise.'

'That if you ever should meet a Shambleau again—ever, anywhere— you'll draw your gun and burn it to hell the instant you realize what it is. Will you promise me that?'

There was a long silence. Yarol's sombre black eyes bored relentlessly into the colourless ones of Smith, not wavering. And the veins stood out on Smith's tanned forehead. He never broke his word—he had given it perhaps half a dozen times in his life, but once he had given it, he was incapable of breaking it. And once more the grey seas flooded in a dim tide of memories, sweet and horrible beyond dreams. Once more Yarol was staring into blankness that hid nameless things. The room was very still.

The grey tide ebbed. Smith's eyes, pale and resolute as steel, met Yarol's levelly.

'I'll—try,' he said. And his voice wavered.

1934

The Supper at Elsinore

'ISAK' DINESEN
(Karen Blixen)

U pon the corner of a street of Elsinore, near the harbour, there
stands a dignified old grey house, built early in the eighteenth
century and looking down reticently at the new times growing up
around it. Through the long years it has been worked into a unity,
and when the front door is opened on a day of north-north-west the
door of the corridor upstairs will open out of sympathy. Also when
you tread upon a certain step of the stair, a board of the floor in the
parlour will answer with a faint echo, like a song.

It had been in the possession of the family De Coninck for many
years, but after the State bankruptcy of 1813 and simultaneous
tragic happenings within the family itself, they gave it up and
moved to their house in Copenhagen. An old woman in a white
cap looked after the old house for them, with a man to assist
her, and, living in the old rooms, would think and talk of old
days. The two daughters of the house had never married, and were
now too old for it. The son was dead. But in summers of long
ago—so Madam Baek would recount—on Sunday afternoons when
the weather was fine, the Papa and Mamma De Coninck, with the
three children, used to drive in a landaulet to the country house
of the old lady, the grandmother, where they would dine, as the
custom was then, at three o'clock, outside on the lawn under a
large elm tree which, in June, scattered its little round and flat
brown seeds thickly upon the grass. They would partake of duck
with green peas and of strawberries with cream, and the little boy

would run to and fro, in white nankeens, to feed his grandmother's Bolognese dogs.

The two young sisters used to keep, in cases, the many birds presented to them by their sea-faring admirers. When asked if they did not play the harp, old Madam Baek would shrug her shoulders over the impossibility of giving any account of the many perfections of the young ladies. As to their adorers, and the proposals which had been made them, this was a hopeless theme to enter upon. There was no end to it.

Old Madam Baek, who had herself been married for a short time to a sailor, and had, when he was drowned, re-entered the service of the De Coninck family as a widow, thought it a great pity that neither of the lovely sisters had married. She could not quite get over it. Towards the world she held the theory that they had not been able to find any man worthy of them, except their brother. But she herself felt that her doctrine would not hold water. If this had been the two sisters' trouble, they ought to have put up with less than the ideal. She herself, on their behalf, would have done so, although it would have cost her much. Also, in her heart she knew better. She was seventeen years older than the elder sister, Fernande, whom they called Fanny, and eighteen years older than the younger, Eliza, who was born on the day of the fall of the Bastille, and she had been with them for the greater part of her life. Even if she was unable to put it into words, she felt keenly enough, as with her own body and soul, the doom which hung over the breed, and which tied these sisters and this brother together and made impossible for them any true relation to other human beings.

While they had been young, no event in the social world of Elsinore had been a success without the lovely De Coninck sisters. They were the heart and soul of all the gaiety of the town. When they entered its ballrooms, the ceilings of sedate old merchants' houses seemed to lift a little, and the walls to spring out in luminous Ionian columns, bound with vine. When one of them opened the ball, light as a bird, bold as a thought, she consecrated the gathering to the gods of true joy of life, from whose presence care and envy are banished. They could sing duets like a pair of nightingales in a tree, and imitate without effort and without the slightest malice the voices of all the *beau monde* of Elsinore, so as to make the paunches of their father's friends, the matadors of the town, shake with laughter around their card tables.

They could make up a charade or a game of forfeits in no time, and when they had been out for their music lessons, or to the Promenade, they came back brimful of tales of what had happened, or of tales out of their own imaginations, one whim stumbling over the other.

And then, within their own rooms, they would walk up and down the floor and weep, or sit in the window and look out over the harbour and wring their hands in their laps, or lie in bed at night and cry bitterly, for no reason in the world. They would talk, then, of life with the black bitterness of two Timons of Athens, and give Madam Baek an uncanny feeling, as in an atmosphere of corrodent rust. Their mother, who did not have the curse in her blood, would have been badly frightened had she been present at these moments, and would have suspected some unhappy love affair. Their father would have understood them, and have grieved on their behalf, but he was occupied with his affairs and did not come into his daughters' rooms. Only this elderly female servant, whose temperament was as different as possible from theirs, would understand them in her way, and would keep it all within her heart, as they did themselves, with mingled despair and pride. Sometimes she would try to comfort them. When they cried out, 'Hanne, is it not terrible that there is so much lying, so much falsehood, in the world?' she said, 'Well, what of it? It would be worse still if it were actually true, all that they tell.'

Then again the girls would get up, dry their tears, try on their new bonnets before the glass, plan their theatricals and sleighing parties, shock and gladden the hearts of their friends, and have the whole thing over again. They seemed as unable to keep from one extremity as from the other. In short, they were born melancholiacs, such as make others happy and are themselves helplessly unhappy, creatures of playfulness, charm and salt tears, of fine and everlasting loneliness.

Whether they had ever been in love, old Madam Baek herself could not tell. They used to drive her to despair by their hard scepticism as to any man being in love with them, when she, indeed, knew better; when she saw the swains of Elsinore grow pale and worn, go into exile or become old bachelors from love of them. She also felt that could they ever have been quite convinced of a man's love of them, that would have meant salvation to these young flying Dutchwomen. But they stood in a strange, distorted relation to the world, as if it had been only their reflection in a mirror which they had been showing it, while in the background and the shadow the real woman remained a looker-on. She would follow with keen attention the movements of the lover courting her image, laughing to herself at the impossibility of the consummation of their love, when the moment should come for it, her own heart hardening all the time. Did she wish that the man would break the glass and the lovely creature with it, and turn around towards herself? Oh, that she knew to be out of the question. Perhaps the lovely sisters derived a queer pleasure out of the adoration paid to their images in the mirror. They could not do without it in the end.

Because of this particular turn of mind they were predestined to be old maids. Now that they were real old maids, of fifty-two and fifty-three, they seemed to have come to better terms with life, as one bears up with a thing that will soon be over. That they were to disappear from the earth without leaving any trace whatever did not trouble them, for they had always known that it would be so. It gave them a certain satisfaction to feel that they were disappearing gracefully. They could not possibly putrefy, as would most of their friends, having already been, like elegant spiritual mummies, laid down with myrrh and aromatic herbs. When they were in their sweet moods, and particularly in their relations with the younger generation, the children of their friends, they even exhaled a spiced odour of sanctity, which the young people remembered all their lives.

The fatal melancholy of the family had come out in a different manner in Morten, the boy, and in him had fascinated Madam Baek even to possession. She never lost patience with him, as she sometimes did with the girls, because of the fact that he was male and she female, and also by reason of the true romance which surrounded him as it had never surrounded his sisters. He had been, indeed, in Elsinore, as another high-born young dandy before him, the observed of all observers, the glass of fashion and the mould of form. Many were the girls of the town who had remained unmarried for his sake, or who had married late in life one having a likeness, perhaps not quite *en face* and not quite in profile, to that god-like young head which had, by then, for ever disappeared from the horizon. And there was even the girl who had been, in the eyes of all the world, engaged to be married to Morten, herself married now, with children—*aber frage nur nicht wie!* She had lost that radiant fairness which had in his day given her the name, in Elsinore, of 'golden lambkin', so that where that fairy creature had once pranced in the streets a pale and quiet lady now trod the pavement. But still this was the girl whom, when he had stepped out of his barge on a shining March day at the pier of Elsinore, with the whole population of the town waving and shouting to him, he had lifted from the ground and held in his arms, while all the world had swung up and down around her, had whirled fans and long streamers in all the hues of the rainbow.

Morten De Coninck had been more reticent of manner than his sisters. He had no need to exert himself. When he came into a room, in his quiet way, he owned and commanded it. He had all the beauty of limb and elegance of hands and feet of the ladies of the family, but not their fineness of feature. His nose and mouth seemed to have been cut by a rougher hand. But he had the most striking, extraordinarily noble and serene forehead. People talking to him lifted their eyes to that broad, pure brow as if it had been radiant with the diamond tiara of a young emperor, or the halo of a saint. Morten De Coninck looked as if he could not possibly know either guilt or fear. Very likely he did not. He played the part of a hero to Elsinore for three years.

This was the time of the Napoleonic wars, when the world was trembling on its foundations. Denmark, in the struggle of the Titans, had tried to remain free and to go her own ways, and had had to pay for it. Copenhagen had been bombarded and burned. On that September night, when the sky over the town had flamed red to all Sealand, the great chiming bells of Frue Kirke, set going by the fire, played, on their own, Luther's hymn, *Ein' feste Burg ist unser Gott,* just before the tall tower fell into ruins. To save the capital the government had had to surrender the fleet. The proud British frigates had led the warships of Denmark—the apples of her eye, a string of pearls, a flight of captive swans—up through the Sound. The empty ports cried to heaven, and shame and hatred were in all hearts.

It was in the course of the struggles and great events of the following years of 1807 and 1808 that the flotilla of privateers sprang up, like live sparks from a smoking ruin. Driven forth by patriotism, thirst of revenge, and hope of gain, the privateers came from all the coasts and little islands of Denmark, manned by gentlemen, ferrymen, and fishermen, idealists and adventurers—gallant seamen all of them. As you took out your letter of marque you made your own cause one with that of the bleeding country; you had the right to strike a blow at the enemy whenever you had the chance, and you might come out of the encounter a rich man. The privateer stood in a curious relationship to the State: it was a sort of acknowledged maritime love-affair, a left-handed marriage, carried through with passionate devotion on both sides. If she did not wear the epaulets and sanctifying bright metal of legitimate union, she had at least the burning red kiss of the crown of Denmark on her lips, and the freedom of the concubine to enchant her lord by these wild whims which queens do not dream of. The royal navy itself—such as was left of it in those ships which had been away from Copenhagen that fatal September week—took a friendly view of the privateer flotilla and lived with it on congenial terms; on such terms, probably, as those on which Rachel lived with her maid Bilhah, who accomplished what she could not do herself. It was a great time for brave men. There were cannons singing once more in the Danish fairways, here and there, and where they were least expected, for the privateers very rarely worked together; every one of them was out on its own. Incredible, heroic deeds were performed, great prizes were snatched away under the very guns of the conveying frigates and were brought into port, by the triumphant wild little boats with their rigging hangdown in rags, amid shouts of exultation. Songs were made about it all. There can rarely have been a class of heroes who appealed more highly and deeply to the heart and imagination of the common people, and to all the boys, of a nation.

It was soon found that the larger type of ship did not do well for this traffic. The ferryboat or snow, with a station bill of twelve to twenty men, and with six to ten swivel guns, handy and quick in emergencies, was the right bird for the business. The nautical skill of the captain and his knowledge of the sea-ways played a great part, and the personal bravery of the crew, their artfulness with the guns, and, in boarding, with hand weapons, carried the point. Here were the honours of war to be won; and not only honour, but gold; and not gold alone, but revenge upon the violator, sweet to the heart. And when they came in, these old and young sea dogs, covered with snow, their whole rigging sometimes coated with ice until the ship looked as if it were drawn with chalk upon the dark sea, they had their hour of glory behind them, but a great excitement in front, for they made a tremendous stir in the little seaport towns. Then came the judgment of the prize, and the sale of the salved goods, which might be of great value. The government took its share, and each man on board came in for his, from the captain, gunner, and mate to the boys, who received one-third of a man's share. A boy might have gone to sea possessing nothing but his shirt, trousers, and trouser-strap, and come back with those badly torn and red-stained, and a tale of danger and high seas to tell his friends, and might be jingling five hundred riksdaler in his pocket a fortnight later, when the sale was over. The Jews of Copenhagen and Hamburg, each in three tall hats, one on top of the other, made their appearance upon the spot quickly, to play a great role at the sale, or, beforehand, to coax the prize-marks out of the pockets of impatient combatants.

Soon there shot up, like new comets, the names of popular heroes and their boats, around whose fame myths gathered daily. There was Jens Lind, of the *Cort Adeler,* the one they called 'Velvet' Lind because he was such a swell, and who played the role of a great nabob for some years, and then, when all gain was spent, finished up as a bear-leader. There was Captain Raaber, of *The Revenger,* who was something of a poet; the brothers Wulffsen, of *The Mackerel* and the *Madame Clark,* who were gentlemen of Copenhagen; and Christen Kock of the *Æolus,* whose entire crew—every single man—was killed or wounded in her fight with a British frigate off Læssø; and there was young Morten De Coninck, of the *Fortuna II.*

When Morten first came to his father and asked him to equip a privateer for him, the heart of old Mr De Coninck shrank a little from the idea. There were many rich and respectable shipowners of Copenhagen, some of them greater merchants than he, who had in these days launched their privateers, and Mr De Coninck, who yielded to no one in patriotic feeling, had himself suffered heavy losses at the hands of the British. But the business was painful to him. There was to his mind something revolting in the idea of attacking merchant ships, even if they did carry contraband. It seemed to him like assaulting ladies or shooting albatrosses. Morten had to turn for support to his father's cousin, Fernand De Coninck, a rich old bachelor of Elsinore whose mother was French and who was an enthusiastic partisan of the Emperor Napoleon. Morten's two sisters masterfully assisted him in getting around Uncle Fernand, and in November 1807, the young man put to sea in his own boat. The uncle never regretted his generosity. The whole business rejuvenated him by twenty years, and he possessed, in the end, a collection of souvenirs from the ships of the enemy that gave him great pleasure.

The *Fortuna II* of Elsinore, with a crew of twelve and four swivel guns, received her letter of marque on the second of November—was not this date, and the dates of exploits following it, written in

Madam Baek's heart, like the name of Calais in Queen Mary's, now, thirty-three years after? Already on the fourth the *Fortuna II* surprised an English brig off Hveen. An English man-of-war, hastening to the spot, shot at the privateer, but her crew managed to cut the cables of the prize and bring her into safety under the guns of Kronborg.

On the twentieth of November the boat had a great day. From a convoy she cut off the British brig, *The William*, and the snow, *Jupiter*, which had a cargo of sail cloth, stoneware, wine, spirits, coffee, sugar and silks. The cargo was unloaded at Elsinore, but both prizes were brought to Copenhagen, where they were condemned. Two hundred Jews came to Elsinore to bid at the auction sale of the *Jupiter*'s cargo, on the thirtieth of December. Morten himself brought in a piece of white brocade which was said to have been made in China and sent from England for the wedding dress of the Czar's sister. At this time Morten had just become engaged, and all Elsinore laughed and smiled at him as he walked away with the parcel under his arm.

Many times he was pursued by the enemy's men-of-war. Once, on the twenty-seventh of May, in flight from a British frigate, he ran ashore near Aarhus, but escaped by throwing his ballast of iron overboard, and got in under the guns of the Danish batteries. The burghers of Aarhus provided the illustrious young privateersman with new iron for his ballast, free of charge. It was said that the little seamstresses brought him their pressing-irons, and kissed them in parting with them, to bring him luck.

On the fifteenth of January, the *Fortuna* had, together with the privateer *Three Friends*, captured six of the enemy's ships, and with these was bearing in with Drogden, to have them realized in Copenhagen, when one of the prizes ran ashore on the Middelgrund. It was a big British brig loaded with sail cloth, valued at 100,000 riksdaler, which the privateers had, on the morning of the same day, cut off from an English convoy. The British men-of-war were still pursuing them. At the sight of the accident the pursuing ships instantly dispatched a strong detachment of six longboats to capture their brig. The privateers, on their side, were not disposed to give her up, and beat up against the British, who were driven away by a fire of grapeshot and had to give up the recapture. But the ship was to be lost all the same. The prize-master on board her, at the sight of the enemy's boats with their greatly superior forces, had put fire to the brig so that she should not fall again into the hands of the British. The fire spread so violently that the ship could not be saved, and all night the people of Copenhagen watched the tall, terrible beacon to the north. The five remaining prizes were taken to Copenhagen.

It was in the summer of the same year that the *Fortuna II* came in for a life-and-death fight off Elsinore. She had by then become a thorn in the flesh of the British, and on a dark night in August they made ready, from the men-of-war stationed on the Swedish coast, to capture her. Two big launches were sent off, their tholes bound with wool. The crew of the privateer had turned in, and only young Morten himself and his balker were on deck when the launches, manned by thirty-five sailors, grated against the *Fortuna*'s sides, and the boarding pikes were planted in her boards. From the launches shots were fired, but on board the privateer there was neither time nor room for using the guns. It became a struggle of axes, broadswords and knives. The enemy swarmed on deck from all sides; men were cutting at the chain-cable and hanging to the figurehead. But it did not last long. The *Fortuna*'s men put up a desperate fight, and in twenty minutes the deck was cleared. The enemy jumped into its boats and pushed off. The guns were used then, and three canister shots were fired after the retreating British. They left twelve of their men dead and wounded on the deck of the *Fortuna II.*

At Elsinore the people had heard the musketry fire from the longboats, but no reply from the *Fortuna.* They gathered at the harbour and along the ramparts of Kronborg, but the night was dark, and although the sky was just reddening in the east, no one could see what was happening. Then, just as the first light of morning was filling the dull air, three shots rang out, one after another, and the boys of Elsinore said that they could see the white smoke run along the dark waves. The *Fortuna II* bore in to Elsinore half an hour later. She looked black against the eastern sky. It was apparent that her rigging had been badly crippled, and gradually the people on land were able to distinguish the little dark figures on board, and the red on the deck. It was said that there was not a single broadsword or knife on board that was not red, and all the netting from stern to main chains had been soaked with blood. There was not one man on board, either, who had not been wounded, but only one was badly hurt. This was a West-Indian Negro, from the Danish colonies there—'black in skin but a Dane in heart,' the newspapers of Elsinore said the next day. Morten himself, fouled with gunpowder, a bandage down over one eye, white in the morning light and wild still from the fight, lifted both his arms high in the air to the cheering crowd on shore.

In the autumn of that year the whole privateer trade was suddenly prohibited. It was thought that it drew the enemy's frigates to the Danish seas, and constituted a danger to the country. Also, it was on many sides characterized as a wild and inhuman way of fighting. This broke the hearts of many gallant sailors, who left their decks to wander all over the world, unable to settle down again to their work in the little towns. The country grieved over her birds of prey.

To Morten De Coninck, all people agreed, the new order came conveniently. He had gathered his laurels and could now marry and settle down in Elsinore.

He was then engaged to Adrienne Rosenstand, the falcon to the white dove. She was the bosom friend of his sisters, who treated her much as if they had created her themselves, and took pleasure in dressing up her loveliness to its greatest advantage. They had refined and decided tastes, and spent as much time on the choice of her trousseau as if it had been their own. Between themselves they were not always so lenient to their frail sister-in-law, but would passionately deplore to one another the mating of their brother with a little *bourgeoise*, an ornamental bird out of the poultry yard of Elsinore. Had they thought the matter over a little, they ought to have congratulated themselves. The timidity and conventionality of Adrienne still allowed them to shine unrivalled within their sphere of daring and fantasy; but what figures would the falcon's sisters have cut, had he, as might well have happened, brought home a young eagle-bride?

The wedding was to take place in May, when the country around Elsinore is at its loveliest, and all the town was looking forward to the day. But it did not come off in the end. On the morning of the marriage the bridegroom was found to be missing, and he was never seen again in Elsinore. The sisters, dissolved in tears of grief and shame, had to take the news to the bride, who fell down in a swoon, lay ill for a long time, and never quite recovered. The whole town seemed to have been struck dumb by the blow, and to wrap up its head in sorrow. No one made much out of this unique opportunity for gossip. Elsinore felt the loss its own, and the fall.

No direct message from Morten De Coninck ever reached Elsinore. But in the course of the years strange rumours of him drifted in from the West. He was a pirate, it was said first of all, and that was not an unheard-of fate for a homeless privateer. Then it was rumoured that he was in the wars in America, and had distinguished himself. Later it was told that he had become a great planter and slave-owner in the Antilles. But even these rumours were lightly handled by the town. His name was hardly ever mentioned, until, after long years, he could be talked about as a figure out of a fairy-tale, like Bluebeard or Sinbad the Sailor. In the drawing-rooms of the De Coninck house he ceased to exist after his wedding-day. They took his portrait down from the wall. Madame De Coninck took her death over the loss of her son. She had a great deal of life in her. She was a stringed instrument, from which her children had many of their high and clear notes. If it were never again to be used, if no waltz, serenade, or martial march were ever to be played upon it again, it might as well be put away. Death was no more unnatural to her than silence.

To Morten's sisters the infrequent news of their brother was manna on which they kept their hearts alive in a desert. They did not serve it to their friends, nor to their parents; but within the distillery of their own rooms they concocted it according to many recipes. Their brother would come back an admiral in a foreign fleet, his breast covered with unknown stars, to marry the bride waiting for him, or come back wounded, broken in health, but highly honoured, to die in Elsinore. He would land at the pier. Had he not done so, and had they not seen it with their own eyes? But even this spare food came in time to be seasoned with much pungent bitterness. They themselves, in the end, would rather have starved than have swallowed it, had they had the choice. Morten, it was told, far from being a distinguished naval officer or a rich planter, had indeed been a pirate in the waters around Cuba and Trinidad—one of the last of the breed. But, pursued by the ships *Albion* and *Triumph*, he had lost his ship near Port of Spain, and himself had a narrow escape. He had tried to make his living in many hard ways and had been seen by somebody in New Orleans, very poor and sick. The last thing that his sisters heard of him was that he had been hanged.

From Morten's wedding-day, Madam Baek had carried her wound in silence for thirty years. The sophistries of his sisters she never chose to make use of; she let them go in at one ear and out at the other. She was very humble and attentive to the deserted bride, when she again visited the family, yet she never showed her much sympathy. Also she knew, as was ever the case in the house, more than any other inhabitant of it. It cannot be said that she had seen the catastrophe approach, but she had had strange warnings in her dreams. The bridegroom had been in the habit, from childhood, of coming and sitting with her in her little room from time to time. He had done that while they were making great preparations for his happiness. Over her needlework and her glasses she had watched his face. And she, who often worked late at night, and who would be up in the linen-room before the early summer sun was above the Sound, was aware of many comings and goings unknown to the rest of the household. Something had happened to the engaged people. Had he begged her to take him and hold him, so that it should no longer be in his power to leave her? Madam Baek could not believe that any girl could refuse Morten anything. Or had she yielded, and found the magic ineffective? Or had she been watching him, daily slipping away from her, and still had not the strength to offer the sacrifice which might have held him?

Nobody would ever know, for Adrienne never talked of these things; indeed, she could not have done so if she had wanted to. Ever since her recovery from her long illness she seemed to be a little hard of hearing. She could only hear the things which could be talked about very loudly, and finished her life in an atmosphere of high-shrieked platitudes.

For fifteen years the lovely Adrienne waited for her bridegroom, then she married.

The two sisters De Coninck attended the wedding. They were magnificently attired. This was really the last occasion upon which they appeared as the belles of Elsinore, and although they were then in their thirties, they swept the floor with the young girls of the town. Their wedding present to the bride was no less imposing. They gave her their mother's diamond earrings and brooch, a *parure* unique in Elsinore. They had likewise robbed the windows of their drawing-rooms of all their flowers to adorn the altar, this being a December wedding. All the world thought that the two proud sisters were doing these honours to their friend to make amends for what she had suffered at their brother's hands. Madam Baek knew better. She knew that they were acting out of deep gratitude, that the diamond *parure* was a thank offering. For now the fair Adrienne was no longer their brother's virgin widow, and held no more the place next to him in the eyes of all the world. When the gentle intruder now walked out of their house, the least they could do was to follow her to the door with deep courtesies. To her children, later in life, they also for the same reason showed the most excessive kindness, leaving them, in the end, most of their worldly goods; and to all this they were driven by their thankfulness to that pretty brood of ornamental chickens out of the poultry yard of Elsinore, because they were not their brother's children.

Madam Baek herself had been asked to the wedding, and had a pleasant evening. When the ice was being served, she suddenly thought of the icebergs in the great black ocean, of which she had read, and of a lonely young man gazing at them from the deck of a ship, and at that moment her eyes met those of Miss Fanny, at the other end of the table. These dark eyes were all ablaze, and shone with tears. With all her De Coninck strength the distinguished old maid was suppressing something: a great longing, or shame, or triumph.

But there was another girl of Elsinore whose story may rightly be told, very briefly, in this place. That was an inn-keeper's daughter of Sletten, by the name of Katrine, of the blood of the charcoal burners who lived near Elsinore and are in many ways like gypsies. She was a big, handsome, dark and red-cheeked lass, and was said to have been, at a time, the sweetheart of Morten De Coninck. This young woman had a sad fate. She was thought to have gone a little out of her head. She took to drink and to worse ways, and died young. To this girl, Eliza, the younger of the sisters, showed great kindness. Twice she started her in a little milliner's shop, for the girl was talented and had an eye for elegance, and Eliza advertised it herself by wearing no bonnets but hers, and to the end of her life she gave her money. When, after many scandals in Elsinore, Katrine moved to Copenhagen, and took up her residence in the street of Dybensgade, where, in general, the ladies of the town never set foot, Eliza De Coninck still went to see her, and seemed to come back having gathered strength and a secret joy from her visits. For this was the way in which a girl beloved and deserted by Morten De Coninck ought to behave. This plain ruin, misery and degradation were the only harmonious accompaniment to the happenings, which might resound in and rejoice the heart of the sister while she stopped her ears to the words of comfort of the world. The two were together for long days. The broken woman was without speech, except for asking three or four times a day in what quarters the wind were, a question which the erect and elegant lady at her bedside would ever answer without hesitation or mistake. Eliza sat at Katrine's deathbed like a witch attentively observing the working of a deadly potion, holding her breath to catch the last breath of the dying girl of Sletten.

The winter of 1841 was unusually severe. The cold began before Christmas, but in January it turned into a deadly still, continuous frost. A little snow in spare hard grains came down from time to time, but there was no wind, no sun, no movement in air or water. The ice was thick upon the Sound, so that people could walk from Elsinore to Sweden to drink coffee with their friends, the fathers of whom had met their own fathers to the roar of cannons on the same waters, when the waves had gone high. They looked like little rows of small black tin soldiers upon the infinite grey plane. But at night, when the lights from the houses and the dull street lamps reached only a little way out on the ice, this flatness and whiteness of the sea was very strange, like the breath of death over the world. The smoke from the chimneys went straight up in the air. The oldest people did not remember another such winter.

Old Madam Baek, like other people, was very proud of this extraordinarily cold weather, and much excited about it, but during these winter months she changed. She probably was near her end, and was going off quickly. It began by her fainting in the dining-room one morning when she had been out by herself to buy fish, and for some time she could hardly move. She became very silent. She seemed to shrink, and her eyes grew pale. She went about in the house as before, but now it seemed to her that she had to climb an endless steep hill when in the evenings, with her candlestick and her shadow, she walked up the stair; and she seemed to be listening to sounds from far away when, with her knitting, she sat close to the crackling tall porcelain stove. Her friends began to think that they should have cut out a square hole for her in that iron ground before the thaw of spring would set in. But she still held on, and after a time she seemed to become stronger again, although more rigid, as if she herself had frozen in the hard winter with a frost that would not thaw. She never got back that gay and precise flow of speech which, during seventy years, had cheered so many people, kept servants in order, and promoted or checked the gossip of Elsinore.

One afternoon she confided to the man who assisted her in the house her decision to go to Copenhagen to see her ladies. The next day she went out to arrange for her trip with the hackney man. The news of her project spread, for the journey from Elsinore to Copenhagen is no joke. On a Thursday morning she was up by candlelight and descended the stone steps to the street, her carpetbag in her hand, while the morning light was still dim.

The journey was no joke. It is more than twenty-six miles from Elsinore to Copenhagen, and the road ran along the sea. In many places there was hardly any road; only a track that went along the seashore. Here the wind, blowing on to the land, had swept away the snow, so that no sledges could pass, and the old woman went in a carriage with straw on the floor. She was well wrapped up, still, as the carriage drove on and the winter day came up and showed all the landscape so silent and cold, it was as if nothing at all could keep alive here, least of all an old woman all by herself in a carriage. She sat perfectly quiet, looking around her. The plane of the frozen Sound showed grey in the grey light. Here and there seaweeds strewn upon the beach marked it with brown and black. Near the road, upon the sand, the crows were marching martially about, or fighting over a dead fish. The little fishermen's houses along the road had their doors and windows carefully shut. Sometimes she would see the fishermen themselves, in high boots that came above their knees, a long way out on the ice, where they were cutting holes to catch cod with a tin bait. The sky was the colour of lead, but low along the horizon ran a broad stripe the colour of old lemon peel or very old ivory.

It was many years since she had come along this road. As she drove on, long-forgotten figures came and ran alongside the carriage. It seemed strange to her that the indifferent coachman in a fur cap and the small bay horses should have it in their power to drive her into a world of which they knew nothing.

They came past Rungsted, where, as a little girl, she had served in the old inn, red-tiled, close to the road. From here to town the road was better. Here had lived, for the last years of his life, in sickness and poverty, the great poet Ewald, a genius, the swan of the North. Broken in health, deeply disappointed in his love for the faithless Arendse, badly given to drink, he still radiated a rare vitality, a bright light that had fascinated the little girl. Little

Hanne, at the age of ten, had been sensitive to the magnetism of the great mysterious powers of life, which she did not understand. She was happy when she could be with him. Three things, she had learned from the talk of the landlady, he was always begging for: to get married, since to him life without women seemed unbearably cold and wasted; alcohol of some sort—although he was a fine connoisseur of wine, he could drink down the crass gin of the country as well; and, lastly, to be taken to Holy Communion. All three were firmly denied him by his mother and stepfather, who were rich people of Copenhagen, and even by his friend, Pastor Schoenheyder, for they did not want him to be happy in either of the first two ways, and they considered that he must alter his ways before he could be made happy in the third. The landlady and Hanne were sorry for him. They would have married him and given him wine and taken him to Holy Communion, had it lain with them. Often, when the other children had been playing, Hanne had left them to pick early spring violets for him in the grass with cold fingers, looking forward to the sight of his face when he smelled the little bunches of flowers. There was something here which she could not understand, and which still held all her being strongly—that violets could mean so much. Generally he was very gay with her, and would take her on his knees and warm his cold hands on her. His breath sometimes smelled of gin, but she never told anybody. Even three years later, when she was confirmed, she imagined the Lord Jesus and his long hair in a queue, and with that rare, wild, broken and arrogant smile of the dying poet.

Madam Baek came through the East Gate of Copenhagen just as people were about to light their lamps. She was held up and questioned by the toll collectors, but when they found her to be an honest woman in possession of no contraband they let her pass. So she would appear at the gate of heaven, ignorant of what was wanted of her, but confident that if she behaved correctly, according to her lights, others would behave correctly, according to theirs.

She drove through the streets of Copenhagen, looking around—for she had not been there for many years—as she would look around to form an opinion of the new Jerusalem. The streets here were not paved with gold or chrysoprase, and in places there was a little snow; but such as they were she accepted them. She likewise accepted the stables, where she was to get out, and the walk in the icy-cold blue evening of Copenhagen to Gammeltorv, where lay the house of her ladies.

Nevertheless she felt, as she took her way slowly through the streets, that she was an intruder and did not belong. She was not even noticed, except by two young men, deep in a political discussion, who had to separate to let her pass between them, and by a couple of boys, who remarked upon her bonnet. She did not like this sort of thing, it did not take place in Elsinore.

The windows of the first floor of the Misses De Coninck's house were brightly lighted. Remembering it to be Fernande's birthday, Madam Baek, down in the square, reasoned that the ladies would be having a party.

This was the case, and while Madam Baek was slowly ascending the stair, dragging her heavy feet and her message from step to step, the sisters were merrily entertaining their guests in their warm and cozy grey parlour with its green carpet and shining mahogany furniture.

The party was characteristic of the two old maids by being mostly composed of gentlemen. They existed, in their pretty house in Gammeltorv, like a pair of prominent spiritual courtesans of Copenhagen, leading their admirers into excesses and seducing them into scattering their spiritual wealth and health upon their charms. As a couple of corresponding young courtesans of the flesh would be out after the great people and princes of this world, so were they ever spreading their snares for the *honoratiori* of the world spiritual, and tonight could lay on the table no meaner acquisition than the Bishop of Sealand, the director of the Royal Theatre of Copenhagen, who was himself a distinguished dramatic and philosophical scribe, and a famous old painter of animals, just back from Rome, where he had been shown great honour. An old commodore with a fresh face, who had carried a wound since 1807, and a lady-in-waiting to the Dowager Queen, elegant and a good listener, who looked as if her voluminous skirt was absolutely massive, from her waist down, completed the party, all of whom were old friends, but were there chiefly to hold the candle.

If these sisters could not live without men, it was because they had the firm conviction, which, as an instinct, runs in the blood of seafaring families, that the final word as to what you are really worth lies with the other sex. You may ask the members of your own sex for their opinion and advice as to your compass and crew, your cuisine and garden, but when it comes to the matter of what you yourself are worth, the words of even your best friends are void and good for nothing, and you must address yourself to the opposite sex. Old white skippers, who have been round the Horn and out in a hundred hurricanes, know the law. They may be highly respected on the deck or in the mess, and honoured by their staunch grey contemporaries, but it is, finally, the girls who have the say as to whether they are worth keeping alive or not. The old sailor's women are aware of this fact, and will take a good deal of trouble to impress even the young boys towards a favourable judgment. This doctrine, and this quick estimating eye is developed in sailor's families because there the two sexes have the chance to see each other at a distance. A sailor, or a sailor's daughter, judges a person of the other sex as quickly and surely as a hunter judges a horse; a farmer, a head of cattle; and a soldier, a rifle. In the families of clergymen and scribes, where the men sit in their houses all their days, people may judge each other extremely well individually, but no man knows what a woman is, and no woman what a man is; they cannot see the wood for trees.

The two sisters, in caps with lace streamers, were doing the honours of the house gracefully. In those days, when gentlemen did not smoke in the presence of ladies, the atmosphere of an evening party remained serene to the end, but a very delicate aromatic and exotic stream of steam rose from the tumblers of rare old rum with hot water, lemon, and sugar, upon the table in the soft glow of the lamp. None of the company was quite uninfluenced by this nectar. They had a moment before been conjuring forth their youth by the singing of old songs which they themselves remembered their fathers' friends singing over their wine in the really good old days. The bishop, who had a very sweet voice, had been holding up his glass while giving the ancient toast to the old generation:

> Let the old ones be remembered now;
> They once were gay and free.
> And that they knew to love, my dear,
> The proof thereof are we!

The echo of the song—for she now declared that it was a five minutes' course from her ear to her mind—was making Miss Fanny De Coninck thoughtful and a little absent-minded. What a strong proof, she thought, are these dry old bodies here tonight of the fact that young men and women, half a century ago, sighed and shivered and lost themselves in ecstasies. What a curious proof is this grey hand, of the follies of young hands upon a night in May long, long ago.

As she was standing, her chin, in this intensive dreaming, pressed down a little upon the black velvet ribbon around her throat, it would have been difficult for anyone who had not known her in her youth to find any trace of beauty in Fanny's face. Time had played a little cruelly with her. A slight wryness of feature, which had been an adorable piquantry once, was now turned into an uncanny little disfigurement. Her birdlike lightness was caricatured into abrupt little movements in fits and starts. But she had her brilliant dark eyes still, and was, all in all, a distinguished, and slightly touching, figure.

After a moment she took up again the conversation with the Bishop as animatedly as before. Even the little handkerchief in her fingers and the small crystal buttons down her narrow silk bosom seemed to take part in the argument. No pythoness on her tripod, her body filled with inspiring fumes, could look more prophetic. The theme under discussion was the question whether, if offered a pair of angel's wings, which could not be removed, one would accept or refuse the gift.

'Ah, Your Right Worshipfulness,' said Miss Fanny, 'in walking up the aisle you would convert the entire congregation with your back. There would not be a sinner left in Copenhagen. But remember that even you descend from the pulpit at twelve o'clock every Sunday. It must be difficult enough for you as it is, but how would you, in a pair of white angels' wings, get out of—' What she really wanted to say was, 'get out of using a chamber-pot?' Had she been forty years younger she would have said it. The De Coninck sisters had not been acquainted with sailors all of their lives for nothing. Very vigorous expressions, and oaths even, such as were never found in the mouths of the other young ladies of Elsinore, came naturally to their rosy lips, and used to charm their admirers into idolatry. They knew a good many names for the devil, and in moments of agitation would say, 'Hell—to hell!' Now the long practice of being a lady and a hostess prevented Fanny, and she said instead very sweetly, 'of eating a roast white turkey?' For that was what the Bishop had been doing at dinner with obvious delight. Still, her imagination was so vividly at work that it was curious that the prelate, gazing, at close quarters, with a fatherly smile into her clear eyes, did not see there the picture of himself, in his canonicals, making use of a chamber-pot in a pair of angels' wings.

The old man was so enlivened by the debate that he spilled a few drops from his glass on to the carpet. 'My dear charming Miss Fanny,' he said, 'I am a good Protestant and flatter myself that I have not quite failed in making things celestial and terrestrial go well together. In that situation I should look down and see, in truth, my celestial individuality reflected in miniature, as you see yours every day in the little bit of glass in your fair hand.'

The old professor of painting said: 'When I was in Italy I was shown a small, curiously shaped bone, which is found only in the shoulder of the lion, and is the remains of a wing bone, from the time when lions had wings, such as we still see in the lion of St. Mark. It was very interesting.'

'Ah, indeed, a fine monumental figure on that column,' said the Bishop, who had also been in Italy, and who knew that he had a leonine head.

'Oh, if I had a chance of those wings,' said Miss Fanny. 'I should not care a hang about my fine or monumental figure. But, by St. Anne, I should fly.'

'Allow me,' said the Bishop, 'to hope, Miss Fanny, that you would not. We may have our reasons to mistrust a flying lady. You have, perhaps, heard of Adam's first wife, Lilith? She was, in contradistinction to Eve, made all out of earth, like himself. What was the first thing that she did? She seduced two angels and made them betray to her the secret word which opens heaven, and so she flew away from Adam. That goes to teach us that where there is too much of the earthly element in a woman, neither husband nor angels can master her.

'Indeed,' he went on, warming to his subject, his glass still in his hand, 'in woman, the particularly heavenly and angelic attributes, and those which we must look up to and worship, all go to weigh her down and keep her on the ground. The long tresses, the veils of pudicity, the trailing garments, even the adorable womanly forms in themselves, the swelling bosom and hip, are as little as possible in conformity with the idea of flying. We, all of us, willingly grant her the title of angel, and the white wings, and lift her up on our highest pedestal, on the one inevitable condition that she must not dream of, must even have been brought up in absolute ignorance of, the possibility of flight.'

'Ah, la la,' said Fanny, 'we are aware of that, Bishop, and so it is ever the woman whom you gentlemen do not love or worship, who possesses neither the long lock nor the swelling bosom, and who has had to truss up her skirts to sweep the floor, who chuckles at the sight of the emblem of her very thraldom, and anoints her broomstick upon the eve of Walpurgis.'

The director of the Royal Theatre rubbed his delicate hands gently against each other. 'When I hear the ladies complain of their hard task and restrictions in life,' he said, 'it sometimes reminds me of a dream that I once had. I was at the time writing a tragedy in verse. It seemed to me in my dream that the words and syllables of my poem made a rebellion and protested, "Why must we take infinite trouble to stand, walk and behave according to difficult and painful laws which the words of your prose do not dream of obeying?" I answered, "Mesdames, because you are meant to be poetry. Of prose we think, and demand, but little. It must exist, if only for the police regulations and the calendar. But a poem which is not lovely has no *raison d'être*." God forgive me if I have ever made poems which had in them no loveliness, and treated ladies in a manner which prevented them from being perfectly lovely—my remaining sins I can shoulder easily then.'

'How,' said the old commodore, 'could I entertain any doubts as to the reality of wings, who have grown up amongst sailing ships and amongst the ladies of the beginning of our century? The beastly steamships which go about these days may well be a species of witches of the sea—they are like self-supporting women. But if you ladies are contemplating giving up being white-sailed ships and poems—well, we must be perfectly lovely poems ourselves, then, and leave you to make up the police regulations. Without poetry no ship can be sailed. When I was a cadet on the way to Greenland, and in the Indian Ocean, I used to console myself, on the middle watch, by thinking, in consecutive order, of all the women I knew, and by quoting poetry that I had learned by heart.'

'But you have always been a poem, Julian,' said Eliza, 'a roundel.' She felt tempted to put her arms round her cousin, they had always been great friends.

'Ah, in talking about Eve and Paradise,' said Fanny, 'you all still remain a little jealous of the snake.'

'When I was in Italy,' said the professor, 'I often thought what a curious thing it is that the serpent, which, if I understand the Scripture, opened the eyes of man to the arts, should be, in itself, an object impossible to get into a picture. A snake is a lovely creature. At Naples they had a large reptile house, and I used to study the snakes there for many hours. They have skins like jewels, and their movements are wonderful performances of art. But I have never seen a snake done successfully in a picture. I could not paint it myself.'

'Do you remember,' said the commodore, who had been following his own thoughts, 'the swing that I put up for you, at Øregaard, on your seventeenth birthday, Eliza? I made a poem about it.'

'Yes, I do, Julian,' said Eliza, her face brightening, 'it was made like a ship.'

It was a curious thing about the two sisters, who had been so unhappy as young women, that they should take so much pleasure in dwelling upon the past. They could talk for hours of the most insignificant trifles of their young days, and these made them laugh and cry more heartily than any event of the present day. Perhaps to them the first condition for anything having real charm was this, that it must not really exist.

It was another curious phenomenon about them that they, to whom so very little had happened, should talk of their married friends who had husbands, children, and grandchildren with pity and slight contempt, as of poor timid creatures whose lives had been dull and uneventful. That they themselves had had no husbands, children, or lovers did not restrain them from feeling that they had chosen the more romantic and adventurous part. The explanation was that to them only possibilities had any interest; realities carried no weight. They had themselves had all possibilities in hand, and had never given them away in order to make a definite choice and come down to a limited reality. They might still take part in elopements by rope-ladder, and in secret marriages, if it came to that. No one could stop them. Thus their only intimate friends were old maids like themselves, or unhappily married women, dames of the round table of possibilities. For their happily married friends, fattened on realities, they had, with much kindness, a different language, as if these had been of a slightly lower caste, with whom intercourse had to be carried on with the assistance of interpreters.

Eliza's face had brightened, like a fine, pure jar of alabaster behind which a lamp is lighted, at mention of the swing, made like a boat, which had been given her for her seventeenth birthday. She had always been by far the loveliest of the De Coninck children. When they were young their old French aunt had named them *la Bonté*, *la Beauté*, and *l'Esprit*, Morten being *la Bonté*.

She was as fair as her sister was dark, and in Elsinore, where at the time a fashion for surnames had prevailed, they had called her 'Ariel', or 'The Swan of Elsinore'. There had been that particular quality about her beauty that it seemed to hold promise, to be only the first step of the ladder of some extraordinary career. Here was this exceptional young female creature who had had the inspiration to be, from head to foot, strikingly lovely. But that was only the beginning of it. The next step was perhaps her clothes, for Eliza had always been a great swell, and had run up heavy debts—for which at times her brother had taken the responsibility before their father—on brocades, cashmeres, and plumes ordered from Copenhagen and Hamburg, and even from Paris. But that was also only the beginning of something. Then came the way in which she moved, and danced. There was about it an atmosphere of suspense which caused onlookers to hold their breaths. What was this extraordinary girl to do next? If at this time she had indeed unfolded a pair of large white wings, and had soared from the pier of Elsinore up into the summer air, it would have surprised no one. It was clear that she must do something extraordinary with such an abundance of gifts. 'There is more strength in that girl,' said the old boatswain of *La Fortuna*, when upon a spring day she came running down to the harbour, bareheaded, 'than in all *Fortuna*'s crew.' Then in the end she had done nothing at all.

At Gammeltorv she was quietly, as if intentionally, fading day by day, into an even more marble-like loveliness. She could still span her waist with her two long slim hands, and moved with much pride and lightness, like an old Arab mare a little stiff, but unmistakably noble, at ease in the sphere of war and fantasias. And there was still that about her which kept open a perspective, the feeling that somewhere there were reserves and it was not out of the question that extraordinary things might happen.

'God, that swing, Eliza!' said the commodore. 'You had been so hard on me in the evening that I actually went out into the garden of Øregaard, on that early July morning, resolved to hang myself. And as I was looking up into the crown of the great elm, I heard you saying behind me, 'That would be a good branch.' That, I thought, was cruelly said. But as I turned around, there you were, your hair still done up in curling papers, and I remembered that I had promised you a swing. I could not die, in any case, till you had had it. When I got it up, and saw you in it, I thought: If it shall be my lot in life to be for ever only ballast to the white sails of fair girls, I still bless my lot.'

'That is why we have loved you for all your life,' said Eliza.

An extremely pretty young maid, with pale blue ribbons on her cap—kept by the pair of old spiritual courtesans to produce an equilibrium in the establishment, in the way in which two worldly young courtesans might have kept, to the same end, an ugly and misshapen servant, a dwarf with wit and imagination—brought in a tray filled with all sorts of delicacies: Chinese ginger, tangerines, and crystallized fruit. In passing Miss Fanny's chair she said softly, 'Madam Baek has come from Elsinore, and waits in the kitchen.'

Fanny's colour changed, she could never receive calmly the news that anybody had arrived, or had gone away. Her soul left her and flew straight to the kitchen, from where she had to drag it back again.

'In that summer of 1806,' she said, 'the *Odyssey* had been translated into Danish for the first time, I believe. Papa used to read it to us in the evenings. Ha, how we played the hero and his gallant crew, braved the Cyclops and cruised between the island of the Laestrygones and the Phaeacian shores! I shall never be made to believe that we did not spend that summer in our ships, under brown sails.'

Shortly after this the party broke up, and the sisters drew up the blinds of their window to wave to the four gentlemen who helped Miss Bardenfleth into her court carriage and proceeded in a gaily talking group across the little iron-grey desert of nocturnal Gammeltorv, remarking, in the midst of philosophical and poetic discussions, upon the extraordinary cold.

This moment at the end of their parties always went strangely to the sisters' hearts. They were happy to get rid of their guests; but a little silent, bitter minute accompanied the pleasure. For they could still make people fall in love with them. They had the radiance in them which could refract little rainbow effects in the atmosphere of Copenhagen existence. But who could make them feel in love? That glass of mental and sentimental alcohol which made for warmth and movement within the old phlebolitic veins of their guests—from where were they themselves to get it? From each other, they knew, and in general they were content with the fact. Still, at this moment, the *tristesse* of the eternal hostess stiffened them a little.

Not so tonight, for no sooner had they lowered the blind again than they were off to the kitchen, making haste to send their pretty maid to bed, as if they knew the real joy of life to be found solely amongst elderly women. They made Madam Baek and themselves a fresh cup of coffee, lifting down the old copper kettle from the wall. Coffee, according to the women of Denmark, is to the body what the word of the Lord is to the soul.

Had it been in the old days that the sisters and their servant met again after a long separation, the girls would have started at once to entertain the widow with accounts of their admirers. The theme was ever fascinating to Madam Baek, and dear to the sisters by reason of the opportunity it gave them of shocking her. But these days were past. They gave her the news of the town—an old widower had married again, and another had gone mad—also a little gossip of the Court, such as she would understand, which they had heard from Miss Bardenfleth. But there was something in Madam Baek's face which caught their attention. It was heavy with fate; she brought news herself. Very soon they paused to let her speak.

Madam Baek allowed the pause to wax long.

'Master Morten,' she said at last, and at the sound of her own thoughts of these last long days and nights she herself grew very pale, 'is at Elsinore. He walks in the house.'

At this news a deadly silence filled the kitchen. The two sisters felt their hair stand on end. The terror of the moment lay, for them, in this: that it was Madam Baek who had recounted such news to them. They might have announced it to her, out of perversity and fancies, and it would not have meant much. But that Hanne, who was to them the principle of solidity and equilibrium for the whole world, should open her mouth to throw at them the end of all things—that made these seconds in their kitchen feel to the two younger women like the first seconds of a great earthquake.

Madam Baek herself felt the unnatural in the situation, and all which was passing through the heads of her ladies. It would have terrified her as well, had she still had it in her to be terrified. Now she felt only a great triumph.

'I have seen him,' she said, 'seven times.'

Here the sisters took to trembling so violently that they had to put down their coffee cups.

'The first time,' said Madam Baek, 'he stood in the red dining-room, looking at the big clock. But the clock had stopped. I had forgotten to wind it up.'

Suddenly a rain of tears sprang out of Fanny's eyes, and bathed her pale face. 'Oh, Hanne, Hanne,' she said.

'Then I met him once on the stair,' said Madam Baek. 'Three times he has come and sat with me. Once he picked up a ball of wool for me, which had rolled on to the floor, and threw it back in my lap.'

'How did he look to you?' asked Fanny, in a broken, cracked voice, evading the glance of her sister, who sat immovable.

'He looks older than when he went away,' said Madam Baek. 'He wears his hair longer than people do here; that will be the American fashion. His clothes are very old, too. But he smiled at me just as he always did. The third time that I saw him, before he went—for he goes in his own way, and just as you think he is there, he is gone—he blew me a kiss exactly as he used to do when he was a young man and I had scolded him a little.'

Eliza lifted her eyes, very slowly, and the eyes of the two sisters met. Never in all their lives had Madam Baek said anything to them which they had for a moment doubted.

'But,' said Madam Baek, 'this last time I found him standing before your two pictures for a long time. And I thought that he wanted to see you, so I have come to fetch you to Elsinore.'

At these words the sisters rose up like two grenadiers at parade. Madam Baek herself, although terribly agitated, sat where she had sat, as ever the central figure of their gatherings.

'When was it that you saw him?' asked Fanny.

'The first time,' said Madam Baek, 'was three weeks ago today. The last time was on Saturday. Then I thought, "Now I must go and fetch the ladies." '

Fanny's face was suddenly all ablaze. She looked at Madam Baek with a great tenderness, the tenderness of their young days. She felt that this was a great sacrifice, which the old woman was bringing out of her devotion to them and her sense of duty. For these three weeks, during which she had been living with the ghost of the outcast son of the De Coninck house, all alone, must have been the great time of Madam Baek's life, and would remain so for her for ever. Now it was over.

It would have been difficult to say if, when she spoke, she came nearest to laughter or tears. 'Oh, we will go, Hanne,' she said, 'we will go to Elsinore.'

'Fanny, Fanny,' said Eliza, 'he is not there; it is not he.'

Fanny made a step forward towards the fire, so violently that the streamers of her cap fluttered. 'Why not, Lizzie?' she said. 'God means to do something for you and me after all. And do you not remember, when Morten was to go back to school after the holiday, and did not want to go, that he made us tell Papa that he was dead? We made a grave under the apple tree, and laid him down in it. Do you remember?' The two sisters at this moment saw, with the eyes of their minds, exactly the same picture of the little ruddy boy, with earth in his curls, who had been lifted out of his grave by their angry young father, and of themselves, with their small spades and soiled muslin frocks, following the procession home like disappointed mourners. Their brother might play a trick on them this time.

As they turned to each other their two faces had the same expression of youthful waggishness. Madam Baek, in her chair, felt at the sight like a happily delivered lady-in-the-straw. A weight and a fullness had been taken from her, and her importance had gone with it. That was ever the way of the gentry. They would lay their hands on everything you had, even to the ghosts.

Madam Baek would not let the sisters come back with her to Elsinore. She made them stay behind for a day. She wanted to see for herself that the rooms were warm to receive them, and that there would be hot water bottles in those maiden beds in which they had not slept for so long. She went the next day, leaving them in Copenhagen till the morrow.

It was good for them that they had been given these hours in which to make up their minds and prepare themselves to meet the ghost of their brother. A storm had broken loose upon them, and their boats, which had been becalmed in back waters, were whirled in a blizzard, amongst waves as high as houses. Still they were, in their lappets of lace, no land-lubbers in the tempests of life. They were still able to manoeuvre, and they held their sheets. They did not melt into tears either. Tears were never a solution for them. They came first and were a weakness only; now they were past them, out in the great dilemma. They were themselves acquainted with the old sailor's rule:

> *Comes wind before rain—Topsail down and up again.*
> *Comes rain before wind—Topsail down and all sails in.*

They did not speak together much while waiting for admission to their Elsinore house. Had the day been Sunday they would have gone to church, for they were keen churchgoers, and critics of the prominent preachers of the town, so that they generally came back holding that they could have done it better themselves. In the church they might have joined company; the house of the Lord alone of all houses might have held them both. Now they had to wander in opposite parts of the town, in snowy streets and parks, their small hands in muffs, gazing at cold naked statues and frozen birds in the trees.

How were two highly respected, wealthy, popular and petted ladies to welcome again the hanged boy of their own blood? Fanny walked up and down the linden avenue of the Royal Rose Gardens of Rosenborg. She could never revisit it later, not even in summer time, when it was a green and golden bower, filled like an aviary with children's voices. She carried with her, from one end of it to the other, a picture of her brother, looking at the clock, and the clock stopped and dead. The picture grew upon her. It was upon his mother's death from grief of him that he was gazing, and upon the broken heart of his bride. The picture still grew. It was upon all the betrayed and broken hearts of the world, all the sufferings of weak and dumb creatures, all injustice and despair on earth, that he was gazing. And she felt that it was all laid upon her shoulders. The responsibility was hers. That the world suffered and died was the fault of the De Conincks. Her misery drove her up and down the avenue like a dry leaf before the wind—a distinguished lady in furred boots, in her own heart a great, mad, wing-clipped bird, fluttering in the winter sunset. Looking askance she could see her own large nose, pink under her veil, like a terrible, cruel beak. From time to time a question came into her mind: What is Eliza thinking now? It was strange that the elder sister should feel thus, with bitterness and fear, that her younger sister had deserted her in her hour of need. She had herself fled her company, and yet she repeated to herself: 'What, could she not watch with me one hour?' It had been so even in the old De Coninck home. If things began to grow really difficult, Morten and the Papa and Mamma De Coninck would turn to the quiet younger girl, so much less brilliant than herself: 'What does Eliza think?'

Towards evening, as it grew dark, and as she reflected that Madam Baek must by now be at home in Elsinore, Fanny suddenly stopped and thought, Am I to pray to God? Several of her friends, she knew, had found comfort in prayer. She herself had not prayed since she had been a child. Upon the occasions of her Sundays in church, which were visits of courtesy to the Lord, her little silences of bent head had been gestures of civility. Her prayer now, as she began to form it, did not please her either. She used, as a girl, to read out his correspondence to her papa, so she was well acquainted with the jargon of mendicant letters—'. . . . Feeling deeply impressed with the magnificence of your noble and well-known loving-kindness . . .' She herself had had many mendicant letters in her days; also many young men had begged her, on their knees, for something. She had been highly generous to the poor, and hard on the lovers. She had not begged herself, nor would she begin it now on behalf of her proud young brother. As her prayer took on a certain likeness to a mendicant letter or to a proposal, she stopped it. 'He shall not be ashamed,' she thought, 'for he has called upon me. He shall not be afraid of ten thousands of people that have set themselves against him round about.' Upon this she walked home.

When upon Saturday afternoon the sisters arrived at the house in Elsinore, they went through much deep agitation of the heart. Even the air—even the smell in the hall, that atmosphere of salt and seaweed which ever braces up old seaside houses—went straight through them. They say, thought Miss Fanny, sniffing, that your body is changed completely within the course of seven years. How I have changed, and how I have forgotten! But my nose must be the same. My nose I have still kept and it remembers all. The house was as warm as a box, and this struck them as a sweet compliment, as if an old admirer had put on his gala uniform for them. Many people, in revisiting old places, sigh at the sight of change and age. The De Coninck sisters, on the contrary, felt that the old house might well have deplored the signs of age and decay at this meeting again of theirs, and have cried: Heavens, heavens! Are these the damask-cheeked, silver-voiced girls in dancing sandals who used to slide down the bannisters of my stairs?—sighing down its long chimneys. Oh God! Fare away, fare away! When, then, it chose to pass over its feelings and pretend that they were the same, it was a fine piece of courtesy on its part.

Old Madam Baek's great and ceremonious delight in their visit was also bound to touch them. She stood out on the steps to receive them; she changed their shoes and stockings for them, and had warm drinks ready. If we can make her happy so easily, they thought, how is it that we never came till now? Was it that the house of their childhood and young days had seemed to them a little empty and cold, a little grave-like, until it had a ghost in it?

Madam Baek took them around to show them the spots where Morten had stood, and she repeated his gestures many times. The sisters did not care a pin what gestures he would make to anybody but themselves, but they valued the old woman's love of their brother, and listened patiently. In the end Madam Baek felt very proud, as if she had been given a sacred relic out of the boy's beloved skeleton, a little bone that was hers to keep.

The room in which supper was made ready was a corner room. It turned two windows to the east, from which there was a view of the old grey castle of Kronborg, copper-spired, like a clenched fist out in the Sound. Above the ramparts departed commandants of the fortress had made a garden, in which, in their winter bareness, lindens now showed the world what loosely built trees they are when not drilled to walk, militarily, two by two. Two windows looked south out upon the harbour. It was strange to find the harbour of Elsinore motionless, with sailors walking back from their boats on the ice.

The walls of the room had once been painted crimson, but with time the colour had faded into a richness of hues, like a glassful of dying red roses. In the candlelight these flat walls blushed and shone deeply, in places glowing like little pools of dry, burning, red lacquer. On one wall hung the portraits of the two young De Coninck sisters, the beauties of Elsinore. The third portrait, of their brother, had been taken down so long ago that only a faint shadow on the wall showed where it had once been. Some pot-pourri was being burned on the tall stove, on the sides of which Neptune, with a trident, steered his team of horses through high waves. But the dried rose-petals, dated from summers of long ago. Only a very faint fragrance now spread from their funeral pile, a little rank, like the bouquet of fine claret kept too long. In front of the stove the table was laid with a white tablecloth and delicate Chinese cups and plates.

In this room the sisters and the brother De Coninck had in the old days celebrated many secret supper-parties, when preparing some theatrical or fancy-dress show, or when Morten had returned very late at night from an expedition in his sailing boat, of which their parents must know nothing. The eating and drinking at such times had to be carried on in a subdued manner, so as not to wake up the sleeping house. Thirty-five years ago the red room had seen much merriment caused by this precaution.

Faithful to tradition, the Misses De Coninck now came in and took their seats at table, opposite each other, on either side of the stove, and in silence. To these indefatigable old belles of a hundred balls, age and agitation all the same began to assert themselves. Their eyelids were heavy, and they could not have held out much longer if something had not happened.

They did not have to wait long. Just as they had poured out their tea, and were lifting the thin cups to their lips, there was a slight rustle in the quiet room. When they turned their heads a little, they saw their brother standing at the end of the table.

He stood there for a moment and nodded to them, smiling at them. Then he took the third chair and sat down between them. He placed his hands upon the edge of the table, gently moving them sideward and back again, exactly as he always used to do.

Morten was poorly dressed in a dark grey coat that looked faded and much worn. Still it was clear that he had taken pains about his appearance for the meeting, he had on a white collar and a carefully tied high black stock, and his hair was neatly brushed back. Perhaps he had been afraid, Fanny for a moment thought, that after having lived so long in rough company he should impress his sisters as less refined and well mannered than before. He need not have worried; he would have looked a gentleman on the gallows. He was older than when they had seen him last, but not as old as they. He looked a man of forty.

His face was somehow coarser than before, weather-beaten and very pale. It had, with the dark, always somewhat sunken eyes, that same divine play of light and darkness which had long ago made maidens mad. His large mouth also had its old frankness and sweetness. But to his pure forehead a change had come. It was not that it was now crossed by a multitude of little horizontal lines, for the marble of it was too fine to be marred by such superficial wear. But time had revealed its true character. It was not the imperial tiara, that once had caught all eyes, above his dark brows. It was the grave and noble likeness to a skull. The radiance of it belonged to the possessor, not of the world, but of the grave and of eternity. Now, as his hair had withdrawn from it, it gave out the truth frankly and simply. Also, as you got, from the face of the brother, the key of understanding to this particular type of family beauty, you would recognize it at once in the appearance of the sisters, even in the two youthful portraits on the wall. The most striking characteristic in the three heads was the generic resemblance to the skull.

All in all, Morten's countenance was quiet, considerate, and dignified, as it had always been.

'Good evening, little sisters; well met, well met,' he said, 'it was very sweet and sisterly of you to come and see me here. You had a—' he stopped a moment, as if searching for his word, as if not in the habit of speaking much with other people—'a nice fresh drive to Elsinore, I should say,' he concluded.

His sisters sat with their faces towards him, as pale as he. Morten had always been wont to speak very lowly, in contrast to themselves. Thus a discussion between the sisters might be carried on with the two speaking at the same time, on the chance of the one shrill voice drowning the other. But if you wanted to hear what Morten said, you had to listen. He spoke in just the same way now, and they had been prepared for his appearance, more or less, but not for his voice.

They listened then as they had done before. But they were longing to do more. As they had set eyes on him they had turned their slim torsos all around in their chairs. Could they not touch him? No, they knew that to be out of the question. They had not been reading ghost stories all their lives for nothing. And this very thing recalled to them the old days, when, for these private supper-parties of theirs, Morten had come in at times, his large cloak soaked with rain and sea water, shining, black and rough like a shark's skin, or glazed over with snow, or freshly tarred, so that they had, laughing, held him at arm's length off their frocks. Oh, how thoroughly had the tunes of thirty years ago been transposed from a major to a minor key! From what blizzards had he come in tonight? With what sort of tar was he tarred?

'How are you, my dears?' he asked. 'Do you have as merry a time in Copenhagen as in the old days at Elsinore?'

'And how are you yourself, Morten?' asked Fanny, her voice a full octave higher than his, 'You are looking a real, fine privateer captain. You are bringing all the full, spiced, trade winds into our nunnery of Elsinore.'

'Yes, those are fine winds,' said Morten.

'How far away have you been, Morten?' said Eliza, her voice trembling a little. 'What a multitude of lovely places you have visited, that we have never seen! How I have wished, how I have wished that I were you.'

Fanny gave her sister a quick strong glance. Had their thoughts gone up in a parallel motion from the snowy parks and streets of Copenhagen? Or did this quiet sister, younger than she, far less brilliant, speak the simple truth of her heart?'

'Yes, Lizzie, my duck,' said Morten. 'I remember that. I have thought of that—how you used to cry and stamp your little feet and wring your hands shouting, "Oh, I wish I were dead."'

'Where do you come from, Morten?' Fanny asked him.

'I come from hell,' said Morten. 'I beg your pardon,' he added, as he saw his sister wince. 'I have come now, as you see, because the Sound is frozen over. I can come then. That is a rule.'

Oh, how the heart of Fanny flew upward at his words. She felt it herself, as if she had screamed out, in a shout of deliverance, like a woman in the final moment of childbirth. When the Emperor, from Elba, set foot on the soil of France he brought back the old time with him. Forgotten was red-hot Moscow, and the deadly white and black winter marches. The tricolour was up in the air, unfolded, and the old grenadiers threw up their arms and cried once more: *Vive l'Empereur!* Her soul, like they, donned the old uniform. It was for the benefit of onlookers only, and for the fun of the thing, from now, that she was dressed up in the body of an old woman.

'Are we not looking a pair of old scarecrows, Morten?' she asked, her eyes shining at him. 'Were not our old aunts right when they preached to us about our vanity, and the vanity of all things? Indeed, the people who impress on the young that they should purchase, in time, crutches and an ear-trumpet, do carry their point in the end.'

'No, you are looking charming, Fanny,' he said, his eyes shining gently back. 'Like a bumblebee-hawkmoth.'–For they used to collect butterflies together in their childhood. 'And if you were really looking like a pair of old ladies I should like it very much. There have been few of them where I have been, for many years. Now when grandmamma had her birthday parties at Øregaard, that was where you would see a houseful of fine old ladies. Like a grand aviary, and grandmamma amongst them like a proud cockatoo.'

'Yet you once said,' said Fanny, 'that you would give a year of your existence to be free from spending the afternoon with the old devils.'

'Yes, I did that,' said Morten, 'but my ideas about a year of my existence have changed since then. But tell me seriously, do they still tie weights to *billets-doux*, and throw them into your carriage when you drive home from the balls?'

'Oh!' said Eliza, drawing in her breath.

> Was klaget aus dem dunkeln Thal
> Die Nachtigall?
> Was seuszt darein der Erlenbach
> Mit manchen Ach?

She was quoting a long-forgotten poem by a long-forgotten lover.

'You are not married, my dears, are you?' said Morten, suddenly frightened at the absurd possibility of a stranger belonging to his sisters.

'Why should we not be married?' asked Fanny. 'We both of us have husbands and lovers at each finger-tip. I, I married the Bishop of Sealand—he lost his balance a little in our bridal bed because of his wings.' She could not prevent a delicate thin little laughter coming out of her in small puffs, like steam from a kettle-spout. The Bishop looked, at the distance of forty-eight hours, ridiculously small, like a little doll seen from a tower. 'Lizzie married—' she went, and then stopped herself.

When they were children the young De Conincks had lived under a special superstition, which they had from a marionette comedy. It came to this: that the lies which you tell are likely to become truth. On this account they had always been careful in their choice of what lies they would tell. Thus they would never say that they could not pay a Sunday visit to their old aunts because they had a toothache, for they would be afraid that Nemesis might be at their heels, and that they would indeed have a toothache. But they might safely say that their music master had told them not to practise their gavottes any longer, as they already played them with masterly art. The habit was still in their blood.

'No, to speak the truth, Morten,' Fanny said, 'we are old maids, all on your account. Nobody would have us. The De Conincks have had a bad name as consorts since you went off and took away the heart and soul and innocence of Adrienne.'

She looked at him to see what he would say to this. She had followed his thoughts. They had been faithful, but he—what had he done? He had encumbered them with a lovely and gentle sister-in-law.

Their uncle, Fernand De Coninck, he who had helped Morten to get his ship, had in the old days lived in France during the Revolution. That was the place and the time for a De Coninck to live in. Also he had never got quite out of them again, not even when he had been an old bachelor in Elsinore, and he never felt quite at home in a peaceful life. He had been full of anecdotes and songs of the period, and when they had been children the brother and the sisters had known them by heart from him. After a moment Morten slowly and in a low voice began to quote one of Uncle Fernand's ditties. This had been made on a special occasion, when the old aunts of the King of France had been leaving the country, and the revolutionary police had ordered all their boxes to be opened and examined at the frontier, for fear of treachery.

He said:

> Avez-vous ses chemises,
> à Marat?
> Avez-vous ses chemises?
> C'est pour vous très vilain cas
> si vous les avez prises.

Fanny's face immediately reflected the expression of her brother's. Without searching her memory more than a moment she followed him with the next verse of the song. This time it is the King's old aunts speaking:

> Avait-il de chemises,
> à Marat?
> Avait-il de chemises?
> Moi je crois qu'il n'en avait pas.
> Où les avait-il prises?

And Eliza took up the thread after her, laughing a little:

> Il en avait troi grises,
> à Marat?
> Il en avait trois grises.
> Avec l'argent de son mandat
> sur le Pont Neuf acquises.

With these words the brother and the sisters lightened their hearts and washed their hands for ever of fair, unhappy Adrienne Rosenstand.

'But you were married, Morten?' said Eliza kindly, the laughter still in her voice.

'Yes,' said Morten, 'I had five wives. The Spanish are lovely women, you know, like a mosaic of jewels. One of them was a dancer, too. When she danced it was really like a swarm of butterflies whirling round, and being drawn into, the little central flame; you did not know what was up and what was down, and that seemed to me then, when I was young, a charming quality in a wife. One was an English skipper's daughter, an honest girl, and she will never have forgotten me. One was the young widow of a rich planter. She was a real lady. All her thoughts had some sort of long train trailing after them. She bore me two children. One was a Negress, and her I liked best.'

'Did they go on board your ship?' Eliza asked.

'No, none of them ever came on board my ship,' said Morten.

'And tell us,' said Fanny, 'which, out of all the things that you had, you liked the best?'

Morten thought her question over for a moment. 'Out of all lives,' he said, 'the life of a pirate is the best.'

'Finer than that of a privateer captain in the Sound?' asked Fanny.

'Yes, it is that,' said Morten, 'inasmuch as you are in the open sea.'

'But what made you decide to become a pirate?' asked Fanny, much intrigued, for this was really like a book of romance and adventure.

'The heart, the heart,' said Morten, 'that which throws us into all our disasters. I fell in love. It was the *coup de foudre* of which Uncle Fernand spoke so much. He himself knew it to be no laughing matter. And she was somebody else's, so I could not have her without cheating law and order a little. She was built in Genoa, had been used by the French as a dispatch-carrier, and was known to be the quickest schooner that ever flew over the Atlantic. She was run ashore at the coast of the island of St. Martin, which is half French and half Dutch, and was sold by the Dutch at Philippsburg. Old Van Zandten, the ship-owner, who employed me then and loved me as a son, sent me to Philippsburg to buy her for him. She was the loveliest, yes, by far the loveliest thing I ever saw. She was like a swan. When she came along, carrying the press of her sails, she was light, gallant, noble, a great lady—like one of grandmamma's swans at Øregaard, when we teased them—pure, loyal, like a Damascene blade. And then, my dears, she was a little like *Fortuna II*. She had, like her, a very small foresail with an unusually large mainsail and high boom.

'I took all old Van Zandten's money then and bought her for myself, and after that we had, she and I, to keep off the respectable people of the country. What are you to do when love sets to at you? I made her a faithful lover, and she had a fine time with her loyal crew, adored and petted like a dainty lady who has her toe-nails polished with henna. With me she became the fear of the Caribbean Sea, the little sea-eaglet who kept the tame birds on the stir. So I do not know for certain whether I did right or wrong. Shall not he have the fair woman who loves her most?'

'And was she in love with you as well?' asked Eliza, laughing.

'But who shall ask a woman if she is in love with him?' said Morten. 'The question to ask about woman is this "What is her price, and will you pay it?" We should not cheat them, but should ask them courteously and pay with a good grace, whether it be cash, love, marriage, or our life or honour which they charge us; or else, if we are poor people and cannot pay, take off our hats to them and leave them for the wealthier man. That has been sound moral Latin with men and women since the world began. As to their loving us—for one thing, Can they love us?'

'And what of the women who have no price?' said Eliza, laughing still.

'What of those indeed, dear?' said Morten. 'Whatever they ought to have been, they should not have been women. God may have them, and he may know what to do with them. They drive men into bad places, and afterwards they cannot get us out even when they want to.'

'What was the name of your ship?' asked Eliza, her eyes cast down.

Morten looked up at her, laughing. 'The name of my ship was *La Belle Eliza,*' he answered. 'Did you not know?'

'Yes, I knew,' said Eliza, her voice full of laughter once more. 'A merchant captain of Papa's told me, many years ago in Copenhagen, how his crew had gone mad with fear and had made him turn back into port when, off St. Thomas, they spied the topsails of a pirate ship. They were as afraid of her, he said, as of Satan himself. And he told me that the name of the ship was *La Belle Eliza.* I thought then that she would be your boat.'

So this was the secret which the old maid had guarded from all the world. She had not been marble all through. Somewhere within her this little flame of happiness had been kept alive. To this purpose—for it had been to no other—had she grown up so lovely in Elsinore. A ship was in blue water, as in a bed of hyacinths, in winds and warm air, her full white sails like to a bold chalk-cliff, baked by the sun, with much sharp steel in boards, not one of the broadswords or knives not red, and the name of the ship fairly and truly *La Belle Eliza.* Oh, you burghers of Elsinore, did you see me dance the minuet once? To those same measures did I tread the waves.

While he had been speaking the colour had mounted to her face. She looked once more like a girl, and the white streamers of her cap were no longer the finery of an old lady but the attire of a chaste, flaming bride.

'Yes, she was like a swan,' Morten said, 'sweet, sweet, like a song.'

'Had I been in that merchant ship,' said Eliza, 'and you had boarded her, your ship should have been mine by right, Morten.'

'Yes,' said he, smiling at her, 'and my whole *matelotage.* That was our custom when we took young women. You would have had an adoring seraglio.'

'I lost her,' he said, 'through my own fault, at a river mouth of Venezuela. It is a long story. One of my men betrayed her anchoring place to the British governor of Port of Spain, in Trinidad. I was not with her then. I had gone myself the sixty miles to Port of Spain in a fishing boat, to get information about a Dutch cargo boat. I saw all my crew hanged there, and saw her for the last time.

'It was after that,' he said after a pause, 'that I never slept well again. I could not get down into sleep. Whenever I tried to dive down into it I was shoved upward again, like a piece of flotsam. From that time I began to lose weight, for I had thrown overboard my ballast. It was with her. I had become too light for anything. From that time on I was somehow without body. Do you remember how Papa and Uncle Fernand used to discuss, at dinner, the wines which they had bought together, and to talk of some of them having a fine enough bouquet, but no body to them? That was the case with me, then, my dears: a bouquet I should say that I may still have had, but no body. I could not sink into friendship, or fear, or any real delight any longer. And still I could not sleep.'

The sisters had no need to pretend sympathy with this misfortune. It was their own. All the De Conincks suffered from sleeplessness. When they had been children they had laughed at their father and his sisters when they greeted one another in the morning first of all with minute enquiries and accounts of how they had slept at night. Now they did not laugh; the matter meant much to them also now.

'But when you cannot sleep at night,' said Fanny, sighing, 'is it that you wake up very early, or is it that you cannot fall asleep at all?'

'Nay, I cannot fall asleep at all,' said Morten.

'Is it not, then,' asked Fanny, 'because you are—' She would have said 'cold,' but remembering where he had said he came from, she stopped herself.

'And I have known all the time,' said Morten, who did not seem to have heard what she said to him, 'that I shall never lay me down to rest until I can sleep once more on her, in her, *La Belle Eliza.*'

'But you lived ashore, too,' said Fanny, her mind running after his, for she felt as if he were about to escape her.

'Yes, I did,' said Morten. 'I had for some time a tobacco plantation in Cuba. And that was a delightful place. I had a white house with pillars which you would have liked very much. The air of those islands is fine, delicate, like a glass of true rum. It was there that I had the lovely wife, the planter's widow, and two children. There were women to dance with there, at our balls, light like the trade winds—like you two. I had a very pretty pony to ride there, named Pegasus; a little like Papa's Zampa—Do you remember him?'

'And you were happy there?' Fanny asked.

'Yes, but it did not last,' said Morten. 'I spent too much money. I lived beyond my means, something which Papa had always warned me against. I had to clear out of it.' He sat silent for a little while.

'I had to sell my slaves,' he said.

At these words he grew so deadly pale, so ashen grey, that had they not known him to be dead for long they would have been afraid that he might be going to die. His eyes, all his features, seemed to sink into his face. It became the face of a man upon the stake, when the flames take hold.

The two women sat pale and rigid with him, in deep silence. It was as if the breath of the hoarfrost had dimmed three windows. They had no word of comfort for their brother in this situation. For no De Coninck had ever parted with a servant. It was a code to them that whoever entered their service must remain there and be looked after by them for ever. They might make an exception with regard to marriage or death, but unwillingly. In fact it was the opinion of their circle of friends that in their old age the sisters had come to have only one real object in life, which was to amuse their servants.

Also they felt the secret contempt for all men, as beings unable to raise money at any fatal moment, which belongs to fair women with their consciousness of infinite resources. The sisters De Coninck, in Cuba, would never have allowed things to come to such a tragic point. Could they not easily have sold themselves three hundred times, and made three hundred Cubans happy, and so saved the welfare of their three hundred slaves? There was, therefore, a long pause.

'But the end,' said Fanny finally, drawing in her breath deeply, 'that was not yet, then?'

'No, no,' said Morten, 'not till quite a long time after that. When I had no more money I started an old brig in the carrying trade, from Havana to New Orleans first, and then from Havana to New York. Those are difficult seas.' His sister had succeeded in turning his mind away from his distress, and as he began to explain to her the various routes of his trade he warmed to his subject. Altogether he had, during the meeting, become more and more sociable and had got back all his old manner of a man who is at ease in company and is in really good understanding with the minds of his convives. 'But nothing would go right for me,' he went on. 'I had one run of bad luck after another. No, in the end, you see, my ship foundered near the Cay Sal bank, where she ran full of water and sank in a dead calm; and with one thing and another, in the end, if you do not mind my saying so, in Havana I was hanged. Did you know that?'

'Yes,' said Fanny.

'Did you mind that, I wondered, you two?' he asked.

'No!' said his sisters with energy.

They might have answered him with their eyes turned away, but they both looked back at him. And they thought that this might perhaps be the reason why he was wearing his collar and stock so unusually high; there might be a mark on that strong and delicate neck around which they had tied the cambric with great pains when they have been going to balls together.

There was a moment's silence in the red room, after which Fanny and Morten began to speak at the same time.

'I beg your pardon,' said Morten.

'No,' said Fanny, 'no. What were you going to say?'

'I was asking about Uncle Fernand,' said Morten. 'Is he still alive?'

'Oh, no, Morten, my dear,' said Fanny, 'he died in 'thirty. He was an old man then. He was at Adrienne's wedding, and made a speech, but he was very tired. In the evening he took me aside and said to me: "My dear, it is a *gênante fête*." And he died only three weeks later. He left Eliza his money and furniture. In a drawer we found a little silver locket, set with rose diamonds, with a curl of fair hair, and on it was written, "The hair of Charlotte Corday."'

'I see,' said Morten. 'He had a fine figure, Uncle Fernand. And Aunt Adelaide, is she dead too?'

'Yes, she died even before he did,' said Fanny. She meant to tell him something of the death of Madame Adelaide De Coninck, but did not go on. She felt depressed. These people were dead; he ought to have known of them. The loneliness of her dead brother made her a little sick at heart.

'How she used to preach to us, Aunt Adelaide,' he said. 'How many times did she say to me: "This melancholy of yours, Morten, this dissatisfaction with life which you and the girls allow yourselves, makes me furious. What is good enough for me is good enough for you. You all ought to be married and have large families to look after; that would cure you." And you, Fanny, said to her: "Yes, little Aunt, that was the advice, from an auntie of his, which our Papa did follow."'

'Towards the end,' Eliza broke in, 'she would not hear or think of anything that had happened since the time when she was thirty years old and her husband died. Of her grandchildren she said: "These are some of the new-fangled devices of my young children. They will soon find out how little there is to them." But she could remember all the religious scruples of Uncle Theodore, her husband, and how he kept her awake at night with meditations upon the fall of man and original sin. Of those she was still proud.'

'You must think me very ignorant,' Morten said. 'You know so many things of which I know nothing.'

'Oh, dear Morten,' said Fanny, 'you surely know of a lot of things of which we know nothing at all.'

'Not many, Fanny,' said Morten. 'One or two, perhaps.'

'Tell us one or two,' said Eliza.

Morten thought over her demand for a little while.

'I have come to know of one thing,' he said, 'of which I myself had no idea once. *C'est une invention très fine, très spirituelle, de la part de Dieu*, as Uncle Fernand said of love. It is this: that you cannot eat your cake and have it. I should never have hit upon that on my own. It is indeed an original idea. But then, you see, he is really *très fin, très spirituel*, the Lord.'

The two sisters drew themselves up slightly, as if they had received a compliment. They were, as already said, keen churchgoers, and their brother's words had ever carried great weight with them.

'But do you know,' said Morten suddenly, 'that little snappy pug of Aunt Adelaide's, Fingal—him I have seen.'

'How was that?' Fanny asked. 'Tell us about that.'

'That was when I was all alone,' said Morten, 'when my ship had foundered at the Cay Sal bank. We were three who got away in a boat, but we had no water. The others died, and in the end I was alone.'

'What did you think of then?' Fanny asked.

'Do you know, I thought of you,' said Morten.

'What did you think of us?' Fanny asked again in a low voice.

Morten said, 'I thought: we have been amateurs in saying no, little sisters. But God can say no. Good God, how he can say no. We think that he can go on no longer, not even he. But he goes on, and says no once more.

'I had thought of that before, quite a good deal,' Morten said, 'at Elsinore, during the time before my wedding. And now I kept on thinking upon it. I thought of those great, pure, and beautiful things which say no to us. For why should they say yes to us, and tolerate our insipid caresses? Those who say yes, we get them under us, and we ruin them and leave them, and find when we have left them that they have made us sick. The earth says yes to our schemes and our work, but the sea says no; and we, we love the sea ever. And to hear God say no, in the stillness, in his own voice, that to us is very good. The starry sky came up, there, and said no to me as well. Like a noble, proud woman.'

'And did you see Fingal then?' Eliza asked.

'Yes,' said Morten. 'Just then. As I turned my head a little, Fingal was sitting with me in the boat. You know, he was an ill-tempered little dog always, and he never liked me because I teased him. He used to bite me every time he saw me. I dared not touch him there in the boat. I was afraid that he would snap at me again. Still, there he sat, and stayed with me all night.'

'And did he go away then?' Fanny asked.

'I do not know, my dear,' Morten said. 'An American schooner, bound for Jamaica, picked me up in the early morning. There on board was a man who had bid against me at the sale in Philippsburg. In this way it came to pass that I was hanged—in the end, as you say—at Havana.'

'Was that bad?' asked Fanny in a whisper.

'No, my poor Fanny,' said Morten.

'Was there anyone with you there?' Fanny whispered.

'Yes, yes, there was a fat young priest there,' said Morten. 'He was afraid of me. They probably told him some bad things about me. But still he did his best. I asked him: "Can you obtain for me, now, one minute more to live in?" He said, "What will you do with one minute of life, my poor son?" I said, "I will think, with the halter around my neck, for one minute of *La Belle Eliza.*"'

While they now sat in silence for a little while, they heard some people pass in the street below the window, and talk together. Through the shutters they could follow the passing flash of their lanterns.

Morten leaned back in his chair, and he looked now to his sisters older and more worn than before. He was indeed much like their father, when the Papa De Coninck had come in from his office tired, and had taken pleasure in sitting down quietly in the company of his daughters.

'It is very pleasant in here, in this room,' he said, 'it is just like old days—do you not think so? With Papa and Mamma below. We three are not very old yet. We are good-looking people still.'

'The circle is complete again,' said Eliza gently, using one of their old expressions.

'Is completed, Lizzie,' said Morten, smiling back at her.

'The vicious circle,' said Fanny automatically, quoting another of their old familiar terms.

'You were always,' said Morten, 'such a clever lass.'

At these kind direct words Fanny impetuously caught at her breath.

'And, oh, my girls,' Morten exclaimed, 'how we did long then, with the very entrails of us, to get away from Elsinore!'

His elder sister suddenly turned her old body all around in the chair, and faced him straight. Her face was changed and drawn with pain. The long wake and the strain began to tell on her, and she spoke to him in a hoarse and cracked voice, as if she were heaving it up from the innermost part of her chest.

'Yes,' she cried, 'yes, you may talk. But you mean to go away again and leave me. You! You have been to these great warm seas of which you talk, to a hundred countries. You have been married to five people—Oh, I do not know of it all! It is easy for you to speak quietly, to sit still. You have never needed to beat your arms to keep warm. You do not need to now!'

Her voice failed her. She stuttered in her speech and clasped the edge of the table. 'And here,' she groaned out, 'I am—cold. The world is bitterly cold around me. I am so cold at night, in my bed, that my warming-pans are no good to me!'

At this moment the tall grandfather's clock started to strike, for Fanny had herself wound it up in the afternoon. It struck midnight in a grave and slow measure, and Morten looked quickly up at it.

Fanny meant to go on speaking, and to lift at last all the deadly weight of her whole life off her, but she felt her chest pressed together. She could not out-talk the clock, and her mouth opened and shut twice without a sound.

'Oh, hell,' she cried out, 'to hell.'

Since she could not speak she stretched out her arms to him, trembling. With the strokes of the clock his face became grey and blurred to her eyes, and a terrible panic came upon her. Was it for this that she had wound up the clock! She threw herself towards him, across the table.

'Morten!'she cried in a long wail. 'Brother! Stay! Listen! Take me with you!'

As the last stroke fell, and the clock took up its ticking again, as if it meant to go on doing something, in any case, through all eternity, the chair between the sisters was empty, and at the sight Fanny's head fell down on the table.

She lay like that for a long time, without stirring. From the winter night outside, from far away to the north, came a resounding tone, like the echo of a cannon shot. The children of Elsinore knew well what it meant: it was the ice breaking up somewhere, in a long crack.

Fanny thought, dully, after a long while, What is Eliza thinking? and laboriously lifted her head, looked up, and dried her mouth with her little handkerchief. Eliza sat very still opposite her, where she had been all the time. She dragged the streamers of her cap downwards and together, as if she were pulling a rope, and Fanny remembered seeing her, long, long ago, when angry or in great pain or joy, pulling in the same way at her long golden tresses. Eliza lifted her pale eyes and stared straight at her sister's face.

'To think,' said she, '"to think, with the halter around my neck, for one minute of *La Belle Eliza*."'

1934

The English Gentleman's Tale — The Gold Bride

CHRISTINA STEAD

There was, in recent years, a Spanish youth of pure race who married a Moorish beauty and took her to Paris, where lived his cousin Ferdinand, a rich man of fashion. The sacrifices that the marriage had cost him, and his wife's youth and ardent beauty, put him into such an extremity of passion that he could never leave her by day or night, but spent his time with her in the house and garden, interrupting all she did with kisses, and sometimes washing her hands and feet with tears. But he was naturally frail and in a few months this peculiar flame had so burned up his blood that he had to take to his bed. Then he sent for a black dress for Zelis, and ordered from a well-known sculptor a statue of her to serve him for a headstone.

When the statue was finished and Zelis came to see it, she saw that it was naked, of full height and cast in gold. At the foot was engraved, 'Death, my Bride.' She cried and begged Carlos to put away his freaks, and to live, and love her with a calmer and more honest passion. But he continued to be consumed by his insatiable love, was reduced to a shadow by these extravagances, and was only cured by an accident.

His cousin Ferdinand, a handsome, lively man, whose rake's progress before marriage had amused all fashionable Paris and Madrid, began to call on Zelis and entertain her. He came every day and they walked in the gardens. A few days after his first visit Carlos was able to get up and look out of the window at the terrace where they took tea, and in a week or so he was so much better that he could walk about the house without help. Zelis was rejoiced at this recovery. Some time after this she brought into the world a son. Ferdinand took a violent fancy to his nephew, was for ever in the house dandling the child, and chatting with its mother, and Carlos was displeased to find him several times standing before the naked golden statue with a lively, covetous expression. Once he said to his cousin, 'I will pay you a very high price for that fine piece of workmanship, when you want to sell it!' Carlos replied, 'You know I do not want to sell it.' 'Why do you call it "Death"?' said Ferdinand, gaily: 'It is liker life than death. Do you call it Death, to veil, with decent melancholy, its imprudent grace?' And Carlos grew anxious and jealous.

One day he was obliged to go out for a few hours and when he returned he heard a loud outcry in the house. He rushed in and found his wife lying on an ottoman, dead, and Ferdinand weeping beside her. With clamour and confused details, his servants and his cousin told Carlos that Zelis had flung herself from the window into the paved court and had so killed herself. Carlos stared at the body and murmured, 'It isn't possible: I can't believe it!' and from that time on for many days did not say a word to his household. He watched with his oldest servant by his wife's body, which was embalmed in their presence. A goldsmith came and took away the gold statue, but returned it on the day of the burial, and there was now engraved at the foot, 'Zelis, my Life.'

Then began a weary time for the household. Ferdinand's wife, forgetting the jealousy which had destroyed her peace in these last days, came and took in charge the ailing and neglected child; and Carlos did not even notice that his son was gone. He dressed in black, put ashes on his head, and day and night scarcely ate or slept. The statue was put behind a thick curtain at one end of a gallery and Carlos slept at the foot of the pedestal on a mattress. He had to walk about on the arm of the old servant, and all were sure he would soon die. The smooth figure he covered with a thousand kisses, ten times repeated, and would often fall asleep clasping it. The right foot of the statue, advanced a little, as if the woman had just taken a small light step on a carpet, was polished by his lips. His hair was white, his clothes hung on him like sacks: the house decayed, his servants robbed him and ran away, his banker neglected to send him notices of his dividends, and his factors his accounts, and his whole estate fell away from him as if it had turned to water.

Presently he had only one servant left him, this old man who had watched with him, and who stayed on because he could without much concealment get rid of the works of art in the house to dealers; he wore Carlos's clothes and kept his own family and friends on the provisions which he was still able to order. He emptied the cellar, the pantry, the attics, the salons and left a bare furniture: and when there was nothing more to filch, and nothing to eat, he disappeared one day, after leaving Carlos a tin box which he put by the statue, and which contained a woollen shirt, a pair of shoes, a cloak and a gold piece. He came back and substituted a silver piece for the gold piece, and then went away altogether.

Presently creditors were knocking at all the doors, and all the doors were opened to them by the wind, and they were said good-day to by the barnyard which had installed itself there. The house was sold. His cousin Ferdinand came to Carlos then and said, 'Where is your golden statue? You must sell it to pay your creditors!' Carlos did not answer. Ferdinand said more gently, 'Carlos, tell me where your statue is and I will put it into my house and keep it for you as security, until you have put your estate in order, and can pay me back the expenses I have been put to!' Carlos looked vaguely at his cousin. 'I offer you a very high price for your statue,' said Ferdinand: 'enough to set you up again in a decent way till your affairs are settled, or to get back to Spain in a proper condition. Listen, Carlos, sell me the statue of Zelis, your dead wife.' Carlos at last spoke softly and said, 'I have no statue, Ferdinand: only my wife. That is all I have in the world.'

But Ferdinand followed him and found out where he had hidden the statue, in a box, buried in a corner of the park: then he took it from him, and had it carried to his own house, reasoning that he was really doing Carlos a service, and that Carlos might some day get back his senses, and be able to redeem it. He then put Carlos in a private lunatic asylum and went home to his wife who was not quite satisfied with the whole business.

Carlos was in that institution eleven years, and did not cease to mourn the loss of his golden wife. He was soft and mild to the attendants, answered the director intelligently and devised a thousand means for escaping. When visitors came twice a week they would delight to talk with this pathetic figure, and when he had their sympathy, he would suddenly fall on his knees, and beg them to get him out, because he was sane and kept there wrongfully by his jealous adulterous cousin, the engineer of his ruin. Then, one day, the visitors who came on a Sunday, left the illustrated Sunday newspaper which featured the social activities of the rich. It was Tuesday by the time it reached Carlos. He scarcely glanced at it, yet he saw immediately as if it had been written in red ink, his wife's name, and above this he found a photograph of the golden statue, garlanded with roses and chains, and at its foot the words 'Zelis, my Life.' It had been chief piece at a fête given to society by Ferdinand on the twelfth birthday of his ward, Carlos's lost son.

After this day, Carlos began to walk in the gardens of the hospital, not affable as before, but holding his hand over his heart as if he had a mortal wound, and often, leaning against a tree or against the wall where plumtrees were trained like Lorraine crosses, he would say, 'My head, heart and entrails are in ashes.' At night they heard him calling to Zelis, to leave her elegant home and sinful love, to come and succour him who had spent his whole life and poured out, on her alone, his passion, affection and intelligence. Sometimes, it seemed, in the night she came, and put her hands on his head and breast, and left them there for an hour or two while he slept.

Now, when the son of Carlos asked where were his father and mother, his adoptive mother said that his father had been killed in a foreign country and his mother had died of grief. When Ferdinand heard this explanation he always made a wry face, but said nothing. His wife begged him many times to return the gold statue to Carlos or Carlos to the statue, and so perhaps restore him to health, but her husband always refused. He kept the statue in his own apartment, draped in a black veil, and only brought it out when, his wife being away, he gave fantastic parties. Ferdinand's wife had always held Zelis in disfavour and now she roundly reproached her husband for the bad influence the Moorish beauty had had on his life, in bringing him back gradually to his former wild ways, and in making him put away his own cousin.

When April came and the household packed up to move to the country house, Ferdinand's wife breathed freer, but the first thing she saw when she went into the newly-aired hall of their villa was the golden statue, standing grave and fine as ever, and at her feet the words, 'Zelis, my Life.'

Then she had an attack of nerves (for the season had been trying), and told her husband she would sell the creature, or have it put in safe deposit for the boy when he grew older. The next day the statue had vanished. Ferdinand began to make long solitary rides, with his gun and dog, into the forested country which surrounded the estate, stayed away all day and only returned at nightfall with the homing birds, his horse looking plump and rested, his gun idle and his bag empty. She followed Ferdinand in a hunter's costume one day, and found that he spent the day in a lonely cottage, heavily shuttered and barricaded, in which was the golden statue. As astonished as angry, she asked him, if he left that priceless thing out all night in the lonely woods, for anyone to steal. 'My servants watch over it,' he said: and as he persisted and became always more gloomy and unnatural, she was obliged to have the strange metal woman back in the house, but she began to fear her unreasonably. Ferdinand now kept the statue entirely in his own apartment and refused to let the growing boy see it, for fear he would learn its history and claim it; and he spent long hours by its side hopelessly desiring the dead woman.

A little later his affliction had increased so that he insisted on having the image to sleep with him, and had it wrapped in a silk sheet each night and put in his own bed. He said that then under its wrappings the body began to breathe gently, and he heard soft sighs as of a young woman gratefully asleep. At other times he heard a voice as if the young woman were speaking, not to him, but to someone at a distance: at last, one night he broke out of his apartment, forced his servants to bring sticks and a dog, and said that Carlos was there, in the dark conversing with Zelis, and begging her to return to him.

Then he acknowledged that for many nights now his ears had been full of Carlos's sobbing, and his head stuffed to desperation with his prayers: and that the statue itself was restless in the daytime and moved about the room, and now at night was as still as a stone, as if its soul had gone elsewhere. To keep the statue at home he would be forced to satisfy it.

Therefore he sent for Carlos and brought him home, and kept him there, under his eye, but never let him speak to or see the people in the house. So they lived together for a short time, Carlos, Zelis and Ferdinand. The blinds were lowered in that part of the house, and the attendants that served them were blindfolded before they entered the room, and guided themselves from the door by ropes placed there for them. Thus nobody knew what went on, but the servants invented a legend, and eventually this spread discreetly, so that the white turrets of the house, behind trees, would be pointed out by travellers from the railway.

The son was now fourteen years old and heard a distorted tale of what happened in the forbidden wing from a servant-girl who had fallen in love with him. He crept in one day behind one of the blindfold servants and saw two old men, both yellow as gold, and both sitting motionless, as if they were paralysed, only moving their white eyes, in the midst of the faded hangings of the apartment. One was Ferdinand his foster-father, and the other was unknown. Yellow dust covered everything in the room, and the summer sun through the windows made the statue glitter inconceivably. As he looked he imagined that the subtle mouth of the golden idol smiled sidelong at him; the old men never moved their heads and he escaped unseen. He thought of it for two days, with his heart beating hard and his dreams troubled, and then he said, 'I will get goldsmiths and have it melted down, and then its fascination, which is entirely a question of lines and contours, will vanish,' for he wanted to restore to his foster-mother her long-mourned husband. At the same time, he was marvellously affected by the statue's grace, and wondered what this personage could be that was so exquisitely modelled.

The next night they crept into the apartment and stole the statue. They took it into the central court of the mansion and there prepared to cast it into a great pot in a portable furnace, before which stood two goldsmiths. The statue touched the crucible as a loud cry rang out: the attendants started back from their work, and looking behind them, began to run, with agitated shouts, towards the house. One of the inmates of the forbidden apartment stood on the brink of the window-sill, and as they ran, threw himself into the paved court. When they reached him, he was already dead, and they saw in him the companion of Ferdinand, the yellow old man who watched with him, unknown Carlos.

The body was laid out, and the priest came. Ferdinand was brought out of his apartment and, shocked by the event, brought together his household and confessed that the dead man was Carlos, his cousin, and the golden statue Zelis, the wife of Carlos, and that Zelis had killed herself by leaping from the window of her apartment when Ferdinand had tried to force her love. 'If you look now at the statue of your mother,' said Ferdinand to Carlos's son, 'you will see a suture down the side. After your mother's death, your father opened the statue: inside the head he placed the ashes of the brain, inside the breast the ashes of the heart, and inside the belly the ashes of the bowels, and thus bound himself for life, to this golden idol.' The boy scarcely understood, but being of his father's blood, he turned his back on the people there and began to weep, swearing to build a memorial to his father and mother that would commemorate their love to his family.

On the day following his father's funeral he went to look at the statue of Zelis which had been locked in a cabinet. The cabinet was empty. Presently a messenger came from the caretaker of the cemetery saying that the golden image had been found on the brink of Carlos's newly-dug grave during the night. They brought it back to the house, and the son put it in his own room. Awaking, towards morning, with a feeling of calm delight and satisfaction, he saw the faded lavender morning light through the uncurtained window and looked towards the statue of his mother. There was nothing there. After considering for a few moments, he dressed quietly, went out without a sound and, going to the cemetery, knocked on the gate until the porter got up, and demanded to be taken at once to his father's grave. There, with the advanced right foot slightly embedded in the new earth, stood the statue. 'Who passed through the gate this night?' asked the boy. 'The gate has been shut since sunset yesterday,' said the attendant. Once more the statue was taken home, yet the next dawn if was found buried in the grave up to the waist.

The son attached it to the pedestal with a padlock and chain, and the next night watched in the room, while a servant waited in the adjoining room, in case robbery or a practical joke should again be attempted.

About one o'clock in the morning the boy heard a slight sigh, and looking at the statue of Zelis, saw the golden eyes move and the breasts heave. Then a soft voice said, 'Why am I chained?' Much moved, the boy made haste to unlock the lock. Then the voice said, 'My son, put out that light!' He was paralysed with doubt and surprise, until the voice said again, 'I am Zelis, your mother, and ask you to put out the light which discountenances miracles.' The boy, softened by the mystery, and by a spring of love for his dead mother, put out the light. The voice of Zelis then said, 'Open the window!' and he did so. 'Close your eyes, my son,' said the voice now, 'and do not come looking for me until an hour after sunrise.' He closed his eyes with regret, heard a light sound of a footfall, presently looked and found the statue gone and the window shut again. He lay down clothed on his bed and waited for sunrise.

An hour after sunrise he called the attendant and said, 'Let us go to the graveyard, the statue is no more here,' and he showed the loosened chain. This time the cemetery was already open and the porter came out and said, 'I have been to look and there is nothing at the graveside: this time a good watch was kept.' 'Lend us two spades, and a hammer and chisel, and shut the public gates for an hour,' said the son, giving the man some money, and the porter did what was requested. When they came to the grave they dug until they reached the coffin and then took a hammer and chisel and opened it. There was a sweet smell mingling with the smell of aromatic oils coming out of the box and the embalmed body had not decomposed. But there lay on it three heaps of ashes, one on the forehead, one on the heart and one on the belly. There was no sign of the golden woman at all.

So the son went home and brought his uncle and aunt to see this miracle, and it was decided to seek no more for the gold statue, but to cover up the grave and leave them in peace. This was done, and there was no further manifestation of so great a love, except that within a few days, and after that, every spring and summer, the grave and every inch of ground surrounding it for some distance, was covered with yellow flowers of every sort that oozed out of the earth; and in three spots, covering the three heaps of ashes, there was nothing at all but the black marble chips which had first been strewn over the earth.

1936

The Mask of Sacrifice

MARGERY LAWRENCE

It was a horrible thing, really. Jack Trelawney picked it up in some old curiosity shop near the Strand, and carried it home in triumph—now it sat tilted up against the inkstand in Trelawney's study, its narrow eye-holes squinting sideways at the firelight, the round red cap on its head a little askew. One wisp of coarse black hair hung straight each side of the long thin face, dull yellow-brown in colour and creased with a thousand lines and wrinkles; huge gilt rings swung from the hidden ears, and the thin-lipped mouth was bitterly sardonic. Maisie Trelawney, bride of a year, stood with her pretty brows wrinkled in obvious disfavour, regarding it with a doubtful finger at her lip, the bright light shining on her curly hair.

'Jack! Another horror—what a beastly old face!'

Trelawney laughed uproariously as he slipped an arm about her shoulders, rising white and round above her black velvet dinner-gown.

'Horror—oh, Maisie, you're incorrigible! Will you never have any sympathy with my craze for oddities?'

She turned a bright face up to him, and tiptoed for a kiss. The fire crackled and flared suddenly, and threw an odd shadow across the pale sardonic face of the mask, almost like a sudden smile, fleeting and cruel; Maisie slipped an arm inside her husband's as she turned again to look at the new purchase.

'Sympathy? Jack, you know I love some of your oddments, but this is—somehow not very appealing—to me at any rate! Sorry, dearest! As long as you like it, it doesn't really matter, and certainly, as a piece of work, it's frightfully clever. An unpleasant face, I think, but immensely well done. Is it Chinese?'

'I don't know,' Trelawney admitted. 'The old villain who sold it to me didn't seem to know much about it—or wasn't in a communicative mood. I got it absurdly cheap, too—only a fiver, and it's obviously worth much more. As a matter of fact, I fancy it's stolen goods—at any rate the old chap seemed deuced anxious to get rid of it, and jumped at my offer. Wish now I'd offered three quid!'

Maisie shook her head.

'I'm not—it was cheap, I admit, but anyway, he seemed satisfied—if you'd beaten him down I shouldn't have liked it. But somehow I don't think . . . .'

'What don't you think, you funny shrimp?' Trelawney's tone was very tender as he kissed the tiny frown between her eyebrows.

'I don't quite know,' she said doubtfully, 'but anyway, I rather wish you hadn't bought it, dear. I have a rather funny feeling about it—I don't like the look on its face when the firelight catches it sometimes.'

The flame flared again, and Trelawney released his wife with a rather irritated little shrug.

'Really, Maisie! I never thought you were superstitious—anyway, I'm sorry I ever got the thing, since it seems to get on your nerves so. I can sell it again if you like.'

His tone was edgy, and Maisie looked a trifle hurt.

'Of course not, Jack—what nonsense! But you always like to hear just what I think—or you always said so . . . .'

There was an edge in her tone, too, and Trelawney hastily changed the subject.

'I like your frock, Maisie. Anyone coming to-night?'

She nodded, sinking into a big leather chair and lighting a cigarette.

'Only Miles. He rang up to say he'd got the Staff appointment he wanted, and was only waiting orders to go abroad now, so might he come and talk it over with us to-night.'

'Miles—good scheme! I haven't seen the old chap for weeks—all right; I'll go and change.'

The door slammed, and the room was silent, save for the occasional leap and purr of the flames flickering up the chimney. It was a charming room, cosy and well furnished, lined with books, an antlered head or two over the door and fireplace, heavy velvet curtains shutting out the cold wind that whistled outside, and a thick Persian carpet, wonderfully coloured, on the polished floor. A regular man's room, the room of a well-bred Englishman of rather bookish tastes, the only incongruous note struck by the mask that now rested on the table, facing the fire, its lined, sallow face oddly and unpleasantly alive in the dancing lights and shadows. Maisie glanced at it again over her shoulder, and shivered a little.

A horrible thing—she loathed it—and Jack was sure to insist on its being put up in the drawing-room, a lovely room stacked with curious and beautiful things, mostly Oriental, from Trelawney's many wanderings.

Many were presents from Miles, too—her cousin, a burly, shy soldier to whom she had always been a second sister. The bell rang sharply, and Miles himself was shown into the room, his square, good-humoured face still red from the sharp wind. Maisie sprang up from her seat and held up her charming face for the usual kiss. At the same moment as he bent towards her, the man's eyes caught the mask, and with a sudden exclamation he raised his head, without kissing her.

'By Jove—what an extraordinary thing!'

He picked up the mask, studying it intently, regardless of Maisie's pout—then as she flounced into a chair again, put it down with a half-embarrassed little laugh.

'Sorry, May! That wasn't very polite, I admit—but all of a sudden I saw this thing, and it almost looked as if—well, as if it was laughing . . . .'

His tone was suddenly shy, and his honest blue eyes, always so completely frank and open about his affection for her, looked oddly troubled—looking away, he sat down opposite her and fumbled for his tobacco pouch, awkward and embarrassed. Maisie herself fell silent—how often and often, before Jack, before anybody, had she not kissed Miles, with the same frank, happy affection that she would have shown towards a real and only brother–now suddenly, this one kiss not kissed, seemed to have changed the whole position. Extraordinary! Why had she never felt this consciousness of sex before towards Miles—she was no child, in this her radiant twenty-sixth year, and he an experienced soldier of thirty-two? The silence grew heavy between them, till resolutely shaking his broad shoulders, the man laughed and turned the old smile of frank good-fellowship upon her, his white teeth gleaming in the firelight.

'Tell me, May—where did old Jack pick up this recent horror?'

'I'm so thankful you think it's a horror too!' The girl laughed in return, as she answered: 'He got it in some old shop in the Strand—you know, the same he got the Algerian knife and those Chinese coffee-cups from. Coffee-cups, now—they're nice useful, charming things—but this!'

Miles' thick, fair brows were knitted.

'Strand? Not near the corner of Southampton Street?'

'Yes. Why?' Maisie was alert at his tone. Miles reached out a hand behind him and fished up an evening paper. Rustling over the pages, he turned to a paragraph, and folding the paper up, passed it over, a brown thumb marking the place. The two heads were bent over the paper, close together, brown short hair against a tangle of fair curls, and Jack Trelawney, entering quietly at the door, stood silent, suddenly struck by a thought that had never entered his happy, straightforward head before. It was an unworthy thought, and he scouted it on the moment, hot with anger at himself, and strode into the circle of the firelight, a cheery greeting on his lips. But the thought had been there—and was to come again. Miles turned a delighted grin to him, and Maisie sprang up and caught him by the arm, waving the crumpled paper.

'Jack! Isn't this your old man—this thing, I mean?'

The paragraph was headed 'Shocking Murder,' and Trelawney's brows went up as he read. The police, hearing groans, had forced their entrance into the back room of the little antique shop where he had purchased the mask, only a short time after he left it, and found the wife of Schroeder, the old proprietor, dying from a dozen knife-thrusts from an old Moorish dagger.

According to the doctor, she must have been dying at the moment he purchased the mask—with a faint feeling of sickness, Trelawney remembered that he had subconsciously noted the old man's hasty and furtive glances at his hands once or twice during the transaction. He must have come to attend Trelawney straight from the awful deed—no reason given, except that the neighbours said that recently the old couple, once devoted, seemed to have done nothing but quarrel. Old Schroeder was dazed, vague, seemed scarcely to realise what he had done. 'Committed for trial . . . .'

'Good God, how ghastly!' Trelawney put down the paper with hands that were none too steady. 'That's really too awful—the police must just have come in only a few minutes after I left! I never heard anything—she must have been lying there. Oh, Lord, it's ghastly. The old brute—I wish I'd known! And he must have come straight out to serve me with this thing!'

'Oh, throw it away—throw it away!' shuddered Maisie. 'It's awful! Fancy what it may have seen—he brought it out from the room behind, didn't he?'

Trelawney nodded.

'I went in to ask about a carved screen they had in the window—he knows I like oddities, and he said he'd like to show me this. No—I won't get rid of it, May. It's an ugly story, but it's nothing to what it must have seen in the old days, if it is, as I suspect, a sacrificial mask.'

Maisie turned away with a shrug, and led the way to the dining-room.

'Well,' she said over her pretty shoulder, 'do as you like, of course—but personally, I can't congratulate you on your taste, Jack. Come on, Miles.'

Dinner was a rather constrained meal—Maisie, presumably by way of marking her displeasure with her husband, talked mainly to Miles, who, unconscious of the strain, ate hugely, laughed bluffly and talked cheerfully all through the courses, to Trelawney's increasing annoyance; he and Miles had always before been inseparable chums, and the younger man's cheery, good-tempered humour one of the joys of life—now that same humour was getting steadily and slowly on his nerves, and heavens, how that perpetual 'Ha! ha!' maddened one!

Trelawney wished to goodness Maisie wouldn't laugh at all his futile jokes. Damn it, she was looking amazingly pretty in that black velvet thing; it was his frock—he'd given it to her, she was his wife, and she should know it, should be made to know it if necessary. Why should he pay for frocks that were palpably being used to attract other men? Why should Maisie sit tilting her face up towards Miles in that fashion that always drove men mad? Oh, well, women were all alike, jades every one—never mind—we should see! With a sudden shock of nausea and anger at himself, Trelawney pulled himself sternly together and joined in the talk, but Maisie was still annoyed, and was so frigid that he relapsed into silence again, and played moodily with his bread till she gave the welcome signal for release.

Afterwards in the drawing-room, a return of the ugly mood seized Trelawney, and he insisted on bringing the mask into the drawing-room. Miles was genuinely interested, and the two men sat studying the thing and discussing it for a long time, but Maisie chose to consider it—as indeed it was!—a deliberate 'slap back' for her behaviour at dinner, and was correspondingly aloof and disagreeable. At last the suppressed acrimony of the situation reached even Miles' non-too-perceptive brain, and he relapsed into awkward silences, until the most uncomfortable evening ever spent in the Trelawney's cheerful house drew to a close, and with a barely suppressed sigh of relief, Miles Burnaby rose to his feet and held out a large hand to his host.

'Well! Must be getting along, old man. Thanks for another awfully cheery evening—' The lie fell like a plummet into the waiting silence, and Miles hurried on. 'Hope this priceless old chap you've got here isn't going to bring you the rotten luck he seemed to land on old Schroeder and Co.!'

'I sometimes wish, Miles,' said Trelawney very distinctly, 'that you would learn to talk a little sense for a change.'

Miles' open mouth of astonishment was a study, but Maisie intervened.

'Jack's got the black dog on his back to-night—all because I hate his ugly old mask,' she said sweetly. 'I'm afraid you've had a rotten time, Miles, you poor dear, with us two in a state of suppressed hostility all evening! Never mind—next time we'll choose an evening when Jack's away! Kiss me, Miles!'

Her charming face lifted towards the soldier's in the firelight, and Trelawney turned suddenly away, sick with the wave of red fury that surged up. The kiss that passed between the two who had loved each other so long and well as brother and sister love, seemed no longer to him the frank and innocent thing it had been till this night, when they kissed under the baleful shadow of the mask . . . .

Standing at the table, his head bent, Trelawney heard Miles cross the room, say 'Good night,' and slam the door. Turning, he surveyed his wife, her slim velvet-shod foot on the kerb, humming a contented little tune as she stared into the fire.

'Maisie.' His voice had an odd harshness, carefully controlled. 'Maisie, I won't have you kiss Miles again. D'you hear?'

The toss of her head was unmistakable, and there was a hint of steel in her voice as she answered:

'My dear Jack! Isn't it rather late in the day to try and come the early Victorian husband over me? I've always kissed dear old Miles—I shouldn't dream of hurting his feelings by stopping now, for no reason!'

'You don't seem to mind hurting *mine* by doing it!' retorted the man.

'Nor you mine by refusing to throw away things I hate like this old mask!' Maisie responded swiftly. 'It doesn't matter now, though. As a matter of fact I've changed my mind. I rather admire the thing. In its horrible way it's rather decorative. I'm going to hang it over the fireplace in the drawing-room. Now you ought to be contented—anyway, stop talking nonsense about Miles and me, and what I'm to do or not to do about him, see?'

The door closed after her, and Trelawney, vanquished, stared moodily into the fire. He did not look up to where the mask was resting, or he might have seen again the odd effect of the flickering flames upon it—almost, again, one might have said that it smiled . . . .

.   .   .   .   .

Jack Trelawney's brow was clouded as he left home for his accountants' office next morning. Things seemed no better between Maisie and himself, despite his tentative efforts at reconciliation. True to her word, Maisie had with her own hands hung the mask above the fireplace in the drawing-room, and pronounced it 'odd, as I said, but rather decorative, after all!'

She was nonchalantly charming to him, bidding him good-bye with a dutiful kiss on the cheek, but Jack's sensitive heart ached for the old Maisie again, teasing, possessive, full of instructions as to how he was to take care of himself this cold day, running after him for another kiss, her warm lips pursed to meet his. With a frowning brow he read through his letters, dictated answers to his secretary, answered telephone calls and interviewed impatient clients, and at last by dint of savage work managed to deaden a little the pain at his heart—lunch-time was almost in sight when a messenger knocked at the door. Trelawney looked up with a brusque 'come in' and jumped, for the blue helmet of a stalwart constable loomed over the glass half-door.

'What on earth . . .' The door closed, and the policeman saluted, moving heavily into the room. Trelawney's face was blank with astonishment and consternation, not lessened when the man in blue fished out a note-book and pencil.

'Excuse me, sir. Only called to arsk a few questions about the murder and sooicide at Schroeder's yesterday—from the hentry in the old man's books, sir, you was the last person served, and it's thought you might be able to help us with a little information, sir?'

'Suicide? I only knew there had been a murder?' interrupted Trelawney, suddenly remembering he had been so preoccupied that he had never seen a morning paper. The constable nodded.

'Old man committed sooicide late larst night in the cell where he was waitin' his trial—strangled himself with his braces. Now what we want to know, sir, do you know anything about a marsk?'

Trelawney jumped—the question was so unexpected.

'Mask? Yes, of course I do. I bought a mask from him that day—a sort of Chinese thing, I think. Why?'

'Don't know where he got it—anything of its hist'ry, like?'

The constable was ponderously ploughing on his official way, regardless of Trelawney's question—the latter shrugged his shoulders.

'No—I don't know a thing. He professed ignorance as to where it came from, even—why do you ask?'

'Why? Because he was calling and screaming out about the thing like a lunatic all the way to the station—and all the time he was locked up too. Going on awful he was—telling it to keep away, or close its eyes, because he'd done all it wanted—awful it was, I give you my word, sir. Seems stoopid, but I was told to c'lect information about it . . . . So you're quite sure you can't throw any light on this here matter, sir?'

Trelawney's decided negative closed the interview, and the constable creaked slowly out. Alone, Trelawney stood frowning, his head on the mantelpiece, thinking. Pretty horrible, what? Telling it to keep away, or close its eyes—come to think of it, the thing's eyes, or rather eye-holes, *were* rather unpleasant; narrow and almost with a beastly sort of laugh in them. Where *did* the thing come from, anyway? Perhaps Maisie had been right, as she often was, and he would have been better advised to re-sell the head.

Poor little Maisie! By Jove, she *had* been upset last night! He had been a bad-tempered brute, anyway, and she deserved a treat to make up.

There was a new show at the Lyric—what about going to-night?

Acting on impulse, Trelawney took up the receiver and rang up his home number. The answer came promptly—the maid speaking. Trelawney's face darkened suddenly as he listened, and with a curse he slammed the receiver home. His square-chinned face was not good to look upon as he flung on his hat and went out to lunch, muttering viciously to himself.

'Out motoring with Miles, eh? Not likely to be back till late, so don't bother about waiting dinner! My God, Maisie, you're playing a dangerous game with me!'

Business suffered badly during the rest of the day, for Trelawney was quite incapable of diverting his mind from its growing obsession of jealousy, and he snapped furiously at his clerks till they wisely put away any further important business matters till the following day, when 'the boss' might have recovered his usual genial temper. Twice he rang up his home, to discover that no further news had been received of Maisie—going home through the driving rain in a taxi, he sat glowering out at the wet streets and hurrying crowds with the dark mood riding his shoulders like the veritable black dog of Maisie's laughing remark, and ate his solitary dinner in a silence that grew grimmer and more grim as the hours wore on and Maisie did not return. Stretched at full length in a huge chair before the fire, the mask above his bent head staring out into the gloom of the big room, only lighted by the flaming heaped coals in the wide grate, the man brooded, chin on hand, seeing in the red heart of the fire endless pictures of the two, Maisie and Miles, each of which added fuel to the fire that was slowly rising in his jealous heart. Pictures, too, of the past year, that had been so entirely happy and blessed till last night, now such untold ages ago. Till their quarrel, the quarrel over that mask—everything seemed to have gone wrong since he bought the wretched thing!

How Maisie had hated it at first, yet now she didn't seem to mind it; she had hung it there above the mantelpiece with her own pretty hands . . . funny, how the firelight leaping up then seemed to give the thing a horrible look of life! Almost as if it smiled, and the eye-slits looked down at him oddly, obliquely . . . whoever it was taken from,

he must have been a horrible old devil, with a taste for blood . . . .
Getting up from his seat, Trelawney stood staring at the head, hung
on a level with his own to the left of the tall mirror that occupied the
centre of the space above the mantelpiece.

'Now what put that into my head, I wonder?' he muttered, as his
troubled grey eyes wandered over the sinister, fine-drawn face etched
clearly in the leaping firelight. 'I suppose it's that murder business.
What did the old man say? "Turn your eyes away" or something of the
sort? "I've done what you wanted"—extraordinary idea! I suppose it
was a mask worn by some priest for sacrifices—perhaps human—who
knows? Anyway, you old brute, I suppose one of those psychic asses
would get a fine yarn out of your "thirst for blood" still fulfilling
itself . . .'

The words died away, and Trelawney's gaze was fixed on the curious,
dreadful hollows where eyes should be—his jaw was dropped, a little
slack, and his eyes were dull and fixed. Holes in a mask—blank hollows
where human eyes had once looked out on horrors unspeakable, orgies
of blood and evil! Holes, blank and black and eyeless—yet *were* they
eyeless, in truth? In the leaping flicker of the firelight, how could one
be sure that eyes no longer hid behind those long slits in that lean and
terrible countenance, wreathing now into a faint but significant grin
of knowledge and understanding as those dark holes, alight now with
horrible life, stared back into Trelawney's own?

Gripping the edge of the mantelpiece with his trembling hands,
the man tried dimly to pull himself together, to withdraw his gaze
from those awful hollows where his very soul seemed to be sinking,
disappearing into some wild, dark vortex wherein sanity, decency,
all that made him a man must inevitably drown and vanish! Wider
and wider wreathed the sardonic grin on the lean, leathern face,
crossed and recrossed with lines of age-old evil, as the blank black
eyes glared into his, and from them seemed to flow a sort of spiritual
miasma, a dark, slow flood of mental poison that was slowly but with
ghastly sureness sucking down, drowning, extinguishing, all that went
to make a sane and well-balanced man!

The clock ticked slowly, distinctly into the dead silence. The
tiny flop of a breaking coal, the cheep and scutter of a mouse
behind the wainscoat—otherwise, not a sound broke the hush of
the waiting-room, where Jack Trelawney, clean, healthy Englishman,
clung to the stone mantel, drawing little sobbing breaths that barely

stirred the warm air, his eyes blank and fixed, his mind wandering at large in strange and dreadful lands!

Dark glades and a lowering sky, and strange figures that followed a faint flickering light to a distant hill-top where, between the twisted trunks of a group of trees, another light glistened, a light blue-green and horrible . . . blue flames dancing on a crude altar about which moved a shadowy throng of horrible shapes! The sound of drums beating, softly, maddeningly, and a voice that chanted, muffled, as though singing from behind a mask . . . a chorus of voices that took up the chant, and at last one high-pitched scream of shrill and dreadful agony as the blue flame leapt high and showed in the flash of a moment a knife dripping blood, held in the hand of a masked figure stooping over a writhing form! Then a mad dancing whirl of cruel faces daubed with a crimson that stained more deeply than any dye, and the rising of the blue flame triumphant into the midnight skies, as the dance waxed wilder and more terrible in that dread orgy of blood-worship wherein, naked, screaming and horribly glad, man forgot he was man and made in the image of God, and returned to his primeval filth! The drums throbbed whimpering throughout the quiet room, the distant voices screamed, hysterical, abandoned, and all the time the masked figure chanted, chanted beside the blue flame . . . . *The mask. The mask. . . .*

The grind of a car stopping outside the house broke across the infernal spell that held the man standing frozen, hypnotised, beside the fire. Livid, shaking, Trelawney released his grip of the mantelpiece and, fumbling for his handkerchief, wiped his wet brow. Yet it was not the old Trelawney, genial, jolly, open-hearted, that peeped between the thick window-curtains at Miles and Maisie ascending the steps, and after rummaging in a drawer at the writing-table, crouched away behind those same curtains, one furtive hand clenched about the butt of a revolver!

Laughing and chattering, Maisie came in, unbuttoning her thick grey motor wrap—for Miles, open-air fiend, insisted on an open roadster. The old Trelawney? Was it the old Maisie who, glancing hurriedly about her, said in a whisper:

'It's all right, darling,' and turning, held out her arms to Miles.

Trelawney's fingers clenched tighter, but he forbore. No! Let her hang herself completely, damn her, and the fellow too! Wait—wait— and he'd get 'em both . . . . Miles, his open brow creased by an anxious frown, switched on the light and came half hesitatingly forward.

'Maisie—I don't know whether I'd better stay. Where's Jack?'

Ill at ease, vaguely uncomfortable, he stood looking down at the girl on the hearthrug. Above them the mask grinned, as she reached up to put her arms round his neck.

'Jack—Jack—he's asleep—fed up with me for running off with you, Miles!' she laughed, drawing her slender length up against the soldier's stalwart frame. Still uneasy, he held her away, frowning, puzzled.

'Wait awhile, May. Look her, old thing, there's something wrong to-night. I swear there is! You—we never acted like this before . . . and you know . . .' The lame sentence was drowned as she laid a slim hand across his mouth and laughed up into his troubled eyes.

'Silly—don't argue! Now you know you never kissed me yesterday— you stopped half-way, you ungallant boy. Kiss me now, Miles—oh, kiss me, kiss me, kiss me . . .!'

A red flame darted before Trelawney's eyes as he saw their lips meet in a wildly passionate kiss. With a hoarse laugh of rage that, strangely enough, seemed to be echoed and surrounded by another and a more terrible laugh that seemed to fill and deafen the very air around him, he flung the curtain aside and stood revealed, the revolver level in his hand. Even as he pulled the trigger he saw the mask, sharply distinct in the light, its cruel mouth all awry with awful merriment, its blank eyes alight and blazing, watching him . . . .

.　　.　　.　　.　　.

'Jack! Jack! Jack, dearest—look at me!' Surely it was Maisie's voice, her old loving, darling voice, shaking with tears and full of love? From a long way off, it seemed to Trelawney, that voice penetrated through a thickness of gloom and dark terror and anguish that had for untold ages hidden him.

With a great effort he opened his eyes, and blinking up in the strong light, looked straight into his wife's anxious face, and above it, Miles' square, honest countenance, fixed in a portentous frown of anxiety. Feebly reaching after memory, Trelawney whispered:

'Maisie—Miles! Why—I thought you—what's happened? Have I dreamt everything?' He struggled into a sitting position, his head against Maisie's knees, and on doing so his foot knocked against something, and he glanced down with a sudden cry. The mask lay in pieces on the hearthrug—he stretched out a curious hand, but Maisie stopped him with a cry of dismay.

'Don't, Jack—don't touch it again! It's horrible—it's wicked!'

Trelawney's eyes, rapidly regaining their old brightness and sanity, widened as he looked from Miles to her and back again. The soldier nodded frankly, and kicked a fragment of the mask away as Trelawney spoke.

'I—can't remember clearly. But I thought—I thought I saw you two . . .'

Flushing a dull scarlet, Miles nodded, and Maisie gripped her husband's hand.

'There's no use lying, Jack, old man. For a crazy moment or two—while this beastly horror was hanging there, only!—something seemed to take us both by the throat! I swear that though I've always been awfully fond of May as a brother, I never had the remotest feeling for her any other way, nor she for me, I'll take my solemn oath. But somehow, as I say, for a moment something happened to us both—but it's gone now, for ever, and everything's clear again. You *do* believe me, old man?'

Trelawney's old, frankly affectionate glance met his, as he held out his hand.

'You don't need to ask, my dear old chap! Now things are coming back to me again. I remember now, faintly, some of the awful things I seemed to see when I was looking at the mask . . . . I seemed to go off into a sort of dream of sacrifices and magic and lust and blood and the Lord knows what sort of horrors . . .'

Maisie broke in.

'I believe you were right all along, Jack. It must have been a thing somehow used to having blood sacrifices before it, and tried to get them again—I believe old Schroeder's murdering his wife was done under the same influence.'

Trelawney shuddered as he put his arms round his wife and buried his head in her soft shoulder.

'Good God! To think that I nearly fed the vile thing with a double sacrifice to-night—how I missed you I don't know!'

'You slipped a little on the polished floor,' supplied Miles, 'and that just saved us all, for your shot went wide and crashed full into the mask. It fell on the hearthrug just as you made for me, and we rolled about fighting each other and rolled on top of the mask—you were still mad, but the minute the mask smashed, May and I got sane at once, and the one thing she was screaming about the whole time was for *me* not to hurt *you!* Well, that scrap of ours finally flattened the thing to smithereens, so all's well. And we're all three out of the most awful danger we're ever likely to meet this side of hell, where I believe that devilish mask was made.'

'How did you know it was the mask that had that effect on all of us?' Trelawney asked curiously.

Miles frowned.

'Once in India I came across something of much the same sort. And, too, I had a funny feeling about the thing directly I saw it,' admitted Miles, for once shedding his English dislike of admitting any belief in the supernatural. 'And what made me bang *certain* was that the second the thing was broken the—well, the sort of passion that May and I had for each other just for that moment when we kissed, all vanished as clean as a whistle, and we were back in the common-sense, cousinly, affectionate atmosphere again, thank the Lord. And all we wanted was to stop *you* hurting yourself till you came to your senses. That took longer with you, I suppose, since you let the thing hypnotise you more or less. Anyway, thank heaven it's smashed up and done for now, and nobody else can suffer what we've been through. Now with your permission, May, I'm going to gather up the bits of the thing and burn 'em.'

Maisie shivered as she watched the shovelful of fragments, carefully collected, placed at the back of the fire. Then gave a sudden cry of fright as with a crackle the electric lights fused, as a huge blue tongue of flame leapt roaring up the chimney!

For a brief second it seemed that a huge wind, fierce and savage, swept the cosy room with a hot breath like the sudden opening of a furnace door, and the ghastly blue of the dancing flames lit up their white faces with an awful radiance, livid and terrible. The roar of the wind and the flames together seemed to soar and scream as if something in frenzied, impotent rage shook an invisible fist at them, shrieking fury and baffled evil as it fled—then in a flash, it passed, and through the windows came peeping in the light of the fresh and wholesome dawn.

Notes on the Authors

Wilkinson, Sarah Scudgell. Born Britain, died after 1830. Author of novels like *The Spectre of Lanmere Abbey* (1829), she is best known for her Gothic chapbooks, stories of ghosts and priories.

Shelley, Mary Wollstonecraft. Born England, 1797–1851. The daughter of writers Mary Wollstonecraft and William Godwin, she married the poet Percy Bysshe Shelley. A prolific author, she wrote a number of tales of fantasy, some in the Gothic tradition. She founded the genre of science fiction with her novel *Frankenstein* (1818).

Bronte, Charlotte. Born England, 1816–1855. This famous author made skilful use of the Gothic tradition in *Jane Eyre*. She also wrote several weird tales when young.

Gaskell, Elizabeth Cleghorn. Born England, 1810–1865. Her novels include *Mary Barton* and *North and South*, which depict the suffering of the 'industrial' poor. She wrote a *Life* of her friend, Charlotte Bronte, and a number of chilling ghost stories.

'Eliot, George', Mary Anne Evans, later Cross. Born England, 1819–1880. A major Victorian author of realist fiction, her best known novel is *Middlemarch, A Study of Provincial Life*. *The Lifted Veil* reveals her interest in telepathy and the Gothic tradition. Eliot scandalised her peers by living openly with George Henry Lewes, a married man unable to divorce his wife.

Spofford, Harriet (Prescott). Born USA, 1835–1921. She began writing to support her invalid parents. Many of her novels and short stories, which show interest in gender stereotypes and the pattern of life in New England, rely for their effect on fantasy and Gothic romance. 'I read Miss Prescott's *Circumstance*,' wrote the poet Emily Dickinson, 'but it followed me in the Dark . . .so I avoided her.'

Edwards, Amelia B[landford]. Born England, 1831–1892. As well as being England's foremost Egyptologist, she supported her family by writing novels, travel books and ghost tales.

'Barnard, A. M.', Louisa May Alcott. Born USA, 1832–1888. An active suffragette, she helped support her family by writing stories and novels, including the children's favourite, *Little Women*. She used her pseudonym to sign her sensational fiction.

Phelps, Elizabeth Stuart Ward. Born USA, 1844–1911. A keen advocate of women's rights, she was a prolific writer and sought through her novels to draw attention to the suffering of women and the poor. Many of her short stories deal with the spiritual world.

Stowe, Harriet Beecher. Born USA, 1811–1896. Best known for her anti-slavery novel, *Uncle Tom's Cabin: or life among the lowly*, which influenced Northern feeling before the American Civil War, she also wrote historical novels and ghost tales. Other work includes a book claiming that Byron committed incest with his half-sister.

Broughton, Rhoda. Born Wales, 1840–1920. The niece by marriage of Sheridan Le Fanu, who has been acclaimed as the greatest writer of the supernatural, she wrote bestselling novels and ghost stories.

Oliphant, Margaret. Born Scotland, 1827–1897. Author of almost 100 novels, some of which qualify as weird fiction, her writing supported her own and her brother's family. She also wrote biographies, criticism of art and literature, two autobiographies and supernatural stories.

Marryat, Florence. Born England, 1838–1899. Author of some 75 books, mostly sensational romances, she also wrote stories about ghosts and the spirit world. She married her first (of two) husbands in Penang and travelled all over India with him. She also toured America, performing a musical monologue she had written.

Molesworth, Mrs [Mary Louisa]. Born Britain, 1839–1921. Author of many novels and children's stories, much of her work draws on fairytales. She also wrote ghost stories.

Schreiner, Olive. Born South Africa, 1855–1920. An active campaigner for women's rights and peace, she also took part in the struggle against the racist and imperialist policies of South Africa. She wrote novels (*The Story of an African Farm* is partly autobiographical), essays and a collection of fantastic narratives called *Dreams*.

Atherton, Gertrude. Born USA, 1857–1948. The great-grand niece of Benjamin Franklin, some of her novels were pronounced immoral because of their sexual frankness. She also wrote memoirs and weird tales.

Nesbit, E[dith]. Born England, 1858–1924. A founding member of the Fabian Society and a friend of the Webbs, she is famous for her children's fiction but little known for her horror stories.

Riddell, Mrs. J. H. [Charlotte Eliza Lawson]. Born Northern Ireland, 1832–1906. When her husband lost his money in 1856, she started writing a stream of novels, often under male pseudonyms. She also published several collections of ghost tales.

Perrin, Alice. Born India, 1867–1934. Most of her novels and short stories are set in India, where she lived for most of her life. Her work is sensitive to the impact on India of British rule.

Wilkins [Freeman], Mary E. Born USA, 1852–1930. Her novels and short stories reveal her interest in the lives and difficulties of women. She wrote many ghost stories, some of which use the techniques of detective fiction.

Hossain, Rokeya Sakhawat. Born Bangladesh [Hossain is considered Bengali although she died before Bangladesh became a separate country], 1880–1942. A feminist and social activist, she helped to promote women's education. She was a bitter opponent of the practice of purdah, which she ridicules in the utopian story, *Sultana's Dream*.

Meade, L. T. [Elizabeth Thomasina]. Born Ireland, 1854–1914. Author of nearly 300 novels, mostly conservative adventures for girls and young women, she also wrote weird ghost tales.

Gilman, Charlotte Perkins. Born USA, 1860–1935. Best known for her tale, *The Yellow Wall-paper*, she wrote fiction and essays about the oppression of women by men. Her fantastic work includes *Herland*, the utopian vision of a community of women without men, and stories in which gender roles are reversed.

Cather, Willa. Born USA, 1873–1947. An author of poetry, essays and fiction, she made her name with novels of Nebraska frontier women. Admired for the intellectual rigour of her work, she wrote some bizarre and extraordinary tales.

Wharton, Edith. Born USA, 1862–1937. A friend of Henry James, she wrote novels about American and European society at the time and about the impact of World War I. She also published short stories, some of which deal with ghosts and the occult.

Mansfield, Katherine. Born New Zealand, 1888–1923. Author of short stories, she was acclaimed for her writing style. Some of her stories achieve their effect through their presentation of the inexplicable.

Woolf, Virginia. Born England, 1882–1941. She wrote several ghost stories and *Orlando*, a novel about a person who lives through four centuries and changes gender. Like all of her work, her fantasy manifests an interest in feminist issues and narrative style.

Sinclair, May. Born England, 1865–1946. A campaigner for women's suffrage, her interest in women's problems and the role of the unconscious influenced the form and content of her fiction. She drew on her knowledge of spiritualism to write many short ghost stories.

Lowndes, Mrs [Marie] Belloc. Born Britain, 1868–1947. The sister of Hilaire Belloc, she established herself as a writer with a fictionalised version of Jack the Ripper's murders. She wrote historical and general novels, as well as weird stories that aimed to terrify their reader.

O'Malley, Mary [Lady]. Born Britain, 1891–1974. Author of many novels drawing on the experience of living abroad with her British diplomat husband, she often signed herself 'Ann Bridge'. Some of her weird short stories were published in Cynthia Asquith's anthologies of ghost and mystery stories.

Moore, C[atherine] L[ucille]. Born USA, 1911. An innovative writer of SF, she created the strong warrior heroine, Jirel of Joiry. It has been claimed (but not demonstrated) that most of her writing from 1940 was in collaboration with her husband, Henry Kuttner, until his death in 1958. They used 'Lewis Padgett' as a joint pseudonym for collections like *Clash by Night*.

Dinesen, 'Isak' [Karen Blixen]. Born Denmark, 1885–1962. After *Out of Africa*, the story of her life in Kenya on a coffee plantation (made into a film in the 1980s), she wrote the fantasy stories in *Seven Gothic Tales*, *Winter's Tales* and *Last Tales*.

Stead, Christina. Born Australia, 1902–1983. Her eleven novels include *The Man Who Loved Children*, which is based on her own childhood. *The Salzburg Tales* is a collection of stories—some wildly fantastic—told by people of different types.

Lawrence, Margery. Born England, 1896–1969. A writer of adventure, romance and weird novels, she also wrote horror tales and stories about an occult detective (collected in *Number Seven, Queer Street*).

Sources and Acknowledgements

The Spectre; or, The Ruins of Belfont Priory by Sarah Wilkinson (London: A. Kemmish, 1806). 'The Mortal Immortal, A Tale' by Mary Shelley, first published in *The Keepsake* (1833), collected in *Mary Shelley: Collected Tales and Stories*, ed. Charles E. Robinson (Baltimore: Johns Hopkins Press, 1976). 'Napoleon and the Spectre' by Charlotte Brontë, completed 1833, first published in 1919. 'The Old Nurse's Story' by Mrs Gaskill, first published in 1852, collected in *The Gentlewomen of Evil*, ed. Peter Haining (London: Hale, 1967). 'The Lifted Veil' by Mary Ann Evans ('George Eliot'), first published 1859, collected in *The Gentlewomen of Evil (op. cit.)*. 'Circumstance' by Harriet Prescott Spofford, first published in *The Amber Cord, and Other Stories* (New York: Henry Holt & Co., 1881). 'The Phantom Coach' by Amelia B. Edwards, first published in Charles Dickens' *All The Year Round* (1864). 'The Abbot's Ghost, or, Maurice Traherne's Temptation: a Christmas Story' by A. M. Barnard (Louisa May Alcott), first published in *The Flag of Our Union* (1867), collected in *Behind A Mask* (London: The Hogarth Press, 1985). 'Kentucky's Ghost' by Elizabeth Stuart Phelps, from *Men, Women and Ghosts* (Boston: Fields, Osgood & Co., 1869). 'The Ghost in Cap'n Brown's House' by Harriet Beecher Stowe, from *Sam Lawson's Oldtown Fireside Stories* (1872). 'Behold It Was A Dream' by Rhoda Broughton, first published 1873, collected in *Twilight Stories*, ed. Van Thal (London: Home and Van Thal, 1947). 'The Secret Chamber' by Margaret Oliphant, first published in *Blackwood's Edinburgh Magazine* (1876), collected in *Margaret Oliphant: Selected Short Stories of the Supernatural*, ed. Margaret K. Grey (Edinburgh: Scottish Academic Press, 1985). 'The Ghost of Charlotte Cray' by Florence Marryat, from *A Moment of Madness, and Other Stories, vol. III* (London: F. V. White & Co.,

1883). 'Lady Farquhar's Old Lady: a True Ghost Story' by Mrs Molesworth, from *Four Ghost Stories* (London: Macmillan, 1988). 'In A Far-Off World' by Olive Schreiner, from *Dreams* (London: T. Fisher Unwin, 1891). 'Death and the Woman' by Gertrude Atherton, first published in *Vanity Fair* (1892), collected in *The Bell in the Fog, and Other Stories* (London: Macmillan, 1905). 'Man-Size in Marble' by Edith Nesbit, first published in 1893, collected in *In The Dark: Tales of Terror* (Wellingborough: Equation, 1988). 'The Banshee's Warning' by Mrs J. H. (Charlotte Eliza Lawson), from *The Banshee's Warning, and Other Tales* (London: Remington & Co., 1894). 'Caulfield's Crime' by Alice Perrin, first published 1901, collected in *Women Writers of the Raj*, ed. Saros Cowasjee (London: Grafton Books, 1990). 'The Wind in the Rose-Bush' by Mary E. Wilkins, first published 1902, collected in *The Best Stories of Mary E. Wilkins*, ed. Henry Wysham Lanier (New York: Harper & Brothers, 1927). 'Sultana's Dream' by Rokeya Sakhawat Hossain, first published in *The Indian Ladies' Magazine* (1905), collected in *Sultana's Dream, and Selections from The Secluded Ones* (New York: The Feminist Press, 1971). 'The Woman with the Hood' by L. T. Meade, from *A Lovely Fiend, and Other Stories* (London: Digby, Long & Co., 1908). 'If I Were A Man' by Charlotte Perkins Gilman first published in *Physical Culture* (July, 1914), collected in *The Charlotte Perkins Gilman Reader*, ed. Ann J. Lane (London: The Women's Press, 1980). 'Consequences' by Willa Cather first published in 1915, collected in *The Short Stories of Willa Cather*, ed. Hermione Lee (London: Virago, 1989), copyright © 1915 by Willa Cather, reprinted by permission of Virago Press. 'Kerfol' by Edith Wharton first published in 1916, collected in *Ghosts* (New York: Appleton Century Co., Inc., 1937). 'A Suburban Fairy' by Katherine Mansfield first published in 1917, collected in *The Complete Short Stories of Katherine Mansfield* (Auckland: Golden Press, 1974). 'A Haunted House' by Virginia Woolf first published in *Monday or Tuesday* (London: The Hogarth Press, 1921). 'The Nature of the Evidence' by May Sinclair first published in *Uncanny Stories* (London: Hutchinson & Co., 1923), copyright © 1921 by May Sinclair, reprinted by permission of Random Century Ltd. 'The Unbolted Door' by Mrs Belloc Lowndes first published in *The Fortnightly Review* (November, 1929), collected in *When Churchyards Yawn: Fifteen New Ghost Stories*, ed. Cynthia Asquith (London: Hutchinson & Co., 1931). 'The Buick Saloon' by Mary O'Malley first published in